AHUITZOTL

A Novel of Aztec Mexico

H. ALLENGER

ARPress
45 Dan Road Suite 5
Canton MA 02021

Hotline: 1(888) 821-0229
Fax: 1(508) 545-7580

Ordering Information:
Quantity sales. Special discounts are available on quantity purchases by corporations, associations, and others. For details, contact the publisher at the address above.

Printed in the United States of America.

ISBN-13:   Softcover   979-8-89389-174-4
           eBook   979-8-89389-173-7

Library of Congress Control Number: 2024914625

To Xochiquetzal

ACKNOWLEDGMENTS

I am indebted to the following sources: Fr. Bernardino de Sahagun (Arthur J.O. Anderson and Charles E. Dibble trans.); Fr. Diego Duran (Fernando Horcasitas and Doris Heyden trans.); Bernal Diaz; William Brandon; Gordon Brotherston; Burr Cartwright Brundage; Nigel Davies; R.C. Padden; Frederick Peterson; Jacques Soustelle; Seattle Public Library; University of Washington Library. Also, I would like to express my gratitude to Judith Zier for her years of continuous support and companionship to Mexico.

PRONUNCIATION AND IDENTIFICATION

Ahuitzotl (Ah-wheet-sohtl); Water Dog, eighth Revered Speaker of Mexico, 1486-1502.

Anahuac (Ah-nah-wahk); Near by the water; Valley of Mexico.

Axayacatl (Ah-shah-yah-kahtl); Water Face, sixth Revered Speaker of Mexico, 1469-1481; brother of Ahuitzotl and Tizoc.

Chalchihuitlicue (Chal-chee-wheet-lee-kwah); She of the Jade Skirt; Water Goddess; consort of Tlaloc, the Rain God.

Chalchiunenetzin (Chal-chwee-nay-nay-tsin); Jadestone Doll, wife of Nezahaulpilli, daughter of Axayacatl, shortened to Nenetzin.

Chimalpopoca (Chee-mahl-poh-poh-kah); Smoking Shield, Ruler of Tlacopan, a city of the Triple Alliance.

Cihuacoatl (See-wah-koh-ahtl); Woman Snake, Chief Minister and Vice-Ruler of Tenochtitlan; also the Earth Goddess.

Cocijoeza (Koh-see-hoh-ay-sah); Ruler of the Zapotecs, a major adversary of Ahuitzotl.

Cuauhtemoc (Kwow-tay-mock); Descending Eagle, son of Ahuitzotl and the last Revered Speaker of Mexico, 1520-1524.

Huactli (Whock-tlee); Hawk, Lord of the Pochteca (merchants).

Huaxtecs (Whash-tecks); people of the Panuco River basin who spoke in a Mayan type tongue and often battled the Aztecs.

Huitzilopochtli (Wheet-see-loh-poach-tlee); Hummingbird of the South, martial patron god of the Aztecs, and specifically of Tenochtitlan.

Maquauhuitl (Mah-kwow-wheetl); war club with embedded obsidian or stone blades, standard weapon for Aztec warriors.

Mictlantecuhtli (Meek-tlahn-tay-ku-tlee); Lord of the place of the dead; God of Death

Motecuhzoma Ilhuicamina (Moh-tay-ku-soh-mah Eel-whee-kah-me-nah); Angry Lord Who Shoots At The Sky, fifth Revered Speaker of Mexico, 1440-1469; grandfather of Ahuitzotl, Axayacatl, and Tizoc.

Motecuhzoma Xocoyotzin (Shoh-koh-yoh-tsin); Angry Lord, the Younger, son of Axayacatl and ninth Revered Speaker of Mexico, 1502-1520.

Nezahualcoyotl (Ness-ah-wahl-koh-yohtl); Fasting Coyote, Ruler of Texcoco, 1402-1472; famed philosopher-king, poet, and patron of arts.

Nezahualpilli (Ness-ah-wahl-peel-lee); Fasting Prince, Ruler of Texcoco, 1472-1515, son of Nezahaulcoyotl, also famed for erudition, poetry, and building.

Pelaxilla (Pay-lah-sheel-lah); Cotton Ball, lover and mistress of Ahuitzotl.

Quetzalcoatl (Kett-sahl-koh-ahtl); Plumed Serpent, God of Knowledge; Wind God; Creator God of Mankind, often depicted as an adversary of the God Tezcatlipoca.

Tenochtitlan (Tay-noach-tee-tlahn); Place by the Hard Prickly-Pear Cactus, the island capital of the Aztecs.

Texcoco (Tesh-koh-koh); capital of Acolhuacan (Ah-kohl-wah-kahn); a city of the Triple Alliance and acknowledged cultural center of the Aztecs.

Tezcatlipoca (Tess-kah-tlee-poh-kah); Smoking Mirror, supreme god of the Aztec pantheon; eternally young god of the night sky; patron god of sorcerers and magicians.

Tizoc (Tee-sock); Bloodstained Leg, the seventh Revered Speaker of Mexico, 1481-1486, brother of Ahuitzotl and Axayacatl.

Tlalalcapatl (Tlah-lahl-kah-pahtl): Earth Medicine? Shortened to Tlalalca, empress, mother of Cuauhtemoc.

Tlaloc (Tlah-lock); He Who Makes Things Sprout, Rain God.

Tonatiuh (Toh-nah-tee-uh); He Who Lights; Sun God.

Xiuhcoac (Shee-uh-koh-ahk); capital city of the Huaxtecs.

Xiuhtecuhtli (Shee-uh-tay-kuh-tlee); Turquoise Lord, God of Fire, Lord of Time.

Xochiquetzal (Shoh-chee-kett-sahl); Flower Feather or Precious Flower, Goddess of Beauty and Love, also of Flowers and Fertility.

Xoyo (Sho-yoh); aged servant woman to Tlalalca.

PROLOGUE

"We fear our Gods!" Our ninth Revered Speaker, Motecuhzoma,-to you Lord Montezuma-is said to have told his captor, the conqueror Cortez. And indeed he was most sincere in his convictions. Even as a young man Motecuhzoma took his religious studies very seriously and early in life formulated strong views in this regard. He was particularly seduced with a notion of the God Quetzalcoatl returning, as promised, to Anahuac in the year One Reed–within his own lifetime-of whose eventuality he needed no pursuasion. But mainly his proclivity was a result of experiences and observations met during the reign of his noteworthy predecessor, the great warrior-king, Ahuitzotl–Water Dog-which infused in him the dreadful trepidations leading to his inevitable ruin when confronted by the foreign invader.

The punishment that our Gods inflicted upon Lord Ahuitzotl is spoken of to this day. That fierce warlord's rise to predominance and then the horrid wretchedness of his last days–the ignominy of it–pitiless and cruel!-and this to the mightiest monarch ever to rule in Tenochtitlan! He was the very embodiment of power and resolution, courageous and resourceful, unequalled and supreme master on the battlefield, but oh, the humiliation. Truly he was humbled. And Motecuhzoma was there to see it all. So certainly he was justified in declaring his conviction, for he had borne witness to its veracity.

But had he? Some say that Motecuhzoma erred in large measure over how he interpreted the misfortunes that befell his illustrious fore-bearer, a serious mistake leading him to his own calamitous end years later. His was, when everything is taken into account, but one of many depictions rendered for those astonishing events forever associated with Lord Ahuitzotl. Although of royalty, he was not one among the elite circle of Ahuitzotl's court, being too young at the time and often away on the frequent far-flung expeditions he was sent on. In fact, insiders to the royal household have given us a different narration of his reign—of how Lord Ahuitzotl generated into motion the events commonly accepted to be the orchestrations of angry Gods. They have spoken of how he was, for the most part, responsible for his own fall, and much of it had to do with his impassioned love of a woman.

Now, let us turn the pages forward and learn of the truths behind the transpired events that so profoundly affected a youthful Motecuhzoma as revealed to us by the All-Seeing, All-Knowing, Eternal Lord of the Night Sky, first among the Gods, Tezcatlipoca. You understand, of course, the need to remain anonymous as this story is related. Our new masters possess no tolerance for our age-long traditions and sacred ways, readily discrediting the importance these rituals held for us in sustaining life, unable to discern its necessity, denouncing these as the Devil's work, and condemning us for basic practices we believed essential for preserving the fifth Sun. They have no insight into our world, being ignorant as they are. But let us proceed.

By your calendar's reckoning, the year is 1486. Ahuitzotl is not yet the monarch. It is his younger brother, Tizoc, who sits on the throne—to the discontent of many, including members of the Council of Speakers, the Tlatoani, who appointed him to rule.

—A priest of Tezcatlipoca
circa 1530 A.D.

PART 1

THE DEATH OF A KING

"Most mighty lord and brave youth; you have inherited the royal seat, of very rich and fine feathers, and the hall of precious stones that the God Quetzalcoatl, great Topiltzin, and the wonderful and glorious Huitzilopochtli have left behind them. This royal throne is only lent to you, and not for ever but for a short while only. The brave rulers who preceded you have exalted and extended this realm, more especially your grandfather, great Motecuhzoma, of high and revered memory, who, in his long life, raised it to a high pitch of glory such as it had never before attained.

"Therefore, my lord, take care not to be of faint heart. Look carefully to what you do Take heed for the orphan and for the widow, for the aged who can work no longer, because these are the plumes, the eyelashes, and the eye-brows of Huitzilopochtli. Most especially you must care for the eagles and the tigers, those brave and valiant men, who act as a rampart of defense for you and your realm, and who extend its boundaries by the shedding of their blood. With these words, my lord, I end my speech."

—Nezahualpilli of Texcoco at the appointment
of Tizoc as Revered Speaker*

* Nigel Davies, 'The Aztecs', University of Oklahoma Press, 1973, pp. 152-153.

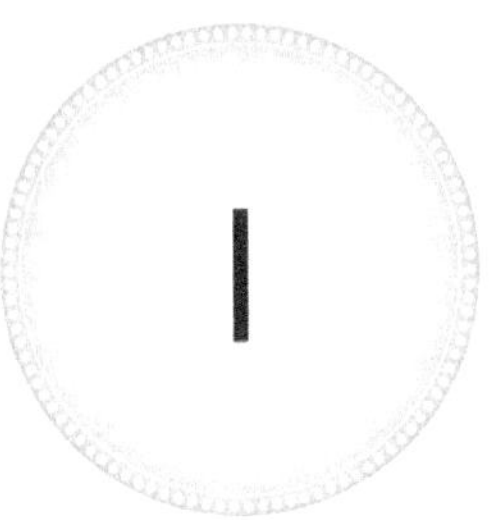

huitzotl stood in all his contradictions before the palace door watching work crews emplace masonry atop the second tier of the future Great Temple in Tenochtitlan. Handsome and possessed of a solid, muscular frame that rose to medium height, an aura of sublime countenance bespeaking of confidence and lordliness embodied his personage. But he was not as elaborately attired as might have been expected, cutting an image of austerity in shunning the profuse embellishments his peers would have proudly, even arrogantly, displayed. He had none of the facial ornaments-the golden earlobes, half-moons, or lip insertions-nor the necklaces of metallic beads and small marine shells that others wore, his jewelry limited to the golden arm bracelets common to the aristocracy. Nothing about his dress, not his golden embroidered breechcloth, or his blue cotton tunic, or his tilmantli, a cape fastened over his right shoulder which hung down in back to knee level, not even his feathery tasseled headband with gold trimmings, made him stand out as a particularly distinguished individual. However, his sandals, of turquoise blue fabric and golden laces, marked him as a member of the highest nobility, that of the royal house, and brother of the reigning monarch. Yet his modest ensemble opposed a reputation for conspicuousness he had acquired among those who knew him. He demonstrated a will of his own and, apart from the rigid conformity demanded by sacred rituals and protocol of courtly life, made a habit of adapting the rules to meet his purposes.

The Great Temple, as gigantic a construction project as ever undertaken by the Tenocha-Mexica, was to be an abode for their chief tribal deity, the war-god Huitzilopochtli, and the rain-god Tlaloc, who would occupy separate shrines upon its uppermost platform, and the crowning achievement of Tizoc, the seventh Revered Speaker, monarch of the realm. Its conception was not Tizoc's, however; that claim belonged to his predecessor, Axayacatl, and it was he, not Tizoc, who had implemented the groundwork. He meant to commemorate his triumph over the ruler of Tlatelolco, Tenochtitlan's rival city on the lake, by erecting this gigantic edifice to symbolize their unification into one metropolis, but he died unexpectedly from wounds received in an earlier war. Ahuitzotl had anticipated the interclan council would appoint him as successor, but it had chosen Tizoc. And now, in his fifth year as Revered Speaker, Tizoc decided to make the project his major priority and directed all his energies toward its completion. Plaudits would come to him for this—as long as Tenochtitlan ruled, Tizoc would be immortalized as the builder of that imposing structure.

Treasonous thoughts raced through Ahuitzotl's brain. They were brothers, all three of them—Ahuitzotl, Axayacatl, and Tizoc—grandsons of the famed Motecuhzoma Ilhuicamina and inheritors of an established tradition of empire building. Since the time of Motecuhzoma's progenitor, Itzcoatl, the Mexica had subdued their rivals and embarked on a trail of conquests which had made them masters of the highland valley, Anahuac, so that now scores of cities rendered tribute to them. What conquerors they were! Itzcoatl, who set the pattern for the rest, subjected Anahuac under his rule. Next came Ahuitzotl's illustrious grandfather, whose very name is uttered in deepest reverence. He had warred on countless tribes, defeating them all, and built the aquaduct from Chapultepec to Tenochtitlan. Then came Ahuitzotl's brother, Axayacatl, a most worthy heir, who fought the powerful Tarascans and isolated Tlaxcala by subjugating the nations around it. He forever ended the intolerable rivalry of Tlatelolco and by so doing established Tenochtitlan's supremacy. That Tizoc should be counted among such giants bordered on insult.

Tizoc! In his opening campaign against Metztitlan, his poor leadership allowed the Huaxtecs, allies of the enemy, to send him into a humiliating retreat. In his wars against the Mixtecs he cowered behind the lines—he said he was afflicted with chills and fever—and it fell upon Ahuitzotl to take command of the situation, secure victory, and win respect for Mexica arms. And yet Tizoc would finish the Great Temple so that all will remember his name and sing praises to his glory. A deception was in progress here—foul and dishonorable.

"You have been standing here for a long time, Lord. Your excessive absorption allows for much conjecture."

His thoughts abruptly broken, Ahuitzotl glanced up to see Cihuacoatl, the Woman Snake, chief minister of Tizoc's court. Cihuacoatl's actual name was Tlilpopocatzin, but he was always addressed by the title of his office.

"Why should it, Cihuacoatl?" replied Ahuitzotl. "The structure is impressive-it doesn't tire one's eyes to observe it."

"True. However, you failed to notice me approaching you-from it. You are looking at the temple, but you see something else."

"I was contemplating its enormity—the suggestion of a single temple serving two of our primary gods. Will this not generate envy between them?"

"When the work is done and the dedication rites begin we shall find out. You are being evasive, Prince. We both know well enough what you were thinking—do I need to say it?"

Such an overture was typical of Cihuacoatl. An adroit minister of the state and Vice-Ruler of Tenochtitlan, he was second in power only to the monarch himself. While he was not particularly liked by Ahuitzotl, or many of the other nobles-a reaction he elicited through an abrasive mannerism-there was significant respect attached to his position. He was a man to be reckoned with, a Tlatoani, one of the principals of the interclan council, that body of chosen speakers which elected the ruler. As the council's ranking member, he exerted major influence, and Ahuitzotl was well aware of a statement made by Cihuacoatl's father, Tlacaelel, the greatest Tlatoani of them all, that there was no reason for him to be king when he himself told kings what to do. Cihuacoatl was, in every sense of the word, the maker of Mexica 'kings'.

"Go on," Ahuitzotl said. "Enlighten me."

"It's not the envy of gods you contemplate, but the envy of brothers. You resent the prestige this magnificent temple will bring to Lord Tizoc's memory. Dismiss these thoughts, Lord. They are not worthy of you."

"Do you think I would trouble myself to deny it?" Ahuitzotl countered after a brief pause. "I'm not alone in questioning if Tizoc deserves this. There is much resentment."

"Enhanced by you, no doubt."

Ahuitzotl was offended over the insinuation. "Chief Minister you may be, Cihuacoatl," he said, "but I remind you to maintain your courtesy when speaking to a member of the royal house. You have no cause to deprecate me. Any feelings I harbor my brother, I've kept to myself. No, minister. If there is dissatisfaction in the realm-and it becomes more apparent at every passing day-the fault lies with Tizoc. Say what you will; it will not diminish the deterioration emanating from the throne. I have no need to proclaim the obvious."

"You may not express it, but your actions make your intentions clear enough, Royal Prince. Your hostility towards Lord Tizoc is well known to us-so well that it no longer merits my attention," said Cihuacoatl, turning to make his departure, but Ahuitzotl brought him to a halt.

"You have wronged me, Cihuacoatl!"

"Indeed! How?"

"I was the rightful heir as eldest brother. Everyone knows this. My conduct in battle is of the highest merit, distinguished and honorable— my bravery unquestioned. I am the ablest of our commanders. Is it not the duty of the council to choose the man most capable of leading us as Revered Speaker?"

"So it is."

"Then how is it that Tizoc sits upon the throne? What has my brother done to earn him that exulted..."

"He sits on the throne," Cihuacoal angrily interrupted, "because the council chose the man best fit to rule. Does this offend you, Lord? If you dispute the council's judgment, be warned! You come perilously close to condemning yourself before the gods."

The stern admonishment momentarily quieted Ahuitzotl, but his eyes glared with an intensity belying his affected composure. "Excuse this pain and bitterness I feel," he said. "My reaction to the disappointment which overwhelms me when I reflect on the council's decision."

"Accept it, Lord! If you do not, it will poison your mind. Rulers are appointed for life and Lord Tizoc is a young man-you will suffer a lengthy torment if you trouble yourself with that."

"It was an injustice to me-I will never forgive the council for that!"

"An injustice?" Cihuacoatl roared out.

"Yes, an injustice! It was I who led the army and won us honors. For this Axayacatl himself granted me command of the Order of the Eagles. And where was Tizoc then? At the school in Calixtlahuaca to study the arts of statecraft. I ask you, did his education save us from the Huaxtecs? Or from the Mixtecs? Did it spare us from humiliation? How many times have I rescued him from certain defeat? You say he is best fit to rule? Nonsense!"

"Enough! Nobody doubts your ability in the conduct of wars, Lord Ahuitzotl, but there is more to running a state than waging war. It might have done you some good to spend more time at Calixtlahuaca."

"I have learned what I most need to know. Mainly how to properly serve Huitzilopochtli, our Sustainer. Am I not his high priest?"

Cihuacoatl was not impressed. "For you, a perfunctory duty bestowed by a royal assignment. Huitzilopochtli does not rule the skies alone, Lord. What of Tezcatlipoca? And of Tlaloc, or Quetzalcoatl? What do the sacred rites of Tlaltecuhtli signify? How would you propitiate these gods? If you cannot tell me, then ask your brother. He would know."

Ahuitzotl remained silent, embarrassed over having his deficiency in these matters stated.

"Hear me, Royal Prince," continued Cihuacoatl. "You are a headstrong and ambitious man, and that is a dangerous combination. Not only for you, but for the realm. Men whose actions are guided by, and directed towards, their own preceived interests place these above the state and rarely attend to the duties of their office. They measure success by their own gratification than by what is beneficial-doing what is preferred to what is required. Did you expect we would imperil our lives by having such a man alienate the gods through impiety or ignorance? You are blinded by your conceit. In praising your accomplishments, to an exaggerated degree I might add, you diminish those of your brother, and are unable to see his worthiness. But I have said enough-it's unlikely you will heed my advice. Be grateful I remain silent on what I have heard."

Ahuitzotl paused as he mused over the minister's words. "You misjudge me," he then said, "but I am thankful for your prudence. Yet note what I say. My time for greatness will come-of this I am certain!-and I shall outdo them all. What my father, and his father, and my brothers have done, I shall do ten times over. The cities they took I shall double, and the captives they took I shall increase a hundredfold. This I swear before all the gods! Tizoc may build his massive temple, but my glory will some day eclipse his. I shall surpass them all!"

Such determination could hardly be dismissed by Cihuacoatl and, for an instant, he even felt a chill come over him as what he heard bore into his mind. But upon further deliberation, he brushed aside his first intuition, recognizing these things are simpler said than done. For one thing, where would such opportunities arise? Ahuitzotl was not the Revered Speaker. Still, an uneasiness remained with him, and he knew that he must now ponder over what possibilities the sheer strength of will can bring to fortune.

"Perhaps-if the gods will it," Cihuacoatl whispered, turning to make his departure.

Ahuitzotl's gaze remained fixed on the minister as he crossed the plaza for the temple complex. Could the Woman Snake be trusted? What was his true standing with Tizoc? There were some in the court who held that Cihuacoatl was highly displeases with his appointment of Tizoc to the kingship, that he even admitted to an error in judgment. But such talk was speculative. It may have been a dangerous miscalculation to speak ill of the monarch.

Ahuitzotl turned his eyes back on the temple and scanned over the sight of sweating bodies laboring upon the wooden ramps and scaffolding. The surge of indignation he felt was overpowering, gnawing at him for seemingly the longest time, until, at last, he was compelled to look away. Beyond the hubbub of activity he saw dark clouds descending on the distant peaks of Iztaccihuatl and Popocatepetl as if congruent with the mood projected by the one thought that dominated him. I shall surpass them all!

At the school in Calixtlhuaca, two of the head priests, who also performed as the principal instructors, discussed the future of one of their more noteworthy students.

"Have you told him yet?"

"I am to meet with him shortly. I shall break the news to him then."

"Does he know?"

"I think he suspects it. Word from the court has a way of reaching the ears of those not meant to hear it."

"Will he be ready to accept the change in store for him?"

"It does not matter whether we think he is ready for it. The Revered Speaker has decided that he is. To be fair, Motecuhzoma has excelled in all his courses here, and although I would personally have him spend another year with us, there are other, shall we say more sinister, aspects of statesmanship to be learned that cannot be taught here. He is brilliant and has a gift for leadership. Such men are rare and it is proper that his further education be acquired in the courts."

"Even so, it's regrettable we could not keep such a talent for service to Huitzilopochtli. There's something disagreeable about only the second best being priests.

"Huitzilopochtli can be better served by the most brilliant becoming the rulers."

"You believe this? If it is the gods who confer their blessings on the state, what can be more important than devoting one's life to them?"

"Even as priests, there are practical realities to be faced. We know how to appease the gods while the strength of the state protects our institutions from those who would not have us-and there are many of them. As long as we have rulers who fear the gods, we shall be able to amply continue serving them."

"You make it seem so obvious."

"The nobility throughout the realm brings its future kings, judges, administrators, and priests to this school. What is essential is that we assure these students leave here with a proper regard for our gods. By doing so, we please them, as well as ourselves."

With that, they parted. The taller priest, attired in the black robe denoting his order, proceeded to his study and sat down to reflect over the many reports he had received on his expected visitor.

His was an impressive record. In all the courses taught at the school, Motecuhzoma excelled. These included the details and functions of government, administration, justice, history, the interpretation of glyphs, astronomy, architecture and engineering, agriculture, genealogies, hunting, and the skills of warfare. His devotion to the religious studies entailing both instruction and temple service, an apprenticeship to priesthood, was flawless. He had mastered reading the calendar, determining and fixing the time of feasts, and performing the required rituals and incantations. He was taught how to interpret dreams, astrology, verses of divine songs, and the counting of the years. His ratings were of the highest category; never had there been a more exemplary record on anyone who resided here.

His full name was Motecuhzoma Xocoyotzin. He was the son of Axayacatl and great grandson of the revered Motecuhzoma Ilhuicamina and a prince of the Royal House of Tenochtitlan. There was little doubt that this student was destined to take his place among the ruling elites. No person of such lineage and such extraordinary achievement could fail to leave his stamp among the chroniclers of Anahuac. He would most likely spend his next two or three years in the lower echelons of the military and in an apprenticeship to key ministersand then be promoted as a personal aide to some ranking official. It fit the usual pattern, except that he was beginning at an earlier age and ahead of his contemporaries. This youth was being groomed for nothing less than a candidacy for the kingship itself. The priest knew he must exercise prudence with this progeny, one who could be an ally of significant importance in years to come.

A rapping on the door announced to the priest that his guest had arrived and awaited permission to enter. This the priest immediately granted and he watched while the tall, lanky youngster briskly walked to the center of the room and stopped when squarely ahead of him. He studied his subject at length, as if groping for a sign of flaw in this seemingly paragon of Mexica manhood, and then began.

"You are Motecuhzoma Xocoyotzin?"

"I am," came his confident reply.

"Do you know why you have been summoned to me?"

"I have heard I am wanted back at the court in Tenochtitlan."

"To come directly to the point, the Revered Speaker, Lord Tizoc, has requested that you terminate your training here so you can assume full-time duties among the ministers, priests, and commanders as an understudy in their professions. Evidently he is of the opinion that your presence is now desireable or required—for what reasons I was not told-and has some specific assignment envisioned for you."

The priest paused to scan the young man's face but detected no particular emotion in it. "You are not disappointed then," he surmised.

"No. I am in need of a change."

"Have the instructions here become stale for you?"

"Perhaps prolonged. I feel I have mastered the subjects taught me and prefer being introduced to new challenges."

"You record certainly attests to that." At this juncture, the priest thought it appropriate to probe his student to the extend of his reverence, not only to determine whether the training had been effective, but also to satisfy in his mind that Motecuhzoma was aptly indoctrinated and would face the world with his convictions properly implanted. "In summarizing your education here, what is your conclusion about our service to the gods? Are you assured that we accede to their wishes in order to secure their blessings?"

"We amply serve them in our rituals. I see no reason for thinking otherwise."

"So you see the gods as the manipulators of our fortunes and arbiters of all that we do."

"Of course! We would risk invoking their wrath through any remission in our obligations to them."

'It is often done, with the gravest consequences afflicted upon us. The chroniclers mention it repeatedly-sickness, fires, the floods, and the deep snows, drought and famine-disasters which have brought great misery and suffering. Warnings from the gods resulting from man's failure to show them obeisance! Take care in your dealings with them, Motecuhzoma. As our providers, they must be nourished and sustained. We live within the fifth cycle. Four previous suns have existed and flowered an age for man, and each of them has been destroyed, and so will this one be destroyed if the gods, who preserve it for us, are weakened. The eternal night demons constantly strive to make their claim upon this world. It is only by the strength of divine Huitzilopochtli embattling them that the path is cleared for the glorious Sun, Tonatiuh, so that life can flourish. It is blood-our blood-that sustains them, and this same substance which assures them life also gives us life. Explain to me why this is so."

"The gods created us from the bones of previous men mixed with their blood, which is the seed developing our being. Since from their blood they created us, it is fitting that we in turn from our blood nourish them. We are, in essence, the harvest from the seed they have sown and are therefore sustenance for them. Our sacrifice assures us their dominion so that all can continue to exist."

'You must appreciate it as a self-perpetuating system, with one surviving to support the other and thus insuring its own existence. Were one element to fail in doing its part, it would cause the others to fail. Our universe would fall into eternal darkness and life would cease. Each deity has a distictive function to perform in maintaining this cycle and none can be ignored. All must be propitiated so that no jealousies are invoked. This does not deter us from having our favorites-many are revered for the services they perform-as long as they collectively have institutions to honor them. The magicians and sorcerers honor Tezcatlipoca because he alone sees all that takes place in the world, and it is through patronizing him that he reveals what he sees to them. As for myself, I feel most indebted to Huitzilopochtli. An excellent choice for our patron god-wouldn't you agree?"

"Surely I cannot diminish his importance to us, but where I to name my own favorite, I should choose Quetzalcoatl."

"Indeed?" a puzzled look came over the priest. "I should have thought Huitzilopochtli. Why Quetzalcoatl?"

"He is closest to me. It is he who searched the underworld for the bones so we could be recreated with his own blood. He gave us corn and taught us how to cultivate it. He taught us to use a calendar and the sacred rituals, and who gave us knowledge of the arts and showed us how to build. He endowed us with the wisdom by which we can honor the other gods."

The priest, not pleased over having his own choice relegated to second place by a mere youth, felt compelled to sway Motecuhzoma from his preference. "But Huitzilopochtli assures us the daily sun," he said. "Is this not greater than what Quetzalcoatl has done?"

"I seek not to minimize this, but if he must receive his nourishment and strength from our blood, than are we not as important to him as he is to us? Must he then not also be indebted to Quetzelcoatl?

The priest was amazed. There is a formidable power in the intellect.

"I see. You make a strong case for your choice, but remember, having already arranged for our creation and tought us how to grow our food and given us our knowledge, he is not tasked with the awesome duties that Huitzilopochtli must do for us. For this reason he does not require the number of sacrifices that we must give to Huitzilopochtli."

"Quetzalcoatl has said that he did not wish to have any sacrifices at all, yet he is a god and must therefore be so served."

"Is that why you favor him?"

"Quetzalcoatl alone among the gods has promised to return to us so that he might teach us how to create a paradise in which to live. What greater honor could befall us than to be visited by a god?"

"Do you expect such a divine intervention?"

"So the sacred texts tell us. He said he would return in the year One Reed-thirty-four years from now-easily within my lifetime, if the gods are disposed to grant me such fortune."

"I suppose. It's clear you are sufficiently regardful in your piety that I see no point in continuing. But be advised, Motecuhzoma. Do not neglect the other gods in your zeal for Quetzalcoatl, for they will know this and punish you for it. Nothing escapes their notice. How well do you know your kinsman, Lord Ahuitzotl?"

This sudden turn of questioning seemed to catch Motecuhzoma unprepared and the priest waited on his answer.

"Hardly at all," replied the youth. "I was very young when my father sent me here and, even before then, I rarely saw him. I have no recollection of him."

"Hmmm," the priest mumbled. It constituted a breach of etiquette for a student to ask Questions unless directed, but the step was not necessary as the priest read Motecuhzoma's impatience. "You are to report to the headquarters of the Order of the Eagles in Tenochtitlan," he said. "You are assigned to the command of Lord Ahuitzotl. He will determine your further disposition and direct you to the duties anticipated for you. You have one month to arrange for your departure before reporting to him. That is all."

Motecuhzoma appeared momentarily dazed, either due to the excitement over his new prospects or an alarm over the seeming abruptness in which the session had come to an end. The priest, ascribing it to the latter, was prompted to make the termination more agreeable. "May the gods protect you, Motecuhzoma," he said.

The youngster turned about and exited from the chamber leaving the priest staring blankly at an austere wall. There was an unmistakably troubled look in his face indicating that he was not pleased with where their conversation had led them. Is it possible, he thought, that this student has received his education too seriously?

III

n Tenochtitlan's royal palace, the ladies of the court sat on cushions chatting over things of common interest and amusement. Amid the elation and laughter arising from hearing about the latest escapades came an appreciation of individual attributes and an admiration for those who best contributed to the gaiety of the occasion. Through these gatherings the wives and mistresses of the monarch created their bonds of friendship. But in spite of the numerous ladies present to serve his sensual needs, there was only one empress, and that was his first or favorite wife who, by commanding most of his attention and affection, attained a position of dominance over her entourage. She was Tlalalca, the beautiful young wife of Tizoc, and she surrounded herself with her courtly favorites to pass the afternoon engaging in the pleasantries of casual conversation.

"How vain our lords are!" she began. "Did you see how they carried themselves at the reception yesterday? Their aloof posturing–and in their most ornate attire. Each one struts prouder and haughtier than the other before our Lord Tizoc, as if he was of such singular importance that the Revered Speaker should take special note of him."

"But that is expected of them," said one of the ladies.

"Yes, but like everything else, it can be overdone until it begins to have an unfashionable quality about it. I'm sure it seemed absurd to Lord Nezahualpilli who was there to see it all. His court in Texcoco is known for its refinement. He must think we come across as quite artificial."

"Nezahualpilli is here?" one more lady interjected with some excitement. "They say he is quite the lover."

"It's said he has over a thousand concubines," added another, "and forty wives. How does he get to each one?"

"I dare say," Tlalalca replied, "such a remark is so typical of you, Nenetzin. You do have a way of getting to the point of a subject."

This sparked an outburst of laughter among the members who appreciated its message. Tlalalca continued, "Perhaps you should ask Nezahualpilli how he manages it. Such straight-forwardness may be pleasing to him over all our affectation. But let's not dwell on this. I do not care to have my afternoon spoiled with this sort of vulgarity."

'As you say, my Lady, but I'm sorry I missed him. Someone will have to point him out to me next time. I should like to see what such a man looks like."

"Come now, Nenetzin, you make this Texcocan seem too extraordinary," another of the ladies broke in. "Surely we also have lords to compare with him."

"And which of our lords might that be?" asked Nenetzin.

"Lord Ahuitzotl," a voice spoke out assertively.

A hush ensued, as if out of an awareness that an apparent error had been precipitated.

"That must be Pelaxilla," Tlalalca said after a brief delay. "We know she has taken a fancy to him."

"It's true I admire him, my Lady," replied Pelaxilla, "but even if this were not so, we are improper in placing our own lords below Texcoco's."

This mild rebuke offended none, for Pelaxilla was fondly regarded. She was seen as one of those endearing personalities who with seemingly effortless ease exude a winsome presence and manage to attract well-wishes out of all who know her.

"Our little one is correct, of course," said Tlalalca. "But let us remind her that we are not talking about all the lords of Texcoco-only of one. And in truth Nezahualpilli is an exceptional man if we are to believe what we hear of him. He is by reputation the wisest man in Anahuac-even Lord Tizoc places the greatest value on his counsel."

"He may be all they say, but I did not even notice him," answered Pelaxilla.

"Of course not," Nenetzin quickly added. "The only person you see is Lord Ahuitzotl."

"With good reason. Is he not the handsomest man in all Tenochtitlan?" Pelaxilla retorted.

"I have seen better."

"Have you? How selfish of you to keep it from the rest of us, Nenetzin. Tell us who so that we might share your opinion."

"Yes, Nenetzin, tell us!" another voice demanded.

Nenetzin pondered over it for a moment not really knowing whom she had in mind when she made her earlier remark. Finding herself on the defensive, she decided to name whoever came to her.

"Take Cihuacoatl for example, there's..."

"Cihuacoatl!" Pelaxilla did not allow her to finish, "That old worn-out beast? You dare to compare Ahuitzotl to him?"

Again the room resounded with laughter.

"Now, Pelaxilla," Tlalalca interceded, "Let's not get personal over this. Cihuacoatl may have his faults, but he assuredly does not merit the lowly appellation that you assign him. Be reasonable, child! You cannot expect everyone to share your enthusiasm for Lord Ahuitzotl. Handsome he may well be, but the real worth of a man lies in more than mere appearances. Even an ugly man can be appreciated, perhaps even loved, when one learns that he possesses noble qualities."

"Excuse my unkind words, my Lady," said Pelaxilla, her embarrassment much in evidence. "They were thoughtlessly expressed."

"You are forgiven, my dear. You are young and in love, and we can understand how that can deprive us of our better judgment. After all, were we not all in the same situation once? Lord Ahuitzotl is indeed fortunate to have so devoted an admirer."

"Why are all these nobles here?" inquired Nenetzin.

"There are movements about that portent another war. The nobles meet in council tomorrow to discuss the matter. Lord Tizoc mentioned something about a revolt in Toluca, I believe."

"Another war? I hope not. It's not very exciting around here when our men are gone."

"For shame, Nenetzin! You risk angering the gods in making light of this, for they ordain these things."

"I only said it in jest, my Lady," Nenetzin retracted.

"Still, it would be better not to tempt them. We should not question the purpose of our men's action as it involves our relationship with them and has great importance," counseled Tlalalca who then chanced to see the ashen look in Pelaxilla. "Is something wrong, Pelaxilla? You seem unduly disturbed by the news."

"I just did not wish Ahuitzotl to be gone again. It's been only a few weeks since he returned from the last war."

"Back to Ahuitzotl? Really, child. You do weary me with your constant preoccupation over him. You must accept that there is a design behind what our Lord Tizoc intends to do. Were it not necessary, I should think it would not be done. But I have heard enough of Ahuitzotl. I shall retire to my chamber for my bath. Perhaps our conversation will be more pleasant tomorrow."

With that, Tlalalca arose and departed from the room, accompanied by her loyal servant, the aged Xoyo, while the remaining ladies were left to puzzle over her annoyance. Nenetzin gave Pelaxilla a wary glance.

"You have angered her, Pelaxilla," she said. "If I were you, I would be more careful."

"I didn't mean to. She asked me what troubled me, and I told her. What have I done wrong?"

"It would be prudent for you not to mention Lord Ahuitzotl's name again. Something about him upsets her."

"But why?"

"I don't know. But it's rather obvious-isn't it?-so please be cautious. We like you and would hate to see you dismissed from the court."

Pelaxilla, not understanding her transgression, was jolted by this, prompting Nenetzin, who sensed her consternation, to embrace her and allay her fears. "Now, now, Pelaxilla. You make too much of it. I made a reckless statement-too harsh. Our lady knows you would never intentionally offend her. Tomorrow you will find her well-composed again."

While Nenetzin was calming a frightened Pelaxilla, Tlalalca took her customary afternoon bath in spring waters piped through stone conduits into a compartment adjacent to her private chamber. Her tub was a squared cistern into which steps had been carved so that she could climb into its depth and immerse herself to the level of her neck. She cleansed herself with the rich lather formed by cakes made from the root of the copalxocotl tree, and when she was finished emerged from her tub into large towels held forth by Xoyo. These she wrapped over her and then entered her chamber where she sat down on the cushions placed abundantly about the floor. Xoyo sank to her knees and began to brush Tlalalca's glossy raven hair. She noticed a disquietude not common for her charge.

"My lady is disturbed," she remarked, giving voice to her observation.

"Does it show?" Tlalalca replied. "I do not hide my feelings well. When I am troubled, people see it instantly. It's not befitting for an empress to reveal herself so."

"May I ask what is the problem?"

"Pelaxilla thinks too highly of him. It is very upsetting to me."

"You mean Lord Ahuitzotl?"

"He is not the man for her."

"He is quite good-looking. Where I younger, I would fancy him myself."

"He cannot be trusted. Have you seen how he glares at my Lord Tizoc? He does not look upon him with respect, or with joy, but rather with a cold, contemptuous gaze. There is cruelty in his eyes. He thinks too much and speaks too little, and I have fears over what thoughts he may have. I find it very discomfiting."

"Perhaps my lady misreads him."

"If so, I should never again be able to rely on my perceptions, for they confirm this to me."

"How can you know?"

"What I say about him I cannot prove. They are things I feel. He bears a grudge against my husband which is often reflected in his behavior. I was told of the extreme vehemence he displayed when the council selected Tizoc as Revered Speaker. They say he flew into a rage and bolted from the scene like a savage beast when its choice was disclosed to him. Such conduct is most unbecoming. And to his brother. To this day whatever communication exists between them is of an official nature only. They do not socialize. There is no cordiality between them, and even though he resides in this palace, he keeps his distance from us. If only I could be certain of his intentions. I fear he means Tizoc harm."

"Surely you are wrong, my Lady. One would never suspect it looking at him."

"It's as if his attractiveness masked his true evil purposes all the more. Yet I tell you my fears are not groundless. To think he should capture the heart of our dear Pelaxilla. Even this amounts to a derogation of Tizoc, for she is pledged to him as one of his mistresses. It's almost more than I can bear."

"This is not a one-sided affair, my Lady. He loves her too."

"He does? I was not aware of it."

I have not only seen it in him, but have heard others speak of it. Those eyes you say glare so contemptuously at Lord Tizoc gaze quite differently upon Pelaxilla. Indeed, they shine like stars when they behold her. He is often at a loss of words when with her, and has been clumsy in his attempts to humor her. Surely these are symptoms of Xochiquetzal's affliction. He is with her on many afternoons-they frequently stroll in the royal garden. From what I make of it, I would say that he loves Pelaxilla more than she loves him."

"What a revelation you have given me. But then, she is such an adorable child, so lovely and charming, and of such cheerful disposition. How could any man resist her? Do you think I frightened her today?"

"If you did, it would matter little. One loving glance from you will mend things for her again."

"Yes, it is amazing what a position of authority can do. I shall put that to work for me next time we see our little flower."

"What does my lady mean?"

"You're convinced that Ahuitzotl loves her?"

"I'm certain of it."

"Then we shall make use of his enrapture. Pelaxilla will find out for us what he is thinking. Would not a man in love give his sweetheart any answer she desired, especially if pressed?"

"Possibly, but isn't this kind of unseemly?"

"Unseemly?" Tlalalca hesitated as she gave this some weight. "I suppose it is. But we do have an important purpose behind this-perhaps nothing less than the safety of our Revered Speaker. I should think that would be all the justification we need. I am correct in assuming we are together in this and that I can count on your cooperation, am I not?"

Xoyo, who had a decided distaste for court intrigue, found difficulty in answering. She felt herself placed as an unwilling accomplice in a scheme she wanted no part of by virtue of her being the queen's attendant. What choice was there for her?

"Yes, my Lady," she consented.

"Good. Then I expect we shall soon discover whether my fears are warranted."

By this time, Xoyo had finished preening Tlalalca who expressed a desire for her usual late afternoon nap. The old woman gently assisted her into the multi-layered mats making up the bed and covered her with a single thin cotton sheet that sufficed as a blanket in the day's comfortable temperature. Then she went about wiping the water from the floor and picking up the towels, and when done, she quietly slipped away leaving Tlalalca in reposed slumber.

IV

In a magnificent profusion of color, nobles from throughout the realm, accompanied by their ministers, ambassadors, counselors, and commanders, stood resplendently arrayed in their finest attire and adorned with their richest jewelry as they met in the reception hall of the royal palace. They were in their feathered tilmantlis, embroidered breechcloths, in ocelot sandals, and in brilliantly plumed headdresses, each adapting to his particular tastes in color and material. Their ornamentation of gold, silver, jade, and other gemstones shimmered at every movement. They constituted a wondrous spectacle, and as was the fashion, their dress and adornment represented their social rankings in the cities and provinces from where they came.

On a raised platform at the end of the hall sat Tizoc in his Eagle and Jaguar Throne. He wore a turquoise blue cape distinguishing him as the Revered Speaker, monarch of the nation, and representing the color of Huitzilopochtli. His jewelry included earplugs of gold and jade and an emerald nose insertion worn by all kings as a sign of their direct linkage to the gods. His headdress was made from feathers of the quetzal bird and from his neck hung an emerald medallion. He was an imposing figure, and anyone present would have readily sorted him out as the leading personage in the assembly. He alone was seated.

Below the platform on Tizoc's right stood Cihuacoatl, wearing a jaguar skin tilmantli and holding a long staff, the symbols of his office. Beside him were the leading officials of Tenochtitlan, including two of its chief priests. To the left was Ahuitzotl, austere in his lack of ornamentation although his clothing was as fine as anyone's, who represented the city's army. He was accompanied by Tlohtzin, his battle-hardened vice-commander. Among them, Tizoc had all his key civilian, religious, and military advisors available to give him appropriate counsel should he request it.

In the gathering grouped by regional realms, closest to Tizoc stood the delegation from Texcoco, headed by its famed king, Nezahualpilli, and that of Tlacopan, led by its own ruler, Chimalpopoca. These were the cities which, along with Tenochtitlan, made up the Triple Alliance that dominated the empire, a compact now dated almost sixty years and having been formed when the empire was in its incipient stages and struggling to rule Anahuac. In addition, the remaining major cities of Anahuac-Azcapotzalco, Chalco, Coyoacan, Culhuacan, Ixtapalapa, Otombo, Tecpatepec, Tenayuca, and Tepeyac among them-had their agents in attendance. In all, the assembly represented the leading administrative and political centers which comprised the realm.

Tizoc motioned his hand to signal Cihuacoatl into commencing with the proceedings. After obtaining silence from the gathering by tapping his staff repeatedly on the floor, the minister called on a priest to recite the usual opening incantations, its purpose aimed at securing the necessary approval of the gods, for no action contemplated by men could proceed without their consent. When the orisons were completed, Cihuacoatl took a roll call of the officials present while a scribe faithfully recorded this in his texts. That done, the floor was ready to hear Tizoc's words.

"We are met here to bring to a decision certain problems that remain unsolved for us," he spoke out. "First, and obviously most crucial, is the matter of Toluca. We have Tecolotl, the ambassador of Toluca, with us so that he might know what is decided here today. As you know, the Tolucans have taken it upon themselves to challenge our dominion over them and are refusing to consign further tributes to us. These are actions which we, if we are to retain any kind of credibility as a power, to say nothing of our standing with the gods, cannot ignore. Not only is this an affront to our authority, but it also extends a dangerous precedence to be emulated by our other subjugated states. That the Tolucans must be punished for their insolence is certain. The question is to what degree. Let us consider what responses should be directed against them. Clearly we can move our armies upon them–that would be the easiest-but is this the wisest course to pursue?"

Answering first was Ahuitzotl. "Why should there be any doubt about what we will do? Toluca has presented us with what, by any account, must be seen as a serious threat–an insidious erosive influence which, while not that significant for one city, can rapidly accelerate into a viable large-scale insurrection. We are only as strong as the hold we keep over our individual states. I see this rebellion as nothing less than a well-calculated assault directed at our very foundations, and it is imperative on our part to make the message clear that we will not stand idly by and watch subversive maneuvers disintegrate the bonds which hold the realm together. I say the punishment against the Tolucans must be severe. Since they, by their actions, have made themselves an example for other vassel states to follow, so let us, by our actions, make them an example of the retribution in store for anyone who defies us."

A commotion of nods and mumblings from the floor indicated that there was general agreement to this.

"So what is your proposal?" asked Tizoc.

"To destroy them utterly," declared Ahuitzotl. "To devastate their city, destroy its army, and enslave its inhabitants, so that all who see and hear of this will have a permanent imprint of our fury lest they likewise contemplate to rise against us."

Ahuitzotl, smirking with satisfaction, glanced toward Tecolotl and saw that the red-faced ambassador was visibly shaken.

Next to speak was Nezahualpilli. "Let Lord Ahuitzotl be reminded that one cannot collect tributes from the dead. We do not dispute that Toluca poses a threat to our dominance, but it must be recognized that the payment of tribute also supports our institutions and is equally important to us. Toluca has supplied us abundantly with these in the past. Shall we now cut off the hand which sustains us because it occasionally presents itself as a fist in anger? I agree Toluca must be made an example, but even in making examples, we can temper our vengeance with some common sense. Since we already know we can destroy it, who shall we demonstrate this to? Ourselves? Do not forget that the Tolucans have previously served us well as allies and, while their present conduct requires our castigation, this should mitigate against their outright slaughter. So let us do what is necessary, but no more. Let the Tolucans feel our punishment, but let it be inflicted upon them by a means of alternatives that will be difficult, yet tolerable, for them to accept."

Again a murmer arose in the assembly suggesting that many supported Nezahualpilli's position. The Texcocan's reputation was well demonstrated.

Tizoc was favorably impressed; Ahuitzotl questioned his own course of action; Tecolotl breathed a little easier.

"What might those alternatives be?" Tizoc inquired.

"One that comes to mind is we should demand that their ruler, and all the nobles who stood behind his cause, surrender themselves into captivity to us, upon the choice of seeing their city taken. For them to submit to this would be a greater demonstration of our power than any army in the field."

"And if they refuse? Would we then destroy them?"

"We would then have to, for your word must be kept. But let us be clear on the advantage this proposal offers. The Tolucans know full well they have offended us and are expecting our retribution. Whatever misgivings many of their lords may have had about their venture, they now believe it is too late for amends. Because they see no other option, all are united against us. But with our proposition, they would again be confronted with a choice and their unity will falter. What previously involved them all now only pertains to a select few who will find themselves isolated from their subjects. Those who entered the scheme with reservations will find their apprehensions greatly enhanced. If they now choose to doom their city, we can exercise our punitive measures without constraint."

"I see," said Tizoc. "Place the decision leading to our retribution into their own hands. We acquit ourselves of the consequences because they chose their fate."

"We can blame them for their own folly. It is a favorable situation for us—demonstrating our willingness to avoid any carnage.

Tizoc and Nezahualpilli understood each other. They were men of an intellectual bent who held similar interests on a variety of subjects. Both enjoyed reputations as master builders, although Tizoc's projects expressed more of a religious proclivity and included such works as the Great Temple, the combat stone, and the giant calendar which would be part of the new temple's fixtures, while Nezahualpilli's were primarily civic in nature involving the construction of aquaducts, dams, and palaces. Both men enlarged their royal gardens and boasted of the abundant plantlife contained in them, and the bloom of a newly bred flower would have been a source of pleasure for either of them. Both enjoyed literature, poetry, and the arts, and in their leisure time often surrounded themselves with men and women of erudition which, in great measure, secluded them from the everyday mundane tasks of state administration. Yet there were some differences between them, and of these the major one was that Nezahualpilli was the heir of a city-state which, through the efforts of his scholarly father, Nezahualcoyotl, had acquired renown throughout Anahuac for its learning, cultural refinement, and artistic achievement, while Tizoc was the inheritor of a city-state which was built on, and placed its greatest value on, military prowess. Tizoc may have envied Nezahualpilli.

"What other alternatives might we consider?" Tizoc asked the Texcocan who had clearly taken the center stage in the conference.

"I recognize that this may not be deemed severe enough in relation to their offense against us, but we could allow the Tolucans to atone for their transgression by imposing increased tributes assessed over a specified period of time."

This time the clamor evidenced a strong disapproval.

"Why should they want to do this when it is our tributes that allegedly gave cause for their rebellion in the first place?"

"Facing possible destruction, their resourcefulness may surprise us."

"That may be, but I see little promise in this proposal. It has a lackluster quality about it, one which fails to impress, and there remains the requirement that an example must be made of them. This conjures up expectations for the dramatic. The terms must be sufficiently high to lend an awe-inspiring aspect to our power."

Nezahualpilli knew what Tizoc was saying. The Tolucans had initiated their revolt before the eyes of all the states under Mexica domination, and whatever countermeasures the Mexica applied, they were necessarily before an audience. The object was not merely to humble Toluca, but to assure everyone of an ability to do it with facility. This kind of demonstration required a sensationalism that would leave a lasting impression on an observer.

Tizoc next scanned the hall seeking out anyone who wished to add to the subject at hand and, finding none, brought the issue to a conclusion. "Of the proposals offered," he said, "how many favor Lord Ahuitzotl's course?"

Approximately a third of the assembly voiced its agreement.

"And Lord Nezahualpilli's?"

A resounding majority gave its consent. The Texcocan had won the day.

"I concur," stated Tizoc. Even at this point, he could have rejected the measure, having that authority, but he was convinced it was the most effective approach to the problem. He called out to the ambassador of Toluca, "Tecolotl! Come forward!"

Tecolotl advanced through the ranks of delegates fully conscious of their contemptuous sneers and glares, and when he halted in front of the Revered Speaker, he felt his knees quivering.

"You heard the proceedings," said Tizoc. "Have you anything to tell us on behalf of your king that we might consider?"

"Great Lord," began Tecolotl. "The venture my lord Zozoltin has embarked upon is fixed. His intention is that Toluca be an autonomous state free from the obligations, duties, and tributes imposed by the Triple Alliance. Nothing I can say will detract from this course. He is as resolved in his purpose as you are in yours, Lord Tizoc."

"Does Zozoltin speak for his subjects as well?"

"There is a consensus among our lords that he is pursuing the correct policy."

"In spite of their knowledge that this insurrection can be effectively suppressed by us?"

"It appears they believe otherwise, Lord Tizoc."

His statement provoked an outburst of derision and anger from the floor, and Tizoc had to motion Cihuacoalt into restoring order with his staff.

"Hear me, Tecolotl," continued Tizoc after attaining silence. "These are the words you will carry to Zozoltin. I direct that he and all the lords and ministers favoring his action denounce their cause and surrender themselves to us by appearing in Tenochtitlan on the first day of the month Ochpaniztli. We give him forty days. You may inform him that we will grant many of them the fate of war captives-an honorable sacrificial death. Our advance parties will march on Toluca in a forthnight, not to engage in hostile activity but rather to keep watch on Toluca so that Zozoltin does not secure allies for himself. We shall move against him in force on the day he is to appear here if he chooses war. Should it come to this, his city will suffer accordingly, with its non-combatants, women and children brought under slavery, and its warriors slain. You are dismissed to begin your journey so that you may inform your master of our conditions."

After rendering a respectful bow, a shaken Tecolotl walked out of the hall amidst shouts of anger, abusive remarks, and gestures of scorn. While a harrowing experience for him, the greater obstacle lay ahead. He had to bring unpleasant news to his master, and no minister could predict the reactions of an angry lord.

"If war is offered," Tizoc said after Tecolotl had gone, "we must determine the contingents for it. Ahuitzotl, how large an army can the Tolucans field?"

"Based on our most recent information, we estimate their strength at seven thousand, perhaps as high as eight thousand, but no more."

"Eight thousand! That's more than I would have thought."

"This assumes they will arm everyone of military age. We think these estimates are accurate and take into account the latest population figures we have on them."

"How many shall we sent against them?"

"Our doctrines prescribe an invading force ought to be at twice the strength of a defender's. I see no reason to deviate from this norm."

"Tecolotl spoke of a consensus behind Zozoltin. We may encounter stiff resistance if they are fanatical in their defiance."

"Perhaps, but as Nezahualpilli pointed out, the choice you offered will create divisiveness among them. Many will face us half-heartedly and lack the resolve necessary for victory. Also we do not consider them as well trained or disciplined as our own warriors. Sixteen thousand will be enough."

Tizoc remained skeptical and glanced at Nezahualpilli to see if the Texcocan agreed with the assessment. "That will require five thousand of your Acolhuas, Nezahualpilli," he said. "Is that sufficient?"

"I believe so," replied Nezahualpilli, "if our information is correct, although I contest the assertion about their being less trained or disciplined. They are surely expecting our attack, having set upon their foolish course, and must be passing their days in constant preparation for it."

Ahuitzotl gave Nezahualpilli a scornful look. He did not appreciate being contradicted, especially in military matters in which he regarded himself the expert. "Are you suggesting our surveillance is faulty?" he scowled.

"Not so," Nezahualpilli answered, recognizing he had annoyed the commander and needed to cool his hot head. "I merely emphasize caution. The situation merits our best evaluation."

"And you have it! You forget we also have strong motivations to impose our will on them. With this determination, not even an equal number of them can stand against us."

"I assumed from the start that our forces will prevail." Nezahualpilli replied.

"What of Tlacopan?" Tizoc asked Chimalpopoca. "Do you agree with the allotment of five thousand?"

"I do, Lord Tizoc," declared Chimalpopoca with great confidence. "We border on Toluca and maintain our eyes on it. From the reports my scouts have delivered, I conclude we have little to fear from them."

"Very well, we will accept a contingent of five thousand from each of the alliance cities. The others will be given their designated numbers by Lord Ahuitzotl as soon as he can determine an equitable allocation. Our staffs will work out the details of the move. As for the advance party, a force of two hundred from each alliance city will be adequate."

With the general application of policy on Toluca decided, Tizoc next addressed his chief priests in order to acquire assurances that their proposed action met its most crucial test. "What say you priests?" he said. "Does our enterprise engage a consent from the gods?"

"They will be pleased enough, Lord," affirmed the head priest, "if our oblations invoke their auspices. To make certain, we will offer appropriate sacrifices and conduct ourselves in submissive obedience to them, with the fastings and self-denials, as they command us to do. Our prayers to them will stress the importance of our intentions."

"Yes, do what you must. Take all the precautions demanded for their intercession. While we speak of this, have any prophecies been received in connection with this undertaking?"

"Not by me, Lord Tizoc, but perhaps by my associate who specializes in such matters. He is skilled in concocting the divine potions which induce these visions."

A second priest stepped forward, and as he chanced to look into the monarch's eyes, a sudden shocked expression came over his face that abruptly halted him. Tizoc was startled.

"Is something amiss?" he fretted.

"No! It is nothing, Lord!"

"But I saw..."

"An uncontrolled reflex, Lord!-an effect of the potions we consume. It strikes us momentarily at certain intervals without warning to numb our senses in the manner you have just observed."

"I would not have deemed it any numbing of the senses. It struck me more like a—a revelation."

"So you may have interpreted it, Lord, but I assure you it was an involuntary reaction."

The priest's assertion did little to soothe Tizoc's troubled composition. What he had just witnessed was not a bodily response to drugs, of which he was familiar enough, but a reflex spontaneously initiated by the priest looking at him. The priest saw something, and whatever it was, it impacted as a profound shock. A grim silence hanging over the council told Tizoc that others had also taken note of this exchange and were similarly perplexed by it. Despite his alarm, Tizoc strove to maintain a dignified countenance and avoided further allusion to the incident.

"You are a seer?" he asked the priest.

"I am regarded as such, Lord."

"Have you had any premonitions in connection with our plans?"

'Only one, Lord. A dream came to me in which I perceived the recognizable features of a city I knew to be Toluca. Above it, I saw an eagle in flight during the early dawn and it was approaching its prey, a quail hiding in some bushes. As the eagle was about to strike the quail, it suddenly reversed itself and was instead pursued by the quail, which, in doing so, left the safety of the bushes. While the quail was chasing the eagle, a second, more bolder, eagle swooped down upon it, seized it, and flew away carrying it in its talons. But it was now dusk. The event had taken an entire day."

"That's all? What does it portent?"

"I believe the quail is Zozoltin, for that is the meaning of his name, and that the eagle represents the Mexica."

"It's a sign denoting the tactics we should employ to defeat Zozoltin," Ahuitzotl calmly interjected. "Some of our forces will lure him from his city by feigning a retreat, and when he has exposed himself, our remaining forces will capture him. A familiar battle plan, not even that imaginative."

"This means," Tizoc said with some concern, "that Zozoltin will not surrender to us. The issue will be decided by arms after all."

"So it would seem, Lord Tizoc, and at first I thought the same thing, but..." the priest paused.

"But what, priest?"

"The interpretation is too simple, one might say deceptively simple. We must give it serious consideration if we are to know the true message so we are not misled. For instance, I am not convinced that the turn about by the eagle is intentional, as Lord Ahuitzotl deduces. Nor, for that matter, can it be said that the intervention of the second eagle is a planned maneuver. Also why is a full day spent in a flight that should be of short duration?"

"It appears clear enough," Ahuitzotl pressed on, confident his was the correct explanation. "An entire day will be required to defeat Zozoltin. It is to be a hard fought contest it seems. I would not have expected this of the Tolucans."

"This is distressing," Tizoc soberly reflected. "If we offer additional supplications, would this alter the vision?"

"No, Lord. What I have seen will be. It cannot change."

"Can the priest give us another account of this vision?" Nezahualpilli asked.

"I cannot. I have related the vision faithfully as I saw it, Lord. What is made of it can apply to anyone as well as me. I can explain what the signs symbolize, but I'm not always able to grasp their significance."

"Then of what use are you as a seer?" retorted Tizoc.

"All I can offer is that perhaps if I take more of the divine potions in the coming days, additional information will be revealed to me by Tezcatlipoca–if he wishes me to have it."

"Do that, priest," Tizoc directed, "and if any other revelations come to you, let me know immediately."

Sensing Tizoc's uneasiness, Nezahualpilli again spoke to the priest, "Since you cannot tell us another rendition, would you not agree Lord Ahuitzotl has given us the best interpretation of your vision?"

"It is the most logical," replied the priest.

Try as he might, Tizoc was now unable to concentrate on the issues at hand as his mind remained preoccupied over his initial encounter with the prophetic priest; the more he dwelled on it, the greater became his consternation. His heartbeat began to accelerate and he became physically unsettled. He sensed the perspiration droplets forming on his brow. He determined that he needed to retire to his private quarters where he might find some diversion from his discomfort.

"I had planned to also discuss the Tlappan affair, but it can wait until a later council," he announced. "This meeting is ended. I shall contact you when I wish to take up the subject."

Ahuitzotl could not hide his disappointment. "Why require another recall when we are already here?" he said. "Let us act on Tlappan."

A hushed strain came over the assembly. Tizoc gave Ahuitzotl an angry glance prompting the commander into a hasty retraction. "Your pardon, Lord." he said, "I have erred."

Tizoc did not respond. Instead he motioned for Cihuacoatl to terminate the session and departed with his escorts through the side door leading to his private chamber. This the minister dutifully accomplished and then also left, but several of the lords and officials remained to talk. With this group was Ahuitzotl and Nezahualpilli.

"You go too far, Ahuitzotl," Nezahualpilli advised. "You had no right to question Lord Tizoc's prerogative."

"I recognized it and did recant," Ahuitzotl replied. "So spare my your reprimand."

"Yes, you recanted, but not before we all witnessed your insubordination. You deprecated Lord Tizoc. I can assure you this will not regarded lightly."

"What can he do? He would be lost without me to manage his campaigns, as you well know," answered Ahuitzotl with a smugness that rankled Nezahualpilli. "I appreciated your occasional support for me in there, Nezahualpilli, but you cross me often, and one of these days it will be you who has gone too far. You and I may eventually come to a day of reckoning."

"I do not fear it."

"Perhaps you should. But let's not quibble over this now. We have need of each other. Who will you sent to lead your Acolhuas?"

"I shall command them myself."

"Splendid. I know I can rely on you. It should be a good fight, if we are fortunate enough to have it come to that. Until then, farewell, Nezahualpilli."

"Farewell, Ahuitzotl. May the gods provide for you."

"They will," boasted Ahuitzotl as he walked away in the company of his trusted captain, Tlohtzin.

Nezahualpilli lingered awhile longer to deliberate over his potential adversary. In spite of the threats, he was not particularly upset; he felt that he understood the impetuous Ahuitzotl and could placate his volatile nature if he had to. Indeed he was actually quite fond of him and admired his demonstrated abilities in leadership and tactics, and, for whatever his faults, Ahuitzotl respected sound logic and learning. With these tools as weapons, Nezahualpilli had no need to fear him. No, he was not frightened by Ahuitzotl's words—what alarmed him was the commander's open flaunting of the gods, his brazen flirting with their patience, the temptations, edging near contempt. He was playing a dangerous game with them, and in such contests, the gods would invariably emerge as the victors.

huitzotl and Tlohtzin walked crossed the city's main plaza passing by the stately Temple of Quetzalcoatl, unique in its roundness representing the whirling wind and surmounted by a conical spire. They were proceeding in the direction of a complex of buildings serving as the headquarters for the city's army and situated along the avenue leading west to the Tlacopan causeway about a hundred paces from the serpent headed wall enclosing the square. Both men, however, were oblivious of their surroundings with their thoughts still on the meeting.

"Did you note the priest?" asked Tlohtzin.

"How could I miss it?" said Ahuitzotl. "I was standing only an arm's length from him."

"What do you make of it?"

"Most disturbing. If not for us, certainly for Tizoc. I think he was correct in believing the priest had come upon a revelation. Whatever it may have been, I am convinced Tizoc himself is the key to its proper translation. The priest knew this. It's ludicrous he actually expected us to accept his explanation about it being an involuntary response."

'He needed a hasty retreat from what was an uncomfortable predicament for him."

"Yes, and if it was uncomfortable for him, it must have been something unfavorable about Tizoc. Good reports are eagerly passed on. It's bad ones that present burdens for us. Isn't that so?"

"It is as you say."

"Accepting that it's undesireable, we must try to determine what it could be. What are Tizoc's most apparent shortcomings?"

Tlohtzin stumbled over how to answer. "You have me at a disadvantage, Lord. The Revered Speaker is your brother; were I to speak freely, I would be incurring, ah, let us say, improprieties."

"Forget that," advised Ahuitzotl. "I can assure you whatever you say will hardly come as a surprise."

"Then I will say that Lord Tizoc lacks a strong will. He does not have the resolve to lead our armies in a capacity expected of a ruler. He has great learning and is skilled in running the state, I suppose, but there is something amiss even in that. Indeed, a weakness reveals itself in all his actions. He leans too much on the counsel of others, mainly Lord Nezahualpilli from whom he seeks constant assurances for his own decisions. His leadership is, to put it bluntly, uninspiring."

"You do quite well when barred from restrictions, Tlohtzin. Certainly he has his faults as a commander. We saw ample evidence of this in Metztitlan. The priest's vision was clearly of a military nature, so we can assume what he perceived in Tizoc involved a connection with the army-perhaps his personal command of it."

"Tizoc did not say he would command it. He has you for that."

"True, but for a nearby operation as Toluca, I suspect that he will. The priest said he did not know if the eagle's turnabout and ensuing flight was intentional. Indeed, I now believe it was not."

"I suspect what you are thinking, Lord, but I dare not say it."

"I shall say it for you. The priest deceived us. The eagle does not represent the Mexica, but rather Tizoc himself. He will attack Zozoltin and then flee from the battlefield, or be forced into a retreat-our remaining units will defeat the Tolucans for him. By the gods, that is it! That's what the priest saw!"

Tlohtzin was alarmed, not so much over this interpretation of the vision as by Ahuitzotl's audacity in relating it.

"You dare to say this about the Revered Speaker?"

"Do you think I'm wrong? It fits together. What else could shock the priest so?"

"You cannot presume this, Lord Ahuitzotl. It's treasonous to even think this of the Revered Speaker, much less speak of it."

Ahuitzotl paid no attention to Tlohtzin; his smirk indicated that he was gloating over what he saw as a brilliant feat of mental cognition. By this time they had reached the headquarters and no reply awaited Tlohtzin as they parted for their own duty chambers. Ahuitzotl was still grinning when he entered and was met by his drillmaster.

"We have a new man assigned to us, Lord. I think you should see him."

"What for? It's not my habit to see newcomers."

"This man is special, Lord."

"In what respect?"

"He comes to us from the royal palace, with instructions from the Revered Speaker himself."

"From the palace you say? What is his name?"

"Motecuhzoma Xocoyotzin, Lord. A royal prince."

Ahuitzotl paused, straining to associate the name with whatever feeble recollection he possessed of him. "Ah, yes," he said, "the son of my brother, Axayacatl. I remember him as a bright-eyed lad, curious about many things and asking frequent questions. He seemed the studious sort to me-very serious-but that was long ago. You say there are instructions?"

"Delivered by the court's official courier, Lord. The Revered Speaker informs us that Motecuhzoma is to be prepared for top-level commands in the shortest possible time allowing for his mastery of the tasks given him. He is to begin at the squadron chief level, a lower position not deemed suitable to his talents. Despite his ancestry, he should be granted no special favors and is to perform his duties, and be rated in these, as anyone else appointed or promoted to such assignments. He expects you to give this your personal attention and to insure Motecuhzoma's advancement based on your assessment of his capabilities."

"What regard for this Motecuhzoma!" Ahuitzotl exclaimed. "A squadron chief commands two hundred, sometimes more, men-no easy assignment for a neophyte, and not necessarily fair to the warriors under him. But Lord Tizoc has spoken, and our duty is to comply. Send him in."

Accordingly, the drillmaster departed and, before Ahuitzotl had enough time trying to piece together any impressions of Tizoc's directive, he returned with the youngster and left him standing alone in front of his commander.

What Ahuitzotl noticed first was his thin features. He was tall and lean, taller than Ahuitzotl himself by at least half a head. His face was more elongated than was typical of the family members comprising the lordship over the Mexica-Tenocha, and he wore his hair short, covering only part of his ears. He did not bear much resemblance to his illustrious father, Ahuitzotl thought, and looked considerably different from the boy he remembered, but his eyes were very expressive and at the moment reflected a calm demeanor. An authoritative countenance embodied his presence: this would assist him in his first command.

"So you left us as a boy and have returned a man," Ahuitzotl finally spoke. "You were at the school in Calixtlahuaca?"

"For the last seven years, Lord." Motecuhzoma answered, his voice reflecting an inner confidence.

"The school of the nobility. Your father gave it that distinction. Did you know that?"

"I have heard it mentioned, Lord."

"Before his time, nobles sent their sons to the local schools in each city. Things were more informal then—we did not have the separation between those who ruled and those who obeyed as we have now. It seems the creation of an empire state has also led to a permanent ruling class which no longer thinks it proper or dignified to associate with the commoners, whom many lords now even hold in contempt."

"You sound as though you regretted it," Motecuhzoma could not resist saying.

"When we are in official contact, as presently, Motecuhzoma, you will not speak unless directed to do so," Ahuitzotl reproached him, but his acerbity quickly dissipated and he went on. "I was merely thinking aloud—not illiciting a response. But since you asked, I may as well tell you. I would not say I regret the order we have carved out for ourselves. No, that would be rash; after all, I have benefited from it as much as anyone-as you have. Still, there are limitations to it. I see it every day in our army, and it becomes particularly evident when we are at war. We have much talent out there among the ranks, and to preclude it from being exercised by denying it access to upper administrative, political, and military posts on the basis of class distinction may be, I think, self-defeating for us. What's your opinion on this?"

"To regulate our realm requires considerable loyalty from these posts," Motecuhzoma replied, happy that he was afforded a chance to state his view. "One questions whether such allegiance would be forthcoming if filling these positions were not based on elite clan lines and family ties."

Ahuitzotl was impressed with this and instantly recognized Motecuhzoma was not the ordinary person to come to him.

"You don't think this loyalty can be obtained from men who fill such posts based upon merit?"

"No," Motecuhzoma hesitated as if wrestling with his intellect. "Merit can be bound by various judgments. Were these posts filled by men who held themselves deserving of them and competed for them, many would not tolerate the performance of those deemed of lesser capability and could make their duties difficult for them. Their loyalty would be to themselves, not the Revered Speaker. We would face endless squabbles-so I believe."

"What you say is that it's better to sacrifice expediency and possible greater efficiency for the sake of stability. It makes sense, especially when you consider the current Tolucan rebellion. No matter, I've gotten off my intent in seeing you. The Revered Speaker has great expectations from you. I am directed to assign you to a squadron command. I must confess that while I had reservations about this initially, I now think this is indeed the proper charge for you. How do you feel about leading a unit of that size?"

"I see it as a challenge, Lord," replied Motecuhzoma eagerly.

"How like a school indoctrinated response. You will find it considerably different here than in school, Motecuhzoma. Once in command, you are expected to know what to do, not to learn. You have a strong presence about you-make use of this by approaching your work with confidence. Be forceful and direct when issuing orders to your warriors. They are inclined to naturally follow the leader they believe knows what he is doing-especially in battle. You come to us at an opportune time and may find yourself leading your unit into combat in in but forty days. We will be engaging the Tolucans-worthy of the challenge you seek. Does that prospect alarm you?"

"No, Lord," Motecuhzoma calmly answered, "I consider it fortuitous."

"Do you?" Ahuitzotl deemed the remark conceited. "You will discover that the first time into battle as a commander will tax your ability to the utmost. Now as to your station. You are to head the Mazatl squadron, in the Tlatelolco section. I will send a messenger to your division chief so he can expect you. Will you be residing in the royal palace?"

"I believe so. I am also to work an apprenticeship under one of the court ministers."

"Then we ought to see each other at times. I now entrust you to my drillmaster. He will give you further guidance."

With their meeting thus terminated, Motecuhzoma left the chamber while Ahuitzotl remained to deliberate over their encounter. His disposition was sober and he speculated over why Tizoc would pull Motecuhzoma out of school now. Certainly Motecuhzoma gave a good account of himself and should manage his squadron well enough, but is this the motivation behind his accelerated advancement? Often the station one occupies when great events are in the offering does more to enhance a career than any individual action one takes. Clearly Motecuhzoma was provided with a good position; what he makes of it will depend largely on his own doing and the benevolence of the gods. But there is the stamp of Tizoc's handiwork present. What could he be planning?

VI

Tizoc sat alone brooding in his chamber. He had dismissed his escorts after he left the conference, expressing a wish to be by himself. Solitude eased his troubled soul, and in the recent months he sought it out more than had been his usual habit. Many moods flashed through him, ranging from extreme vexation when he recalled Ahuitzotl's insubordination and how he failed to take forceful action in castigating him to abject fear at the recollection of the terror in the priest's eyes when he gazed upon him. While he so reflected, Tlalalca entered from behind a curtained doorway carrying a tray of various food items, mainly a selection of beans, and small slices of deer meat and rabbit.

"You are troubled again, Tizoc," she said caringly. "Forgive my intrusion. I thought you might be hungry, but if you want to be by yourself, I shall leave."

"No, Tlalalca," answered Tizoc, pleased at seeing the food and in need to discuss his torment. "Stay. I am spending too much time by myself lately, and although I find it necessary, I know there are risks in this."

"You become so quiet when you are disturbed. Would it not be better to speak about it?"

"As usual, I have your concern to comfort me when despondent–that is precious to me and does much to console me. You are very dear to me, Tlalalca; if I am reluctant to speak of the things troubling me, it's to spare you from the same problems facing me."

His words penetrated Tlalalca to the heart, for she loved him deeply, extending her complete devotion to his care, and she cherished those sentiments that affirmed his own affection for her, even if voiced under duress.

"Oh, Tizoc, if I'm to share your pleasures, why should this preclude my sharing your pain? It's not easy for me to see you so distressed, and not to know the source of your worry makes it even worse. In trying to spare me your problems, you instill more worries in me."

Tizoc gazed into her eyes, fully grasping the anguish she felt and reminded of the selfishness of his disquietude.

"Ah, Tlalalca," Tizoc began, shaking his head slowly and then staring into empty space while his hands cupped his chin. "They are looking for the warrior-king incarnate to lead them to glorious conquests and to bring in captives by the thousands for sacrifice. This is our divine mission-what the gods created us for and gave us abundance for. In my coronation oath I swore to extend our realm by the shedding of our blood so our gods would be propitiated into directing us to even further glories. It's what my grandfather bequeathed to us and what my brother Axayacatl carried to absurd proportions. They look upon me to continue this exercise in lunacy,-that is what it surely must be-so they can boast of their honors while we are much despised by our neighbors, distrusted by our so-called friends, and feared by our enemies. Where is the virtue in all this?"

"Who are they, My Lord?"

"Everyone. The commanders. The priests. The adjudicators. All want war. I am endangering our existence by not securing enough captives to satisfy our voracious gods. Certain priests have been particularly outspoken in their criticism—and look at all the captives we have working on the Great Temple. It amazes me how they can say we are in want of them. Their demands weigh heavily on me, Tlalalca. I have no love for battle. There is much I want to build. I prefer expending my energy on this instead of leading our warriors in these destructive activities they clamor for."

"Destructive? Surely you did not mean this. Are not the priests correct when they say our world is sustained for us by the blood of captives taken in war?"

"I was trained in the priesthood myself, and once even sought to become one, had not Axayacatl's untimely death thrust me upon this throne. The priests themselves establish the quota on the numbers that are sacrificed. These do not have to be increased merely because our conquests are increased. If this were so, we would certainly set a horrid pattern for ourselves. Obviously we acquire no friends with these practices. We can be benefited more by using the captives as I am doing—would the gods resent us building their temples? We've had no signs of their displeasure. Why should they want more victims when they are satisfied?"

"My poor Tizoc. Is there nobody to share your views?"

"No, I am alone on that," Tizoc replied and then, after reconsideration, added, "Perhaps Nezahualpilli does. I think he also tires of our bloodthirsty routine, but aside from him, there are no others."

Tlalalca, by training and inclination motivated to her husband's well-being, began to massage Tizoc about the neck and back in an effort to alleviate his discomfort.

"My conduct is fraudulent," continued Tizoc. "How can I, with my dislike for war, rule over the most martial people in Anahuac? Great Huitzilopochtli instructed our ancestors to keep him and his consorts well nourished. That is our reason for being, yet all my convictions run contrary to this purpose. Am I wrong?"

"No, my Lord," Tlalalca consoled him. "As you said, the gods are not displeased with you. It does not matter what the others say."

"If only my chief minister would speak these words. And then there is my commander-in-chief-my most persistant aggravation. He has a way of belittling me. Even when I know it's not intentional, his actions and ill-chosen words have a humiliating aspect about them that are injurious to me."

"Ahuitzotl?"

"Yes, my brother. He must always dominate the scene. Whether on the battlefield or in my court, he must prevail over everyone else. He has an annoying talent for coming out the master of a situation-people are drawn to him for advice and purpose. It rankles me beyond belief."

"You should be above jealousy, Tizoc. You are more honorable than he could ever be."

"You think it is jealousy?" Tizoc lashed at her. "No, Tlalalca, I say to you it is not. It's much worse-it is fear. He intimidates me."

Tlalalca shrank back, as she had never seen Tizoc exhibit such anger and was startled by it, and he, sensing her alarm, felt compelled to make amends.

"I meant no harm, Tlalalca. It's precisely for these reasons I refrain from revealing my inner conflicts to anyone, lest I be misunderstood. I'm not angry with you, but at my own inability to successfully cope with this. I, as Revered Speaker, should put him in his place whenever he makes a display of his arrogance, but I'm unable to. My mind does not think fast enough as it happens-only afterwards does the reply I should have made come to me. I find myself endlessly humiliated by him. Rightly or wrongly, I magnify my injury when I'm around him so that I cannot confront him with a composed frame of mind. It's as if his very presence is an impediment to me."

"You are too hard on yourself, Tizoc. These fears you have of Ahuitzotl are not baseless. I share your apprehensions."

"You fear him?"

"I sense an evilness about him. I feel he means to harm you—it frightens me."

"Do me harm? Come now, Tlalalca. He may dislike me, but he knows that to wish malice upon the Revered Speaker is blasphemous. He cannot hide such profanity from the gods and would not risk invoking their anger. No, I need not fear bodily harm from him—he would not dare touch me!-it's his derogatory insinuations I fear."

"But if that's what you think, why concern yourself? Words cannot hurt you."

"You're wrong. They can be more damaging and painful than any wound inflicted by arms."

"He is ambitious and young, and you are also young. Am I to believe that he will be content to spend his lifetime as your subordinate?"

"He would not incur the wrath of the gods upon his head."

"He fears nothing. Why should that constrain him?"

Tizoc was silent. Until this moment it had never occasioned for him to consider that he faced any actual physical threat from his brother, in spite of all the deprecation he endured from him. Now this perception was shattered, and its potentiality immersed him in most sobering deliberation. Still he was reluctant to accept this.

"No," Tizoc affirmed, "Only a fool does not dread the gods."

"Perhaps he is a fool."

"Why do you tell me this?" Tizoc again raised his voice. "It's as if I were not afflicted with enough adversity that you should have to add to it."

Tlalalca was astounded that she should be reproached for cautioning Tizoc on what she felt was in his best interest. "But...but I only wished to alert you," she told him. "It's my concern for you that prompted me to say this."

"It has compounded my problem."

"I meant to help you," she lamented, "and I thought you would appreciate it. I am dismayed that you do not."

Tizoc's irritation was mollified by her apparent dejection. "Forgive me, Tlalalca," he was moved to say, "I am such an ingrate. Perhaps I underestimate my brother's aspirations. It's just that this comes to me as an added blow to the one I received in today's assembly. This has not been a good day for me."

At first, Tlalalca was averse to inquiring into the matter as she was no longer confident if she was of any assistance, but then her inquisitive nature demanded an answer.

"What happened?" she asked.

"The priest!" Tizoc trembled as the encounter flashed across his mind again. "I asked him if any prognostications concerning our Toluca operation had been imparted. As he stepped forward to reply, he looked at me and was suddenly overcome with a countenance of abject fright. His panic braught him to a halt. You should have those eyes! Bone chilling they were-as though he gazed upon cruel death. He soon recovered from his paralysis, but too late. Its damage was done. Nothing said in conciliation afterward could have erased the horrifying impression dealt me."

"What did he say?" a tense Tlalalca asked.

"That he was siezed by-by an uncontrolled reflex induced by the potions he drank."

"It's possible. The juices of the ololiuhqui plant, which the priests drink to attain their visions, have such an effect. I learned this when I served the goddess, Tlazolteotl."

"This was different. I know about the divine potions. No drug could have struck him with such immediacy. His alarm was spawned by something he saw-in me!"

"Tizoc, do not frighten me so."

"It's true, I tell you. The face of death could not have terrified him more."

Tlalalca was at a loss for words. His mere description of the encounter infused her with dread-to have actually undergone it, as Tizoc did, and worse, been the object of it, as Tizoc was, would have unnerved her completely. Yet her instincts drove her to allay his fears.

"Perhaps you misread it," she said. "Priests are known to exaggerate. They are a pretentious lot."

"Their interpretations are not subject to our conjecture. They voice the words of the gods."

"It's not the words they receive I dispute, but rather the manner in which they relate them to you. Don't you suspect there is some effort applied in presenting them more dramatically than is necessary?"

"I do not."

"It seems my attempts to alleviate your fears are in vain," retorted Tlalalca in frustration. "I am trying to comfort you and you thwart me at every turn. Must you be so obstinate?"

Tizoc noticed that she was weeping, a sight moving him to pity. "Dear Tlalalca," he said, "I am so callous. Please understand. How can I be master of our realm if I cannot even triumph over my own adversities?"

"There's no disgrace, even for a Revered Speaker, to ask for help when it is needed."

"Privately we know this, but it is a public Revered Speaker who rules. He cannot be with such imperfections."

"If the actions of the priest caused you this distress, why not call him in here and speak to him alone about it. Get a further clarification."

"Protocol will not permit it. The priests are granted their immunity."

"Then there's no help there, but as for your brother, I believe I can learn his intentions concerning you. It's said that he is enraptured with one of your courtly ladies-Pelaxilla. Perhaps through her we can discover what he hides within himself."

"How like him to tamper with my own women-another show of contempt for me! Pelaxilla? The little charmer?"

"You have too many mistresses."

"I'm too often with you to notice the others. She can help us, you say?"

"What man can resist the charms of a woman he loves? Xochiquetzal has given us a curious power in this respect; were a woman inclined to manipulate her lover, she certainly would succeed at it."

"What do you expect Pelaxilla to learn?"

"Ahuitzotl's true regard for you. Whether he schemes against you, or contrives disloyalty among our lords, or encourages disobediance. If he seeks your throne. There's much that could be learned."

"You think the unthinkable," Tizoc rebuked her.

"Because I care for you. If you will not think of these things, I must do it for you."

"By the gods!" groaned Tizoc. "Has it come to this, that I should harbor such fears. If indeed these things are learned, what will I do then?"

Tlalalca was amazed at his timorousness and wondered how she had failed to notice it previously. "Why, you bring him before the Tlacxitlan, the tribunal for the nobles," she said, "with charges of treason."

Tizoc studied the prospect at length, viewing it more as an imposition upon himself than a justifiable cause on which to prosecute Ahuitzotl. Then he gave her his consent. "Very well," he said, "find out what you can. I shall decide what steps to take once I see the kind of information we will get."

By now Tizoc had sufficiently recovered from his earlier despair to turn his attention on the amatory sensations Tlalalca so readily aroused in him. As he caressed her, smelled her exotic perfumes, and felt the soft brushes of her raven hair on his flesh, fire flared in his loins and overwhelmed him with a passion to possess her. He removed her clothing with an adeptness acquired from practice and smothered her body lavishly with kisses and strokes. Then he slipped off his own attire and the two lay interlocked in erotic embrace upon the many layers of matting. While he expended himself in his ardor, Tlalalca gazed blankly at the ceiling and was, for the first time in her memory, unmoved by Tizoc's efforts. She uncovered much from her talk with him and questioned if she ever had really ever known him, and whatever else she may have thought of him, there was one thing she came to realize: he was somehow diminished in her eyes.

VII

Pelaxilla stood nervously and alone before Tlalalca and Xoyo. She had been earlier summoned by the empress and was now obediently in her presence expecting the worst that could befall anyone who evoked her displeasure. Her moment had come, fretted Pelaxilla; she was about to receive sentence that she would suffer expulsion from the court. It meant she would probably return to the city of her parents and live with them in utter disgrace. She was but a child of nine years when she was taken from them, upon the recommendation of a high priestess who, noticing her and taking a liking to her, wanted her for servitude to the goddess Coatlicue. It was the Revered Speaker Axayacatl who, also drawn to her, removed her from the temple and brought her into the royal house-being herself the daughter of nobility made this transition simple-to serve as a future concubine and she became a mistress of Tizoc when he acceded to the throne. Her seven years in the court had been an enriching experience, rewarding and enjoyable, and she knew that she would never be able to readjust to the mundane existence facing her in the place of her childhood. Perhaps, if the empress chose to be kind, she would be transferred back to one of the many temples to again be trained in the duties of a priestess. This was preferable. She could then stay in Tenochtitlan and spare her parents the humiliation they surely would suffer from their peers over having a daughter evicted from the Revered Speaker's palace.

Tlalalca was seated in her royal chair, appearing altogether elegant in her attire and tenor, while Xoyo stood next to her unsmiling as was her usual comportment.

"So, my dear," began Tlalalca in a most cheerful tone, "How are you today?"

"Uh, well enough I suppose, my Lady," answered Pelaxilla.

"Why, child, you are horribly tense. One so young should not be burdened with such stress-it will untimely age you and detract from your beauty. And there's no reason for it. I do not intend to upbraid you. I called for you because I need your help, dear."

"My help?" Pelaxilla was bewildered. "You are not angry with me?"

"Of course not. How could you believe such a thing?" Tlalalca smiled brightly and glanced at Xoyo who remained stone-faced.

"I was told I had offended my lady."

"You did," Tlalalca informed her, "but that was the other day. Now I give you a chance to redeem your transgressions. I do not frequently render such clemency and strongly urge you to take advantage of it."

"I will, my Lady," replied Pelaxilla greatly relieved.

"Wonderful. Now as to my reasons for having summoned you. We already know your sentiments for our kinsman, Lord Ahuitzotl, but tell me, dear, how does he feel about you?"

"Oh, he is quite seriously in love with me-I have no doubt."

"My, are you that certain about it?"

"Yes, my Lady. He has told me this often enough, and I can see it in his eyes. The signs are unmistakable."

"How sweet. I presume he would do whatever you asked then."

"I believe so," Pelaxilla replied while becoming suspicious of Tlalalca's purpose.

"Now listen to me, Pelaxilla," said Tlalalca, "Whether you have knowledge of the things I tell you is of no consequence to me, but you must accept I have ample basis for saying it, else I should not trouble myself with this affair at all. I must add what I say is of a private nature and is not to be discussed with anyone. Is this understood?"

"Yes, my Lady," answered Pelaxilla, sensing a strain in her intuition over what would follow.

"We have sufficient cause to believe that the long-standing animosity between Lord Ahuitzotl and my Lord Tizoc has reached a point where we must give it serious attention. Truthfully, we should have anticipated this. We all remember his bitterness when the interclan council named Lord Tizoc as ruler. That this hostility should attain a new and dangerous direction seems natural enough considering the circumstances."

Tlalalca gave herself a momentary respite in order to assess Pelaxilla's reaction to her allegations; she deemed her expression of disbelief to be sincere. "Does this surprise you, dear?" she asked.

"Why yes, my Lady. I would never have guessed it."

"Really? Ahuitzotl does not speak to you about Lord Tizoc?"

"Yes, he does," admitted Pelaxilla, "but nothing that's bad. I have never heard him speak words I would consider disreputable, and I could not conclude this from his behavior."

"It need not be obvious, dear. There are contrived actions which, while not in themselves a direct confrontation, speak of a derogatory intention-a surliness of manner for example. It does not have to be an open declaration, but in its subtleness still is damaging. Bearing this in mind, do you still believe Ahuitzotl to be innocent of any malicious intent?"

"I do, my Lady."

"That is puzzling," said Tlalalca, not satisfied with what she was hearing, "It contravenes evidence we have received from other sources. Indeed some actually assert that he-the gods forgive my saying it!-schemes to overthrow Lord Tizoc and rule in his place."

"It cannot be true!" exclaimed Pelaxilla, shocked at hearing this. "These are flagrant lies! Ahuitzotl honors Lord Tizoc. He could never be involved in anything so treacherous."

"Has he ever discussed his ambitions with you?"

"No, my Lady."

"I thought not. Since you find this so incredulous, let me ask if he's ever spoken anything political in nature with you?"

"No, there's been no occasion to."

"It's quite apparent, my dear, that you are as much in the dark about this as I am—even more so as you do not receive the reports that come to me-which brings us to the reason I require your assistance. You will find out for me if there is any factual basis to the allegations we have heard. I want to know what he conspires, if anything, against Lord Tizoc."

"You want that I should be an informant on the man I love?" Pelaxilla replied indignantly, announcing her obvious aversion.

"You needn't make it sound so despicable, child. You are not the first person to be placed in such a predicament, I'm sure. And really, dear, would you not do as your empress asked?"

"But it's unfair to me. Why not get one of the other ladies to do this?" squirmed Pelaxilla in her attempt to extricate herself from her quandary.

"Don't be naive, child!" snapped Tlalalca, "And who else should I get? It is precisely because he loves you that only you will do. He trusts you and will confide in you what he would never impart on anyone else. So let us cease this foolishness and do what is required."

"But if he hasn't mentioned such things before, why should he start now?"

"Why, you'll have to be very convincing, won't you? Surely you need no lessons in directing your conversations toward the objectives we seek. I'm certain you will manage it nicely."

"It's so devious," Pelaxilla moaned.

"Indeed, child, you do try my patience!" Tlalalca retorted so angrily she startled Pelaxilla. "I do not see myself offering you an alternative. If you will not cooperate, I shall this very day address your further presence in our court with Lord Tizoc. I can guarantee he will not be kind towards you."

"No! Please don't!" Pelaxilla pleaded as the fear of expulsion hounded her again.

"Then you agree to help us?"

"It seems I must, my Lady," Pelaxilla frowned in resignation, "I am coerced into this."

"The audacity!" fumed Tlalalca. "Did you hear that, Xoyo? You are an impertinent young lady! If it displeases you so much to do something for your empress, then let us forget all that's been said. I will be able to get the information I need-perhaps not as quickly, although I shall still get it-but I will not have a minor palace courtesan insult me!"

Pelaxilla shook with fright, never having previously seen the empress so offended or been so angrily rebuked by her. Tlalalca, perceiving her severe duress, decided to aggravate her tribulations. "We have nothing more to discuss," she declared, "so leave me now! Begone! I do not wish to see you again and will arrange that I do not!"

Completely shattered now, Pelaxilla dropped to her knees sobbing and entreated for Tlalalca's pardon. "Forgive me, my Lady," she blurted out in her tears. "I beg you relent your severity. It is out of fear that I expressed a reluctance to do as you asked-not because I want to displease you."

Tlalalca was both astonished and gratified by her effectiveness. "Out of fear?" she said. "From what?"

"I'm afraid I will lose his love for me if he ever found out what I was doing," lamented Pelaxilla, still trembling. "I could not bear that. And what will happen if what I discover offends Lord Tizoc? How could I live with myself if I brought harm to him?"

Her sentiment touched Tlalalca who had failed to grasp the extent of Pelaxilla's devotion, and she pondered if perhaps she had been too adamant in her demands. "This is not meant to bring punishment on anyone," she said, "but to learn what I should caution Lord Tizoc against. Why, you may not discover anything at all. Our reports could well be false. Lord Ahuitzotl could be entirely guiltless of any conduct prejudicial to the Revered Speaker. But if not, it would indeed be reprehensible and we would be obligated to inform Lord Tizoc of it. Regardless, I give you my personal assurance that no harm will come him."

Pelaxilla was not comforted by this. Her impulse was to press for more guarantees on Ahuitzotl's safety, but her previous fearful encounter, combined with her years of training in the courtesies, made her aware of its imprudence. She felt herself persecuted to the extreme and now longed only to be away from Tlalalca's dominating presence.

"I hope you can sympathize with my necessity for doing this," Tlalalca continued. "Had these reports not come to us, there would be no need for this intrigue. But we would be remiss if we did not determine their accuracy. We owe that much to the Revered Speaker, don't you think?"

"Yes, my Lady."

"Then I shall depend on you. Be skillful, my dear. Try not to extract everything out of him in one meeting and give yourself time so it will all seem natural enough. Convince him you wish to share in his aspirations. That should do it."

"I will do my best, my Lady."

"Very well, I shall call on you again. I hope our next session will be more rewarding. You may go now, dear."

Pelaxilla, still teary-eyed, stood back up and rendered a small but respectful bow and then hurriedly left the chamber while Tlalalca, although sensing a degree of compassion for Pelaxilla's dilemma, nevertheless beamed over her success. Her smile vanished in an instant when she noted the hard, penetrating gaze of Xoyo.

"Why do you look at me like that?" she demanded to know.

"I fear for my lady if she did not tell the truth," answered the old woman.

"It should not concern you."

"It does when I am a party to it, and so you have made me by requiring my presence here, empress."

"You stood quiet. Your conscience should be clear."

"You said much to Pelaxilla that I know was false. She trusts you and yet you will deceive her. I shall remain silent on this out of my loyalty to you, my Lady, but do not tell me that my conscience should be clear."

"There is a bigger issue at stake here than the sensitivities of a mere child, Xoyo-I'll thank you not to lose sight of that. Whatever I will do requires no apology. It is Tizoc's safety I am speaking of. That in itself should mitigate any trespasses you adjudge me of."

"It is not I who judges you, my Lady. The goddess Tlazolteotl heard what you said and knows what you will do. She will decide if your actions deserve mitigation. All my life I have been taught to be truthful lest I offend her. I was told she could afflict us with unspeakable suffering if we made false statements or contrived false purposes. I never imagined we could predispose her into agreeing that our misdeeds can be justified."

Tlalalca grew worried. What Xoyo had stated was consistent with her own convictions and she could not recall a previous circumstance in which she had deliberately misrepresented her intentions. Yet now, with Pelaxilla, she set upon such a direction, and she had no confidence her path was not fraught with hazards. Still, she strongly felt her cause was just and that she could not be faulted for pursuing it. However, there remained an element of concern. Who could say for certain what thoughts possessed the gods?

"We must see," Tlalalca concluded. "I cannot undo what I have already begun. My intentions are beneficent, and Tlazelteotl, in her wisdom, will know this. She will not hold this against me."

Xoyo did not answer. She sensed Tlalalca's disquietude and correctly deduced the empress preferred to dwell on her possible transgressions in silence rather than having attention drawn to these and thereby affirming them as such. Xoyo knew her lady well.

VIII

In his capacity as the Tlacatecuhtli, supreme commander of the Mexica and their allies, Ahuitzotl made it a point to personally oversee those operations viewed as unusual or daring in scope or as a prelude to greater, more promising undertakings. In keeping with this practice, he held a conference with his squadron chiefs of the advance party contingents which had now arrived and were being assembled in Tenochtitlan. With him in the headquarters was Tlohtzin, second in command and his principal assistant, who attentively listened as he imparted his conception of the enterprise.

"It must be understood," Ahuitzotl emphasized, "that you are not to engage the Tolucans in combat; you have neither the strength, nor is that the purpose of your mission. Your duty is to prevent messengers or dispatchers of any kind, be it ambassadors or mere peasant, from making contact with cities which might support them. Control all access from Toluca through constant patrols by day and night. If you spot anyone, he must be turned back. You will be quartered and provisioned in the villages around Toluca. The local chiefs have received their instructions and will arrange for this. Maintain a constant vigilance-make your assignments accordingly-until you are met by our forces, or until you are given orders suspending the operation. Do you have any questions?"

"What if they send out their envoys under escorts that clearly outnumber our patrols?" asked one of the chieftains.

"In such case, send a messenger to where your remaining units are stationed. You will be thinly scattered, but if enough warriors can be gathered, try to intercept them. While waiting for these reinforcements, follow them, marking the trail, to see where they go. If this will not work merely trail them and send a messenger to us."

"Can't we marshall enough warriors from the local chiefs to counter them?" asked another.

"That would not be advisable. For one thing, their loyalty is suspect, being Matlazincas as are the Tolucans. While we may, through their fear of us, badger them into quartering us, to get them to fight for us is another matter. Also, by the time a muster is completed, the envoys would have a substantial lead on you-better to merely scout them out under such conditions. I do not expect the Tolucans to make use of escorts except as a deceptive move, so be wary of that."

Having said what was deemed important, Ahuitzotl dispensed with added details to further encumber his squadron chieftains and dismissed them so they could make their preparation. They assumed their places among warriors massed in formations within the spacious confines between the quadrangle of buildings constituting Tenochtitlan's major military facilities where visiting soldiers were garrisoned. Ahuitzotl and Tlohtzin watched from the command post doorway as the young captains addressed their warriors and disseminated the information they had just received.

"I tell you, Tlohtzin," commented Ahuitzotl who viewed the proceedings with feelings of immense satisfaction, "There's an excitement surrounding all aspects of war I find intoxicating. The organization of men to serve a common purpose, unit emblems rising above the ranks, the exertion of concentrated action, the thrill and confusion of heated battle-I was born for this."

"War is a divine mission ordained to us by Huitzilopochtli, Lord. I see it as a sacred duty, no more, no less."

"It's much more. We were blessed when Huitzilopochtli made us the instrument of his divine will. No people so honored could have served him more competently and with such zeal. It's no accident that we were chosen to maintain life for the gods-Huitzilopochtli knew what he was doing. I regard it as the highest tribute to be his emissary in achieving this end."

"We know each other well, Lord, but you often confound me. You are Huitzilopochtli's high priest and are surely devoted to him, yet you have never displayed the total commitment I see in the other priests. To be truthful, I believed you more pragmatic and lacking the same religious fervor."

"I make an exception for Huitzilopochtli. He is worthy of my esteem."

"You confirm my point. There is a perverse side to your piety. The other priests would say you are sacrilegious in making yourself the arbiter of which god merits your oblations. You honor the gods differently, based upon the degree in which they support your purposes, as if you bargained with them. The others honor them to assure their dominion over us. They fear the gods; one suspects you do not."

"You're quite wrong, Tlohtzin. It is folly not to fear them. They can bring misfortunes on those who offend them, and I assure you I stand in awe of them as much as anyone."

Tlohtzin's skepticism hid an underlying apprehensiveness. He gave Ahuitzotl a leery glance, not pursuaded by his declaration, and was about to add something when he was distracted by a jaguar clad figure advancing across the quadrangle. "Is this our chief minister Cihuacoatl who approaches us?" he said. "He rarely comes here."

"There's an urgency in his pace." Auitzotl noted, "I'd best see to him."

Accordingly, Ahuitzotl left his vice-commander, not entirely displeased over the minister's timely arrival as he had no eagerness to defend his views on devoutness, and walked out to meet his visitor. "Welcome, Cihuacoatl," he greeted him, "How are you today?"

"I have been better. These are not the best of times, Lord. The burden of my office is most preponderant and affects my constitution. A gloominess abounds me, in spirit as well as body."

"Come into my quarters so we can discuss it. Dark chambers are appropriate for dark dispositions, not so?"

A rough grump acknowledged the minister's assent and both men entered the dimly lit room and sat on benches in its center, pausing to relish the interior coolness afforded by thick walls shielding them from the day's glaring sun.

"So, these are not the best of times," Ahuitzotl spoke first. "Your enlightenment does not surprise me, Cihuacoatl. I've said this often enough myself."

"It's not that I've disagreed with the assessment, Lord, but that my deference to my duties as chief minister prevented me from expressing such sentiments."

"Ah yes, the minister's loyalty must be beyond reproach."

"It is essential to the office."

"Even if false?"

"Not false, Lord, but tempered by other considerations seen as more important."

"Such as?"

"Such as," Cihuacoatl glared at Ahuitzotl with penetrating eyes, "the greater glory and prestige of the realm."

Ahuitzotl's countenance turned grim; he met the minister's eyes with equal concentration. "Then you admit we have suffered in this regard," he said.

"More than you would believe, Lord. The reports come to me daily. You think Toluca is the only city in rebellion? It's the only one to have openly defied us, but there are vaccilations and grumblings in numerous other cities now. Chiapa and Xiquipilco are flagrantly reducing their tributes, proclaiming their insolence in this fashion. The Tlappanecs are known to steal produce from our merchants and harass them into taking lengthy detours around their region, at much inconvenience to us. These incidents have multiplied alarmingly as of late."

"So it's come to this-that they now even dare to interfere with the sanctities guaranteed by our treaties."

"They dare because they believe we no longer possess the will to exercise our power. Indeed, they may actually think us incapable of it now. What other explanation can there be? These offenses were inconceivable only two years ago. Would the great Motecuhzoma have stood for such belligerence? Or even Axayacatl? Under their strong leadership no people would have dared to think, let alone attempt, such actions."

"This demonstrates the importance of making an example of Toluca. And I promise you, Cihuacoatl, if it comes to war with Zozoltin, I shall impart a lesson on him such as has never been seen in Anahuac. Even the desolation of Teotihuacan will appear opulent in comparison."

"I do not think so, Lord."

"You doubt my resolve to do that?"

"Not your resolve, Lord," Cihuacoatl replied dejectedly, "but your opportunity."

"I shall be prevented from it? Only the Revered Speaker can do that."

"And he will. Lord Tizoc has decided to lead the armies himself. He values Toluca's tributes too highly and will want them continued after we have chastised it."

While this did not settle well with Ahuitzotl, it was not unanticipated. "Well," he said, "perhaps nothing will come of this, if the Tolucan lords surrender to us as Nezahualpilli expects."

"That is absurd!" snarled Cihuacoatl. "Submit voluntarily to death? Never!"

"You believe this?" Ahuitzotl was astonished.

"Of course."

"So why didn't you say anything at the council?" Ahuitzotl expressed in bitterness. "It would have given me some satisfaction that the chief minister agreed with me. It may even have helped my proposal."

"For me to try and compete with Nezahualpilli for Tizoc's ear amounts to an exercise in futility."

"Tizoc does not respect your judgment?"

"I did not say that."

"You implied it. You were quiet throughout the assembly. It might have been worthwhile to say at least something to influence Tizoc. As it was, Nezahualpilli had a field day with him."

"That is precisely the problem, Lord. Our Revered Speaker has no mind of his own and is too easily pursuaded by the opinion of others, particularly Nezahualpilli's. He lacks the spine for manly resolution."

"You and I seem to have reversed positions from our previous encounter," Ahuitzotl reminded the minister. "As I recall it, then you cautioned me on harboring treasonous thoughts about him. Why the sudden change?"

"It has not been sudden. Events have greatly accelerated on us in the recent weeks. Patterns of unrest are developing everywhere, which I cannot attribute to any other factor except Tizoc's weak leadership. I was blind not to see it earlier. His reign was manageable because he rode on the crest of successes achieved by his eminent predecessors. His fiasco at Metztitlan did not harm him because it occurred in a remote region and word about it spread slowly, but now everyone knows of it. It may even have inspired Zozoltin to proceed with his insurrection. Worse, when I tell him of these exigencies, he is not even interested in them. He ignores my counsel and spends his days with architects and engineers discussing various building projects. There's an irony for you. He plans all this construction while all around him the domain is crumbling to pieces. If he has no concern for the strength of our realm, why should he listen to my warnings about its weakening? Is it any wonder my health suffers?"

"You have my sympathy, Cihuacoatl, but you also told me I must accept this. The Revered Speaker rules for life, and it was you who chose him. How will you resolve your dilemma now?"

"His vaccilation and indecision threaten our empire. Do you agree with that, Lord?"

Ahuitzotl became curious where the minister would lead him and suspected he was about to be introduce to the unthinkable. "I've maintained that for longer than you have," he said.

"Then it should be evident what our sacred duty must be."

"What are you suggesting, minister?" prodded Ahuitzotl.

"By the gods!" Cihuacoatl roared as he sprang off the bench. "Are you that dimwitted? I pray you do not play games with me, Lord, for this is a matter of gravest concern to us both."

"I play no games, minister. Yes, I know what you are alluding to, but instead of my delving on mere conjecture, I prefer that you tell me directly. If you have something to say, come out and say it!"

"The issue is problematic," Cihuacoatl said. "Heresy is one of our most heinous crimes. I'm not yet convinced I am at liberty to say it-no, even think it! I'm trying to make sense out of it, to give it a justifiable basis-that's why all these questions. They are as much for myself as for you. I seek assurances that my contemplations will not condemn me."

"You still have not told me." Ahuitzotl pressed, adding to the minister's apparent difficulties.

"Bear with me," entreated Cihuacoatl, "so that I am able to extract a solution to this predicament. If we accept that our most sacred duty is to protect and preserve the realm because in so doing we sustain the gods, then what happens if it becomes evident our Revered Speaker is unable or unwilling to perform this task? Would this not make it incumbant upon us to remedy the situation? Could the gods object to this?"

"If it's for their own preservation, I don't see how."

"You lighten my burdens, Lord. Acknowledging that Tizoc's reign jeopardizes the realm, I should think there's no longer a question on what needs to be done, is there?"

"No," agreed Ahuitzotl. "Tizoc must be replaced."

"Tell me how, and I will employ the method. I have no more reservations about its necessity."

Ahuitzotl recognized the trap and was not about to advocate treason. "How can I tell you?" he said, "You're the one who selected him. Why can't the same interclan council which made him ruler take the throne away from him?"

"Its decision is irreversible. The permanence of the monarch is decreed by both custom and religion. It cannot be otherwise if he is Huitzilopochtli's personal representative to the nation. The people's faith in the gods, the very foundation of our society, would suffer irreparable damage if we were to suddenly proclaim it is not so."

"It appears you have a problem."

"We have a problem," Cihuacoatl baited Ahuitzotl, "unless, in your complacency, you are resigned to expending your remaining days under Tizoc's ineffective rule."

"I have no choice, as you told me."

Cihuacoatl realized he would not succeed in getting Ahuitzotl to openly declare any kind of seditiousness against his brother. Perhaps he remembered too well the minister's earlier admonishment or, more likely, simply did not trust him. But whatever his reasons, Cihuacoatl concluded that the time was not yet ripe for urging such action. He would try again later, but not without first offering more enticement. "That is regrettable," he said, "especially when the general consensus is that you would manage the realm significantly better than the man who presently presides."

Ahuitzotl proceeded cautiously, averse in confiding too much and choosing his words carefully, wary of their provocative potential. "I have no way of knowing I would take Tizoc's place," he said.

"It can be arranged. As the council's ranking speaker, my declarations carry weight."

"In that case, I'm sure you can apply your talents and station in finding a way to replace him," Ahuitzotl answered, still refusing to be cornered.

"I'll work on it," Cihuacoatl remarked as he prepared to make his leave. He was satisfied that he had implanted the seed which would spawn the serpent, and it was only a matter of waiting for events to unfold and bring it to life. Tizoc himself would see to that, for Ahuitzotl's tolerance had its limits.

"We shall speak more on this some other time," Cihuacoatl said as he departed.

Ahuitzotl stood at the entrance of his command post to watch the minister ambling away and saw beyond him the third tier of the Great Temple embraced in scaffolding and rising preponderantly above its adjacent structures. Once again he suppressed a bitterness he felt surging within him.

IX

Pelaxilla sat on a stone slab serving as a bench in the garden behind the royal palace and anxiously awaited her lover's arrival. In the late afternoon the temperature had cooled sufficiently to require her wearing a shawl over her blouse for comfort. Normally she would have found repose from the tenseness which clouded her recent days amidst the lofty, contorted cypresses, the myriad of green shades in the shrubbery, and the brilliant hues of a thousand blooming flowers. But today she could not relax, and while she usually eagerly longed for these meetings with Ahuitzotl, there was considerable stress in her. Calm yourself, she told her beating heart, or he will detect something is wrong. She repeatedly tried to focus her thought on the beauty surrounding her, but always she came back to how she was going to conduct an interrogation without arousing his suspicion. The empress said it did not have to be consummated at one time, so maybe she ought to forget about it altogether this day and just enjoy herself with him. That's what she should do, Pelaxilla convinced herself; she should abandon her scheme and simply have a good time.

Her cerebration was useless. She could not be distracted from the purpose Tlalalca had instilled in her and, continuing to feel uncomfortable over it, she decided it would be best for her not to see Ahuitzotl today. She was set on leaving just when he came into view. When she saw his gleaming white teeth behind a broad smile and lighted face, all her apprehensions vanished and the elation she always felt at seeing him repossessed her. She rushed into his welcoming arms and they clasped each other in joyful embrace under the gnarled shapes of the stately cypresses.

"Ah, Pelaxilla," Ahuitzotl sighed blissfully, "Your presence so delights me-I cherish it above everything."

Pelaxilla gave no reply, but her cheerful glee and the manner in which she held firmly on to him defined her contentment. They remained locked in their enrapture while relishing the closeness of their bodies and the pleasure of their stay together. Then, after what seemed an all too short time, Ahuitzotl loosened his grasp and released himself from her.

"It's so absurd to surreptitiously keep meeting like this," he said. "The entire court knows how we feel about each other. Why should we continue being separated.?"

"I want nothing more than to share my time with you," Pelaxilla said, "but what can we do when I am pledged to Lord Tizoc?"

"I can ask him to release you from that pledge."

Pelaxilla could scarcely contain her excitement, "Would he acquiesce to such a request?"

"He has an empress of whom he is exceedingly fond, I'm told,-and many other ladies in his court. I am asking for but one of them. Can this be objectionable to him?"

"With all my heart I hope not."

"If he loves Tlalalca so much, he should understand. Has he any special regard for you?"

"Special?"

"Does he favor you above his other mistresses?"

"Not that I can tell. He does not make use of his mistresses as you would expect. Many complain how he ignores them. He is always with Lady Tlalalca."

"That helps. For such a person, how can one less mistress be of any consequence?"

"When will you ask him?" Pelaxilla asked eagerly.

"After the Tolucan affair is ended-in about five weeks."

"That long?" Pelaxilla was unmistakably disappointed as she thought Ahuitzotl spoke of a nearer date.

"You must be patient, Pelaxilla," he advised her. "The timing at present is inappropriate. The Tolucan problem preoccupies all his thinking. It won't take long to crush this revolt, and when he is rejoicing in our victory, that's when I'll ask him. Better to wait than proceed now and have all our hopes dashed because we caught him in poor temperment."

"Yes, that makes sense," sighed Pelaxilla as she slipped back into his clutches. "He hasn't been in a good mood lately, owing to Toluca I think, and has shunned all contact with us."

"The time will pass quickly enough," he assured her.

They sauntered slowly along the garden's pathway, happy in each other's arms and enjoying the peace and pleasure which comes when love's glow pleases the heart and spirit. Their situation was delicate. Ahuitzotl had his share of mistresses, as a noble of his station was expected to, although he never mentioned these. As far as Pelaxilla knew, he was not emotionally involved with any other woman except herself. He had been married for four years but had preemptorily divorced his wife when she failed to produce an heir, as the law allowed in such cases, and made no further attempt to secure another one. For a man of his age-a year under thirty-to be unwed was extremely rare and generally frowned upon by the nobility, but this seldom troubled Ahuitzotl as he was not typically constrained by the dictates of convention. Most men needed to be married out of economic necessity-it took hours to make bread from corn and a wife was necessary to perform such chores-but Ahuitzotl, being of the royal house, had his servants for this and his mistresses to provide for his sensual desires. If anything, he was 'married' to the army; it occupied most of his time and energy and gave him pleasures that few women could. He was able to take them or leave them at will with no preference for any particular one of them. They satisfied his evenings, but his days belonged to the military. This was so until he met Pelaxilla.

Ahuitzotl had on occasions seen Pelaxilla among Tizoc's ladies, and from the beginning was struck by her beauty, but it was not until he attended a dinner with Tizoc and Tlalalca somewhat over a year ago where she happened to be one of the guests that he chanced to speak with her for the first time and was immediately captivated by her charm. He initiated his advances slowly and did not begin visiting her regularly until six months later, usually in the royal garden, but at times in the market place or central plaza when she told him she would be there. Not long after that it became evident their meetings amounted to more than mere casual get-togethers, and this complicated matters because a Revered Speaker's mistresses were not for sharing. So while they loved each other, they could not become intimate in their affection, and as yet, both had honored this formality.

Custom specified that mistresses belonged to the noble who had acquired them, through prizes of war, payment of debts, purchase as slaves, voluntary submission, or, as for many in Tizoc's case, inheritance. No particular inducement existed on his part to consider giving up Pelaxilla, nor was it appropriate for Ahuitzotl to make such a request. Were Tizoc to grant such a concession, it would be more out of gratuity or benevolence than any other motivation, and Ahuitzotl had not done much lately to render himself any kind of endearment out of his brother. A chill ran through him when he reflected on this.

"I'm puzzled by you, Ahuitzotl," Pelaxilla broke the long silence. "You don't strike me as someone who is content to let things be as they are at present."

"An odd thing to say. What do you mean?"

"Oh, I don't know for sure," she mused, "I often wished things were somehow different-that I had a more meaningful existence. I thought you might have similar thoughts."

"I suppose I do, but I don't think it wise. Cihuacoatl once advised me this can poison your mind. He's right."

"When you do ponder over such things, even if infrequently, what do you wish for?"

"Many things-all of them foolish, for they can never be."

Pelaxilla detected his reluctance to be specific and decided to proceed in a different manner. "So do I," she said. "Often I see myself as a head priestess so that I am honored by worshippers and am able to instruct them and have them obey me."

"I didn't know you had those kind of aspirations."

"Oh yes. I do. I have even loftier ones. I wish to be the empress some day."

"Indeed?"

"What do you suppose that means? That I hunger for recognition or power?"

"Do you?"

Pelaxilla paused momentarily, satisfied that she held his interest, then answered, "I would say so. Yes, I aspire for glory. The longer I am at the court, the more that prospect appeals to me. I feel as if I'm beckoned to become her. Don't you think I'ld make a good empress?"

"Such talk is foolishness, Pelaxilla."

"Yes, but it's entertaining."

"Also dangerous, if anyone hearing you takes it seriously."

"Nonsense! They know I say it in jest. You haven't told me if I would make a good empress."

"Must you persist? How should I know?"

"Well, I think I would. There is a seductiveness in ordering the ladies of the court around, in being attended at my bath, in having all my cares and desires provided for. Yes, I would take a fancy to that."

"You do persist."

"Really, Ahuitzotl, I only pretend. There's no harm in it. I well know my wishes are but dreams. You're the one who is too serious about it."

"Perhaps, but if so, it's because your pretensions closely mirror certain realities I grapple with daily. For this reason, I'm probably oversensitive about it."

"What do you mean?"

"Nothing. Forget what I said."

Pelaxilla was taken aback by the abrupt manner in which he cut her off; yet his defensiveness fueled her curiosity-she had obviously struck a raw nerve. "As you say, Ahuitzotl," she continued. "Apparently what I consider merely frivolous has some serious overtones for you, but I have no desire to pry into your personal affairs."

"Then don't!" he insisted.

"You don't have to get irritable about it," Pelaxilla reacted critically. "If I offended you, I apologize for it. It's quite unintentional."

Ahuitzotl halted to face Pelaxilla and gazed directly into her eyes. A worrisome visage in his features almost gave her regrets over having attempted her inquisition. Yet she found the notion that Ahuitzotl somehow may be involved in a scheme against Tizoc, as Tlalalca alluded to, strangely fascinating and would have wanted to learn more about it, but not at the risk of alienating him-that was too costly for her.

"If I appear offended," Ahuitzotl told her, "understand it's not directed at you. These things you talk about, what you wish for and pretend to be, make me uncomfortable, not only because your are at risk for saying it, but because I am guilty of possessing similar damaging ideas. However, there is a big difference between us, which causes me to view this entire affair in a more sober context."

"What difference is that?"

"To you, it is merely playing," came his answer.

Tlalalca was right, Pelaxilla thought in amazement. The implication was clear, even if Ahuitzotl had not come right out and actually said it. She was convinced that whatever was going on, he was a crucial element in it.

"It isn't to you?" she pressed on.

"I'll speak no more on the subject, so please stop your prying."

"Very well," Pelaxilla said. "At least I learned what certain court ladies say about you is true, and I appreciate that."

"What do they say?"

"That you are ambitious and will go to great lengths to get what you want. Some say you are vain and seek the adulation of others."

"You like that?"

"Yes I do. I prefer someone who professes high-minded goals to one who is content to let things be as they are. There is a drive in such men-something very stimulating to me. I find myself attracted by an aura of excitement that surrounds them."

"I didn't know you felt that way."

"See what you can discover when you open yourself to someone? You should tell me more about yourself-it may surprise you what I think."

"Perhaps."

"Will you tell me what your plans are?"

"Plans? There are no plans, Pelaxilla," he sharply reproved her. "Let the matter rest."

She had to be careful, Pelaxilla thought, so as not to draw erroneous conclusions about what he imparted in the course of their conversation. All she really knew was that Ahuitzotl admitted to having thoughts suggesting a possible desire for the crown, and even this was vague. She knew nothing in terms of details—certainly nothing concrete to relate to Tlalalca. Clearly he had no intentions of revealing any more about this and she decided not to press him further. In time, she would discover more.

As for Ahuitzotl, he thought their entire exchange perplexing and was trying to reconstruct the topics discussed which led up to what he deemed a careless disclosure on his part. He had never previously heard Pelaxilla speak about political subjects-he was unaware that she even possessed an interest in these. It was unusual, although not unknown, for women to express a proclivity towards such matters. Nezahualpilli had his famed Lady of Tula, one of his many mistresses renowned for her wisdom, who advised him regularly on political and judicial issues, but she was a rarity and, in general, women did not involve themselves over what was held as a predominantly male domain. It could be that Pelaxilla was also an exception, but Ahuitzotl remained skeptical about this as it had never come to light previously; he concluded that he needed to exercise greater restraint over what he related to her.

They continued walking in silence, but now felt some tenseness in it. Whereas before the stillness afforded them a serenity which permitted them to absorb the warmth of each other's presence, it now presented them prolonged moments to ponder over their predicament, and each reflected on what the other had said, questioning the motivation behind it and giving rise to both suspicions and bewilderment. The conversation had to some degree tarnished their relationship and placed a barrier between them. These doubts were transitory, but for the present, they beset the two lovers and reinforced uncertainties about the durability of their enrapture, and as of this day, both were relieved to bring their meeting to a close and go their separate ways.

Warriors by the hundreds were entering Tenochtitlan daily as the deadline given Zozoltin was nearing. They came in under colorful standards designating their units and dressed in full battle gear, wearing the ichcahuilpilli, a tunic of thick reinforced cotton fibers serving as body armor, and helmets made of wood, reed, bone, and animal hides molded into shapes resembling the fearsome appearances of jaguars, eagles, and snakes. Many wore plumed headdresses of various bird feathers with distinctive designs and hues identifying their clans. Each day their numbers increased so that they soon crowded the facilities available to them in the capital.

They carried an assortment of weapons depending on the posts assigned them in battle. The principal combatants held the tepuztopilli, a lance six to ten feet in length with a sharp obsidian head ornamented by feathers, with a maquauhuitl slung over their shoulders or attached with thongs to their waistbelts. This club, three feet long with honed stone blades embedded along its edges, was the primary armament used in closed combat and could be wielded with lethal efficiency. Their shields, of wood, cane, and animal hide, were trimmed with tassels or feathers and painted with group insignia and clan emblems. There were slingers and archers, more lightly clad than their infantry counterparts, and also spearthrowers armed with the atlatl, a short wooden staff holding a groove and projecting peg into which was inserted a dart about half the length of a lance. With such armament, the Mexica carved their way to supremacy.

In addition to the warriors came a multitude of priests. These were also impressively attired in magnificent plumages, ornaments, long cloaks or robes marked with sacred symbols denoting their particular order. Their importance could not be underestimated, for through their oblations were gods disposed to influence the outcome of a struggle, and they always accompanied the armies to war, usually a day's march ahead of the main body, carrying the idols of their dieties on their backs or in litters. They required no escort and advanced by themselves-no mortal would have dared to touch them out of fear of incurring the wrath of the divinities they served.

Most of the soldiers and priests came from Acolhuacan, east of Lake Texcoco, and from the southern lakeshore cities who had to make a stopover in Tenochtitlan on the route to Toluca. Across the western causeway, elements from numerous Tepaneca cities were filtering into Tlacopan to merge with forces already assembled there and, as in the capital, their arrival was heralded by cheering throngs and the tossing of flowers. The people knew these processions as preludes to missions imparted by demanding gods and demonstrated their support. The presence of so many warriors generated much excitement and children gaped wide-eyed and in wonder, some running alongside them as they marched, and many an old man glanced enviously at their passing.

They were in the final week of the tenth month, Xocotlhuetzli; activity was mounting as preparation for moving on Toluca was in its finishing stages. The eleventh month, Ochpaniztli, was rapidly approaching and nowhere was its arrival more eagerly anticipated than in the headquarters complex where Ahuitzotl and Tlohtzin reviewed the situation with considerable perplexment.

"Dispatches are coming to us twice a day now," Ahuitzotl commented, "and still there is no movement afoot in Toluca. They have made no attempts to secure allies. It's as though they regarded this impending war as utterly inconsequential-no threat whatsoever."

"Do they mean to surrender to us?" Tlohtzin asked.

"There are no indications of that either. Our scouts haven't been able to determine what Zozoltin has decided. The townspeople say nothing."

"That is mystifying. Evidently they do not realize what's in store for them."

"It would be difficult to conceal. The restrictions imposed by our advance parties should have alerted them to us and prompted them to press their leaders for an explanation. No, they are fully aware of what is going on. It seems their ambassador, Tecolotl, was correct when he told us Zozoltin has a consensus in his defiance. Imagine that-a show of courage from the Matlazinca."

"All the better I say. We shall have our battle and punish them accordingly for it."

"We owe it to ourselves," Ahuitzotl emphasized. "They are adding to their insolence by demonstrating, through their complacency, that they need not fear us or heed our warnings. Such an insult cannot be ignored."

"Clearly. What preparations are they making for our expected battle?"

"The usual training-nothing we would think extraordinary. No special drills, maneuvers, or exercises, no massing of units, no close-order combat, no production of any additional weapons, not even extra training for the inexperienced boys. If these activities are actually taking place, they're out of sight from our observers."

"What you say is astounding. Have they no fear at all?"

"They're Matlazinca-they mask it. At any rate, we shall have to teach them, won't we?"

"Quite so. Does Lord Tizoc know about this?"

"I've informed him of the reports. As Revered Speaker, he cannot view these actions with sympathy. Even his moderation must be tested over this."

Just then, coming as an interruption to their discussion, the air was pierced by blaring drones of numerous conch shells and the rhythmic beat of drums. "It's the main column from Texcoco," Ahuitzotl surmised, "led by Nezahualpilli I expect. Let's welcome him."

No sooner had they stepped to the front portal when they were met by Nezahualpilli who walked with his trumpeters and drummers ahead of his army marching as an endless line of six warriors abreast toward the complex where most of its soldiers would be billeted.

"I had a premonition you changed your mind," Ahuitzotl greeted the Texcocan, "but I see your eagerness for battle overrode all else. Better than a dull surrender, wouldn't you say?"

"The choice was difficult for me-between this and my poetical compositions," retorted Nezahualpilli knowing that his answer would be disdainfully received by Ahuitzotl. "I spoke with Lord Tizoc as we came through the plaza. He bids we join him at dinner to discuss this operation with him."

"It is near evening now."

"Then let's not dally here. The march has famished me."

The sun was slowly sinking below the western mountains when Ahuitzotl and Nezahualpilli crossed the central square on the way to the royal palace. It cast a brilliant reddish glow upon the unplastered masonry of the Great Temple, outlining its austere features in sharp shadows. In reflected light, the structure appeared even more gigantic, looming in massive splendor above the two men gazing up at it. Ahuitzotl paused to fully absorb the spectacle.

"An imposing temple," declared Nezahualpilli. "There is none like it in Texcoco, or any other city for that matter."

"Huitzilopochtli and Tlaloc shall reign magnificently over Tenochtitlan."

"I assume Tizoc is already planning for its inauguration."

"He hasn't mentioned it, but why should he? It will not be finished for another year."

"A temple of such size and grandeur will require a proportionately large dedication. The ceremony will have to be well thought out, involving lords and dignitaries from many realms. invitations must be sent out; facilities set up; priests will have to give long incantations, orisons must be memorized, and sacrifice offered. It must all be flawlessly executed and cannot be marred in any way-that would be an affront to Huitzilopochtli and Tlaloc both."

"One would think this structure, as large as it is, ought to gratify them amply."

"A building itself, no matter how impressive, is not that significant. It's what we do with it, the honors we render it, and the priests we assign to its keeping, which will do most to please the gods. You've seen Teotihuacan? It is said the people who built it failed in granting their gods appropriate homage and perished as a consequence. Even that city, with all its monumental sights did not satisfy them, else they would never have permitted its builders to be destroyed."

"A terrible price for their oversight," Ahuitzotl concluded. "We must not ignore the message. Huitzilopochtli is most demanding."

Their eyes remained transfixed on the temple for some time after light ceased to reflect from it and dusk descended on them. Not until it stood before them as a shadowed mount and after braziers had been lit in adjacent buildings, casting their flickering glow upon the stonework, did they proceed. Arriving at the palace, whose interior brightness received them as a warm welcome, attendants escorted them to one of the smaller rooms where they were cordially greeted by Tizoc and Tlalalca. After washing their hands and faces in bowls of water and drying themselves with towels, a particularly refreshing observance for Nezahualpilli following his day's march, they took their place upon soft cushions in the manner prescribed by court etiquette and were brought trays of food and drink by servants of both sexes.

The meal was of the usual good quality conjured up by the palace chefs. Beginning with a vegetable plate containing a dozen varieties of beans, pepper, and squash, as well as a mixture of onions, tomatoes, yams, and an assortment of nuts, their main fare was a meat dish consisting of small bite-size slices of flesh from duck, grouse, quail, and turkey, with a complimentary plate of iguana meat, a delicacy. Side dishes included variations of corn bread, some with flowers added into the dough to enhance the flavor, and spices for seasoning the treats to please even the most severe culinary critic. Chocolate blended with vanilla and honey served as their main drink.

During the course of their dining, one topic dominated their discussion–Toluca-and Tizoc, already appraised on much of the information by Ahuitzotl, was both confused and annoyed over the conflicting reports which gave overall indications this issue was to be decided by the usual means-a force of arms.

"Have all the contingents arrived?" Tizoc asked.

"We expect the last of them tomorrow, Lord," answered Ahuitzotl. "The ones from the farther outlying cities are here."

"And the same for Tlacopan?"

"Yes, Lord."

"So it's only a matter on waiting for Ochpaniztli to arrive."

"Are we to wait for it here?" questioned Ahuitzotl. "Would it not be better to proceed on Toluca now so when Ochpaniztli comes we will be ready for them there?"

"We told the Tolucan lords to come to Tenochtitlan," Tizoc curtly reminded Ahuitzotl.

"So we did, however that should not place any constraints on our own movements. We would not interfere with their coming here if they still decide on that. I want to be prepared to attack if they refuse your demand."

"And have your Revered Speaker known as a treacherous bargainer?" Tizoc rebuffed his commander.

"The plan has some merit, Lord," Nezahualpilli interjected. "If the Tolucans were to see our armies move on them, they might be more inclined to give our ultimatum further consideration. It will then be obvious there will be no more time for second thoughts."

"This would not be dishonorable?" Tizoc wondered.

"It may be just the tactic needed to give Zozoltin the incentive to do as we ordered. As things stand now, we have nothing to suggest that he intends to comply."

"Nor have his envoys told us anything," added Tizoc. "Indeed it would seem that Zozoltin wishes to have this war. Still, we must honor the word we gave him."

"We will," said Ahuitzotl, "by not attacking before Ochpaniztli."

"Very well. It's settled. Tomorrow we'll send a messenger to our ambassador at Zozoltin's court to learn of his intentions. Pending his reply, we will move our armies. This will have us in position when the time comes. I trust this stipulation is not undermined by your impatience to have this war, Ahuitzotl, for you have forced my hand. Yet you say all the signs are that Zozoltin makes no preparation for war. Surely he means to surrender. What else can it be?"

"I think he mocks us, Lord," said Ahuitzotl.

"Mocks us?"

"He is a dead man no matter what choice he makes, and since everyone is watching this, why not make us appear the villain in the process?"

"Interesting, if true," commented Nezahualpilli. "It makes sense in some ways. He is using our need to make an exhibition of our punishment, so that others will be awed, as a weapon against us. Zozoltin is a greater man that I credited him."

"You see greatness in this?" Tizoc asked in amazement.

"Consider the setting, Lord. The world is watching us and, in a peculiar but effective way, he is shouting out for everyone to hear that death is preferable to living under the rule of his overlords. It's as if a prisoner about to be sacrificed were to spit in the face of the priest ready to cut him open-a final, deliberate act of defiance-of utmost contempt!-one we obviously cannot afford to have others emulate. We have unwittingly offered Zozoltin that opportunity."

"What of his people? Has he no regard for them?"

"I think he refuses to believe we would actually carry out our threats against them."

"Either that," added Ahuitzotl, "or he has their support."

"That's preposterous!" exclaimed Tizoc, alarmed. "Do you realize what you're saying? It means his people would share his preference for death or enslavement. No mortal man has such a hold on his subjects."

"If he did," concluded Nezahualpilli, "he would be a most remarkable leader indeed."

"Impossible!" declared Tizoc. "He is a man, not a god!"

"I am merely giving you our interpretations of the reports we received," stated Ahuitzotl who felt a revulsion over Tizoc's apparent timidity-already he was cowed by Zozoltin-and resented how everything he agreed to required Nezahualpilli's prior affirmation. "Make of it what you like, but for reasons we do not know, they are unconcerned about their impending fate."

A quietness fell over the room as its occupants, unfamiliar with this seeming contradiction, groped for answers.

"It is puzzling," Tizoc finally said, "but does not confirm the people are behind Zozoltin. Surely he has kept them ignorant of our ultimatum."

"We discounted that," said Ahuitzotl. "Seeing our advance party would have prompted them to insist on being told."

"He could have deceived them," Nezahualpilli surmised.

"That's possible," conceded Ahuitzotl.

"It may have been necessary," Nezahualpilli continued. "How could he let them know he was placing their lives in danger if he and his lords refused to surrender? Conceivably this could have led to a revolt among his people."

"To be sure," Ahuitzotl grinned. "They would have insisted he surrender, perhaps even turned him over to us bound hand and foot."

"Such a deception cannot be continued," Tizoc remarked. "When our armies approach, they will have to be told. I should like to see how Zozoltin manages that."

"Whatever he does, it won't save him," quipped Ahuitzotl.

"If it comes to a battle I want him taken alive for eventual sacrifice. The gods should be gratified over receiving such a captive."

"Why render him that honor?" scowled Ahuitzotl contemptuously. "He has created a lot of trouble. I see no reason for any generosity by granting him entrance into the Eastern Paradise."

"What would you do with him?" Tizoc asked.

"I agree he should be taken alive, but I would cage him up without food or water and let him die on his own accord. This will offer him ample time to brood over his mistakes."

Tizoc and Nezahualpilli glanced at each other in disbelief.

"That is too harsh!" declared Nezahualpilli. "By all indications Zozoltin is an opponent we can respect-and he is a king! It's proper to give him the honor he is entitled."

"A king who dared to oppose us!" Ahuitzotl replied. "He does not merit our clemency."

"We can determine that later," said Tizoc. "At least we are agreed he will be taken captive. I think we've said enough on this and I'll welcome a change of subject. I'm sure Tlalalca has felt herself ignored all evening."

With that, their conversations turned to lighter themes, with Tizoc and Nezahualpilli speaking of their latest garden blooms and construction feats while Ahuitzotl and Tlalalca talked occasionally about Pelaxilla. Ahuitzotl detected some hostility in her terse responses but dismissed these for the sake of congeniality-he knew she bore no love for him. In this way the evening passed until gradually fatigue overtook them and they, disinclined to further discussions, finally requested retirement to their chambers, bringing the day to a close.

XI

All that afternoon couriers, running in relays with each one covering a stretch of approximately five leagues, carried eagerly anticipated words from the Mexica ambassador at Toluca for his monarch in Tenochtitlan. His message, written on paper in the pictographic style of the scribes, was transported in a deerskin pouch slung over each runner's shoulder. In this manner, the distance between Toluca and the capital was traversed in less than half a day and as the sun was setting, a final runner crossed the Tlacopan causeway and entered the central plaza heading in the direction of the royal palace. He nearly dropped from exhaustion when he handed his pouch to the court orderly who immediately took it to the main hall where Tizoc was in conference with his major priests and commanders; Nezahualpilli and Cihuacoatl were present when the receptionist entered.

"Your message from Toluca, Lord!" he said as he transferred the pouch to Cihuacoatl. Everyone stood still as the minister removed the papers and gave them to Tizoc; all eyes were focused on him as he unfolded the codices and read them section by section without a trace of emotion. Finally, when his spellbound audience was at its breaking point, he looked up.

"It is confirmed," Tizoc announced. "Our ambassador offered Zozoltin a final plea for surrender and was rejected. He properly reminded the Tolucan that his refusal amounted to war and has given him the appropriate signs. He presented Zozoltin with a shield, bow and arrow, and the protective tunic, and told him that we will march on him to engage in battle."

"Excellent!" rejoiced Ahuitzotl. "At the sun's rising tomorrow, we shall sound the war drum to assemble our warriors."

"Let a priest dress himself as Painal, Huitzilopochtli's messenger, and proclaim this war to everyone with his rattle and shield," Tizoc added. "There can be no more delays."

The priests hurriedly imparted these instructions to one of their lot who immediately left to begin the ritual call to arms.

"I see no point in protracting this already overextended conference," continued Tizoc. "You have your work to do. We will meet at early dawn before the palace."

Tizoc, whose lack of enthusiam for this venture strained his audience, wished to be alone and soon those in attendance acceded to his desire and hastily departed. Only Nezahualpilli remained. Long after the hall had been emptied, the brooding monarch sat quietly in his throne, absorbed in his cogitation, while leaving his guest to pace the floor at much discomfort to himself.

"If my lord will tell me what troubles him," Nezahualpilli at last spoke out, finding the silence intolerable, "perhaps I could be of some assistance."

"It is nothing," replied Tizoc.

"Nothing? You are usually more generous with your hospitality, Lord. Am I to just stand here over nothing?"

"You know the way to your chamber. Do not stay here on my account."

"It is too early."

"If you wish to be entertained, go to one of my mistresses. I am not disposed towards amusing anyone this evening."

"I have more than enough of them so that they no longer entertain me. No, Tizoc, I prefer that we should speak. We do not see each other often and when we do, we should conduct ourselves in a manner befitting the lords that we are and share our mutual concerns. What can be so burdensome for you that is not of some consequence to me? Are we not together in this?"

"Yes, you're quite right-excuse my contemplation if it seems rude. I am thinking about this entire sordid affair. It appears what you and I considered a prudent alternative to Toluca's destruction is seen as a monumental joke by its own ruler. Where did we go wrong?"

"There were weaknesses in the plan that we failed to give due regard. The more one thinks of it, the more they come to light. We cannot be certain if their ambassador, Tecolotl, even related our ultimatum. Zozoltin may be of such temperment that vents fury upon envoys bearing ill tidings. Tecolotl, knowing this, may have said nothing, or distorted your words to him. It's one of many ways in which our intent could have been miscarried."

"True, but the Tolucans knew, when they refused their tribute quotas, war was inevitable. Whatever we may have decided subsequent to that ought not have surprised them."

"Maybe Ahuitzotl is correct in thinking that they indeed want this war."

"What madness! How can Zozoltin possibly believe he can stand up against our might?"

"That I can't tell you. He may well be demented."

"And all his nobles too, I suppose."

"Under a delusion, Tizoc-expecting they can escape our wrath. They miscalculated our intent to maintain the domain established by the revered Motecuhzoma and Axayacatl."

"Is this because I am the Revered Speaker?"

"I'm not clear what you allude to, Tizoc."

"There are those who say that because I prefer seeking other solutions to conflicts than war, I am perceived as weak by our enemies-that this even may have inspired Zozoltin to carry out his rebellion, and accounts for his present defiance. You have not heard this?"

"I do not place much value on such talk. Revolts against the imposition of our tributes have been happening since our realm was founded. Axayacatl waged many wars on people he had previously conquered. It is nothing new."

"What of my aversion for wars?"

"Is this true?"

"I do question their usefullness. There's no denying we achieved great power through our aggressiveness, and no doubt have ingratiated ourselves to the gods for this, but we haven't generated any amiability among our neighbors. Ultimately this will prove disastrous for us. It would be beneficial for all if we struck a more favorable accord among us; our ceaseless wars contribute nothing to this."

"You contest our reason for being, Tizoc. As a ruler, it is your sacred duty to discharge our divine obligations."

"Do you actually believe this?"

"It's what the priests tell us."

"Then it must be so!" Tizoc exclaimed sarcastically.

"It is so, Tizoc! And it's dangerous for you to challenge this. A Revered Speaker cannot relinquish himself from these ordained responsibilities-he is sworn to uphold them! I'm not that fond of wars myself–they disrupt my devotion to the arts-but I accept them as necessary for our well-being."

"You are by reputation the most learned man in the realm, Nezahualpilli," Tizoc said, unable to hide his disappointment over the Texcocan's counsel, "but you speak to me as if I were a lower ranking chieftain whose obediance you are trying to extract. We are both kings and understand the demands of our office, especially when it comes to preserving our priestly institutions and their credibility with the people. As a scholared man, I cannot accept you haven't speculated over this web we've spun for ourselves and find ourselves trapped within. Do you know of what I speak?"

"You have my attention."

"The priests say our divine mission is to sustain the gods, and so we make the sacrifices they prescribe for us. We are told that the more nations we conquer, the greater a favor we are asking of the gods and must accordingly make more sacrifices in order to propitiate them into granting our requests. Each nation we subjugate, we add its gods to our own, and so increase our requirements for sacrifice even more. The question that comes to mind is: why was it once sufficient to sustain our world with the sacrifice of hundreds when it now requires thousands to do the same thing? These nations existed before we came upon the scene and our gods managed to survive with our previous meager offerings. What have we gained from all this, aside from the need to now wage war for no other purpose except to obtain captives for sacrifice? Where will it end?"

"Take my advice, Tizoc, and do not dwell on such questions. They will not ease your burdens. We were chosen kings to enhance the expectations of those who appointed us. We must satisfy many institutions-all interlocked by our relationship with the gods. We commit ourselves to this sworn duty when we accept the crown."

"You've said that before."

"You must not lose sight of it."

"Somehow I expected more from a man of your reputation. I speak of issues I see as eventually leading to our downfall, which we must face sooner or later, irrespective of what others tell us. As kings, we cannot ignore them."

"Hear me, Tizoc, because what I tell you is for your safety. Not only is it unheard of for the Revered Speaker to proclaim himself a pacifist, but it is intolerable. It threatens our very existence. A state polity, religious and civil, has been constructed, and has flourished, under a belief that it thrives on, and is sustained by, the shedding of blood. The sinews of our nation are centered on war. To challenge that which is arranged and regulated does not fall within our prerogatives. You cannot undo the the policies and direction initiated by a succession of rulers who preceded you. These are not matters of individual discretion-these are accepted practice. You have no choice in this, and if you wish to torment yourself in trying to make sense out of it, that is your personal affair. But do not-and I strongly emphasize this!-do not even think of putting a stop to this. That would be the greatest folly."

"Then such is to be our destiny," Tizoc concluded, still not satisfied with his colleague's advice. "Oh, I shall do my part, Nezahualpilli. You needn't worry about that–after all, It appears we're going to destroy Toluca over it. The tradition must be preserved."

"It would be better if you really believed it, Tizoc, otherwise it may affect your performance. It's not enough that battles must be waged, they must be fought with great zeal; as Revered Speaker you are instrumental in injecting such fervor among our warriors. You trouble me; I caution you— do not approach this war half-heartedly. Your actions will be detected."

"Do not fear, Nezahualpilli. They'll get a good performance out of me."

"Worthy of a Revered Speaker. That is all we can ask."

"Come, let's go to the garden before complete darkness overtakes us so we can forget about the grim tasks facing us tomorrow. I want to show you my latest creation-a unique flower of soft vermillion texture. Its aroma will delight your senses."

And so they ambled into the garden. Tizoc, Revered Speaker of the Mexica-Tenocha, seeking relief from duties he considered distasteful, was showing his guest a new strain of flower which bore his interest. In his garden Tizoc discovered his most pleasurable moments, experimenting with many forms of plantlife and developing fresh varieties through cross-breeding techniques. This was his refuge-a haven which granted him the solace he needed to get away from the pressing demands of an office he increasingly despised. Nezahualpilli, although similarly possessing a predilection towards gardening, was not quite as prepared to block out the coming events from his mind, and as he listened to Tizoc expounding his successes with flowers, he heard little of it owing to his reservations over the ease in which his friend dismissed the approaching campaign. He wished Tizoc would embrace the venture with more enthusiasm and was not misled by a diversion which he recognized as an attempt at escapism. A long evening awaited him, he thought.

XII

KA-RA-BOOM! KA-BOOM!

In a succession of deafening dull thuds, the panhuehuetl, an enormous war drum, shattered the morning bliss as its deep reverberations thundered out the call to arms heard in every quarter of Tenochtitlan. Within minutes after it first beat, soldiers began to assemble in the plaza, coming from its connecting streets and avenues and entering through the four gates of the serpent's wall. They formed their stations under each standard bearer and soon stood as armies comprised of separate and distinct organizations representing their cities and clans, thousands of them massed in units, one following another while quartermaster and supply squadrons brought them their weaponry from the city's arsenals-a sublime spectacle.

Ahuitzotl, resplendant in his eagle-headed helmet, with his maquauhuitl slung over his left shoulder and a shield strapped to his back, strutted proudly in front of the warriors to take his position at the head of the legions as Supreme Commander. In passing before the Tlatelolco component, he noticed Motecuhzoma standing stiffly before his mazatl squadron. A smile came to him and he halted upon reaching the young officer.

"Your first command in battle-if the gods favor us, Motecuhzoma," Ahuitzotl remarked.

"I am eager for it, Lord," beamed Motecuhzoma.

"No doubt. I shall keep my eyes on you. Perhaps your deeds will match those of my noble brother, Axayacatl."

Reinforcing Motecuhzoma's spirit through this encouragement, Ahuitzotl next proceeded to his post. On arriving there, he turned to face the warriors, looking them over unit by unit as if they stood for inspection and relishing the glory of this moment, and shortly thereafter began to address them.

"Mexica, Tenocha, Allies! The Lord of Battles, under whose domain we live, honors us! A war is in the making and the gods are rejoicing in want of those who are to die! Already they are choosing those among us who must kill, and those who must be killed whose rich blood will give them life, as we are once again called upon to carry our divine mission. Oh Great Lord! Let those warriors who die be received by the sun and earth who are the mother and father of all. We know that you wish them to die because that is why you sent them to this world-so that they can give life to the sun and earth-and we implore you to accept them in your house, with love and respect, to take their place among those eagles and tigers who have gone before them and are now serving our lord, the Sun. Let them depart from us to the greater glory of your realm, where happiness abounds and there is no more pain. We go to war, Mighty God, secure in our faith that you will do what is best for us."

When he finished his oratory, the thousands cheered wildly and lifted their spears and shields over their heads to demonstrate their approval and determination. Their roar echoed through the palace halls just as Tizoc and Cihuacoatl were preparing to enter the square and came upon Nezahualpilli who had observed the proceedings from the doorway.

"What means this outburst?" asked Tizoc.

"Ahuitzotl has just spoken to the warriors, Lord," Nezahualpilli said. "A speech worthy of Huitzilopochtli's high priest."

"He has a way with them-that I will grant him."

"Wait until we join them, Lord. A path has been well set out for you."

And so it had, for when Tizoc emerged from his residence and came into view, he was met by a tumultuous reception even louder than earlier. His presence unleashed a torrent of applause, thunderous as a roaring cascade, rendering hearing difficult.

"Will my lord speak to them?" Cihuacoatl asked.

"Ahuitzotl has done admirably enough," Tizoc said. "There's no need for me to add more."

While the cheering continued, eight bearers came with the monarch's litter and, after Tizoc climbed into its canopied couch and was lifted upon their shoulders, the acclamation accorded him attained an even greater intensity. Not until he was being carried off did Ahuitzotl, who thoroughly enjoyed this show of exuberance, raise his hand and quiet the square.

"Commanders!" he bellowed forth. "Begin the march!"

A flurry of subordinate directives ensued as individual unit chieftains ordered their warriors into march columns. One trailing the other, they filed out of the plaza through its west gate until it stood in emptiness except for a few observers too old or too young to participate in the venture who had risen early enough to witness the procession.

Once the armies broke into their route step, they progressed quickly and quietly, as talking was minimal in the ranks, and crossed the causeway to Tlacopan where Chimalpopoca had his own Tepaneca army waiting to join them. These were readily merged and the composite force–sixteen thousand-advanced in a broken column with three to four men abreast.

Leading the host was a detachment of chieftains and selected warriors noted for their bravery who formed the reconnaissance party. Normally ahead of the main force by a full two day's march, the proximity of Toluca negated the logistical and security problems typically entailed with such movements. Soldiers carried their rations in netted sacks, and because the area had been well covered by the advance elements sent out weeks ago, many of the precautions ordinarily applied, such as scouting out the canyons, ravines, and adjacent hills and forests, were not required. Consequently, only a half day's march separated it from the next unit.

The main body advanced in four primary components, each separated from the other by a distance of approximately twelve leagues. Heading it was a company composed of priests who moved by themselves, requiring no protection as their sanctity was all-encompassing and extended them safety even in hostile regions. After it came the Army of Tenochtitlan with its Tlatelolco subdivision and led by its elite Order of the Eagles, a unit comprised of a thousand teuctli–knights-the boldest and most courageous warriors of the realm. Behind it was the court entourage with Tizoc in his litter; Cihuacoatl, who in a longer campaign would have remained in the capital to rule in the monarch's absence but left this duty in the hands of a subordinate, and a few other counselors; Ahuitzotl with his primary staff, and Tlohtzin in front of the Order of the Jaguars-a unit of the same strength level and nearly equally prestigious as its Eagle counterpart. The bulk of the soldiery, divided into squadrons based on the their quarter of the city, formed the rear. With its congregate units and intervals, the Army of Tenochtitlan extended to a length of ten leagues. The Army of

Acolhuacan, led by its own Eagle and Jaguar Orders under Nezahualpilli, trailed Tenochtitlan's, and was, in turn, followed by the Army of Tepaneca commanded by the seasoned Chimalpopoca.

In this sequence the Mexica advanced on Toluca, the peculiarities of the campaign dictating their abnormal tactics. Under more typical operations each army would have been separated by a day's march so the other's overnight facilities and food caches could be used—all armies arriving simultaneously at a camp would have exhausted the available resources and their replenishment. However, some regular measures were executed, and as the armies snaked into the valleys, flanking patrols were sent out to prevent anyone from nearing the column and to provide early warning, more in adherence to established doctrine than out of any expectation of hostile activity.

All that day the column moved steadily forward and as evening drew near, a suitable campsite was selected by each army which afforded some protection for its overnight stay. Ahuitzotl secured an elevated knoll for Tenochtitlan's army with guards posted in a defense perimeter. Soldiers erected shelters and campfires for their chieftains while they themselves slept on blankets spread over a plot of earth covered with leaves stripped off the shrubs and trees in the vicinity. Each unit, down to the squad level, set up its own fires, and when darkness settled in, hundreds of burning lights dotted the landscape in clusters marking the location of its army. Upon one such bonfire was roasted a deer caught earlier for Tizoc and his notables who enjoyed the venison eaten along with fruit, nuts, and other food items carried in their ration packs.

"There's something to be said for a meal under a night sky," commented Tizoc. "Even the dried fruit has a succulence I rarely notice. Regrettably Nezahualipilli is at his own camp. His company would be most agreeable now."

"Tomorrow we'll be as one before Toluca," said Ahuitzotl. "Zozoltin will gaze out from his palace and see a thousand burning fires in the distance-a sight to stop his heart."

"Just the thing to make him consider surrendering to us."

"You would still allow him to do that?" sneered Ahuitzotl.

"Those were our original terms," Tizoc bluntly reminded his commander. "Why should they change?"

"They should change because the conditions under which they were granted are no longer the same," answered Ahuitzotl.

"Indeed. How are they different?"

It became evident to everyone seated around the fire that a confrontation was developing; the ensuing tension created some discomfort, not only for those observing it, but also for Ahuitzotl who had not intented that his words should lead to this.

"The terms were made before we assembled our armies and moved on Toluca," said Ahuitzotl.

"That's your reply?" countered Tizoc with appreciable agitation. "But we anticipated this–I should not have to remind you of it. Why are you making an issue of this now?"

"It is different now that we have come this far," Ahuitzotl said, seeking to extricate himself from the controversy he had unwittingly generated. "A momentum is in progress. Warriors are itching for battle-we should not disappoint them."

"And who determines our policy? An assembly of our council leaders or our warriors?"

Tizoc could be a formidable antagonist if he so chose. He was not made Revered Speaker for any lack of abilities or alternative choices and often had moments of brilliance, particularly on the intellectual plane, which impressed those who witnessed it displayed. Ahuitzotl realized that he had underestimated him and now found himself pressed to make a face-saving retreat.

"Perhaps you misunderstand," he squirmed. "I merely meant to point out that our soldiers should be rewarded for having undergone this journey. Their efforts should not be expended over nothing."

"I see. You suggest that a bloodless victory is an insufficient reward-that it is nothing."

"You demean my purpose, Lord. They wish to serve the gods. Their valor must be tested so their true worthiness can be demonstrated. It's necessary that they expose themselves to dangers. Captives must be taken."

"Is this your opinion, or are you speaking for them?"

Ahuitzotl was beginning to feel vexed displeasure at Tizoc's pointed line of questioning and was struggling to maintain his composure. "I speak for the army," he said.

"Do you? So were I to ask each warrior if he agreed to have battle rather than capitulation, he would choose to fight them."

"Perhaps not all of them," Ahuitzotl corrected himself, "but most. There are always those, even in our army, who have no heart for fighting. But a true warrior must, and wants to, have a good battle in which to exhibit his worth."

Tizoc saw that Ahuitzotl remained persistent in his obstinacy and deemed it useless to continue this verbal exchange. By now the tension had settled so heavily over the group that any relief, however slight, would be welcomed, and Tizoc, sensing the worriment of his ministers, decided to prudently alleviate their apprehensiveness.

"They may still get their chance," he said. "It appears unlikely Zozoltin will surrender peaceably to us, but he shall nevertheless be given his opportunity. We promised him that, and I am obligated to abide by our words. We know you opposed this, Ahuitzotl, but a majority in our council believed it the correct decision. I see no point in carrying on with this debate. My position should be clear to you."

Ahuitzotl, seeing that Tizoc had offered him an opening to end their standoff, gratefully grasped for it. "It is, Lord," he said, "I retract any suggestion that I disapprove of the council's policy. My duty is to serve it."

"It pleases me to have you say as much," Tizoc beamed in a rare smile. "I consider the matter closed."

Their reconciliation was received as a heavy burden lifted from the backs of everyone seated there and, in more than one instance, a low sigh of released nervousness was heard over the crackling fire. On each face could be read the thoughts possessing its bearer: Tizoc was gratified-for once he had faced up to Ahuitzotl without backing down and had, in a small but significant way, gotten the best of him; Cihuacoatl glanced at the monarch in a perplexed state, mystified by what he must have regarded as inconsistencies in Tizoc's behavior, and was reminded of the reasons he had appointed him to succeed Axayacatl, and it had been a long time since he held such notions; Tlohtzin exhibited no particular emotion beneath his stoic expression except perhaps some relief that things did not get out of hand; Motecuhzoma gaped wide-eyed and was obviously impressed. As for Ahuitzotl, he fluctuated between moods of irritability over finding himself disadvantaged in front of the group and a genuine, although begrudging, respect for his brother. He was on the verge of erupting into an explosion of fury which he would not have been able to contain and, in all probability, come to regret, and Tizoc spared him from that. In spite of his seeming faintheartedness, the Revered Speaker could be aroused into opposition that was threatening: it would be remembered.

With tensions eased, conversation drifted to more trivial subjects which entertained the group through the remaining evening until, worn out by the long day's march, individual members left one by one for their tents. Soon only Ahuitzotl and the chief minister remained beside the gradually fading fire.

"An interesting exhibition," Cihuacoatl remarked. "It's not often that you are bested by the Revered Speaker."

"Bested?" Ahuitzotl snarled. "Is that what you think?"

"It appeared as such."

"You misread it."

"I think not."

"Do not anger me," Ahuitzotl cautioned the minister. "If that's your intent, be advised I will not tolerate it."

"There's no need for me to anger you-Tizoc has accomplished that quite satisfactorily."

"I will not be pushed like this!"

"That is your problem, Lord. You are a bolder and stronger man than your brother, and you are better at leading men, but you allow your turbulent nature to rob you of good judgment. If you are ever to rise above your station, you must learn to control your rash temperment-at least have us believing you are master of it."

"I am the Tlacatecuhtli. Only the Revered Speaker is more powerful-and you. What is this talk of rising? Have you found a way of arranging this?"

"I'm still working on it. Have you given any additional thought to our last conversation?"

"No. This Toluca affair has kept me busy. As things presently stand, I see no solution to the problem."

"Events could create a solution for us. It's always possible the Revered Speaker could be killed in battle."

"But not very likely. Revered Speakers do not move in the front lines. They are protected by bodyguards and security squads. An enemy arrow might strike him down, but that would have to be a remarkable shot indeed, guided by the hands of the gods themselves."

"Did I allude to an enemy arrow?"

Ahuitzotl recoiled in dazed silence, and Cihuacoalt instantly realized that the commander was not ready for such extreme measures and still distrusted him. He was at a loss on how to advance this delicate subject. Resigned that he was overstepping his bounds with such provocative suggestions and unable to ascertain where Ahuitzotl stood on them, he simply sat quietly by watching the now barely glimmering fire grow dimmer.

"It would never work," Ahuitzotl at length broke the long silence.

"What wouldn't?" Cihuacoatl inquired with a sudden renewed interest.

"Having one of our own warriors fire on the Revered Speaker."

"Then you did not ignore what I said."

"I heard you. But why even think it? Who would dare? The fear of retribution from outraged gods is a most potent deterrant."

"True. It would take someone who did not fear the gods."

"Is there such a man?"

"I once thought there was, but now I'm no longer certain."

"You knew no such man," Ahuitzotl informed him. "Every man fears them—if not all, then some. No, Cihuacoatl, we must rely on the orchestrations of the gods if Tizoc is to fall in battle. Look for another solution."

"I shall."

"Why so determined? Tizoc is on his way to punish Toluca. Depending on how we do this, it ought to settle your fears about our ability to maintain our dominance."

"Toluca is one of many cities now openly defying us. I told you of them. Will he punish them all?"

Ahuitzotl did not answer.

"And why your complacency?" continued Cihuacoatl. "You once had me believing I was restraining you from traitorous ideas; now it is you who checks me. Am I to accept you have suddenly had a change of heart and now approve of the manner in which Tizoc rules us? Do not play the loyal noble subject with me, Lord. I know you better than that."

"You do not know me," Ahuitzotl corrected the minister. "I haven't disagreed with what you've said, nor have I censured you for your blasphemy. This should tell you we are not out of accord with each other."

"You dare to admit that much?" Cihuacoatl gloated. "I'm gratified that I've managed to make you see things my way."

"Don't flatter yourself, Cihuacoatl. You base it on false presumptions. What I do is on my own account. Answer this for me: if a Revered Speaker were to commit an unspeakable act, one offending lord and peasant alike, resulting in clamor to get rid of him by one and all, could it in fact be done?"

The question aroused curiosity in Cihuacoatl, not merely because of his puzzlement over what Ahuitzotl was leading to, but as a matter of speculation. He knew of no circumstances giving rise to such a consideration in the past.

"We have no precedent for this," he finally said. "I suppose if the demand were strongly pressed, the interclan council would have to take up some measure, although what that might be I couldn't say. I find such a possibility even more remote than my suggestion. What do you infer?"

"I was merely dwelling on the improbable. Do not concern yourself over it. Now leave me, Cihuacoatl. I wish to be alone-to think things through."

Cihuacoatl did not object in spite of his inquisitiveness; he was quite wearied by now and fought off the surges of drowsiness hastening to overwhelm him. "I go, Lord," he said, "but we shall have more to say on this."

Ahuitzotl rendered his farewell gesture with a wave of his hand and remained seated in solitude beside the glowing embers of a once bright fire. Many ideas raced through him during this quiet time, but mainly he resented the way in which Cihuacoatl constantly fueled his exasperation and envy of Tizoc. The slightest hint, the merest suggestion, the smallest of clues revealing a bitterness in him was seized upon by the minister and cast back at him for clarification and definition. He felt himself constantly prodded, and he still did not know where Cihuacoatl's allegiance led, which increased his reluctance to confide anything in him despite the severe actions he advocated. It may all be a ruse to snare Ahuitzotl committed to an act of treason with the minister actually obeying Tizoc's instructions by offering temptation in the form of these wild proposals.

What the minister advanced was contrary to all their ethical standards. The monarch's person was inviolable-to declare even the remotest insinuation of a threat against him constituted seditious conduct punishable by death. And if that were not enough, the gods also would seek their own penalties, denying a soul entrance to the nine levels of paradise, and keeping it forever confined to the underworld. No, Ahuitzotl thought, to harm Tizoc entailed the gravest peril. His own approach-Tizoc perpetrating an outrage which would lead to a universal condemnation and demand for his ousting-held the only real promise. And yet...! What of the minister's conjecture that if a Revered Speaker fails to adequately serve the gods, does it not become a matter of duty to replace him? If he cannot be forced to abdicate, then how? Would gods punish someone for seeing to their needs? No, it is not up to Ahuitzotl, or Cihuacoatl, or anyone else-Tizoc must bring about his own undoing.

At last, Ahuitzotl felt a need for sleep, having attained a degree of contentment in his conviction that events would arise that will render Tizoc the blow which would lead to his demise. Spent of energy, he slipped into his tent and retired for the day.

On the following dawn, the armies resumed their march, passing through a number of villages along the route where they drew a few admiring glances from children thrilled by the spectacle and the general hostile stares of adults who bore no friendliness for the Mexica, viewing them as aggressive belligerants out to subdue another unfortunate people. Once out of Anahuac, the Mexica were rarely received with warmth by a local populace which was kept under their yoke by force of arms and threats of destruction. Unlike many of the previous conquerors who had contributed to the general welfare of a subjugated people, the Mexica offered no particular benevolence or enlightment and instead invoked great fear through the excessive demands of their bloodthirsty gods. They inspired no loyalties or sense of pride and were, on the whole, much despised. Not that this troubled them any; their entire history had been one marked by humiliating degradation at the hands of their neighbors until they finally, through adopting policies of overt aggression cloaked in a religious fervor, managed to gain superiority over their former tormentors. They were dealing out no more than they had for so long received, they reasoned, and if people resented it, so much the better, for it gave them a taste of what the Mexica had so bitterly endured. Tizoc may have been the singular exception among them to genuinely trouble himself with this animosity and to truly desire an improved relationship with his neighbors.

It was still morning when the Army of Tenochtitlan made contact with some patrols of the advance parties and, after the fanfare of a joyful reunion had worn off, they regrouped with the ranks of their fellow warriors and together proceeded on the march. They had by now entered the fertile valley of the Tolucans and noticed that most of its farms and community centers had been abandoned—unmistakable evidence that Zozoltin was marshalling his people and resources so he could field as large an army as possible-signs increasingly indicating that Toluca would have to be taken by force.

Shortly after the sun had crested along its daily path, the Army of Tenochtitlan arrived upon a green plain criss-crossed with innumerable plots of irrigated land edged by forests and dense brushes and lying between two widely separated mountain ranges, and its warriors espied the distant towering mounds overlooking the surrounding countryside.

"The temples of Toluca, Lord!" Cihuacoatl shouted.

"I see them!" replied Tizoc. "We shall be there well before the day is spent."

They were soon met by chieftains of the reconnaissance detachment and the priests who had advanced ahead of them and had assembled beneath the shade of a cypress grove only two leagues from Toluca at the site selected for their camp. Ahuitzotl stepped forward and carefully scanned the plain, noticing its cleared ground and gradually descending slope to the city which would make any troop movements visible and afforded open fields of fire for his archers while also easing the control of unit deployment. He nodded his assent on the well-chosen location.

The next few hours constituted a frenzy of activity as the encampment was being prepared for its occupants. Field directors constructed drainage and drinking facilities; unit locations were spotted; waste disposal areas set up; subordinate and command headquarters were established with shelters erected for the lords, ministers, priests, and chieftains; guides were posted to direct the trailing armies and remaining contingents to their designated sites. Much of the campground was still being laid out when the Army of Acolhuacan made its appearance and, with its additional soldiers to help, the work progressed rapidly. By the time Army of Tepaneca arrived at dusk, everything was in place and only a minimal amount of extra labor was required to provide for it.

After the camp was settled, and everyone had partaken of their evening meal, Tizoc called on his expected command meeting around a bonfire set up in front of his headquarters where the battle plan was reviewed. Tizoc declared his intention to give Zozoltin until noon for his surrender before initiating an attack. In spite of the evidence that Zozoltin had massed his people in Toluca, the Mexica believed that he remained in a numerically inferior position, a view strongly held by Ahuitzotl. As a result, Ahuitzotl proposed attacking on a broad front thereby requiring Zozoltin's stretched lines to be spread even thinner and making any part of his force vulnerable to penetration. With everyone agreed on this, Tizoc allowed Ahuitzotl and his chieftains to go and work out the details while he stayed with his ministers, head priests, and the rulers of Texcoco and Tlacopan to participate in informal conversation with them. He longed to speak with his esteemed friend, Nezahualpilli, whose counsel he valued above all others, but this opportunity came late as the group dispersed slowly, and, not until the two of them were alone, did he open himself to a subject of deep concern to him.

"What manner of man can this Zozoltin be?" Tizoc pondered aloud. "To have a city choose enslavement or death rather than submission for his sake?" Tizoc pondered aloud.

"You're still disturbed by this?" Nezahualpilli said. "Why is it so important to you?"

"Perhaps because of its novelty. I've never heard of such a thing."

"I'll make my assessment of him when I see him."

"To have such a hold on his subjects–and devotion. He willingly receives an obedience the rest of us must attain through threats and force. There's power in that. Would the Acolhuas accept death for your sake?"

"I doubt it."

"That's my point. Surely you must be impressed by what Zozoltin has achieved."

"I am not. You make too much of him, Tizoc-a mistake. He is no greater king than you or I, and if he has the consent of his subjects, it's because they are unified in their opposition to us. Such circumstances magnify a leader's greatness in the eyes of his people, but it does not mean he is so superior a man that the rest of us should stand in awe of him. Do not make him into more than he is or it will cause you to be intimidated by him. Tomorrow we shall see that he is a king like any other king, nothing more."

"Yes, and you will see something unique about him. No ordinary man defies his overlords with such a flagrant disregard of their retribution."

"Tizoc, I have heard enough. I will not have you extolling some arrogant king to exaggerated proportions-a king you have never met to know if he even merited so lofty an acclaim out of you. You are the Revered Speaker of the greatest power in the world. There are none mightier than you-it is Zozoltin who should stand in awe of you. That is our reality—believe it. I shall see in the morning. Think on what I said."

This was one of the rare times Tizoc had seen Nezahualpilli in anger and it imparted an unsettling effect on him. Seated alone by the fading fire, he shuddered over the possibility of alienating his ally, the only person he could still call a friend. He was becoming increasingly unsure of himself and correspondingly relied more on his colleague to assist him in his decision-making, and this realization alarmed him. Nezahualpilli was right in asserting there was no greater ruler than the Revered Speaker of the Mexica, Tizoc was thinking, and he had to act the part. Absorbed in such introspection and unhappy about what he saw in himself, and ever more self-conscious over what he perceived as grave shortcomings in his ability to rule, Tizoc was to spend a long drawn-out and sleepless night abusing himself with torments he could neither ignore nor face.

XIII

"Ochpaniztli is here!" Ahuitzotl scornfully related to Tizoc while the Mexica leaders were gathered before their armies to await the arrival of Zozoltin and his delegation. A messenger had been sent into Toluca at early dawn to carry word of a desired conference to its monarch and his presence was soon expected as decreed by custom regulating the intercourse among nations.

"You've served your purpose in coming here," Tizoc sarcastically countered. "Without your declaration, I'm certain I would have forgotten."

Ahuitzotl was left bewildered over Tizoc's seeming unfriendliness and noticed, when he glanced at Nezahualpilli, that the Texcocan's expression intimated a similar puzzlement. He refrained from saying anything further, deducing that the monarch's unusual behavior was in part due to his impatience over meeting an antagonist who, for some inexplicable reason, held a strange ascendancy over him.

If Tizoc was anxiously anticipating this encounter, the same could not be said for his adversary, for half the morning had already elapsed before a band of dignitaries was spotted emerging from the city.

"He comes!" announced Tizoc. "It is Zozoltin!"

Their eyes strained to distinguish the Tolucan monarch from among the group slowly ascending the steady incline toward the Mexica lines, but at this distance, they could not tell.

"At last we will see Zozoltin," Ahuitzotl scowled, "this self-appointed insurgent who would deliver his city from our domination."

"Will you be silent!" Tizoc sharply rebuked his commander. "He comes to us with the burden of his personal doom and the fate of his people upon his shoulders. At the least, you can render him proper respect."

"As my lord commands," replied Ahuitzotl, embarrassed.

By the time the party advanced to within a hundred paces from the Mexica, its leader could be readily discerned as he was taller that his compatriots and walked in a bold and proud manner indicative of his station. The nearer he came, the more distinctively declared stood the regal countenance in which he bore himself, and when he finally presented himself in front of Tizoc, his commanding presence clearly denoted him as an authoritarian figure born to rule his nation. He wore a tilmantli of blue feathers and a silver embroidered breechcloth, and his headdress was adorned with the long plumes of the prized quetzal bird emanating from a golden crown. Jade and gold ringlets extended from his earlobes. His stance was calm before Tizoc and for several minutes the two rivals mutely gazed upon one another as each assessed the other's apparent attributes. Then he spoke.

"I am Zozoltin, Lord of Toluca, here under the protection of the Revered Speaker's word."

Tizoc was impressed; the deep, assured inflections of his opponent's voice signified a practiced familiarity to issuing commands that could only have been borne out of its habitual usage.

"I, Tizoc, accorded you this pledge so that we might speak about the conditions exacted on you."

"Speak, Lord Tizoc!"

"You have opposed our dominion over you by your failure to meet our assigned tributes quotas, and you have done this openly and defiantly in view of all our subject states, thereby necessitating our action against you. You were told by your ambassador of the terms imposed by our council, and also failed to comply with these. In this opposition you have set Toluca apart as an example to be emulated which constitutes a threat to our power and demands retaliation. This we must do; however, in conformance with the accords existing between our realms, we are obliged to once again offer you these terms-the lives of your supporters and yourself in exchange for your city's salvation. You have until noon to reconsider. If no answer is received by then, we will commence our attack."

"I need no time to reconsider," Zozoltin proclaimed. "The issue is decided. If you want Toluca, you will have to take it."

"Surely you grasp the consequence of this," Tizoc said worriedly. "Your people will fare badly for this."

"We have chosen to accept our fate"

"Indeed!" Tizoc replied, greatly disturbed by a response that reinforced the awe in which he held his adversary. "Can it be so miserable to live under our rule? Are we such inhuman beasts that death is preferable to living in our servitude?"

"You rob us of our dignity, our autonomy, and our bounty. Your voracious gods take from us our most promising young men and women. You sneer at us and hold us in contempt, and flagrantly flaunt your imagined superiority over us. We are men as good as you, and not deserving of your shameful treatment and endless degration. Yes, Lord Tizoc, it is indeed that miserable to live under your yoke, and for these reasons we have, to a man, decided to challenge you and take our chances in battle."

"And your women and children? Don't you care what happens to them?"

"Of course we care! But if we are to continue our existence oppressed by the policies and dictates of the Mexica, which strangle us, then no acceptable future exists for them. It's better to control our own affairs than to have those whom we despise determine this for us. As this is not possible while we remain under your domination, death is favored by us and by them."

"What you say is absurd, Zozoltin!" Tizoc burst out indignantly. "We have not been unduly harsh on Toluca. The tributes we demand from our subjected states are not excessive and place no undue hardships on them."

"It's not that they can't be met, Lord Tizoc," Zozoltin said, sensing Tizoc's legitimate concern on this matter, "but by submitting to them we are constantly reminded that we are not masters of our own house. It represents an incessant humiliation for us–as it would for you!-which we, as worthy and honorable men, will not permit ourselves to endure any longer."

"Do you think by your action you can change all this? That is the way of our world. There will always be masters and those who must serve them. Gods created this-it is according to their fashion this has been so made."

"No, Lord Tizoc, that is the work of men! We have lived for a long time within the confines of this valley. Our gods have been good to us. They have blessed us with rich lands and have brought us good harvests and fresh waters, and all this they gave us with no demands for us to make war on our neighbors beyond our valley. They were pleased-our sacrifices were sufficient to for them and insured us life and prosperity. Then you came to us, a vile intruder, and you told us it takes a hundred times-no, even more!-our sacrifices to satiate your gods into doing for you-not us!-what ours have done for so long. I see this and am to listen to you say it is their work that things should be so. You are wrong, and I do not accept that."

Tizoc gazed at Zozoltin, astounded that the Tolucan monarch so accurately voiced his own sentiments. "Accept what you will, Zozoltin," he said after a lengthy pause, "but understand this: in our eyes a divine calling brings us here and my warriors will fight with the zeal invoked by such a belief. Once we are embattled, it will be difficult to restrain them. If you fail to surrender by noon, certain destruction awaits you. Now go and think on this."

"I have already given my answer."

"I know, but you have until noon to ponder its wisdom. Discuss it again with your lords and subjects. Should your position remain the same, then bring forth your army at that time."

"I thank you for permitting me this opportunity to speak," Zozoltin said. "May the gods grant victory to whom they favor this day."

"So be it," Tizoc nodded his assent, and added, "It's a pity you have chosen to direct your talents against us, Zozoltin. I would rather have men of your ability as allies."

Zozoltin gave Tizoc a comprehensive glance and knew him to be sincere. Then, maintaining his lordly comportment, he turned about and proceeded back to his city with his ministers trailing behind.

"So this is Zozoltin," Ahuitzotl said to Nezahualpilli standing beside him. "He has a noble bearing, if nothing else."

"Why shouldn't he?" Tizoc injected, having overheard his commander. "He is a king."

"An enemy king, Lord," declared Ahuitzotl, "and so shall he be treated."

Nezahualpilli, noting the Revered Speaker's vexation, grabbed Ahuitzotl by the arm in an attempt to prevent him from further inflaming the situation, but his efforts came too late.

"What does it take," fumed Tizoc, "to get you to understand that a great man can be respected and yes, even admired, in spite of being your enemy? A lord of such worth deserves honors, no matter what cause he espouses."

"What you say is alien to me," answered Ahuitzotl. "I have not said I did not respect him."

"You certainly have a poor way of showing it. Now, remember, I want Zozoltin taken alive! Make sure our warriors know this."

"So do I," Ahuitzotl affirmed. "It shall be as you say."

"Good. You may proceed assembling our forces."

Thundering drums and blaring conch shells marshaled the warriors into their prearranged battle configuration, a long line arched slightly inward in the middle and extending for nearly three leagues. The Army of Tenochtitlan constituted the right wing with its Tlatelolco section closest to the center while the Army of Acolhuacan stretched from there to the left with the Army of Tepaneca at the extremity. In addition, selected squadrons from each of the armies comprised a reserve element that was positioned along a second line about a hundred paces behind the first. A heavy squadron of four hundred Order of the Eagle knights was posted around Tizoc to function as his bodyguard.

As for their composition, squadrons of archers, intermingled with smaller detachments of sling-throwers, formed the first row of warriors. Immediately behind them were infantrymen, carrying their spears and shields and standing four to six ranks deep with one squadron averaging a sixty man front Stationed behind these warriors stood two ranks of capturers-newly initiated youths and older men-whose task it was to bind the enemy soldiers disarmed and taken by the combatants. Each squadron was separated from the other by an approximate twenty pace gap.

Ahuitzotl presented himself on the right halfway between the his army and directly ahead of his Order of the Eagles division, and with him was Tlohtzin, whose Jaguar knights extended further right. Nezahualpilli and Chimalpopoca remained with Tizoc, centered amid the armies a short distance behind the forward wall of bodyguard warriors, also Eagle knights, and allowed their commanding generals to lead their armies. Also with Tizoc stood Cihuacoatl and the other ministers, as well as most of the priests. Motecuhzoma was in front of his mazatl squadron which made up the left flank of the Tlatelolco section and was thus nearest to the Revered Speaker, with the young officer standing but a hundred-some paces from him.

Like silent sentinels they stood, eagerly waiting for the sun to arrive at its daily apex and watching what appeared to them a deserted city with no signs of life detectable from within its confines. Then, and with startling suddenness, they heard the rapid pounding of drumbeats, followed by repeated deep drones of trumpets. All eyes were riveted on Toluca which abruptly sprang into vitality, bursting forth with armed warriors brilliantly clad in battle array. Within minutes, the opposition took up a similar line, covering nearly an equal length as the Mexica's, only that their ranks were more shallow with but three rows deep and they appeared to have no units in reserve as far as Ahuitzotl could see. They whistled, whooped, and clashed their spears against the massive shields they carried as they marched out to take up their battle stations.

The Mexica, not to be outdone, responded in kind, beating their own drums and sounding trumpets, and likewise rapping their weapons against their shields so that the entire field resounded with the clamorous collision of arms and the shouts and whistles of men in an endless tumultuous bluster. This fanfare was allowed to continue until the Tolucans were solidly emplaced along their line, at which point Ahuitzotl raised his clenched first over his head and motioned his warriors into obedient silence. Zozoltin's army followed this example and soon an eerie stillness, very daunting to an observer, encompassed both forces standing poised to strike upon the given order.

The strained quietness rankled taut nerves as it attained an unbearable peak, acting as a leashed restraint on impulses and sinews itching to spring into action. At last Tizoc nodded to his chief priest signifying that the battle should commence. Directly, the priest raised a huge shell horn, pressed it to his lips, and pierced the stillness with its deep resonance. Its blare was echoed and re-echoed by additional votaries spotted at specified intervals throughout the force, and upon hearing the blast nearest them, warriors roared out their repressed eagerness to fight and moved forward. Archers opened fire, launching arrows toward the enemy lines with an intent not so much to inflict injury as to lay down a protective cover for the advancing ranks, and after releasing several volleys, they stepped aside so as not to impede the drive of their attacking compatriots.

First and most zealous to rush on the Tolucans was the right wing under Ahuitzotl whose exhibited enthusiasm for the engagement had a contagious effect on his soldiers. When it closed on them, the stonethrowers and slingers hurled their projectiles into the enemy rows to create confusion and consternation among them while, at the same time, inhibiting their ability to counter the assault. An instant later, the first wall of warriors collided with the opposition in a vociferous crunch and the clash of shields, clubs, and swords. Screams and shouts of angry combatants rang out along the lines. Within minutes, the whole of the force was locked in fearsome battle.

Warrior fell upon warrior, crashing shield into shield, parrying and thrusting swords, bashing clubs, and stabbing with spears as each attempted to gain the upper hand over the other, all amid the painful and terrible cries of those cut down and the exultant cheers from the triumphant. The maquauhuitl, wielded by powerful arms, smashed through helmets and crushed skulls; lances penetrated armored tunics and tore into vital chest cavities; clubs hacked at exposed limbs, tearing flesh and breaking bones, and blood spewed profusely forth from horrible wounds. And almost as quickly as contact was initiated, enemy captives were seized and dragged behind the lines by groups of priests, prowling about like ravenous wolves, who stripped a number of them naked, flung them over improvised altars, and cut out their hearts to let the hot blood spill on the field as an offering to Huitzilopochtli for his aid in securing a victory.

On the right, Ahuitzotl seemed everywhere present in the thick of the fighting, directing one squadron to replace another, issuing commands and shouts of encouragement to his embattled warriors, and striking down opponent soldiers daring enough to reach him between the ranks with deft blows of his maquauhuitl. Under his ferocious assault, marked by an exuberance bent on speedy conquest, the weaker Tolucan lines began to crumble as the boldly led Mexica attackers broke their resistance. At that moment, Tlohtzin, fighting alongside his commander, happened to glance behind him and saw a startling sight.

"Look!" he roared out. "A large force attacks Lord Tizoc!"

To the amazement of Ahuitzotl and all the Mexica, Zozoltin had assembled more than a thousand of his strongest warriors into a massed wedge formation which plunged forth from Toluca under his personal command and charged headlong toward the Mexica center. In a tactical move borne out of utter desperation-the greatly outnumbered Tolucans had little chance of defeating their enemy-Zozoltin risked everything on this one bold stroke aimed at capturing Tizoc in the hope that they could bargain for their sovereignty with his life. Never before had anyone seen such a maneuver applied.

"Send our forces to the center!" shouted Tolhtzin in his alarm. "We must reinforce it!"

"Wait!" Ahuitzotl countermanded him. "It could be a ploy. Let's see what develops."

"What?" Tlohtzin could not believe it.

"I said to wait!" repeated Ahuitzotl sharply-he thought of the priest's vision and instantly perceived he could bring about its reality. "Continue to press our right!"

At the Mexica center, an insufficient front wall of warriors could not hold their positions against the heavy concentration of Tolucans presented by their formidable wedge and one by one were beaten back, falling in writhing heaps where they dared to stand their ground. Tizoc stood aghast as he watched this fearsome juggernaut hammering its path through the ranks and bearing down on him, and while his bodyguard Eagles took up a half-circle in front of him, they were clearly at a numerical disadvantage and he could see that they would never be able to hold up against such an overwhelming host.

"They've broken through!" Nezahualpilli warned Tizoc. "We must make a stand!"

"There are too many!" Tizoc yelled back.

"There's no choice! We must fight!"

"No!" Tizoc was now frantic. "We cannot allow ourselves to be taken."

"We only need to hold them for a short while. Reinforcements will be sent."

"Don't be a fool, Nezahualpilli! Come on!"

"Stand fast, Tizoc!" Nezahualpilli shouted as sternly as he could. "A Revered Speaker cannot leave the scene of battle!"

That instant, in a deafening crash, the point of Zozoltin's wedge met the bodyguard force; Nezahualpilli and Chimalpopoca, shield and club in hand, ran forward to join their embattled Eagle knights trying to repulse the fanatic horde caving in on them. Heroically, the Mexica kept their place, furiously determined to protect their monarch, but fell in increasing numbers under the spears and swords of their wildly screaming attackers, dying beneath advancing feet. Their blood soaked the ground as it came gushing out of severed veins and smashed skulls. Still, they inflicted severe losses, unwilling to yield in the slightest measure, and as both Mexica and

Tolucans were furiously cut down, the advance was slowed when soldiers tripped and climbed over the bodies of their fallen comrades.

Panic-stricken, Tizoc could no longer contain himself; with the situation desperate, and believing his capture imminent, he issued a stunning order.

"Move behind the right wing!" he commanded. "There we'll be safe."

No argument came from the alarmed priests and ministers who were with him. Only Cihuacoatl hesitated, recognizing the gravity of this decision, but he was too startled to say anything and found himself caught up in the group's frenetic attempt to escape as it hastened away to the astonishment of everyone observing its flight.

"The Revered Speaker flees!" shouted someone from the bodyguard force fighting for his life.

"Tizoc flees!"

Like a rampaging fire, these electrifying words raced through the ranks, striking as a shock-wave the Eagle squadron warriors in their deadly struggle. Almost immediately their resistance faltered: Nezahualpilli and Chimalpopoca were extremely pressured to encourage continued fighting and strove by their courageous example to sustain it.

At the very same instant that Tizoc chose to retreat from the field, Motecuhzoma, whose squadron had already smashed its opposition guarding the city, saw the fearsome battle being waged in the center. He accurately assessed the situation and, in a flash of initiative, directed his warriors to come to the Revered Speaker's assistance. Responding to the order, his unit rushed toward the beleaguered center to strike at Zozoltin's rear-a move that did not unnoticed farther on the right.

"What squadron is that?" snarled Ahuitzotl.

"By it's banner, the mazatl squadron, Lord!-from Tlatelolco," answered Tlohtzin.

"They have broken the battle order."

"They're doing what we should have done moments ago," Tlohtzin bitterly reproached his commander. "They're trying to save our Revered Speaker!"

Unaware yet of Tizoc's fateful decision, Ahuitzotl seethed as he saw his plans go awry. With the possibility of Tizoc's imperilment snatched away, he could no longer hold back and ordered his entire wing, which by now had totally crushed its resistance, to wheel inward and attack the Tolucan wedge from behind. Even as the Mexica saw their ruler fleeing the center, Tenochtitlan's army was coming back to entrap Zozoltin's force.

In the course of a few minutes, the Tolucans, who had Tizoc's capture within their grasp, now found themselves hemmed in between the bodyguard force which was holding its ground under the valorous efforts of Nezahualpilli and Chimalpopoca and the right wing, first under Motecuhzoma and then Ahuitzotl, which fell upon their rear. They knew it was over for them; their all-out drive to seize Tizoc had failed, primarily because of an unexpectaedly strong defense put up by his protective Eagles which robbed them of critical minutes and permitted reinforcements to arrive. Had they succeeded, they could have used the monarch's person to keep his rescuers at bay, retreated back to their city, and obtained acceptable terms for his release. Zozoltin's entire plan rested on this single daring move. Now all was lost.

Doomed, the Tolucans refused to concede defeat and faught tenaciously against captivity, enraging the Mexica who resented this break in convention-battles were waged to acquire prisoners for eventual sacrifice-and now were forced to beat them into submission. They hacked viciously at their attackers, who came at them from all sides, and struck them down in great numbers, only to be compressed tighter and tighter until they were too cramped to wield their weapons. Many, in their death throes, leaped at the nearest assailant and furiously embraced him, biting and clawing to immobilize him so he could be slain by the others. Into this constricted heap of battered bodies, the Mexica hurled and jabbed their lances: obsidian tipped projectiles gored necks, chests, and abdomens of entrapped warriors. Everywhere the blood ran, spurting over bodies and spilling to the ground; the dying, squirming in pain, choked in it. This gruesome slaughter, while ferocious and intense, lasted but a short time until more than half of Zozoltin's force lay in gory piles about him.

"Stop the killing!" Zozoltin roared out. "We yield to you!"

"Hold off!" responded Ahuitzotl. "We want them alive!"

Shortly thereafter the fighting ceased and the Tolucans dropped their arms, offering no more resistance as they stood shocked and dazed, hearing the moans of their wounded and dying all about them. Their conquerors quickly took hold of them, binding their hands behind their backs. Zozoltin was brought before Ahuitzotl who had by now learned of Tizoc's flight.

"So this is how you planned to win," Ahuitzotl taunted his captive. "It explains everything-the deceptions, the failure to seek allies-a truly bold design. It almost worked-Tizoc will vouch for that. You've made it difficult for us. For that, your city will pay the price."

"You are a mad dog!" raged Zozoltin. "It is Lord Tizoc I wish to appeal to."

"Unfortunately-for you!-you have chased him from the field so it is I, Ahuitzotl, who will enter Toluca. By the time he returns, my work there will be finished. Take him away!"

"Monster! May you be cursed!" screamed Zozoltin as he was being dragged off. "May the gods damn you!"

Ahuitzotl had commenced issuing orders directing his units to regroup for their assault on the hapless city when Nezahualpilli, thoroughly exhausted from his arduous ordeal, came forward.

"What took you so long?" he puffed angrily.

"We were heavily engaged on the right," replied Ahuitzotl, "I couldn't come any earlier."

Nezahualipilli's intense glare told Ahuitzotl that the Texcocan did not believe him. "Their lines were thin," he said, "and they employed the bulk of their force in their drive upon our center. You could have easily sent half your army to relieve us when you first saw this."

"Leave me be!" Ahuitzotl growled, "We have unfinished work to do!" and with that, ordered his attack.

Nezahualpilli, outraged but spent of energy, felt in no mood to restrain him and, even as the reservists were taking their bound prisoners to the Mexica camp for internment, Ahuitzotl and his remaining front line squadrons stormed into Toluca.

The carnage that arose was absolutely frightful. Soldiers, infuriated over the stiff resistance encountered earlier and its resultant unexpected high losses, were given a free hand to vent their fury upon a defenseless populace and cruelly sacked the city. Unusual for the Mexica, whose ethical standards and discipline prohibited rapine and slaughter of noncombatants, this resultant brutality, which arose almost spontaneously, was more due to a loss of restraint over hot-headed individuals than out of any intentional design yet nonetheless proved disastrous for Toluca's inhabitants. Defenseless women were dragged screaming from their homes by howling warriors to satisfy their carnal appetites, and when they resisted, were clubbed to death or strangled. Houses were set on fire, with some still holding occupants too frightened to come out of hiding who perished in the flames shrieking horribly, and everywhere looting prevailed. The rampaging soldiers ran into pockets of resistance where priests and old men, and even some women, armed themselves to make a stand against them. These they quickly dispatched, the fearsome maquauhuitl slicing their bodies open, but when they reached the central temple, hundreds of armed priests awaited them at its front steps.

Motecuhzoma's squadron was the first to come upon them and unchecked, without waiting for specific instructions, it charged headlong for them. In a horrid scene straight out of an unspeakable nightmare, amidst the blackened smoke and glowing fires of a city in destruction about them, Motecuhzoma and his frenzied warriors hacked their way step by step up the temple's platforms, killing the priests opposing them and dodging the bodies rolling down beneath their feet. The priests were no match for the better armed and better trained warriors and fell in rapid succession before the stone eyes of the god they were pledged to protect, a butchery that continued unabated to the upper stage and into the temple's shrine until the last of them was struck down directly in front of the idol while desperately pleading to it for a divine last instant intercession. Then the Mexica toppled the statue from its pedestal, carried it through the narrow doorway, and rolled it across the platform to the steps where it bounced down in dull thuds over the bodies of dead and dying votaries until it crashed into pieces at the bottom. Next, they set fire to whatever would burn inside the shrine-this was the work of one squadron out of an army run amok.

Ahuitzotl, horrified over the extreme violence he had unleashed, called forth his leading commanders. "Stop your men from this madness!" he shouted.

"But we thought you sanctioned this," answered one of the captains with surprise.

"Fool! Do you think I would condone this kind of savagery? I had no idea it would come to this-the people were to be enslaved—not brutalized! We must put a stop to this!"

"It's impossible now-they are beyond our control!"

"I said to stop them!" Ahuitzotl raged. "Do what you must, but, upon pain of death, obey my orders!"

Frantically, the captains ran from unit to unit, bellowing out commands to subordinate chieftains who, after tremendous effort that included actually dragging soldiers from out of houses they were looting and threatening them with punishment by death, eventually managed to attain some semblance of discipline. Gradually order was restored and the warriors, their heated passions enervated, now stood red-faced and ashamed of their gruesome conduct and gathered up the remaining prisoners-mostly weeping women and children and a few old men-and sheltered them from additional abuse as they were assembled in a group.

All this was taking place during the time span in which Tizoc and his entourage fled towards the protection of the army's right flank and, upon seeing the danger passed, returned to their former position where Nezahualpilli and Chimalpopoca were still standing, fatigued from their hard fight. At seeing the monarch, Nezahualpilli's disdain heightened.

"You have committed the gravest error!" he denounced Tizoc. "Today's action will forever be held against you!"

"I did what was prudent," Tizoc answered, vigorous in his attempt to minimize the blunder. "Had I been taken, there would have been no victory for us this day."

Nezahualpilli may have perceived the truth in this, but also knew such a justification would never be acccepted. As for Chimalpopoca, he said nothing in his embarrassment and refrained from eyeing Tizoc.

"You should have stayed!" Nezahualpilli said. "I told you we could hold them."

"I could not have known that at the time. I do not wish to belabor the point. I see the city is in flames. Who authorized this destruction?"

"Who do you think authorized it?" Nezahualpilli replied in bitterness.

Tizoc gazed over the devastation in disbelief, fearing the worst. Huge black billows of smoke from raging infernos clouded the afternoon sky, blocking out the sun and darkening the surrounding plain, and he heard the horrible and repeated distant screams of women and children arising from the conflagration. He shuddered as every painful cry impacted on him.

"So he got his way after all," Tizoc thought aloud, a coldness gripping him as one particularly terrible shriek pierced the setting, and then turned to his colleague and added, "We may as well investigate this and learn first hand what he has done."

The three monarchs, along with Cihuacoatl, their ministers and head clerics, on entering Toluca's streets, were greeted by an appalling spectacle, the likes of which they had never witnessed before, with naked bodies of slain women, young and old, grotesquely twisted where they fell, and blood-soaked children wailing next to their dead mothers, and corpses of old men and priests strewn about smoldering wrecks of houses and temples-sights which stunned them into grim reticence. A massacre contrary to all standards of accepted decency, it imparted as a profound shock on them. Tears of rage and remorse flowed from a petrified Tizoc who viewed the ruin of this once proud city in abject horror, and he cursed himself over and over for not having been present to prevent this atrocity.

When they came to the main plaza, they met the first group of warriors escorting lines of captives from the vicinity-Tizoc could not look upon them. Then, at seeing the stacked bodies of the priests on the temple tiers and steps and the shattered fragments of the statue which had been hurled from its upper platform, their revulsion was heightened; the Mexica priests babbled nervously among themselves, exhibiting shocked expressions, especially when they saw the broken idol. A short distance from there, they noticed Ahuitzotl with Tlohtzin appearing to give out orders to a number of his chieftains standing about, and Tizoc, not disposed to dismiss this slaughter, headed straight for him, his vehemence mounting at every step. Ahuitzotl, who knew he faced condemnation, observed his approach in soberness.

"I see you've done your work well," muttered Tizoc when he reached his commander; he was so enraged that he trembled even as he spoke. "Are you satisfied now?"

Ahuitzotl, himself still aggravated and nerves on edge, was in no mood to receive further criticism but, for the moment, held back from answering.

"Is this how our warriors must demonstrate their bravery?" Tizoc stormed on. "Were we in such need of our exhibition that we had to inflict it upon innocent women and children and enfeebled old men? This is what you led them to?"

"I'll not endure this insult!" Ahuitzotl suddenly exploded. "I did not intent this, nor did I order it! I am as sickened as you over what happened here, so do not prod me, Lord, else I shall forget myself and commit my own act of brutality-against you!"

Tizoc recoiled, stunned over his commander's open indiscretion, as was everyone else witnessing this outburst, including Nezahualpilli whose patience with Ahuitzotl was running out.

"You dare threaten the Revered Speaker?" he interjected in his apparent shock.

"You will pardon my ill-chosen words," Ahuitzotl backed off, aware he had overextended his authority. "They were spoken in haste out of my disgust over this massacre. I will not be made the villain in this!"

"Then how do you account for it?" Tizoc pressed.

Ahuitzotl deeply resented this sort of interrogation coming from a man he regarded as his inferior, but he remembered his obligations and was not about to add another transgression above an already untenable breach of conduct. "We lost control," he admitted, "and what you see here is the result. Our warriors were mad with rage, due to our near humiliating defeat incurred by Zozoltin's refusal to fight conventionally, and could not be constrained. By the time I could get order reinstated, it was too late. This is the truth—I swear it before Huitzilopochtli."

An oath such as this was unquestioned and convinced Tizoc of Ahuitzotl's sincerity, and although his anger abated, he remained horror-stricken over the wreckage around him.

"By all the gods in heaven!" he cried out. "How can we face our allied rulers and speak of honor after this? What a day this has been! How will I tell my people I forsook the battlefield in order to assure our victory? Who will believe it?"

"We have both done damage to ourselves it seems," replied Ahuitzotl, "so let's absolve ourselves of our misdeeds and draw no more attention to it, if that is acceptable to you."

"Forget this?" Tizoc faltered.

"Yes, as I must forget your fleeing before Zozoltin."

After a lengthy pause, Tizoc nodded his agreement, not because he felt he could dispel any repugnance over what he had witnessed-his nature would never permit this-but that he knew his was a far graver infraction than Ahuitzotl's. He knew himself to be false, which bore heavily into his consciousness. Even how he rationalized his flight, as necessary for their triumph, was deceitful, for he fled out of fear, perpetrating an unspeakable act of cowardice which, had it been committed by a lower ranking noble or warrior, constituted an offense that demanded execution. Nezahualpilli was correct in saying this would forever be held against him.

While Ahuitzotl and Tizoc were agreeing to their mutual concessions, Nezahualpilli, also greatly troubled over the magnitude of the carnage, was not as assured of the commander's probity as was Tizoc and questioned Tlohtzin about it. "Is it true," he asked, "that Lord Ahuitzotl did his best to put an end to this butchery?"

"It is, Lord!" replied Tlohtzin. "I was with him through it all and can attest for it. Indeed, only after he threatened his chieftains with death did he managed to end it."

"Then I misjudged him. I am gratified I was wrong," said Nezahualpilli who next detected a nervousness in Tlohtzin. "Is something amiss?"

Tohtzin was reluctant to answer.

"You know something," Nezahualpilli perceived, "and I believe I have an idea what it is. I refer to events occurring earlier in the day." He paused to peer directly into Tlohtzin's eyes and knew he had struck a sensitive case. Tlohtzin wanted to say something but could not find the words.

"No matter," the Texcocan determined, "I'll not pursue it. It's better that I leave this field with some degree of trust for Ahuitzotl left in me through doubts than to find myself alienated by the certainty there has been treachery afoot in which my own life was at risk. Such knowledge would surely strain my relationship with him. I'll say no more on this."

The rest of the day was spent in mopping up operations which entailed taking the wounded to physicians, accumulating the dead, counting them, and burning them on pyres, and amassing weapons taken from the defeated. The captives, including most of the city's residents and surviving warriors, among them Zozoltin, were gathered into a containment area guarded by sentries. A long debate ensued among the victors about the wisdom of leaving Toluca in desertion and in the end they decided that a majority of local citizens, along with a number of soldiers, should be released and permitted to rebuild their city with the help of their neighboring tribesmen. Even Ahuitzotl concurred with this, largely out of misgivings he felt over having been responsible for the cruelty inflicted on the city, and there were no objections by the warriors who ordinarily could have made claims on individual prisoners but were still shamed by their conduct and found it awkward to insist upon this right under the circumstances. Zozoltin, while grieved over the ruin of his city, nevertheless was able to give thanks to Tizoc for what he deemed an act of atonement for the Mexica's excessively ruthless vengeance. When all was done, the Mexica had counted three thousand captives, several of whom were women who had either chosen to remain with their taken husbands or were selected as desireable for slaves or sacrificial victims.

So ended the first day of the month Ochpaniztli. In the passing of a single afternoon, the Mexica exacted their punishment and in the process the lives of the principals who had taken art in this drama were inexorably altered. For Zozoltin and his followers, it forged a climactic finish to what they had dreaded the most-the inevitable outcome of challenging a superior power in an attempt at sovereignty against almost all hope. For Tizoc, already unpopular, it added one more stain on his effectiveness as a ruler and appeared to portend a beginning, rather than an end, to greater difficulties. For Nezahualpilli, it festered lingering doubts and supicions towards men he once regarded as true friends and whom he thought he had understood. As for Ahuitzotl, it exposed how fragile his control over his forces was in its reality, how easily it could be lost, and, more importantly, the dangers of injecting his own solutions into events decreed by greater powers. The vision of the priest had been fulfilled, but not at all as expected, and worse, Ahuitzotl could not capitalize on it, as he might have wanted to, because of his own misdeeds. For all of them, it had been a most memorable day.

XIV

Toluca had been a costly enterprise for the Mexica, with nearly seven thousand casualties that included twenty-five hundred dead; it was predictable that the reception accorded the returning armies in their respective cities would be subdued, if not at first, when the details of the battle unfolded. Still, custom called for a runner to be sent to Tenochtitlan with his hair neatly braided who would race through its streets waving his maquauhuitl and shield joyously bespeaking of their triumph. No sooner had he set out on his way when the rest of the force began its two day march back with the prisoners and wounded, an uneventful journey.

When the armies of Tenochtitlan and Acolhuacan entered the capital, the populace was out to greet them. Incense burners were lit and shell trumpets sounded, reeds and flowers were spread on the main avenue over which the soldiers trod, and there were roars of appproval when the people saw the number of captives being led by the guards. But amid the fanfare came also the disappointments and shock for many who sought out their sons in the returning squadrons and discovered they were not among them. Although male children were born for battle, and significant honor was attached to their falling in war as this assured one's place in Tonatiuhichin, the East Paradise of the Sun, there remained the initial horror all parents feel upon learning that they will never again see their sons until this deprivation is reconciled as being for the greater good of all things ordained. They bore their reversal in fixed solemnity, restrained by the knowledge that they would receive no sympathy from a crowd which believed their sons had arrived in a happier place, and intent on contributing to the general spirit of celebration so as not to mar the gaiety of the event.

Zozoltin and his warriors were placed in strong wooden cages hastily assembled from various storage areas and located in the central plaza. Three to four men were fitted into these, but Zozoltin was confined alone in his on Ahuitzotl's orders as a kind of mockery of his kingship. Certain townspeople were assigned to feed the Tolucans at regular intervals and to replace their waste containers, a task by no means regarded demeaning because, as potential sacrificial victims, the prisoners attained a somewhat sacred status as divine messengers to the gods and deserved good treatment. Nevertheless, a few guards were kept around them in case there should be an attempted escape, however remote that possibility existed.

Before being dismissed, the soldiery gave up its armaments to collecting quartermaster sections which amassed them for storage in arsenals to be duly refurbished and prepared for the next campaign, and soon everything returned to a state of normalcy except that the Acolhuas stayed for the night and would not resume their journey home until the following day. The work of the commanders, however, was not finished. There remained the usual grievances to be heard, the recommendations for awards to those warriors who distinguished themselves, the assessment of the battle plan to determine where it had been effective and where it proved faulty, and there were the special tribunals which had to be ordered to sit in judgment over those who were accused of cowardice before the enemy and other military crimes, such as failure to obey orders, dereliction of duty, insubordination, malingering, or so on. Ahuitzotl directed these affairs from the headquarters complex; after listening to the reports of his chieftains, he told them he would evaluate each one and make a decision on them in the succeeding days and then dismissed them, except for Tlohtzin who remained in consultation with him.

"A strange case we have on Motecuhzoma," he said to Tlohtzin.

"In what way, Lord?"

"Contradictory. Certainly his bravery was exemplary-in that respect his conduct is beyond reproach-yet he broke the battle order, led the assault on the temple priests, and, according to a number of sources, was most averse to stopping his men from ravaging Toluca, even after my orders to do so. What do you say to this?"

"As to the first charge, I would say his actions demonstrated good initiative-something we should place more emphasis on."

"Not when it entails a disruption of our tactical plan. Discipline is the key factor differentiating us from our opponents-from the top levels to the lowest so that every facet of a battle can be controlled. Our failings in this at Toluca aside, which must be deemed an anomaly, it is the most basic ingredient leading to our successes."

"To be sure, but his motivation-coming to aid Lord Tizoc will provide a solid case for him and could lead to embarrassment for anyone charging him with misconduct for this. The court will never prosecute him."

"What of the other charges?"

"Who makes them against him?"

"His division commander, not that this makes a difference."

"It doesn't. I just thought for a moment that it might have been you."

"Would that have offended you?" Ahuitztol asked, curious over Tlohtzin's response.

"When you consider all that happened that day, yes. You had the occasion to relief our heavily pressed center but delayed in doing so. Indeed, I had suspicions you actually desired that the Revered Speaker would be killed or captured. Whether this is so I don't know, but if it is, it would be no less a violation of our military codes than those alleged against Motecuhzoma."

Ahuitzotl blushed over the insinuation but ignored additional reference to it. "It's not my conduct that's being disputed, but Motecuhzoma's," he said. "What is your recommentation on the charges against him?"

"He is new to his duties. Novices are reluctant to force decisions on their men which are seen as unpopular. It takes time for a youthful commander to develop the inner strength and fortitude to lead authoritatively."

"You were not asked to plead in his defense, but for a recommendation. What do you advise?"

"Dismiss them!" Tlohtzin answered without hesitation.

"On what grounds?"

"Mitigating circumstances. His squadron was not the only one to commit anton outrages, nor was he alone averse to stopping his warriors from their, ah, diversions. Why should he be singled out to bear the brunt for all that? Either we share in this burden or we disdain from seeking scapegoats for it."

"Will this satisfy his division commander?" asked Ahuitzotl.

"If it doesn't, it creates a dilemma for him. Can he swear before the court that he issued specific instructions prohibiting attacks on Toluca's civilians? If he did not, then what is the basis of his charges against

Motecuhzoma? And if he did, why are his other squadrons, equally guilty, not accountable for it?"

A smile came to Ahuitzotl; such an order was rarely given as there was no expectation of the abnormal brutality that had occurred in Toluca. "Now that would be interesting," he mused. "I can see him squirming. We shall have to save him from the indignation he will undergo if he persists in his allegations. I will recommend a dismissal of all charges against Motecuhzoma, but we must find a new assignment for him. It's counterproductive for anyone having to retain a member of his command against whom he has initiated charges. That creates uncertainty about issuing more orders to him and weakens one's ability to lead."

"I agree. Do you have one in mind?"

"He will be assigned to this headquarters-to become my personal aide."

As Motecuhzoma's future was being determined at the headquarters, another conversation was underway in the royal palace between Nezahualpilli and Tizoc. Although he never would have thought that unfavorable circumstances could stand between him and a truly good friend, Nezahualpilli found his association with Tizoc strained as a consequence of the events in Toluca and their discourse suffered accordingly. He had lost much of his esteem for Tizoc and tried his best not to let this affect his comportment, but doubted if he succeeded at this. Tizoc was keenly aware of his colleague's reservations, as well as the cause for it, but refused any allusion to this, realizing he could not negate what the gods had ordained, and repressed it, however difficult. The future of someone else was being decided.

"What will you do with Zozoltin?" asked Nezahualpilli.

"What we agreed to from the start," replied Tizoc. "He shall be offered to the gods."

"I thought perhaps, as a king, you might allow him to fight for his freedom upon your ceremonial stone. It's an honorable gesture considering his courageous performance against us."

"We give him ample honor by sending him to the gods."

"If you say so. When?"

"In twenty days, during our festival to Tlaloc. I trust you will attend the rites."

"If that is an invitation, of course."

"You know it is," Tizoc confirmed. "You're unduly formal, Nezahualpilli. We've always been good friends, and I had believed we understood each other, but tonight you make me feel as if I am imposing on you. Since when have you needed to ask for an invitation?"

"I'm sorry, Tizoc. The Toluca affair has placed a barrier between us and it will take time to remove it. I ask you to abide with me until I'm able to recover from my inhibition."

Tizoc delayed in answering. He knew that his damage was irreparable and did not want reminders of it. "It does weigh heavily on me, Nezahualpilli," he finally stated. "I shall have problems enough facing our people once they learn of what happened, but to also suffer the scorn of friends, that will make my burden unendurable. I appeal to your sense of justice–afford me a chance to redeem myself. I cannot change what has happened. I can only continue from where I stand now; for this I need the support of friends, not their derision."

His was an impassioned plea, and Nezahualpilli was not left untouched by it, sympathizing with Tizoc's tribulations which he knew tormented him, and he felt obliged to offer some consolation.

"You face a serious setback, Tizoc; I'm not at all sure the people will permit you to forget it. But as for me, be assured my friendship is true. Whatever misgivings I presently feel will pass. I regret your misfortune, but with perseverence, you will overcome this disparity. Trust me on this."

"You have satisfied me. Your assurance is convincing–I'm certain I can surmount this crisis."

On this amiable note, the two kings retired for the evening. No restful night was in store for Tizoc, however; he remained extremely discomforted over his recollections of the campaign and his yearning that things could have been different. He wanted to suppress these, but they kept resurfacing to disrupt his efforts at relaxation. In this half asleep, half awake state, he passed the excruciating long hours in wretched misery and turmoil.

The rejoicing which met the armies after they returned from their venture was tarnished considerably when news of what actually had transpired became known. By word of mouth, primarily from the very warriors who had participated in the operation, people learned of the brutal manner in which Toluca was taken, of the flight of their monarch, and of the breakdown of discipline which had permeated the ranks and led to the city's destruction. They reacted with mixed emotions, combining feelings of outrage, disappointment, and humiliation, and shortly thereafter one could hear derogatory words expressing contempt for the Revered Speaker-seditious words which would have been unthinkable earlier and still ran punitive risks. Clearly the prestige of Tizoc was dangerously diminished, and there were many lords who openly began to discuss if something should be done about it.

Under the rising of this dark cloud Nezahualpilli and his Acolhuas left Tenochtitlan, and already, even as they were making their departure, they could hear derisive remarks said to them and the cheers they received only yesterday were significantly subdued. To the Texcocan it came as a confirmation of what he had suspected-it would indeed be a severe storm that Tizoc must withstand.

As Tizoc watched the procession leave from the second-level quarters of his palace, a sense of loneliness came over him, for this was a time when he was very much in need of Nezahualpilli's companionship to console him and help him through his adversity. He could confide things in the Texcocan he dared not tell anyone in Tenochtitlan-his innermost feelings and apprehensions-and know he would receive an understanding ear and not be censured or ridiculed for it. Who could he trust here? Cihuacoalt was a sycophant, loyal enough, but cold and insensitive and forever preoccupied with the dignity and status of the monarch's office. He was a capable minister, an advisor, but not a friend. As for his brother, Ahuitzotl, there was no kinship between them; he despised the ruler and was envious of him. His counsellors, intellectual friends, and the builders he often distrusted-they served him well in an official capacity, but not a personal one. Indeed there was not a person in Tenochtitlan with whom he could discuss his case, and this greatly added to his frustrations.

At this point, while Tizoc absorbed himself in his reflections, Tlalalca entered the room and gingerly snuggled up to him, as together they saw the last elements of the Acolhuacan column departing through the serpent gate. She was familiar enough with Tizoc's mannerism to know when he wished quietness and said nothing, but he, warmed by her close presence, longingly glanced at her. Perhaps he was wrong, he thought; he could talk to Tlalalca, yet there were things he dared not tell even her. What would she think of him if she knew?

"I wish Nezahualpilli had stayed a while longer," he finally said, his despondency revealed in his voice.

"He has his own city to rule," replied Tlalalca. "It never made a difference to you before–why should it matter now?"

Tizoc frowned; hers was the kind of question devoid of the sensitivity he solicited and it left him unsettled. He did not reply.

"I can see you are in no mood for my company," Tlalalca noted. "I shall leave you in peace."

"I want you to stay, Tlalalca."

"Shall I speak to myself then?"

"No need to feel indignant," Tizoc weakly smiled. "I merely meant that after the unusual operation we just completed, I would have preferred talking with someone who took part in it."

Tlalalca intuitively understood that something had gone wrong and her searching eyes beckoned for details.

"I may as well tell you," muttered Tizoc uneasily, "You will learn of it anyway. You're going to hear from many sources that I, lord of our nation, ran from the enemy in the heat of battle and retired from the field. It's true-I did!-although the circumstances will undoubtedly be reported falsely to you."

Tlalalca paled; in spite of wanting to appear sympathetic, she found it difficult to conceal her alarm. Tizoc dismissed her unease and went on.

"The Tolucans surprised us by a concentrated attack on our center after we had thinned our lines over a wide area. I was there with Nezahualpilli and Chimalpopoca-also my ministers-when they came at us. Believing my bodyguard would not be able to withstand them, I withdrew from there, with my ministers and priests, to avoid being captured, which might have given the enemy a chance at winning. To make it worse, Nezahualpilli and Chimalpopoca remained to fight and, as it turned out, reinforcements came in time to repel the attack. So my flight amounted to nothing and could only be construed as the act of a recreant by all who observed it."

Tlalalca was dumb-struck. She needed no explanation on the severe nature of Tizoc's action as it was common knowledge that soldiers who exhibited such cowardice were usually tried and sentenced to death so they did not contaminate anyone else with their defilement. But for a Revered Speaker-her husband-to have done this came as a jolt.

"What will you do?" was all she could think of saying.

"What can I do?" he moaned bitterly. "I'll have to ignore it-pretend that it never happened, I suppose. If I dwell on it, I will surely lose my mind."

"Will anything happen?" Tlalaca worried.

"I don't think so. Nobody knows what to do, and this will probably work in my favor. By the time the fact-finding committees and inquiry boards are formulated, if such a move is being contemplated by the interclan council, much of this will have faded or at least seem dated and lose its relevancy. The priests will be my strongest allies, for they hold this office as inviolable. I must do my best to foster their friendship."

"And who is your strongest enemy? Ahuitzotl?"

"Not this time," Tizoc pondered aloud. "He has his own burden to carry. He allowed–inadvertently he says-our warriors to commit cruel excesses upon the Tolucans and to desecrate the temple of their patron god, which shocked our priests into revulsion. For the time being, he could not get their cooperation against me."

"This operation grows more bizarre at every word."

"It was unusual," Tizoc reflected with sober introspection. "None of us escaped unscathed from it in some way. No wonder Ahuitzotl pledged his word to make no mention of it."

"You believe him?" Tlalalca raised her voice in exacerbation. "He hates you. How can you possibly go by what that animal tells you?"

"He is my brother, and of royal lineage. Whatever you may say about him, he is a man of honor and will stand by his word. He would not deceive me."

"He is your greatest foe! Everyone speaks of his ambitions, and these events in Toluca–I speak of your conduct!-have certainly granted him an opportunity to press for an advantage. You would be well advised to fear him!"

"Fear him?" Tizoc bellowed. "No! By the Gods, that is one thing I will no longer do! If there's anything I've learned from this affair, it's that I was a fool to ever have let him intimidate me with his arrogant ways, but no more."

Again Tlalalca was astonished. At no time previously had she heard Tizoc repudiate Ahuitzotl with such mettle, as if the campaign had transformed his character into a more aggressive temperment, much in contradiction to his earlier confession, and she was perplexed over the inconsistencies. "I stand corrected," she said. "Do not fear him, but rather eye him with suspicion and due caution. Brother or not, he bears you ill-will."

"You know this? Is this what you discovered from Pelaxilla?"

"No, I've learned nothing from her—yet. It's what I feel."

"I should prefer something more solid, but I will heed your advice and maintain an eye on him. At present, I don't think it's so crucial. He has disgraced himself, as I have, and will also need some time before attaining the respect of influential lords."

Tizoc felt his confidence returning as he spoke with Tlalalca, a quality she seemed to invoke through her presence, which he appreciated. He grew more assured he could regain the respect and trust of his ministers and people. It would be mostly a matter of ignoring the temporary denigration, generating a dynamism by expanding his construction projects and asserting his leadership, and pleasing the large caste of priests and their multiple cults by planning an impressive ceremony for the upcoming feast of Tlaloc-this he could accomplish with the sacrifice of Zozoltin and his Tolucans.

XV

Ahuitzotl met Pelaxilla at their favorite rendezvous point, the gardens behind the royal palace, in as joyful a reunion for two lovers as could be imagined, with smiles, laughter, and even tears of happiness streaming from Pelaxilla's eyes as she was beside herself with rapture that he had safely returned. They smothered themselves in long affectionate embraces and tender caresses, and for Ahuitzotl these moments reinforced a deep felt yearning for comforts and pleasures only a woman loved could provide and he understood how empty his life was without Pelaxilla. His incessant longing for her was becoming obsessive; she would have to be his—if not presently, soon.

"How little you men understand," Pelaxilla said, "what grief you bring to us when you go on your wars-the anxieties we endure over whether we shall ever see you again. Is this what our life together will be like?"

"The requirement exists, Pelaxilla," he told her. "Huitzilopochtli's work must be done."

"Yes, I shall have to accept that. At least you've come back to me."

"So let's enjoy our moments together. They are not that frequent and should be relished to the fullest."

"The goddess Xochiquetzal will be envious."

"Of me? You flatterer."

"No, silly, of me," Pelaxilla teased, "for the pleasures you give me."

"See? You are a flatterer."

"Why shouldn't she? Am I not with the handsomest man in Anahuac?"

"Of course," Ahuitzotl grinned, "as I am with the most beautiful woman. We complement one another perfectly."

They laughed and walked in the delight of each other's company along the familiar footpath, but the merriment was short-lived as Pelaxilla could not hold back the question burning within her. "Will you do as you promised?" she asked. "Will you speak to Lord Tizoc now about releasing me from his pledge."

"I shall, however..."

In her excitement she did not allow him to finish, finding the prospect too stimulating, "It's so thrilling. Can you imagine it? You and I together from now on-and this with but an approving nod from Lord Tizoc."

Pelaxilla's elation evaporated when she was suddenly struck with the realization he did not share it; she knew something was wrong about this. "What is it?" she inquired, her demeanor turning somber.

"You interrupted me," Ahuitzotl said, displaying some nervousness. "Lord Tizoc is not in the best of spirits at present. I don't think he will be amenable to granting me any favors for awhile. I guess what I'm trying to say is that I must wait before speaking to him about you."

"Oh, no!" Pelaxilla moaned, unrestrained in her disappointment. "No!"

"Please, Pelaxilla," Ahuitzotl begged, "You know this is as painful to me as it is to you, but it is extremely risky to ask him for anything now."

"I can't believe this! How long must I wait this time?"

"I don't know. Perhaps another month."

"This is incredible!"

"You are angry with me," Ahuitzotl reacted to her indignation with some acrimony of his own. "That is unfair to me, especially when I have our welfare at heart. If I were to ask Tizoc for anything now, he would refuse me out of spite-things did not go well between us at Toluca. I won't have your impatience jeopardizing our future."

"What sort of duplicity is this? You are supposed to be the bravest of men, but are afraid to face your brother. Give me evidence of your boldness!"

"I'm doing what is prudent at this time."

"Allowing a cowardly ruler to deprive us our happiness?"

"Cowardly? Then you know?"

"All Tenochtitlan knows. The rumors are rampant."

"What do they say?"

"That your brother, our Revered Speaker Lord Tizoc, if he may still be called that, fled from the enemy to the disgrace of all who saw it. Everyone has heard of it."

Ahuitzotl marveled over the speed in which word had spread, somewhat skeptical if they truthfully portrayed the actual events. "Anything else?" he asked. "About me?"

"Yes, I've also heard that you threatened Lord Tizoc."

At first Ahuitzotl eyed Pelaxilla in utter amazement, then his demeanor turned to anger. "You knew this," he glowered, "and yet you insisted I should confront him and ask for a favor?"

"Because I thought you had a higher regard for our happiness and deemed the risk worth taking. Evidently I was wrong."

"I swear there are times I think I hardly know you. Beneath that lovely face of yours lurks a deviousness I find dismaying. All this time I believed you were sincerely distraught, you were merely exercising your pretensions over me. Isn't that so?"

"Only partly," she admitted, worried about how he might react. "I was very despondent on hearing of more delays. Those were my true emotions you saw. I could not have feigned the disappointment I felt. How can it be that this weak brother of yours should stand between our being together?"

"This 'weak brother' of mine happens to be the Revered Speaker, in case you've forgotten."

"He certainly did not act the part in Toluca, did he?"

Until this moment, Ahuitzotl had no idea that Pelaxilla held such low esteem for Tizoc and this revelation did not please him. Tizoc was still a royal lord and, while it may have been acceptable for him and the ministers to find fault with their monarch, for a mistress, whose dealings with Tizoc were of a personal nature rather than an official one, to declare him in contempt was quite another matter. Ahuitzotl's own hostility for Tizoc was centered on the ineffective manner in which he ruled the state and a bitterness over not having been bestowed the throne himself, and as far as knew, Cihuacoatl's animosity was based upon his legitimate concerns over the realm weakening under Tizoc. These were justifiable reasons for despising Tizoc, but to resent him and ridicule him out of mere personal dislike, such as Pelaxilla seemed to do, was distasteful to Ahuitzotl; it had a jaundiced aspect to it which he thought offensive. Tizoc did not deserve this kind of deprecation over his personal qualities, for he was essentially a good man-he was just not a good ruler. It troubled him that the woman he so loved should possess such negative notions.

"That does not change anything," Ahuitzotl finally replied.

"I think it should," she countered.

"Of course it should," Ahuitzotl's ire mounted, "but you've overlooked a major obstacle. Tizoc cannot be replaced while he lives-that's objectionable to the priests. They believe his office and the person filling it is divinely ordained. As long as this is the case, I must appeal to him for your hand. There's no point in demeaning his character-I'll still have to go to him."

"But you won't!"

"Did I say I won't?"

"You keep putting it off!"

"All right!" Ahuitzotl shouted, "All right! It's against my better judgment, but if it means so much to you, then-very well!-I'll see him about this tomorrow."

"Please don't be upset with me," Pelaxilla pleaded. "I wish for us to live together. It's because of my love for you that I'm unable to wait any longer. I should not be castigated for this."

"It will be a mistake," Ahuitzotl said, still feeling uneasy.

Pelaxilla found his recalcitrance exasperating, but she saw that she was perilously close to provoking his volatile temperment and instead brooded over her unpromising predicament. She meant nothing to Tizoc. The number of times he had requested sensual pleasures from her she could count on her fingers in spite of all the years he ruled. Yet this man wielded the authority to prevent her from obtaining what she desired above all else. She hated Tizoc for this and, if she had to, and by whatever method she had available, she would press Ahuitzotl to instill a similar loathing in him.

"Why are you so intractable?" she languished. "I thought you loved me."

"You know I do."

"What will you do if he refuses to give me to you? Be content to let the matter rest?"

"What do you suggest I do? Steal you from him?"

"That's not a bad idea, but I have a far bolder scheme in mind. You were once surprised when I told you I preferred men who had great aspirations. I've always believed you to be such a man-indeed, that may even be why I'm so attracted to you."

"Get to the point, Pelaxilla."

She decided to risk it all on a most daring proposition, one she had never previously considered and deemed quite horrible yet felt it necessary to put forth in order to force his hand.

"Why should you beg for me and crawl like a dog before Tizoc? You are a better man than he is. If a Revered Speaker cannot be replaced while he lives, then, if you are ever to rule, his life must be shortened."

Ahuitzotl was stunned. He could not believe this was Pelaxilla speaking, the darling of the court whom everybody adored, who charmed them all and who possessed not a single disparaging bone in her body. There was a time when he was assured that he was the only person alive to think such thoughts, and now it seemed as though everyone was inferring this. But from sweet Pelaxilla? She must be playing her pretending games, he told himself, or perhaps she was testing him for some purpose or other.

"I see it now," he responded, "You're acting out the things you wish for. Tell me when you do this, Pelaxilla, so that I'm not unnecessarily shocked."

"Is that what you think?" she asked, amazed at his reply.

Pelaxilla fretted if she had not overextended herself. The court rumors must have been wrong in their allusion that Ahuitzotl aspired for the throne. But then, why did Tlalalca fear this so much? There must have been sonething to it-why else would she have been implored by the empress to ascertain what he planned?

"You are serious," Ahuitzotl concluded to his astonishment. "How can you hate him so? What has he done to you?"

"I have you to thank for that. Had we never met, and had I not fallen so in love with you, I should have been happy enough to expend my days in service to him. Because you have engendered this desperate expectation in me-for our being together-you have also instilled a loathing for that which would prevent this. Yes, you created this abhorrence I bear for Lord Tizoc. And all this since our last meeting in this garden!"

"I did this to you?"

"By promising we would be united after this war. I was thrilled beyond belief! What hopes you gave me! And now you tell me it may not be? Oh, you have most severely wounded me! But it is Tizoc who holds our future in horrid abeyance and who, from all you have said, stands in our way. Why should it be a surprise I now possess such evil wishes upon him?"

Distressed, Ahuitzotl groped for words which momentarily eluded him. It seemed that every aspect of his life somehow entailed a connection to Tizoc, and he grabbled if he would ever be independent of the monarch's ever-present predominance over him, viewing this as increasingly oppressive, and irritated that he could not function within its confines. It was as if all the pressures directed him towards one incontrovertible conclusion-against Tizoc.

"I didn't realize you would become so obsessed by what I told you," he finally answered. "Certainly that was not my intent."

"Not your intent?" Pelaxilla nearly wept in her despair. "How could I have helped it? I am a mortal woman-I have frailties."

"So I see," Ahuitzotl said, reluctantly making up his mind. "I won't prolong your anguish by deferring this. It's best that I face him and get this issue resolved."

They continued ambling along when the laughter of several ladies of the palace, who had just entered the garden, came upon them as an intrusion. Both would have wanted to linger in their conversation and regarded this distraction as an unwelcome interference, but could not require the women to leave. With his need for her additional companionship frustrated and greatly discouraged by the hopelessness of the situation he found himself in, Ahuitzotl drew on the occasion to leave Pelaxilla in the company of her friends and departed. No longer was it possible for him to postpone the inevitable request and so, with the gravest of misgivings, he determined his course: he would talk to Tizoc.

XVI

Ahuitzotl saw the drillmaster waiting for him when he entered his headquarters after having left the garden.

"You sent for Motecuhzoma, Lord?" he asked his commander.

"Ah yes. Is he here?"

"In your chamber, Lord!"

When Ahuitzotl walked in, the young chieftain braced himself in an erect stance; his countenance was one of intense sobriety, reflecting a nervousness quite unusual for him which the commander instantly noticed on seeing him.

"You may relax, Motecuhzoma," Ahuitzotl directed. "We have no more need for such formality as we'll be seeing a lot of each other. Favorable fortune brings you here-you're being assigned to this headquarters to assume duties as my aide. I believe congratulations are in order."

Motecuhzoma's confusion was clearly in evidence; he did not expect these news and, until now, had been under the impression he faced a reprimand for his conduct at Toluca. But a change of command assignment after only a few weeks as squadron leader–that was severe, Ahuitzotl's comments to the contrary.

"You look bewildered," Ahuitzotl noted, "and not too pleased. I don't take kindly to bestowing privileged positions on ingrates. What disturbs you about this?"

"I don't know what to make of it, Lord. I've been led to believe a command assignment is desirable for a young chieftain. You congratulate me, and yet I sense that this is a blemish on my record. Has my command been considered unsatisfactory?"

"Have you cause to think it might?"

"I'm aware of having taken certain discretions at Toluca which at the time I thought proper and in conformance with my duties, but have since been told they were against procedures and contravened orders."

"You thought your actions in conformance with your duties?" Ahuitzotl adjudged his answer reckless. "How did you reconcile your squadron's attack on the temple as such?"

Motecuhzoma, puzzled that the exploit he had considered his most daring was regarded his worst mistake by his superiors, pondered over this. He had already been censured for it by his division commander and now anticipated that he faced the same denouncement from Ahuitzotl.

"The priests were armed and gave every indication they meant to fight," Motecuhzoma finally said. "It may be true I miscalculated their purpose when we attacked them, but in the heat of battle, I was not inclined to question them about it."

"Slaying the priests, while unfortunate, did not constitute a violation of orders. It's unlikely they would have surrendered to you; your initial estimate that they meant to fight was undoubtedly correct. But why was their god toppled from his pedestal and hurled from the temple?"

Motecuhzoma delayed in his search for an acceptable answer; his division commander had offered no adequate explanation over his indignation and this was the first time he was asked about the idol.

"I suppose I failed to exercise proper restraint," he said.

"A mistake!" Ahuitzotl was quick to point out. "It has generated significant condemnation from our priests for which I was accountable, and for which I have been subjected to considerable rebuke. Our priests profess to honor the gods of all nations with the same reverence they hold for ours and are inclined to readily accept these into our pantheon. You should have know this, having been schooled in Calixtlahuaca. Isn't that what they teach you there?"

"They do, Lord." acknowledged Motecuhzoma, quite red-faced.

"That's all you can say about it?"

"What else can I say? I've already admitted that I failed to take due care. Am I supposed to grovel in the dirt and beg for forgiveness?"

"Certainly not to me," Ahuitzotl smiled, amused by Motecuhzoma's sarcasm, "but perhaps to the priests of the god you offended. He was the patron god of the Tolucans, the equivalent of our revered Tonatiuh, the Sun. The priests are adamant in their contention that you have committed a sacrilege and expect you to properly atone for it. As a matter of practicality, I advise you to adhere to their wishes-do some act of repentance which will please them."

"What should I do?"

"You ask me that? I find our panoply of deities confusing enough without knowing the ceremonial demands of each particular one of them. I propitiate my favorites and tell myself that by pleasing them, I please all the rest. For the others I rely on the priests to keep them content. Go to the priests of Tonatiuh; they will instruct you on what they want. Perhaps they expect you to fast in their temple for a number of days-how should I know?"

Motecuhzoma still had a befuddled look about him, "Is it at the request of the priests then that I am being reassigned?"

"No, it is at my request," Ahuitzotl told him.

"Forgive me if I am confused, Lord. It strikes me odd that you should want me after making it apparent you are annoyed over what I had done. I don't know what to say."

"You needn't say anything for the moment. I have my reasons for your transfer. But for now, settle this account with Tonatiuh's priests. When you go to them, do not allow them to impose excessive conditions on you that will keep you from your duties here."

"Am I to argue with them if they do?"

"Whatever, but use tact. I can't afford to have them oppose me again."

Motecuhzoma then left the chamber to proceed for the temple of Tonatiuh. Originally Ahuitzotl was bent on chastising him for breaking the battle order, but he recognized that this was a delicate issue. As a royal, Motecuhzoma had easy access to Tizoc-to have censured him for coming to the monarch's rescue would have been a monumental blunder. He did the correct thing in referencing the problem to the attack on the temple; this way, should Tizoc conduct his own interrogations, he would not be found in a compromised position.

Ahuitzotl remained deeply troubled over his earlier encounter with Pelaxilla. Theirs was, in many respects, a frustrating relationship: when they were together, they argued a lot, exposing more than they should of their inner passions, yet, when apart, he was constantly preoccupied with thoughts of her. He often felt uncomfortable when with her, but then even worse when without her-a sort of sweet misery, desired and yet disagreeable, cherished yet regretted, but it endlessly gnawed at him and prevented him from attaining the peace of mind he felt much in need of these days. If this is love, he thought, then he was certainly a happier man without it. This could not be what poets elevate to such lofty scales: it is entirely too painful. While he was thus absorbed in his contemplation, the drillmaster returned and informed him of still another visitor.

"Our chief minister, Cihuacoatl is here to see you, Lord."

"What does he want?" Ahuitzotl muttered to himself in his agitated state, not enthusiastic over this call. "Very well, send him in."

Cihuacoatl entered and took his place on the bench now familiar to him while Ahuitzotl studied his features with a critical eye; he had a good notion why the minister came. "Twice here in a month?" Ahuitzotl said. "Something draws you to this place."

"Don't trifle with me, Lord!" exclaimed the minister grimly. "There are portentous movements afoot! A sense of urgency consumes many of our leading lords. Did you not see what happened at Toluca?"

"A lot happened at Toluca. What incident to you refer to?"

"The one incident to which all others are miniscule in comparison, and of which you well know. I speak of the overt act of cowardice by Lord Tizoc."

"If I remember it correctly, Tizoc did not run by himself. You were next to him the entire way, so if you will condemn the Revered Speaker, then condemn yourself along with him."

"In compliance with his orders, Lord!" fumed the minister. "Am I hearing correctly? Of all our lords, the one I would have sworn to be most outraged, who would have deemed Tizoc's flight as most intolerable, is you! Did I err in my judgment?"

"Not necessarily, Cihuacoatl, but what exactly did you expect I would do? Storm the palace with my Order of the Eagles and throw him out?"

"You are being impertinent, Lord."

"Then explain what you want."

"Action! But not the kind you insult me with. Tizoc can no longer remain our Revered Speaker. He has disgraced the office and is not worthy of it. Men of influence, myself among them, are resolved to bring this matter to a close, but we need a commitment from you."

"What sort of commitment?"

"Approval for what we propose to do."

"Do what you like. I shall not stand in your way."

"Listen to me, Lord!" Cihuacoatl's comportment turned so serious that Ahuitzotl felt himself becoming taut. "We intend to terminate Tizoc's reign. Because you stand to gain most by this, for in all probability the council will select you as his successor, it is crucial that we have your consent to this. Indeed, without it there will be no measures taken at all."

"Why is my consent so important?"

"As a guarantee you will seek no retribution against us for having slain your brother."

"Slain?" Ahuitzotl winced. "You mean to slay him?"

"We have explored all the possibilities and see no other option. Do you think we take this task lightly? It is under the dread of our very lives that we conspire such a drastic step–many of the priests, not to mention the gods, will denounce us or punish us severely for it. Despite this, we are uniformly in accord that the deed, however foul, must be done."

Ahuitzotl stood motionless, pausing to overcome his initial shock. "What assurance have I of being appointed his successor?" he then said "Is this why you need my approval?"

"No, it does not matter. We still need your consent. If perchance you were not appointed, you could, as the supreme commander, be capable of avenging Tizoc's death. Be certain I will do my part to secure your succession, but, like it or not, you are intrinsically connected to this effort and truly hold its implementation in your grasp."

"They will accept my mere word on this?"

"If sworn before Huitzilopochtli, yes."

Ahuitzotl had expected a startling proposal, but was nevertheless stung by the extreme action being precipitated. But then, when all things were taken into account, this stood as the only solution possible and had to be eventually faced, even though he sought to avoid it. Yet it constituted a heinous crime in the eyes of the gods and entailed enormous risks.

"There's no other way?" Ahuitzotl demurred in the hope there might be.

"No. Believe me, Lord, we have exhausted the question."

"How will it be done?"

"Poison. It must be an unseeing death that comes upon him; we have to take precautions so as not to arouse the suspicions of the priests. A number drugs function in this manner, making it appear as though he is suffering from but a common ailment. We haven't decided which one to use, but we'll make it as painless as possible."

"When?"

"Assuming we have your consent, after the Tlaloc festivals. Tizoc has immersed himself too deeply in arranging these rites with the priests to permit it any earlier."

"Then I have time to think on it," Ahuitzotl was relieved to point out.

"Are you mad?" Cihuacoatl shouted out, jumping to his feet in agitation, "Everything we talked about–the disillusionment!–the declining prestige of the realm! A chance to finally do something about it is being offered-and you hesitate? What is holding you back?"

"He is my brother!" Ahuitzotl declared. "We are speaking of murdering him. A horrendous deed!–certainly not what I had in mind. I need time to digest this unsavory proposition."

"Fine!" Cihuacoatl said, still fuming, "But be warned. Do not delay for long. The problem is one of giving support to those committed to our deed. A long wait will cause them to reconsider and, if they think you are wavering in your backing, change their resolution."

Ahuitzotl knew the point was valid. A hazardous venture involving great personal dedication towards its completion had to be seized upon at its rising moment, when all conditions favored success, or otherwise it would disintegrate if its inertia was not maintained. Tomorrow's planned meeting with Tizoc, he told himself, would help make up his mind, affording him one more opportunity to ascertain the need for his elimination. Maybe Tizoc will give some evidence that he will reform the manner in which he has ruled and thereby prevent this horrible measure from being implemented. But why hope for this? He was only deceiving himself; after all, is this not what he had long wished for? The nation was within his grasp; all he had to do was let others act, with nothing more than his assent. The throne was never closer. Still, there remained the gods-what if they should disapprove?

"Give me one week," Ahuitzotl answered, "and I will know."

While highly disappointed by this postponement, Cihuacoatl decided not to aggravate his demands. "I take my leave then," he said as he proceeded for the door, "assured that I shall hear from you."

"You will," Ahuitzotl reaffirmed. "In one week."

XVII

Tizoc, accompanied by his court sycophants, stood by watching an enormous ceremonial stone rumbling over log rollers toward its permanent emplacement in in the central square behind the tow of thirty-some workmen. A huge circular slab of volcanic rock, eight feet across and weighing several tons, meant to be centered about fifty paces in front of the steps to the Great Temple and replace a similar but smaller stone already there; its purpose was to provide a base platform for warriors engaged in gladiatorial combat. Sculptors walked alongside the monolith, for they still had some finishing touches to complete on the frieze chiseled into the block's lateral surface. The carvings depicted a superbly engraved scene which saw the Revered Speaker Tizoc holding a number of captives by their hair, each symbolizing a conquered city identified by its respective glyph. To Tizoc it had special signification as it commemorated his triumphs and, like the Great Temple when completed, would stand as an enduring monument to his reign.

The stone represented one of two gigantic sculptures advanced by Tizoc. In addition to this combat piece, there existed an even more massive calendar, already finished, which would be housed in Huitzilopochtli's shrine atop the Great Temple. Tizoc felt justly proud of these accomplishments, not only for their important functional roles in the many rituals, but also as works of art. The stones were exquisitely designed and carved out by the finest artisans in the realm who were specially recruited for this task and, to any observer, they instilled a sense of awe by their overwhelming crushing energy and epitomized the most magnificent examples of Mexica creativity.

With extreme pride, Tizoc viewed his ceremonial stone being shifted into position when a messenger rushed up to him and told him that Ahuitzotl wished to see him. "Must my finest moments be spoiled by his presence," Tizoc mumbled to himself, his disposition turning sour. But he duly informed the messenger to go and fetch his brother.

No sooner had Tizoc consented to seeing Ahuitzotl when he was already standing next to him, having hastily maneuvered through the cluster of builders and counselors surrounding the Revered Speaker. Before giving him a chance to speak, Tizoc initiated the conversation.

"What do you think of my masterpiece?" he asked as he extended his open hand toward the stone.

"It is magnificent," Ahuitzotl replied.

"A fitting piece to adorn our most glorious work of all, the Great Temple. Do you like the side carvings?"

"Beautifully executed, but the scene is perhaps an exaggeration," Ahuitzotl tactlessly remarked, more as a joke in bad taste than out of any maliciousness.

"If you mean to humiliate me, brother," an unamused Tizoc commented, "then know that this stone represents a well-conceived deprecation of you."

Ahuitzotl turned red over his poorly received raillery, but also held a curiosity over Tizoc's meaning. "How so?" he asked.

"You say the stone depicts an exaggeration? Of course it does. You and I both know this, but will anyone a generation from now? They will look upon it and remember my reign as far more glorious than any other, and this perpetually burns you, doesn't it? I shall disregard your last remark, satisfied with the knowledge that by this single stone, I'll gain far greater renown than you ever will with all those excursions I send you on. Your victories will fade in time and eventually be forgotten altogether, but this stone will remain, as will my Great Temple—my endowments to the world."

Ahuitzotl sizzled, and only with utmost self-restraint did he avoid doing even more damage to himself. "I spoke without thinking," he apologized. "I hope, in your wisdom, you can see this and excuse my carelessness, Lord."

"That's more like it. You can be quite civil when you put your mind to it, but I'm sure you didn't come here to speak of my achievements. What did you want?"

"A private matter. I wish to speak to you alone on it."

"Is it so important that it warrants my leaving here?"

"It is to me, Lord. If you would condescend to hearing me, I will be most appreciative."

"Do not overindulge me with your flowery words, Ahuitzotl. It's not in your character—I know you too well to be deceived by them. I've seen enough here and was about to leave anyway, so come, I shall give you an audience."

They headed in the direction of the palace, having separated themselves from the monarch's coterie, and once alone saw no reason to delay their discussion.

"Now, what is it that's so important?" Tizoc began.

"Something very personal to me, it concerns one of your mistresses—one named Pelaxilla."

"I was curious when you would ever get to her," Tizoc dryly mentioned.

"You know about us?"

"Come now. You two haven't been exactly discreet with your afternoon meetings—really."

Ahuitzotl sensed an uneasiness over Tizoc's apparent lack of sympathy. "Then you are aware how much I desire her," he said. "As your mistress, she is pledged to you, and I have honored this with her, but I now humbly ask that you release her from these obligations and allow her, on her own volition, to choose the man she wishes to serve."

"Why should I?"

It became obvious to Ahuitzotl that he was going to face complications in securing his request, but, having already declared his purpose, he persisted. "You have many mistresses," he replied, "What can one less mean to you?"

"So do you. One more should be of no concern."

"Pelaxilla is special to me—else I should not be here. Indeed, I would willingly give up all the others just for her."

"I'm touched," Tizoc responded without projecting a hint of compassion. "And if I give her to you, what will you do with her?"

"Why, marry her, of course."

"I thought so, and am compelled to inform you that you cannot. It's not possible."

His words impacted as a thunderbolt on Ahuitzotl, startling him, and he reacted with shock. "What are you saying?" he asked.

"I said you cannot marry her. You have forgotten what our laws decree."

"What do you mean?"

"Unhappily for you, Pelaxilla is not of royal lineage. She is not of the Toltec or Tepanec family, which any priest will tell you is a prerequisite for any union involving our ruling elites. I correct myself-not any priest, since you, as Huitzilopochtli's high priest, evidently did not. I must remind you that this has been a mandatory condition since the reign of Itzcoatl in order to keep the royalty in domination over our other nobles. Even if she was of nobility in her own city, this is not sufficient to qualify her for the House of Tenochtitlan."

How could he have ignored this? It had never occurred to him that an inquiry into Pelaxilla's background was in order; by her mere presence in the palace, he had assumed that she had the qualified ancestry. Tizoc was correct; the nobility, to be eligible for the kingship, had to belong by bloodlines to the Toltec or Tepanec families to which was claimed a divinity that descended from the gods themselves. A marriage to Pelaxilla constituted an impurity of this legacy, a defilement, and was unacceptable, particularly to the priests whose abstractions entailed an obsession for the proper lineage among Revered Speakers and their heirs.

"Can this be true?" gasped Ahuitzotl in disbelief.

"It is. Deny it all you want, but no priest will perform the sacred rites for you."

"The priests. Always it is the priests. They must approve of this, they must condone that, but always they must have their say. Is there not one aspect of my life that is not controlled by these infernal priests?"

"There isn't, and it will do you no good to blaspheme against them. They are a sacrosanct lot and ever remind you of it. A Revered Speaker has little power over them, and certainly no measures by which to dispense with the laws they have decreed for us."

The world had crashed down upon Ahuitzotl. Any hopes he sustained for himself and Pelaxilla were eclipsed by this one cruel revelation Tizoc had presented. After he finally recovered sufficiently enough from his initial jolt, he probed for another solution to his predicament.

"If it's proclaimed that I can't marry her, so be it, but I should like to have her just the same. My love for her will not be wanting just because she cannot be my wife."

"In exchange for what?" Tizoc now had his turn to disclose long held frustrations, "Your never-ending insults? Your open contempt for me at every opportunity presented to you? Why should I do anything at all for you?"

"I have served you loyally..."

"Loyally! Everything you've done for me had to be extracted out of you, and even this accompanied by your derogatory slurs and abusive and disrespectful gestures towards me. When have you ever said anything–anything!-that was not in direct opposition to me, or not contradictory to my wishes? You have the nerve to ask me for favors? You are a greater fool than I imagined."

"So this is how I'm to be treated for appealing to your magnanimity!" Ahuitzotl stormed back. "Have I not given you enough victories to allow you to expand this realm, and more, to boast of them as your own on your stone? Had I suspected you would turn on me for so small a request-small for you because I know Pelaxilla means little to you-I would certainly not have taken the time to seek your audience. I expected more out of you."

"I treat you no different than you have behaved towards me. Not very pleasant, is it? I have justifiably reacted adversely to it. In truth, at times I felt loathe to issue orders to you out of disdain over hearing your negative replies. Do you see the trepidation you have caused me?"

"The interpretation is yours. I've never intentionally tried to degrade you; if you perceived me in this light, you should have brought it to my attention so I might have corrected myself."

"What do you take me for? Maybe your actions are unintentional as you say, but they have a way of occurring in the presence of my ministers and lords-always in public-which makes them suspect and also more detrimental for my reprimanding you because you would resent such castigation in front of others and would become hostile. As Revered Speaker, I ought not be placed in such a situation to begin with. By publicly disagreeing with me, you announce your lack of respect and dispute my authority."

"You're overly sensitive to this. It leads you to magnify my resistance to you. Usually I oppose you on matters of policy where you yourself have solicited a different point of view, so do not censure me for your misreading my purpose."

Tizoc gave this argument some judicious consideration, but after weighing all the factors dismissed it as unlikely. "If I have indeed overreacted, there were ample reasons for it," he concluded. "But let's not dawdle over this. Back to Pelaxilla, what can you offer me for her?"

Ahuitzotl did not anticipate Tizoc's new approach and had to study the possibilities it presented. What Tizoc wanted, he envisioned, was what he most loathed to do-he was to humble himself indignantly before him as an act of repentance for his alleged transgressions. It was to be as Pelaxilla told him: he was to grovel underneath his feet in pleading for her hand.

"I can guarantee a mending of my ways," Ahuitzotl asserted reluctantly. "Give you my full support in as compliant and respectful manner as possible."

"That's not offering me anything," Tizoc retorted, taking satisfaction in having his brother at a disadvantage. "I can demand this by merely ordering that you honor me properly."

"Is it because you also desire Pelaxilla that you wish to keep her?"

"She is quite lovely, but no—she means nothing to me."

"And yet," Ahuitzotl now sensed the strain impacting on his composure, "knowing my regard for her, you would deny her to me. I can accept that you have cause to be offended with me, but must your displeasure be directed at her? She's done you no harm. What about her happiness?"

Tizoc brooded over this. It contravened his basic sentimentality to have others suffer because of one's personal vindictiveness and yet such was the fate he now imposed on Pelaxilla. "It's regrettable that it should be so," he said. "You've done nothing to make this harmonious reign for me, so why should I now try to please you. If this means depriving her of happiness, then such must be the case."

"I implore you to reconsider. For her sake, please soften your harsh stand. She has often told me how she needs me for her contentment."

"Are you suggesting I cannot make her content?"

"That's not what I meant!" Ahuitzotl's voice rose proportionately to his mounting exasperation. "If she means so little to you, then allow her the joy every woman seeks from a man she loves, who also loves her."

"Stop it, or I shall break out in tears and soil my new feather tunic. Now, if you have anything else to speak about, say it. Otherwise I bid that you leave me to my privacy. Tlalalca waits or me."

In his duress, Ahuitzotl could feel his heartbeat hammering away as the failure of his attempts sank in. Reaching a point of desperation, he advanced one final plea.

"Will you give her to me?" he entreated.

"No!" Tizoc emphatically declared.

Ahuitzotl's eyes vibrated; his face turned red and his body trembled. He glared intensely at a startled Tizoc, then hastened about furiously and without another word stormed from his presence. In long frenzied strides, he paced across the stone pavement, seeing and hearing nothing, and muttering curses between his heated, forceful breaths. Vessels protruded from his neck and brow under the pressure of his exorbitant fury. His hatred knew no bounds, surging forth from his inner depths, dispossessing him of all reason to encompass his every thought and motion. This was his worst setback, and he was not used to having many of them; his indignation was beyond appeasement, his vehemence above constraint. He could not believe it! Over and over he assailed himself with these words as he stomped heavily across the plaza.

He was still blazing hot when he reached his headquarters, passed by his perplexed drillmaster, and shut himself up in his chamber. There he sat, both hands holding up his chin, huffing laboriously while stewing in his wrath. So this was it! Tizoc had decided! He told Pelaxilla this would be a mistake. What was he to tell her now? And as he so raged, he was also gripped by a cold shiver as the stark realization came to him that Pelaxilla would never be his. In this tortuous state, he continued to froth for most of the remaining day until he was drained of energy, and when at last he calmed himself enough to consider his next move, the course he would take was fixed in his mind.

"Drillmaster!" he shouted into the adjacent room.

Responding immediately, the obedient soldier rushed in to see what his commander wanted.

"Do you know where Cihuacoatl, the chief minister, resides?"

"Yes, Lord."

"Send a messenger to him," Ahuitzotl directed, "to tell him that I wish to see him."

XVIII

N o words could have more effectively described her utter despair than the shocked expression on Pelaxilla's face when Ahuitzotl told her of his meeting with Tizoc. After listening to what he had to tell her, she sat dazed on the stone bench staring blankly into the flower beds in front of her. There were no tears; her astonishment was too great for that, and the full impact of this reversal had not yet totally implanted itself. To Ahuitzotl, her quietness seemed overpowering and he was very discomfited by it.

"The news is terrible," he said, "but you must not let it demoralize you like this. It's not as though we will never see each other again. We can continue to meet here and enjoy our company."

She did not answer and retained her vacant focus on the flower patch.

"Everything went wrong," Ahuitzotl said on. "This was not the time to see him. I should have abided by my instincts and not allowed myself to be swayed of my better judgment."

Still she said nothing, and her silence unnerved Ahuitzotl who strove to end her dejection. "Don't think of this as final," he offered in consolation. "If I wait for a day when he is in better disposition, he may accede to our wishes. There's always a chance I can perform some feat he will appreciate and grant my request for you. When you think about it, the possibilities are numerous, so end your gloominess, my pretty one, all is not lost. You shall yet be mine."

"Can't you see what you are doing?" she at last was aroused into voicing her dismay. "In everything said to me, you've consigned yourself to a lowly subservient affiliation to your brother, crawling beneath his feet like some beaten dog before its master—and this from a man of your repute. Someone certainly assessed you wrongly."

"Do not irritate me, Pelaxilla! I have already endured enough injury from Tizoc.

"Have you? His injury must have been painful indeed, since you will not confront him again, but rather choose to wait until his bite is softer before you see him to beg some more."

Ahuitzotl resented her provoking him like this but reminded himself that she was deeply upset, as he had been when with Tizoc, and resolved not to let it offend him.

"He is the Revered Speaker, and if you want to believe that I grovel to him, then fine. I do what I am honor-bound to do. We are all servants of our ruler."

Pelaxilla knew this, and it was only because of the bitterness felt over her disappointment that she still attempted to precipitate some kind of action out of him. "How long will it be," she asked, "before you speak to him again?"

"There's no definite time. It depends on circumstances, but certainly not until after the Tlaloc festival."

"Another three weeks-if you dare. Well, that's not as bad as I had expected. I suppose I'll have to resign myself to that, but what will you do if his answer remains the same?"

"I don't want to think about that now."

"You could have said something more positive. How am I to know you'll do anything at all with such a response?"

"I'll do something."

"I should hope so. It's most unpleasant to have you acquiesce to such treatment from a lesser man-even if the Revered Speaker, a countermeasure is in order. I will not spend my life relegated to a minor courtesan for him. No, not anymore! Not after the promises you have aroused in me."

Ahuitzotl gave her a despairing look, and for Pelaxilla, it penetrated to her very core and she feared she had carried her prodding too far.

"It's best that I leave for now," he determined. "Things will be clearer after you've given more thought over what I've told you. Presently you are too distressed."

"Yes," she agreed, relieved that he kept control of is temperament. "The news has been very upsetting."

"Then you don't mind."

"No. It's as you said—I need to think on this."

With their discord seemingly settled, they parted. Ahuitzotl worried about Pelaxilla as he walked back to his headquarters. He had only told her about Tizoc's refusal to release her from his services-what will she say when she discovers that he cannot marry her? He shuddered over this reflection. Perhaps he should have mentioned it to her, but that would have been too great a shock for one day. He would tell her some other time.

On arriving at his command quarters, Cihuacoatl was already there waiting for him; together they proceeded to a secluded corner of the inner courtyard where no-one was able to approach them without being seen.

"I came as quickly as I could," Cihuacoatl began eagerly. "I assume you've come to a decision."

"I have."

"Then you will give us your support?"

"Before Huitzilopochtli, I swear it."

"Excellent. I shall immediately notify those involved. We will speak to the physicians on what method we should employ to accomplish our end."

"I thought the method had been decided."

"The poison? Oh yes, we're agreed on that, but we need to find out which ones will function best in the manner we desire."

"Can you trust the physicians?"

"Rest assured, the ones we talk to will have our confidence. They won't be told for what purpose we seek our information and, after the deed is done, if they suspect a connection, we can always dispatch them."

"Them too? This scheme grows more nefarious as it moves along."

"What did you expect, Lord? Evil feeds upon evil, and it is after all an evil crime we conspire. You must remind yourself constantly of its necessity. Are we not agreed that the present situation cannot be allowed to continue?"

"We are."

"Then dismiss any reservations about it. It has to be done, and if in the process, one or more unfortunate individuals pay the price for having unwittingly become ensnared in this web of intrigue, so it must be. If you're concerned about them, you will make us question your dedication to this cause. Perhaps I should ask, to ease my own apprehensions, why your sudden change?"

"Let's just say that Tizoc has given me the incentive to hasten his own demise."

"Aptly put. I won't press for an explanation. I will arrange for the preparations and, if all goes well, we shall have a new Revered Speaker soon after the Tlaloc festivities."

A chill came over Ahuitzotl; it seemed inconceivable that notions he so long harbored were about to transform themselves into reality. Cihuacoatl took note of his troubled demeanor.

"Is something amiss, Lord?"

"Everything we do here is amiss-I must catch my breath to absorb it all. Has anything like this ever been done?"

"Not since Maxtla killed his brother Quetalayatzin fifty-some years ago."

"What became of Maxtla?"

"A war ensued, which he lost, and he had his heart cut out after he was captured by none other than Nezahualpilli's famed father, Nezahualcoyotl."

"Should this serve as a warning?"

"The conditions surrounding that affair were different. For one thing, Maxtla was never selected to be ruler and slew his brother in anticipation of being so appointed, looking upon him as a potential rival. As a result, the council appointed Itzcoatl as the new head of state so he could pursue Maxtla until he was finally caught. No, Lord, we face a considerably distinctive situation. Ours is a greater obstacle."

"As you earlier, I'm now struck by the gravity of our venture. Will the gods approve of it?"

"I've agonized over the same question. I came to the conclusion that I served them in a far greater capacity by assuring the strength of the realm. It took me some time to accept this premise, but having finally done so, I now believe it to be correct."

"So it is possible to overcome this uncertainty."

"Oh, absolutely. Be assured of it. It will happen as soon as you are convinced what we do is required for the greater good."

Ahuitzotl was heartened by the minister's confidence and dispelled his previous qualms with remarkable ease.

"Well, that's it then-Tizoc brings this upon himself."

"His days are short. If no complications arise, Lord Tizoc will not outlive the next month."

The impossible was almost within Ahuitzitl's reach, and his eyes gleamed as he deliberated on it. He thought about how he would begin his reign-with an attack on the cities of Chiapa and Xiquipilco to teach them the same lessons imparted on the Tolucans. No nation would rise in opposition to the Mexica while he ruled as they had done under Tizoc: he would see to that. As for his Pelaxilla, even though she could not be a wife, she nevertheless would remain as his courtly favorite in much the same way as Nezahualpilli had his Lady of Tula. Whether she was actually married to him was less important than having her present so he could continue to enjoy her beauty and companionship without restrictions. And the Great Temple-it would now be completed under his reign and stand as an enduring monument to his glory. He could see it all: how he would expand the kingdom, rule over his subjects, and have his private life life with Pelaxilla-the prospect loomed tantalizingly before him to fill him with eager anticipation. Already, to Ahuitzotl, Tizoc was discounted.

XIX

Excitement abounded in the streets of Tenochtitlan as the first day of the thirteenth month, one of three during the year honoring the god Tlaloc, arrived. Nezahualpilli and Chimalpopoca, along with numerous other rulers, princes, and dignitaries, had made their appearances in response to invitations from Tizoc; both were expected to participate in the sacred rites to the Rain God, second in importance after Huitzilopochtli.

Tizoc contrived two major ceremonies, each one lasting a day, to initiate the month. The first, a sacrifice of the waters, was to conform to traditional demands imposed by Tlaloc's priests by which they would propitiate the god into delivering them continuous fresh rains. The second ritual entailed sacrificing a representative number of Tolucan captives. The priests had determined that one in ten, three hundred of them, amounted to an ample supply for Tlaloc as well as several other deities, with those remaining reserved for future rites, enduring until then as laborers on Tizoc's abundant projects. Both observances required the active involvement of the sovereign whose primary duties included initiating the cutting.

The sacrifice of the waters commenced at early dawn with a procession of lords and priests marching slowly by way of the northern causeway avenue from the central plaza to the lake's edge where hundreds of rowers waited for them in canoes. Upon their shoulders, two priests bore a canopied litter within which sat a little girl six years old and dressed in blue garments representing the water. They sang songs and chanted prayers to Tlaloc as they ambled along accompanied by music from flutes and drums. When they reached the shore, the priests carrying the litter boarded one of the canoes, the boat that was to lead the others from the city. Each lord, escorted by his principal aides, took his own canoe and followed. Many of the townspeople crowded into extra vessels in order to observe the rites making a flotilla of hundreds of canoes that moved out on the lake.

Propelled by many rowers, the canoes rapidly skimmed over the water for a place known as Pantitlan, near the lake's northern end, where it drained amidst strong currents forming a large whirlpool. All along the route, a ceaseless chanting of intones coupled with the haunting melodies of numerous flutists and dull thuds of drums marked their passage. After arriving at the sacred spot, they waited, still singing and playing their instruments, until the whirlpool attained its maximum strength and width. At this point, Tizoc raised both hands over his head, holding them parallel to each other with palms extended forward, and by this signal brought the chanting and music to an abrupt halt. He nodded to the foremost priest who shared his canoe and the ceremony began.

"Lord Tlaloc!" chanted the priest, "Protector of our Fields and Provider of Fresh Waters! We beseech you and pay our debt for the gift of life you bestow on us. We ask for your dominion over us, your continued abundance, and that you accept our offerings to you and your glory. Receive these, Oh Lord of Waters, and grant us your bounty!"

With his invocation thus completed, drums were beaten in rapid succession as other votaries broke out in more incantations of praise to Tlaloc. Faster and faster rolled the percussions until they approximated the thunderclap of a rainstorm-Tlaloc's voice! Then, after building up to a crescendo of deafening rumbling, the chief priest raised his hands and all fell silent again.

In the canoe bearing the litter, one of the priests next took their gift to Tlaloc from its covering and lifted her over his head for all to see. The second priest removed a small spear from his sash and, as his companion brought the girl down, slashed its sharp obsidian point across her fragile throat and sliced open her jugular veins. She gave out a brief whimper when her flesh was penetrated and was quickly extended over the canoe's edge so that the hot blood gushing forth fell into the water, and, upon striking it, her dying body was cast into the eddy and disappeared from sight as if Tlaloc had swallowed it up.

After she vanished beneath the swells, music and singing resumed as the lords passed the spot into which she had been thrown and tossed their jewelry, precious stones, necklaces and bracelets into it. One by one, the canoes rowed by and were lightened of the valuable belongings and when the last of the lords had delivered up his gifts, an eerie stillness ensued as all voices ceased and all instruments stopped playing; under this blanket of reverential solemnity they returned to the city.

By the time they disembarked from their canoes, most of the day had been spent and the notables were invited to a banquet held in the royal palace that evening. As protocol dictated, Tizoc sat centered at the hall's end with the rulers of Texcoco and Tlacopan on his immediate right and left; Ahuitzotl was next to Nezahualpilli and Cihuacoatl beside Chimalpopoca; the remaining guests were circled around this group. No ladies were in attendance. They dined lavishly, enjoying succulent dishes prepared with care by the cooks which the bounty of the land watered by the grace of Tlaloc offered, while in the god's temple, his priests fasted to demonstrate their devotion and reverence. The feasting had gone on for an appreciable length of time before Nezahualpilli deemed Ahuitzotl's conspicuous silence, brought on by his apparent brooding, as somewhat disconcerting.

"You are strangely quiet tonight, Ahuitzotl," he commented, "unusual for a carouser like you. Did the ceremony displease you?"

"It went well enough," said Ahuitzotl, "but since you speak of it, there is a puzzling feature in it. Tell me, as a point of curiosity, how is it that the child sinks so quickly at Pantitlan?"

Nezahualpilli turned grim. "The currents are strong, the waters deep, and the child is dead. I would expect her to sink."

"Odd. I would have expected her to swirl around the surface for awhile before submerging out of our sight."

"Tlaloc has approved of our offering and has readily accepted her into his domain."

"No doubt you are correct. Ignore my foolish fancies. I entertained a notion that the priests may have weighted her down with stones concealed underneath her pretty garments."

Nezahualpilli, always suspicious of Ahuitzotl's religiousness, glared hard at him, his displeasure obvious. "How dare you blaspheme like this. On the very night we dine to honor him, you dare to mock Tlaloc?"

"Not Tlaloc, Nezahualpilli, for I revere him as much as Huitzilopochtli, but perhaps his priests."

"You are a dangerous man."

"Forget what I said. It was but idle speculation-my private rebellion against the constraints I find the priests have placed upon me. Do not take it seriously."

"It has spoiled my evening."

"For that, I am sorry. I should not have disturbed you with my personal grievances."

"You already have, and by so doing have invited my counsel. Be warned, Ahuitzotl! Never try to separate the priests from the gods they serve; they are one and the same. The gods speak through them and impart their knowledge and demands on them. If you scorn one, you also scoff at the other. You will be well advised to heed my counsel, for if you do not..." Nezahualpilli paused to take a bite of the grouse on his plate.

"Yes?" Ahuitzotl was eager to hear him finish.

"You will bring calamitous misfortunes upon yourself, if not on our people."

"For their devotion to the gods, I respect them, and for their services to them, I honor them, but I think they too often meddle into the affairs of men that go beyond the requirements of their office. Do not ask me to refrain from questioning their integrity-I haven't as lofty an opinion of them as you do."

Tizoc, who spotted Nezahualpilli deep in conversation with Ahuitzotl, noticed how it left his colleague in obvious discontent; uneasy over what subject matter could impugn such an impression, he was compelled to know its cause.

"What does my brother say to you, Nezahualpilli, that so affects you? I see your alarm."

"We were discussing today's ceremony, Tizoc. A small disagreement over it, nothing more."

"Surely not small-it had an unsettling effect on you."

Nezahualpilli caught a glimpse of Ahuitzotl's impassioned eyes and felt himself pierced by them; he perceived something more was involved here than he supposed. But it was clear to him that Tizoc was bent on having a reply and he saw no reason for withholding it.

"We were questioning the role of the priests. Ahuitzotl is of the belief they go further in their duties than is necessary or demanded by the gods they serve, and I opposed him on that issue."

"I see," grinned Tizoc, relieved that it was nothing worse. "He is still angry at them over the revelation I gave him."

"What was that?"

"He hasn't told you? Our chief commander is angry with the priests because their laws forbid him to marry outside of the required royal families."

"So that's it," Nezahualpilli laughed. "Now it all begins to make sense. I presume we speak of the Lady Pelaxilla."

"You have heard about her?" asked Ahuitzotl in amazement.

"Only by name. See?-your amorous escapades have reached even my court in Texcoco. She must be quite a woman to have turned your head so. I should like to meet her."

"She is agreeable, but not extraordinary," Tizoc noted. "My brother's tastes favor the mundane. There are dozens of royal princesses who wish to be claimed by him, but he wants none of them. He has eyes only for my mistress."

"That's understandable," Nezahualpilli concluded. "Cheer up, Ahuitzotl. It should be no barrier to you. You are in a similar position I'm in. I have my wives, and I have my Tula Woman, whom I prefer above any of them. The priests also say I cannot marry her, but if you asked any of my wives, they will tell you I already am."

The group resounded with hearty laughter, except for Ahuitzotl who deemed his situation serious, and Cihuacoatl who regarded a feast in honor of Tlaloc a more solemn occasion.

"Come now, Ahuitzotl," Nezahualpilli continued after seeing him in his somberness, "No woman is worth all this trouble. In the dark, they are all alike."

"Is that why you have so many of them?" Tizoc added, bringing on even more laughter.

"At least your Tula Woman is not denied to you," Ahuitzotl related to Nezahualpilli.

"Pelaxilla is denied to you?"

"She belongs to Tizoc, and he has no inclination to give her to me."

"What's this?" Nezahualpilli intuitively recognized his initial supposition was accurate and that he had stirred up a hornet's nest. "Tizoc keeps her even though he says she is nothing extraordinary? Does he realize how you covet her?"

"He does."

"Then there's something unsavory here; you two play a game I want no part of," Nezahualpilli said. He judiciously avoided additional comments on the subject as he had no liking for clandestine schemes and certainly no wish to get embroiled in any personal dispute between Ahuitzotl and Tizoc.

Tizoc was perturbed that Ahuitzotl had taken his denial of Pelaxilla so severely and ruminated if he might not have been unreasonable about it. There always remained the possibility for him to relent, he thought, and it may be wise to do so. His brother's services were valuable to him and could be easier obtained with more kindness. As he pondered over this, he glanced aside and noticed an irritated look in his minister.

"What! You too are disturbed, Cihuacoatl?" Tizoc remarked.

"This feast is supposed to bestow our gratitude to Tlaloc–a solemn occasion!" Cihuacoatl replied. "Yet none of you have regard for this and engage in merriment. I find this demeaning and irreverent."

"As usual, I have you to remind me of my obligations," Tizoc said, vexed over the minister's incessant preoccupation with the monarch's duty requisites but conceding a validity in his claim. "You're quite right of course, and we are properly admonished for it, but don't worry about displeasing Tlaloc. Tomorrow we shall satisfy him amply when we offer him the Tolucans."

"Will Zozoltin be among them?" asked Nezahualpilli.

"He shall be the first."

"So you have not yielded your stand; you will not permit him to fight on the combat stone."

"No. He is to die on the altar. I shall personally send him on his journey to our East Paradise. This ought not offend you any–we accord him the highest honors by doing this."

Nezahualpilli's objection to having Zozoltin sacrificed was not so much based on it being any less honorable fate as that he felt it undignified for a monarch to be paraded naked before his subjects in the fashion of the offered victims. An exhibition of this sort reflected unfavorably on the kingship in that it debased an office which he believed should reserve a certain sanctity to a commoner's level. He was mystified why Tizoc, who professed to admire the Tolucan, persisted in this choice of death for him—perhaps he found this a necessary measure in order to put the doomed adversary out of his life.

Nezahualpilli was not the only one thinking of Tizoc; Ahuitzotl likewise had the Revered Speaker on his mind, but with sentiments considerably less favorable towards him. Enjoy this feast, Tizoc, he was thinking; there shall not be many more of them for you. You have mocked me and this love I bear Pelaxilla for the last time. Had you not so basely deprecated my desires for her, things might have gone differently for you, but now it is too late. You should have given her to me.

Ahuitzotl's deliberation was interrupted when the feast came to a close with a chant to Tlaloc in whose honor it had been held. When it was over, the lords left for their private chambers in the various guest quarters and, for those who had made the request, were met by mistresses. So ended the first day of festivities dedicated to the Rain God.

Early that following morning, priests probed among the cages of Tolucan prisoners and selected the three hundred who were to be honored this day. These were led into a nearby building for their ceremonial preparation where they were divested of their clothing, bathed, and painted yellow over their entire bodies. Their last sumptuous meal was laced with drugs which numbed the senses, making their movements lethargic and inducing anesthesia to destroy much of the pain felt from the knife. The priests gravely spoke to them, giving them messages they wished carried to Tlaloc, often repeating them until the words were memorized and could be recited back. Sedated, counseled, and otherwise conditioned for their final journey, the Tolucans were next marched to the Temple of Tlaloc in columns of two escorted by sober priests and a few guards.

Crowds had gathered at the base of the structure, standing quietly by as the captives entered the square and listened to repetitive incantations voiced from the numerous votaries accompanying them while a lone drumbeater walked along pounding out a cadence. The occasion was an extremely solemn one, and this was patently evident in the grim countenance of the spectators who viewed the procession with hushed veneration.

Tizoc waited on the temple's upper tier in front of the techcatl, the altarstone, emplaced directly ahead of Tlaloc's shrine at the very edge of the steps. On his right was Nezahualpilli and on the opposite side Chimalpopoca—all wore brilliant plumages and colorful attire with the typical copious adornments. Also standing with them were Cihuacoatl and the chief priests of Tlaloc. Gravely, they gazed down on the square to observe the lines of victims approaching them, and when Tizoc noticed the once-proud Zozoltin, tall and naked, heading one of the columns, looking not at all like the noble king he had been, he blushed, feeling regret that he had not taken Nezahualpilli's advice. At least that would not have presented the ill-fated monarch in so pitiful an exposition.

Ahuitzotl was standing with Tlohtzin at the bottom of the temple's steps when the Tolucans arrived and he was quick to notice Zozoltin leading his line. "A great day for you," he said as Zozoltin passed by. "Today you enter paradise."

In spite of his sedation, Zozoltin's mind was lucid. "It's no paradise of mine, madman!" he sneered to emphasize his contempt.

"Defiant to the end, Zozoltin? Most unfortunate. If you believed as we did, you would consider yourself highly honored-more than you deserve."

"Damn your beliefs!"

"No, Zozoltin. Thanks to them Tizoc has granted you the stone-a warrior's death. Had it been left up to me, you would be rotting away in your cage like the lowliest criminal."

Zozoltin was not afforded an answer as a priest prodded him to proceed up the steps.

"Why do you taunt him like that?" Tlohtzin objected. "Can a man not be allowed to meet his fate in peace?"

"By the heavens!" Ahuitzotl countered. "Don't you defend the enemy to me now! You heard the man condemn the very tenets permitting him entry into our sun's house. Tizoc has no business extending such a privilege to him."

Soon the Tolucan lines ran up on both sides of the steps and Zozoltin was halted on reaching the uppermost level. He glowered fiercely at Tizoc who avoided looking at him and yet felt his overpowering presence. Next, on taking his cue from the Revered Speaker, the chief priest raised his arms and thereby activated a thunderous roll of the giant panhuehuetl, beaten by many clubs and booming as Tlaloc's invocation across the square leaving its multitude of spectators awestruck. Then, a short time later, he dropped his hands and, as abruptly as it had begun, the drum was stilled.

The chief priest recited his prescribed age-old chants, invoking Tlaloc's blessings and entreating him into granting abundant rains by which the nation was assured another successful planting season. When he finished and stepped back, his subordinates tossed a powdered substance into the decorated braziers placed at each of the temple's five tiers which emitted dense clouds of smoke when it struck the fire. Again the huge drum shattered ears and rattled nerves with its deafening rumble. Four priests strode up to the techcatl where Tizoc was standing and after they posted themselves, he lifted his hands to once more silence the drum.

"Oh Tlaloc!" Tizoc shouted out as he peered into a partially clouded sky, "Accept these offerings-warriors honorably taken in battle-we are about to send you! Welcome them into your house and hear their messages from us!"

This completed, he nodded to the four priests and they quickly seized Zozoltin, each grabbing one of his limbs, and dragged him to the altar. He was thrown on his back upon the curved block so that it arched his chest upward, elevating it above the rest of his body, and as each priest tightly held him down, a fifth one stepped up and threw a strap under his chin that forceably yanked his head back. His chest heaved up and down under his heavy respiration and his eyes never left Tizoc's.

Tizoc raised his flint knife a full arm's length over his head, holding it there momentarily for all to see, then plunged it with all his power into Zozoltin's chest. It cut into the flesh directly under the rib cage and was forced in one strong horizontal stroke across the width of the chest, opening it in a broad slash as the blood gushed forth. With his free hand, Tizoc reached into the gory cavity and pushed his fingers ahead until he felt them encircling the pulsating heart. He then violently jerked his hand back, ripping the organ, which for an instant still clung to attached veins, from its snug enclosure. As red blood spurted volumously over the altar, he lifted the heart into the air, then passed it to Cihuacoatl who transferred it on a plate to the arperture of the stone idol within the shrine and dropped it in. Tizoc stood acutely aware of the glassy, sightless eyes of the corpse still fixed on him as it was raised from the block by the four priests and flung over the steps. It rolled down like a heavy log leaving a thin streak of blood to mark its path. At the bottom, the body was taken by more priests who cut off its head, arms, and legs, setting these parts aside for later use-the limbs to be cooked and eaten-while the torso was set on a stretcher and placed away from the temple's base for eventual removal by boat, either to a burning ground or to the zoo for the animals. Thus did Zozoltin enter paradise.

Without any delay, the four priests grabbed their next captive from the opposite row, spreading him over the altar, and the operation was repeated. The trail of blood widened along the steps when this body plummeted down. Then the priests went back to the first row and carried their new victim to the block, and in this fashion, moving back and forth between the two lines, the Tolucans met their end under blood-soaked knives wielded by Mexica kings. After about an hour of cutting, Tizoc's arms began to weaken, strained in his efforts, and by the time he came to his fortieth captive, his work was becoming sloppy, with the gashes not as deep and more tugging to rip the heart from its tendons. Nezahualpilli next resumed the arduous task, to be later followed by Chimalpopoca.

This slaughter lasted throughout most of the day, and when the last of the victims had finally been dispatched, the temple stairs rested thoroughly splattered with coagulating blood and at its base, where the corpses had been dismembered, a large pool of it lay stagnated and sticky in the sweltering heat. After all was done, a signal once again directed the panhuehuetl to thunder out its earsplitting rumbling and when it fell silent, the ceremony was concluded and the Mexica lords descended the stairway along its lateral edge, the only section remaining clear of blood.

Even as the dignitaries left in preparation for the evening's banquet, clean-up crews were already beginning their strenuous task of refurbishing the temple, carrying containers of water up the steps and scrubbing the stonework clean of its congealed, pasty blood. The torsos they dumped into barges after reserving a few for the zoo. The priests themselves collected up the edible limbs and took them, along with basketloads of hearts recovered from the idol, to the kitchens to be boiled in large vats for eventual consumption, while the heads were amassed so that they could be stripped of flesh and mounted on the skull rack located in the main plaza. In its entirety, the rehabilitation work of the sacrificial ritual entailed a major constructive effort involving crews of hundreds toiling late into the night, if not all the next day.

The feasting that evening, observed to give the commemoration of Tlaloc its closing sequel, was, in contrast to the previous night, an affair conducted under a cloud of serious contrition, and when small cuts of cooked flesh were served to the guests, each of the participants spoke a solemn prayer before he began to eat. In this way he shared the sacrifice with Tlaloc and maintained a mutual connection to him.

As Tizoc bit into a piece of meat that had been placed on his platter, a recollection of Zozoltin's piercing eyes suddenly flashed through his mind. He turned pale. "It is the flesh of Zozoltin!" he gasped.

"What?" Nezahualpilli replied, staggered by this. "How can you be sure?"

"I know!" Sweat appeared on Tizoc's forehead.

"I don't see how you could, but even if it were, why an aversion in digesting it? He was a gallant warrior-you respected him when alive-and if Tlaloc accepted him, so should you."

"I will not eat it!"

"Why not?"

"Out of misgivings. He never believed we sent him to paradise. Until his end, he remained convinced we merely exacted our revenge on him. Doubts prevail whether this is palatable."

"This stops you? Don't be so squeemish and accept that he was a good offering."

"Even so, I will not partake of this flesh. It is tainted."

"Suit yourself, but know it's not the flesh that is contaminated. The defilement exists in your lack of piety about our purpose in eating it and you announce it to everyone here. You always manage to bring harm to yourself, Tizoc, even if it's unintentional. You must display a greater regard for our customary practices. Your office demands this."

"I did not ask for this counsel from you."

"I recommend you abide by it. My intent was to prevent you from spoiling this feast for everyone else."

"My not eating this affects the others in a like manner?"

"Yes," came Nezahualpilli's reply, which he deemed sufficient in getting Tizoc to grasp the ramifications of his behavior.

Tizoc eyed the meat on his plate, noting its grayish appearance from having been boiled, and reluctantly picked up a small portion of it, placed it slowly in his mouth, and started to chew on it. It had a sweetlike taste and, in spite of his efforts to suppress sensations of revulsion, he did not find it unsavory. The gesture met a silent approval from several guests seated in his vicinity who had apparently stopped eating in anticipation of his next move; when they saw that he proceeded with his meal, they heartily resumed cleaning up their own plates. For Tizoc, it stood as another reminder of how closely his actions were scrutinized by his subordinates: an aspect of being ruler he found difficulty adjusting to. By nature he was a private man, and he held a distinct aversion for the public role demanded of his title. Once again, Nezahualpilli had given him the correct advice and again he resisted in taking it. Yet he felt no compulsion to thank him for it; a satisfied look in the Texcocan's face combined with the fact that Tizoc was now eating the meat spoke well of their relationship.

That night, after the feasting, the parties retired to their chambers without engaging any of the available mistresses, for the occasion was too grave for activities which might be considered pleasureable and thereby detracted from its sobriety. The gods could be aroused to jealousy and, in their ensuing anger, could abrogate all the oblations rendered them this day. It had been a lengthy undertaking for them, one which they were not likely to soon forget as no festival to Tlaloc had ever previously provided so many victims, and one could only wonder, while they slept, what dreams they might have had.

XX

A few days later, Cihuacoatl paced the floor of his ministry anticipating the arrival of one of his more obscure friends, the physician Alotl. These were anxious times for him and his nervousness was evidenced in the long hard strides he took as he walked back and forth within the narrow confines of his chamber. With the hour of his contemplated action approaching, he wavered and had to constantly assure himself of its essentiality to bolster his flagging resolve. The burden strained him severely, exacting its toll in weight lost and stress endured; he endlessly deliberated over it, but always he came to the same conclusion-it had to be done!

At last he heard footsteps echoing in the corridor. He walked to the door and glanced out just as Alotl came up to him.

"You are alone?" Cihuacoatl asked.

"Do you see anyone else?" replied Alotl sardonically.

"Then enter. I have been much inconvenienced by this delay. I expected you earlier."

"An unfortunate aspect of our lives-one must always wait on physicians."

"Well, let's not meditate on it. Have you what I requested?"

"Oh yes, and in ample amounts too."

"Splendid." Cihuacoatl declared as Alotl handed him a deerskin pouch. "Can you describe its effects to me?"

"It begins with a headache, followed by sensations of dryness in the mouth and excessive thirst. There is a burning and swelling in the throat, the pupils dilate, and the victim suffers delirium. Finally, after nausea and convulsion, he will go into a coma, and then-death!"

"That is how it acts?" Cihuacoatl blanched in alarm.

"It will not be pleasant."

"I thought you would bring me something that was painless—not this."

"You told me to get the poison that was most effective, and that's not the most painless one. I see you are distraught–shall I take it back and get another?"

Cihuacoatl hesitated; the prospect of deferring his plan to a later time was not desireable. "No, this will have to do," he replied at length. "I can't have any more delays. My nerves would never withstand it."

"It is guaranteed to bring the desired result. Who did you say it was for? Some relative in pain of a lingering sickness?"

"Yes. That's why I had hoped it would be a painless drug, but even so, he has suffered so much already; this could not make his pain any worse."

"I don't approve of using this for such purposes, but that's only my opinion. I shall not stand in your way if you are set on its application. No doubt you have agonized over this before resorting to these desperate methods."

"Indeed I have, Alotl. The decision has caused me horrible despair."

"Such resolutions are never easy. You have my sympathy."

"Thank you for your condolences, but back to the drug. Which is better for it-food or drink?

"Both are well suited for it, but perhaps it would be a somewhat quicker reaction if he drank it. Also, if given to him in a cup, you have greater assurances that only he would drink it. The chances of someone else accidently consuming it are minimized."

"I was just thinking the same thing. Now, how much of this should I give him?"

"That depends. If he is old and feeble, it will not be necessary to use more than a fourth of the bag's contents. If you wish to put him out of his misery quickly, then pour all of it into a cup. It disssolves readily and had no peculiar odor to it-he will never be able to distinguish it from whatever else he drinks."

"How precise you physicians are. If I use all of this, there will be no chance of escaping the drug's lethal effect?"

"None!"

"Remarkable. This is what I needed to know-not the medical analysis. I shall put this to use at the earliest opportunity."

"Such haste," Alotl wryly commented. "The situation must be unbearable-for you. You are certain you do not want me to get something less potent?"

"No, this will do nicely."

"Nicely? I should hate to be your relative. Then you are satisfied?"

"You've done well, Alotl. Perhaps some day I can do you a favor in return."

"I'm not so certain I would ask you for one. However, if you need anything else, I'm always at your service."

With his business thereupon concluded, Alotl departed, leaving Cihuacoatl alone in the chamber as he had found him. A cynical man, the physician had long ago determined there was nothing more in life that could surprise him, but when he left the minister, he must considered his conclusion sorely tested.

Now that Cihuacoatl had the poison, a more complicated task lay ahead of him as he thought about over how he would administer it and discovered few alternatives existed for him. If he placed the drug in food, many could become affected by it, and there was a need for him to be in the kitchen or Tizoc's dining quarters–to accomplish this unseen required a magician. A more promising possibility was to corner the monarch alone somewhere and, with the aid of accomplices, force him to consume the potion. The perfect situation was if the minister were alone with Tizoc without anyone knowing of it; there had been such occasions, but they were quite rare. One thing he was clear on: if the deed was to be executed, he would have to create the conditions permitting its consummation.

Fortunately Cihuacoatl had already managed to secure abettors in the scheme-Tizoc's lack of popularity extended through many circles making that recruitment easier than he had imagined. He decided it might be beneficial to seek them out for ideas on how to continue from here. He walked from his ministry feeling confident the problem would unravel itself; no sooner had he cleared the door when he was intercepted by a messenger. "Our Revered Speaker requests your presence, Lord Minister," the courier reported. "He desires a private meeting-in his royal garden."

"When?"

"At noon."

The gods themselves have arranged this, Cihuacoatl thought in amazement. They beckoned him to proceed.

He still had enough time to meet with his accomplices to finalize their strategy and, after dismissing the courier, hastened off for the trading center to make contact with Lord Huactli who ruled over the pochteca, the merchants. It was perhaps to be expected that he would be involved in plotting against Tizoc, for no other sector of the society was more adversely affected by the monarch's timidity than the pochteca. Their trading routes, once sacrosanct, became increasingly hazardous to traverse as a result of banditry which they blamed on Tizoc's failure in policy enforcement and his acquired reputation for weakness. Only the military may have held the monarch in lower esteem, but there the command and authority of Ahuitzotl acted as a steadying influence against drastic action, preventing any escalation of opposition.

Cihuacoatl was met at the center by Huactli's personal guardians who informed their master of the minister's visit and, after receiving the lord's consent, bade him to enter and left him alone in a chamber with Huactli.

"You breathe heavily," Huactli observed, "and have come in great haste. Does this portent what we have so long desired?"

"I think this is the day," Cihuacoatl affirmed.

Huactli sat motionless, needing time to fully appreciate the news. "What would you have us do?" he finally asked.

"I am to meet Tizoc at noon in his garden. I have the poison with me, and I believe we will be by ourselves. If he has a drink available, I should be able to slip it in his cup; however, in case he doesn't, I want you and the other conspirators to appear with a goblet filled with water. We can then force him to drink it."

"But if he is to meet only you, how will we explain our presence to him?"

"Do not make your appearance until I give you a sign-I'll rub my arm across my brow as if wiping off perspiration. You have access to the garden. Hide yourselves in the shrubs and await my signal. Once I call for you, it will be too late for him and it no longer matters what he thinks."

"And if he is not alone."

"Then we'll have to postpone our plan until another occasion presents itself."

"How will we know the poison will be allowed to do its work? He could drink it, and then regurgitate it, annulling its effect, or maybe even take some kind of remedy to counteract it."

Cihuacoatl studied this possibility for a moment, then continued. "The poison begins to have an affect shortly after it is ingested. We'll simply have to stay until the first symptoms appear-by then nothing will save him."

"We could be seen if we stay."

"Perhaps, but who would interrupt a Revered Speaker in conference? Even if we are spotted from the palace, I doubt if anyone will come close enough to identify you. Besides, we have the sworn word of Lord Ahuitzotl there will be no retribution against us."

Huactli was not as enthralled over this as the minister. "I do not trust him. The priests say he does not show the gods proper reverence."

"He will keep his word."

"Then I must believe you. Still, it is better if we were not seen. Even as Revered Speaker, he could not keep the justices from us if we were positively identified as having slain Tizoc."

"We must risk it if we are to see this through. I tell you this opportunity is god-sent. They must surely approve and will protect us. We shall not get a chance like this for a long time if we fail to act on it."

Huactli was agreed that they could ill afford to lose such an auspicious moment. Further delay posed dangers as it might present Tizoc with favorable circumstances in which he could redeem himself and regain the people's good graces, and each day lost meant more trade losses for his merchants on the road.

"Very well," he determined, "I shall gather my partners and proceed to the garden with them. It will not take long."

Cihuacoatl left the trading center shrugging off the last instant doubts that resurfaced to plague him. The time was beyond possessing any reservations about this scheme, he said to himself. The machinery had been set into motion and was now rolling ahead under its own inertia. Still, there was considerable tension in the minister as the moment drew near; he felt his heart pulsating in his jugulars when he entered the garden through its main portal. He saw Tizoc at its farthest extremity apparently engrossed with some of his flowery plants. The monarch stood by himself, and as Cihuacoatl approached him, he looked about and noticed that no-one else was in the vicinity-another indication for him that providence guided him to this climactic conclusion.

"You sent for me, Lord?" said Cihuacoatl on arriving.

"Ah yes," Tizoc acknowledged, still absorbed in his flowers. "Look at this delicate plant here. Have you ever seen a more magnificent bloom?"

It was typical of him to seek an agreement from his visitors on things he admired, and for the minister, who cared little about plants, it amounted to a meaningless diversion. Had he exhibited as much interest in maintaining the realm as he did in his garden, Cihuacoatl conjectured, there would have been no necessity for this conspiracy.

"Indeed not, Lord," Cihuacoatl said in a strained attempt at showing some fascination. "It has a brilliant luster."

"Also a remarkably soft texture. Nezahualpilli would appreciate it. I should send him one of these lovelies."

Cihuacoatl was too tense to share in the adoration, and Tizoc sensed his impatience. "I had forgotten," he said, "you don't have the same enthusiasm for gardening as Nezahualpilli. It's a pity; there are enormous pleasures that can be derived from it, but I'll not bore you with my recreations. I summoned you so that we might discuss the Xiquipilco situation. It's worsening and I think some sort of remedial action is in order. What's your assessment?" Cihuacoatl was by this time in such a state of strained agitation over his next anticipated move that he could not focus on anything said to him. He felt a weakness in his knees.

"What's wrong?" Tizoc voiced his concern when he noticed the minister's discomfort. "You are quite pale, and you sweat profusely. Are you ill?"

"I feel a dizziness. Do you have something to drink?"

"No, but let me call my servants."

"No!" Cihuacoatl sharply reacted. "Perhaps if I rest for a moment, it will go away."

"It's no problem. I shall call them."

"No! It's not necessary!" the minister exclaimed as he slowly wiped the perspiration from his forehead.

He gave the signal. Huactli and three other associates, who had arrived only a short time ago, were concealed behind a thicket of bushes a few paces away when they saw it. They broke from their foilaged cover and, carrying a goblet and pitcher of water with them, proceeded for Tizoc and the minister. Tizoc saw them coming.

"Why are they here? I called no meeting."

"They come at my request, Lord!" Cihuacoatl exclaimed.

Apprehension came over Tizoc who had never known his minister to take on this kind of prerogative without his consent.

"What does this mean?" he said in his consternation.

"Your end!" Cihuacoatl grimly informed the startled monarch.

"What!"

"Do not yell out! Listen to all I tell you and obey my instructions. If you do not, Tlalalca, your sons, and your daughters will perish this day. Do you understand?"

A dazed Tizoc stared unbelievingly at his minister whose words struck him with devastating impact. He was too stunned to say anything, and when at last he regained a degree of composure, he was surrounded by the other conspirators.

"You must be mad!" Tizoc gasped.

"Mad you say? Oh no, Lord. Not at what I'm doing now, but perhaps I was mad when I appointed you to succeed your worthy brother Axayacatl. You have disgraced your office, and I have stood by to observe it happen, doing nothing, and all the while seeing our realm deteriorating under your spineless rule. Indeed I was mad, Lord-mad at not having sought this solution earlier!"

"I did not ask to be the Revered Speaker!" Tizoc angrily retaliated. He now grasped the severity of his situation and fully understood that the steps taken by the minister and his accomplices were irreversible. It was clear to him that he was fighting for his life. "You apppointed me," he raged on, "with no regard whether I wanted the title or not. Now you want me to bear the brunt of your erroneous judgment. The blame rests with you!"

"And so does this remedy we now seek. We must put an end to you if we are to reverse the realm's decay-the rot from within."

Tizoc's nervousness increased, and his knees were shaking so badly that his tilmantli could be seen quivering. His heart palpitated at a frightening pace.

"I knew I wasn't meant to be Revered Speaker soon after having assumed those duties," Tizoc whimpered now, "But how could I abdicate? The priests would never permit it—nor would you!"

"You could have refused the appointment. Surely you must have had some indications even then about your abilities to run a state."

"How was I to know? I did not comprehend the demands of this office."

Cihuacoatl was not impartial to Tizoc's impassioned defense and for an instant even wished that he could somehow overturn the events which carried him to this point. He had certainly been most responsible for Tizoc being named Revered Speaker and now he doomed the young man over this misjudgment-not an easy thing to dismiss. Yet his own life and those of others were placed at stake here and this awareness led him to quickly dispell such notions.

"It's most unfortunate, Lord," Cihuacoatl sympathized. "Perhaps you can take comfort in that we undertake this at the peril of offending the gods and may suffer greatly for it. Such is the distress you have driven us to."

Tizoc understood. Somehow he had suspected that this was the only possible way it could have ended, and his lamentation was more over the dismal circumstances, including his own woeful inadequecy, which directed him to this fate than out of any resentment for his minister. Fearfully, he watched the potion being stirred in the goblet held by Huactli, and after it had dissolved in the water, Cihuacoatl took the cup and handed it to his distraught master.

"Here, Lord. Drink this."

"And if I refuse?" Tizoc asked in a broken voice. "You cannot be so cruel as to extend your crimes to my family."

"Drink it!" Huactli demanded, becoming irritated over the delay. Cihaucoatl placed his hand on Huactli's shoulder to indicate his annoyance over the interruption.

"Know our position, Lord," the minister explained. "We are desperate men and have nothing to lose by whatever measures we take, for we are doomed if we fail here. It is to be your life alone or that of your entire family. Have courage, Lord, and take the reasonable option. You will enter Tlalocan, the South Heaven, a much better place than is in store for us who will most likely go to Mictlan for having committed this heresy. Take the cup and drink."

With his hand trembling, Tizoc reached for the goblet but stopped before taking a hold of it.

"No! I will not drink it."

Cihuacoatl glanced at Huactli and readity discerned what he was thinking. "He is a coward to the end," Huactli sneered. "What sort of man would have his wife and children die with him?"

"He will drink," Cihuacoatl assured him. "Give him a little more time to ponder on it."

"I have waited long enough. Let us kill him now!" Huactli said as he pulled a knife from under his cloak.

"Wait!" Tizoc cried out. Huactli replaced his weapon.

The game was over for him. At last, no longer seeing any possibility of relief, Tizoc resigned himself to the inevitable. Tears of anguish came to him as he clasped the goblet with his shaking hands; he trembled uncontrollably and felt as if his heart would stop under his duress.

"Will it be painful?" he uttered weakly.

"For a short while," Cihuacoatl answered. suddenly overcome with remorse.

"What will happen to Tlalalca?"

"She will be taken care of, as will your children, but only if you retain your silence about us after we leave you. I promise you this."

Tizoc gazed straight into the minister's eyes and, despite his intense nervousness, seemed to sense the sorrow which had struck Cihuacoatl. In his acuity, he apprehended how troubling this step must have been for him, and his dismay that the minister was part of this conspiracy left him. "I believe you," Tizoc told him. Then, with no more hesitation, he brought to cup to his lips and drained it while the conspirators held their breaths.

Cihuacoatl was so deeply touched by Tizoc's expression of faith in him, even though he had betrayed his lord, that he could scarcely hold back his tears, and as he watched his pitiful monarch empty the cup, he had to repress urges to intercede on his behalf by calling for help. When Tizoc had finished, and it was too late for any productive countermeasure, Cihuacoatl felt as if his heart would break.

Feeling faint over the knowledge of his imminent death, Tizoc had to sit down on one of the stone slabs he so abundantly emplaced through the garden while the conspirators remained about him awaiting an appearance of the first symptoms like vultures hovering over a dying animal. He knew why they stayed, and if he withheld any hopes of getting to a physician, they were shattered as effectively as the world which had collapsed on him this afternoon. Still he retained some concern over what was to come.

"Who will reign after me?" he asked Cihuacoatl in a somewhat calmer voice than earlier.

Cihuacoatl delayed in his response as he was reluctant to inform Tizoc, wishing to spare him any additional duress.

"Is it Ahuitzotl?" Tizoc insisted on knowing.

"We will recommend him," replied the minister. Contrary to what he had expected, there was no sign of objection in Tizoc.

"Is he also part of-of this?"

"Indirectly, Lord. He promised he would seek no retaliation against us."

"But he did not contrive this...death."

"No, Lord."

"That's good," Tizoc winced as the headaches began. "He will make a better ruler than I have been. He is...much....stronger."

His speech became sluggish as a dryness enveloped his mouth. Headaches now pounded his brain violently in heavy, painful throbs; he felt his throat burning and he was nauseous. For Huactli this presented conclusive proof that the poison was acting on Tizoc. "He is dying," he said. "Our work is done. Let us leave him."

Cihuacoatl was immobilized in his compunction. When, after a moment, Huactli's words took hold of him, he arose to depart but was held back by Tizoc who clutched at his cloak.

"Help me..to..my...quarters," Tizoc begged of his minister.

"Yes, Lord!" Cihuacoatl answered, his practiced sense of obligation overriding all other considerations, and he motioned for Huactli and the others to go.

"You're not coming?" Huactli resisted.

"No."

"But you'll be seen."

"My meeting with him is already known. I shall say I found him becoming ill as we engaged in it. They will believe me-I have served him loyally. Now go!"

They left without hesitation, requiring no pursuasion to dally at the scene of this obvious misdeed, while the minister raised Tizoc's arms over his shoulder and half-carried him into the palace where astonished servants ran to assist him. They carried Tizoc into his private chamber and lifted him upon layers of mats, covering his shaking body a blanket.

"I'll fetch a physician," an attendant said to Cihuacoatl.

"No!" Tizoc muttered, "Please...let...me...see...Tla....."

"He asks for Tlalalca," Cihuacoatl told the attendant, "Bring her here-quickly!"

At near panic, the servant raced frantically through the corridor for the other end of the palace and barged into an interior courtyard where Tlalalca was employed in her afternoon chats with her ladies; he startled everyone.

"My Lady," he panted, "It is Lord Tizoc. He is gravely ill."

Abject fear gripped Tlalalca and, leaving her group in stunned confusion, she immediately followed the valet back to Tizoc's chamber where she saw him lying in bed quivering under his cover.

"Tizoc!" she cried out in horrified shock, tears coming to her eyes, "Oh, my Lord!" She rushed up to him, embracing his trembling body while weeping uncontrollably in her despair.

Tizoc gazed at her and strained to say something but was now no longer able to speak; he wanted to wipe the stream of tears from her cheeks but was too weak to lift his arm. So in his last moment he beheld Tlalalca's lovely face contorted in its anguish; his eyes shone for one more brief instant, and then they closed as he lapsed into a coma.

The bereaved empress could not be consoled. Sobbing hysterically, repeating his name over and over, she clung tenaciously to him, refusing all attempts by Xoyo, who had followed her to the chamber, and the others to wrest her from him, and while she so held fast to him, his breathing stopped. And thus, in the arms of his adored Tlalalca, did Tizoc end his life.

Cihuacoatl staggered from the palace a broken man. Torn between his years of dedicated servitude to Tizoc and the desperation that drove him into being the instrument of his murder, he must have questioned the forces which led him to this. Devastated by feelings of intense guilt over having been responsible for selecting that young man to the kingship and then inflicting on him the ultimate penalty when the office proved too much for him, he knew he could never escape his own complicity in this and would forever carry this burden with him. Fainthearted while he lived, Tizoc exited from the world with wholesome dignity, casting a shadow of doubt over the necessity for his end and adding greatly to the minister's commiseration. As he came to the front steps, his legs weakened and he paused to rest. He sat down and, for the first time in his recollection, openly wept.

Ahuitzotl, in session with his aide, Motecuhzoma, and Tlohtzin at the headquarters complex, was mapping out various strategies the Mexica meant to apply against Chiapa and Xiquipilco in their next anticipated campaign. Making a bold departure from previous such proposals, Ahuitzotl took it upon himself to preempt Tizoc's authority and directive towards implementing this action, a move scrutinized with more than minor suspicion by Tlohtzin.

"Tizoc plans another war so soon after Toluca?" he commented with skepticism. "Isn't that a bit unusual for him?"

"He did not say when," replied Ahuitzotl, "but wanted us to come up with some ideas for his evaluation, namely a credible motivation. It appears certain these cities are targeted as our next objectives."

"No doubt you will urge him to take to the field again."

"Of course!" Ahuitzotl declared, discerning Tlohtzin's mistrust. "And why not? Sometimes you puzzle me, Tlhotzin. They have pursued the same course as Toluca and, while I'm not advocating a similarly cruel retribution, punitive measures are appropriate."

"There's no need for you to get angry, Lord! I did not say I opposed you."

"The manner in which you said it indicated your disapproval."

"I protest!" Tlohtzin rebuffed him. "I will not be held in charge for how you construe what I say—not when my intent was far from your estimation."

"Disregard it," Ahuitzotl hastily retracted. "It was rash of me."

"If that is an apology, I accept it. I'll give greater care to I say so I'm not misunderstood.

"Don't do that. You are my watchdog, Tlohtzin. I prefer having strong men under me who dare to challenge my views when they perceive them to be wrong than those who, out of lack of courage or will, agree with everything I say."

Tlohtzin did not comment on this as he accepted the apology more readily in words than on faith. Their friendship was reaching an ebb and Tlohtzin was painfully aware of it. Ever since Toluca when he had witnessed Ahuitzotl's reluctance to send reinforcements to the monarch's aide, a move he considered wholly contrived, he regarded his commander's actions less than sincere. He developed a critical eye, questioning much of what Ahuitzotl said, and he had reservations if he could ever trust him again.

"To continue the assessment," Ahuitzotl went on, "It is time we send out scouts to survey the activities of both cities so…"

At that instant, the drillmaster, looking pale and visibly shaken, broke into the room. "A message from the palace, Lord!" he exclaimed. "The Revered Speaker, Lord Tizoc, is dead!"

"What?" Ahuitzotl was genuinely startled, not because he never expected such news would eventually come to him, but over the suddenness in which it struck.

"Lord Tizoc is dead!" repeated the drillmaster.

Tlohtzin and Motecuhzoma glanced at each other in disbelief. For the latter, the news was particularly jolting. New to Tenochtitlan and still impressionable in his youth, Motecuhzoma had not apprehended the general discontent over Tizoc's rule and stood in awe of him because he was the monarch and thereby inspired great veneration. Although Tizoc had been an even more remote figure to him than Ahuitzotl, this served to make his person all the more mysterious and imposing. In fact, he looked upon the Revered Speaker as almost a living god, to be honored and revered as a god, and it struck him as a profound shock that he could perish so readily-as any mere mortal.

By contrast, Tlohtzin was wily to the court intrigues and immediately suspected foul play. Fully knowledgeable of the poor regard Tizoc commanded from his principal lords and ministers, he had long marvelled over the patience in which they endured their disdain. Yet he himself had refrained from openly displaying enmity towards the monarch and always rendered him the respect his title deserved, unlike Ahuitzotl who attained notoriety for a lack of courtesy for him. Indeed, had he not seen the alarmed expression in Ahuitzotl's face, Tlohtzin could willingly have believed him to have had a hand in it. Tizoc's demise came to Tlohtzin as that of a familiar personage to whom he had become accustomed, and he was not without sorrow.

After recovering from his initial amazement over the haste in which Cihuacoatl had set out to do his work, Ahuitzotl was mystified that he should be saddened by the news. It was one thing to oppose Tizoc, to scheme against him, and to hunger for his eventual downfall, and quite another to be confronted by its actuality, and it seemed that despite all his anticipation for this event, its happening nonetheless caught him unprepared. He sincerely deplored that his brother should come to such a tragic end but remained adamant in his belief that Tizoc had brought this fate upon himself. Dispirited, and sharing the melancholy hanging over their meeting, Ahuitzotl had no inclination to continue it and ordered its termination.

The chieftains arose and proceeded for the door, but there Tlohtzin halted and turned to face Ahuitzotl again. "What will happen now?" he asked.

"I expect a summoning of the interclan council-to appoint a new Revered Speaker."

"Is it not Cihuacoatl who presides over this council?"

"He does," Ahuitzotl replied; his eyes narrowed as he tried to ascertain the purpose of this inquiry. "Am I to draw something from this?"

"I was merely curious."

"Curiosity is spawned by a supposition. You're keeping something from me."

Tlohtzin was annoyed over Ahuitzotl's overly demanding reaction to mere speculation but he clearly saw there was no escaping it. Indeed, it might be better if he actually told him, for an openness of suspicions bespoke of trust and affirmed their friendship, far preferable to risking his alienation and falling out of favor with him.

"I was wondering about the minister's frequent visits to our headquarters as of late-you yourself said this was unusual for him. For a moment there I was struck by a notion that there may have been a connection between that and the news we just heard."

"What sort of connection?" Ahuitzotl asked, a disagreeable visage coming to him and twisting his face in grimness.

"Must I endure this interrogation?" Tlohtzin snapped, finding Ahuitzotl's obstinacy vexing. "I said it was but a passing fancy. Is it any surprise I dislike confiding anything in you when you always heighten it to exaggerated levels."

"I know what you are thinking, Tlohtzin, and I caution you to be assured of it before making certain allegations."

"Making allegations? To who, Lord? What I discuss with you does not reach beyond this room. I don't need this admonishment!"

Ahuitzotl knew this and was alarmed over his own behavior regarding his compatriot's fidelity-he had no reasonable grounds for questioning him. That he did came as another indication over the state of iniquity his complicity had taken him, arriving at a point where he trusted nobody and had to be certain about every implication. "Would it amaze you," he said, "if I were chosen to succeed Tizoc as Revered Speaker."

"Not at all!" responded Tlohtzin without the slightest hesitation. "Who is more fit to rule?"

Ahuitzotl fancied that, assuaged by the certainty in which Tlohtzin said it, and in this single statement he redeemed all his earlier indiscretionary remarks.

"Be assured, Tlohtzin," said Ahuitzotl, a wide grin brightening his face, "should this be the case, there will be great things in store for you."

Tlohtzin departed feeling relief that their conversation had ended on a satisfactory note, but was becoming increasingly unsettled in his association with Ahuitzotl. He feared his mercurial temperament and, as he proceeded for his quarters, was not at all convinced if there would indeed be great things in store for him.

XXII

Word of Tizoc's death did not imbue the people of Tenochtitlan with the same depressing sense of loss as had marked the passing of previous monarchs. To a large extend, Tizoc's personal habits contributed to this, for in his fervor for a private life which gave him greater leasure in working his garden than in attending to his ministers, he isolated himself in his palace more and more. As a result, he became an incrementally remote figure to them. During his last year, and especially following the Toluca campaign, he was rarely seen in public, appearing only when ceremonial duties required his presence, which made a majority of the populace easily susceptable to the circulating rumors claiming that Tizoc had long been ill. After all, this explained his frequent absence from them. There was thus no undue difficulty in reconciling that he had died as a consequence of his ailment.

And there remained also the tarnish of Tizoc's cowardice which greatly detracted from his character and rendered him a figure of derision and public scorn. Not one individual resided in Tenochtitlan who had not learned of the monarch's performance at Toluca; it stood as a hot topic discussed repeatedly by many warriors, and after every retelling was magnified to more pronounced dimensions until anyone hearing of it could only react in an outburst of angry revulsion or shame. Tizoc had therefore become a singularly unpopular leader among his subjects; for many there was acute embarrassment in admitting that he was their Revered Speaker. Some may have actually believed that providence saw to his untimely end so that they no longer had to endure further indignity and humiliation. Even the priests, whose reaction was so greatly dreaded, seemed to uniformly accept the explanation offered.

Although disfavored, Tizoc nevertheless had been a Revered Speaker and this required the appropriate funeral rite; protocol demanded it, even if it was to be subdued. It fell upon Cihuacoatl, Vice-Ruler, to announce

Tizoc's death, and he summoned the principal lords, magistrates, ministers, commanders, and ambassadors to the assembly hall on the following day and confirmed what most of them had already heard from unofficial sources.

"It is my umpleasant duty," the minister soberly told his assemblage, "to inform you of the truth behind the rumors circulating our city. Lord Tizoc died unexpectedly of unknown causes yesterday afternoon. It is believed that he had been ill for some time, although he never spoke to anyone about this, and that the sickness had finally taken its toll on him. Send messengers to your cities to notify your rulers of this unfortunate event."

A respectful show of silence for the departed monarch encompassed the gathering; there were some in attendance for whom the news was received with genuine sorrow, but for most it was met as not perticularly disturbing. Then Cihuacoatl continued.

"Inform your lords that they are enjoined to participate in the funeral rites as is customary. We are aware this notice is short, and if they cannot themselves attend, their representatives will be acceptable. Also inform them that the interclan council will meet afterwards to take up the matter of naming a successor. This concludes my announcement."

Accordingly, the personages departed to make their preparations and reflect over the situation. Most concerned themselves with the meeting of the interclan council, for its decision was of more immediate importance to them. The prospect of a new Revered Speaker had an appealing, and yet apprehensive quality to it: it portended changes and, as had been the case in Tizoc, these may not necessarily be for the better.

In the House of the Dead, Tizoc's body was being readied for its final ceremonial function. First it was bathed thoroughly in clover water and then dried out and scented with exotic perfumes. Next, it was dressed in the royal robes which he normally wore on important occasions and bedecked with rich jewelry; locks from the top of his head were sheared off to be retained as a memorial and emeralds were placed in his mouth. The body was then cloaked in seventeen different mantles, each delicately woven and representing a deity, with Huitzilopochtli's the outer wrap, and it was set on a mat in a sitting position. A lifelike turquoise mask conforming to Tizoc's prominent features was fastened over the face: the body was now prepared for its last observance.

Soon, dignitaries arrived in the capital to send Tizoc on his journey, among them Nezahualpilli and Chimalpopoca of the Alliance cities as well as a host of monarchs from the nearby urban centers and ambassadors of those rulers too distant to personally attend. They brought with them gifts for offerings. Nezahualpilli came with two slaves, a man and a woman, exquisitely adorned in attire and ornaments who carried his gifts and would serve as benefactions themselves. For Axayacatl's funeral, he had brought four of them, as did every other ruler among the clans, but this was an uncertain situation for him; Tizoc's lack of popularity might have made even these seem extravagant to the remaining princes. As it was, only he and Chimalpopoca, who also provided a slave of each gender, came with such presents while the rest of the potentates arrived merely with containers of ornaments. food, and drink. Such was the decline of respect spawned by Tizoc.

Tizoc's beclad body was set upon the throne and the official ceremony began by each lord in turn speaking to it in the presence of his peers as if it were still alive and could hear his words. Nezahualpilli initiated this series of orations.

"Most noble ruler, Tizoc. I look upon you for the last time and wish you a successful journey to the heavens. You have by now come to the place where you shall find your fathers and the lords who preceeded you, and you now enjoy the glory of the Lord of Creation, of the day and the night, and of the air and fire. So that you might spend your time in greater happiness, I present you with this gift. I hope you will favor it."

With that, Nezahualpilli led his slaves carrying the rich presents before the body and stepped aside to make way for the next speaker, Chimalpopoca.

"My son, distinguished lord, and ruler. The glory and happiness you sought in life, and were so often denied to you, presently surround you in the place of your kinsmen and ancestors. Even as I speak to you, you are already standing before the house lit by the splendor of the Sun where you will meet those who have taken this journey before you. I, too, give you an offering which should make your future time more pleasant for you. May you repose in serenity, my son."

And so it continued, ruler after ruler, while the remaining participants listened to each speaker impart his memories and final comments, until the last of them had their say. After this observance, professional mourners entered and sang dirges to the body as food and drink were placed about it in a variety of containers. Then the lords slowly passed by and deposited their jewelry and other prized belongings beside the gifts already there while criers continued with their sad songs until the entire room overflowed with presents.

When all the gifts had been presented, all the songs sung, and all the eulogies rendered, the body was then placed into a covered litter and carried across the plaza toward the Temple of Huitzilopochtli in a solemn procession, imposing in its staid expression, with dignitaries trailing the bearers to the slow intermittant beat of a single drum. Decked out in their finest attire of colorful array, carrying their batons and insignia, the kings, nobles, kinsmen, and ambassadors chanted sacred hymns for the fallen monarch, some even weeping for him. Behind them walked the servants and slaves who would be sacrificed to die with their lord so that they might accompany him in his afterlife.

By the time they arrived at the temple, laborers under the direction of priests had already completed erecting a pyre for the body, and the litter was set upon it along with the many containers of gifts. An altarstone had been temporarily positioned in front of the mound around which stood the usual five priests required to perform the operation. After Cihuacoatl assumed his stand directly behind the block, the four slaves and five of the monarch's favorite household menials took up a single line to await being reunited with their lord. Cihuacoatl addressed them.

"My sons and daughters, highly honored to continue in the service of your lord. May you happily reach him in the other life which will greet you with its richness and all the delights of the world. Do not lose the things that belonged to your lord, but deliver them safely to him so that he might enjoy them in his new life. May you relish with him the blessings of this paradise."

One by one, they removed their garments, setting these in the hands of a priest, and assumed their place upon the stone while Cihuacoatl cut out their hearts and put these in a receptacle held by a subordinate to be later fed to the Death Goddess. Their bodies, along with their clothing and adornments, were stacked next to the monarch's on the pyre and, this completed, Cihuacoatl then signalled the torch bearers to light it.

In minutes it roared forth fully ablaze and all the bodies and gifts that had been cast upon it were engulfed in the flames while the votaries and dignitaries stood quietly by watching their donations comsumed therein.

After the pyre had been finally reduced to a glowing, smoldering heap, Cihuacoatl thanked each of the tribal rulers for having attended the rites and gave them their leave. They would now fast in their respective cities for a number of days as an act of individual bereavement for their departed monarch. With their departure the funeral of Tizoc came to a close.

Later that night, two soldiers rapped on the door of a house along one of the city's side streets. They wore eagle-crested helmets which extended over their eyes and noses making it impossible to identify them. An elderly man, looking haggardly from just having been aroused from his slumber, came to the door, opened it, and was startled to find himself facing the masked figures.

"What is it? Why do you wake me at this time of night?"

"Are you the physician, Alotl?" asked one of the soldiers.

"Yes, I am Alotl."

"Take him!" the soldier said to his comrade.

They pushed the bewildered physician against one of the upright posts supporting the roof and while one of them pinned him there by wrapping his arms around the beam, the other pressed his free hand over the physician's mouth to muffle any screams as he plunged a dagger deep into his chest, penetrating the heart. They continued to hold him fast until he grew weary in their arms, then let him fall to the floor dead. As furtively as they had come, the soldiers then disappeared into the darkness.

That night seemed darker than usual in Tenochtitlan, and the braziers lit before the steps and tiers of the temples and palaces cast an eerie glare upon the masonry, bathing it in a glimmering subdued light. The city was shrouded in stillness, and through it could be heard the rustling of a wind sweeping the lofty trees and whistling out its song to whoever might have remained awake to listen. But in the royal palace, the solitude was periodically interrupted by the piercing shriek of a singular lonely voice crying out in despair within the empty, gloomy corridors. Always it began as a loud painful wail which then drifted into muffled whimpering sobs, and anyone who perchanced to hear it would have felt his heart torn by its mournful protraction. The cries arose from Tlalalca, staggering about overcome in her grief and giving expression to the loss of Tizoc through her flowing tears. Although living, she felt as if she had died with her husband and during those long, horrible hours of her anguish, no one could have told her that such unbelievable sorrow would eventually pass.

One Revered Speaker's reign had come to an end; the world awaited the beginning of another's.

PART 2

———

THE OUTRAGE

"This will be your indispensable food, this you will live by, so that you proceed striking terror. The payment for your breast and heart will be your conquests, your overrunning and destroying the common people, the dwellers in all the places you reach, and when you take captives you will cut open their chests with a flint on the sacrificial stone and you will offer their hearts to the Brilliant Movement in the sky. As soon as the heart, rich with blood, is thrust out, you will offer it in the direction of Huitzlampa, the Thorn Place, as a sacrificial object, and the blood too, and the bloodiness. And when you have done this, I shall be there. Towards Tlaloc also, and then to all my friends, those gods known to you. And you shall eat the flesh unsalted. You may add to it only a little cooked maize, so that it might be eaten."

—Huitzilopochtli's instructions to
the Mexica from Nahua texts.
Cristobal de Castillo, Historia*

* Gordon Brotherston, "Images of the New World", Thames & Hudson Ltd, London, 1979, p 201

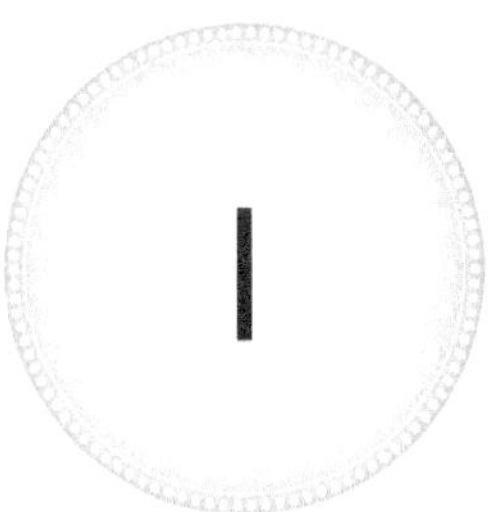

Four days after Tizoc's cremation, the nation's leaders were gathered in the royal palace to make their determination who would succeed him as Revered Speaker. A serious conference was in session: the situation was grave for them as five years of rule under Tizoc had left the realm unsettled, its policies in confusion, and its predisposition towards conquests ill-defined. In addition, whenever there occurred a change in Mexica leadership, many subjugated states experienced a restiveness and their natural proclivity for throwing off the conqueror's yoke came to the forefront and manifested itself in numerous rebellions. With the death of Tizoc, this activity was heightened under a general perception that the power of the Mexica was entering a declining phase which would carry over to his successor. The occasion was a momentous one: they could not afford another mistaken choice as in the case of Tizoc.

The Tlatoani, principal speakers of the member clans, were represented, among them Nezahualpilli, Chimalpopoca, and Cihuacoatl, the presiding official. Even before the official roceedings had started, their council was already divided into two distinct camps with each one strongly opposed to the position of the other. There were those who favored having an older, wiser man appointed the Revered Speaker; Chimalpopoca sided with this group and became its chief spokesman. Against them stood those who held to the customary passing of the throne within family lines in order to secure the royal descendancy; for them there existed but one choice, Ahuitzotl, and Cihuacoatl advocated their cause. Nezahualpilli leaned toward Ahuitzotl, but was open to hearing the opposition, and with their demarcation thus drawn, the council began to hear the arguments presented by each proponent. Chimalpopoca spoke first.

"As we all know, we have endured a less than satisfactory five years which have created many problems for us, and the fault for this ought not be blamed entirely on Lord Tizoc, but rather should be placed on his youth and lack of experience in handling state affairs. He was simply not alert to the devious ways in which such affairs are conducted because he was too young to know. We therefore urge the council to consider someone who is older and more venerable who would be held in greater esteem by rival lords. Even great and revered Motecuhzoma Ilhuicamina was over forty when appointed Revered Speaker."

"This is true," Cihuacoatl countered, "and we have never had so able a ruler, nor are we likely to again. But we must accept that such a man is a rarity in any age and should ask ourselves if there is one here today who could serve us as well. I, for one, do not know of anyone. We should recognize that no matter who we appoint as ruler, we cannot expect the greatness that came from Motecuhzoma."

"You enhance my cause," Chimalpopoca told the minister. "If we cannot find a ruler like him, then at least we can name one who possesses similar qualities, one who has acquired the skills that age and experience provide and who has matured to the fullest. I am weary of being led by mere youths who make repeated mistakes and command no respect."

Chimalpopoca's supporters appreciated his comment and gave him a resounding approval, surprising Cihuacoatl by their numbers. He had no idea that so many backed the Tepanecan and feared he faced an uphill struggle to get Ahuitzotl selected.

"You look for an older man," Nezahualpilli joined in, "yet one who will lead us to victories in numerous battles?"

"That can be delegated." countered Chimalpopoca. "It is his will to wage them that counts. But if he is respected, there shall be no need for numerous battles—only enough to meet our sacrificial requirements."

Again there were voices of approval.

"You are wrong," Nezahualpilli silenced the hall. "Quite the contrary, that will be the major task facing our new Revered Speaker after the way things have deteriorated. I do not wish to discredit Tizoc's memory and would add that much of his adversity happened inadvertently, perhaps owing to his youth as you say, but nevertheless, the damage has been done. With our affairs as muddled as they are-cities in rebellion, tributes denied to us, our merchants abused and threatened-I say to you it will take more than mere respect to set hings in order. It will require action! We need a dynamic ruler who has the ability and the energy to lead us on many campaigns so that the prestige of the domain established by the great Motecuhzoma is restored to us. Can an older man do these things?"

"Motecuhzoma did these things," Chimalpopoca pointed out.

"But we have no Motecuhzoma to guide us now. It is useless to bring up the dead past in face of our present situation. Do you know of anyone who is able to do what will be required? An older man? If so, name him for us."

Chimalpopoca hesitated. While no shortage of distinguished individuals existed to fill the post, there were no unique personalities with demonstrated drive which clearly set them apart from their contemporaries-none except Ahuitzotl, a younger man than he desired. He sensed his position weakening.

"Why do we deceive ourselves?" continued Nezahualpilli. "Why must I inform you of what you all know? There is only one possible candidate. Our needs increasingly direct themselves to Lord Ahuitzotl as the proper choice."

"It is said he is impetuous and hot-headed," Chimalpopoca replied, resisting the suggestion. "Also fond of carousing and entertaining the women. Should this be the man to rule us?"

"True, he is all these things, but also a brilliant leader of men, an outstanding commander, and possessed of a natural talent for decisive action. While we may have regressed under Tizoc, can anyone here declare that Ahuitzotl has not effectively led our armies? Indeed, whatever modicum of prestige remains for our realm, we owe to him."

There was no disputing this; everyone knew Ahuitzotl was the ablest of commanders, and to many the very embodiment of the warrior ideal-courageous, resolute, competent, and energetic, devoted to the mission of Huitzilopochtli. Chimalpopoca realized his cause was no longer tenable under this kind of barrage from his formidable Texcocan adversary.

"Who among us would fear going into battle with Ahuitzotl leading him?" Nezahualpilli added. "Why, then, should we fear to have him lead us as ruler? Why this ingratitude to him when his efforts kept us intact through our recent dark times?"

Once again it appeared that Nezahualpilli had carried the day as the speakers deliberated over his words and indicated a general concurrence.

"The council also believed this of Tizoc," Chimalpopoca said. "A lesson should have been learned from this. What assurances have we that we will not undergo a similar ordeal with Lord Ahuitzotl?"

"Have you such assurances with anyone else we appoint?"

"There's no basis for this inordinate fear about the age of our ruler," Cihuacoatl injected. "Axayacatl was but a boy of nineteen when we made him Revered Speaker. Was not his reign glorious? Not as great as Motecuhzoma's to be sure, but most certainly there was cause to rejoice in it. Were we not all struck with grief over his untimely death? If you will attribute Tizoc's dismal rule to his youth, how do you explain Axayacatl's? It's not youth, but the man himself, wherein lies the fault."

That determined the issue, and Chimalpopoca, already at a disadvantage, was not about to desecrate Axayacatl's memory over an argument that was lost. "I concede the point," he declared, "I was wrong to make an issue of age."

"It is best that the ruler be retained in the royal lineage," Cihuacoatl informed him. "They, by training and ability, are best fit to rule."

With the debate concluded, Cihuacoatl and the four primary Tlatoani retired into a smaller adjacent chamber to discuss the matter further in private. Few doubts remained as to who they would select, but the occasion afforded deeper review of the arguments presented and lent an appropriate aura of mystery and sanctity to the proceedings, and there have actually been times when a consensus among the assembly was overturned. In this case, however, Cihuacoatl's pursuasive powers were not required: the decision was uncontested. Having concluded their business, they returned to the reception hall where those who met had awaited the outcome. Cihuacoatl issued the official proclamation.

"It is decided. Let word be sent to the far reaches of our realm, to our allies, and our enemies as well, so all may know that the sun has risen anew. Lord Ahuitzotl is our Revered Speaker."

A runner was hastily dispatched to the headquarters building where Ahuitzotl was pacing the floor in the presence of Tlohtzin and Motecuhzoma eagerly anticipating the council's results when he entered. He sank to his knees before Ahuitzotl.

"Great Lord, chosen as Revered Speaker!" he began, "Cihuacoatl, Chief of Ministers, requests that you appear at the palace among the gathered lords for the initiation. I am honored to be the first to tell you this."

Ahuitzotl, strained and relieved in spite of having expected such a message, felt ecstatic on hearing it and a broad grin lit up his face. "I'll not detain them," he beamed. "Inform the Lord Minister I am coming."

Taking time only to receive congratulations from his subordinates and fasten his tilmantli over his shoulder, Ahuitzotl then proceeded to his place of destiny. All eyes were fixed on him as he entered the hall and confidently approached the raised platform at its far end where the throne was situated with Cihuacoatl and the kings of the alliance standing around it. On reaching it, Cihuacoatl quieted the assembly with his staff and everyone's attention focused on them. Nezahualpilli opened the ceremony by addressing the new monarch in his characteristic style.

"Oh Mighty Lord! You have been chosen to inherit the royal throne. To you we offer this seat, left to our care by the gods, most especially the high and glorious Huitzilopochtli, so that you might carry on his divine charge, the mandate he imparted upon us. You must faithfully and courageously fulfill this duty, for now is the time in which the foundation is embedded for our realm to flourish. We are living under a darkened sky, a time of peril, and we look for a new ascendancy, a fresh rising, out of the troubled depths into which we have sunk. We seek the glory that marked the passage of our honored forebearers, an eminence that has been lost. Our eagles must soar! Never before have our jaguars been so in want of their former fame and warriors, born to battle, must have their day. Our rising must claim its dominion over nations and kings as in the beginning the divine Huitzilopochtli instructed us to do so that Tonatiuh, the Sun, can once again grace us with his splendor. The firmament, the great movement, beckons this! We look to you, Great Lord, to provide for us and to achieve for us that which we have forsaken, that which we have lost, and that which we have been denied."

Following Nezahualpilli's stirring oration, Cihuacoatl stepped towards Ahuitzotl and placed his left hand under the monarch's chin to bend his head back. With his right hand he pierced Ahuitzotl's nostrils with a sharp thorn, carving out a hole large enough to allow for the emplacement of the emerald plug which denoted a Revered Speaker's divine linkage to the gods. The flowing blood was absorbed in white linens applied to the wound by Nezahualpilli.

Next two nobles came forward carrying the royal finery of the office and handed these to Cihuacoatl and Nezahualpilli who together unfolded them. A mantle of netted material, turquoise blue-the color of Huitzilopochtli, Lord of the Southern Sky-and studded with jewels delicately interwoven into the fabric, was draped over Ahuitzotl. An emerald diaden, embossed with precious stones, was hung around his neck to cover the front of his chest. Throughout the donning of the robe and official insignia, priests chanted out hymns to Huitzilopochtli lending a solemn dignity to the event.

After this formal dressing, the monarch was led to his blue feather and jaguar skin throne and when he was seated, the princes, lords, ministers, and ambassadors stepped forward in sequence and presented themselves before him rendering him words and gestures of respect and avowing their allegiance. Cihuacoatl stood adjacent to the throne and introduced each of these dignitaries to Ahuitzotl who became annoyed when one of the lords coming forward broke into a faint, but noticeable smile as he bowed.

"Who is he?" Ahuitzotl asked, "And why does he smirk like that?"

"He is Huactli, Lord of the Pochteca," Cihuacoatl replied. "He smiles, I believe, because he is grateful there is a new ruler. The pochteca have not fared well under Tizoc."

"I find it disrespectful. He makes it appear as if I owe him something. See to it he is informed of my displeasure."

Cihuacoatl was tempted to reveal Huactli's complicity in the plot against Tizoc but held back, thinking it best that Ahuitzotl be kept ignorant of who the conspirators were lest he should one day, out of anger, seek revenge on them. He was incensed over Huactli's audaciousness and would later admonish him for it, but at present he needed to placate his master.

"We must excuse his insolence, Lord. The pochteca are crude and earthly in their habits. It is understandable that they should behave awkwardly here and hold themselves in undue regard."

"I suppose you're right-I am indebted to their services. They provide useful intelligence on our enemies. Disregard my last statement, but advise Huactli of our courtly etiquette so that he does not err again."

The honors heaped upon the new monarch lasted throughout the afternoon and became quite tedious for Ahuitzotl, and while he maintained his lordly bearing and demonstrated an attentiveness, he greatly appreciated seeing the last of the dignitaries finish. He then motioned for Cihuacoatl to close this affair therewith ending the initiation rites. The actual coronation was still months away, as all monarchs had to be crowned on the day, One Dog. Custom dictated that new rulers use this interim period for conquests in order to exert their influence and obtain captives for sacrifice at this formal event. Ahuitzotl already had his victims selected.

That evening, a feast was held in the reception hall, hosted by Ahuitzotl for the potentates who had come to witness his initiation. Like most such fetes, the occasion had to be engaged in adherance to accepted protocol and constituted a requirement rather than a prerogative for both sponsor and guest. Ahuitzotl, however, desired his parties to be gala events, even if there was a deeply ingrained concern that excessive merriment could provoke certain gods to envy, and nearly detracted from their somber quality. He was generous in his compliments, sparing no effort towards making his visitors appreciate their stay and seeing to their needs. In this fashion, he spent his first evening as Revered Speaker performing his obligatory duties with considerable relish and attending to his subject lords.

lalalca sat tensely upon cushions within her chamber while Xoyo preened her in preparation for her sleep. Uncertainty defined her present condition. Possessing no notion of what was to become of her, she could take some solace in the knowledge that as a royal widow her needs would be cared for, but she harbored no illusions about expecting her days as empress to end. Time after time she pondered if it was possible to adjust to having one of her former ladies in court now sit in domination over her or if she could join their ranks subordinated to a new first lady coming from elsewhere. Neither prospect held any appeal, offering no preclusion from personal humiliation for her. What did it matter, she told herself; her life was already permanently shattered and without hope- the loss of Tizoc was unendurable, tormenting her immeasureably: to lose her title as empress was insignificant compared to that. Word of Ahuitzotl's accession had come to her earlier in the day-news she received with feelings of utmost disdain in spite of having conjectured it-and this added grievously to her distress.

"Were it anyone else but Ahuitzotl, I would not feel such dread," she fretted, "but he is justified in despising me and would relish exacting his vengeance on me."

"I think my lady misjudges him." answered Xoyo. "His own women say he is quite amiable."

"Not to his enemies. He's the unforgiving sort, and certainly has ample cause to hold me in that regard. I've never been particularly kind to him. Were he to learn from Pelaxilla how I tried to use her to..." she halted, leaning her head into Xoyo's shoulder, and softly wept as she was again struck with the stark reality that Tizoc was forever gone.

"Please, my Lady," begged Xoyo, torn over Tlalalca's disconsolation and worried that nothing helped to alleviate her pains. "Tizoc is in the company of the gods; you should not suffer like this when he now enjoys his paradise. I truly fear for you at times-for what you may do in your grief."

"It seems so useless now," Tlalalca wiped her tears. "All my attempts to protect him, to learn of the things I believed threatened him, coercing Pelaxilla into discovering them for me. Everything was for naught. He was taken from me just the same."

"My lady should not dwell on it. There can be no relief in continuing this speculation. Perhaps it is best never again to mention his name."

"I know you mean well, Xoyo, but what you ask is beyond my volition. How could he fall ill so suddenly and die? Things just do not happen like that; there's an unnatural aspect to it."

"Please, empress, is this wise?"

"Tizoc's habit was to seek solitude in the garden; he bade his servants not to disturb him when there. This certainly would have made it easy for his murderer-yes, I say murderer, for I truly believe this."

"Does my lady suspect anyone?"

"My inclination is to say Ahuitzotl, based on his years of demeaning my lord, his expressed discontent and known ambition, and indeed, who has gained more from Tizoc's death? He is now the Revered Speaker."

"You must be careful not to let him know of your suspicions."

"I can't avoid it. He will assuredly conclude this once Pelaxilla reveals what I tried to do."

This was a chilling thought for Tlalalca. Facing termination as empress was dismaying enough, but even that prospect was not as frightening for her as being exposed by Pelaxilla. Ahuitzotl's tempestuous nature was well known. "Oh, Xoyo," she lamented, "I do fear his wrath. What shall I do?"

"Things have a way of working out, my lady. You may find yourself surprised."

Xoyo's words afforded some mollification for Tlalalca; she was reminded why she had retained the aged woman as her personal attendant, and with her anxieties temporarily eased, her thoughts dwelled on another consideration.

"He has no wife," she pondered aloud. "Soon he will learn he must have one, especially if he wishes to lead by example as he is so fond of boasting. The lords will put him to the test on this. They will not appreciate their own lives constrained by marriage vows while their leader romps merrily about free from such impositions. He must appease their dissatisfaction. I'm curious who he has in mind."

"Why, the woman he loves I should think."

"Pelaxilla? He cannot. She is not of royal descent. Tizoc told me about having to deny his request to marry her. The priests will not sanction such a marriage, nor regard a child born to her as a claimnant to the throne."

"Then he knows."

"Oh yes. He reacted extremely adversive to it."

"I should expect so. I assume he has told Pelaxilla."

"What a shock that must have been for her," reflected Tlalalca, her empathy for Pelaxilla heightening as she recalled how she had made the young maiden's life far from comfortable in the palace. "As much as she loves him, and then to be told she can never be his wife–she must have suffered horribly."

"But then one never knows about Ahuitzotl. He is prone to do things his way. It would not be beyond him to marry her in spite of these restrictions."

A long quietness ensued as Tlalalca sat engrossed in her contemplation, and for Xoyo, inconvenienced by a muteness she deemed oppressive, it seemed an eternity before her lady spoke again.

"He would not dare," Tlalalca concluded. "Even a ruler faces limitations on what he can do. He will learn that a Revered Speaker can be more effective by maintaining a cordiality between his ministers, priests, and himself. Doing things against their wishes will not be of any help to him. Ahuitzotl may not favor their dictates, but he is wise enough not to alienate them."

"I hope my lady is right."

Tlalalca wanted to believe this, but felt insecure over the frequent unpredictability which characterized Ahuitzotl's methods, and yet, even while this caused her significant worries, it also possessed her of a strange fascination, and she fluctuated between these changing moods with repeated frequency as he was being discussed.

"I have to be," she said. "I could not tolerate being a subservile to that young girl. Oh no. That would simply be too much. But enough on this; it's late and I am ready to retire."

Taking her cue, Xoyo removed Tlalalca's robe and covered her with linen sheets after she took to her bed. Following this, the old woman saw to a few minor tasks remaining, then placed her lady's morning dress on a bench opposite the corner from where Tlalalca lay on her mats. This completed, Xoyo doused the torches and quietly slipped out.

Contrary to her earlier supposition, Tlalalca had difficulty falling asleep as her mind was too active allaying ever present fears and coping with repeated bouts of grief. She was in a most wretched condition, tormented over her indefinite future status, and she lay awake for what must have seemed an endless period of time, alone in the silent darkness and stung by recurring pangs of horror over Tizoc's absence from her side. Suddenly she was startled to hear heavy footsteps in the corridor apparently coming to her chamber; her heart began to pound furiously and she trembled under her sheets. Increasingly pronounced came the steps, and when they were directly before her chamber door, they stopped. Tlalalca froze.

Abruptly the drapes covering the doorway were flung aside and there, to her astonishment, was Ahuitzotl, clearly distinguishable in the light emitted from the brazier he was carrying. He merely stood there looking at her and not making a move. At first, she was inclined to feign sleep, but she knew that would never work—she was shaking too much and breathing too heavily. Surely he must be hearing her throbbing pulse! There was no choice but to confront him. "What is the meaning of this intrusion?" she inquired without further hesitation.

Ahuitzotl said nothing for the moment and instead walked across the total length of the chamber to place his brazier on one of the furnishings set there. Then he turned around and stepped up to the bed until he was standing next to Tlalalca. She was numb with terror.

"I intrude," he finally said in a low but assertive voice, "because it is my chamber you are in, and I wish to look it over."

"Your chamber?" Tlalalca said, bewildered but lightened of her fears after he spoke out.

"This is where the Revered Speaker sleeps, isn't it? And as I am he, I ask you, where else would I go?"

"What manner of cruelty is this?" stammered Tlalalca in a quivering tone with tears of both anger and pain swelling in her eyes. "If you meant to sleep here, you might have said something so I could have made other arrangements. Instead, you barge in here in the middle of night, like a vile thief, and subject me to base harassment. Is it not enough for you that I have suffered the loss of my husband?"

"Duty requirements prevented me from such niceties. Having been with Tizoc all these years, you know how it is. But I'm here now and, like it or not, here I will stay."

That was clear enough for her; she looked to where Xoyo had placed her clothing. Her heart sank when she saw her dress draped over a bench on the other end of the room.

"Very well, stay!" Tlalalca said. "I shall go elsewhere. Will you hand me my garments?"

"You're the one who wants to leave. Get them yourself."

Tlalalca was appalled at his rudeness, announced as though he desired the abhorrence in which she regarded him and did his best to elevate it. She did not move.

"What are you waiting for?" he asked with apparent pleasure. "Surely you did not expect me to play handmaiden to you?"

"I will not have you gawking at my nakedness," she retorted angrily.

Ahuitzotl burst into a hearty laughter. "Why not?" he said, grinning widely. "I'm sure you are not that different from my other women."

Her face flushed in embarrassment, but she was quickly overtaken by indignation, augmented by his obvious delight in seeing her discomfited. She began to rise from her bed, keeping one of the sheets wrapped about her body, but Ahuitzotl halted her by pressing its trailing end against the mats.

"Do not soil my sheets by sweeping them across the floor," he said.

Frustrated, Tlalalca fell back on the mats. What had she to fear, she said to herself; he was only toying with her and will go when he tires of his sport-she must not let it upset her. But then, to her horror, he began removing his tunic-he was undressing! "What are you doing?" she said, disputing the act.

"I'm getting ready to go to sleep."

"You mean here?"

"In my chamber, yes. You chose not to leave, and I have no objections to your staying."

"You have no ob...! You must be mad to think I would spend the night with you! I shall take my leave!"

"Go. Do not stay here on my account."

"Indeed I shall not!" she snapped.

Angrily, she flung aside her sheets and sprang from the mats. She was completely nude, and as Ahuitzotl observed her walking to the bench, he felt his body overwhelmed with hot and cold tingling sensations in his aroused state. The blood surged in his phallus, raising it to a jade-hard erection underneath his breechcloth.

She had an exquisitely shaped body, slim and tantalizing, and all the more accentuated by her long raven hair extending down to her narrow waist. The graceful rounded folds of her buttocks swayed deliciously from side to side enhanced in softness, yet the flesh was firm with not an unsightly wrinkle in it. Her skin shone silky smooth under the dim light; Ahuitzotl's heartbeat raced feverishly as he beheld her loveliness. She was a strikingly beautiful woman, and if she did not arouse him to the same exhilarating heights that only Pelaxilla could, she nevertheless induced an enthralling stimulation of her own which quite intoxicated him. Seeing her naked for the first time left him with an insatiable appetite to possess her.

"Wait!" he directed.

"Yes?" she turned about to offer him full sight of her bare front, making no attempt whatever to cover any part of her as she feared it would only add to her shame.

He was transfixed in wonder over her enticing figure. His eyes scanned her entire body from head to toes, lingering as they focused on her private features to fully savor their magnificence; with the subdued light emphasizing her curvatures and giving them an appealing soft texture, she was irresistible. She was taller than Pelaxilla, but noticeably thinner. Her head was ovaline and featured large glowing eyes with a straight, narrow nose; the lips were small but well rounded, and the shadows revealed high cheekbones. She had a smooth neck, slender and elongated, which rested on shapely shoulders. Her breasts were not particularly voluminous, but sturdy and beautifully molded, with somewhat diminutive nipples protruding solidly forward. Her body tapered to a small waist and then widened to alluring hips in perfect symmetry with the little dark indentation of her navel drawing attention to its shapeliness.

His eyes focused on the shaded furrow between her voluptuous thighs, seductively folding inward and yet hardly discernable. Ahuitzotl's pulse palpitated in his throat. Absorbing as much of her as he could, his gaze proceeded downward noticing the lean solidness of her long legs, her thinly proportioned knees, and the shapely contours of her calves reaching to slender ankles. Her toes seemed small and fragile to him.

Tlalalca was visibly perturbed over having her body so thoroughly scrutinized. Yet, for an instant, she entertained a notion that he actually might have found her desireable, but she hastily dismissed this fancy as her vehemence for him was remembered.

"Pitiless man," she protested, "Why do you taunt me so?"

"I had forgotten what I wanted to say," Ahuitzotl slowly replied. "I was so distracted by your-your obvious charms. I must say that Tizoc had good taste in making you his wife."

He then approached her. She trembled in her anticipation over what he would do next, unable to calm her stress. When he was next to her, he became enflamed in his ardor, her proximity arousing him to anxious heights. Stepping around her, he admired her figure up close, and noticed the folds of her bottom quivering: it was apparent that she was extremely frightened.

"Why are you so afraid?" Ahuitzotl asked, perplexed over what he deemed an exaggerated reaction to his advances. "I've never tried to hurt you."

She was too numb to render a reply and he, propelled ahead by powerful urges, ran his hand under her glossy raven hair, feeling its lightness. He then touched her skin, marveling at its velvety essence, and stroked his fingers down the length of her spine and through the cleavage of her buttocks, savoring the pressure of her flesh on them. He extended his palm across her rounded cheeks, delighting in their weightiness and resilience. When he again caressed her front, he cupped his hand over one of her breasts, occasionally tapping on the nipple with his finger as if trying to push it in—he liked the sensation of resistance this offered him. Lowering his hand, he came to her navel and inserted his little finger into it as if to measure its depth. He continued his descend, touching lightly upon her genital area when he abruptly stopped his stroking.

"There's no need for you to get dressed." he proposed, clinging to a vague hope that she might consent to this. "Stay here."

"I will not spend the night with you!" she exclaimed without as much as a moment's pause.

"So you say, but you ought to reconsider. You might not find it that disagreeable."

"I would abhor it!"

"You don't have to get offensive about it," he reacted with agitation. "Is this an example of the graciousness I can expect from you? You need to improve on your manners."

No longer feeling threatened, Tlalalca's indignation rose commensurately to her loss of fear. "You dare speak to me of manners?" she shouted. "You steal in here late at night, contrive to see me naked, and take indecent liberties with me, and you dare to talk of manners? What a despicable beast you are!"

"Nobody speaks to me like that!"

"Really? I should think it quite the opposite-you behavior certainly invites it."

"What rashness! Instead of being thankful that I refrain from forcing myself upon you, you insult me and sorely test my restraint. I should take you here and now."

She stared into his glaring eyes and in her wrath failed to take into account how far she could venture with her inflammatory censure: she was bent on denouncing him.

"You don't have the balls!" she snapped recklessly at him.

"By the gods!" he roared out, lunging out at her. Tlalalca's anger instantly turned to panic as she was lifted off the floor in his powerful arms and flung half the distance across the room upon the mats. She landed on her backside, and before she could recollect her thoughts, Ahuitzotl had torn off his breechcloth and pounced atop her in one long leap.

He smothered her with vengeful ferocity. Using his broad chest pressed against her upper body to anchor her in place, he devoured her face and neck with repeated kisses as he held her head steady with one hand while, with the other, he forced her legs apart, gripping the flesh to tightly that it bruised. He rammed his rigid shaft into her juicy opening until it felt firmly enclosed within its heated membrane walls and then began his vigorous motions, merging the rhythmic oscillation of his movements with the natural contractions of hers so they blended into a simultaneous surging current of mounting intensity that strove for a climactic conclusion. He gasped for air, his heart pounding at a triple-pace, his muscles so taut he thought they would crush his bones. Then, when his body was so strained that it convulsed under the pressure, in an overwhelming eruption of frenzied pleasure he felt the spasmodic release of his fluids shooting forth. He lavished on that exquisite gratification of all his senses. Not until he had expended himself did he become aware of Tlalalca's hot dampness beneath him and the moaning she emitted.

He rolled off her and lay on his back savoring the night air drape his sizzling frame like a cool blanket. Breathing heavily to relieve his exertion, his pulse still throbbing furiously, he heard Tlalalca's own heavy inhalations and felt the heat from her body. Neither of them spoke, too spent of energy to apply the effort, and preferred remaining oblivious to further contact as their excitement began to dissipate. At last sufficiently recovered, and now riddled with an awkwardness over having violated Tlalalca when he was initially set against this, Ahuitzotl felt uncomfortable over prolonging his stay and rose to depart.

"I shall sleep in my old chamber," he said, putting on his clothes and flinging his tilmantli over his shoulder, and then picking up the brazier. "It's what I meant to do before you hurled your insults at me. You provoked me and I will not apologize."

She did not say anything, but a look in her eyes momentarily left him with a yearning to remain with her-he had the impression they entreated him to stay. He was wrong, he told himself; if anything, she had even more reasons for despising him now.

"You drove me to it," he emphasized. "Remember that!"

Then he was gone. Tlalalca continued to lie atop the mats in complete darkness permitting the breezes to cool her still heated flesh. At first, she thought of nothing except the gentleness in which she was physically stroked by the soft breath of the wind. Then, a mixed aggregation of emotions swept over her, varying from feelings of outright repugnance over what had happened, to relief that she had not fared worse for it, to self-loathing over her inability in better handling the situation, to guilt that she derived some exhilaration in it, to condemnation that she herself produced the provocation for it. Yet, there was no denying that Ahuitzotl held a degree of fascination for her, and if she was unable to adequately give it definition, she nonetheless felt its impulses surfacing amid her general attempts to reinforce the antipathy she sustained for him. She suppressed this attraction, but the mere fact that it arose at all alarmed her. Finally, after an indeterminant length of time had elapsed, she felt a chill come over her. She slipped under the covers, and not long thereafter, spent by the ordeal, she was asleep.

More than mere curiosity caused Pelaxilla to consider when Ahuitzotl would speak to her about the plans he had envisioned for them. Now monarch for several days, he had, as yet, not given her any indication of his intentions, very much as if he wished to defer it, she thought, and she was both mystified and disturbed over his hesitancy. Her waiting seemingly fruitless, it became evident to her that if she was to obtain an explanation, she would have to take the initiative. She had seen little of him lately, which she attributed to his newly acquired duties, and believed herself neglected, and while she thus moped groping for a means to confront him, a servant girl entered her chamber.

"My Lady," the girl began, surprising Pelaxilla who had been so engrossed in her brooding that she failed to notice her enter. "Lord Ahuitzotl requests that you see him."

Pelaxilla was temporarily speechless, and then immeasurably thrilled; her desires were suddenly answered and all her earlier worries instantly vanished. Brimming with excitement, she followed the girl through several narrow passages until arriving at a restricted doorway draped by woven curtains. She was motioned to enter, and no sooner had she passed the threshold when she found herself facing her smiling hero. Eagerly, she ran into his embrace.

"Oh, Ahuitzotl," she moaned, nearly in tears, "you have not called on me-and for so long. You can't imagine. I feared you had forgotten about me."

"These are demanding times for me. I've spent days listening to the tirades of angry priests, discontented ministers, and demanding ambassadors. I'm weary of their endless complaints, but Cihuacoatl informs me it is what I must do. Tomorrow I'll tell them of my own plans-many will be shocked. Anyway, this is what kept me from you, contrary to my wishes."

"You could have let me know. I was worried sick."

"I'm sorry. That was very inconsiderate of me."

Ordinarily, Pelaxilla might have deemed his curt dismissal of so flagrant a remission as unacceptable, but another, more serious issue preoccupied her, and with his mood now drawn to her concerns, she decided this was the proper time to have her main question answered. "Since you speak of plans," she said, "what are they for us?"

He readily knew what she was after, having long regretted not mentioning it before in spite of seeking to alleviate her depression on those occasions. This omission arose to haunt him again and again, and the more he postponed it, the more unsettled he became, so that he was left considerably troubled over how to proceed.

"Why, you'll be my favorite mistress, of course," he ventured to say. "You will share my bed more often than anyone else and we shall have each..."

"Your mistress?" interrupted a stunned Pelaxilla, "Not your wife?"

There was now no escaping the subject, and Ahuitzotl greatly feared her reaction over what would surely be received as a most severe jolt. "There's a complication," he muttered nervously, "and it stands as a major obstacle to our plans. The House of Tenochtitlan, as you may know, must claim an ancestry to the gods. This was a measure instituted a long time ago as a means of keeping the proliferation of our nobility in check and excercising control over them. It is accepted doctrine-there is no compromising it. A priestly structure exists in support of this; it is assumed to give stability to our social order and indespensible to our welfare. Only two families, the Tepanec and Toltec, are by bloodlines associated with this connection and are the sole legitimate link to our divinities. It turns out you are not of these families, Pelaxilla. Owing to this, the priests will not condone a marriage between us."

Pelaxilla stood dazed, her mouth open, unable at first to grasp the full significance of what she had just heard, and when it finally sank in, her disillusionment was total.

"It-it cannot be," she gasped.

"I'm afraid it is. Tizoc was the first to tell me-when I tried to get you released from him. Since then, I have checked with others, desperately hoping to hear a denial, but they have all confirmed it. I'm truly sorry, but the condition is stipulated by our laws."

"How can the gods be so cruel?" she cried out, nearly panic-stricken as his words imparted their full implication and she felt her standing with him seriously threatened. "I don't know what to do."

"There's nothing you can do-nor can I."

"You've crushed me!" Pelaxilla lamented, ignoring his statement in her self-pity as she openly wept. "You have destroyed all my dreams in one single stroke. Everything I hoped for, and lived for, is shattered for me. Don't you realize that!"

"What have I done?" Ahuitzotl replied, resenting her insinuations. "It's not my law that prevents our marriage and I'll not be censured for it."

Pelaxilla was quieted as she reflected over this latest setback. Again the shock of another reversal bore into her, but this time it struck with far greater severity, coming when she had anticipated an ending to her problems, and she was utterly forlorn in the hopelessness of her situation. While her nature was to rebel against accepting adversity, she knew that in the present case this was futile and her mood changed from angry disappointment to utter dejection, which in her always manifested itself in an unnatural silence. For Ahuitzotl, her depression was a more difficult barrier to surmount.

"I know your anguish," he said. "I reacted as you when I was first told. But after all my agonizing, I came to the conclusion it didn't matter whether we're married or not. We can still love each other and there will be nothing to separate us."

"Except a wife!" she declared.

"She would not stand between us," he assured her. "I'll make that clear to her. It will be like Nezahualpilli and his Tula Woman; even though he has many wives, he spends most of his time with her, and they understand."

"I should hate to be a wife under such conditions. Why bother having one?"

"Unfortunately, if I am to have a legitimate heir, one who can succeed me on the throne, I must have a Tepanec or Toltec wife-another of the trappings by which the loyal lineage is preserved."

Once more Pelaxilla was stung. She knew that the kind of arrangement such as Ahuitzotl suggested had troublesome aspects to it and was fraught with potential adversities for both herself and an empress, but to request that he forego an heir for her sake was out of the question.

"How can I serve under your lady knowing that she may be envious of the position I hold with you?" Pelaxilla forwarded. "She will make my court life miserable for me-out of sheer jealousy."

"If she did, you need only mention this to me. I will put a stop to it."

"Such things can be done subtly enough, in a manner calculated to make my complaining about it appear foolish to everyone, perhaps even to you. I can easily envision it as a humiliation for me."

"You worry too much."

"With good reason-the prospect is not a happy one."

"It works fine with Nezahualpilli. I think what upsets you is that you can't be empress. You'll just have to make that adjustment, disagreeable as it may be."

Pelaxilla refused to comment on that, aware there was some truth in his assertion; at the same time she was perplexed how, on the one hand, he could accurately relate on her disposition while, on the other, so grossly minimize the threat his proposed arrangement held for her.

"Everything said so far has been unpleasant for me," she related, "and I seriously doubt if I could be shocked any further. May I ask who we can expect as our next empress?"

He should have expected this, Ahuitzotl thought. He did, in fact, have a prospective mate in mind but was unwilling to impart this on her, at least for the present, as his own certainty over the matter still lay unresolved. How should he answer her?

"There are some who fit the requirement," he answered.

"Do I know her?"

"Fairly well, I think. You are bent on hearing it, so I'll tell you. I had considered Tlalalca, Tizoc's wife, to be, or rather should I say, to remain empress."

"Tlalalca!" Pelaxilla was wrong-she could still be shocked; her outburst and stunned expression also startled Ahuitzotl.

"Why is this so alarming?" he questioned. "She's of the Tepanec family and has performed admirably enough as empress. I though she was popular among you ladies."

"But Tizoc's wife-so soon after his death?"

"That does not matter."

"But I was under the impression she loathed you. I know she does. You would marry someone like that?"

"That makes it convenient for both of us. Don't you see? No matter who I marry, it's you I'll love. Better for her that she loathes me; she won't be offended if I spend all my time with you, nor will she be a threat to you. The situation is perfect for us."

Pelaxilla was skeptical and clearly preferred having someone unknown to her as she had been intimidated by Tlalalca before and, even if Ahuitzotl's declaration of love remained fixed, of which she was by no means assured, the resultant relationship was certain to be strained. But even more importantly, Tlalalca was, by any measure, an alluring woman, even regarded by many as an exceptional beauty, and this frightened Pelaxilla to a greater degree than any fear of enmity. She was determined to dissuade him from his present course.

"I've had my problems with her," she said. "She wanted me to learn what evil schemes you planned against Lord Tizoc. She feared you meant to harm him. This seems strangely empty now, but at the time it gave me horrible anxieties, especially when she threatened to have me ousted from the palace if I did not carry out her instructions. As it was, I found out little from you and did not tell her anything at all, and events then outpaced both of us–who knew Tizoc was so sick? The experience was terrifying for me."

"So this was the source of your pretending games."

"Yes-she was behind it all."

"Frantic efforts of a fearful wife trying to protect her husband. Surely you can appreciate that."

This was not the answer Pelaxilla wanted to hear, and there was a studied concern in her curiosity over why Ahuitzotl should try to defend Tlalalca after what she had just related to him. As often before, he baffled her.

"Perhaps so," she conceded, "but I felt it was extremely unfair for her to use me like that, especially from her position of power. It left me with no defense whatsoever. I don't think I would be comfortable if she remained the empress."

"She won't threaten you again. I guarantee it."

"Why are you so bent on her being the empress?" Pelaxilla declared in frustration. "It seems nothing I tell you will detract from that purpose, as though you've suddenly consigned yourself as her champion."

"You're quite mistaken. In fact, I'm not yet convinced if I ought to select her. Her aversion for me, after all, presents a deterrent and is certainly nothing to be cherished. She is merely a candidate should pressures be exerted on me to secure an empress, nothing more yet."

"If only I could believe that."

"It's true, and until I decide, keep this to yourself. What we discussed is not known to her-I wish it to remain so, else you will hasten my decision, something I'm sure you don't want."

"Obviously not, but what difference does it make? What have I to be cheerful about? My hopes are dashed to pieces. Is this why called for me?"

"Actually I wanted to ask that you join me in my quarters tonight, but it's evident enough our conversation has left you quite distraught. I will understand if you refuse."

A myriad of thoughts raced through Pelaxilla's troubled mind as she dwelled on his request. She was demolished by the weight of all she had heard, and demoralized to such an extend that she feared her companionship would be wanting. Yet there cried out within her an overwhelming yearning to be with Ahuitzotl, to fulfill long sought urges, to spend a much desired night with him and be deluged by his attention and caresses. This is what she had so passionately craved for, more than anything else, and now it came as an utterly spoiled conjuncture by his devastating disclosure. Tears of pain and anguish streamed from her as she bemoaned her cruel fate.

Ahuitzotl was badly shaken by her quiet weeping. His last expectation was to bring sorrow to her, especially when he meant to enjoy their first entire night together, and he inflicted silent denunciations upon himself for having been so careless in his omission about the royal prerequisites and, even worse, over having tactlessly alluded to Tlalalca as the preferred choice for his wife. Unhappy over Pelaxilla's depression, even while he stood confused over how their conversation had gone awry, he was reconciled to do without her for a few more days until she overcame her grief.

"I won't insist on it," he told her, his dejection visibly straining his features. "I know your despair, having felt the same agony. Perhaps it's best to allow additional time to absorb all this."

"No!" her aching heart answered for her, "I don't want to be without you anymore. I will stay."

Rejuvenated by her consent, he clutched her tightly against his solid frame and kissed her lips, and knew in its sweetness that it was Pelaxilla alone who gave meaning to his life. All was well.

IV

"Speak, priest!" Ahuitzotl's voice thundered out over the hall where his assembled principals were met on the following morning. "What is a propitious time to begin our campaign?"

"Now is an auspicious time, Lord." replied the head priest, "Ripe for an undertaking. The stars portent opportune events for us. There is no adversity indicated in their readings."

"Splendid. Prepare yourself and the others for the journey."

The priest recoiled, not over the instructions he received, for it was the habit of newly appointed rulers to embark on campaigns before their actual coronations, but rather in the manner Ahuitzotl's style contrasted from his predecessor's. Tizoc would have held lengthy deliberations, sought approval, and obtained a consensus for his proposed activity whereas Ahuitzotl declared his plans. Five years under Tizoc have left their mark.

"Against whom do we march, Lord?" the priest inquired.

"Against the Matlazinca. Specifically, Chiapa and Xiquipilco. The time for reconciliation is over. They must learn a new Revered Speaker now rules."

"You will not call for a council of the allied lords?" Cihuacoatl asked.

"They expect me to engage in this operation, as is customary, so why should I seek their advice on it?"

"What about their assistance?"

"We've dispatched our couriers to direct them to join us. I will wait two days for them to arrive, then begin our move."

"You do not give them much time, Lord. Are we strong enough to undertake the venture by ourselves if they fail to join us?"

"Our pochteca have acquired ample information to enable us to proceed without much trouble. The Matlazinca are still in low spirits over the fall of Toluca, but they believe that together they have the strength to continue their resistance. I will make them realize their error-even united, they are no match for us."

Ahuitzotl's words instilled the assembly with eagerness, demonstrating a confidence most had not heard from a monarch for a long time and received as a refreshing change. He was granted a hearty round of applause when he closed his first council. Almost immediately thereupon, the ambassadors of Chiapa and Xiquipilco sent messengers to alert their lords of the impending danger.

"You have a good beginning," said Cihuacoatl, who remained to learn more of his master's intentions, "but is it wise to embark on this venture in such haste?"

"We've studied our enemy carefully and know what they can do. I have a dual purpose in mind for waging this campaign. The primary motive is to strike with sufficient expediency so as to invoke fear at the mention of my name and to prevent their merging forces. They are our weakest opponent. It's not out of any threat I do this. Rather, I wish to impress our neighbors with this exercise-so they understand who they are up against. What better way than for me to acquire some speedy conquests."

"You are certain of victory?"

"Of course."

Cihuacoatl was too seasoned to be taken in by this kind of overt bravado and remained skeptical. He had heard such talk before and too often the resultant performance fell short of his expectations. But he also knew that Ahuitzotl had the ability and that his approach differed. For one thing, he undertook detailed studies of his enemies and learned of their capabilities before embarking on them. Also, the minister appreciated how there seemed to be an ulterior purpose in Ahuitzotl's planning, directed typically at more than one objective. Tizoc struck him as having been single-minded in his aims.

"I am compelled to remind my lord than even Tizoc began his Metztitlan campaign boldly enough," Cihuacoatl said. "A single action, however extensive or fruitful, will not restore our former glory."

"Restore?" Ahuitzotl scornfully replied, giving the minister such a cold, derisive glare that he shuddered at having delivered his previous utterance. "No, Cihuacoatl, I have far bolder schemes in mind than merely to restore what has been. I once told you that I would surpass them all. That was no idle boast. Now that I have the power, I shall fulfill this pledge."

"The lowly Matlazinca will serve as a start. A modest one, to be sure."

"Still a start, which brings me to my second purpose. Our warriors must be tested in this campaign. Not their physical stamina, you understand, but their resiliency. Their responsiveness to new ideas–challenges to long held practices. I need to ascertain this if I am to prepare for the other ventures I envision."

"Your words are ominous."

"Well they should be. I plan to march into regions where no Mexica have set foot. I've been told there is a great sea to the west of us, beyond Michoacan-as large as the one east of Totoneca. Have you heard of this?"

"Yes, a number of times."

"You've never mentioned it."

"Oh, I've been curious about it, but subsequent reports have dampened my enthusiasm for that region. It's populated by tribes which call themselves the Huitlateca and Yopetzinca–both are an impoverished lot with no wealth to be found among them. There are no rich cities to speak of."

"How do you know these reports are true?"

"I don't, but if richness were there, word of it would abound. In absence of this, I presume their accuracy.

"Still, I want to be the first to see for myself."

"This is what you wish to prepare the army for? I hope, for your sake, the rewards will justify the effort. Our warriors expect their booty. There will be major disappointment if none was forthcoming from there."

"It deserves our attention even if no riches are acquired. If nothing else, at least we can satiate Huitzilopochtli. Can it be right that these people out there should escape serving him?"

"I didn't know you concerned yourself with that," Cihuacoatl stated, aware this was a side of Ahuitzotl he had ignored.

"I was indicating what should motivate our warriors–above mere looting-which ought to make such a quest worthwhile."

"But you hold no such views yourself."

"I did not say that."

"No, but others have said it for you."

"It's best not to listen to others speak for me. I honor Huitzilopochtli above all and am his most devoted servant. I will do whatever he asks of me. Why do you look at me so strangely?"

"Do you expect him to talk to you?"

A smile came to Ahuitzotl; it amused him to send his minister into befuddlement. "Indeed yes," he said, "and only to me."

"That is most convenient. As ruler, who could dispute it?"

"Precisely."

There was a double-edged meaning to all his thinking, Cihuacoatl noted; he would have to take that into account in his dealings with him. It made the Revered Speaker mystifying, and also dangerous-even now the minister was unable to determine whether Ahuitzotl's statement on his supposed devotion was sincere. In truth, he possessed no conception of how deeply the monarch's allegiance to the gods ran, and this troubled him.

Ahuitzotl's smirk seemed to confirm Cohuacoatl's estimation, and to the minister's further annoyance, he refused to speak any more on this, moving instead to a topic totally different. "What are the demands on my having an empress?" he asked. "Is there criticism for not having one?"

"Not openly–yet. Undoubtedly our lords speak of it in private. You will eventually have to take that step, however; they will begrudge you your liberties from the conventions binding on them. Also it is wise if you are to maintain an order among your own women. You are correct in bringing this up-the matter must be given sober deliberatioin."

"For reasons you are aware, I cannot take Pelaxilla for my wife. What is the view of the priests if I were to take Tizoc's wife as my own?"

Cihuacoatl was impressed that his master had even contemplated such a move; he saw no grounds to oppose it as he professed a fondness of his own for Tlalalca-one of the few palace women he actually favored-and had an interest in her welfare. "It's somewhat out of the ordinary," he said, "but I don't see how they could object. Certainly there's no prohibition against it. Unlike this Pelaxilla, she meets the lineage requisites they are obsessed with."

"I see it as a formality to please everyone. My time will be spent with Pelaxilla."

"That is problematic," Cihuacoatl cautioned, disillusioned in Ahuitzotl's reply. "The empress will be envious if your attentions are directed elsewhere."

"I don't think so-not in this case."

"Would an empress be content to be a mere figurehead?"

"Tlalalca would."

"And not be able to have her affairs with you? She'll not be overly fond of you for that."

"She's not overly fond of me now."

"Indeed? Then how is it you wish her for a wife?"

Stated as such, the notion did carry an absurdity about it and Ahuitzotl paused to ponder on it. He was not quite certain why he wanted her, other than that she met the lineage demands, except that his previous encounter with her somehow left him with a strange yearning for her. He could see that he again baffled his minister and was prompted into providing an answer.

"There's something about her that appeals to me, aside from her beauty, although I can't exactly place it. Perhaps it's even her loathing for me. Does that make any sense to you?"

"Since you ask, no."

"Nor to me. There are mysteries to these thing we cannot explain-the contrivances of Xochiquetzal and not meant for our comprehension. All I know is I find her very intriguing. She presents a challenge to me."

"She may indeed do that. She is a hot-blooded young woman, and if you don't give her any affection after making her your wife, you may force her into an adulterous relationship. that will truly present you with a challenge. I suggest you forget about her and stick to your Pelaxilla-the spurns of our lords are a less formidable obstacle."

"I will not deprive myself of an heir. I think that Tlalalca, because of her dislike for me, would willingly perform as my empress without harboring any resentment for Pelaxilla. She will not be envious of her."

"Do not overlook one key factor-Tlalaca's physical needs. By making her empress, you place her in servitude to you-by law! No one else can have access to her—you impose a lonely existence on her. You will have to do your part in keeping her satisfied."

"I can do that on occasions."

"So charitable of you. I should have to make such painful decisions. When will you announce this-this arrangement."

"I haven't decided yet-perhaps after the coronation. Do not mention this to anyone."

"So you have time to think on it; I would give it serious consideration indeed. I can't see anything productive coming out of this kind of concoction. It has all the potentiality of a disaster."

"I'm prepared to risk it."

"In that case, the only advice I can give you is not to allow your tumultuous personal life-and tumultuous it will surely be!-to interfere with your performance of duties as Revered Speaker."

"It won't. You can be certain of it."

These assurances were sufficient for the minister, but when he departed the palace, he surely had to wonder how a person so capable of mounting vast large-scale military operations could conduct his personal affairs in such a haphazardous manner. To think that such an arrangement as Ahuitzotl envisioned for himself could actually work out defied all common logic and ran counter to every instinct and conviction he possessed on the subject. As usual, Ahuitzotl was a source of bewilderment to him, whose impulses edged on the unfathomable, and while he knew he had not been much help to his master, he felt himself at a disadvantage when giving counsel outside of state functions. Certainly he was no expert on love-no man was as far as he knew-and besides, men in love are not prone to listen to advice, especially when it regarded the object of their affection, and Ahuitzotl, headstrong as he was, warranted no exception to this assessment. Yet his experience taught him to be cautious of men whose domestic lives were in turmoil, for rarely had he seen this work to anyone's benefit and, more often than not, the ensuing chaos proved detrimental to them. It was with a sense of deepest foreboding that Cihuacoatl left the monarch to brood over his dilemma.

V

Once again the Mexica army was on the march. The short call to arms gave Nezahualpilli some irritating moments, and he almost decided to abstain from participation, but he decided that ignoring an imperative by the new Revered Speaker was tantamount to an offensive display of contempt and thereupon arrived within a day at the head of his complement of five thousand Acolhuas. His force could rest in Tenochtitlan as this operation was launched in the orthodox pattern with an entire day separating each singular army. For Chimalpopoca, while he received the news with equal disdain, the situation was less taxing as Tlacopan lay directly en route of the advance and his army of four thousand was already on its way. On this day, Tenochtitlan's army, sixteen thousand strong with its combined Tlatelolco component, departed, proceeding for the Toluca basin where the Matlazinca dwelled.

Unlike Tizoc, Ahuitzotl refused to be carried in a litter. Inseparable from his army, even as Revered Speaker, he firmly adhered to his belief in leading by example and willingly endured the same hardships borne by each warrior. He walked amid his entourage of ministers, head priests, and chief staff members comprising the command section and located between the army's two major divisions. With him were Tlohtzin, now Supreme Commander, and his aide Motecuhzoma. Cihuacoatl remained in Tenochtitlan to perform his duties as Vice-Ruler.

On the second day, the Army of Tenochtitlan entered the valley of the Matlazinca, using a more northern route which bypassed the previously destroyed city of Toluca, and in marching toward Xiquipilco entered a number of abandoned villages, many of which had been reduced to charred remains.

"It's the work of Chimalpopoca," Ahuitzotl commented as he surveyed one such wreckage. "He obeys my instructions faithfully."

"You ordered this?" Tlohtzin asked. "This was not covered in our preliminary planning."

"The idea came as an afterthought. I told him to ravage the countryside and drive its inhabitants to Xiquipilco so they would be waiting there for us. I must have an audience if I am to leave a lasting impression of my passage through here."

"Evidently you're not worried about their strength."

"These villagers are no warriors. They'll be more of a hindrance than help to the city dwellers. My prediction is that they will get in their way, consume their stored food supply, and make things uncomfortable for the ruler by insisting that he protect them."

"You are formidable, Lord."

"You affirm the very purpose I seek when my name is mentioned. Under my reign, no city will dare rise against us."

By noon on the following day, with Xiquipilco's temple structures rising into view only a few leagues from Ahuitzotl's advancement, guides posted by Chimalpopoca directed him to the main campsite where their armies merged for consolidation. Like previous rulers, Ahuitzotl ordered the command posts of the allied forces placed adjacent to his own as this promised unified control and allowed for coordinated planning and actions to be formulated. He then expended the evening tending to personal needs, visiting among his widely scattered units, giving encouragement to his warriors through both his presence and speech and inspiring in them eagerness over tomorrow's events by the confidence he exuded. Not until he obtained satisfaction that his efforts were adequately rewarded, an achievement he measured by the martial spirit exhibited by his soldiers, did he retire that night.

The next morning, while the Mexica engaged in training exercises as they waited for the Acolhuas to arrive, Ahuitzotl called on his emissaries to send the customary surrender appeal to the lords of Xiquipilco.

"Give them the usual verbal pursuasion," he told his envoys, "but do not expound on it. If they refuse our terms, refrain from increasing your threats. How can I impress anyone if I am denied a good battle?"

"Then why send them at all?" Tlohtzin interjected.

"A good point. It's risky enough adhering to this formality-what if they should accept? I may dispense with it when we get to Chiapa. It counters my purpose in coming here."

Tlohtzin, who placed high value on the conventions established through generations of interaction among states, questioned this. Compliance to these accords amounted to more than merely an adherence to custom for him: it remained a matter of honor. "Is it wise," he asked, "to capriciously cast aside our long standing practices for temporary convenience?"

"I do not do this capriciously," Ahuitzotl barked, displeased over his commander's obvious aversion for the directive. "Nothing I do is without a design. You are here to advise me, Tlohtzin, and so you have done, but always remember, I make the final decision."

Ahuitzotl then motioned for his envoys to proceed, and they, not in a position to contest this mandate even though it belittled their roles in the process, departed for the city to inform its ruler of their ultimatum. In the meantime, Ahuitzotl stood restlessly by in anticipation of the response.

He did not have to wait for long. The emissaries were soon sighted coming forth from the city in their practiced haughty gait; Ahuitzotl endured some uneasy moments as he watched their approach. He worried the appeal may have been accepted, a contingency presenting a major setback for him. Tlohtzin observed the monarch's impatience with misgivings of his own: a new doctrine was being promulgated here, portending unfamiliar changes.

"Well?" Ahuitzotl inquired after the emissaries had arrived.

"We gave their lord the usual warning to surrender." answered their spokesman, "declaring he could keep his life and property but would have to acknowledge our ascendancy and pay the tributes we exacted from him. If he did not, we told him, we would enslave his people and burn his..."

"Yes, yes, I know the conditions. What did he say?"

"He said he did not fear us and was weary of our demands. We asked him if this was a refusal of our terms and he replied that it was. We then turned around and left his presence without saying another word."

"Excellent," Ahuitzotl beamed. "We shall have our battle."

But if Ahuitzotl rejoiced that morning, his euphoria faded as the day wore on, for it was well into the afternoon, later than he had presumed, before the standards of the Army of Acolhuacan were spotted nearing the camp.

"Another day is lost to us," he scowled as he watched the distant force. They'll be too exhausted for any use today. This will give the Matlazinca additional time to shore up their defenses. We'll have to alter the battle plan somewhat–I do not wish to be delayed by a strong resistance."

"What do you propose?" asked Tlohtzin.

"I'm thinking we should send part of our army to the other side of Xiquipilco during the night-to attack them from the rear after we've mounted our frontal assault. I want you to lead it."

"Gladly, but how will I know when to attack?"

"We'll spot trumpeters within hearing distance of each other; they will relay a specific signal, let's say three short blares, to differentiate it from the normal battle calls. When you hear it, begin your attack."

"Shall I proceed to ravage the city, or do I aim for the rear of their army?"

"Go for their army. After it is defeated, we can lay waste to the city at our leisure, if we choose to."

"It seems cowardly to strike them from behind."

"Yes, I'm sure I will encounter protests when I cover this in tonight's conference, but our object is a speedy triumph. I'll not be detained by the niceties of protocol."

"How large of a force do I take with me?"

"Take ten squadrons-two thousand warriors should suffice. It is the shock of being struck from behind, not your numbers, which will defeat them. You'll need to send out scouts this afternoon to mark your trail for tonight. As this is a departure from our normal tactics, I won't inform the commanders of it until the last possible moment. Swear your men to silence. Haste must take precedence over honor tomorrow."

With that, Ahuitzotl excused Tlohtzin to search out the members for his scouting party, which he quickly succeeded in accomplishing, and the patrol was well underway by the time the Acolhua army had arrived. Ahuitzotl cordially greeted Nezahualpilli, dispelling the earlier irritation over his ally's slowness, and while the Texcocan settled in at the command post, he finalized his battle plan with Tlohtzin. Only at his council meeting later that evening did he disclose his strategy to his colleagues even as Tlohtzin was already moving his squadrons to Xiquipilco's opposite edge. Just as he had predicted, objections abounded over it.

"A dishonorable way to fight!" exclaimed Chimalpopoca. "I see no virtue in attacking a worthy opponent from behind–it's disgraceful! Not the work Huitzilopochtli ordained for us."

"What do you think he meant for us to do?" asked Ahuitzotl.

"A battle is not supposed to be a mere brawl. It is meant to test our courage and strength. Each warrior must engage an enemy warrior so that when he has taken him captive, he can rejoice at having accomplished this through his own efforts and because the gods favored him this day. That is how the gods determine our worthiness and decide who will join them in paradise. It's what we teach our young men in the schools."

"Battles are faught to be won, Chimalpopoca," Ahuitzotl countered. "Huitzilopochtli meant for us to defeat our enemies in order to impose our will upon them. If this little maneuver insures us a victory, it will meet with his approval."

"It is contemptible! There is no honor in defeating the Matlazinca through treachery."

"We seek to defeat them-how it is done is inconsequential."

"How can it be of no import?-the outcome of a battle is a matter they preside over. You make it a prerogative dependent on what methods we apply. That is heresy. What do you say to this, Nezhaulapilli?"

The Texcocan lent judicious consideration to the issue, keeping both Ahuitzotl and Chimalpopoca, who expected his response to favor their point of view, in a state of temporary suspension. When he at last spoke out, the council's attention was riveted on him.

"I do not see this as an extreme deviation from our prescribed doctrines on warfare," Nezahualpilli said. "It is but an application on a larger scale what we do consistently on a smaller one. Our tenets specify ambush techniques as an acceptable method of fighting, especially when our outnumbered units must face a greater enemy force. I regard this deployment as a kind of ambush we are setting up, nothing more."

"There's no need for me to persist in my rejection of it," Chimalpopoca moped, frustrated that his perspective, which he deemed solidly based, was so thoroughly dismantled. "It's quite evident you are set upon its application regardless of what I say. I am wasting my time."

"Your views are of interest to me, Chimalpopoca," Ahuitzotl informed the Tepanecan in an attempt to soothe over his revealed dejection. "If I felt as you say, I would not trouble myself to open this kind of discussion. I had hoped, however, we could pursuade you of the plan's practicality and had your agreement on it."

"You have, Lord," Chimalpopoca thereupon declared, breaking into a smile. "As usual, our Texcocan friend presents a strong case. I confess I am not free of stubbornness, a trait common among older dogs such as I."

Contented that harmony had been restored, Ahuitzotl commenced to explain the details under which his plan would be implemented and, by the time the meeting came to a close, not a man among them needed convincing that tomorrow's engagement would result in certain conquest.

VI

Few spectacles could match the brilliance and color of warclad Mexica armies assembled in their various formations in readiness for attack and this morning's preparation for battle, amid a blaring of trumpets and rolling of drums, offered that imposing display at its most exemplary best. As in Toluca, Ahuitzotl arranged his forces along a line covering a broad front with several ranks in depth, positioning the Tepaneca army on his right and the Acolhuas on the left while he located himself immediately behind Tenochtitlan's first row of warriors near the center. He was accompanied by Motecuhzoma and kept his priests and other court officials with the reserve elements some distance further to the rear. Cimalpopoca and Nezahualpilli stationed themselves with their respective armies.

Facing them, equally magnificently arrayed, stood thousands of Matlazinca warriors massed in a battle configuration similar to the Mexica's, waiting only for priests to complete their rites and deliver their oblations. Methodically, designated votaries set small fires and threw powders into these causing thick smoke to rise, a signal that the onslaught was imminent. Each exhorted his god to grant a successful day for the combatants, then watched the flames die out, when they spread the coals along the whole of the army's line to symbolize its impending scattering of the enemy.

With the battle's onset but a short time away, Ahuitzotl glanced over both flanks of his force, engulfed by the excitement that must have possessed every soldier in the ranks at that moment. "You will remain by my side throughout," he told Motecuhzoma. "and when I direct it, you'll run to our stationed messenger and order him to relay our signal to Tlohtzin."

"This ought to be entertaining," grinned Motecuhzoma. "I would like to see their faces when Tlohtzin falls upon them."

"Entertaining? You are misled by your exuberance-this may still be a hard faught contest."

"Not if Tlohtzin makes a timely appearance."

"Do not expect him too soon," Ahuitzotl said very gravely. "He'll be called into action only at the height of battle when all the enemy force is committed to it. He doesn't have enough men to be met by any reserves."

His smile vanished; Motecuhzoma still had much to learn.

At that moment, Matlazinca trumpets echoed forth from across the field, immediately followed by those of the Mexica, and warriors bellowed out their battle cries, their jubilation resounding over the ranks. Orders ensued, sending both armies into an advance and shortly thereafter, in a tempestuous collision, they consummated their bloody encounter, becoming entangled in fearsome combat.

As always, the object was to take an opponent captive and the battle, once contact was initiated, transformed itself into individual confrontations between combatants to secure this end. They met to disable or disarm their adversaries so that the specialists with ropes trailing their ranks could take them prisoner. Death resulted to the extent that a warrior offered resistance and refused to be taken, but it remained a secondary aim. Propelled forward in confidence fueled over expecting a rear attack on their foe, the Mexica edged forward with fanatic determination, hacking out paths through the Matlazinca rows embracing them. Additional warriors joined those already embattled until, by sheer weight in numbers, the aggressors slowly but steadily overpowered the opposition and forced it to fall back.

Meanwhile, rapacious priests flocked about the lines and seized any enemy soldier who happened to find himself unarmed or injured and unable to fend them off. They were dragged to makeshift stone altars, their clothing was torn off, and their chests were expeditiously cut open as swift hand yanked out pulsating hearts, lifting these into the air with bloodied arms amid frantic exhortations appealing to the gods for victory. As long as the Matlazinca lines held, the priests persisted in their search for offerings so that they might tip the balance in favor of the Mexica.

Ahuitzotl kept a sharp eye on the defending force as he called more warriors forward to pressure it into a gradual withdrawal. Responding to this drive, the Matlazinca commander, on seeing his lines faltering, directed his back-up elements out from their rear stations to assist the beleaguered front squadrons. This was the moment Ahuitzotl had waited for. "They've committed their reserves!" he shouted at Motecuhzoma. "Run back and have our message sent to Tlohtzin. He is to attack without delay!"

Immediately, Motecuhzoma scurried back and relayed these orders to a selected trumpeter who blasted forth three successive blares above the clatter of arms. No sooner had he finished when the signal was repeated some distance away. Over and over the call resounded until it traversed the area separating the divided army and reached the ears of Tlohtzin's warriors who, thirsting to hear it, were itching for a fight.

"There it is!" exclaimed Tlohtzin. "Let the enemy feel the claws of our jaguars! Let's go!"

Enthralled warriors roared out their approval and raced full speed from their hiding place toward the distant conflict. Screaming wildly in their moment of glory, they came bearing down on the startled opponents like a crushing tidal wave.

"We are lost!" shouted one of the Matlazinca captains when he saw them coming. "They have us surrounded!"

At once, the frightened defenders lost heart, and most of them strove for a means of escape while, in direct contrast, the attackers sensed their triumph within grasp and were inspired with renewed vigor. With the Matlazinca morally defeated and the Mexica rejuvenated, the outcome was inevitable.

Tlohtzin's men crashed into the reservists, slicing a gory passage into the less experienced force and breaking it apart as if it scarcely existed. Within minutes, they had their opposition scattered over the field and were striking the front line warriors at their rear while, at the same time, Ahuitzotl spurred his battalions onward squeezing the Matlazinca between them. Crushed in spirit, most of the defenders simply stopped fighting and permitted themselves to be taken captive; however, certain individual squadrons fought on in isolated pockets and had to be beaten into submission. Ahuitzotl left this task to his subordinate chieftains while he sought out the enemy ruler for the surrender. He found him amidst a circle of soldiers in one of those units still resisting.

"Stop the fighting!" Ahuitzotl ordered. "I wish to speak to their leader."

Instantly the Mexica stepped back, exposing the Matlazinca warriors huddled among themselves in a last-stand posture. Ahuitzotl boldly confronted them. "Your army is defeated and scattered," he shouted into the group, "and your city is in our hands. It is pointless to continue your fight. Yield to us now, or we will slay you all where you stand."

"What does it matter?" answered the Matlazinca ruler. "We are all dead. Fight us!-so we can die nobly-as men."

"Not so. Most of you will live and even be allowed to remain in your city. Your deaths are unimportant to me and I'll not grant you a warrior's end. I will simply surround you with archers and bring you down under a hail of arrows."

"A coward's way of fighting–dishonorable!-unworthy of warriors! I should have expected it from one who so treacherously attacked us from behind."

"Be cautious, Matlazincan. I do not offer you clemency in exchange for insults. Surrender now and Xiquipilco will be spared."

"How can I believe you? We know what you did to Toluca."

"I am Lord Ahuitzotl, Revered Speaker, and I pledge my word of honor."

Such a promise, delivered by no less a personage than the Revered Speaker himself, undeniably carried weight; it did not take long for the Matlazincan to reach a decision. "Upon your word then," he assented. "We surrender to you."

At their lord's command, the reluctant defenders threw down their arms and complied with the directives of their conquerors who proceeded to line them up and bind their hands behind them, tying the prisoners to each other with strong cords. With their leader now taken, all opposition ended.

In the meantime, Ahuitzotl summoned his chief commanders together and issued orders of his own for their units. "Get word to the lowest squadron levels," he announced. "There will be no abuse of the people or looting, and no fires set. Round up the captives for transfer to Tenochtitlan under the usual escorts and then assemble your forces at the campsite."

They responded, but not without grumbling over how their warriors would react to what was an undoubtedly unpopular directive. Messengers carried it to the allied armies which, reluctantly and with copious vocal agitation, forsook their intended activity and regrouped at the main camp, each bringing its share of taken prisoners to be herded into a containment area and placed under guard. Chimalpopoca was outspoken in his displeasure over the Revered Speaker's order whereas Nezahualpilli said little but revealed his dissatisfaction in the lines of his face.

"Might I inquire," the Texcocan asked Ahuitzotl, "why you spared the city? I find this contrary to your methods."

"You know I seek to accomplish many things on this campaign. How much time would be lost if we permitted our units to engage in their after-battle activities?"

"A day perhaps-not excessively long."

"And another day to regroup. Maybe even a third day to resolve disputes arising over the spoils. You could say Xiquipilco is spared out of my haste to advance on our next target."

"I knew it was not out of benevolence."

"I shall overlook that remark-for the present; we have much to do."

"Now that you have us here, Lord," growled Chimalpopoca, still fuming in his discontent, "what do you want from us?"

"Prepare your armies to move out."

"What! You mean today?"

"That is precisely what I mean."

"Lord, I protest!" Chimalpopoca reacted angrily. "We've just faught a hard battle–the men are exhausted. We must see to our wounded and consolidate our gains."

"Our reserves will keep a squadron here to administer the wounded and clear the field. I shall appoint a nominal ruler-one of their local officials from the captives-over the city with a squadron of our warriors to maintain control until we determine its disposition and tributes. As for the men, they can rest until noon before breaking camp."

The order was clearly objectionable and many of the subordinates were displaying an aversion in executing it. "What of the prisoners?" one of the chieftains decried, "Who will see to them?"

"They'll be taken back to Anahuac by part of our force. Two squadrons should suffice for this-we won't take all of them."

"One squadron stays here, two accompany the captives," said Chimalpopoca, "You deplete the strength of our armies, and yet you will have us take on more cities. You ask the impossible."

By now, Ahuitzotl had reached the limit of his tolerance over their reluctance to comply with his orders and he sternly cautioned them. "I weary of these attempts to further delay my plans; if it becomes necessary for me to invoke penalties for failure to obey me, I shall do so. I've heard enough of your endless bickering and will hear no more of it. I promised victories on this campaign and will bring these to you, but if this is insufficient for you, say so now; otherwise do as you are told."

None dared confront the angry monarch, and even Chimalpopoca, the most defiant, knew when to desist from fomenting increased agitation. Once resolved to advocacy of their instructions, the camp quickly transformed into a hive of activity as the armies prepared for their march. Advance parties were sent out; priests formed into their sections and closely followed them; the warriors disassembled the shelters and packed their gear and rations. This time the Army of Tenochtitlan would depart first; Ahuitzotl deemed the measure useful as a demonstration to his allied lords that he asked no more of them than he was willing to take on himself.

While this hubbub was in progress, Ahuitzotl met with the captives in their confinement area and selected a noble, along with some officials, who would temporarily rule in Xiquipilco until the kingship was reinstated under Mexica guidelines. As it turned out, the man appointed was the son of the present reigning king, a move adjudged prudent by Ahuitzotl in that it promised future cooperation, provided he retained a hope of eventual release for a good portion of the prisoners, including his father. The tributes imposed on the city could be worked out later. With the issue settled, Ahuitzotl returned to his command post where his shelter had already been stowed for its journey.

"Are we set to move out?" he asked Tlohtzin.

"As you ordered, Lord."

"Then let us proceed-to Chiapa."

Ahuitzotl left word for the combined Acolhuacan and Tepaneca armies to follow him later that afternoon and, as Chimalpopoca and Nezahualpilli looked on in awed wonder, the Army of Tenochtitlan silently departed for its next targeted destination.

VII

Chiapa was a day's journey north of Xiquipilco and possessed only half of the latter's population, but it stood amid hilly surroundings and could be more easily defended. Only one side permitted an attack by massed warriors, the city's southern approach, with the terrain restricting such movements from the other directions, and to Ahuitzotl this presented a troublesome feature as it meant a smaller force had the capability of mounting a stronger resistance. And so, while his army marched on the city, he reviewed his reports and studied the possibilities on how he might conquer it, and he listened attentively to the information delivered by the pochteca.

"The thing to note is that there's internal dissension among the people," Ahuitzotl told Tlohtzin. "We must make use of the situation. We may be able to turn the dissidents against their overlords, perhaps by bribing them into assisting us."

"What will we offer them?"

"I'm not sure how far we should go. We can be generous and offer them power—the throne or other lofty assignments-or we can merely grant them their lives in exchange for their help."

"Go with the latter. If you promise them titles and positions, you will have to leave them a city to rule over—preferably intact. Can we deny our warriors plunder for a second time?"

"I have no qualms over how we leave Chiapa for them-nor any compulsion to inform them on it. Consider it an appropriate reward for their disloyalty."

At his camp that night halfway en route, Ahuitzotl came into additional reports from his scouts highlighting the nature of the existing discordance in Chiapa. Local village chieftains appeared to still demonstrate an allegiance to the Mexica and had apparently disapproved of Chiapa's lords defying their authority and forming an alliance with Xiquipilco on that basis. moreover, there were indications that many of the people viewed the conditions imposed on them by the Chiapans as even more oppressive than the tributes demanded by the Mexica, a situation very much favorable to Ahuitzotl's aims for another easy triumph.

"The dissension is widespread," Ahuitzotl told his commanders during his evening conference around the fire, "particularly among the villagers. Some could provide us with assistance."

"Can they be trusted?" questioned a captain. "Why would they turn on their own people?"

"Who knows? Out of fear what we might do to them, or maybe it's true their own ruler is a tyrant who exacts extreme hardships on them. The point is we can make use of them, if we are tactful, to supplement our own shortages."

"I thought we outnumbered them."

"We do, but Chiapa is well defended. They've made masterly use of their natural barriers, transforming it into a stronghold, and will fight from behind walls. Taking it will pose a major obstacle. It's in our interest to win the dissidents over and, if possible, secure them as allies."   " Y o u mean treat the Matlazinca as our equals?" another of the chieftains sneered.

"Repulsive as the notion may be to you, cast aside your derision, at least temporarily, and advance our effort. Simply treat them with courtesy and respect, and promise them what we can to get their support. They must look at us as a benevolent conqueror—their deliverers if you will. Make sure your warriors understand this."

With that, Ahuitzotl terminated his meeting, aware of the resentment his policies aroused among the commanders but steadfast in his determination to execute the unorthodox measures he advocated. Only Tlohtzin and Motecuhzoma remained with him, the priests and ministers having retired in exhaustion after this longest of days. At first, they sat in silence, but their thoughts bore heavily on them and beckoned to be stated, and finally Tlohtzin was compelled to give release to his restraint.

"Your methods become increasingly alien to our accepted standards of warfare," he advised. "The attitude of our warriors are not as flexible as these changes you demand from them."

"I see that," affirmed Ahuitzotl. "Some of their presumptions will have to be met. We'll give them free reign of Chiapa after we take it."

"What of the battle itself? You know it is demeaning allowing local warriors to fight for them."

"They must learn there are other ways in which to wage war."

"This contravenes a primary tenet, including your constant reinforcement of it, that they are asked to do the divine work of Huitzilopochtli. You deny this to them when you negate their deeds before his eyes. We are taught that the gods are who determine a battle's outcome, yet through your manipulations you undermine this precept and make yourself the arbiter of it."

Understanding Tlohtzin's point, Ahuitzotl knew he could not persist in his unconventional measures for long; eventually the contradictions would manifest themselves in disaffection, if not outright rebellion. "What you say is true," he said, "Somehow they must be made to realize that victory is what Huitzilopochtli wishes the most-all their individual courage and feats of daring are of little account if they have not won the battle."

"You attack our entire belief system with that kind of a statement. All our lives we've been told that valor in battle is everything, and that there is no greater honor than to fall in service of gods who have chosen which among us they wanted. You challenge all this with your emphasis on trickery-contriving the situation. It is dangerous."

"We must reconcile these conceptions. Our successes, not only in this campaign, but future ones, will depend on it."

Tlohtzin was up against a wall; he could no more budge the monarch from his views than he could move a mountain, and seeing a futility in protracting his efforts, he feigned tiredness as a means to escape it. Ahuitzotl, aware of his commander's recalcitrance in accepting the deviations he offered, felt obligated to caution him on his obtuseness.

"You are my right arm, Tlohtzin," he said, "and I depend on you above the others to enforce my decisions. I place significant reliance on your ability to do so. I want you to know this."

"Have I ever disappointed you?"

"No. I'm of the opinion we make a good team."

"You should not have to remind me of it, Lord. I do as you direct me, and if I fail in this, I'll be the first to accept responsibility for it."

Feeling some smugness over having clarified his position, Tlohtzin left for his bedding while Ahuitzotl watched him fade into the darkness beyond the fire's glow. When he turned his head back, he was conscious of Motecuhzoma's eyes fixed on him, and he knew what was on the aide's mind.

"Tlohtzin is a good commander," Ahuitzotl said. "I trust him implicitly in the conduct of our operations, but he has a sharp tongue which requires sheathing on occasions."

"He wasn't wrong in interpreting your statement as a warning to be more obedient, was he?"

"No," said Ahuitzotl, impressed by Motecuhzoma's acuity, "his interpretation was correct."

Ahuitzotl gazed at length into the fire, leading Motecuhzoma to believe he detected turmoil in him. When he finally ceased his contemplative staring, he appeared quite fatigued and in no mood to continue the exchange. Enervated of strength, he arose without uttering another word and left for his shelter, leaving his aide to puzzle over what he might have been thinking.

Shortly after dawn, the Mexica resumed their march. Driven relentlessly by the example of their warlord, they moved at a rapid pace with few periods of resting and many a warrior must have been incensed over the tireless energy of Ahuitzotl who seemed never to slow his gait in spite of all the ground covered. Some of the youthful soldiers, not to be outdone by someone older, quietly bore their encumbrance, unwilling to admit that even they were becoming exhausted, but others, not bound by such restraints, muttered out their irritation loudly enough to be heard by their squadron leaders. Yet onward they marched until, when the sun arrived at its apex, they at last spotted the numerous temples soaring upwards against a hazy background of surrounding mountains. It came as a welcome sight.

As they progressed on to the city, they were met by the advance party halted at a nearby village, and when Ahuitzotl and Tlohtzin came to its square, the commander of this unit rushed up to them in obvious excitement. A number of local lords were with him.

"Lord!" began the captain, "These are leaders of a group of defectors. They say they will help us."

Ahuitzotl surveyed them with unusual intensity, intrigued over what sort of situation would drive men to turn on their own people.

"Why will you do this for us?" he asked their spokesman.

"To put to an end to a corrupt regime, Great Lord. Chiapa's ruling circles have long ceased to concern themselves with the needs and interests of the people. They regard these as unwarranted impositions on them while holding their subjects in contempt and abusing the powers they wield over them. They care only about enhancing their wealth and privileges, and have increasingly alienated themselves from their obligations, forcing us on a path against our wishes. We were once members of the city's council who opposed their refusal to render tributes to you. We have been punished for this act of prudence by having our property taken from us and our lives threatened."

"It seems your act of prudence is seen as traitorous."

"The council is entitled to voice its objections without being subjected to harassment for it. Our long-standing traditions permit such opposition."

"Why did you oppose them?"

"We knew their decisions would lead to war-one which we could not hope to win."

"Ah, you were seen as cowards then."

"Is it cowardice to have stood against them in the council? We knew the cause they were advocating, and yet chose to denounce them for it."

Ahuitzotl thought this answer reasonable, comprehending that courage can manifest itself in diverse ways, but a betrayal of one's people, however sound the justifications, was a notion he viewed with absolute repugnance and he naturally mistrusted anyone capable of such conduct. "What can you do for us?" he said, hiding his disdain.

"We can augment your force with warriors of our own who are loyal to you."

"Chiapa is strongly fortified. You may lose many of your followers in an assault on it."

"We know of a way to strike the city through the mountains. There is a path."

This caught Ahuitzotl's attention, and his mind immediately grasped the possibilities suddenly presented. "Now that is useful to me," he said. "What will you want in return for this?"

"Guarantees for our safety. A promise of protection from you, and a restoration of our properties and titles once the city is reclaimed. We will obediently serve you if allowed to rule after the present regime is ousted."

Ahuitzotl pondered over that. He regarded their conduct contemptible and their demands arrogant, but he favored the prospect of another speedy victory, and knowledge of that pathway all but assured him of this. Let them have their titles and rule over the city, he thought-after my warriors have sacked it.

"We will be ready to attack at dawn," he told their spokesman. "Assemble your men and have them meet us here, and bring the guide who will show us the trail."

Having struck their accord, the defectors set about tending to their own affairs and, in the meantime, Ahuitzotl established his base camp only a short distance from the village but still a two-hour's march from Chiapa. He chose this site after learning about the pathway so that his enemies could not detect which units of his army were missing from the battlefield while moving through the mountains: his own patrols would prevent them from coming close enough to ascertain this information. Not until the actual attack were they to know his true strength.

Just prior to dusk, the merged Acolhuacan and Tapeneca armies arrived and, after settling into their designated sites, Ahuitzotl held his usual evening conference with his commanders. There he disclosed the day's events to them and his intent to use the local forces in the frontal assault while his own army would strike from behind. This time a general consensus prevailed-Chiapa's daunting fortified position made its application prudent-and all agreed that the combined allied armies would remain with the local contingent, a step considered necessary not only to bolster their numbers but also to make certain the dissidents did not renege on their word or falter in their resolve. With the critical decisions concluded and details worked out, the meeting was ended, permitting an earlier than expected retirement for its participants, a gesture highly savored after the grueling pace of their march.

Familiar commotion surrounded the impending commencement of battle the next morning as men were busy sharpening their weapons, adjusting each other's equipment, preening themselves so that the gods might take due note of them, and trying to ease the underlying tension with raw humor and boasts about what they would do. The sun had broken over the horizon for some time now before guards sounded the approach of the local contingent. Ahuitzotl thought them late but also fortuitous that they came at all: the Matlazinca were not known for their dependability.

"You have the guide with you?" he asked their leader.

"I shall take you there myself," came his reply.

"You bring more men than I expected."

"Nearly three thousand-a measure of the tyranny imposed on us."

"So it is. Call forth your commanders so we may explain our battle plan to them. Nezahualpilli, Lord of Texcoco, will command the forces attacking from here-yours will be among these. I will accompany you."

Through a succession of orders, the battle configuration was completed, commanders were briefed, and the stage for today's activity was prepared, and by mid-morning, the armies began their advance on Chiapa. They were still a considerable distance from the city and its defenders, even though anticipating their attack, could not have reckoned that a divided force neared them. Long before coming into view, Tenochtitlan's army had branched off and was presently snaking through a narrow defile between rugged crags, a passage Ahuitzotl felt oppressive as he could neither see much area ahead of him nor maintain good contact with his units extending far behind him while the repeated turns of the trail seemed endless.

Nezahualpilli willfully created a preponderant spectacle of his approach, marking his presence with voluminous beating of drums and multiple exchanges of trumpet calls, all designed to rivet his enemy's attention on the impending threat. Upon reaching Chiapa, he quickly formed his army into its attacking configuration, grouping it in a linear pattern covering the southern access to the city in full. The defenders, conforming to their practices strategies of engaging in warfare, had earlier sallied forth from behind their barriers and were waiting for their opponents to initiate the assault. Both sides stood in readiness, restrained now only by the priests finalizing their rituals, an observance intermittently broken by the warriors who cheered and hurled abusive declarations and gestures upon their adversaries as if venting release to pent-up energies through this verbal exertion.

"We have done our part," the head priest then told Nezahualpilli. "It's in your hands now."

"Very well," Nezahualpilli replied, "Sound your trumpet!"

The ensuing distant blares could be faintly heard by Ahuitzotl and his squadrons within the canyon walls and they knew that the battle was underway. Instinctively they hastened their pace in nervous agitation that they might miss out on most of it.

"How much further?" Ahuitzotl asked the guide, impatient at not being able to see beyond the terrain flanking him.

"About a fourth of our distance remains," the guide answered. This was more than Ahuitzotl had wished.

Meanwhile, before the city, leading squadrons of Mexica warriors made contact with their Chiapan opposition and quickly sent it scurrying into retreat behind the safety of the fortifications. In response, Nezahualpilli issued orders directing his archers into several lines. He scanned the walls with his keen eyes and noted a weak point between two buildings where a wooden barricade had been erected at a lower level than its adjacent walls and, while undoubtedly heavily manned, could be breached under a well-coordinated assault.

"Have our archers concentrate on that spot," he pointed out to his commanders. "Fire on it in rapid succession so the defenders are forced to keep low. We will storm it under the protection of our arrows."

While squadrons were being deployed to implement this action, Ahuitzotl and his army emerged from the ravine, entering into a short clearing at the city's unprotected rear. Instantly, trumpets signaled his units into their attack and rapacious warriors, in eagerness for action and spoils, charged along the main streets, the bulk of them racing for the center temple precinct, Chiapa's stronghold, and cutting down anyone unfortunate to stand in their way. Screams from panic-stricken inhabitants alerted the soldiers on the walls of the danger behind them. Too late, the Chiapans tried to counter the pressure from their rear: it was like trying to stem the flow of floodwaters.

Frightened townspeople, fleeing from the on-rush of their fervid assailants, impeded the advancing Chiapan warriors who sought to mount a resistance, and by the time they reached the central plaza, a Mexica squadron had already stormed the main temple, killing the priests on the stairway and setting fire to its upper shrine. Other soldiers were torching the abodes of the nobles, but what shocked the Chiapans most was that they found themselves facing as large an army within their city as met them outside the barricades. Surrounded by Ahuitzotl's warriors, they took the only prudent option left for them under the circumstances-they dropped their shields and weapons and capitulated.

Dark smoke rising skyward from inside Chiapa told Nezahualpilli that the defenders were finished. Surmising their plan had come to fruition, he deemed it unnecessary to direct an assault on the city and simply ordered his units to enter it in massed formation, correctly assessing that the Chiapans had lost the will to continue fighting. With parts of the city burning about them and its inhabitants rushing to make their exit through the front gates, and the shouts of enemy soldiers ahead of them as well as behind them, confusion and dismay prevailed among the defenders. As there remained no hope of affecting the outcome, or even a standoff which might have led to acceptable concessions, their units surrendered one after another and all resistance disintegrated. Chiapa was taken.

The beaten army was herded into the central plaza, placed under guard, and retained there until its eventual disposition could be assessed. In the meantime, Mexica warriors were permitted their liberties and they rampaged through the streets and ransacked the residences, plundering items of value from them and frightening their occupants. Here and there a woman was raped and a recalcitrant old man assaulted, and a few of the houses were set on fire, but it had been an easy conquest and, as a consequence, none of the spontaneous and unchecked explosion of rage which marked the destruction of Toluca occurred. For the most part, the local populace escaped unmolested.

Ahuitzotl took approximately one-fourth of the Chiapan army captive, making certain that among these were included the lords, ranking officers, and officials who were pointed out by others as the principals responsible for having advocated a policy of hostility towards Tenochtitlan. The leaders of the dissidents who had assisted him he appointed to official positions to exercise control over its citizens. He had no particular sympathy for their stunned disappointment over his having left much of Chiapa a smoldering ruin.

"They deserved this," he told Nezahualpilli. "It's a fitting reward for their disloyalty."

"But an ingracious one. They will remember you for it."

"They will also remember never to rise against me. I shall hear no more of Chiapa."

Like a whirlwind that descends swiftly upon a place, sweeping everything before it in a torrent of violence, and then disappears as suddenly as it came, so it seemed to the Chiapans that the Mexica had struck them. The following morning, when they looked about the charred remains of their homes and public facilities, and then saw the abandoned campground of the host who had wreaked this havoc upon them and now was gone, they greatly lamented over how it could have been possible for a world they had always known to be so abruptly altered. With a quarter of their warriors in captivity, a third of their city in ruin, many of their priests slain, and the temple of their patron god gutted by fire, the defectors who had helped bring about this disaster and were now to restore the wreckage left them unquestionably felt themselves betrayed and in bitterness cursed the name of Ahuitzotl.

VIII

Xilotepec was next to fall. At the northern extremity of the Matlazinca domain, Xilotepec was targeted by Ahuitzotl for shock effect on neighboring cities and states rather than out of any distinct animosity. The city had not failed in submitting its allocated tributes, nor had it joined the alliance of Xiquipilco and Chiapa in opposing the Mexica, but Ahuitzotl had achieved two major triumphs and adding a third important city to the list was sure to create an indelible impression. Also he believed it appropriate to instill a total confidence on the part of his soldiers in his ability towards leading them to successes: one more certain victory was thought useful in accomplishing this end. Some were not as convinced of the requirement as others.

"Why Xilotepec?" Nezahualpilli demanded to know. "Is it punishment we wish to inflict on it?"

"You may consider it as such," Ahuitzotl scoffed.

"What offense have they committed against us?"

"Does that matter to you?"

"It would ease my reservations about attacking them and make it, shall I say, more palatable to me."

"In that case, I'll give you a reason. They have rendered, morally and materially, support to Chiapa and Xiquipilco in their rebellion against us. They encouraged them and provided them with arms and supplies. Our reports indicated this."

It amounted to the flimsiest of excuses and was nothing more than a pretext, and if Nezahualpilli could understand its purpose, he nonetheless found it personally disreputable. "Indeed?" he replied sarcastically, "I must have failed to hear of it."

"Do not make it seem so detestable. We'll merely chastise them; I have no desire to destroy Xilotepec. We shall all benefit from this."

"Some things I hold in honor, Lord. That means more to me than whatever gains I might obtain from them."

"That's your mistake, Nezahualpilli. There can be no affairs of honor between us and the Matlazinca."

"To you perhaps-I disagree."

"I don't. But I expect you to render your assistance as our alliance demands. This attack on Xilotepec will once and for all end the Matlazinca's perpetual defiance, which will profit you and your Acolhuas as much as the rest of us. I would not appreciate you sharing this favorable outcome after your aversion to bringing it about."

"You've made your point," exclaimed Nezahualpilli, somewhat vexed over being lectured. "I won't oppose this attack; no doubt the purpose for it has been well calculated."

"There's a design to everything I do," Ahuitzotl advised his colleague. "Try to remember that."

A two-day's march separated Xilotepec from Chiapa and the Mexica armies advanced on it divided by shortened intervals so that the entire force arrived there on the same afternoon. Brazenly adding insult to their belligerence, they set up their base camp within sight of the city and made it clear to its startled populace that they meant to do battle with them. When, the following morning, they prepared to commence with fighting, they were confronted by a haggardly-looking army of defenders which had been hastily assembled to meet its host The Xilotepecans were greatly outnumbered and this, along with their bewilderment that the Mexica had come upon them at all, aroused feelings of extreme uneasiness among them as they waited for the enemy's assault, their disposition exhibited by a general lack of spirit and quietness.

By contrast, the Mexica were bursting with enthusiasm which they readily demonstrated by their jubilation and hearty whooping. The roar emitted from their ranks was deafening–even amazing Ahuitzotl by this display-and when the priests scattered the smoldering embers of fires started earlier, such was their thunderous applause that it drowned out all voices. Nezahualpilli and Chimalpopoca glanced at each other in wonderment. Never in their memory had their armies displayed such an outburst of exhiliration.

"Do you hear them?" Ahuitzotl shouted to his allied rulers, his face gleaming. "Have you ever witnessed anything like it?"

"I can't believe it!" Nezahualpilli yelled back. "What brought this on?"

"Who cares? With such exuberance, how can we possibly lose? Let's make use of it while it lasts. Priest! Sound the attack!"

Distinctly audible over the clamor, a deep blare rang across the field provoking an even louder cry of approval out of the warriors that thundered forth in ear-splitting resonance. Stepping ahead at a normal pace initially, they gradually picked up their momentum until they burst into full speed and raced unchecked toward the frozen Xilotepecan lines.

Fear gripped the defenders when they saw the impatient fury of their aggressors rushing upon them like a giant wave—nothing could have stood in its way. They collided headlong into the leading wall of Xilotepecan warriors and literally crashed through it like a battering ram penetrating a barricade and shattering it in place. Wherever the defenders stood their ground, they were smashed by the shields of rampaging Mexica, speared and smitten by the deadly maquauhuitl, and fell under the ferocious contact to be trambled underfoot by successive wave of attackers. Panic seized them when they saw their lines crumbling without being able to sustain any significant opposition and many lost heart, cast aside their armaments, and ran from the field.

In the briefest of moments, the battle turned into a rout. Incapable of mounting a stand against such a violent onslaught, and abetted by the example set for them by their fear-ridden comrades, even the most steadfast of the Xilotepecan ranks bolted to escape capture. With no resistance remaining to challenge them, the Mexica poured into the defenseless city ravenous for its spoils and proceeded to plunder the palaces and temples, even private abodes, tearing precious stones from the idols and inhabitants and stealing whatever was not tightly secured.

"So much for your treating them with moderation," Nezahualpilli wryly commented.

"It's incredible!" exclaimed Ahuitzotl, still astonished. "How do we stop it?"

"With difficulty. My recommendation is to let it run its course until it has expended itself of energy."

Ahuitzotl, annoyed over having things out of control, even if it led to a dramatic defeat of his enemies, said nothing, but his vexation was visible to his companions. While he passed through Xilotepec's main street surveying the damage, several of its citizens rushed up to him, some dropping to their knees, and begged for clemency.

"We beseech you, Great Lord!" their leader pleaded. "Spare us your ravages! Save our city!"

"Why should I trouble myself?" Ahuitzotl replied.

"We sought no war with you and are unjustly punished. Xilotepec is clearly yours as you have scattered our army; we have no protection available save what you, in your mercy, can give us. We beg of you-have regard for us."

His was a plea borne out of desperation, and Ahuitzotl was significantly touched by it. He already viewed the situation out of hand and now, with its victims desparately entreating for his benevolence, felt a personal culpability over the chaos having been unleashed. "Motecuhzoma!" he shouted to his aide. "Send word to all commanders that I want this looting, destruction, and abuse of the people halted immediately! Let me know who refuses to comply!"

The order was hastily disseminated to the various sections of Xilotepec where the pillaging was in progress and again, as in Toluca, the chieftains saw their abilities taxed to the utmost in enforcing a directive repugnant to their men. After considerable exertion, discipline was eventually restored. Some chieftains had to drag their soldiers from houses laden with booty, and many of them came dangerously close to sealing their fate by resisting the efforts to halt their plundering. In the end they obeyed; failure to do so meant a certain and dishonorable death by judgment of the tribunal presiding over their conduct.

Less captives were taken than might have been expected from such an overwhelming triumph. In their eagerness for the bounty of an undefended city, the Mexica did not bother with a strong pursuit of its defeated army whose soldiery dashed into the distant hills; only those warriors brave enough to make a stand fell into their hands. In an odd sort of way, Ahuitzotl found it amusing that his easiest victory should yield the least number of prisoners.

"Not much of a gain," he commented as he looked the captives over. "It demonstrates the drawbacks when there is a breakdown of discipline and order. We should have taken all of them."

"True," agreed Nezahualpilli, "but you do not appear that upset over it, considering your wishes were overtly countermanded."

"It poses an awkward dilemma. We can't single out any instigators. Not one commander claims to have authorized it. What am I to do? Punish my entire army?"

"Indirectly you have-by stopping their looting."

"My one consolation," ruminated Ahuitzotl. "Such chaos may have led to beneficial results, but never again do I want to be placed in this situation. I do not like things out of control."

As it was, Ahuitzotl did not even take most of the few captives, settling only for a minor handful of lords and chieftains who were most vocal in their resentment, and left these soldiers behind to the gratitude of some townspeople and the shame of others who believed the act disgraceful. And in truth, this was not done entirely out of generosity, for Ahuitzotl doubted whether the gods deemed warriors who fell so easily as worthy offerings. Ironically, the zeal exhibited by the Mexica had spared their victims from the flint.

With Xilotepec's fall, Ahuitzotl was satisfied over his incursion into Matlazinca. Conforming to the usual pattern, he named a high ranking local official to rule nominally over the city on a temporary basis until the appropriate kingship could be restored. At times, this involved nothing more than a re-education of one of the resident nobles, or even the former monarch, at Tenochtitlan for a certain period of time after which he was allowed to return and resume his powers-with a clear conception of the obligations owed to his masters. And so, for the Xilotepecans, who stood about numbed but grateful that their lives and city had been spared, the Mexica whirlwind had come and gone.

IX

Tenochtitlan's army was accorded an exultant reception after an absence of two weeks. Many years had elapsed since a Revered Speaker scored a series of glorious victories and everyone was favorably impressed. On three separate occasions runners had entered the capital with their hair braided and waving their shield and maquauhuitl to announce three important conquests, and these were followed by the lines of captives from Xiquipilco and Chiapa brought in under their escort squadrons. Now the main body itself was arriving and most of its elements were intact; this time there were no excessive casualties to dampen the crowd's enthusiasm, and they appropriately greeted their returning warriors with abundant incense burning, shell trumpeting and roaring applause.

In the central square, the soldiers remained in their formations to hear speeches of welcome and appreciation, and when these were completed, they stacked their weapons and were dismissed, most of them into the arms of their waiting relatives and friends. Reserve components, which had stayed behind in the capital, saw to the more routine tasks yet to be performed, including housing the captives, collecting the belongings of the fallen and sending these to surviving relatives, and assisting the wounded in whatever way they were able to. Quartermaster units collected the weaponry for refurbishing and storage in the city's armories. The Acolhuas, who accompanied Tenochtitlan's army, had their billeting facilities prepared for the night.

Nezahualpilli went with Ahuitzotl and Motecuhzoma to the palace, and after having spent the last few day marching over dusty trails under a hot sun, the darkness and cool comfort of its interior rooms were joyously received even as their faces continued burning from the long exposure. Ahuitzotl directed one of his servants to bring sweetened chocolate drinks for his guests as they sank into soft cushions in their exhaustion.

"In all respects, a remarkable campaign," Nezahualpilli declared. "Far more successful than I dared hope, and I credit you for that, Lord Ahuitzotl. What a way to start a reign."

"It served its purpose," Ahuitzotl said. "The Matlazinca will trouble us no more."

"You're being too modest. It was your tactics–the speed in which we moved-which led to our spectacular wins. They had no time to unite against us, in spite of their alliance."

"Many opposed my methods. Chimalpopoca for one."

"Chimalpopoca clings to the old ways-which to him have been time tested and worked. But even he was delighted over our successes, although he will probably never admit to this."

"I've come to expect his opposition, but to his credit, he always does what I ask of him. Yet I would prefer if he did things more quietly."

"It's not his nature to be accommodating," chuckled Nezahualpilli. "He has his own style."

They laughed heartily, but soon Ahuitzotl ached from tiredness and was disinclined to continue the conversation, wishing only to bathe and wash the grime from his body. He arose to excuse himself, and by this gesture released his grateful guests to likewise pursue their own pleasures. He entered his private chamber where he instructed his menials to prepare the bath.

"Bring me the Lady Pelaxilla," he directed one of the women, "and leave us. I wish to be alone with her."

While the woman went to fetch her, other attendants saw to his request, filling the cistern with water and placing soap, towels, wash cloths, and various cosmetic effects on the adjacent bench. A moment later, Pelaxilla entered, her eyes gleaming and a bright smile illuminating her face, and as soon as the servants had all gone, she and Ahuitzotl locked themselves in a passionate embrace with him lavishing kisses on her while his groping hands ran up and down the fabric of her dress.

"You're covered with dirt," she teasingly protested when at last he gave her an opportunity. "It has rubbed off on me."

"That's why you are here. I'm about to take a bath-you will join me."

Her smile told Ahuitzotl that the notion was wholly agreeable and he, already undressed, walked down the cistern's indented steps as Pelaxilla went to the bench. There she unfastened the clips extending along one side of her skirt and let it drop to the floor boldly exposing her naked charms underneath. What a magnificent nakedness it was, Ahuitzotl thought as he watched her stoop down to pick up the skirt and set it on the bench, the narrowed cleavage of her bottom folding deliciously between her rounded flesh. She then straightened up with her backside still facing him and took hold of the edge of her cotton blouse and in one swift stroke pulled it over her head. Completely nude now, Ahuitzotl scanned over the back of her seductive body enthralled by what he saw. After neatly arranging her blouse on top of her skirt, she turned around to give him a full view of her frontal features. His dazzled look made it very evident to her that he obviously found her appealing and she hesitated before advancing to give him full satisfaction of the sight.

She had a wonderfully proportioned frame and her skin was drawn tightly over it so hardly a wrinkle revealed itself in it. Her breasts were firm and voluminous, with the small brownish nipples at their tips enticing in their projection. Her waist was narrow and below it her hips widened harmoniously to beautifully shaped legs; between her thighs was that exquisite mound so invitingly alluring. She was noticeably shorter than Tlalalca, but more voluptuously composed.

After allowing him to glance her over thoroughly, Pelaxilla then walked leisurely to the cistern and delicately stepped into it, keenly aware that her every movement had its titillating effect on her lover. He took her once more in his arms, kissing her repeatedly as he pulled her in, and caressed her body under the water, and when he let go of her, she moved behind him and began to massage the back of his neck and shoulders.

"Ah, Pelaxilla," Ahuitzotl sighed, savoring her applications, "Being away from you is truly a hardship—but, oh, the return. So rewarding."

"Take me with you next time," she suggested playfully. "I've seen those long baggage columns that follow the armies. Do not deny it-are they not the wives of the soldiers?"

"Mistresses mostly-of the lords-but not on my campaigns, at least not those of short duration. On a prolonged operation I may permit it, but never for a lady of the court."

"You consign me to a cruel fate-I must suffer your absence continuously. Oh well, as you said, it allows for a more inviting homecoming."

"I'll make it so," Ahuitzotl grinned. "This is only the beginning, you will see."

"Promise me that," she giggled while she began scrubbing his back with a soapy washcloth, then moved over the rest of his body, "for we must make the most of the short times we have together."

"I'll be here for awhile. My coronation must be planned."

"Your coronation?" Pelaxilla was reminded of something he had told her earlier. "It's then that you will declare your empress, isn't it?"

"Afterwards, yes."

"And you will name Tlalalca?"

"Yes, but don't worry; my love for you will not be diminished due to this. My affections are confined to you-the others will find my attentions incidental."

"How long do you think Tlalalca will put up with that? What if she becomes jealous?"

"There's no chance of that. Everyone knows she dislikes me. She might even appreciate this arrangement-it offers her that much less time she would have to spend with me."

"Perhaps now, but eventually she may regard you differently."

"Believe me, that possibility is extremely remote-in fact nonexistent."

"Is my conquering hero such a loathsome person?"

"To Tlalalca, yes. She believes I had something to do with Tizoc's death and will always hold this against me."

"Did you?"

Ahuitzotl glanced contemplatively at her momentarily. They had talked enough about their mutual dismay over the former monarch that she certainly could not be blamed for suspecting his involvement, he thought. She had as much as proposed doing away with him herself, so it should not alarm her to learn of his complicity in such an affair. Still, he felt it better if she never knew; that would prevent any likelihood of the matter ever being spoken out of turn.

"I was told he died of an unknown illness," he answered.

"I believed that-once. Now I'm not so sure."

"It's best that we continue to believe it."

Pelaxilla briefly stopped her scrubbing, which led him to consider if he disappointed her by shattering certain romantic illusions she might have held, but then she resumed it, apparently accepting that the answer would forever remain a mystery for her.

"Speaking of Tlalalca," Ahuitzotl went on, "How are you two getting along?"

"Well enough, I suppose. It's difficult to say. She hasn't been making any appearances."

"Oh? She no longer holds her afternoon chats with you ladies?"

"No, not since the death of Lord Tizoc. She has become a recluse within the walls of her chamber. Occasionally she is seen walking in the garden with Xoyo, but she will not speak to any of us. It's quite eerie."

"She is afraid to exert her authority when she does not know what will happen to her."

"I had thought it was her mourning over Lord Tizoc."

"She must have seen something in him that escaped the rest of us. It's not good to cling to that which is over and gone."

"What a heartless thing to say, Ahuitzotl. She loved him."

"Is this what love can do to you? Then it is a frightening thing."

"Oh no, it's beautiful," Pelaxilla corrected him, a touch of sadness coming over her. "She can't help herself-Xochiquetzal has seen to that. Where it not for Tlalalca, who would even think of Lord Tizoc now?"

"Why are you defending her? You viewed her with disdain the last time we spoke."

"Tlalalca does not make herself empress. I have you to blame for that."

Ahuitzotl was taken aback by the sudden angry inflection in Pelaxilla's voice; he turned to face her. "If you wish," he said gravely, "I can get someone else. Would that be preferable to you?"

Even in her disgruntlement, Pelaxilla had the sensibility to recognize that her chances of remaining Ahuitzotl's favorite were improved by his having an empress who disfavored him than one who loved him. "Don't be upset," she entreated him. "Were she less beautiful, I could more willingly accept her as your wife, yet she's more agreeable to me than if you chose someone else."

"Dear Pelaxilla, what must I do to convince you that none can take your place in my heart?" he smiled and exuded a warmth from his glowing eyes that she felt penetrating through her.

"My womanly passions," she said softly, captivated by the radiance emanating from him. "I fear losing you-it makes me say these horrible things. I don't want to share you with anyone, even if it is selfish of me."

"You must lose such fears-they're groundless."

He inched closer, until his lips met hers; the sensuous contact enflamed him and he could feel the burning in his loins. His arms ran down her back, caressing the folds of her bottom, and he blazed in heated excitement, even though submerged in water.

"Come!" he exclaimed. "We have bathed enough!"

He lifted her up with an effortless sweep of his muscular arms and emerged from the cistern carrying her. Without taking the time to dry himself, he spirited her away to the adjoining bedroom where together they fell on the sheeted mats, their bodies still dripping wet. Pelaxilla laughingly protested.

"Ahuitzotl, the bed will be soaked."

"Let it. As hot as I am, it should soon be dry."

As he lay over her, he lapped the water droplets on her skin with his tongue, sensuously sliding from her neck across her heaving breasts; he tightened his lips over her nipples, moving from one to the other and savoring them in his open mouth. Then he probed lower, halting temporarily to fully encircle her navel and feeling its small indenture on his tongue's moist surface. Her excitement mounted and she gasped for her air and began to quiver in delight. Still he moved lower, until he reached the dampened cleft between her twittering thighs; he spread her legs apart and kissed that tender flesh, softly brushing the ripples within. Her heart palpitated at an accelerated intensity and she moaned out in her ecstasy.

While he continued working his kisses back up her body, Pelaxilla ran her hands up and down his back, enflaming him with her soft touches. Stirred to exhilarating heights, his breathing quickened to short, gasping pants and his muscles tightened until he trembled under the strain. His phallus felt so enormous that he thought it would spring itself free of its confines; he deftly maneuvered it toward her juicy orifice until he knew by the snug fit that he was properly within her. Instinctively, he generated his oscillations, feeling his fluids inch ahead as his body tensed under the venereal strain, until, in an explosive release, his seed shot forth, followed by the involuntary spasmodic surges of his organ draining itself: it was indescribably pleasureable.

Pelaxilla moaned in delectable gratification and, even after he had expended himself within her, she clung tightly to him in an effort to protract his penetration. But at last, he released himself from her encircling arms and rolled over on his back, and as he lay there enjoying the subsiding relief of his strain and its ensuing relaxation, Pelaxilla snuggled up to him, her skin rubbing his. The moment was one of extreme contentment, and not long after their blissful conjugation, they fell asleep in each other's arms.

ays later, preparations for the coming coronation rites were much in evidence throughout Tenochtitlan. Craftsmen and artisans set about busily creating their variety of products and accumulating them for distribution to the notables expected to make their appearances. Carpenters and masons toiled on the public facilities, inspecting them for structural soundness and insuring each was well repaired and freshly painted. Jewellers, goldsmiths, and weavers worked into late hours fashioning the ornamentation and finery required for the dancing and feasting, and florists adorned the temple steps and facades of buildings with colorful blooming decorations. The bustle of activity was ceaseless, going on day and night.

In the palace, Ahuitzotl passed his days receiving the dignitaries and representatives of nobles who had been invited to attend the ceremony. He took great pains to compile the list of rulers who were to be contacted and made it a specific point to summon those who were not as yet under Mexica domination, wishing to impress them with a prodigious giving away of innumerable items of wealth as a sign of the power he wielded. Messengers were sent to the farthest regions to carry their important words to these distant lords; now Ahuitzotl sat in session to receive the dignitaries arriving daily with their responses.

"Who is scheduled for me today?" Ahuitzotl asked Cihuacoatl.

"The Tarascans, Lord," the minister replied, red-faced and obviously embarrassed over having to report this.

"Ah yes, our old enemies from Michoacan. They did not dally in coming here, but judging from your face, I will not be pleased with their message."

"They remember too well having defeated your brother Axayacatl, and I suspect they'll make a show of it in front of you."

"That was many years ago. We are stronger now."

"They believe themselves also stronger, Lord."

"Then we may find ourselves tested again. Refusal of a royal invitation is tantamount to an open insult–providing us with our pretext for it. The Tarascans know this and should take the precautions not to provoke me."

"They fear us not," Cihuacoatl advised Ahuitzotl.

"No matter. My duty is to hear them. Bring them forward."

Cihuacoatl rapped his staff on the floor to quiet the hall and motioned for the Tarascan emissaries to come before the Revered Speaker. They strutted haughtily up to him, elegantly dressed with ornaments dangling all about them, and when they reached him, bowed their heads respectfully and waited to be addressed by him, protocol requiring the ranking lord to initiate any verbal exchange.

"Do you have your lord's reply to my invitation?" Ahuitzotl asked the ambassador.

"We do, Lord, and we are instructed to cite him verbatim."

A sober countenance came over Ahuitzotl; he looked at Cihuacoatl who returned his gaze with one of equal seriousness. Both expected an unwelcome response.

"I presume he means to reject my invite," Ahuitzotl surmised, "and if so, does he wish to accomplish this in the manner of a public humiliation for me?"

"He does reject it, Lord, but as to his intent on how the message is received I am not in a position to say. Only the recipient can judge that."

"Dismiss them now!" Cihuacoatl urged. "It's evident they mean to degrade you before the assembly."

"And reveal to everyone that we fear their lord? It's better we listen to his words, however insulting they may be, than to demonstrate that we can be frightened by them."

"They have cunningly attained their platform. I do not like this."

Ahuitzotl grimly faced the ambassador preparing himself for the anticipated deprecation. "Proceed then," he said, "Let us hear his words."

"My lord says 'Indeed you must be mad; once you wanted war and now you want peace. How am I to feel safe, eating and drinking in your presence, after you have mistreated me in such a way? I am not deceived by your motivations; your envoys say it is time to set aside our hostilities and that we should honor our neighborly obligations, but I know that you cannot be trusted and that, in your heart, you despise us for what we have done to you and wish to bring us under your domination. You may have your coronation whenever and wherever you like, but do not expect me or my people to be present.' These are his words to you."

Ahuitzotl's face flushed after having heard them; they announced a rebuke of his good intentions in having offered an invite to begin with. Rejections were seldom made, and when they were, it was always with the customary and profuse deliverances of sincere regrets so that a host was not offended, but the tone of this one was clearly aimed at insult, and what especially incensed Ahuitzotl was that the Tarascans were able to get away with it.

"My lord has requested I not attend the rites," the ambassador continued, "in conformance with the design of his message. It is with apologies, Great Lord, that I must adhere to his wishes."

"I see no choice for you," answered Ahuitzotl. "Your duty is to obey your lord. We do not hold your absence against you."

"Is there anything else you wish from us?"

Ahuitzotl paused in his typical fashion when searching for an appropriate response to things that disturbed him. He felt the eyes of the assembly fixed on him and pondered if he should try and deliver some face-saving declaration, as Tizoc might have done, or simply dismiss the matter. He decided a reply was in order.

"Inform your lord," he said, "that we are sorry he cannot allow our past differences to be set aside for a temporary period of rejoicing. Remind him that since it was we who had suffered most at his hands, we should be the ones to bear the greater hostility, but we chose to forego this anger by sending our invitation. It had been our hope that he could do likewise, reciprocating our gesture of friendship with a courteous act of his own, but as he is incapable of doing so, we shall take this into regard and will consider his abstention as excusable."

A smile came to Cihuacoatl who thought the reply brilliant. Now the Tarascans stood red-faced in the hall as Ahuitzotl motioned that they should depart with a flick of his wrist. They rendered their bows, turned about, and proceeded for the exit keenly aware of the angry stares centered on them. The ambassador knew that his arrogance had been put in place—also that his lord would be interested in learning that this new

Revered speaker, unlike the previous one, had a potential for greatness and bore watching.

Ahuitzotl had no reason to congratulate himself, in spite of the praise he received from his elated minister, for as the days progressed it became patently clear that a Mexica monarch no longer held the position of awe and respect which had once existed. The Tarascan lord's refusal was soon followed by a second rebuff-this time from a traditional enemy, the Tlaxcalans.

"Why should we bother ourselves over this?" their lord replied. "We can arrange a feast any time we like in our own city. Your coronation of a new ruler is of no particular interest to us and we do not expect it to affect any policies between us."

Even more rejections succeeded this one, and Ahuitzotl was rapidly reaching his breaking point towards receiving them. "It's inconceivable!" he fumed, pacing the floor in front of his minister after he summarily dismissed his visitors following the latest disappointment. "Have any of the independent state rulers accepted our invitation?"

"Only a few, the most notable among them the ruler of Cholula, and then only after we promised him gifts and entertainment."

"This defies all comprehension. It's as if the kingship of the Mexica, the most powerful of nations, had no significance whatsoever. My Matlazinca incursion hasn't impressed anyone."

"That was a short time ago, Lord! Word of it may not have circulated, particularly to the independent states."

"No, Cihuacoatl; if anyone would have heard, it's them—they must keep their watch on us if they are to maintain their free status. They have their spies and scouts just as we do. What of the conquered states, or the one's we've defeated in battle? Are their rulers coming?"

"All but one, Lord!"

"Even a beaten nation dares reject us. Why was I not told?"

"The fault is mine, Lord. I wanted to spare you additional irritation."

"Never do that again!" Ahuitzotl sternly warned his minister. "You spare me nothing by withholding such information—eventually I will learn of it. It only complicates things, and I don't expect this to be repeated. Now, which state was it?"

"Huaxteca, Lord." Cihuacoatl hastily replied, embarrassed over his blunder and resultant berating.

"The Huaxtecs!" Ahuitzotl bellowed. "By the gods!"

Cihuacoatl expected this; the sight of an enraged monarch was a fearful enough spectacle, and if he felt that he had erred in failing to report the news, he also deemed his reasons for it excusable. Now Ahuitzotl's reaction substantiated it.

"What unmitigated audacity!" Ahuitzotl stormed on. "Why, I personally have defeated him when he came to the assistance of his ally at Metztitlan."

"It's been five years, and a new lord now rules the Huaxtecs," Cihuacoatl sought to placate his master. "Evidently he is ignorant of his obligations."

"No, minister!" Ahuitzotl always addressed Cihuacoatl by that title when he was offended by his remarks. "Our envoys would have made the requisites apparent to him. He is well aware of his conduct. It is a calculated snub."

Cihuacoatl, uncertain about his answers, feared he might displease the monarch again and concluded his only safe course was to agree. "I am most astounding he should be so rash," he said. "What can he hope to gain by it?"

"A test of my will I believe. Who is he?"

"He is called Xaman Utec. He is the son of the former ruler. It was his father, you will recall, who made things difficult for Tizoc in his first campaign."

"I remember. Like many of Tizoc's operations, he botched it up. No doubt his father had much to do in indoctrinating him with a healthy contempt for us-a good reason against keeping a ruler in his position after defeating him. Xaman Utec had best tread lightly. I will not be trifled with."

Again Ahuitzotl ruminated on the number of rejections he had received, both agitated and depressed over it. That his coronation, which he had hoped to use as a platform to display the authority at his command, should be minimized and dishonored by the contemptuous actions of his peers stung him severely.

"So this is how low we have fallen," he groaned. "Tizoc's legacy to me. I am to bear the burden of his ineptness. Our Matlazinca campaign was supposed to reverse this situation, but it appears to have failed me. By the gods, that galls me. My splendid victories left no imprint whatsoever on our enemies. They still regard me with-with impudence, as they did Tizoc. How can I nullify this indignity he has made us suffer?"

"I said once before you cannot erase the damage of five years in a single operation," Cihaucoatl stressed, "but you are wrong if you think it has been of no use. I was told of the spirt that infused our warriors at Xilotepec. You have instilled a confidence in them never equalled, and with such men, you will be able to march to the ends of the world. It is indeed a good beginning!"

Ahuitzotl's moodiness abated on hearing this, and his attention turned to the planned ceremony, primarily over its prestigious aspects which now held a paramount importance in his mind. "We need to stage an impressive exhibition," he said. "While it may be that many powerful lords think our invitation is unworthy of their time, word of our celebration must reach their courts so that they will regret having stayed away. It must be a grand spectacle."

"So it shall be. We have amassed more wealth to be dispensed than ever before. The festival will last four days."

"We must also impress the gods-with much blood-letting. Huitzilopochtli must look favorably upon my accession; I have much to ask of him."

"I see no problem. There are ample captives available."

"Let us sacrifice a thousand of them over the four days—that ought to satisfy even the most demanding of them."

Cihuacoatl gulped, unsuccessful in concealing his astonishment; the number was far greater than he imagined.

"Does that figure shock you?" Ahuitzotl responded when he noticed his minister's startled expression.

"It is no small quantity, Lord."

"You've demonstrated my reasons for doing this," Ahuitzotl said, smiling for the first time that afternoon in his amusement over Cihuacoatl's reaction. "Make certain the priests comply."

The course of their conversation had them ambling to the doorway and, after Ahuitzotl directed the minister outside, both men stood in long pause staring at the enormous edifice of the Great Temple now nearing completion. Looming gigantically over Tenochtitlan's central plaza, the massive structure gleamed in its freshly plastered walls and dwarfed all surrounding buildings. Its four tiered base section was done and scaffolding now rose upward about the two shrines whose dimensions were already taking shape, their entrances and main chambers being finished and all remaining work concentrated on the huge trapezoid roof combs jutting to almost a third of the entire structure's height into the sky. This temple differed from previously raised ones in that it was higher than its base width, a feature which, coupled with its inordinately tall roof combs, created an impression of illusionary loftiness from the perspective of an observer at ground level. A divided stairway of one hundred and fourteen steps led to each shrine and was bordered by smoothly coated balustrades. The overall emphasis was one of awe and dramatic power, and anyone viewing it felt himself humbled by its immensity.

"In my current depression," Ahuitzotl confided in his minister, "my one consolation is that this magnificent temple will be finished under my reign and will stand as a lasting monument to its glory. Just as we now look with wonder upon the Temple of the Sun at Teotihuacan, so future Revered Speakers will see this temple and marvel at the power of the lord who built it. It is fitting that it should be completed under my rule-Tizoc was not deserving of such acclaim."

"There's no disputing that, considering the humiliation we are now undergoing."

"Yes, but that will end-I promise you. Huitzilopochtli's monument will not stand for a reign unequal to the tasks he has conferred upon us. My reign must shine as brilliantly as this temple under Tonatiuh's rays: the glory of one must complement the glory of the other."

"That means the temple's inauguration must be under the most favorable auspices. We will plan a ceremony to match its dimensions when we dedicate it. I'll task the priests with that as soon as we are done with your coronation."

With that, they entered the palace again to carefully review all the processions and rituals which were to take place; not until darkness enveloped Tenochtitlan did Ahuitzotl, satisfied at last that everything had been properly prepared, permit his minister to retire to his quarters. After he had gone, Ahuitzotl once more stepped out to fix his gaze upon the Great Temple's darkened outline under the night sky. Appearing even more gigantic then, the overpowering sense of preponderance it projected enthralled him and he never wearied of seeing it. Finally, however, other urges came to him and he left for his chamber where he knew Pelaxilla was waiting.

XI

Gaity and rejoicing were the bywords in Tenochtitlan on the opening day of Ahuitzotl's coronation. Guests who had arrived were lavishly provided for, housed in splendidly redecorated palaces and catered the finest food and drink by cordial servants instructed to satisfy their every need. They were graciously received by Ahuitzotl himself who entertained them opulently in his palace hall. A noted longtime carouser, he had an appreciation of what his visitors desired and proved a hospitable host. Many were present, most of them lords from the Mexica and allied cities, and the turnout pleased the monarch whose preference ran towards large audiences, especially when the occasion involved his own exultation. And even if the lords of the principle enemy states failed to have a representation, there came enough of them from the 'free' states-those kingdoms which were neither subjugated by, nor at war with, the Mexica-to still allow for an impressionable show of omnipotence.

"How did you manage to get them here?" Tlohtzin asked Cihuacoatl as they watched Ahuitzotl greet the latest lordly retinue that had arrived. "I thought most were bent on not coming."

"They were," confirmed Cihuacoatl. "It required skillful inducements to make them change their minds."

"What sort of inducements?"

"The promise of many gifts, rich prizes, and an abundance of women, food, and ample entertainment."

"They were bribed then," concluded Tlohtzin.

"Essentially that is correct," the minister glowered-he did not like shrewdness coming from a professional military man, "but the Revered Speaker was determined to have a respectable showing, so I did what I could to provide him with one."

"I assume he knows of your method."

"Only in some cases, as with the lord of Cholula. For the most part, he does not. It's important you keep this to yourself. We have both seen him in anger-clearly something to avoid."

"I'm familiar with what you say. I have offended him before and would not risk doing so again, not over something like this."

The first day's events began with a parade of the Revered Speaker and his celebrated luminaries through Tenochtitlan's main avenues in the accompaniment of a band of musicians, principally of flutists and drummers. Starting out at the palace, they circled a major section of the city, returning to the central plaza where bleachers had been erected beneath those temples from where they would observe the scores of activities scheduled, including the day's chosen sacrifices. The march was aimed at introducing the dignitaries to the people who were thronged along both sides of the streets to view them, affording the lords the chance to ostentatiously exhibit themselves in their most bedecked adornments and costumes, dazzling in color and indicative of their exultant stations in their realms. Ahuitzotl, attired in gold and turquoise, led the retinue with Chimalpopoca and Nezahualpilli, partners of the Triple Alliance, but a pace behind.

After thus displaying themselves, the dignitaries took their place in the bleachers which were canopied to shade them from the glaring sun; each lord had his seat marked and an attendant standing by to see to his needs and refill his drinks for refreshment. When all were seated, the first of many groups of dancers appeared, entering the square in their rhythmic movements and flowing banners to the playing of music by an accompanying band.

Brightly clad in red and white, the dancers, both male and female, glided gracefully with interwoven fluctuations between each other in circular motions. The men wore rattles around their ankles whose sound paralleled the drumbeats to which they stomped in pace. As the music changed its tempo, the dancers varied their patterns, flailing their colorful streamers to create a rippling effect of synchronization and beauty. They executed a number of styles, each with its own particular music and depicting the variations popular through the realm, and when they were finished, the lords applauded and hooted out their approval.

Next came a band of warrior dancers, whose introductory number thrilled the crowd with its rapid tempo accentuated by the beat of many drums. They clashed their weapons and struck the pavement with their spears in harmony with the rolling percussions, much to the excitement of the spectators. Their successive scores were characterized by equally furiously paced rhythms with dynamic movements to represent the action of warriors locked in combat and the maneuvering of squads into battle formations-passages with which most of the audience could identify. These were flawlessly executed, stirring in their presentation, and when it was over, vigorous applause ensued: clearly martial music and dancing was a crowd-pleaser.

After the all-male military dancing entered an all-female party of the auianime, ladies chosen to serve the nobles and notable warriors as concubines. Less accentuated with percussions and more melodic, their music inspired them to move in slower but more elegant manner; their intent was less to delight the audience with their graceful movement than it was to draw attention on their individual beauty and tease it into a selection game of picking out a favorite with whom one preferred to spend the night. Successful in their pursuit, the lords could be heard actively debating amongst themselves which dancer appealed to them, stressing the merits and assets of their particular choices. Even Ahuitzotl thought one of the performers sufficiently captivating that he held his eyes on her through the duration of the show. Their final score was an exceedingly erotic rendition which strongly suggested sexual encounters and literally had members of the audience squirming in their seats, even sweating, and at its completion, the lords loudly proclaimed their satisfaction.

Having spent the morning gratified by this seemingly endless procession of entertainers, an interlude of free time followed in which the lords attended to some of their personal concerns and wandered about to do their socializing while servants brought trays of drink and delicacies to them as they mingled with each other. This present carnival-like atmosphere served as a prelude for the more somber affair that was to follow.

"A good show," the king of Cholula told his host. "What comes next?"

"Just as we delighted our guests this morning," Ahuitzotl replied, "so we must delight our gods this afternoon."

"I presume you speak of sacrifices. A bloody business, I expect; that should please most of the lords here, although I do not count myself among them. You Mexica have carried this thing to far more monstrous proportions than we Cholulans are accustomed to. It's a problem when you have too many gods–you must placate them all."

"Many are the gods of people we have subjugated. Can you deny that they exist?"

"No, I suppose not."

"Nor could we; we found it necessary to place them alongside our own–at least those for whom we had no counterparts. Many were the same ones that we worship, and only had other names, but there were also new ones."

"Yes, I can see how it can lead to all this. But your own gods have always been more demanding than ours, and your sacrifices shocked us in the earlier days by their numbers. Of course, we've now adjusted to it and understand your need for it."

"We've always had more to ask from them–we were not content to remain a small state–and I, in particular, have much to request from them, especially from Huitzilopochtli."

The Cholulan did not press for an explanation; the implication was that conquests would mark this Revered Speaker's reign. This meant an increasingly powerful and bellicose neighbor was to border his kingdom, which he considered threatening to its future 'free' status. A less than satisfactory countenance featured the Cholulan when he returned to the stands.

KA-RA-BOOM! The abruptness in which the giant drum echoed across the plaza caught the dignitaries unaware, startling them. They scrambled back to their seats knowing what was to occur; suspense ensued–most of them eagerly anticipated the prisoners' arrival.

The Mexica rulers left their guests to assume their stations beside the priests atop four of the five temples situated in the square. Ahuitzotl and Cihuacoatl climbed up the steep steps of Huitzilopochtli's present temple; Chimalpopoca and Nezahualpilli took their station at the Temple of Quetzalcoatl, south of the unfinished Great Temple; the rulers of Chalco and Azcapotzalco went to the Temple of Xipe Totec at the west end of the square, while the lords of Coyoacan and Ixtapalapa were at the Eagle

Temple adjacent to it. Each of these monarchs was to initiate the offerings; other rulers accompanied them to assist so the rites could be sustained without interruption until all of the day's allocations were dispatched.

Conch shells announced the parade of victims into the plaza, under a light escort and in four columns, each going to its respective temple. There were one hundred of them in each line, with its leading member draped in a feathered cloak which he spread out by extending his arms as instructed to signify the soul's flight into heaven; about half of them were painted yellow, all were naked. They walked calmly to their destiny, sharing their conqueror's convictions that, highly honored, they would this day enter the East Paradise of the Sun, and only a handful of guards guided them.

After the captives had lined up to the uppermost tier of each temple, the pounding panhuehuetl sounded out the call to commence. Incantations bellowed forth from priests entreating the deities they served, and when they were done, they leaped upon the first victim and carried him to the block. As he was spread-eagled over it, the ruler walked up to it, raised his flint knife high into the air, and then plunged it forcefully into the heaving chest, slashing it open so he could reach into its goriness to tear out the still pulsating heart. Such was the scene repeated over and over with tedious regularity atop each temple and lasting until late afternoon when the last body plummeted down the steps into the tiring arms of priests who quickly cut it apart.

When the sacrifice were over, the lords retired to their quarters for a resting period before attending an evening feast in the palace hall. This was a time they had to themselves, much desired after spending almost an entire day in a ceremonial capacity, either as spectators or participants, and each made use of it in accordance to his habit. The more amorous occupied their time with the concubines available to them; others forsook their relaxation, choosing instead to stroll the city's streets for sightseeing or visiting the gardens and zoo; still others simply went to sleep, the day's activity having worn them out.

That evening, after the sun had set, the first of many feasts honoring the new monarch was held. A gala event in which all the exotic dishes created by palace chefs were served in ample quantity, and while the dignitaries dined, musicians played, adding their pleasure to the occasion. Their meals consumed, more entertainment was in order, mostly on a smaller scale, of individual or group singing, juggling acts and acrobatics, and instrumental solos. While sweet and alcoholic beverages were poured in abundance, the lords expended their late hours enjoying these shows until, overcome by the effects of their drinking and drowsiness, they gradually filtered out of the hall. Even Ahuitzotl, one of the last to leave, was staggering somewhat as he limbered through the corridors trying to find his chamber.

A similar sequence of activity marked the second day, with more dancing and singing in the morning and sacrificial offerings afterward, and concluding with another banquet which ended earlier so that the visitors were permitted opportunities to engage in their own escapades during the later period. The estimation was that by this time, most of them had selected their favorites among the auianime and wished to partake of their companionship. For some this fulfilled part of the promises which had induced them to make their journeys in the first place.

On the third day, however, the schedule of events changed with sacrifices in the morning, but instead of dispatching captives in the usual fashion, many were offered a chance at life by battling on the combat stone. Considerable suspense surrounded these gladiatorial contests with many lords often betting enormous sums on those warriors whom they selected as their champions. Victors who impressed the spectators won their freedom, and more than one of them went on to serve in employment for the noble who had wagered on him; those who won through suspected foul play or an uninspired performance were saved from the altar but remained as slaves or captives. The losers, if not slain in the fighting, were taken away and decapitated.

As it chanced to happen, one particularly enterprising warrior won the admiration of his audience by slaying all of his opponents in rapid succession-two of them simultaneously-and even Ahuitzotl who, until seeing this, had a general low regard for the Matlazinca as fighting men, found the action to his liking.

"A noteworthy achievement!" he exclaimed. "You have proven yourself a most valiant warrior. Honor us by revealing your name."

"I am Nopaltzin," the warrior answered, "from Xilotepec."

"Xilotepec! The easiest of my triumphs-I thought you a city of lowly recreants. How did you escape my notice there?"

"I was hampered from wielding my weapon by our own warriors rushing by me. Before I was free to move, I was struck down from behind, and when I awoke discovered myself a captive."

"No matter," Ahuitzotl smiled, looking with favor on the Xilotepecan, "You have done remarkably well today. You are released to return to your city."

"If my lord pleases, I would not shame my name and family in such a manner. It is the fate of captives to be sent to the gods, and I do not wish to be denied this honor."

"A noble gesture, Nopaltzin, but one which I will deny you. I have need of warriors such as you; if you will not return to Xilotepec, then I ask that you remain here to serve in my army. This is not to refuse paradise to you, but to postpone it; should you still be disposed to meet the gods later, we can grant your request then. Will you consent to this?"

"If my lord desires it, I shall be his loyal servant."

"That is my wish," declared Ahuitzotl amidst the approbations given him by approving lords.

Nopaltzin was next surrounded by several Mexica chieftains who eagerly accepted him as a highly distinguished warriors into their ranks. Courage was valued by them and stood as no barrier to social status or promotion, even for a former enemy.

Following this fare, the afternoon was left free for the visitors to carry on as they pleased, and Tenochtitlan hosted them graciously, with people everywhere greeting them in respectful and open friendliness. Canoes were made available to ride the canals and view the city from the lake; guides led them along the streets and apprised them of the latest changes and construction in progress; priests explained the extraordinary features of the Great Temple to their awestruck audience. And also many enjoyed musing in the royal garden admiring creations owed to Tizoc-a pleasant respite from the endless rituals.

After another morning of sacrifices, the afternoon of the fourth day was hailed as the actual coronation in the palace assembly hall. Everyone present stood attired in their most impressive array, leaving an aisle between their rows from the entrance to the platform where the throne was emplaced. Here Cihuacoatl, wearing his jaguar skin cape, was standing when Ahuitzotl, flanked by Chimalpopoca and Nezahualpilli, approached in a slow but steady gait through the passageway while a male choir comprised of young votaries was singing. He stopped upon reaching the minister, and this in turn led the singers into a cessation of their renditions, bringing the floor to complete silence.

"Mighty Lord!" Cihuacoatl's booming voice rang out, "Chosen our Revered Speaker! Now is the time when we entrust the keeping of this royal seat to you. We seek that you uphold the obligations and duties which this exulted position, proclaimed by glorious Huitzilopochtli, Lord of the Southern Sky, entails; that you protect and defend us; that you see to the great tasks lying undone and bestowed upon us. Take this mission to heart, see to its fruition. Do these things in the spirit of your illustrious fore-bearers, Great Lord, so that you will assure the blessings of the gods upon our realm and live forever in the hearts of your people. I now decree you, from this time forth, until you are beckoned to the greater glory of the heavens, Revered Speaker, Lord of the Mexica"

Ahuitzotl was then draped with a bejeweled turquoise cape, symbol of his office, and the royal diadem was hung over his neck; a richly adorned gold and feather headdress was set on his crown. He next partook in rites of personal sacrifice, piercing his ears and thighs with a sharp golden-handled jaguar bone and allowing his red blood to flow freely onto white linens applied to the cuts by Cihuacoatl. This completed, he took his place on the throne while priests again chanted out their sacred songs and received the numerous well-wishing orations presented by the lords.

After the coronation began the most dramatic, and for many the most anticipated, highlight of the celebration-a prodigious giving away of riches by the Revered Speaker as a demonstration to its recipients how great was the abundance of the nation he ruled. The show was meant to impress, and Ahuitzotl was not one to do things haphazardly: all of the accumulated wealth equivalent to an entire year's tributes was to be dispensed to the guests and people.

The summation of the quantities of items distributed was of staggering proportions. No other ruler had gone to these lengths towards making such an ostentatious display of his capacity to rid himself of his treasures. The list included over two hundred thousand mantles, skirts, blouses, loincloths, and sandals; thousands of handfuls of feathers; thousands of weapons and shields; loads of cocoa, corn, and beans measured in volumes too vast to count; jewelry-necklaces, bracelets, diadems, earlobes, half-moons, ankle trimmings, lip insertions, belts, headbands, rings-and feathered ornaments, also numbering also numbering in the thousands. Even slaves, nearly a thousand of them, were among the presents given away.

While the richest and most elaborately adorned items were offered to the guests first, an ample amount remained on hand for the populace at large which patiently waited its turn at public facilities converted into distribution points to share the outpouring of Ahuitzotl's generosity. This was altogether proper; after all, it was the potentates whom the Revered Speaker sought most to influence; they had to view his power with envy and considerable apprehensiveness, for the extravaganza was intended to inspire fear as well as astonishment and set the tone for a future relationships between states. Ahuitzotl and Cihuacoatl carefully examined each ruler's reaction and made their evaluations on what sort of enterprise would be forthcoming from him.

"For this I most wanted my enemy lords here," said Ahuitzotl. "Their absence tarnishes this affair."

"Then why persist in this lavish dissipation?"

"In the hope that they will hear of it, and marvel at what has taken place this day."

"How are we to know it has this effect on them?"

"Men's imagination will accomplish this well enough for us. Never has there been such a dispensation of wealth, and the lords who partook of it know of its uniqueness and will long boast about it. I expect, in their bombasting, they will exaggerate this to even greater levels. All things considered, how can they fail to be awed?"

"You have more faith in this than I, Lord!"

"I have faith in the manner of men's action. You will see I am correct when they make their appearance for our next scheduled celebration-the Great Temple's dedication."

Ahuitzotl held one more function on that final night and the contented lords, laden to the hilt with the prizes they had received earlier, were well disposed to spending an evening in discussions over their acquired riches and the magnanimous distribution from which they so wonderfully benefited. Their slaves would start the trek back to their cities tomorrow carrying these gifts laden on their backs and, for most of them, it would not be a light load. But tonight they relaxed and dined, and related their satisfaction over having made the trip to Tenochtitlan. For the majority, the rewards they had reaped for their efforts had been beyond their wildest dreams, and yet, there prevailed an underlying uneasiness over the occasion. The lord of Choluca, on the morning of his departure, rendered the best definition to this apprehension when he spoke to Cihuacoatl.

"With such riches at your disposal," he said, "to be so effortlessly dispersed, how will anyone dare to oppose you? I may have been well paid in coming here, but, indeed, so have you."

Long after his guests had gone, Ahuitzotl remained seated in his throne and deliberated over the extraordinary course of events which had brought him to this point. Among other emotions felt as he so contemplated, he was still smarting over the derision his enemies held for him by snubbing his invitation. His coronation had failed in some aspects, but overall, it had gone quite well, for if he was unable to awe his adversaries, at least he succeeded in intimidating the lords of the independent states. They would think twice before attempting to align themselves with his opponents and in effect were neutralized by this restraint. If nothing else, it assured him that, should he one day decide to avenge this humiliation, his foes would stand alone and unassisted against him. So while the 'free' states may bear no love for the Mexica, at least they now did the next best thing-they feared them. His objectives had therefore been attained in great measure even if not that apparent at first: it had been a successful coronation.

XII

several days later, Ahuitzotl, becoming increasingly restive over Tlalalca's seclusion and her conspicuous absence from the remaining ladies of his court, sought her out in order to put an end to her self-imposed isolation. When his servants reported that she was not seen in the palace, he surmised she had ventured into the garden and, on continuing his search there, noticed her sitting on one of the slab benches in the company of Xoyo.

"Do not be distressed now," Xoyo said to Tlalalca, "but it is the Revered Speaker who approaches us."

"He means to castigate me for ignoring him. I have expected it for some time-indeed, my surprise is that he has taken this long."

"Shall I go, my lady?"

"I beg you do not; with both of us here, his fiery temper will find itself checked."

Ahuitzotl calmly strode up to them and paused momentarily to assess their demeanor. Clearly Tlalalca was unsettled-she refused to look at him and her eyes groped anxiously for something in the garden to fix themselves upon.

"Leave us, old woman," Ahuitzotl presently directed. "I wish to be alone with Tlalalca."

"My lady has instructed me to stay," Xoyo replied.

"Your Revered Speaker insists that you leave," he countered.

"My allegiance is to my lady. Revered Speaker you may be, but I shall not leave her."

"What?"

"Withhold your anger, Lord," Tlalalca interceded, sensing his irritation rising and fearing for her handmaiden's safety, "Xoyo is sworn to my servitude. Even as Revered Speaker, you cannot revoke this loyalty."

"Then you order her to go. I don't want to make an issue of this."

Hesitating briefly, Tlalalca worried over having another face-to-face confrontation with Ahuitzotl, but she dreaded the wrath her refusal might invoke even more. "It's all right, Xoyo," she said. "No harm will come to me. I shall see you later."

"As my lady wishes," the devoted woman answered and dutifully left them.

"Such fidelity," Ahuitzotl commented as he watched her go, "But highly mislaid. No one disobeys the Revered Speaker; you would do well to enlighten her of that."

"She is old and fixed in her ways; nothing you can say will frighten her."

"That can be risky."

"You would harm an old woman?"

Ahuitzotl felt foolish persisting in this exchange, and he was puzzled why his conversations with Tlalalca always seemed to direct themselves toward a confrontative posture. "No, I suppose not," he conceded. "At any rate, I did not come her to discuss the merits of Xoyo's loyalty to you-it means nothing to me."

"Why did you come?"

"To speak with you. I haven't seen you since our last, ah, encounter and am questioning why you avoid me like this?"

"You think I have no cause to shun you? Our last encounter, as you call it, did not exactly endear you to me."

"You will recall that I had sufficient provocation to do what I did. I don't owe you an apology for it."

"I provoked you into coming to my bedchamber? Really, Lord, you have quite deluded yourself if that is your belief."

"I was prepared to leave when your glib tongue invited me to-to stay. You well know this."

"I do not wish to discuss it. I find its recollection revolting."

"Revolting?"

"Utterly so."

"I suppose you mean it in every respect."

"That is precisely my meaning."

"You do rather nicely in offending people yourself-a natural talent for you I assume. It makes me curious how Tizoc bore your presence for so long."

That remark hurt her; Ahuitzotl perceived this from her moistening eyes and he was prepared to retract it. Yet she faught back.

"Unlike you," she retorted, "Tizoc knew how to handle me."

"Then that's all he knew. Certainly he lacked understanding on how to rule his nation."

"Say what you like against him; you will not succeed in diminishing him for me. He was a good man-better than the one who now sits on the throne in his place."

Now she had pushed him to the limit. This was all Ahuitzotl could take from her and he exploded in an outburst of rage that stunned Tlalalca.

"By the gods, I will not be insulted like this! Do you know of the humiliation I underwent at my coronation? Of all the lords who rejected my invitation and refused to come? Do you realize the significance of that? It amounts to an overt degradation of our people-a willful act of contempt hurled upon us! Six years ago none would have dared commit such insolence. And who do we have to thank for this? Your good Lord Tizoc! Under him, we have fallen to such lowly depths that even lords we have defeated venture to treat us with surliness. So do not speak words of praise for Tizoc to me. It will take me years to undo the damage he has done."

Tlalalca was quieted. Had she believed his words fallacious, she might have countered them in her usual acerbic manner; however, she remembered only too well how many of her own discussions with Tizoc had led her to a similar conclusion. For once, and much to her surprise, she felt a degree of empathy for Ahuitzotl.

"My deprecation is enhanced by your absence from my palatial dinners and other social affairs," he went on, although more subdued now. "The ladies of the court talk, and when they see you staying away they say you are displaying scorn for me. It is enough that I have sustained insults from these lords, but I will not be subject to them in my own palace."

"They are wrong if they say that."

"I think not. You have mourned for Tizoc long enough. He is happy in his paradise; why should you persist in hurling misery upon yourself over him? No, you do this to degrade me."

"If so, I have adequate justifications. You haven't treated me with any respect."

"I know this," he admitted, his anger subsided. "That's why I came looking for you. I had hoped we could forget about our past mistakes and start anew with each other."

"Forget our past mistakes? Was the death of my husband one of them?"

Ahuitzotl glared at her on the verge of another outburst but checked himself, having no desire to strain this already bad start towards mediation any further. "I was thinking of the night I forced myself on you," he said. He was being honest; he did not consider the death of Tizoc a mistake.

"I can dismiss that easily enough," replied Tlalalca, "and certainly would not permit it to impede a reconciliation between us. It is Tizoc's death I cannot forget."

"Why hold that against me?"

"Because I believe you are implicated in it."

"I will not even comment on such a preposterous allegation. He died of a sudden illness-that's what Cihuacoatl told me."

"Don't be absurd!" Tlalalca asserted. "A healthy young man does not, in the course of a single afternoon, succumb to any kind of illness and suddenly die from its effects–such circumstances are unknown to us, even if ordained by the gods. He met with foul play."

"Nobody saw him for weeks before his death-except at the Tlaloc feasts. How do we know he was healthy?"

"I saw him–daily."

Ahuitzotl discerned that he was not getting anywhere with her on this subject. He could have advanced a case for the necessity of Tizoc's death, but decided such an expenditure of effort would be wasted on her. "You're a hard woman," he said. "You make it difficult for me to improve our relationship, as I wanted to do when I came here."

"I'm sorry."

"I doubt if you really are, but regardless, I do admire your spirit, even if it is exercised in poor judgment. It's imprudent for you to offend the man who holds your future life in this court in his hands. If you have any desire at all to remain here, you are advised to make a better effort in acceding to my wishes."

"I see," Tlalalca concluded after giving his warning some weight. "You are unable to attain my acquiescence, so now you must threaten me. What will you do to me? Expel me from the court? That will not please some of the lords who hold my royal lineage in high regard."

"Aren't you the clever one. Don't rely on it, Tlalalca; if I'm so inclined, I can oust you this very day."

"If that's supposed to frighten me, you are mistaken. I have expected this since the day you were named Tizoc's successor."

"Understand that's not what I want; I'm driven to this by your caustic tongue."

"What do you want, Ahuitzotl?"

Seemingly this was an opportune moment to disclose his plans to her, as she practically invited him to it, but he found himself pondering its wisdom. He had hoped for a more amiable interchange-the argumentative tendencies of their encounter made it highly questionable. Nevertheless, he decided the risk had to be taken.

"I want you to remain at the court," he said, "as empress."

"What?" Tlalalca was in shock.

"I want you as my empress."

Tlalalca was wholly unprepared for this. Her immediate reaction was one of incredulity; then she became suspicious, but still she could not find the words to give expression to her amazement.

"Did you hear me?" said Ahuitzotl.

"Why do you mock me like this?" she finally answered.

"Mock you?" he grew furious again. "I endure the barbs and slurs you heap upon me ceaselessly, and it is I who mocks you? I ask you to be empress, and this is all you can say? By the gods, woman! What does it take to get a favorable response out of you?"

"What game do you play with me?" she snapped back equally angry. "Why would you even consider me, unless you had some devious scheme in mind to cause me further injury?"

"Don't be ridiculous! If that were my intent, I could do it without asking you to be empress."

"I can't believe this! You and I aren't even friends-there is treachery afoot here. Everyone knows of your love for Pelaxilla. How could I possibly measure in your plans?"

"She cannot be empress," replied Ahuitzotl bitterly. "I am not permitted to marry her for reasons you already know."

His reminder gave her pause as she was again struck with pity over their unfortunate circumstances, aware of how much they adored each other. She was beginning to see Ahuitzotl differently; beneath his seemingly surety in doing things and confident bearing, he also had his share of obstacles to surmount.

"I assume Pelaxilla knows what you ask of me," she said. "She does not object?"

"Of course she objects. But what can she do?"

"But why me? There are ample candidates available, some are within this very palace."

"None that I would have but you."

"Me? You would have only me? To what end? Certainly not out of any affection."

Ahuitzotl looked oddly at her, fascinated that she detected no other purpose in his request. In fact, he thought her very appealing and frequently repressed urges of desire for her; it would be wrong to say he had no affection for her, and he wished that he could attain her willing friendship. Indeed he meant to have her, and if that entailed coerciveness or subterfuge, so be it, but she was going to be his.

"It's for Pelaxilla that I do this," he continued, now realizing how the situation increasingly favored his design. "She knows of your loathing for me and sees a comfort in it, preferring me having an empress who won't threaten to take me from her. She thinks you as safe."

"I begin to understand. You want me an empress in name only-to appease offended lords-while you remain with Pelaxilla, much like Lord Nezahualpilli with his Lady of Tula."

"Yes. I thought it would be to our mutual advantage and could work."

"How did you think it would be to my advantage?"

"It's rather obvious. Since you're not in want of me, you should not be troubled by my loving Pelaxilla even while empress. It would be a marriage of convenience, nothing more."

"I don't see it as convenient for me. It places me in bondage to you if I give my wedding vows. What if I should fall in love again? I could face a threat of punishment for adultry, whether consummated or not."

"If that happens, you have only to tell me and I'll grant you a divorce. There will be no need for adultry."

"You make it appear so simple, and yet I see a complexity in this. There are things unseen, possibilities not considered, that lurk behind such schemes. What about us? How will I know you won't force yourself on me again?"

"I will not-I swear it. But I'll expect you to perform your duties as a wife when I call for it. It will not be frequent."

"What you say is you mean to have me as well as Pelaxilla."

"And the many other mistresses at my disposal, as is customary for a ruler. Your Lord Tizoc made as much use of it as anyone."

Tlalalca knew this was not true, but also that it was immaterial as the practice prevailed among nobles and was not only considered a prerogative, but a right. There was no point in challenging it.

"What will you do if I say no?" she asked.

"Keep you here and do with you as I please. I needn't remind you that it's proper for me to keep mistresses of the royal lineage available in case my wife, whomever that might be, fails to provide me with an heir. I'll fully exercise this privilege."

Somehow she counted on hearing this from him; she knew Ahuitzotl could not be accused of moving in half measures. "You are intent on having me no matter what," she decided. "I see no particular benefit in your proposal."

"No? Remember, you have been empress for almost six years, and it will be awkward, even uncomfortable, to find yourself among the same ladies you have for so long placed demands on. They will not hold you in the same regard."

"Perhaps not, but what of Pelaxilla? My association with her, knowing she is your favorite, will be problematic at best. How would I reproach her, if such action was required, when she has your attention? I see difficulties for both of us."

"Interesting-she voiced almost the identical concern. All I can do is promise you I will be as objective and fair-minded about this as is possible so whatever complications come up will be minimized. Will you consent to this arrangement?"

"I hardly feel as if I have a choice. I should like some time to think on it."

"I want an answer now," Ahuitzotl demanded.

"But it's so soon after Tizoc's death," Tlalalca demurred in an attempt to defer a decision she felt unable to make at present. "What will everyone think?"

"Everyone expects me to do just this. A woman such as you, of royal lineage and..." he was about to add fairly attractive but refrained from it, "and a former empress still young in her years, could not be seen remaining a widow for long. The people will consider this an agreeable gesture and give it their approval."

She was beset with doubts; it was happening too fast for her. The entire conversation had seemed so inconceivable, beyond anything she had dared to ever contemplate or imagine, and now she was prodded to fulfill a committment to the man she had heretofore despised above all others. But what did it matter, she thought; he already declared his intentions on keeping her as a mistress anyway, as was his inherent right. Whether she became empress or not, he would still exert his dominance over her. Besides, he was beginning to reveal certain qualities that held a degree of attraction for her. He was not the merciless, uncaring and dispassionate person she had previously always thought him to be-he could occasionally demonstrate a rare sensitivity-and he certainly was handsome enough. Who could say for certain what fortune held in store for them under his proposed arrangement? It might even be possible for her to eventually change her feelings toward him and tolerate him. The prospect of remaining an empress was not without its appeal; in fact, it was quite enticing. Also to be spared the indignity that a consignment to an inferior standing among the court ladies presented was a reward in itself.

"Well?" he pressed, "Must you keep me waiting like this?"

What had she to lose by it? He promised, after all, to abrogate this obligation if she acquired another lover and, whatever else, Ahuitzotl was a man of his word. All things considered, this was the prudent thing to do.

"By thunder!" Ahuitzotl exclaimed, exasperated at her stalling. "Can it be so troublesome for you to make this decision? Will you consent to being my wife and empress?"

"Yes," she said softly, genuinely relieved over having arrived at her conclusion, "I consent."

He stood there motionless and stone-faced for what seemed an immeasurably long time to her, and then, when it appeared her answer had finally struck him, he flashed a wide smile and his brightened eyes exuded an intensely warm glow. She had never seen him gleam like that, with such captivating penetration, and felt herself being drawn irrepressibly towards those shining eyes. Her face inched closer until their lips nearly met; at the last instant she withdrew, alarmed that she actually possessed thoughts of drowning in the sweet rapture of their anticipated contact.

XIII

For a man inclined to do things on a grandiloquent scale, Ahuitzotl's wedding to Tlalalca was an uncommonly subdued affair and somewhat contrary to the prescribed rituals. He in effect decreed his own marriage and underwent a private ceremony in his palace consisting of the traditional tying together the tilmantli cloaks worn by bride and groom amid the ritualized accompaniment of chants and speeches presented by priests and kinsmen. In attendance were Cihuacoatl, Motecuhzoma, and several lords and ladies related to the families of either the monarch or Tlalalca. Also present were the palace ladies, including an unhappy Pelaxilla who undoubtedly viewed the proceedings with much discomfort.

Had it been the first wedding for both of them, there would have been notable fanfare attached to the rites with formal announcements and invitations sent to the neighboring cities, but as it was, even Tenochtitlan's residents learned about it after the event had already taken place-through an official announcement given by Cihuacoatl. Few seemed that attentive, their attitude being fairly much as Ahuitzotl had guessed; here and there could be overheard a favorable comment on his taking Tizoc's widow for himself, but overall none saw this as of any special significance. It was incumbent upon a monarch to have a wife-that this should be linked to romance was generally not considered.

Yet for Tlalalca, the entire affair was clouded with a distressing amount of embarrassment as she felt it had been willfully downplayed by Ahuitzotl to minimize his own distaste for it, and she possessed appreciable misgivings over ever having consented to it. But now too late for any regrets, she bore her resignation, maintaining a quiet dignity throughout the procession. Still, it did not portent for better tomorrows.

Ahuitzotl spent that night with Tlalalca, deeming his action proper, and she acquiesced to his demands as any dutiful wife would have, but she lamented the apparent emptiness of their conjugation and its lack of approbation. After having concluded their sexual activity, Ahuitzotl noticed her tears betrayed by a brazier's light and heard her muffled whimpering.

"Why are you crying?" he was moved to comment, sounding as if a protest. "Isn't this what you wanted?"

"I thought so when I gave my consent," she replied brokenly, "But now this-this false relationship-is tormenting me. I've always believed marriage a sacred kind of bond to be highly venerated; I feel as though I've belied my deepest convictions. I have offended Xochiquetzal."

"There's no need for your compunctions; ours is not the only marriage of convenience ever conceived. Indeed, it appears to be quite the norm among our lords."

"That's no comfort to me. I was not raised in that fashion."

"You'll get over it soon enough," Ahuitzotl assured her with assumed capriciousness, "and when you do, it will sit well with you-you may even find it to your liking."

"I suppose you're right," she wavered, wrestling with ideas so vividly contradicting the values ingrained in her since childhood. "Considering what we agreed to, I should perhaps count myself fortunate that you are here with me at all." She emitted a soft sardonic laugh as she lingered over her last words. "Imagine that," she mused, "a bride thinking herself lucky that her husband spends the wedding night with her."

Ahuitzotl thought this altogether comical and could not help snickering as he grinned. "Put that way," he said, "it does have an absurd ring to it. But we both know the conditions governing our union-you're not particularly fond of me, and I am quite enamored with Pelaxilla. When this is taken into account, it makes sense."

Tlalalca gazed at him with visible strain over his description of their conjunction and repressed a surging pain, for against all expectations, she was consumed with a yearning for him, a craving to be possessed by him, which she never dreamed as possible. This defied all her sensibilities and she faught its acceptance, telling herself repeatedly of its folly. Yet she could not deny her urges and, incredible as it seemed, she was attracted to him.

"Why do you keep saying I loathe you?" she asked. "I've never said that to you."

"It is common knowledge; others have related it often enough."

She wanted him to believe otherwise, and if she gave cause for such an impression in the past, she now regretted it and wished him to know this. "It's possible to change one's mind," she said.

"Yes, but in this case, I don't advise it," Ahuitzotl replied soberly. He became perturbed over her insinuations and was set on discouraging her from acquiring any notions about a romance blossoming out of their situation. True, he thought Tlalalca very attractive, and was not beyond believing that he could even develop an interest in her, but she could not replace Pelaxilla, and that she understood this was imperative. "It will lead to complications for you," he continued, "as well as for my relationship with Pelaxilla. She must believe that you dislike me."

This was the first night of their so-called arrangement with each other and already Tlalalca was beginning to feel envious of Pelaxilla, a realization very alarming for her as it held frightening ramifications over what it could lead to. "Some things cannot be helped," she remarked.

"Fight it!" he cautioned her. "It can only bring you sorrow."

She said nothing more and preferred having another sexual encounter with him, his overpowering masculinity intoxicating her, but she knew this was now unlikely as she had apparently dissuaded him from applying additional effort in that regard and had to content herself in passing the rest of the night merely reposed beside his warm body. Sadly, she resigned herself to the stark reality that she would enjoy only those moments he allowed her, and she was suddenly fearful that there might not be many of them.

As for Ahuitzotl, he repressed his compulsions to possess her a second time. Her revealed change in attitude towards him aroused a consternation that his calculated scheme might turn against him. He never foresaw that Tlalalca could possibly develop any degree of affection for him-the idea was so remote that he had not even considered its potentiality. Yet he wanted her, regarding her a most alluring woman, and was challenged by her resistance to him, but it had to be on his terms. He could not afford to feed fire to her passions and fuel possible romantic illusions, and so he abstained from whetting his sexual appetite in the hope this would remind Tlalalca of their arrangement. Neither of them was to have a blissful night.

The next day, Ahuitzotl was intercepted by Pelaxilla as he was on his way from his quarters to one of the frequent meetings now engaging his time. She had waited most of the morning for a chance to confront him; her seriousness bespoke of her displeasure with him, and he suspected the reasons for it.

"I assume you had a good night," she began, more than a little piqued.

"Not especially, if you must know," Ahuitzotl informed her.

"You haven't spoken to me in over a day. Is this because your wife has you so occupied that you no longer have time for me?"

"Come now, there are proprieties to maintain. Am I to shun her on our wedding night?"

"You could have said something instead of leaving me to worry that she was gaining your favor. It's not as if I'm out of your reach. I reside in this same palace, you know."

She was clearly upset, her voice denoting a frenetic nervousness in its inflection, and Ahuitzotl, who viewed her inquisition with some disdain, knew he had to alleviate her anxieties. "I'm sorry for causing you undue alarm," he said. "You are right in being angry with me, but if it's any comfort for you, I want you to spend the next few nights with me."

"Why the next few?"

"I need to emphasize a point to Tlalalca; she must understand it's you who is foremost in my heart-nothing will change that."

"Should I be flattered by that?"

"What do you mean? I say it with sincerity."

"Why must you emphasize this to her? Are my worst fears being realized-that she no longer loathes you?"

"I don't know what to make of it, but she speaks of late as though she has had a change of heart. You have no reason to worry, however; I'll do my best to discourage her from these ideas."

His words were not willingly received by Pelaxilla; she had taken solace in the knowledge that Tlalalca disliked him-the slightest hint suggesting this was not the case was threatening to her. She had always considered Tlalalca an arresting beauty and was appalled by a likelihood of having to compete with her for Ahuitzotl's attention. She could not refuse his request.

"What will you do-oust her from her own bedchamber?"

"I'll have another room prepared for us."

"Should I appear in your bedroom tonight and tell her I am here to take you to one of the adjacent chambers?"

He did not appreciate her sarcasm, feeling the strain of his predicament now implanting itself. "Why are you so caustic?" he snapped. "It's unbecoming of you."

"I'm sorry," she recanted, "I meant to illustrate the awkwardness of my situation, admittedly in poor taste."

"A servant will inform you which room we shall use," he said, ignoring her retraction. "We'll make it a permanent place for us-there will be no inconvenience for you."

Pelaxilla nodded her concurrance, but when she looked into his eyes, she keenly sensed his disappointment in her. A sudden apprehensiveness came over her, as she had given him ample reason for umbrage and now worried about having jeopardized her standing with him. "What's wrong?" she asked nervously, "Are you angry with me?"

"Dismayed is more accurate. I'm disturbed that you doubt me when I say you're the only woman for me. We've known each other for some time now. Have we ever denied our love for one another? You must pardon me if I am disheartened by your lack of trust in me. I shouldn't have to justify my activities with Tlalalca to you-it should suffice that I say I love you."

She recognized this for the admonishment it was; he succeeded in making her feel as if she had contracted to an irreversible sin, and after her initial embarrassment, she was overcome with horrible pangs of remorse and exceedingly miserable.

"I'm afraid of losing you," she replied in a trembling voice. "This leads me to say things I then regret. I ought not have such fears, but I do, in spite of your assurances."

"If you won't believe me when I say I love you, what else can I do to convince you of it? You must not doubt it."

"I'm not strong enough to accept that as readily as you are. Don't you ever dread losing my love for you?"

"It never enters my mind. I'm that certain of your love."

She questioned if such a faith was possible, and even thought he perhaps did not love her as deeply as she loved him. Or maybe his was an expression of true affection, based on trust and confidence, while hers was deceptive, not love at all but a longing to be loved. She did not understand the reasons for her affliction, but she knew her fears were real-and she feared losing him.

"The goddess Xochiquetzal has victimized me," she moaned. "I'm at the mercy of her cruel fancies."

"You will fare better if you attained a hold of these feelings yourself."

She indicated her agreement through a stream of tears now flowing from her eyes, and in her fruitless attempts to keep from crying so magnified the wretchedness of her condition that Ahuitzotl was moved to great pity.

"Dear Pelaxilla," he said caringly, "Am I the cause of such sorrow?" He placed his hand behind her neck and gently drew her into his shoulder. With his other hand he wiped the tears from her cheeks while warming her with a gleaming smile as he continued. "Never forget it's your love that is my greatest source of happiness and sustains me—nothing will ever change that. Desist in your tears, my pretty one, and be consoled by the certainty that you are the most precious to me, my only love."

She was much encouraged by his words and felt an elation reassert itself in his adoration. Her anxieties seemed suddenly lifted from her and left her exhilirated in its aftermath. In those moments when he held her close to him and soothed her with his gentle stroking and soft deep voice, she found the contentment she so ached for, and when he at last relinguished his embrace to resume the day's business, he left her overjoyed in eager anticipation of the promised evening's engagement.

XIV

Ahuitzotl met with his principal engineers and architects to discuss a project he had contemplated since even before he was appointed monarch. He had long considered the present palace built by the revered Motecuhzoma Ilhuicamina as inadequate for the kind of receptions and living quarters he envisioned for himself. Its dining facilities could not accommodate the number of guests he desired to host; the assembly hall was too cramped for the lords of adjacent cities who periodically came for council; he wanted a more spacious setting for his private gatherings and his ladies and household staff. In addition, like his renowned predecessors, he wished to leave his personal stamp on the growing metropolis. Today was his first meeting with these craftsmen in as much of the proposal was only in its initial stages of conception, and he possessed his own strong ideas about where he wanted his new palace located, to the vexation of his experts who viewed the desired area too confining for the size of structure envisioned.

"But my lord," one of the engineers advised, "It's not possible to build this palace on the north side of the Great Temple. There's not enough space if you want it to measure the dimensions you indicate. The canal restricts this."

Ahuitzotl studied the model of the layout presented to him: it depicted the central plaza with its encompassing temples and buildings matched to scale. The engineer's assessment was evident at first glance, but so also were other possibilities. "It's not the canal that restricts us," he said, "but rather your limited conceptions on how this palace should be constructed."

The chief engineer was irked over this statement; he may be the Revered Speaker, but he was no master when it came to building. "Indeed?" he reacted, "Perhaps we did not understand you. Did you propose that we should fill in the canal with earth to create the space required?"

"It's possible, isn't it?"

"Yes, but I would not recommend it. That will stagnate the waters about the palace and lead to sanitation problems, also a potential breeding ground for insects."

"Agreed, but the size of my palace will require an area north of the canal. What about the building spanning over it?"

The idea was novel, intriguing the engineers as well as the architects who gazed at one another contemplatively. "It's feasible," said the leading engineer after studying the parameters, "It would entail an immense support structure to cover the flooring over the canal, that is, if we don't place uprights into it as buttresses, but it can be done."

"I prefer that the canal be left unimpeded."

"Some sturdy crossbeams anchored into strong masonry would allow for the proper weight distribution. I assume this will be a double storied building as the present palace."

"Yes. Have your designers complete their plans on it. I want some choices so I can select one that appeals to me."

At that instant, the chief minister came rushing wildly into the chamber. Nearly breathless, having raced to get there, he startled everyone with his bold entry.

"Cihuacoatl!" exclaimed Ahuitzotl. "What is the meaning of your haste?"

"A most serious matter, Lord!" the anxious minister replied. "I must inform you of it immediately!"

In that nothing more remained for discussion with his artisans which was of significance, and obviously distracted by his minister's exhibited duress, Ahuitzotl bade them their leave. "You should not be so stressed," he said after they had gone, "Remember, it affects your constitution."

"When you hear this, it may affect yours, Lord. We have just received word that the Huaxtecs have attacked Metztitlan-allegedly to punish it for acknowledging us as overlords and to divert its tributes to themselves. They have captured our emissaries and have slain a number of our pochteca trading in the region. One of our legates, who escaped from them, has just brought us these shocking news."

Ahuitzotl was stunned into grim visage, staggered by the import of the message, and when he recovered from his amazement, he exploded in a momentary eruption that had the minister holding his breath. "He has dared!" Ahuitzotl roared. "Xaman Utec has dared to raise his hand against me! It was not enough that this upstart insulted me with his refusal to attend my coronation; now he has also committed outrages upon me by slaying my merchants."

"He is ambitious and has designs on expanding his own realm."

"He could have moved on other regions-Totoneca is ripe for plucking, although eventually he would cross me over that too. Metztitlan was ours and can have only one master. His attack is meant as a direct challenge to me-an affront both deliberate and damaging."

After his initial outburst, Ahuitzotl calmed down and paced the floor as he studied the situation and groped for the means by which to avenge the injury inflicted by his audacious Huaxtecan adversary. "This requires a bold response on our part," he continued. "No doubt by now they have consolidated the fruits of their attack and secured Metztitlan as an ally against us. We must account for this in our plans. Send out messengers to our allied lords; inform them of the nature of our recall in the most urgent terms. Fortunately, the gravity of this situation will not require lengthy explanations or pursuasion-they will see the need for speedy retaliation. Also sent word to Tlohtzin to have him and his commanders meet me here–immediately!"

Cihuacoatl quickly left the monarch and instructed his subordinates to carry out the declared requests. Within minutes, couriers were dispatched from Tenochtitlan to transfer their messages to the cities in Anahuac.

Tlohtzin arrived with his chieftains soon after having received his directive; other principals, including head priests, ministers, and numerous lords, who were also summoned. In addition, Cihuacoatl returned to control the proceedings and there was Motecuhzoma who, as the monarch's aide, was rarely absent from high level meetings in spite of his youth. Ahuitzotl wasted no time in getting to the point of the gathering; he had Cihuacoatl repeat the words reported earlier to him and then briefed them of the preliminary steps which had been implemented. He viewed this upcoming campaign as a matter of deep personal commitment, seeing the impending struggle as a duel between himself and his Huaxtecan counterpart–a battle of the powers-and impressed his own sense of urgency upon them. After informing them of the favorable omens delivered by the priests, he stressed the particulars he meant to apply towards this operation.

"Xaman Utec thinks he is secure by the distance separating Huaxteca from Anahuac," he said, "and that he has the time to prepare his defenses if indeed he believes we will come at all. Despite this obstacle, I say we can still catch him off guard if we act promptly-and do the unexpected. This means a swift deployment of our armies and a forced march, but not against Metztitlan, which he thinks is his buffer. Let him keep his appendages-we will strike at the heart-Xiuhcoac, his capital."

"Xiuhcoac!" Tlohtzin gulped. "That is nearly three hundred leagues. Yet you speak of a forced march."

"I expect it to take us two weeks. We will rely on the support of our subject states along the way so we are not unnecessarily encumbered by our own slow moving logistical units. Only by freeing ourselves of our supply chains can we proceed at that pace."

"That will not be easy."

"But we can do it-and surely surprise the Huaxtecs. After our meeting, Tlohtzin, prepare our advance parties to go to the regions we must traverse so they can arrange for our provisioning with their lords. Huaxteca is extensive, but by striking at its core, we should minimize the overall protraction of this campaign. For certain this will be the greatest operation we have conducted since the days of Axayacatl. I anticipate a total force of close to fifty thousand men-the largest we have fielded in over ten years. I have informed our allied rulers that it is my will they personally participate in this war by commanding their own armies."

Great excitement imbued the gathering, as Ahuitzotl well knew it would; men born to warriors could not be restrained from taking part in such a bold massive-scale enterprise—the mere scope of it had an enthralling aspect to it and assured its invitation. The more hardships he promised them, the more he whetted their appetites and instilled an enthusiasm for its implementation. No man better understood what truly motivated soldiers-that they clearly preferred the warlord who led them to adventure and danger over him who took the cautious route and preoccupied himself with their safety. He excelled in his judicious application of words, gestures, and, above all, a projection of unshakable confidence which contributed to their morale and zeal. Still, other concerns were raised.

"What of the feasts to Xipe Totec?" a minister queried. "This is the month we honor him?"

"So it is," answered Ahuitzotl, annoyed that this should have a priority in the minister's thinking. "You needn't concern yourself. The priests and I have worked out an acceptable means of seeing to these rites."

"Do they not require the presence of the Revered Speaker?"

"Cihuacoatl will preside over the occasion. There will be no ignoring the feast."

Having touched upon the details surrounding this venture, Ahuitzotl ended the meeting with a warning to his commanders. "Understand this," he advised. "This campaign has critical importance to me, and I expect to have Xaman Utec sitting in one of the cages standing in the square when it is over. I will not endure the kind of bickering I was besieged with on our Matlazinca operation. Impress upon your soldiers and junior commanders, as well as yourselves, that anyone who does not apply his best effort towards achieving my purpose shall be deprived of rank and office–perhaps even sold into slavery. There can be no shirking of duties on this expedition."

None dissented. The monarch was asking for nothing more than what was expected from them–the Mexica were a disciplined force and an insistence on what was deemed virtuous posed no controversy. With that, Ahuitzotl dismissed his council, instructing Motecuhzoma to go with Tlohtzin so that he might learn more about the initial phases of this kind of massive undertaking. Only Cihuacoatl remained.

"You did not tell the ministers that I would preside over the Xipe Totec rites," Cihuacoatl mentioned. "I noticed even some of his priests appeared unaware of this."

"In truth, I had forgotten about it. To their credit, they did make an issue of it; however, advise them to keep me better informed on the dates of their rituals–there are so many of them."

"Even had you known, Lord, I suspect it would have made no difference. No ceremonial duties will keep you from avenging Xaman Utec's transgressions."

"I see no need to be present in their endless affairs. You know that I revere Huitzilopochtli as much as any man, and he himself has told us that by honoring him we also see to the other gods who are his friends. Why should I personally attend each of these functions when I accomplish the same thing by seeing to him?"

"They will not accept that answer, even if it makes sense."

"They have become a large and obtrusive lot, and they all vie for the Revered Speaker to give them equal worth before the people and the deities they serve. I tell you, I often think we were better off when we had only our own gods to attend to."

"Yet publicly you espouse their claims-so you told the Cholulan lord."

"It's prudent to have them believe I hold them in high regard. I need them as my allies; much of the support I request from our subject lords is attained through their offices."

"It's practicality you speak of, and in this same context, I think it might be worth your time to learn more of the priestly craft-not just those of Huitzilopochtli's. An oversight such as you admitted did not escape the notice of the priests in question-it has not endeared them to you."

"I'll consider what you say. Still, this war should be more favorably received by them, without their being vexed over my determination to wage it. When I return, the Great Temple will be finished and we'll have the captives to honor its dedication.

"If we make the inauguration a memorable affair, it ought to satisfy even the most fanatical of them."

"I intend for it to be a grandiose event," Ahuitzotl affirmed, "but perhaps you can come up with some additional ideas. Think on it while I'm away and give me some answers when I return."

Pelaxilla had waited in the specified chamber for a considerable time, expecting Ahuitzotl's arrival long before this. Impatient at being left by herself, she was already imagining her lover having gone to Tlalalca, and it came with enormous relief that she at last heard him coming. She had removed her clothing in preparing for him and greeted him in a loving embrace with only a linen bed sheet wrapped about her, and this she let readily slip to the floor when she held him. Her welcome had the desired effect, kindling his passions to frenetic levels.

"By the gods!" he gulped. "You certainly can't be accused of wasting any time."

His hand eagerly glided along her smooth back, feeling its softness on his fingertips and delighting in passing the contours of her flesh, especially in the velvety firmness of her delicious behind. His gasping heightened; he burned in his loins, and his shaft rose to maximum size, straining in its confines. He kissed her profusely, covering every part of her face and then proceeding down to her neck and breasts; her savory peaks jutted forward as hard as rock as he enclosed his lips over one, then the other, causing her to moan in delight.

"Come," he gasped, "let us consume ourselves in this fire."

He frisked her to the multi-layered mats and gently deposited her there, and while she lay searing with erotic desire, he hurriedly slipped out of his own clothes, leaving them scattered about the floor in his haste, and pounced next to her, again resuming his caressing and kissing. He carried on this activity until she, no longer able to contain herself, clawed into his back and literally dragged him atop her as he entered her.

His urges aroused to utmost intensity, he began his motions and had her groaning in ecstatic rapture, and even after he had completed his own function, she, with a strength that astounded him, rolled him beneath her and positioned herself atop his body, all the while retaining his penetration. There she rested in her deep respiration as her moans gradually abated to mere whimpering, contented sighs. At last, fully satiated of the pleasure, she slid off him and lay beside him delighting in the wonderful sensations she had just undergone. Her satisfaction was also shared by Ahuitzotl for whom nothing compared to lovemaking with Pelaxilla as all his bodily perceptions seemed so much more intensified, every touch more pleasureable, every movement more scintillating, every response more intoxicating. He may have found his sexual encounters with Tlalalca gratifying, but they fell considerably short of the sensual highs he experienced with Pelaxilla.

"What satisfaction," he beamed. "My days would be depressingly dreary If not for our splendid way of ending them."

"I was beginning to fear you would not come," she said.

"Important business detained me."

"More important than this?" she teased.

"Certainly not," Ahuitzotl stressed between a wide grin, "but nonetheless substantial. We must take to the field again-to take on the Huaxtecs."

"The Huaxtecs? In that remote northern region?"

"Yes."

"But-but that means you'll be gone for a long time."

"Yes, perhaps two, maybe three months."

Pelaxilla made no effort to conceal her disappointment. "Is this how much my love means to you?" she moped. "That you can just decide to leave me for months without as much as a shred of regret?"

"Regret? I don't understand."

"I don't detect the slightest sorrow in you."

"What do you want me to do-burst out in a flood of tears?"

"At least that would tell me something. As it is, it doesn't seem to matter to you."

"It does, but I have my duties to perform. We've discussed this enough times; I see no point in repeating myself."

She remembered and knew how fruitless it was to confront him on it again. "When will you leave?" she asked.

"In four, perhaps five days-whenever Nezahualpilli arrives here with his Acolhuas."

"That soon?" she decried, her earlier bliss now displaced by melancholy, and as she nestled her body close to his, resting her head on his shoulders, and not uttering a sound. Ahuitzotl, typically discomfited by her quietness, deemed it useless to attempt uplifting her downcast spirit and was relieved she did not weep.

"After this war," she finally said, breaking a long silence, "will you go on another? Is this the fate of your women-to see you off from one campaign to the next?"

"There will be others," he calmly replied.

He offered no solace for her, and while she continued to deplore the situation, her eyes suddenly brightened as if she was was struck with a flash of insight. "Didn't you say that slave women and others accompany our armies on these long ventures?" she asked.

Ahuitzotl knew what she was aiming at but nevertheless answered her question. "Some serve as cooks and assist the surgeons; a few see to their masters, but yes, we have women who go with our armies-in the supply units that trail the main elements."

"And this entourage includes the mistresses of nobles?"

"True."

"So why not take me with you?" she eagerly proposed. "I could cook for you, among other things."

"Out of the question!" he emphatically rejected her notion, the tone of his reply patently uncompromising. "I object to my warriors bringing women on campaigns, even the long ones-I lead by example. What I deny them, I also deny myself."

"But you said the nobles do it."

"Not under my command. I won't have the Revered Speaker's mistresses parading themselves before hungry warriors. Ladies of nobility in particular must retain a dignity if they are to be respected. You know this well enough."

"Yes, but they say you do not abide by the conventional methods," she mentioned, even though realizing she was unlikely to dissuade him from his resolution.

"Those reports are exaggerated," Ahuitzotl informed her.

"Evidently they are."

"Are you disappointed?"

"I guess not," she sighed in resignation, accepting his answer as final, "I was grasping at wishful dreams."

He gave no comment, but continued holding her near to him and stroking his hand repeatedly along her back. Pelaxilla, however, wanted one more reply before taking her repose. "Will we spend our remaining time together?" she asked with some reluctance, fearful of another setback.

At first, Ahuitzotl was of an opinion that he should perhaps spend some of the time with Tlalalca, mindful that she also had her needs. But on further deliberation, he convinced himself it was better if he stayed away from her awhile longer, for he did not want anything to distract from his blissfulness with Pelaxilla. "Yes," he responded at length. "That's what I want."

She was overjoyed in her relief. She thought it inconceivable that he should choose to deny his wife his company before departing on an enterprise that could last for months. Truly this had to be a positive expression of his love for her.

"You mean it?" she looked for a confirmation, "You will stay with me—not with Tlalalca?"

"Yes, I want to be with you."

Her happiness was complete. She cuddled up to him in her elation wearing a broad smile that brightened her beautiful face; she giggled gleefully while she ran her fingers teasingly across his chest, over his navel, and down about his genitals. Poor Tlalalca, she thought; you may be his wife and empress, but it is I who has a claim on him.

Ahuitzotl was somewhat unsettled over her obvious euphoria; it revealed a vindictive side to Pelaxilla he adjudged as edging on a cruel callousness which manifested itself in a delight over Tlalalca's reversals and deprecation. But he soon dispelled these reservations, at least for the present, when she again aroused him with her playfulness. Immediately after her nimble fingertips made their dainty contact with his organ, he felt the blood surging into it and bringing it to a powerful erection. As he once again quivered in erotic agitation, his heart palpitating at a triple-pace, he pursued the natural outlet for his intensified state and rolled his body over hers to end the wakened period as he had begun it—enraptured in her flesh.

XVI

arly at dawn after the day Nezahualpilli and his Acolhuas, augmented by fighting units from all the eastern lake cities, had entered Tenochtitlan, the capital's own force was called to assembly by the thunder of the panheuhuetl. Its warriors stood in formation to await the arrival of their warlord while being armed and provisioned for the long journey to Huaxteca. Ahuitzotl and his Texcocan colleague emerged from the palace on their way to meet with the army when the monarch suddenly jerked to a stop.

"Have you forgotten something?" Nezahualpilli asked.

"Yes, I'll rejoin you in a moment."

He had not seen Tlalalca and considered this in poor taste. Even if not infatuated with the empress, he thought it shameful behavior to forego offering her at least his farewell; after all, there were no guarantees he would come back. After entering her chamber where she was sitting alone on cushions, he noticed a sad expression dominated her and her eyes were moist, but she said nothing and revealed no particular surprise at his coming to her.

"I regret I didn't see you as of late," he spoke first, "but that doesn't mean I did not think of you."

"You needn't apologize to me," she replied weakly. "I assumed you would spend the time with Pelaxilla. This was the arrangement we agreed upon and I must learn to cope with it."

"You don't appear to have slept well," he was moved to say, detecting her sorrow as she glanced longingly into his eyes.

"I didn't, but that should not cause you any disconsolation."

She was wrong. He may have relished his pleasures with Pelaxilla, but he certainly had no desire to see Tlalalca in sadness over this. Their affair was more complex than he had reckoned; he wished that somehow he could love them both without invoking feelings of jealousy between them but knew this was not possible. Pelaxilla's distrust compelled him to devote his attentions toward her, yet he also wanted to be with Tlalalca and was not without caring for her.

"I wish to say goodbye before leaving," Ahuitzotl said. "It probably means little to you, but there you have it."

Her mouth opened slightly as she glared wide-eyed at him; she wanted to reveal her deepest felt yearnings to him, but to what avail? She had for so long spoken ill of him, openly indicating her disdain for him, even coerced his ladylove to betray him-how could she now tell him of her aching longing for him? She could not even admit this easily to herself.

"I suppose you want me to thank you for that. I haven't seen you in five nights and you come to me just prior to embarking in a lengthy expedition to say your farewell. I'm gratified that you remember your wife."

"Let's not deceive ourselves, Tlalalca. You are my wife, to be sure, but we are not exactly a married couple to be envied. Neither of us loved the other, a condition we knew existed when we agreed to our arrangement. It's out of courtesy that I come to you, not out of sentimentality."

He lied and stood puzzled why he could not bring himself to reveal his true purpose, and his words came painfully to Tlalalca. She tried to tell herself he could not be blamed for believing as he did, even if she thought it cold-hearted of him to confess that his visit had no tender regard.

"Then out of courtesy I will tell you that I appreciate your concern for me," she slowly answered.

He was about to add something else but appeared frustrated, perhaps out of an inability to find the appropriate words; instead he turned around and proceeded for the door. Her eyes followed him across the room.

"Ahuitzotl," she said as he was stepping into the corridor.

"Yes?" he stopped, eager to hear what she wanted.

They faced each other as if able to penetrate their inner souls in search of some means by which they could free themselves from the restraints that kept them from expressing their emotions.

"I wanted to tell you..." she hesitated, not yet ready for any intimate disclosures. "May the gods protect you."

He gave her a longing glance. This was the closest she had yet come to wishing him success and he momentarily wrestled with an impulse to hold her in his arms in gratitude. Amazed, his only reaction was a nod of approval. Then he left; he never saw the tears trickling down Tlalalca's face. But whatever feelings Ahuitzotl might have had were eclipsed when he exited his palace and reviewed his magnificent warriors in their brilliant battle array facing him. Nezahualpilli had waited at the entrance and walked with him to his station among the units.

"Three armies stand before you," boasted Ahuitzotl as he gave his ally a smirk, "One left from Tlacopan yesterday. Your own leaves tomorrow. Xaman Utec will shake with fright when he sees the numbers marching against him."

"He has large armies of his own," Nezahualpilli cautioned his colleague, "and the Huaxteca are stronger than the Matlazinca-we will not easily frighten them."

Ahuitzotl disliked being contradicted, especially when he meant to inject confidence in the coterie around him. "I haven't overlooked the possibility of a strong resistance," he said to impress Nezahualpilli. "That is why we are making a forced march on them. Have you been told I intend to be at Xiuhcoac in two weeks?"

"I have, and sincerely hope our warriors will be in condition to do battle after such a strenuous pace."

"It's calculated to dispirit the enemy, and should give us the advantage when we face them."

"I'll not dispute it. You have a talent for accurately assessing these situations."

They had now reached the Revered Speaker's post, centered in front of the massed troops, where Tlohtzin met them. "Will my lord address the warriors?" he asked.

"Indeed I shall." said Ahuitzotl who favored such occasions.

A dais was brought to him and when he ascended it, the plaza resounded with the clamorous roar of twenty thousand warriors-they remembered their previous operation. Ahuitzotl raised both hands over his head and signalled the armies to quiet. He scanned across the field of color, surveying each individual squadron from one end of the square to the other, and he smiled. Then he spoke.

"My brave and worthy warriors! A mighty task lies before us! You will be asked to undergo great hardships, but you will not be alone. My chieftains and I will be with you every step of the way. The Huaxtecan lord,

Xaman Utec, has taken it upon himself to openly insult us by attacking people that we have conquered, who have conceded us their overlords, who pay us tributes, thereby challenging our authority over them. He has taken our emissaries captive and has slain our brother pochteca in defiance of all existing standards of decency-laws divinely ordained! More than that, he has hurled his contempt upon our glorious Huitzilopochtli in whose name we subjugated these people, reviling the sacred work he entrusted to us. The honor of Huitzilopochtli, and the honor of your Revered Speaker, sworn to defend him, and of our people, must be avenged. Look upon this mission as a personal quest for honor. Look to the day when the head of Xaman Utec will adorn our skull rack before the Great Temple! I will drive you hard. I will ask you to do more than your fathers have done and your grandfathers have done, but I promise you, your rewards will be great. Serve me well, brave warriors, and I will lead you to your most glorious victory. This I promise you!"

His speech, unlike any ever heard before, left the warriors spellbound, and when he stepped from the dais, such was the applause that broke loose that even the panhuehuetl could not have been heard above the deafening roar.

"Remarkable!" exclaimed Nezahualpilli, marvelling at the monarch's ability to infuse such fervor among his soldiers–yet another electrifying demonstration of their trust in his noted leadership. "At this moment, you have them totally within your grasp."

"And so I shall at Xiuhcoac." beamed Ahuitzotl. "My victory is assured."

"How can I deny it? I am seeing Xilotepec all over again."

Ahuitzotl took his station behind his Eagle knights when a dozen conch trumpets blared out: the signal for their march to commence. "I trust you'll keep pace with us," he goaded his colleague.

"Whatever your Tenocha can do, my Acolhuas can do as well; I stake my reputation on it."

"So you have-by uttering those words."

Ahuitzotl's teeth flashed behind a widened smile. He had offered his rival a challenge he knew now imposed a personal face-saving requisite for him to uphold, and he fully expected the Acolhuas to make their appearance on the agreed upon time. "Until Xiuhcoac then," Ahuitzotl cheerfully proclaimed his farewell, "in a fortnight."

Nezahualpilli nodded his assent as he stepped back to allow the marching columns their passage. In its usual colorful spectacle, battle-clad warriors proceeded singing martial tunes and chanting in rhythm to the drumbeats that guiding them from the city. In succession, first the Army of Tenochtitlan, then the Army of Tlatelolco, separated from its twin city on this campaign, and lastly a third army from elements of the southern lakeside cities under Tenocha control, left the plaza in a seemingly endless procession. Nezahualpilli kept observing them even after returning to the palace, engrossed in the exhibition, and only after a lengthy time had elapsed did he realize that Cihuacoatl stood next to him watching the parade with equal fascination.

"You look upon it in the same wonder as I," Nezahualpilli said.

"An extraordinary transformation has taken place since we chose Lord Ahuitzotl to rule us," beamed the minister with obvious pride. "A new spirit prevails over us."

"He is an exceptional leader."

"More than that. He is destined for greatness; Huitzilopochtli favors him and will grant him honors-all the signs denote this to me."

"Perhaps you are too eager for it."

"Not so, Lord Nezahualpilli. Can you not feel it? I see it in the warriors. Even the great Motecuhzoma could not have drawn such devotion from his men. These are exciting times for us-a time of promise, even glory—and to think I should live to see it."

"I do not wish to disenchant you, nor to say I have no high regard for Ahuitzotl-no ruler is more able to restore our former eminance than he. Yet there are enough times when he acts rashly rather than upon sober reflection, as is appropriate for a Revered Speaker. He does things I find alarming."

"What? I would dispute it."

"I cannot positively identify it, but there's something deceptive about his maneuverings-the way he honors the gods, even Huitzilopochtli, whom he says he reveres above the rest. He plays a devious game with them. Often I think he comes within a hair's breath of mocking them. Even the speech he just gave announced his personalized view of them."

"This is a dangerous thing you say."

"Did you feel comfortable with the numbers we offered in sacrifice at his coronation? The thousand warriors were not slain to please the gods-I know better!-but to impress and frighten our neighboring rulers. This may have been expedient, and perhaps even making for good politics as it met his aims, but it still amounted to a show of irreverence; it was not for the gods that we did this."

"You're quite wrong, Lord. He was very much concerned with pleasing them. I was with him when he planned the activities and can attest to this. You misjudge him."

This contravened what Nezahualpilli believed substantiated and he viewed the minister's words with considerable skepticism, but he knew he had to be cautious around him. He was the monarch's loyal advisor and was certain to relate any opinions, particularly those of a derogatory or threatening nature, to his master.

"Maybe you're right," Nezahualpilli eased out of his predicament. "If I erred, I will be the first to apologize. For the sake of our people, I hope such is the case."

"And if it isn't?" Cihuacoatl questioned, concerned over the Texcocan's meaning.

"I should expect that the gods will remedy the situation," answered Nezahualpilli. He detected the nervousness in which the minister reacted to his statement and deduced that he would never have asked the question unless he feared a similar possibility; it reinforced his supposition that his initial estimation was accurately based.

"We need not worry," Cihuacoatl seemed to be telling himself as well as Nezahualpilli. "Lord Ahuitzotl is favorably graced by the gods. His successes on the battlefield will affirm this. You'll agree when you see his triumphant return."

"As you say," commented Nezahualpilli as he headed for his chamber. "You know the man better than I."

Cihuacoatl appeared lost in his contemplation as Nezahualpilli disappeared behind the corridor's walls. The Texcocan's words had shaken him significantly more than he had revealed in his conversation; they carried many of his own concerns, and if others held such reservations, the matter was not altogether inconsequential. When he departed for his own quarters, the minister remained sufficiently perturbed over their brief interchange so as to suffer from another bout of indigestion.

XVII

Trampling forth under their blazoned banners, the Mexica host crossed the mountainous region north of the Toluca basin and skirted the western border of Metztitlan. True to his word, Ahuitzotl pushed his warriors to their endurance levels and covered twenty-five to thirty leagues a day over tortuous and dry terrain, but surprisingly, few complaints were voiced among them. He moved in a northwesterly direction, traversing the Panuco River plain between Metztitlan and the land of the Chichimeca, and planned to come upon Xiuhcoac from the west while Nezahualpilli was to bring his army around the eastern edge of Metztitlan and approach the enemy capital from the south. They were to converge before the city.

By the end of the fifth day, Chimalpopoca, leading his Tepaneca and western lake armies, noticed the lights of a thousand campfires glowing like a cluster of stars in the distant darkness.

"Have we sent a patrol out there to discover who it is?" he asked one of aides.

"They are already back, Lord. It is the Army of Tenochtitlan, encamped twelve leagues from here."

To Chimalpopoca's utter astonishment, Ahuitzotl had caught up with his army in spite of it having left Anahuac a day earlier. He did not have to be told of the logistical problems this presented if the armies merged before reaching their destination-they would severely strain the capabilities of the subject lords tasked to supply their provision. This meant he had to increase his rate of march and try to maintain the full twelve leagues between himself and the Revered Speaker, a prospect that filled him with chagrin.

"I assume Lord Ahuitzotl knows by now who we are," Chimalpopoca grumbled. "I know he'll send a messenger in the morning to prod us into moving faster. I thought we marched at a rapid enough pace, yet there he is!"

"He is tireless. No one could keep up with him."

"Are you blind?-his entire army just did. Send word to our commanders that we will move out before dawn tomorrow. We'll have to keep him at this distance for the rest of our trek. By thunder, I'm getting too old for this sort of thing."

He faced no respite for the remaining journey and Chimalpopoca cursed under his breath. Still that was preferable to having the Revered Speaker overtake him and reproach him for his laxity. By the time Ahuitzotl's force began breaking camp the next day, his scouts informed him that the Tepaneca army had already cleared out.

"Bear witness to this, Motecuhzoma," Ahuitzotl grinned, "The motivation invoked by a healthy rivalry. Chimalpopoca will spend the next week in such haste he'll probably shorten his arrival in Xiuhcoac by a full day."

"He fears losing face, Lord."

"Yes. But it is me he is up against–there's no disgrace in that. It must be rough on the old warrior. At any rate, what's important is that our advance will be accomplished as I estimated."

"It proved effective; that's what I will remember."

Ahuitzotl leered at his aide with a touch of annoyance; Motecuhzoma was learning fast but was too serious-minded for him, and he definitely favored a more lighthearted companion for enterprises such as this requiring a close and lengthy presence of one another. The trek was arduous enough without having to share it with someone of dour disposition who contributed nothing cheerful to its passing.

As the armies proceeded on their objective, they increased their numbers, for the subject cities traversed not only were detailed to furnish provisions, but also volunteered to add their own complements of warriors. Of particular value was a force of nearly three thousand offered by the Lord of Huachinango under his personal command. Ahuitzotl welcomed these additions because his latest reconnaissance reports now indicated that a major augmentation of the Huaxtecan army was being promoted by Xaman Utec.

"They seem eager to serve us," said Motecuhzoma, sitting with Ahuitzotl around a bonfire late into the night. "Our influence has remained stronger here than I imagined."

"That's unlikely," replied Ahuitzotl. "Their willingness to help us is prompted out of a greater fear of Huaxtecan authority than of ours."

"Why should they?"

"They live much closer to them, and Xaman Utec has expansionary visions of his own, as his attack on Metztitlan demonstrated. His next step could be directed towards subjugating these lords. Never be taken in by offers of willful cooperation-there are always ulterior purposes to these-you must be mindful of them."

In drawing closer to the lower coastal flatlands, the heat and moisture endemic to this region became more oppressive for the Mexica who had difficulty adjusting to it, especially during nights which offered no respite to the humid conditions such as they were accustomed to in Anahuac's higher uplands. Not only did the temperature make things uncomfortable, but evidence mounted that Xaman Utec was marshalling his forces for a strong stand at the capital. Village after village was inhabited only by women and children, and when these were asked on the whereabouts of their men, the answer was repeatedly the same—they had been recalled to Xiuhcoac by their ruler. The element of surprise no longer existed for the invading host.

"Xaman Utec has an effective intelligence network," Ahuitzotl grimly informed Tlohtzin. "He's learned of our plans and is moving to consolidate his position. If he concentrates all his units at Xiuhcoac, what size force will he have at his disposal?"

"His strength would equal ours-fifty thousand warriors."

Ahuitzotl drew a deep breath. The developments were discouraging and he concentrated on how he might swing the odds into his favor with the opposing powers in balance. "There's a possibility that our advance along the river has masked Nezahualpilli's southern approach," he determined. "This is the most direct route to Xiuhcoac and Xaman Utec would have posted his informants along it. If that's the case, we may yet manage to confuse him."

"It's likely if, after spotting Chimalpopoca's armies, they next sighted ours and think we adhere to our usual marching procedures. Do you suggest that we attack Xiuhcoac with our weaker force?"

"It may be necessary. Xaman Utec must believe us the total force. We shall send a messenger to Nezahualpilli explaining this to prevent him from uniting with us until we call on it. He will understand the need for this."

"But Xaman Utec will expect three separate armies to merge."

"He shall see it," affirmed Ahuitzotl. "With the Huachinangos, we have a complement of nearly five thousand additional warriors. We will bolster these with our lakeshore army under the Lord of Chalco-to have them make their appearance a day after our own arrival at Xiuhcoac. They shall be our third army. This will conform to Xaman Utec's surveillance. Once he exposes all of his force in the belief that he will defeat us, we'll call on Nezahualpilli to rescue us."

"That could be days-we'll have to hold them off until then."

"More than that," said Ahuitzotl somberly. "We must, as the aggressors, initiate the battle so Xaman Utec does not suspect a deception is taking place."

"A risky plan. Our coordination with Nezahualpilli cannot be flawed."

"True. We will have to dispatch messengers to each other at frequent intervals. We must know at all times where he is located in case we need his assistance earlier than anticipated."

Early the next morning, two couriers were selected to carry Ahuitzotl's decision to Nezahualpilli. Sworn to secrecy, their words were to be imparted on the Texcocan lord only; each was to bear the identical message but over a different route. Ahuitzotl personally briefed them, emphasizing the importance of their words, and each was made to recite the message back in its entirety so that he was assured they clearly understood it.

"The enemy must never know of the message you carry," Ahuitzotl stressed. "If you fall into their hands, you must die rather than divulge its contents."

The runners nodded their comprehension. They were no ordinary couriers, but trained Eagle knights who had full knowledge of the terrain features and routes which would lead them to Nezahualpilli, and each could be depended upon to give up his life rather than betray his Revered Speaker.

"Go then," Ahuitzotl directed, "and when I see you again, you should be giving me words from Lord Nezahualpilli."

They quickly left, running across the open field around the encampment until they disappeared into the distant forest, carrying the fortunes of their compatriots on their feet. Later, Ahuitzotl's force broke camp and began its march while leaving the lakeshore army with its complements of Huachinango and the other subject cities resting about their grounds. Now but three days from Xiuhcoac, Ahuitzotl knew that his movement would be carefully monitored by enemy patrols from this point on. However, they never spotted these through the remainder of their trek and things appeared quite normal when Ahuitzotl crossed the low-lying plain where Xiuhcoac was situated and was met by the guides Chimalpopoca had posted to steer the monarch to his location. His Tepanec ally had chosen an excellent site affording a clear line of vision over an open meadow extending toward the outer perimeter of the Huaxtecan capital.

"You did well in keeping ahead of me," Ahuitzotl cheerfully met his colleague.

"Not well enough," replied Chimalpopoca. "You gained half a day-even less-on me."

"Yet you perservered, and in this insufferable heat too."

"It wasn't easy-I speak for myself, not my warriors who will match yours on any level. I'm not as young as you."

Instinctively they diverted their attention to the distant city, glancing over its features and quietly assessing its avenues of approach and the field conditions of their future battleground.

"Have you made an estimate of Xaman Utec's capability?" asked Ahuitzotl.

"All morning we scouted the area to survey his force, both within and outside Xiuhcoac-as close as we could get. He has a large army encamped on the northern edge of the city."

"What do you think?"

"He seems confident enough. I expected him to attack us before you came, but evidently he feels he can take us on even when united. And little wonder; my guess is he has over fifty thousand warriors-an awesome opposition to say the least. Our hasty march did not appear to have surprised them any, as you probably know."

"I underestimated their use of spies. What is the composition of their forces?"

"In general, much like our own, with most of their units fighting men; however I noticed they have more archers than we do, and also more of the long spears. They are well trained and undoubtedly better adapted to fight in this miserable heat. They do not wear any body protection–I think these are too cumbersome for their climate. They look most fearsome, tall as they are, and with their noses perforated to hold large decorative inserts."

"Have you observed their battle drills, or heard of these?"

"They approach an opponent with their shielded warriors in a solid line carrying their long spears, usually six or seven rows deep, and keep a reserve in case of counterattack. It appears the archers are stationed on the flanks and used only to discourage anyone from striking their main body from there, strictly in a defensive posture as far as I can tell. We will have our hands full. They are warriors, and will not be easily daunted."

That evening, as they relaxed around a bonfire after having eaten their meals, Ahuitzotl appraised Chimalpopoca of his plan to detain Nezahualpilli until Xaman Utec was pressured into applying all his forces against the Mexica. The Tepanecan regarded it with overall favor, but expressed some insecurities over their ability to counter the Huaxtecs, particularly if they mounted a frontal attack in full strength. "If they come to know our true numbers, we will be in trouble," Chimalpopoca commented. "As long as they believe we are stronger, they will fight a defensive battle and won't wander far from their city, or attempt any bold movements."

"We can maintain our deception by a show of aggression and by taking the initiative," said Ahuitzotl. "What worries me more is their archers protecting the flanks-that's where I wanted Nezahualpilli to strike. Be wary of them. We must neutralize them somehow."

"How do you propose to do that?"

"I'm not certain-yet! But it will come to me."

"Let it be before you call for him; I should hate to see his anger if he comes upon a hail of arrows."

Late into the night, after the other chieftains had retired, Ahuitzotl still sat about the fire groping for the answer which remained elusive to him. In spite of his temporary failure to see a solution, he retained a confidence that it would eventually come to his mind if he wrestled with it long enough.

XVIII

Three days elapsed before the Mexica armies stood ready to commence their hostilities. Although their third component under the lord of Chalco arrived two days ago, Ahuitzotl adjudged it prudent to grant them a full day's rest before going into a battle he believed would be rigorously faught and disdained in sending enervated soldiers to fight it.

The Huaxtecs were assembled on the plain ahead of Xiuhcoac, appearing awesome and overpowering with their densely packed lines of shielded warriors holding up their long pointed spears. They had sallied forth from their city in obvious elation, singing martial tunes and whooping noisily, and the orderly fashion in which they gathered themselves suggested to Ahuitzotl that he faced a highly regimented and disciplined adversary. Everything was set; the priests had concluded their divinations and were only waiting for the flames of their sacred fires to extinguish so they could proceed scattering the embers; the messengers sent to Nezahualpilli had returned and informed Ahuitzotl where the Acolhuacan army was halted, the Texcocan signifying his understanding of the plan. Ahuitzotl had by now devised a scheme to minimize his numerical disadvantage. Eagerness to engage in combat prevailed among both forces.

Earlier, Ahuitzotl sent his emissaries into the city to give Xaman Utec the customary appeal to capitulate, thereby saving Xiuhcoac and its inhabitants from unnecessary destruction. He told them to be extremely forthright in their demands and to make a dramatic display of his ability to destroy it. This they accomplished in their typical fashion, following the pleas to surrender with threatening verbage, and as he expected, they returned with word that the ruler was resolved to fight, deeming their entreaties as laughable. He then sent his spokesman back to request a meeting with Xaman Utec; he preferred seeing his antagonists face-to-face in order to assess their character and will to oppose him. Xaman Utec agreed, but only if he and Ahuitzotl met at a point halfway between the armies with only the chief commanders accompanying them. Ahuitzotl consented to this and presently waited for his opponent to appear from amid his rows of warriors. Tlohtzin was standing beside him, having been instructed to participate in the conference.

"He's taking his time," Tlohtzin said, revealing a rare impatience. "Perhaps he's changed his mind."

"He will come," replied Ahuitzotl confidently. "He and his commander will want to make a personal estimate of our strength."

"I don't like it. They will guess it and learn they have little to fear. This meeting can only serve their advantage; I see no benefit in it for us."

"Not so. We can also survey his army at a closer range. I want you to scan over their units, particularly where they have positioned their archers."

"Do you think they would try the same trick you plan to pull on them?"

"No. Don't worry-they won't see the archers we've set directly behind our front ranks. They will think them as part of the complement of warriors making up our forward wall."

"I hope so. It's an unusal plan you have come upon; nobody has ever heard of anything like it before."

"We have to negate the shock effect of their long spears. They wear no protection and their shields are not large enough to cover their entire bodies. We shall do great damage by this ruse."

At that instant, two figures emerged from the Huaxtecan formations and proceeded toward the Mexica. "There he is!" exclaimed Ahuitzotl. "Let's see what sort of man this Xaman Utec is."

While both parties neared, the two monarchs eyed each other continuously as if they could make a determination of their abilities from the manner of their appearance or gait, and when they finally stood face apart, Ahuitzotl found his rival to be a most puzzling individual.

There was nothing distinguishable about Xaman Utec to Ahuitzotl. He was of small stature, not even average height for the Huaxtecs, but nonetheless sturdily composed and had a disproportionately large and broad head; his nose was aquiline and somewhat oversized, and his eyes seemed wider apart than might have been considered normal; he had narrow lips and a massive jaw which jutted out with noticeable prominence. He was plainly dressed and, like Ahuitzotl, wore little in the way of adornments.

He possessed none of the natural dignity or commanding presence that had so characterized Zozoltin of Toluca, thought Ahuitzotl. How could it be that this rather homely individual could inspire his nation to take on the Mexica?

Ahuitzotl noticed the Huaxtecan commander glaring through his narrow-slit eyes over the Mexica positions, but his own eyes came repeatedly back to that slight man who called himself the lord of Huaxteca. It seemed an absurdity that this should be the ruler to oppose him–the sheer slightness of the man was enough to disincline anyone into following him. The more he dwelled on this, the more repugnant became the whole idea, and he found himself despising the Huaxtecan for his unmitigated insolence.

"You wanted to speak," Xaman Utec's deep voice rang out, accenting his unfamiliarity with the Nahuatl tongue. "I am prepared to hear what you have to say."

Once he spoke, Ahuitzotl gained a different perspective of his adversary; he uttered his words with such an aura of assuredness that it now was at least comprehensible how it might have been possible for this outrageous figure to acquire the adherancy he obviously attained from his subjects.

"You have rejected my attempts to deal mercifully with you," Ahuitzotl told Xaman Utec, "and it's evident you are not interested in having us treat you with clemency. How is it you regard our threat so lightly?"

"When one does not fear the Mexica, there is no difficulty in dismissing your bombasting; we feel no compulsion to comply with your demands."

The answer offended Ahuitzotl and he made no effort to hide this behind a mask of diplomacy; his lips tightened and he evinced a frown bespeaking of his irritation. "Many lords have said the same thing and came to regret it," he scowled. "It might have benefited you to learn from their mistakes."

"They were weak-we are strong. Had they had the Huaxtecs to protect them, they would never have come to regret their words."

"Your faith in the strength of your warriors is admirable, but falsely based; they will not be able to stand against us. I called on this meeting to offer you one more chance to reconsider and redeem yourself, so you will not doom your people for the sake of your foolish pride. I suggest you accept this alternative."

Xaman Utec burst out in a long contemptible laugh, to Ahuitzotl's extreme vexation. He then spat on the ground to further demonstrate his low regard for the Revered speaker's warning. "This is what I think of your offer, Mexicatl," he sneered.

Ahuitzotl seethed; never before had he been addressed with such surliness-and it came from a king! Xaman Utec's conduct amounted to a serious breach of etiquette, especially of the courtly behavior regulating the affairs of nobles, and Ahuitzotl raged beneath his affected composure. At first, he thought his antagonist had perhaps planned a similar type ruse he devised for the Huaxtecs and that this afforded him the security to dispense with proper courtesy-he deemed the Huaxtecan's offensiveness that incredulous-but after scrutinizing his enemy's lines, he saw no evidence of it, and this rendered Xaman Utec's impudence even more annoying.

"I did not offer this to have you scoff at me," Ahuitzotl declared, "but by your actions you have made your contempt obvious. Now I promise you this: before we leave your city in ruins and enslave your people, for that we will surely do, you will pray to your gods a thousand times for having offended me like this. Know also that when you are taken captive, as you surely will, you will not be honored by a dignified sacrificial death. I will reserve a special fate for you which will afford you endless opportunity to regret this moment in which you insulted me."

"Hah!" Xaman Utec snarled. "I came out here because I believed you had something important to say; instead I hear you babbling the same nonsense that your idiot emissaries confronted me with earlier. I have wasted my time. You can threaten me all day with your wagging tongue, but I will let my warriors speak with their clubs and spears."

"By Huitzilopochtli!" Ahuitzotl fumed, "I shall teach you some humility."

"Do that!-if you can! But when the scattered remnants of your defeated army return to your city, if they manage to escape us, remember that it was I, Xaman Utec, who did this to you, and do not stand in the way of my ambitions again."

Ahuitzotl glanced at Tlohtzin in absolute amazement–his commander was equally stunned-and before he could recover from his astonishment, Xaman Utec and his captain turned about and headed back to their lines, and only after they had gone several paces did it dawn on Ahuitzotl that their conference was abruptly ended.

"He is demented!" Ahuitzotl concluded. "Have you ever seen the like? The man has no grip on reality."

"It had to be ploy," replied Tlohtzin. "He meant to frighten us with his brazen display."

"He would be more convincing were he less of a runt. Has he some trick in store for us? Did you notice anything unusual in the placement of his squadrons?"

"Nothing we did not expect. He appears to stake his hopes in those long spears."

"He'll soon learn of his foolishness. Still, we must be prepared for any unanticipated moves. Have all our chieftains been briefed on what to do?"

"They have, Lord. Your plan will be faithfully executed."

"Then we're ready for him. He will regret having crossed me."

By the time Ahuitzotl and Tlohtzin had returned to take up their battle stations, the fires had gone out and priests were solemnly moving up and down the field delivering their chants and dispersing the embers. This completed, Ahuitzotl then motioned for the leading priest to sound the attack. The drone from his conch trumpet blared sonorously over the wide plain, followed instantly by the rhythmic pounding of deep-toned drums. A series of repeated commands burst over the clamor, heard from one end of the field to the other. Responding to the orders, the Mexica lines advanced.

Opposite them, before Xiuhcoac, fervid Huaxtecs lifted their shields and spears high over their heads, shouting out their readiness to engage the foe. When their own trumpets sounded out the battle cry, they initiated a charge, keeping their rows so even that they ran up as a solid wall of forward thrusted spears cropping ahead between connected shields. Then, when the adversaries were only a hundred yards apart, the front row of Mexica warriors suddenly dropped to their knees and exposed three lines of archers ready to fire. The first order released its missiles, followed immediately by the second, and then the third, so that one continuous flight of deadly arrows descended as a dark cloud upon the shocked Huaxtecs.

Horrid screams resounded everywhere as the darts pierced Huaxtecan eyes, necks, and chests. Those warriors who managed to cover their heads and upper torso with their shields after spotting the initial flight coming were struck in the thighs and groins by succeeding volleys. With blood gushing from their terrible wounds, the first row of warriors uniformly crashed to the ground dead or wounded and slowed the advance of the next ranks which had to sidestep or climb over their bodies. These were then likewise struck down by succeeding volleys coming so thickly that they nearly blocked out the sun. Confusion predominated as combatants by the hundreds fell incapacitated, collapsing in gruesome heaps and opening wide fractures amid their ranks as units tried to maneuver around them.

Ahuitzotl, quick to notice the disorder, called out for the warriors who knelt ahead of the archers to resume their attack. "Strike there!" he shouted, "Where the line is broken, and divide their force!"

His squadrons reacted in an instant, charging furiously toward the gap, but Xaman Utec, alert to the danger, at once directed one of his flanking units to bolster it. What should have dealt a decisive blow against the Huaxtecs instead turned into a ferocious slugging match as units collided head-on with warrior crashing upon warrior. The Mexica maquauhuitl was parried by Huextecan stone clubs, shield smashed into shield: spears were thrust fiercely into the massed concentrations of embattled soldiers causing great damage as many fell screaming when gored by the hard obsidian tips, cupping their hands over gaping holes to hold back the pouring of red blood. More warriors were ordered into the conflagration as squadrons relieved each other and rear elements were sent forward to augment the front-line units, but neither side gave way.

Ahuitzotl stood in the thick of the fighting, accompanying his Eagle knights, and tried to rally his heavily engaged warriors into breaking the resistance and forcing a penetration. He and Motecuhzoma, ever at his side, wielded their maquauhuitl with brutal efficiency and cut down any attackers standing in their way. They hacked relentlessly at the onrushing Huaxtecs, skillfully dodging their sword thrusts and jabbing spears, and smashed their skulls open when they failed to recover from their lunges. But their lines held. In spite of fresher units brought into the melee and the ferocity of enraged warriors slicing and cutting their opponents under, the Mexica were unable to forge a spearhead through the constantly reinforced enemy lines. Xaman Utec had capably recovered from his initial setback and was now holding his own against them.

All day the battle raged, and while Ahuitzotl concentrated his major effort in the unsuccessful attack on the enemy's center, Chimalpopoca led his Tepanecs and auxiliary elements on the right and was similarly bogged down in vicious man-to-man combat. Shortly after noon, however, he broke through the main line that stood against him and led his squadrons in a furious assault on his opponent's left flank which began to falter under the incessant pressure applied to it. In his eagerness to gain a tactical advantage on the field, he forgot the warnings Ahuitzotl had given him about the enemy archers positioned to guard against any envelopment and ran headlong into them just as they fired their arrows into his ranks.

In a stunning reversal of events, it now chanced for the Tepanecs to fall under a rain of thousand missiles released by hundreds of bowmen. On seeing his leading warriors collapse, Chimalpopoca belatedly remembered the words of the Revered Speaker but for an instant was too severely shaken to countermand his previous order.

"Fall back!" Chimalpopoca shouted frantically after regaining his senses. "Withdraw from the trap! We must regroup!"

By the time his commanders could execute the order, nearly a thousand Tepanec warriors lay wounded or dying in pools of their own blood. In extreme bitterness, Chimalpopoca paid the price of his oversight and he wept tears of frustration and anguish at the horror of seeing his magnificent tigers fallen before him. "I have lost my finest warriors!" he cried out. "Cruel gods! How will I replace them?"

Throughout this carnage, priests from both sides busied themselves snatching up those soldiers who had been dragged behind the fighting lines into their ravenous arms and speedily flung them upon the nearest stone that could serve as an altar and cut out their hearts. In their blood-soaked hands they held these to the sun as they shouted out exhortations which would dispose the gods into granting them victory. As the battle hung in balance, more and more captives were sent to carry messages imploring the gods to declare in their favor. This pursuit attained frenetic proportions when neither army was able to make inroads leading to a breakthrough, and many priests openly expressed their worry that the gods may have abandoned them.

By late afternoon, the struggle remained deadlocked and warriors on both sides wearied at battling for so long when trumpets emanated forth from the Huaxtecan section and their soldiers moved to disengage themselves. They fell slowly back as a sign to the Mexica that they wished the fighting ceased for today. Ahuitzotl welcomed the call. "Sound a cessation of hostility!" he directed. "We need a respite so we can tend to our wounded."

With a swiftness unusual in dislodging combatants from their endeavors, the antagonists separated themselves in exhaustion and retired to their unit standards. Soon an eerie silence permeated the battlefield with only the painful moaning of the injured and dying left to be heard. Xaman Utec paced to the forefront of his retreating squadrons and spotted Ahuitzotl opposite him ahead of his own units.

"Let us consider today's battle a draw," the Huaxtecan lord yelled to his counterpart. "If this is acceptable to you, return your army to your camp and I will send mine into our city."

"I consent to this," Ahuitzotl shouted back. "Allow our medical teams to gather up our wounded and dead. We will accord the same sanctions to yours."

"Agreed. What of the captives we have taken?"

"They must remain as such, yours as well as ours."

"So be it. Today's battle is ended."

With that, both armies returned to their respective camps and the rest of the day was spent combing the field for survivors and in gathering up the dead. Not until then did Ahuitzotl learn of Chimalpopoca's folly, and he was not at all pleased. "I told you of it," he roared, "and it was of no avail! You call yourself a commander?"

"Do not upbraid me as if I were a mere schoolboy!" Chimalpopoca snapped back angrily. "The loss was grievous to me, and I am heartsick over it. I do not need this further injury."

Ahuitzotl paused; he saw his ally in such an awful state of dejection that he decided it served no useful purpose to persist in censuring him. "How many did you lose?" he asked sympathetically.

"Nearly eight hundred dead, and over two thousand wounded, perhaps five to six hundred captive. We haven't accounted for all of them yet."

"I've lost more than that in the center-this has not been a good day for us. Xaman Utec is abler than I had believed. We must take this into account from now on."

After darkness settled on them, Ahuitzotl received the final figure on his losses. The first day's battle cost him close to two thousand dead and five thousand wounded, with another thousand lost as captives-a frightening beginning-but the number of Huaxtecan casualties, as reported by his medical teams, was far greater, with four thousand in dead alone. Ahuitzotl knew he had inflicted painful injury on his opponent, and while the Huaxtecs had all their forces committed in the struggle, he still retained a large army in waiting. He sensed an assuredness that victory would come to the Mexica, but it was not going to come as easily as he had estimated.

Later that night, Ahuitzotl reviewed the battle plan with his commanders, retracing the day's events in order to ascertain where things went awry.

"The use of our archers worked well," said Tlohtzin. "They sustained most of their losses in that initial encounter, yet they closed the gaps in their lines before our warriors reached them."

"They drew units from their left flank to accomplish this," Ahuitzotl informed them. "Xaman Utec knows how to wage a battle. He won't fall for the same trap twice. I suspect tomorrow's contest will be fought more cautiously, with many of his units held back to see what develops. He may devise a trick of his own."

"Will you commit the Acolhuas?"

"Only if the opportunity presents itself. We'll probe his stronger lines tomorrow, not to penetrate them, but to learn how he maneuvers his squadrons in providing a back-up defense."

Ahuitzotl terminated the meeting when the chief priest told him that that the funeral rites were about to begin. A most solemn occasion, this observance required that the lords give it its proper distinction. Accordingly, Ahuitzotl and his chieftains walked to the encampment's outer edge where thousands of warriors had gathered to sing mournful dirges around several huge pyres upon which the dead had been stacked. He took his post before one of the mounds; Chimalpopoca took another; Tlohtzin a third, with various lords at each of the others. Twelve Huaxtec prisoners were lined up adjacent to each pyre awaiting their deaths as offerings to their captor's gods. After the orisons had been delivered, the priests grabbed them one by one, stretched them over improvised altar-stones, and held them down while the lords cut out their hearts. Their bodies were then placed atop the mounds alongside those of the slain comrades. Next, amid continuous chanting and singing, the pyres were ignited, and soon their brilliant blaze lightened the surrounding spectators in reddish hues as the corpses were consumed amid the sizzling and crackling combustion.

Much later, when the fires were reduced to smoldering embers and darkness once again encroached on the field, the Mexica could see a glow emanating from beyond the shadowed outlines of buildings in Xiuhcoac. It came from the pyres of the Huaxtecs who were burning their own dead in the city's square, and as Ahuitzotl and his officers ambled back to their command post, they heard the low base-like drones of a thousand Huaxtecan voices weeping and singing out a final tribute to their fallen-an unearthly sequel to a day marked by extreme and brutal violence. Thus came to a close the opening round of their battle: the gods had called many into paradise.

XIX

The conflict began later than usual on the following morning with both antagonists confronting themselves in a verbal standoff for most of the early hours as if attempting to frighten each other from the field through excessive shouting and shield rattling. Neither side showed an inclination to initiate any action, distrusting the other's intentions, until Ahuitzotl, finally tiring of the exposition, ordered numerous squadrons into a concentrated drive against the enemy center, an attack designed to reveal Xaman Utec's countermeasures as keen eyes scanned his units on what they would do.

The assault was mounted by tightly closed units, too heavily massed for the extended Huaxtecan lines to hold, and when they pressed ahead holding this advantage, other squadrons advanced along both flanks to create an impression that the entire Mexica army was attacking simultaneously. Ahuitzotl, Tlohtzin, and Motecuhzoma watched the action from an elevated platform a few hundred paces away.

"He does not move out to meet our advance," Ahuitzotl noted. "He's being cautious and taking a defensive posture."

"We must have stung him badly yesterday," concluded Tlohtzin.

"Look!" declared Motecuhzoma, "He's maneuvering some of his units."

Their eyes strained to make out what was happening. Xaman Utec was providing reinforcements by taking away units from his left flank and moving them in to shore up his weakened center under a belief that a major attack was being precipitated against it.

"He makes the same move as yesterday," observed Ahuitzotl. "It appears to be a well-rehearsed deployment. I suspect he calls on the same units every time."

"Just what I was thinking," said Tlohtzin, "Presumedly he has squadrons designated on his right to react in the same way."

Ahuitzotl remained absorbed in the battle developments that unfolded before him. His attacking force was now heavily engaged in the center; it cut a swath through the front line of defenders as expected, but then was brought to a halt by the reinforcements Xaman Utec had drawn from his lateral position. During that same time, the Mexica right under Chimalpopoca once more broke through its opposition; however, this time he did not pursue the retreating enemy to fall prey to Xaman Utec's archers and instead sharply turned inward to relieve the embattled center. His unexpected move revealed an interesting feature to Ahuitzotl.

"Do you see this?" he said to Tlohtzin. "The archers stay in their position even though Chimalpopoca threatens their center."

"They are leery of another attack on the flank."

"I don't think so. I believe they have but one function relegated to them–to protect the flanks. They will not deviate from this assignment. Look now. Xaman Utec is moving up his reserves to augment his center in order to counter Chimalpopoca. He calls on them rather than moving his archers."

"Perhaps his archers are not capable of engaging warriors in a man-to-man confrontation–they may be inadequately trained."

"Also insufficiently armed. They have little protection, carrying no shields or clubs. I have a plan for tomorrow; as for the present, recall our forces. I've seen enough."

The call for a general withdrawal came as a source of extreme irritation to Chimalpopoca who believed his Tepaneca were making notable headway against the enemy center. "Lord Ahuitzotl trifles with me!" he decried bitterly and then ordered his reluctant warriors to fall back.

Extricating his units from the fighting without giving the enemy an impression that it was winning the battle required a delicate operation, and it gave Chimalpopoca some anxious moments as he ordered his retreat. But when he looked behind him, he saw that Ahuitzotl had sent out his archers to lay down a protective fire as discouragement for any pursuit by the Huaxtecs. At first angry, and now grateful, Chimalpopoca hastily accomplished his withdrawal.

Xaman Utec suspected another trap and refrained his Huaxtecs from chasing the retreating Mexica, and when he noticed the archers Ahuitzotl had stationed behind the retiring force, he congratulated himself for having made the correct assessment. He next regrouped his cohorts in anticipation of a counterattack and kept these at their stations until evening when he finally accepted there would be no more assaults. At dusk he at last ordered his army into the city while maintaining a rotating guard force on duty to keep watch on the foe Even though the battle lasted only an afternoon, it concluded nonetheless as another costly encounter with the Mexica losing over two thousand in dead and wounded, but again the Huaxtec losses were counted as higher. Each side was now accumulating a large number of captives whose containment required a sizable commitment of warriors; more could have been offered in sacrifice for this night's funeral rite, but Ahuitzotl limited them to twenty, considering this quantity adequate in relation to the proportion slain. As for the Mexica prisoners taken by the enemy, he could only guess on how many of them served the Huaxtecan gods. This was an honorable fate for captives and there was no reason to lament it-to be in the presence of the gods in paradise was reward enough, and the living may have envied them.

Ahuitzotl held his usual evening meeting with the chieftains and went over his plans for the succeeding day, informing them of his observations on Xaman Utec's moves during the battle and how he meant to put the Huaxtecan to the test once again. He covered in detail how he hoped to accomplish this, indicating individual unit deployments and objectives, and when the conference was over, every commander had a clear conception of what was to transpire. By all indications, morale was still markedly high with optimism prevailing among these veterans. Their consensus was that Xiuhcoac's fall was inevitable-the only question was when.

Shortly after sunrise, trumpets once more resounded to call the warriors into their battle configuration. This time Ahuitzotl positioned his archers on the right behind the leading Tepanecan squadrons; he sought to use them in an all-out endeavor at crushing the Huaxtecan left. He massed his center with his Tenochtitlan and Tlatelolco armies while the lakeshore army with its allied contingent constituted his left wing. He would attack on a broad front as on the previous days, but in addition, he planned to divert a large section of his central component against the enemy's left to reinforce Chimalpopoca. He chose to lead this attack personally.

Xaman Utec, who must have now worried about the losses he sustained and could not replace, brought his squadrons into their typical formation, also along a wide front, but concentrated mostly on the center. Twice he had been caught off guard by Mexica maneuverings-the first time by Ahuitzotl's hidden archers when he initiated his opening assault, and then again yesterday by Chimalpopoca's unanticipated turn upon his midsection-and by the time he had recovered from both, he endured horrible costs. He sensed that his own losses greatly exceeded the enemy's and had to take precautions over how he deployed his units to prevent any repeated setbacks, and when he saw Ahuitzotl's densely assembled interior, he knew he had correctly deduced that a major thrust would be exerted from there. He instructed his commanders to expect such an assault and alerted his flanking units to be prepared to reinforce the center.

All stood in readiness when Ahuitzotl ordered the attack to commence. Blaring trumpets echoed across the multitude and with an outburst of unbridled cheers, the Mexica warriors moved forward, first slowly, then faster, and finally at full speed, advancing uniformly along the whole front so that all units made contact together in one horrific clash of weapons and impacting shields. The point of decision at present was the center where the bulk of the forces converged and there the fighting was the fiercest. Ahuitzotl, amid his Eagle knights, hacked a path into the unyielding Huaxtecan line, bringing down one soldier after another while listening for a trumpet call from Chimalpopoca-the predetermined signal to diverge on Xaman Utec's left.

Chimalpopoca attacked with his usual aggressiveness behind the strength of his Jaguar squadrons and, after facing some early strong resistance, began to penetrate his opponent's ranks. Xaman Utec's bowmen foresaw another field day as they recognized a repetition of the first day's battle evolving ahead of them.

"Now!" Chimalpopoca shouted to his commanders, "Fall back to expose our archers!"

Ensuing orders brought the Tepanecs to a halt; they stepped to the rear of numerous squadrons of archers who had assembled in full readiness to fire. The Huaxtecs had just enough time to be shocked when a shower of deadly arrows descended unerringly upon them. Screams arose as their ranks were struck, and before they were able to return a volley, most of their lot had fallen in gory heaps. Men writhed in agony, coughing and spitting up blood, their unprotected bodies resembling pincushions from the many penetrating missiles; their painful cries sickened comrades who were trying to scatter the Mexica with their own firing.

"Sound the trumpet!" Chimalpopoca shouted to his priest.

A conch shell blared forth its familiar drone, and Ahuitzotl immediately reacted. "We have our call!" he declared. "Move against their left!"

Word quickly reached the chieftains whose squadrons had been designated to carry this assault; almost instantaneously, a wave of warriors rushed madly toward the enemy's flank, urged ahead by the shouts of their monarch. Stunned, the Huaxtecans comprising the left wing hastily huddled together to make a bold stand to counter the raging Mexica hordes swarming at them. In an instant, the forces collided; weapons lunged fiercely at moving bodies, ripping soft flesh, and powerfully wielded warclubs crashed down on exposed skulls, splitting them open with cold efficiency. They were beaten down where they stood, falling under trampling feet, unable to hold off their attackers.

Xaman Utec's archers turned to fire on Ahuitzotl's advancing corps, only to discover themselves assailed from two sides as Chimalpopoca had rallied his Jaguars to resume the frontal assault. Wedged between Ahuitzotl's attack on the right, Chimalpopoca's on the left and front, and with their own cumbersome reserves on their rear, there was no place to run. Unprotected by body wear or any shields, and poorly equipped with arms, they nevertheless pounced on their rapacious assailants out of desperation and sought to down them their clawing hands. Swift strokes of the maquauhuitl left them mutilated, incapacitated to stop the lifeblood from gushing out of their hacked-off limbs. Hemmed in by their own reserve units moving up to counter the Mexica drive and incapable of countering their attackers, the archers suffered appalling losses. As a last resort, they dropped their bows, declaring their intent to yield, but Ahuitzotl did not have the time to set about taking them captive, for the reservists now initiated contact with him. Although no seasoned warriors, they compensated for their lack of training by their sheer numbers, coming in the thousands, and suddenly Ahuitzotl and Chimalpopoca found themselves in a dire situation.

"We're not enough for them," Chimalpopoca yelled at Ahuitzotl who had fought his way to the Tepanecan's position. "We have badly hurt them—there's no disgrace in retiring now."

"Not yet!" Ahuitzotl shouted back. "They're amateurs-we can do greater damage if we stay awhile longer."

But Xaman Utec was not about to let his left flank fall to pieces, and if he was shocked at first when he saw Ahuitzotl's assault against it, he quickly recovered and directed elements from his center to come to the assistance of his beleaguered wing. Within minutes, Ahuitzotl was met with veteran squadrons advancing on him; he turned his units toward them, leaving Chimalpopoca to hold the reserves at bay, and they collided in a sickening crunch of arms.

Ahuitzotl sidestepped a Huaxtecan soldier who had charged up to him and swung his maquauhuitl into the back of the assailant's neck, nearly cutting off his head. Just then, a stone flung by a slinger glanced off the monarch's shield and struck his helmet with such force that it crushed the wooden layers of its rim. He felt as if hit by a sledge; his head reeled in throbbing pain and dizziness came over him. He fell, shocking Motecuhzoma who had just slain another enemy warrior.

"The Revered Speaker is struck down!" Motecuhzoma shouted in alarm. "We must carry him to safety!"

Ahuitzotl could see Motecuhzoma standing over him through the blackouts that came and went as he lay nauseous on the ground; his aide evaded a blow from an opponent and smashed the soldier's skull with his club. More ran at him; he struck down a second one, and then a third, and when he was about to be overwhelmed by several more, a tall and powerful warrior leaped to his side and together they held their adversaries at bay. They killed one attacker after another, deftly avoiding their blows and striking them dead as they tried to recover themselves.

Still more of them attacked. The tall warrior slew the first one to reach him with such a heavy blow of his club that it crashed through shield and helmet and the soldier fell with his brains and blood oozing down his sightless face. He then dodged a second soldier and imbedded the obsidian blades of his maquauhuitl into his back, severing the spinal cord. He killed a third, and a fourth, and the next group of warriors halted in hesitation over what they should do. They rushed at him all at once; he killed two more and then cried out in pain as a spear was thrust into his side, cutting a gaping hole in his ribcage. The blood spewed forth, and he staggered as he weakened from his vital fluids pouring out of his body, yet he swung his club once again and crushed the skull of the soldier who skewered him. Then a second spear gored his chest, and blood spurted from his mouth as he coughed and choked on it. His eyes rolled back in their sockets and he collapsed to the ground; he was dead before he crashed upon it.

By this time, a number of Eagle knights surrounded the fallen Ahuitzotl and formed a tight bodyguard about him as he was being lifted into a stretcher and carried from the field. Despite his faintness and blackouts, he had seen everything and thought of the warrior who so heroically defended him. "Who was he?" he asked Motecuhzoma in a slurred speech.

"The man you spared from the battle stone," came the reply, "Nopaltizin, of Xilotepec."

He knew him in an instant and marvelled at the workings of the gods who turned his one time antagonist into his protector. Now seized with such pain that he felt his head would split open; he glanced up at the warriors carrying him away, seeing their worried expressions, and then everything went black.

When he next opened his eyes, he saw it was night and that he was lying on a cot beside the campfire with a ring of lords and chieftains around him. Broad smiles appeared on their faces when they saw their master had regained consciousness. Chimalpopoca and Motecuhzoma were closest to him, kneeling directly in front him, while Tlohtzin stood directly behind them; all exuded heartfelt relief that he was well.

"How long have I been here?" Ahuitzotl asked, his tongue heavy in a mouth that felt dry.

"Since late afternoon," Chimalpopoca answered, nearly delirious in his happiness. "It's now close to midnight."

Ahuitzotl still experienced a dull throbbing in his head that seemed to come and go at intervals, but they were now less intense and he recalled the earlier events.

"The Xilotepecan, Nopaltzin; what became of him?"

"He was burned on a pyre earlier this evening. We rendered him many prayers, and honored his departure with several captives."

Ahuitzotl gave out a long sigh; he would have wished to speak to him before he entered paradise-to acknowledge his gratitude.

"And the battle?"

"We retreated after you were carried from the field, but we inflicted a horrible toll on the Huaxtecs-a devastating defeat for them. Your plan proved very effective; we estimate that we destroyed or captured nearly a quarter of their entire force."

"That many? Then we have indeed done well. I don't suppose Xaman Utec has decided to surrender?"

"He won't now that he thinks you dead. It has given him encouragement that we might leave."

"We shall have to surprise him again," Ahuitzotl smiled, to the delight of his chieftains. He was feeling the pain less frequently and, after being administered a medicated drink, sensed his full vigor returning to him. "What of our own losses?" he asked.

"Three thousand five hundred, including twelve hundred dead; by any measure, today was a major victory for us."

"If Xaman Utec has lost as many as you say, there's no need to keep Nezahualpilli waiting any longer. His appearance will totally demoralize the Huaxtecs, perhaps even induce Xaman Utec into conceding defeat."

After messengers were briefed and sent on their way to connect with the Acolhuas, Ahuitzotl was informed on how the day's events had deeply impacted on the disposition of his warriors. Their morale was at a low ebb, believing their warlord was seriously wounded or dead, so when Ahuitzotl began making his rounds to their unit campfires for visitations, and the word spread that he would lead them in tomorrow's action, a transformation ensued nothing short of miraculous. In an immense outpouring of emotion, a great jubilation arose and resounded into the night far beyond the confines of their camp.

XX

Xaman Utec placed his force back in line facing its opponents the next morning. No longer confident of victory, he had his defenses propped up along the city's edge by his reserve complements which erected barriers of stone walls and picket fences, and other fortifications. He lived in the hope that Ahuitzotl met his death in yesterday's battle, but this was shattered when reports reached him that the Revered Speaker was preparing himself for the fight. His heart sank; somehow he suspected it when he heard all the commotion coming from the enemy's encampment last night, but until this moment wanted desperately to believe otherwise. Although set for the attack, he was puzzled why it had not yet been initiated; the Mexica stood opposite him but did not advance-surely they did not expect his Huaxtecs to open the hostilities. He strode atop a platform he had ordered built directly behind his strong center and nervously surveyed his enemy's lines, mystified by its inactivity and trying to surmise the cause of it.

By midday, the horrified monarch had his answer when, at a distance amid far-off echoes of blaring trumpets, he spotted another army nearing his city. He discerned its hundreds of insignia standards and it appeared to him that as large a host as he had fought these last few days was coming for reinforcement. The Huaxtecan's demeanor was one of fright, and his own anxieties were mirrored in the faces of his warriors who gaped disbelievingly at the advancing fresh corps. Wholly dispirited, their dismay was manifest in all of them, from their supreme lord to the lowliest bowman. Xaman Utec now realized that Xiuhcoac's fall was imminent and thoughts of escape dominated him.

Meanwhile, in the Mexica camp, revelry abounded as the Acolhuas neared, and opposite his adversary, the Anahuac warrior now anticipated victory and this uplifted him to new determination. He became imbued with an eagerness to bring this conflict to a finish and, with the help of his Acolhua ally, meant to accomplish this today.

Nezahualpilli had already been told about the Revered Speaker's close encounter with death when he arrived to greet him, and Ahuitzotl, pleased at seeing his confederate, handed him his crushed helmet. The Texcocan examined it carefully, wondering how anyone could have survived such a blow. "You have a hard head, Ahuitzotl," he said with a grin, returning the helmet. "But this should teach you to leave the forward lines to our warriors. As a ruler, you are too valuable to be exposing yourself to such dangers."

"I should be a poor king if I cowered behind the protection of others," said Ahuitzotl. "There is a lesson though: we must be wary of their slingers-they evidently disperse them among their warriors so they are not seen. I am relieved you are here. This has been a bitterly faught contest-I would like to see it end."

"You should have called for me sooner. My soldiers hunger for a fight."

"Give them a short rest and they shall have it. Xaman Utec has taken enormous losses, but he is a powerful opponent. Your abilities will be taxed in subduing him."

While Ahuitzotl was briefing Nezahualpilli on how he meant to destroy his foe, Xaman Utec was meeting with his chief advisors to discuss when they should consider capitulation. They debated long over this and as they were unable to arrive at a decision resolved to let today's outcome determine the issue. The Huaxtecan monarch, who harbored little hope for success, reluctantly agreed with his lords although he believed the appropriate course at present was to appease the would-be conqueror with rich gifts and an appeal for mercy. He was reminded that he himself was doomed for having so foolishly offended his Mexica counterpart; he recognized this but thought it more important to secure his people's safety. A series of trumpet calls brought the conference to a halt; their enemy was preparing for his assault and the commanders were required to be with their units. Yet even the most stouthearted of them must have felt a queeziness in his stomach as he observed a reconstituted line assembled a short distance from Xiuhcoac's defensive works. He consoled himself with the notion that they could move behind the barriers if things went badly for them-to hold the enemy off perhaps another day.

Ahuitzotl kept the Tepanec army on his right but augmented it with the complements of his former third force. The fresh Acolhuas he placed on his left while his own army retained its center position. After the priests had dispensed with giving the impending struggle its necessary prerequisites, the action was resumed. Rejuvenated, the Mexica attacked with spirited vigor, and everywhere along their line, warriors raced for the Huaxtecs as if competing for the honor of being the first to come in contact with them. Under such inspired motivation, no power in the world could have withstood them, and the enemy's first inclination was to take cover behind their bulwarks, but their commanders had them hold their ground. They watched in fear as death charged at them.

Typically, Ahuitzotl's center engendered the first contact, his warriors hurling themselves upon Huaxtecan shields, breaking down the front rows almost immediately in their onslaught. An instant later, the whole of the line met in combat, the clash of impacting weapons echoing from one end of the field to the other, and again a cacophony of shouts and screams congested the air as men became entangled in bloody conflict.

On the left, the Acolhuas, angry over having been left out of the battle all these days, furiously hammered against their opposition and sent it reeling back under the charge. They viciously cut down the defenders, many individual warriors grabbing an enemy soldier they had disarmed or beaten and dragging him to an eagerly waiting priest. The Huaxtecan commander on the flank, on seeing that it was impossible to stem this flood, ordered his bowmen behind preset barricades to lay protective volleys while his fighting men retreated.

Xaman Utec, when he observed his right units leaving the field for the barriers, knew the the Acolhuas would next turn on his center. And on his left, he noticed his lines also faltering with the Mexica making penetrations all along them. In only a matter of time would they succeed in falling on his position. "Sound a retreat!" he shouted to his trumpeter. "We shall fight them from behind our walls!"

For the Huaxtecs, the signal to withdraw came not a moment too soon; all along their front the lines were crumbling and panic ran quickly through their ranks. When they heard the call, they fell back in extreme haste, breaking their battle order and leaving the stragglers to be taken captive. Yet in the center, one of their elite squadrons refused to give up its station and offered to provide cover while the rest of the army fell back. It formed into a square and held steadfast as attackers charged on it from all directions; there its warriors fought to the death, their bold stand witnessed by comrades who now manned the walls, but they had succeeded in delaying the advancing Mexica long enough to permit their remaining warriors to complete the retreat.

"Bring your archers up to keep their heads low," Nezahualpilli told Ahuitzotl after they had regrouped the armies following the enemy's withdrawal, "and I will make an assault there, where they have constructed a wall between the buildings."

"Is it necessary?" Ahuitzotl questioned. "They know they're beaten and may surrender without further effort on our part."

"Do not rob my Acolhuas of their moment to demonstrate their valor, Lord. Yes, it is necessary."

Ahuitzotl understood. Also, such a move might frighten the Huaxtecs into conceding defeat if they recognized that their walls would not be sufficient to protect them. He ordered his bowmen into a line about a hundred paces wide and four rows deep. This carried out, they were instructed to fire two rows at a time; as the first restrung, the second two were to fire so their arrows flew uninterruptedly until the Acolhuas reached the walls.

"Beware of Xaman Utec's archers!" Ahuitzotl cautioned his ally, "He makes good use of them, as Chimalpopoca can well tell you."

"We'll be fighting at close quarters once we've breached the walls. They won't be able to fire without striking their own men."

"Then good fortune. Give us a signal when you have carved out a path for us. I'll order my units to follow."

On Ahuitzotl's command, the archers unleashed their repeated volleys on the fortifications. The deadly fire had its effect—not one Huaxtecan warrior dared to lift his head over the ramparts-and under its screen, Nezahualpilli launched his assault.

Each Acolhua soldier knew he was being observed by his allied comrades, including the Revered Speaker, and took it upon himself to put on an inspiring performance. Like wild beasts voraciously pouncing upon a wounded prey, the warriors charged at the barriers, running full speed at them, while missiles continued to keep the defender's heads down.

With precision timing, when the leading combatants reached the walls and were about to storm over them, the archers ceased firing. The Huaxtecs arose to confront frenzied battalions of screaming Mexica ahead of them.

The first soldier to leap over the barricades met immediate death, as did the second, and also the third and fourth, but these were quickly followed by comrades who burst on the scene as water spilling over a dike. A handful made it across, and were instantly engaged, then more, and finally scores sprang over crashing into the Huaxtecans; they proceeded pouring over in increasing numbers, hacking through the defending squadrons and then spreading out in both directions to take on more.

Xaman Utec ordered warriors from elsewhere within the walls to counter the breakthrough and repel the attackers; these arrived in huge numbers and fought with a determined fanaticism that startled the Acolhuas. The Huaxtecan monarch personally led one of the charges just as Nezahualpilli had scrambled over the wall to join his soldiers in their attempt at securing a breach in Xiuhcoac's fortifications. Compressed on three sides by ferociously resisting defenders, the Acolhuas were now forced into a protective stance even as more of their men streamed over the walls.

"Form a circle!" shouted Nezahualpilli. "We cannot lose the ground we've gained!"

At the same time his warriors set about complying with their directive, Nezahualpilli sent a messenger back to Ahuitzotl carrying an urgent plea for assistance. The runner leaped over the walls as fast as his legs allowed and raced across the field where the remaining Mexica stood watching their allies with keen interest. His message was explicit to Ahuitzotl who readily grasped the value of gaining a toehold within the city's perimeter and he immediately called on his nearest squadrons to follow him in an attack.

In the meantime, Nezahualpilli was in dire circumstances. He positioned himself in the center of his circle while the Huaxtecs assailed them savagely, attacking without personal regard for safety against their shielded ranks and thrusting spears into their constricted mass in an attempt to force them apart. Many Acolhuas screamed out in their agony, blood choking off their cries as the deadly lances tore into their chests; they were falling in staggering numbers and Nezahualpilli was experiencing extreme anxiousness when the whoops of a thousand warriors reached his ears.

Ahuitzotl's squadrons broke upon the scene, howling in their exuberance, and flung themselves on the Huaxtecs who had nearly smashed the Acolhua circle into fractured parts. The monarch, accompanied by the intrepid Motecuhzoma, forged a pathway to where Nezahualpilli was in heated struggle fending off his assailants and joined in the effort to secure a salient inside this section of Xiuhcoac.

"I feared you might not come in time," Nezahualpilli greeted his deliverer in complete exhaustion, gasping for breath.

"I had to give you a full taste of the battle-as you wanted." Ahuitzotl chuckled behind his wide smile.

"I've had enough of it."

In spite of their access within the city, and a numerical superiority, the Mexica encountered savage resistance in trying to advance their gains, and if they progressed at all, every step was earned with the life of a warrior. The defenders fought tenaciously, refusing to yield an inch of ground, but the attackers were relentless in their drive and kept up their incessant pressure. Yet for every building taken, hundreds of them fell in the attempt.

Darkness encroached with undesired haste after the sun had set and both forces remained locked in deadly combat; many a warrior inadvertently wounded his own comrade when he failed to properly judge the distance available for swinging his warclub in the dim visibility. Huaxtecans hid in the shadows of their structures and swooped on Mexica squadrons which had become separated from the main body, killing as many as they could before scurrying back into pitch-black recesses offering them sanctuary or escape. The advantage was now theirs, possessing a familiarity with the buildings and street pattern of their city, and Ahuitzotl, fearing an ambush, held up his drive and ordered his units into a strong perimeter capable of repulsing any counterattack.

In the moonless night, with only stars to send a faint glimmer of light on the blackened shadows of the city, neither side dared move on the other out of fear that an entrapment was waiting for it, nor did anyone risk retrieving the wounded whose painful screaming periodically disrupted the scene. Yet, throughout it, the Mexica transferred more of their army into the sector of Xiuhcoac seized in the day's fighting and tore down the walls and barricades restricting their passage. Nervous defenders could see their activity by the distant torchlights which guided them into the interior and could do nothing. For Xaman Utec, the situation was hopeless, and his mood was as gloomy as the darkness that surrounded him. With the enemy in control of nearly a quarter of the city, and more of them pouring into it unchecked by the hour, he knew tomorrow's battle would be his last. By now his army had been so depleted of its strength that he estimated his opponent outnumbered him at least three to one and he lamented over having unwittingly insulted the Revered Speaker; it amounted to a calamitous mistake and he groped for ways in which he might make amends, if that was even possible.

By midnight, the bulk of the armies of Tenochtitlan, Tlatelolco, and Acolhuacan were within Xiuhcoac's perimeter while those of Tepaneca and its allies maintained their base in the encampment. Messengers freely transferred reports between the two forces and by this procedure the plan for tomorrow's engagement was coordinated. Ahuitzotl determined that every available unit was to attack simultaneously so that the outmanned defenders had to scatter their remaining meager elements over an extensive area to mount an opposition in all directions. This would enable his own combined force to break through their final wall of resistance and bring the contest to a close. No longer was the issue in doubt; it entailed only a mopping up operation and getting Xaman Utec to capitulate.

The day's fighting had been intense and bloody, and the Acolhuas, who bore the brunt of it, made a sufficiently respectable showing to be satisfied if the conflict came to its end. Although no funeral ritual was possible for the fallen as the battle raged until dark, the bodies strewn within the Mexica controlled section were gathered up all night long and stacked in piles for subsequent disposal. Nezahualpilli counted over two thousand Acolhua dead and three times as many wounded-and this did not include a thousand unaccounted warriors lying somewhere in the unsecured areas whose fate was unknown to him: they had indeed done their part. But once more it appeared that the Huaxtec casualties exceeded those of the Mexica; each successive day they had suffered a greater loss and lost ground, and every Huactec soldier must have understood that the end was near, and yet they remained stoically at their duty-stations with their lords accepting the fate decreed for them. If they were destined to fall, it was because angry gods willed this: men were but manipulated pawns in their greater scheme of things.

XXI

The expected fifth day of battle began inconspicuously enough with the sun gradually rising over the horizon spreading its glistening warm rays over the green plain and bathing Xiuhcoac's stone buildings in a brilliant golden hue. Birds sang in melodic profusion to greet its arrival, oblivious to the restlessness of the human activity taking place. This was going to be another cloudless and beautiful day, hot as the others had been, but quite confortable in these early hours for the highland Mexica-the Huaxtecs might have thought it cold.

Ahuitzotl peered down the city's main avenue from the forward edge of his line thinking the place deserted and dead, as lifeless as the many corpses seen lying about in grim testimony of yesterday's horrific slaughter. He saw no Huaxtecs and assumed that they were in hiding inside the numerous surrounding buildings ready to pounce on his columns if they moved ahead. Maintaining a vigilance, the Mexica nourished themselves with dried breakfast foods and made preparations for the fight. They expressed confidence in their conversations, most believing this would be their last day of battle. It seemed as if they had been at it forever, and they longed for a change of scene. Having finished polishing their weapons, repairing broken shields, and replacing damaged spears warclubs, and helmets, they now stood assembled in their formations waiting only for the sound of conch shells to spur them into action. No easy day faced them; Ahuitzotl balked at the prospect of waging a battle in city streets from building to building-such engagements invariably led to high casualties and he preferred to avoid them. He moved ahead with Nezahualpilli and once again scanned the emptiness.

"It's strangely quiet out there," he said. "One could almost believe the Huaxtecs have abandoned Xiuhcoac."

"I saw a few of them between those structures," Nezahualpilli discerned, "but they're not making a sound. It has all the markings of a funeral."

"I hope not Xaman Utec's."

"He has faught you valiantly for days-a noteworthy achievement I would say. Yet I suspect you seek revenge on him."

Ahuitzotl glanced whimsically at his ally when his attention was diverted on the Huaxtecs who suddenly came into view and were lining up in an attack formation at about a block's distance. "He means to fight some more," he remarked with clear disdain. "He's lost half his army and part of his city, and yet he will fight."

"What would you do in his place?"

"The same, I suppose. I may judge the man harshly, but you will see he's not one to like. His rudeness will offend even you."

As the Huaxtecs completed their configuration, Ahuitzotl motioned for his priest to prepare sounding the attack. He raised his hand and was about to initiate the contest when a colorfully clad group of nobles stepped ahead of the enemy ranks and boldly neared the Mexica, and behind them trailed a hundred servants who were carrying fine cloths and containers of other valuable items. Ahuitzotl took note of the parrots, macaws, and other exotic birds-all highly prized-carried in cages. The entourage halted when it reached the Revered Speaker, all its members standing silently before him as if awe-struck by the presence of their conqueror.

"Speak!" Ahuitzotl told their leader.

"Our lord, Xaman Utec, asks that you accept these present we bring you and take this gesture of courtesy and submission into regard when he offers to surrender to you."

At first, Ahuitzotl was skeptical-his previous encounter with the Huaxtecan lord had him convinced that Xaman Utec was incapable of any sort of civility-but that hesitation soon turned to delight. He particularly liked the macaws brought to him. Birds of colorful plumage were valued not only for the beautiful feathers they offered for clothing and adornments, but also as objects of admiration in the aviaries. He looked the gifts over item by item, and then his thoughts turned to the question at hand. "An agreeable gesture," he said. "Tell Xaman Utec that I am pleased with his presents, but that I would be even more pleased if he did in fact surrender to me."

"He wishes to do so this very day, but asks that you accept certain conditions before taking this step."

"Even in defeat he dares to suggest terms to his victors. So what are these?"

"He requests that you save his city from destruction, that you not make captives of his warriors when they yield to you, and that you treat the women and children with respect."

"No captives? He negates a major purpose in my having warred on him. Indeed this lord of yours is mad. I am the one who has him on the run and he wants to impose conditions on me. What does he think I am to gain by accepting his offer?"

"He reasons that you will spare yourself the multitude of losses today's fighting will surely cost you and that your warriors will be gratified to have this bloody business concluded. He promises to fulfill whatever tributes you will exact on him and will double the presents he has given you, and he vows to show proper allegiance and obedience to you. Additionally, he promises to entertain you and your warriors royally and will provide just compensation for their efforts and journey to Huaxteca."

"What is just compensation?"

"Feasting, for days, with an abundance of the finest food and drink, presents, and women."

The latter certainly would have appealed to many, especially his Texcocan ally, and Ahuitzotl did not fail in noting a bemused smirk on him before again facing the emissary.

"And himself? Does he ask nothing for himself?"

"He asks that you grant him and his lords life and their positions so they will be able to serve you."

"The man has unmitigated gall. I will now tell you what my terms are. You will inform your master that his people I will carry off into slavery, his city I will lay to waste, his warriors I will take captive, and he and his lords I will put to death."

The shocked distress of the emissaries was apparent; nevertheless, their red-faced spokesman applied one more exertion towards obtaining some kind of reconciliation. "Shall I tell my lord these terms are final?" he inquired. "Is there any possibility for compromise?"

Ahuitzotl thought it over, impressed by the ambassador's determination to secure the best condition for his people. Also, Nezahualpilli demonstrated such visible shock over hearing his terms that it made him reflect their severity.

"Very well then," Ahuitzotl retracted, "I will spare his city, and its inhabitants will not be harmed. Even many of his warriors will be spared from captivity, but he and his leading lords and commanders will not be permitted their freedom. They must be among our prisoners. I'll await his answer before beginning today's battle."

As the envoys returned toward their lines, Ahuitzotl still noticed a disapproving look in Nezahualpilli and was somewhat irked by it. "You object to the terms?" he scowled.

"You speak to me of Xaman Utec's rudeness, but who is the uncivilized one now? Those are harsh conditions; indeed, your first proposal would have rendered it better for him to fight to the death than capitulate. I do not think it very honorable."

"Can it be that a single day's fighting has been too much for you Acolhuas?"

"Do not mock me or my warriors! We will fight as long as you-with the conditions you gave him, that is what we will undoubtedly have to do. It seems pointless to lose more warriors when they want to surrender, but it's a mistake I make to think you have our welfare at heart. He offended you, and you must have your revenge on him. irrespective of what price."

"I'll not deny I seek vengeance, but would never permit this to endanger the lives of our warriors. Do not worry about Xaman Utec refusing my terms. He will accept them."

"If he does, will you still reward him with a cruel death?"

"He has invited it."

"You're a hard man, Ahuitzotl. Whatever he has done to you should have been mitigated by his valorous conduct in battle and his gesture of submission. At the least, you can honor him by sending him to the gods."

"He shall be denied that honor."

Ahuitzotl's obstinacy disturbed Nezahualpilli, but the Texcocan knew when to stop—to have persisted would only have made him more determined to carry out his plans for the nfortunate Huaxtecan monarch.

"Look! The emissaries return!" exclaimed Ahuitzotl. "And Xaman Utec is with them."

"You were right. He plans to surrender."

"Pay more attention to what I say. I know how my opponents think."

Not only did the approaching party include the Huaxtecan monarch, but also his chief ministers, priests, and commanders, as well as the ambassador, and it was evident their burden wore heavily on them as they walked with their heads lowered, displaying a most sorrowful demeanor. Ahuitzotl was startled when he saw the haggardly disheveled appearance of Xaman Utec; his eyes were darkened from lack of sleep and seemed to have a glassy hue over them, and his lips were downturned to give him a very sad expression, and he was shabbily dressed. He was a man drained of energy and, for a moment, Ahuitzotl was even struck with some campassion for his adversary as he thought of the difficulty posed in ceding over a nation to a conqueror. For the first time, however short-lived the sentiment was, Ahuitzotl actually saw a measure of dignity in his beaten foe.

Both lords then glared intensely at each other; even at this moment there was an apparent loathing between them, but the Revered Speaker beamed in his confidence while his counterpart revealed a tense uncertainty. Ahuitzotl spoke first.

"So the man who would sent me and the remnants of my army back to Anahuac, the man who spits at my offers, and the man who does not fear the Mexica now comes to me-to plead for clemency I suspect."

"Not for myself," Xaman Utec answered, "but for my subjects. I entreat that you do not wreak your vengeance upon them because I have offended you."

"They followed you, and approved of your actions, mainly your seizure of Metztitlan. Why should I be merciful to them?"

"I was their lord, and they were sworn to my obedience, as your people are sworn to obey you. Would you have them reject their monarch's commands?"

A sensible reply, thought Ahuitzotl, and not entirely groundless; he would have to give it consideration. "The fire is gone from your speech, Xaman Utec I see that we have taught you some humbleness."

"Of what use is further resistance? My army is depleted of its warriors and much of Xiuhcoac is taken; I have no capacity for reclaiming either. We cannot hold out against your combined attack. It has been a fair contest, and you have justly won it."

Grinning from ear to ear, Ahuitzotl directed his chief priest to sound the trumpet proclaiming that the battle was finally ended. When it resounded across the city and its outer walls where Chimalpopoca's army stood poised in readiness for another assault, a lengthy vociferation arose from the thousands of warriors; this had been a bitterly waged struggle and not one among them regretted having it over.

"Your terms," Xaman Utec expressed with concern, "Will you compromise on them."

"Some, but not all," declared Ahuitzotl as his Eagle knights encircled the Huaxtec party. "Take them away!"

Once the Huaxtec soldiers saw their lords and leading commanders taken, their resistance was completely broken and their units filled into the city's main plaza to deposit their shields and armaments in large piles on orders from their conqueror. They were then taken to the Mexica camp where a containment area had been set aside for captives since the first day of battle.

Ahuitzotl kept at least one of his promises and spared Xiuhcoac from the torch, not entirely out of feelings of benevolence, but primarily because he wanted to use its facilities for a period of well-deserved resting and feasting for his exhausted combatants. They were fed by the townspeople, the soldiers in private residences and the lords and chieftains in Xaman Utec's palace, and there was great rejoicing everywhere among the victors. So while Xaman Utec and his nobles sulked on the grounds of their compound, the Mexica celebrated and dined regally late into night and finished their gala by being individually entertained by Huextecan mistresses in their private palace chambers. Ahuitzotl and Nezahualpilli made no exceptions for themselves.

The conquerors remained for another month in Xiuhcoac before deciding to make the return journey. That amount of time was required to consolidate their gains, set up administrative control, send out punitive expeditions into nearby cities whose recalcitrance demanded correction, receive vows of allegiance and obedience from the lords appointed to succeed those captured, and cement the basis for future relations with Anahuac. Throughout this period, Nezahualpilli quarreled with Ahuitzotl over the fate of the Huaxtecans, the Texcocan favoring a degree of leniency and proposing that Xaman Utec be left to rule in Xiuhcoac, an idea vehemently opposed by the Revered Speaker. In the end, they agreed to let Chimalpopoca make the final decision and he sided with Ahuitzotl; he was still smarting over the losses his army sustained in the bloody struggle.

The captives were well treated during this interval with the townspeople permitted to feed them and tend to their needs; wives repeatedly visited their doomed husbands and wept over their fate; relatives impassively accepted the inevitable end-what else could they do? This was ordained by vengeful gods into whose disfavor they must have fallen. Xaman Utec continued to be attended by his servants who lamented profusely over the misfortune that befell their noble lord. Ahuitzotl had occasion to see this, marveling at what loyalty the deposed monarch commanded out of his subjects, but it did not shake his resolve to punish the king for his insolence.

After their necessary period of consolidation, the Mexica, now anxious to return to Anahuac, made their preparations to leave. Ten thousand captives were selected for the journey, among them Xaman Utec and his principal leaders. In addition, the women and children widowed or orphaned in the battle were also taken-this was a compromise between Ahuitzotl who wanted to take nearly half of the populace and Nezahualpilli who desired no part of such an affair. They would make good slaves for Mexica households and compensation for the families whose sons perished or were severely wounded in the campaign. Ahuitzotl came by the compound to observe the prisoners being assembled for their trek when a scuffle arose between one of them and the guards trying to bind his hands.

"What is the trouble?" he asked the squadron chief supervising the guard detail.

"They do not like being bound, thinking it a slur on their honor, Lord."

"It may besmearch their honor, but it provides security for my guards."

Ahuitzotl walked up to the resisting captive, a tall warrior who rose to nearly a full head above him, and was struck by his disproportionately large aquiline nose and the size of the perforation in it-he could have easily run his little finger through it. The feature was peculiar to the Huaxtecan people he thought, to have bigger than normal heads characterized by enormous noses. He looked at the thongs binding the warrior, and an idea came to him.

"Very well," Ahuitzotl said, "We shall not bind their hands. I have a better method of securing them. Run these thongs through their noses so that a dozen warriors are connected by a single strand. Tie only the hands of the first and last captive in each group. That ought to keep them under control."

This novel approach delighted the captors; when word of it spread through the ranks, they jeered the prisoners, goading them to attempt an escape, while they fastened them together in the prescribed manner. To their discomposed captives, it constituted an embarrassing mockery of their customs bordering on insulting humiliation, and even Xaman Utec was not spared the indignity, being threaded together with his lords as the rest of the warriors.

The women and children were secured by thinly wooden collars placed around their necks, an act more symbolic than out of worry they might try to escape. They would not have fared well had they managed to get away; vicious predators, not excluding nearby wild tribesmen, would more than likely have committed outrages on them rather than grant them sanctuary. Even ambassadors and couriers faced bodily risks when venturing into foreign lands–defenseless women and children had no chance against criminal elements which freely roamed the hills.

Prior to leaving, Ahuitzotl imparted his exactions on the lords left in charge of Xiuhcoac; the local populace was to continue its existence under an imposed tribute requirement. He demanded an initial portion of it to be paid within half a year, and then the usual eighty day allocations submitted by all subjugated states. The Lord of Huachinango he rewarded with a sizable amount of the levy for his assistance; not that his contribution was so great, but in a typical pattern, Ahuitzotl was more interested in impressing on people the benefits gained by loyally serving the Mexica than in making any representative distribution of the spoils. Huachinango was sure to remain a staunch ally for him, having profited substantially for its effort.

After replenishing their exhausted provisions, the armies assumed their march with the prisoners arranged in long columns of three men abreast, first the warriors and then the women and children, and divided equally among the major components on the lengthy trek back to Anahuac, expected to take twice as long as their march on Huaxteca.

When everyone was accounted for, the lines began to slowly move out, initially to a cadence of drumbeats, and then to loud lamentations from the captives who rendered mournful songs depicting their misfortune. To a passerby, the lines seemed endless, and had he stood in one spot, an entire day would have elapsed for the total column to march by-a fitting closure for the Huaxtecan campaign.

XXII

Runners had already informed the local population of the enormous victory attained in Huaxteca, and when the armies at last came to the capital, after a twenty-four day march, all of Tenochtitlan greeted its triumphant warriors with a tumultuous welcome. Flowers and reeds were strewn over the pavement of the avenues upon which they entered; joyful songs and cheers, and a thousand fired braziers and trumpet calls added to the festive spirit. Young girls ran out to give the soldiers blooms as they marched by, and when they reached the central square within the serpent's wall, speeches of gratitude were announced with the usual fanfare accompanying such occasions. The proud warriors were given food and cups of cocoa, a beverage generally reserved for the ruling elites.

By any measure, it had been a spectacular triumph. In a single bold operation, an entire province heretofore unconquered had been subjugated and brought under the Mexica heel in an exceedingly rapid and convincing fashion. In what might have been expected to drag on for months, the enemy was subdued in a total period of only eleven weeks-a spectacular achievement-and if the Mexica losses were heavier than had been experienced for many years, when the scope of the campaign was taken into account, with its measured rewards in tributes and captives, there remained no question that the enterprise had been one of stupendous success. And for those nations which failed to notice the Matlazinca campaign, there was absolutely no doubt that this latest expedition would receive their full attention. Ambassadors assigned to Tenochtitlan could no longer look with disinterest on the activities of this new Revered Speaker-indeed they now had to watch his every move: he was a man to be reckoned with.

A stand was brought to Ahuitzotl, and when he mounted it, as on the day he left the city, his multitude of assembled warriors gave him a resounding ovation. He expended some time absorbing the applause rendered, smiling across the sea of soldiers facing him and savoring their appreciation, and then raised his hand over his head and silenced them.

"My magnificent warriors! What a feat we have accomplished! Poets will long praise our achievement and songs will proclaim our triumph. Never since the days of our revered Motecuhzoma has there been so glorious a conquest! When we first embarked on this venture, I asked that you undergo the greatest hardship-that you would be driven harder than ever before. I asked that you look upon this noble mission as a matter of personal devotion to our divine Huitzilopochtli and that you seek to avenge the insult the enemy had cast upon him. In all this you have done what I asked-and more! No Revered Speaker was ever better served. For your splendid effort and faithful service to me, I salute you!"

They would have died for him. So tremendous was their outburst when he stepped from the dais that the very walls of the temples trembled under the roaring applause. This was far. far more than merely an approval of Ahuitzotl's leadership: it amounted to a prodigious proclamation denoting an emotional bond he had acquired out of his warriors—he was their god.

When the acclamation at last subsided, the commanders dismissed their units. Arms were stacked for collection and storage and the square gradually emptied as soldiers dispersed to join their waiting relatives and friends and the quartermaster squadrons set about distributing the captives to the various wards of Tenochtitlan where suitable containment areas had been arranged for them. Ahuitzotl was met at his palace by a highly pleased Cihuacoatl who could scarcely restrain the joy he felt over the expedition's success.

"The news has amazed everyone," he excitedly informed his lord. "Days before you arrived word was already being sent everywhere about your conquest. I tell you, Great Lord, the glory of our empire is restored. This campaign has done more to bring this about than anything yet done by you. The ambassadors were amazed when they heard of it."

"My boldest step so far," Ahuitzotl beamed, "and I shall do more than merely restore our former glory-I shall expand it."

Ahuitzotl glanced toward the Great Temple. He had noticed that the tall roof combs were completed when he entered the city across the western causeway, and now that he stood in close proximity to it, was stuck by the impression this imparted on an observer. They gave the structure a vertical emphasis overpowering in grandeur as if it was reaching for the heavens. The exterior was now finished in its entirety, and only the inside of the two shrines housing the idols of Huitzilopochtli and Tlaloc remained to be done. Not that this was a small task; it entailed several more weeks of work and required the skillful hands of numerous artisans to adorn it properly.

"How are the dedication plans going?" Ahuitzotl asked. "Is everything in order?"

"It is, Lord. We shall soon be sending out the invitations. Your great success in Huaxteca will certainly give impetus to making it a memorable event. Who would be so foolish as to reject your invitation now?"

"They would," Ahuitzotl smirked, "only at great peril to themselves."

"The ambassadors are aware of this-you should have seen their faces when word of your triumph reached us."

"I expect that our relations with the other realms—our enemies!-are significantly changed over this. Have you any indications of this yet?"

"Regrettably, no. The Tlappanecs still restrict use of their region for our pochteca, and along the southern frontier, the Mixtecs and Zapotecs harass them at will, charging them excessive duties for access to local trading routes and occasionally stealing their wares, although none have been physically harmed so far."

"It's a problem we must eventually come to terms with; perhaps now is the time to press our claims, while the Huaxteca campaign remains freshly implanted in their minds. I shall discuss it with you in the morning. For now, I wish to retire and attend to personal affairs. See to it I am not disturbed."

Cihuacoatl nodded his consent, his joy remaining boundless.

While the minister was thus engaged in conversation with his master, two women waited anxiously in different chambers within the palace, each wondering with whom the monarch would spend the night. Both had watched him address his warriors from an upper window of their separate rooms; both sensed a mounting excitement at his return, brought on by an eager anticipation over what each dearly wished would ensue.

Pelaxilla's eyes gleamed in delight on seeing her hero, looking as noble and handsome as ever, perhaps even more so. Her heart fluttered in anxiousness and her body ached for his touch, and she had the utmost difficulty repressing her rising passions. Yet interspersed with her periods of intense rapture came also horrible concerns when she feared her lover might go to his wife's chamber instead of her own. How nonsensical, she kept telling herself when seized with such fears; had he not made it repeatedly clear she was his only love? Why did she find it so hard to believe him? Look at how he spent the nights before setting out on his venture with her-not the empress, but with her. Was this not certain proof of his love? Of course it was, and her glee returned as she suppressed her underlying stress through such assurances. Once again a glow emanated from her eyes, and a cheerful smile adorned her beautiful face while she waited on his arrival.

In an adjacent chamber, another woman had quietly observed the monarch's speech in the presence of her devoted servant. For Tlalalca there was greater uncertainty, and she held no illusions about her standing with him, but somehow she wished, against all odds, that he might come to her. What foolishness!-she reproached herself. How could she even believe that after such a lengthy absence he would deny himself his beloved Pelaxilla. Yet she remembered all too well his longing glance when he left-it remained vividly set in her mind as if it had occurred but yesterday. Surely it must have bespoken of something sincere; no man gazes at a woman in such a way unless it had real meaning.

"Why do you so yearn for him?" Xoyo asked her lady. "He will not bring you happiness."

Tlalalca glared at the old woman with considerable amazement. "How did you know?" she said.

"I've tended to you since you were a small child. You cannot keep any secrets from me. Why does my lady torture herself with such vain wishes? You have changed. It wasn't that long ago when you held him in great contempt and blamed him for your husband's death. We are not assured he was guiltless in the matter."

Tlalalca did not reply immediately. What Xoyo said was true enough, and even if she may have still believed this, she was not as certain about is as she had once been. She never actually told the old woman that she had, for reasons remaining quite mystifying and incomprehensible to her, developed a fondness for Ahuitzotl. No, not just a fondness; her affections ran much deeper than that-she now loved him, and she wanted him. But the old woman knew; nothing escaped her.

"I have the goddess Xochiquetzal to blame, or should I rather say to thank, for this transformation. She contrives such schemes against us."

"To thank? I think my lady reads it wrongly, and I fear you will suffer for it. How can you find contentment in loving a man who loves someone else? What can result from this except untold grief?"

"I know this, but I cannot deny my feelings. Yes, I have come to love this man despite all my efforts to resist it. I keep asking myself how this can possibly be, and criticize myself for such fancies, but always the longing for him comes back to me. It makes little sense, and I've given up searching for an explanation. I cannot help myself."

"Then nothing I can tell you will be heeded."

"You cannot tell me anything I haven't already told myself."

Her response saddened Xoyo who was convinced that this relationship would culminate in tragic consequences for her lady. She could readily grasp why Tlalalca had chosen to accept the marriage proposal; in her predicament she might have done the same thing, as the arrangement offered comfort and security during a time when she was under severe duress. It would have worked out well had the empress accepted it as a convenience as Ahuitzotl did, but now, with her admission that she loved the man, the situation was dramatically altered. With powerful emotions now involved, someone was going to be painfully hurt, and she feared it would be Tlalalca.

"Can you not see what this affliction of yours will do to you? Do you really believe you can replace Pelaxilla in his heart? If you know you cannot, why go through all this suffering?"

"Yes, I do believe it," replied Tlalalca. "That is the terrible aspect of this-this affliction, as you aptly name it. You do not understand, Xoyo. Xochiquetzal makes you believe that what you desire the most must eventually be granted to you-you live for this, and suffer because you want to: it is a sweet misery."

"You have lost me in that, Lady."

"Have you never been in love? Surely you must know of what I speak?"

She did not. A slave woman all her life, Xoyo spent her entire existence in the servitude of royal ladies with limited exposure to men. Those she met, she cared little for-not that this disturbed her any; she was quite content with how she had lived her days, but she could not have understood.

"I'm sorry, my Lady, but indeed I do not."

"Then I should be the one to grieve for you, Xoyo. A life without love is filled with emptiness."

"To you perhaps, my Lady, but I have not considered it a bad life. I have seen several ladies come to ruin from Xochiquetzal's curse-some even met their deaths for having engaged in adulterous affairs-and often thanked myself that I was spared such a fate. I've managed well enough without it."

The notion seemed inconceivable to Tlalalca; yet, in some way, she sort of admired Xoyo's immunity from love's torments. Xoyo may actually have lived so long because she avoided the pain and duress which comes to those women who succumb to Xochiquetzal's 'curse'.

But in spite of her deepest wishes that Ahuitzotl would come to her, it was not to be. No sooner had the monarch entered his private quarters when he directed one of his valets to bring the Lady Pelaxilla to him. Oddly enough, he had momentary reservations about it, and he was not altogether without some guilt when he determined to pass up his wife in favor of his mistress-feelings he never possessed previously. Even as the bath water was being prepared, he paced the floor nervously thinking he may have made the wrong decision. His worries, however, vanished the moment he beheld his young beauty enter, and as soon as he dismissed his servants, Pelaxilla rushed to him and they united in joyous rapture.

After lovingly clutching her and caressing her for a lingering period of time, he saw that his dirtiness from the trek had soiled her clothes and skin. "Come, take off your garments and join me in my bath," he said as he stepped Back to remove his tunic.

Smiling, and more than willing, she readily complied and together they entered the sunken tub. They played like children in the water, laughing and teasing each other, splashing themselves, and indulging in the pleasures of their enrapture and the sensuous contact of their bodies. He could not resist running his fingers over her most intimate features, and she delighted in her fondling of his erection, and somehow, amid this frolicking and merriment, she managed to scrub his body with soap and wash him, interspersed by his frequent embraces and kisses.

When at last he wearied of this, he lifted her in his arms and carried her from the cistern to a nearby bench where towels had been neatly arranged for them. He vigorously rubbed her dry, then she took her turn on him, and throughout this an occasionally misplaced hand took hold of a sensitive body part and fully savored its area before finally moving on amid giggling and pleasurable gratification. "You shall know more of that later on," Pelaxilla teased as she removed his groping fingers.

"It is my impetuous nature," Ahuitzotl laughed. "I must know all things first hand."

She appreciated the pun, and her eyes glistened temtingly behind a wide smile. "You should have ample opportunity to do your explorations," she said, "as you'll be staying here for awhile now, won't you?"

"Yes. There's much I want to do here."

She scarcely believed it; always it seemed he had ventured off before she could get her full satisfaction from his company. "What is it you must do?" she asked, feigning her true interest.

"A number of things. Mainly I want to oversee the groundwork for the new palace I wish to build. The city's becoming more populous; our water supply is insufficient to meet this growth. I must consult with my engineers on how to grapple with this. Then there is the dedication for the Great Temple."

"It's interesting," she mused, "that you did not mention Tlalalca. She does not figure prominantly in your plans?"

"Why should she? Our arrangement has been in effect for some time now and has posed no major obstacle for us-why should there be any plan for her?"

This was precisely what Pelaxilla wanted to hear, and while he appeared slightly flustered over her bringing up the subject, she nevertheless took satisfaction in his response.

"I had thought, as your wife, you might have given her as one of your reasons for staying here."

"I've told you many times that when I'm with you, I rarely think of her. Sometimes I think you don't listen to me."

"Oh, but I do," she hastily reacted. "My need for assurances compels me to make these foolish inquiries. I meant no harm."

"I have come to you," he soberly reminded her.

"Yes, you did. Come, let's go to bed."

He lifted her with ease and carried her into the adjoining bedchamber where he meant to drown himself in her sensuousness, for no one could satiate him as Pelaxilla, and theirs had been a long separation: an exhausting night awaited them.

In another bedroom, a lonely woman lay by herself, despondent that her deepest desires would not be fulfilled this night. Not wanting her servant to witness her depression, Tlalalca had dismissed Xoyo earlier in the evening and spent the later time by herself in great frustration and restlessness. Unable to sleep, she remained hounded by an incessant expectation that Ahuitzotl might yet make his appearance at her bedside, but as the hours wore on excruciating slowly, she had to gradually accept the dismaying realization that nothing was to materialize for her tonight. Recurring feverish flashes swept over her as she thought of the pleasures he was giving Pelaxilla and the surface of her skin felt burning hot. Sadly she turned over in resignation, burying her head in the sheets, and she wept.

XVIII

The next morning, while on his way to meet with Cihuacoatl, Ahuitzotl was strangely troubled that he omitted seeing his wife yesterday. He had no idea what he should tell her, but felt a compulsion to render an apology for his neglect although he could not explain why this so obsessed him. He remembered how Tlalalca had wished him a safe journey and how this moved him to sincere sympathy for her condition. He fought off these urges to see her; in many ways he desired her, not in the same manner as Pelaxilla, but with a fascination which attracted him to her. He enjoyed conversing with Tlalalca and admired her sardonic wit; he felt deep compassion for her, and even though he knew his conduct often edged on insensibility, it was not his wish to cause her sorrow and he was frequently angry at himself for producing such a result when he did not intend it. Succumbing to his uneasiness, he entered her chamber and caught her just as she was rising from the mats to get dressed. She was startled at his sudden appearance but quickly regained her composure and flung a blanket over to cover herself. She looked quite weary, and Ahuitzotl knew she had slept poorly.

"You make a habit out of intruding on my private moments," Tlalalca said. "I must be more careful."

"I wanted to see if everything was well with you," Ahuitzotl answered.

"You would have done that better by seeing me last night."

"I suppose so. The problem is I'm in a peculiar situation where I cannot see you without offending Pelaxilla, or rather, without hurting her."

"Certainly you would not want that."

"She means much to me. But why do I tell you what you already know? I'm not here to speak about her; I want to know how things are with you."

"Do you care?"

"Of course I care," he declared, somewhat vexed over her seeming coldness, "else I would not trouble myself to come here."

"I'm touched by your concern."

"You don't sound like it."

"What am I to make of this? That there is some hope you will eventually treat me as a wife?"

"Not that again. You could be a little more ingratiating; after all, I did not ignore you altogether and, in spite of what you may believe, I do worry over you."

"Pardon me if I'm not overwhelmed by your nobleness-perhaps I am remiss in failing to appreciate your efforts."

"Must I endure this?" he grew flustered. "You have a way of making my best intentions appear as though they were a derogatory slur. Why am I always made the scoundrel by your twisting my words?"

"Can it be you reveal yourself to be just that-a scoundrel?"

"Listen to me, Tlalalca. You know full well I have proper regard for you, and it's only out of my fears over causing Pelaxilla grief that I do not come to you as often as I would like."

"Why is she so insecure about your love for her? It seems apparent enough."

"Would I had an answer to that. She's obsessed with a fear that I will fall for your–your, ah charms, and love you instead of her."

"What?" this astounded Tlalalca. "You can't be serious."

"Damn it, woman!" Ahuitzotl retorted angrily, "Does it look like I am joking?"

Tlalalca stared wide-eyed at him, his dilemma suddenly making some sense to her. "That's why you stay away from me?" she asked.

"I've never seen anything like it–she demands I prove my love by remaining with her."

"And you adhere to her wishes. What would she do if you did not comply with what she wants?"

"I don't exactly know," Ahuitzotl muttered in hesitation; he had never questioned that possibility, and now that it was presented to him, he had no answer. "I imagine she would be terribly upset. Perhaps she would avoid me and refuse to allow me to see her."

"Why would she if she so craves your affection?"

The logic never occurred to him. Listening to Tlalalca, one could easily believe it made no difference at all. "What do you suggest I do?" he inquired with genuine interest in what she would tell him.

"Act like a Revered speaker," she curtly replied.

"What is that supposed to mean?" his anger returned.

"You may be a conqueror of innumerable cities and monarch of our people, but you accede to the fancies of a mere mistress like an obedient slave to his master. Instead of catering to her whim, order her to come to you as befits your title and station."

"You tell me this because you want her to look upon me with disfavor. That would make things convenient for you."

"Don't be absurd! I say nothing more to you than what you already know for yourself."

"I did not come here to discuss Pelaxilla. I wanted to see you," he said as he inched closer and placed his hands on her bare shoulders, but she moved quickly away.

"Don't touch me!" she warned.

"What?" he reacted indignantly, "You would reject me?"

"I reject any man who wantonly shows such disregard for me in favor of a mistress. I will not have you treating me as one of your minor concubines-not if I am to remain your empress."

She could see the fury in his eyes and almost panicked, believing she might have provoked him again to uncontrollable action; she hastily sought a retraction for her outburst. "What did you think?" she strained to say. "You admit to me that I am neglected because you fear you will displease Pelaxilla. Where does that leave me? Am I to be endlessly ignored whenever she requires proof of your love? Do you think I have no feelings? If you will always do her bidding, when will you ever come to me?"

To Tlalalca's surprise, he seemed genuinely affected by her lamentation. He lowered his arms and backed away, his eyes never leaving hers as if captured in her gaze. "I didn't think it mattered to you," he said. "I had no reason to believe otherwise, and it wasn't what I anticipated when we agreed to our arrangement. To be truthful, I had little consideration for your feelings then. I must remind you that at the time we both consented for similar reasons-we felt no need for each other's company."

There was no denying this. How much easier things would be now had she retained her past attitude towards him-Xochiquetzal truly conspired against her. But he said something else which caught Tlalalca's attention, and she wanted a verification.

"You said then," she stated. "Are things different now?"

"They must be, else I would not undergo this kind of duress."

To her, his words came like a spark of hope. This may be as close as she would ever come to hearing him admit that he professed a degree of affection for her, she thought, but at least it was something. Foolish woman, she reproached herself; of what use was it to become excited by his mere words when Pelaxilla would continue to enjoy his presence? And yet.

"So tonight?" she asked, "Will you spend it with me?"

"We shall see," he replied after a long pause suggesting the difficulty he was having in wrestling with this problem.

"Oh, excuse me," she retorted, annoyed that her request posed such an apparent burden on him, "I had forgotten. You will require Pelaxilla's consent for that!"

He glared fiercely at her, repressing his manifest anger, and then almost tore the drapes covering the chamber's doorway when he turned about to make his exit. Tlalalca watched him storm down the corridor on the verge of tears, embittered at herself for letting her reckless tongue destroy what appeared to be a developing thaw in their tempestuous relationship.

Ahuitzotl was still fuming when he entered the reception hall where Cihuacoatl had been awaiting his arrival. The minister deduced from his lord's fast-paced gait that something obviously irritated him, but he refrained from saying anything lest it be wrongly received; he was never certain on how to approach his master when in an angry state. The best tactic was to simply stand by until the monarch himself initiated the conversation, which he knew would soon be forthcoming. He was correct.

"I can't believe that woman!" Ahuitzotl growled. "She makes a fine art out of offending me!"

"Your empress?"

"Yes. Her tongue is sharper than the keenest edged knife and she wields it with a dexterity any warrior would envy."

"I have always maintained that scholarly women are dangerous."

"They are cunning-deviously conniving. You must ever be on your guard against them. They excel in striking masterly strokes when you least expect it."

"Would you prefer if we met later? You are presently not disposed towards discussing state affairs."

"No, stay here. I'll soon recover from my indignation. You spoke of problems on our southern frontiers," he promptly seized on a topic, his anger abating as he began talking; "that our pochteca are still being harassed by the Mixtecs and Zapotecs. Don't we have a pact with them allowing all merchants free and unobstructed passage?"

"The treaties permit them to exact a reasonable rate for such passage, but also require them to make it a safe one."

"And that's not what is happening, from what you've said."

"No. Thieves raid our parties at will. Some reports indicate that the cargo stolen has actually turned up in the hands of certain city officials, even rulers."

"Do we have proof of this?"

"The evidence strongly suggests it. Lord Huactli can cite specific examples of singular articles, highly valued, which have been found on a number of their lords. Indeed, in some cases they make no effort to conceal this and even desire that the traders take note of it."

"An agreement among lords and nations is sacrosanct. To infringe on such an accord is an offense of the highest order. I have long wanted to march on our southern neighbors–the Tlappanecs have always been a thorn in my side."

"At least their conduct has been consistent in prohibiting our merchants access across their lands. The others are two-faced, promising passage and then imperiling us when we take it."

"Yes, but by doing so, they have regularly impeded a steady flow of merchandise and tributes to Anahuac, requiring us to travel lengthy detours. It's time we dealt with their insolence. I'm considering sending an expedition to Tlappan and to the periphery of the Mixtec and Zapotec regions-a sort of probe, if you will, to ascertain how they fight and pave the pave the way for subsequent full-scale operations if they fail to get the message."

The idea held an increasing appeal for Ahuitzotl as he delved on it. Not only would it obtain good intelligence on these nations for future enterprises, but also would furnish more captives for the dedication of the Great Temple. He was not in particular need of them, but it offered a cross-section of all people in the region, and if Huitzilopochtli meant for the Mexica to rule over them, certainly he would appreciate sacrifices to represent them all. Also, his reputation as a monarch to be respected, as well as feared, would greatly be elevated among friend and foe alike. There existed many sound reasons for deeming such an operation a worthwhile undertaking.

"Will you lead this expedition?" Cihuacoatl asked.

"Perhaps part of it-against Tlappan. I shall allow Motecuhzoma to lead a force against the Mixtecs and Zapotecs. He has been under my tutelage long enough to give a good account of himself. Besides, it's not an all-out drive, but only a minor incursion: it will be a profitable exercise for him."

"You trust him with that kind of responsibility? He is controversial-many consider Motecuhzoma a vainglorious upstart who is too abrasive to be appreciated. The very meaning of his name, Angry Lord, adequately describes his sober disposition."

"He is a gifted leader and inspires confidence. He may be of a serious comportment as you say, but he also possesses exceptional abilities and, being of royal descendent, must be given his opportunities to properly prepare him as a potential future supreme commander–or even monarch."

"Need I remind you that you yourself had to impose disciplinary measures against him after the Toluca campaign?"

"An impetuosity that comes with youth. He saved my life in Xiuhcoac–perhaps you haven't heard this yet-and has demonstrated his worth repeatedly to me. When he is in actual command, he will gain a new perspective of the skills this entails, but I expect it will be well suited to his talents."

"You make it appear as though he has no faults."

"He has them. For instance, I do not like the way he covets Chalchiuhnenetzin."

"Axayacatl's daughter?"

"Yes, his sister! It would be better if he ogled at other women with as much interest."

"You're not suggesting there might be a, an..."

"An incestuous relationship? No, not that, but then with that strumpet one can never be sure. I must do something about her escapades one of these days."

"I haven't heard of them."

"She masks them well, but there are ample indications she is a corruptive influence on the court ladies. They frequently speak about her many lovers."

"I see. She prefers being an concubine to a royal princess."

"Most concubines serve but one master. Nenetzin must be told that she is a lady and is to act the part. As for Motecuhzoma, do not underestimate him. A day may come when you will find yourself considering him as the next Revered Speaker."

"That will take an exemplary showing on his part."

"We will afford him that opportunity. Reserve your judgment until you have seen with your own eyes what he can do."

They talked on many subjects and Ahuitzotl particularly absorbed himself with city projects being contemplated, including his new palace. Tenochtitlan was a rapidly increasing community whose bulging population was beginning to strain its resources. In the last twenty years, it doubled in size to become the largest city in Anahuac. Earth-fill had been used extensively to connect it with its northern twin city, Tlatelolco, so that, while presently one urban center, that section retained its own central square surrounded by a nucleus of public structures, palaces, and temples. Once separated islands, buildings, streets, and canals now merged the cities to form a single huge metropolis.

With Tenochtitlan's unrestricted growth also came the accompanying urban problems. Refuse and human waste had to be collected and sanitary standards maintained. There were enormous logistical requirements; food and supplies had to be brought in, mostly by boat, in stupendous quantities, and the chinampas, floating farmed plots of earth encased in reeds, were inadequate to sustain the requirements of the city. But mainly there was a shortage of fresh water, and the daily consumption rate did not allow its usage for such former 'luxuries' as washing the city streets, plazas, and public buildings. The aquaduct from Chapultepec built by Motecuhzoma Ilhuicamina was incapable of serving present needs; another one had to be constructed and Ahuitzotl pondered harnessing the natural spring at Coyoacan, off the western shores of the lake. While himself no engineer, he was intrigued by their kind of problem-solving methods, and a conduit extending from Coyoacan to Tenochtitlan represented these techniques at their grandest level and was bold enough a project to fire his imagination. He would think more on this.

And they spoke of the inauguration conceived for the Great Temple. The specific date had now been fixed-only six months away-and a list of honored guests drawn up. For Ahuitzotl, this ceremony had special significance; not only was this the temple of his most revered deity, Huitzilopochtli, patron god of the Mexica, but it represented for him the driving force that lay behind his now being the monarch. Was it not largely out of envy of this awe-inspiring structure, the glory it would impart on its builder, that he turned against his own brother? Its commemoration demanded a unique spectacle, conducted on a monumental scale to match the enormity of the edifice itself, and only after he was informed on the smallest details entailing the proceedings, and was given a satisfactory explanation for every purposeful act surrounding these, did he finally cease questioning his minister and terminate the meeting.

When Ahuitzotl later returned to his private chamber, his troubles with Pelaxilla and Tlalalca surfaced to the forefront again and he almost yearned to be on his campaign, as far away as possible from this unmanageable situation. Compared to the pressures he felt arising within his palace walls, those of a far-flung campaign had all the aspects of tranquility about them.

XXIV

Gradually, in incrementally progressive steps, Tlalalca began to reassert her dominance as empress among the court ladies. Painfully difficult for her at first, damaging as it was to her esteem, she had to blame herself for much of her reluctance because her own conduct contributed largely to the alienation she had felt. In her weeks of seclusion following the death of Tizoc, she had avoided contact with her entourage, spending her time either in solitude or in the company of her loyal servant, Xoyo. Her trepidation was compounded by the uncertainty of her status before Ahuitzotl decided to retain her in her place as his wife. In time, she recognized that she could no longer hide from the obligations that her standing demanded and slowly she was moved to surmount the fears possessing her in resuming her duties.

Her vulnerabilities had been horribly exposed in the aftermath of the life-shattering events marking her last year; this had been her greatest fear in the recovery process, adding deeply to her insecurities, and she was often beset with the worst anxieties over whether she could still acquire any respect out of her household. Would she be seen as the frail, whimpering, woman who had been panic-stricken and crying helplessly when faced with a calamitous situation? If so, how could she possibly enforce her will, or place demands on others who now held her in lower regard. The circumstances were problematic for Tlalalca, but she realized she had to apply the effort in re-establishing her control over them. Eventually, her strengths began to supercede her weaknesses. She was a highly educated woman, with a thorough command of the language, possessed of a sharp wit, and she bore herself in a regal manner that revealed itself in courtly behavior and civility. And she was beautiful, which contributed to an overall impressionable portrayal that worked decidedly in her favor.

Pelaxilla's presence in the now resumed afternoon gatherings existed as both a help and hindrance in Tlalaca's resurgence of dominance. It encumbered the empress by placing constraints over the subject matters under discussion and enhancing her misgivings over how she should voice her opinions. She knew Pelaxilla held Ahuitzotl's ear and owned most of his off-duty time, an access not as available to her, and this placed into question the entirety of her effectiveness as the leading lady of the court, frequently filling her with hesitations and indecisions when conversing with her ladies. Also Pelaxilla was eight years younger, further complicating Tlalalca's estimation of how to maintain an authoritative relationship when she was, in actuality, Ahuitzotl's preferred woman in the court. Pelaxilla, with the charm and charisma of her appealing personality making her the most favorite among the ladies, stood as a competitive rival to the empress; everyone knew of her closeness to the monarch.

Yet Pelaxilla, to her credit, also helped Tlalalca in some measure. She maintained her cordiality whenever in the presence of the empress, upholding a decorum of respect and formality when speaking to her, and thereby assisted her emotionally in overcoming her earlier reservations. Pelaxilla did not do this out of sheer kindness of heart, nor due to having been properly educated in courtly etiquette, but rather because she still lived in awe of the empress, unwillingly clinging on to the fears Tlalalca had instilled in her at one time. And now that she saw herself in contention with the empress for Ahuitzotl's affections, she became increasingly conscious of Tlalalca's attractiveness and was much intimidated by this, deterring her from open confrontations at which she felt disadvantaged.

As for the ladies in the court, they welcomed the return of Tlalalca to her former status. Without her erudition, which led them into a variety topics for stimulating discussion, they had floundered in essentially meaningless and drab conversations with no one to steer them toward more diversified subject matters. They longed for someone to take charge; by themselves, they had no direction as none of them stepped forward to assume this role.

"We wearied hearing about Nenetzin's endless escapades," one of the ladies told Tlalalca.

"I should think so," replied Tlalalca. "Like all things overdone, they become tediously boring to everyone. Really, Nenetzin! You must be more discreet. You run the risk of acquiring a sordid reputation."

"They are jealous of me," said Nenetzin, beaming with pride. "I have my lovers while they do not."

"You are a royal princess," admonished Tlalalca, "and as such, there is a certain propriety you must uphold. I should not have to remind you of this! Your future lies in the households of nobles, involving requisites and duties. A disreputable image will jeopardize this."

"In that case, my Lady, I will just have conduct my affairs in private," Nenetzin responded, still smiling, "and in silence."

This brought forth an outburst of laughter from the ladies, except for Tlalalca who viewed the matter as more serious, understanding that Nenetzin was achieving a notoriety which extended beyond the walls of their gathering place. "You may make jest of this, Nenetzin," she said soberly, "but these things have a way of catching up with you and, eventually, you will find yourself unwanted. I strongly urge you to change your ways."

"I'm not worried about that," said Nenetzin. "I will simply refrain from my number of local lovers—and look for new ones visiting our city."

Again there ensued some laughter, but this time more hushed, for most of the ladies recognized that the advice of the empress was not only well-intended but also held a degree of accuracy. Nenetzin's comments were now regarded as an overt recalcitrance that was not appreciated.

As for Tlalalca, she readily identified Nenetzin's obstinacy for what is was and refused to add further fuel to bolster it. Yet she had an unsettled look reflecting her concerns over Nenetzin's alleged promiscuity that touched upon everyone in attendance, even Nenetzin herself.

"I exaggerate a lot, my Lady," she was moved to say. "In truth, you have no cause to be troubled."

"It pleases me to have you say so," Tlalalca answered, then smiled as she went on, "and since you speak of visitors, we shall see ample of them during the dedication of our Great Temple. I trust you will keep your passions under control."

The gathering broke out in laughter again, including Nenetzin, who felt herself purged from her inflated transgressions, and with that, Tlalalca, who had acquired some respect in the exchange, excused herself so she could stroll in the garden with Xoyo. After some period of silent ambling, she felt the need to converse.

"Pelaxilla has been unusually quiet," she told Xoyo. "I sort of miss her contributions to our discussions, and yet I am also relieved over it, fearing what she might say. Does this make sense to you, Xoyo?"

"Your predicament is delicate, my Lady," Xoyo said. "I can understand why you might have your hesitations. She does spend a lot of time with Lord Ahuitzotl."

"But why should this stop her from talking to me?"

"Perhaps she still fears you, my Lady."

"What? Over my attempts to have her inform on Ahuitzotl? That was some time ago—and never came to fruition-surely that can't be it."

"You badly frightened her, empress, and she was very much the child then."

"Even if I did, she should have gotten over it by now. Besides, she now appears to have the upper hand. I don't think that's it. You are right, Xoyo, in saying she still fears me, but it is for a different reason. She is afraid that I might take Lord Ahuitzotl from her."

"Then she is right, my Lady. You do favor him now."

"Yes, but he certainly does not crave me. She has no cause to worry."

"She may not know this."

That possibility could exit, thought Tlalalca. She had no idea what the two of them talked about privately, but the fact that Pelaxilla feared that prospect told Tlalalca there had to be a basis for it. She suddenly found her hopes resurging that Ahuitzotl might possess more than a casual interest in her; in her elevated bliss, she wanted to absorb it by herself and no longer desired her servant's presence. "Go and prepare my bath for me, Xoyo" she said. "I shall be there shortly."

Xoyo dutifully departed, leaving Tlalalca to delight in the glow of her momentary spiritual rapture. But then, starker realities presented themselves again. Stop this absurdness, she told herself; what if he did indeed fall in love with her—would that simplify her situation? How would she maintain any relationship with Pelaxilla then? Can it be possible to love two women with equal intensity at the same time? Could they abide by this?—without invoking jealousies and hostility? Riddled with these self-doubts, Tlalalca decided she should proceed for her bath and left for her chamber when it chanced to happen that she met Pelaxilla head-on coming from the opposite direction in the narrow corridor. Involuntarily, her heart sank and she thought about reversing her steps; a worried look in Pelaxilla told her that she was similarly disposed. Neither of them spoke at first.

"Pelaxilla, how are you today?" Tlalalca finally said after regaining her composure.

"Well enough, my Lady," Pelaxilla responded.

"And Lord Ahuitzotl? I haven't seen much of him lately; I attribute this to your keeping him occupied."

Pelaxilla was taken aback by Tlalalca's direct approach to the crux of the division existing between them, thinking it tactless, and she withheld no reservations about restraining her feelings. "He's mine!" she blurted out. "And I shall do everything in my power to keep him! You are not going to take him away from me!"

Tlalalca stood stunned; she paused in her realization that she had so totally struck upon a raw nerve–that the fears she suspected possessed Pelaxilla were very real. In this rash outburst, the young mistress revealed to Tlalalca that her earlier hopes had actual potentiality. She fixed her eyes on Pelaxilla as her mind grabbled for an appropriate response.

"Do not raise your voice to me, Pelaxilla!" Tlalalca replied sharply. "I am your empress and will be treated as such!"

"Forgive me, my Lady," Pelaxilla quickly retracted, being instinctively reminding of the court formalities, and then continued. "No one can love him more than I. I could not bear to lose him."

Again Tlalalca had to think before answering, as Pelaxilla's sentiment touched her. "But he loves you," she said after a lengthy pause. "He always has. You really do not have to worry about losing him–and most assuredly not to me."

"Why do you say that?"

"What do you mean? I am being straightforward with you."

"Are you?" Pelaxilla said, tears welling in her eyes, "Lord Ahuitzotl has told me that you have had a change of heart–that you no longer despise him as you once did. Isn't this true?"

Once more Tlalalca paused before answering, having to give weight to what she should say. "It may be true I have changed my mind about him," she then said, "but he certainly has not changed his feelings for me, I can guarantee you that. He does not love me."

"How do you know this?" Pelaxilla murmured, wanting most desperately to believe her.

"Isn't it obvious? Look at all the nights he spends with you. He does not come to me—not voluntarily anyway. I must prod him into coming—this as his wife! Believe me, Pelaxilla, it's not the kind of marriage I would wish upon anyone."

Pelaxilla was comforted to some degree by Tlalalca's words, but needed extra clarification to soothe her troublesome nature. "But what about your feelings for him," she said. "Do you love him?"

Tlalalca thought the question highly intrusive. "What does it matter?" she said. "If he does not love me, of what avail are my sentiments?"

"You do love him," Pelaxilla reacted in her consternation. "How can this be possible? After what he has done to you?"

"What's this you say?" a shaken Tlalalca responded. "Do you suggest that he is implicated in Lord Tizoc's death? You knew this?"

"No!" Pelaxilla quickly declared, aware that in her frustration she had alluded to more than she knew. "I did not."

"Has he told you this?" Tlalalca demanded to know.

"No, my Lady! He has not told me anything."

"If he did not tell you, then how do you know?"

"I don't know!" Pelaxilla truthfully replied, trying to extricate herself from the quandary she had indadvertantly created. "There were certain signs—inferences that gave me the idea he believed something might happen. But he never told me what. I could not relate this to you, my Lady, because I had nothing to go on."

Tlalalca gave Pelaxilla a protracted stare. She surmised the mistress was being honest; what she said did not differ much from what Tlalalca herself had presupposed. There remained the doubts, the allusions, the suspicions, in that shadowy realm of probabilities, but when everything was added together nothing was certain. All was conjecture. And, in truth, it no longer bore any relevance for her; her own passion for Ahuitzotl had by now eclipsed whatever affections remained for her former husband so that, even though her present situation was far from perfect, she no longer possessed any preference for her earlier life. She decided to let the matter rest.

"I believe you, Pelaxilla," she finally said. "Now, if you will excuse me, I must see to my bath. Xoyo has been kept waiting."

"Thank you, my Lady," a relieved Pelaxilla responded, grateful that her interrogation was not extended. She then hastily passed by the empress and departed.

In summation, the conversation had altered nothing in their convoluted interconnection with each other. Tlalalca still found herself in a secondary footing with Pelaxilla for the attention of the monarch; she would remain in her lower priority for his affection and would continue to have to plead for him to spend more time with her. She shuddered over the prolongation of her undesireable predicament, questioning if she could continue to endure it, and yet she retained a hope that things might eventually improve for her. As for Pelaxilla, she dwelled on with her worries that Tlalalca presented an obstacle to her undivided adoration from Ahuitzotl; if anything, her anxieties were even heightened by Tlalalca's admission of now bearing an actual love for him. And there prevailed the subject that was unmentioned during their brief exchange: the singular beauty of the empress, ever present to prey on Pelaxilla's apprehensions. Nothing was changed between them.

XXV

In contrast to his Huaxtecan venture, Ahuitzotl's march south was a much smaller undertaking in which the armies recruited from the Triple Alliance were at but one-third the strength of their previous operation. He did not set out against these nations to conquer them, but only to test their capabilities for what he anticipated would be a future movement on them-the object at present was to 'chastise' them for violating the trading agreements, meant as a sort of intimidation, not to destroy them. Spurred on by his desire to add captives from these inhabitants to satisfy Huitzilopochtli at his temple's dedication, Ahuitzotl conducted this campaign with the determination of a zealous priest out to convert the sinning masses.

As usual, Nezahualpilli commanded the Acolhuas and Chimalpopoca his Tepanecs. Neither was enthusiastic over beginning a new campaign so soon after having completed their last one, especially the latter, who pleaded old age as the cause of his reluctance. However, once the operation was underway, their fervor returned to them and they were in the forefront of stirring their units onward so as to bring this enterprise to a speedy conclusion. Motecuhzoma was given command of his first army and assigned to lead it against the Mixtec city of Coyolapan. This he accomplished readily, executing a rapid incursion into the region and catching the opposition by surprise; he destroyed its army with a skillful envelopment that amazed even the old veterans who accompanied him.

They achieved phenomenal success. Ahuitzotl moved on the enemy in his characteristic style, striking fast and tailoring his maneuvers and tactics to counter the particular situation facing him. He first attacked Tlappan and, routing the army sent against him, accepted the gifts of its ruler who sued for peace and regaled him with offers of rich prizes. He left the city intact but imposed substantial tributes on it. He next proceeded south to Teopuctlah and Quetzaltepec where he met the Zapotecs for the first time and handily defeated them as they easily fell prey to his deceptive moves which lured them into repeated traps. He received their offers for peace without much deliberation, demanding only the number of captives taken in the actual fighting and promises of safe conduct for the merchants and compliance with the Mexica regulations governing their activities. When, after three months of ceaseless campaigning, the Mexica returned to Anahuac, Ahuitzotl's reputation was firmly established: he was heralded as the greatest warlord since Motecuhzoma Ilhuicamina.

Now his fame extended to the farthest reaches of the realm, and when the dignitaries arrived to answer the invitations sent to their lords bidding them to attend the inauguration of the Great Temple, none bore messages declining this offer. Under these auspicious developments, Ahuitzotl was seated in his royal jaguar skin throne in the crowded assembly hall where the envoys were called in to relate the words given them by the many lords they had visited. Already he had received a favorable reply from those envoys sent to Michoacan, and now he listened to the ones from Tlaxcala.

"The Tlaxcalan lord sends his greetings, Great Lord, and he accepts your invitation. Indeed, he offers his apologies for not attending your coronation and regrets having been so remiss in his obligations. He asks your pardon for this oversight."

"Do you hear this, Cihuacoatl?" Ahuitzotl beamed. "He even apologizes. Things are significantly different in the year I have ruled."

"As in the days of Motecuhzoma and Axayacatl," affirmed an equally elated minister, "but hear, our envoy wishes to say more."

"The lord will attend, Mighty One," continued the emissary, "but requests to know how he can make his appearance without being noticed, and thereby not raise the people to hostility."

"His concern is valid," answered Ahuitzotl. "The people must believe we are enemies of the Tlaxcalans, as ever, and that there can be no truce between us even for such an important event as this dedication. To learn that we abide his presence is certain to diminish their martial ardor-a risk neither of us can afford. Inform him we will allow for the customary passage into our city."

"Forgive me, Lord. I am not familiar with this passage, being newly assigned to this post."

"He and his ministers will be escorted into our city at night and in canoes from the eastern shores of the lake by guides sworn to secrecy who can be trusted. Once here, they shall be housed in the old palace under the care of my guards. Canopies will be constructed for their viewing of the rites before the Great Temple from where they will not be seen by the townspeople. And throughout its duration, they will be under my personal protection."

Their exchange concluded, Ahuitzotl permitted the envoys their leave and was beside himself with joy as he watched them go. "Can you believe this?" he gleamed with pride. "Both the Tarascans and Tlaxcalan lords, our most powerful foes, pay homage to me."

"They fear us now, Lord," said Cihuacoatl, "having been daunted by your stunning exploits. They must see for themselves what sort of ruler was able to do such feats."

"They will be even more awed when they leave Tenochtitlan afterward. Who comes before me now?"

"The envoy we sent to the Zapotecan lord, Cocijoeza, from the city of Zaachila."

"Zaachila? I've never heard of it."

"We call it Teotzapotlan. It's far to the south-far indeed, more than five hundred leagues."

"I didn't know the Zapotec realm stretched to that distance."

"It reaches even farther. Cocijoeza is presently moving his capital a hundred leagues more to the south-a place called Tehuantepec."

This interested Ahuitzotl. He long questioned whether there was anything worth pursuing in these forested southern regions and thought if the Zapotecs were extending in that direction, they had ample motivation for it. Perhaps the stories he heard related by the pochteca were true-that rich and powerful kingdoms abounded in those remote jungles. He motioned for the envoy to speak.

"I bring you the words of Lord Cocijoeza," he declared. "He reports that he has already begun his long journey to Anahuac so that he might repay you for the services you have rendered him, for which he is most grateful. That is why he will honor your invitation, in spite of the many leagues he must travel."

His words befuddled Ahuitzotl, "You have me at a disadvantage. What services have I delivered for this Cocijoeza?"

"He has, over the years, been crowded out of his native lands by the ever increasing Mixtecs, who have pushed his own people more southerly-that is why he is moving his capital to Tehuantepec. In your defeating the Mixtecs during your recent operation, you have eased some of the pressures on him, which in turn gave him time to regroup and score his own decisive victory over them. He thus is indebted to you and wishes to express his gratitude by seeing you."

"We also attacked the Zapotecs in that operation. Why should he be grateful for that?"

"You defeated those of his people who have turned against him and sided with the Mixtecs in order that they might be permitted to remain in their former cities. They are regarded as renegades and traitorous to his cause."

"Ah, the Zapotecs are then at war with each other."

"Not open warfare, which is reserved for the Mixtecs, but there is animosity between them."

"I'm unclear what to make of this. It's not my purpose to have others profit from my enterprises. Yet I must acknowledge his desire to honor me. How did the Zapotecs treat you?"

"Opulantly, Great Lord! They are gracious hosts and entertain their guests lavishly with fine foods and beautiful women."

"What are their customs, and what gods do they worship?"

"They are an ancient people and proud of their heritage; many of their current festivities entail recalling their earlier days of glory. Much of their time is spent honoring the dead—they revere the god of the dead highly, devoting their arts and ceremonies to him. But they hold the sun god as their principal deity and have great respect for the rain god-most of their temples are dedicated to these two. They seem a jovial lot who delight in relating happy and humorous stories-more so than other people we have met."

"It would seem that this detracts from a martial spirit. Did you happen to observe their armies in action?"

"Unfortunately no, Lord. In fact, I was prevented from seeing anything connected with their military."

"Cocijoeza understands that envoys are used as intelligence gatherers and took the necessary precautions to keep his operations secret-it says something of the man. I thank you for your report and should like to hear more, but there are others I must yet see."

This exchange was typical of the ones which were to follow. Ahuitzotl had a keen desire to learn about people he knew little of, not merely out of an inquisitive nature which aroused his curiosity in them, but also because he saw them as potential adversaries and looked for clues suggesting their military prowess and capabilities. Many of the envoys he dispatched were specifically trained to make such assessments and their mission was more often to conduct a clandestine surveillance under the guise of diplomatic purposes than to carry mere messages.

Activity was mounting in preparation for the coming events. Now, in the end of the year Eight-Reed, the Great Temple was at last completed after nearly ten years under construction. Braziers, flowers, and other adornments were being emplaced on its tiers for the sacred rituals and, below it, bleachers with draped stands were in process of erection for the potentates whose arrival was shortly expected. Everywhere energy was expended marking the coming celebration; specialists were assigned to create their products for sale or presentation as prizes; streets and buildings were scrubbed clean and, in some cases, painted; Axayacatl's palace, serving as the guest house for the visitors, was made ready by hundreds of workers who set up the rooms, leisure facilities, and kitchens; cooks and stewards devised their recipes and supervised the storage of the enormous quantities of food brought into the palace.

In the different wards of the city where thousands of captives taken over a full year's campaigning were quartered, priests initiated their visitations to instruct them on the divine messages they should transmit to the gods. They were provided with the best food and all the material comforts that local citizens could give, including periodic companionship of women if they requested it, and understood the fate in store for them. The very act of capture, especially on the battlefield, dictated this inevitable destiny. Honored to be granted entrance into paradise, most of them eagerly awaited these sessions with the priests and did their best to memorize the passages they were given.

All the prisoners were visited by the priests, even though only a handful of them were expected to be honored during the dedication. All but one, that is, for Xaman Utec, on orders from Ahuitzotl, rotted away in his cage, fed only at infrequent intervals and then barely enough to keep him alive so that he might witness the ceremonies but until then languish over having so audaciously offended the Revered Speaker. He suffered terribly, becoming more and more emaciated in his slow starvation, but no one dared to show him compassion by giving him an ample amount to eat-to disobey the monarch meant certain and painful death.

Ahuitzotl absorbed himself in his tasks and often worked into darkness with his ministers and priests in overseeing the activity. A major reason for his doing this was as a consequence of the less than comfortable relationship with Pelaxilla and Tlalalca which was quite burdensome for him. Despite all the assurances he could give Pelaxilla, and spending most of his private time with her, it seemed insufficient, and each night she pleaded that he again spend the following one with her. And when he went to Tlalalca, perhaps twice a week, he found her disconsolate over his rare appearances. He was unable to satisfy either of them, and the strain was having its telling affect on him, souring his disposition and causing him to seek out pretexts for avoiding the two women altogether. He therefore welcomed the workload associated with the coming ceremony, and even if there was no requirement for him to supervise it, he often did so because it afforded him a degree of relief from the currently insoluble pressures besieging his personal life.

On the final day in which he received envoys, Ahuitzotl had his planners, ministers, administrators, priests, and chief commanders present in the main hall so he could cover with them all the measures which had been implemented to provide for the comfort, security, and entertainment of the arriving guests. When the last of the legates was dismissed, the meeting began in earnest as every item requiring attention as discussed.

"It appears all is arranged," Ahuitzotl declared after hearing what they had to say. "Our visitors should be amply impressed by what they see here. Will there be enough time for them to view the singing and dancing between the sacrifices?"

"With the recommended two thousand captives sacrificed over a four day period," the head priest responded, "there will be no interference with the entertainment."

Ahuitzotl grinned, revealing his gleaming white teeth in satisfaction, when he noticed that one of his advisors wished to add something. He beckoned him to speak.

"How many townspeople from the mainland cities shall we allow to witness our dedication to Tizoc's temple?" he asked.

Ahuitzotl's smile instantly vanished; he turned ashen pale and eyes blazed. "What did you say?" he demanded sharply.

The advisor became frightened over this sudden change in his master's countenance and his icily issued request; he froze, unable to speak.

"What did you call it?" Ahuitzotl shouted.

"Why, Tizoc's temple, Lord. The people so name it."

"Tizoc's temple! Do you hear this, minster? He said that's what the people call it. Is this true?"

Cihuacoatl grew numb with fear and felt his knees buckling underneath his cloak.

"Well?" Ahuitzotl's fury mounted, "Do I have to repeat myself? Answer truthfully!"

"I have heard it called such-it is indeed so, lord!" replied Cihuacoatl nervously.

Ahuitzotl sprang out of his throne, his face twisted in rage, vessels protruding from his brow; he wildly paced the floor back and forth in front of an assemblage that cringed in abject fright. "Will I never be rid of that accursed name?" he stormed. "What must I do to erase that man's memory? I am forever hounded by him! Are my brilliant conquests to be overshadowed by accrediting the greatest event of our time to his name? By the gods! I won't have it!"

He continued stomping about in his agitation while his audience held its breath as it grimly beheld this frightening spectacle. Suddenly he stopped-a cruel flash came to his eyes: he had come upon an idea.

"I know how to rid myself of his memory once and for all, and when the people speak of this temple, they will forever think of my name. I shall make then forget Tizoc!"

"How will you do this?" Cihuacoatl risked asking.

"What is the total count of all the prisoners we have taken since the Matlazinca campaign?"

"About twenty thousand, Lord."

"Sacrifice them!"

"What!" a much alarmed Cihuacoatl could not believe what he had heard.

"I said that we shall sacrifice them!"

"Twenty thousand of them?"

"Are you daft, minister?" Ahuitzotl exploded, "Am I to repeat myself endlessly for your comprehension? Yes, I want them all sacrificed! Forget about the singing and dancing you have planned; the dedication will consist entirely of the sacrifices. Make use of the adjacent temples if you have to."

His directive led to considerable murmuring among the assemblage and it stood apparent that this was received both in shock and disfavor, even to the point of offending many in spite of his being their monarch.

"But-but how will we dispose of that many bodies?"

"Figure something out. Discuss the matter with the various commanders. The occasion will be one to remember, eclipsing anything we have ever done. No one will ever again call it Tizoc's temple after this!"

"And all that has been arranged? The escorted tours? And feasting?"

"Change what you must, but do not attempt to make me reconsider what I've said. I am resolved on this matter."

The shock could still be read on Cihuacoatl's face as his mind grappled over the enormity of the task confronting him in altering the ceremony's scheduled sequence of events. He was not alone; even the priests of the gods to whom the temple would be dedicated stood spellbound and aghast. They could not help but view their lord's plan with the greatest consternation and feared how the gods might react to such a carnage-even they could be overfed.

"It shall be done," Cihuacoatl answered, feeling the gravest misgivings.

"There is more," said Ahuitzotl.

"More?" Cihuacoatl gasped, wondering how that was possible.

"Every man, woman, and child old enough to walk in Anahuac is to attend the rites at least one out of the four days. Select them by cities and rotate them, but require them to attend-and I want them counted! This event must be indelibly forged into their minds-forever ingrained into their memories. Do not fail me. Let no one refuse these orders!"

"Be warned, Lord!" protested Huitzilopochtli's highest priest angrily. "Do not contrive to make this dedication a monument to your own glory-it is for the gods!"

"Is it to be for Tizoc's glory then?" Ahuitzotl shouted at the priest, alarming everyone. "I tell you, priest, do not deprive me of my greatest achievement!"

Ahuitzotl heard the grumbling and discontent expressed from the floor and became annoyed over the recalcitance he saw in evidence. "This remonstrance will cease!" he glowered. "You've heard my instructions. Let the person who objects to them speak out now and state his reasons for opposing them."

None dared contest the Revered Speaker; he anticipated this and applied his approach to silence their criticism. "No one objects?" Ahuitzotl scowled, contemptuous of their apparent pusillanimity. "Then we are wasting our time remaining here-there is much to do. This meeting is terminated."

The parties thereupon hastily departed, a most sober demeanor about them. They were confused in their reaction to the monarch's proposal-certainly a sacrifice of this magnitude would impact on the visitors, and that in itself may be a good thing. But what of the gods? How would they perceive such an immense slaughter, especially when considering the base motivation behind it? And there remained the monstrous disposal problem entailed is such a killing; no one knew how to get a grip on dealing with this. But whatever else they might have deliberated over, one thing was clear to them: this dedication would be a spectacle never equalled.

XXVI

The great day had arrived. Already, before the rays of Tonatiuh, the Sun, cast its intense glow on the colossal roof combs of the Great Temple, a throng was gathering in the open plaza until everyone stood abreast each other in a sea of humanity. All of Tenochtitlan congregated there, complying with the Revered Speaker's directive; children were lifted upon the shoulders of their parents so they would not be compressed or trampled and could get a better view of the proceedings. Eyes focused on the monolithic structure and excitement prevailed in eager expectation of what the rumors had told them-that this was to be the spectacle to end all spectacles.

The nobles and invited guests of the allied nations were seated in bleachers constructed close to the Great Temple so that nothing obstucted their view, while the lords of the enemy states, or their delegation, sat in screened enclosures where they remained hidden from the crowd. Most entered the city late last night, secretly having crossed the lake, and were met by Ahuitzotl who hosted a splendid reception for them, furnishing them with an initial installment of gifts. Organized to display the greatness and power of the Mexica state and to instill a sense of awe over the opulence offered and readily available to them, this constituted an appropriate introduction for them and sufficiently whetted their curiosity over what was to ensue. As they sat in their canopied stands, they eagerly awaited the promised commemoration to the gods.

Sunlight bathed the temple's smoothly stuccoed surface, first breaking on the dual trapezoid roof combs which towered like twin peaks above the shrines of Huitzilopochtli and Tlaloc, and then gradually descending until its glare reflected the distinct outline of four stone altars emplaced at even intervals where the topmost step adjoined the upper platform. The shadows receded as rays dropped tier by tier until the entire temple stood in glaring brilliance before the spectators: the time was almost at hand.

Silence imbued the crowd when it espied a party of colorfully decorated figures ascending the temple's stairs. It was Ahuitzotl, adorned in a brightly feathered cloak and flowers, accompanied by Nezahualpilli, Chimalpopoca, and Cihuacoatl, and trailed by a multitude of priests wearing their traditional black robes with their hair falling loosely to their shoulders. Rising above the hushed throng until they covered all one-hundred and fourteen steps, they paused on reaching the upper tier to gaze down on the masses beneath them. As far as the eye could see, all about the square, into its connecting streets beyond the serpent's wall, and on the platforms of the adjacent temples and buildings, people were flocked to observe the rites. After spending several minutes in exhiliration over this marvelous sight, Ahuitzotl removed his cloak and positioned himself behind the sacrificial block nearest the center baluster in front of Huitzilopochtli's shrine. Nezahualpilli took his place on the techtacl to the emperor's left while Cihuacoatl stood behind the one on the right, and Chimalpopoca was on the far right. Priests stationed themselves about each ruler and awaited the signal to activate the bloodletting.

Ahuitzotl glanced in the direction of the head priest, giving him a grave look, then nodded to indicate the ceremony's commencement. The priest pressed a conch to his lips and drowned the plaza in its blare. Atop a nearby temple, subordinates responded and began beating the giant panhuehuetl with huge clubs. Its shattering thunder startled the spectators; their hearts pounded in unison to each drumbeat as if it had physically struck them. Then, just as suddenly, stillness.

Solemnly, the captives entered the square from four different directions at once, escorted by knights from the Eagle and Jaguar orders who opened a path for them through the crowd. The leading members in each line had their yellow painted bodies draped with embroidered and feathered cloaks in the colors that represented the deity to whom they were to carry the divine messages-turquoise for Huitzilopochtli and a deep blue for Tlaloc. More than half of them were in bare skin, their numbers being too great for the vats of paint available. They were led up along the edges of the balustrades until their queues reached from the temple's base to its upper tier. From there, three of their lines extended across the plaza into the city's major avenues reaching to the causeways, while the fourth stretched eastward to the lakeshore. Shorter lines led to six other temples. The people gazed gravely at them, and many offered a prayer of their own that they wished relayed to the gods: the mood was one of sober reverence.

KA-RA-BOOM! Again the dull thuds from the panhuehuetl numbed senses, and the chief priest moved to the edge of the temple's dividing baluster. Called Tolpiltzin, he wore a red mantle over a black tunic and a conical headdress of green and yellow feathers; from his ears protruded gold plugs inlaid with green jade and a labret of blue stone protruded from his lower lip. Black paint was smeared on his face in a wide streak extending from his lips to his ears to amplify his fearsome appearance, and he awed those who looked upon him. In a booming voice that roared out over the square, the Tolpiltzin shouted out his sacred chants to Huitzilopochtli whom he served. Then he stepped back and was replaced by another priest, just as frightening in apprearance with his black robe and tasseled conical hat. He was Tlaloc's chief priest and proceeded to present his own intones in an equally boisterous voice, and when he finished his orisons and returned to his post, trumpets once again blew forth. This was the call to begin the sacrifices.

Immediately, as if spurred onward by extreme desperation, four of the black-smeared priests about each alterstone grapped the first captive in each line and flung him over the arched block; a fifth stretched a wooden yoke under the victim's chin, yanking back the head so his body was in a taut arc with its chest jutting up to the highest level, reaching to the waist of the rulers who were ready to begin. Nezahualpilli, Chimalpopoca, and Cihuacoatl looked at the Revered Speaker to wait until he cut out the first heart before starting on their own captive.

Ahuitzotl lifted the hand wielding his flint knife above his head and paused momentarily to take measure of the hushed silence below. He glanced at the victim eagle spread before him and noted the vacant stare in his glassy eyes, an effect of the drugs given him earlier. Then, in one swift powerful stroke, he plunged his knife into the chest, striking it just under the right breast, and slashed it across in a broad sweep; he reached into the goriness, forcing his fingers through the hot flesh until they circled around the pulsating organ at which point he glasped on to it. He heard the heart tear loose from its connecting tendons as he yanked it out and elevated it into the air, still beating, with his bloodied hand. He then gave it to a priest who placed it on a tray and hastily carried it into the shrine where he dropped it into the idol's open mouth. His votaries in the meantime raised the body from the block and hurled it over the stairs and as this was occurring, the monarch's colleagues and chief minister followed his example and dispatched their victims with equal dexterity.

No sooner was this first victim tossed from the temple when the priests seized the next one and in line dragged him over the same block. Instantly he joined his comrade in the next world; his body was flung down, the trail of blood widening, when the third victim was taken; the haste in which he was sent off suggested a self-imposed nervousness that Ahuitzotl must have felt over the enormous task he had set upon himself. One after another, without pause, the captives met their end at the hands of a monarch who did not appear to tire of the bloody exercise, and by mid-morning, the path of the gore on the stairway spread to nearly its total width leaving it coated in red. Not wanting to be outdone by the Revered Speaker, as if a fierce competition had ensued between rulers, Nezahualpilli and Chimalpopoca kept up at his gruelling pace. However, Cihuacoatl, who started out as fast, became exhausted and asked to be relieved by a ranking priest: he had lasted for almost two hours.

Below, the disposal details toiled feverishly to keep apace with the plummeting bodies. Finding it impossible to dismember them in the prescribed manner at the rate in which the captives were being dispatched, the crews cut off only the head, to be later displayed on the skull rack, while lifting the remainder into barges for subsequent transport to the burning grounds. All the city's resources were strained to maximum capacity in preventing the corpses from accumulation in the hot sun.

By noon, Ahuitzotl had enough. Expended of energy, his arms aching from the long hours of cutting and tearing flesh, he finally requested a substitute for his laborious work. Long before this, the priests who seized the victims for the cutting and flung them over the temple's edge had rotated their lot, and only Nezahualpilli kept at it as long as the monarch, the older Chimalpopoca having retired from his duties shortly after the minister. All were replaced by other lords who kept up the gory business without as much as a minute's interruption.

A wearied Ahuitzotl descended the temple with his colleagues. They had to take each step with precaution so as not to slip on the bloodied stones as gore now stained the entire stairway, coagulated and sticky on parts of it, and wet and slick elsewhere. And at the base, bodies lay in contorted heaps where they had landed, piling up faster than the crews could remove them; a pool of blood spread outward from the grim stack—Ahuitzotl could not avoid stepping in it when he left the temple.

The stench of death permeating the square was overwhelming as blood mixed with defecating and urinating corpses to reek in the midday heat and make the work of the disposal squadrons exceedingly miserable. At length, even the spectators became restless, nauseated by the putrid smell and tiring of the monotonous repetition; children were crying while men and women became agitated as they felt themselves trapped amid the throng. Although they could move about to use the public conveniences, their large numbers imposed restrictions and inhibited ready access to these, and this led to general irritation. Nezahualpilli was not blind to these signs.

"Your people grow weary of this," he told Ahuitzotl. "I recommmend you allow them to go and have others take their place."

"That's agreeable to me," replied Ahuitzotl. "There are many more from the cities across the lake who must see this. We can't have one group staying here all day."

With that, Ahuitzotl directed Cihuacoatl to begin rotating the populace, a step the minister had already implemented after having perceived the crowd's disquietude in accordance with his arrangements. Fortunately, the nobles and visiting dignitaries had all the essential services available to them in their stands, being catered to by attendants, and could freely move about to seek a respite from the ceaseless slaughter. A covered passageway led from the guest palace to the bleacher area, erected specially for the enemy lords to avoid their being a captive audience. Yet, surprisingly few of them made use of it, restrained by the demands of protocol which imposed an attentiveness to the activities offered by a host.

Taking these rules of etiquette into regard, Ahuitzotl and his colleagues thought it a prudent gesture to sit with their foreign guests in their canopied section during the afternoon and, after taking a brief interlude to refresh and see to personal needs, joined them there. The dignitaries greeted their host graciously and seemed appreciative that he and his allied rulers chose to stay with them. After having seated himself, Ahuitzotl took note of the different lords about him and the man he surmised might be his faroff visitor, Cocijoeza.

"Is that the Zapotecan?" he asked Cihuacoatl who was seated next to him. "I cannot remember having received him."

"That's him, Lord," affirmed the minister after trailing his master's eyes to the target.

Not a handsome man by any measure, indeed quite ugly, thought Ahuitzotl as he made an assessment of him. He was overweight and his face reflected this with its fleshy folds; it was dominated by a large hooked nose and his eyes were hidden behind two narrow slits. Ahuitzotl took an almost instant dislike for the Zapotecan but checked himself for his unseemly behavior. The man had, after all, come a significant distance to express his indebtedness to him, and he ought to be appreciative for that. Cocijoeza abruptly turned his head to glimpse at the Mexica monarch through his slits and smiled; Ahuitzotl responded by nodding, acknowledging this silent greeting, then focused back on the temple's activity while his mind remained fixed on the Zapotecan.

The carnage seemed doubly intense in the afternoon sun when its heat enhanced the fetidness more prominantly about the square. What thoughts ran through the captives as they stood on the steps waiting for their turn could only be guessed, but the ceremony's sanctity had to be spoiled by its excess. Although glassy-eyed and lethargic, they nevertheless appeared confused and frightened over the sight of their comrades piling up ignominiously below them. How could their entrance into paradise be a unique event when so many joined them in this? Would the gods listen to their messages when others had already related the same words to them?

Only when the sun had dropped below the western mountains after rendering everyone a final reminder of the day's accomplishment by reflecting a brilliant reddish hue off the temple's bloodstained masonry did the slaughter come to an end. Trumpets signaled its conclusion and the captives still left were led back to their quarters while the square emptied of its occupants who had been saturated with the bloodletting. The lords retired for their palaces to ready themselves for the evening's feasting while priests remained at the temple to supervise its cleaning and the emptying of the Thorn's Nest, a depository for the hearts cast through the mouths of the idols.

Cleanup crews labored under torchlights to rid the area of the dead still heaped about beneath the temple's stairway. They scraped off caked blood from the stones and washed them clean as best as they could to remove all traces of the day's butchery; reeds and straw were used to absorb the ankle-deep blood at the base. The corpses were carried to canoes anchored in the canals bordering the plaza just beyond the serpent headed wall and transported to the selected chinampas for burning. Earlier in the day, the zoos had been supplied with all the flesh that could be stored in its facilities-flesh cut from the bodies of the dispatched victims. The heads of the corpses were sliced off to be later stripped of their flesh and contents and thoroughly cleaned so that they could be mounted upon poles on the skull rack located about a hundred paces west of the Great Temple.

While this activity was proceeding in the square, Ahuitzotl entertained his guests in his palace, hosting them regally with delicious foods while they were being amused by jugglers, singers, and various musicians. He seized upon the occasion to learn as much as possible about the kingdoms his many visitors represented, ambling among when they were at leisure after their dinner and speaking to them, questioning them on numerous subjects and eliciting their reaction to the rites they had witnessed. It chanced during this period of repose that he, accompanied by Nezahualpilli, met with Cocijoeza who knew the Nahuatl tongue.

"I must congratulate you on your triumph over the Mixtecs," Ahuitzotl said to the Zapotecan. "We did not know your people were at war with them."

"We have been for many generations," Cocijoeza informed him. "They have deprived us of our ancient lands and forced us to vacate our sacred capital, Zaachila. But we are starting to strike back at them. Your recent victory at Coyolapan greatly assisted us."

"So I have heard."

"They had to send their armies north to counter your threat there, which weakened them in our vicinity and enabled us to defeat them. You must realize this was our first major victory over them in many years, but it will not be the last. We now know it can be done; this in itself gives us the incentive to face them again."

"It is our belief that the gods determine such outcomes. You may have to make the kind of offerings we do in order to dispose them into granting your wishes-the victories you seek."

"You mean a sacrifice such as I have seen today?" Cocijoeza turned pale at the suggestion, a reaction quickly discerned by Ahuitzotl who was perplexed that his grandiose show should be so distastefully received.

"You are appalled by it?" he asked.

"It was, shall I say, more than I had expected-a startling presentation to say the least."

"You are impressed then."

"Impressed? Yes, that would be an accurate description. All those captives-I've never seen anything like it."

"They were all taken honorably in battle-the noblest offerings we can give the gods."

"There were so many."

"We have much to ask from them."

"But, Mighty Lord, you have already scored many victories. If it is incumbant upon you to make all those offerings for things to be granted to you, then what does this portent?"

Ahuitzotl eyed Cocijoeza cautiously; that he harbored a distrust over the purpose of this sacrifice was apparent enough, and he may even have suspected what ambitions the Revered speaker concealed within himself. The realization came awkwardly to Ahuitzotl who now strove to dismiss any implications without giving offense.

"You have nothing to fear," Ahuitzotl assured him, "Just as the Mixtecs are your traditional enemy, so we have ours. But be advised, Cocijoeza, do not allow your wars to jeopardize our trades in your region. We place great value on our agreements."

Cocijoeza did not find much in the Revered Speaker's words to ease his suspicions; they amounted to a virtual admission that he meant to expand the Mexica hegemony, something even the distant Zapotecs could not view favorably. He refrained from making his inner perturbation known so as not to provoke or tempt his host. "I appreciate hearing you say so," he answered. "As for the pacts existing between us, they serve my people as well as yours. You could easily reciprocate in kind were we to infringe upon these-that will benefit neither of us."

"So we understand each other. I trust I have your word that our pochteca will meet with no interference while in your regions."

"You have it," affirmed Cocijoeza.

With this averment, Ahuitzotl and Nezahualpilli walked off, proceeding for the exit to engage in personal pursuits.

"I was curious how you would extricate yourself from that," said Nezahualpilli. "Your tongue was too loose in his presence."

"True, but I didn't know how else to divert his mistrust except to draw attention to the pochteca. He's a clever man; you saw how quickly he deduced a threatening situation—not altogether inaccurate I might add—yet he kept his calmness in spite of it."

"He is safe enough, isn't he?"

"If you mean by that whether I have my eyes on his realm, the answer is no. Zapoteca is too far from Anahuac for my tastes. It poses a major supply obstacle for an army to venture into so remote a region."

Ahuitzotl's response told Nezahualpilli that he had indeed given such an enterprise some consideration. The Texcocan sensed that he was being deceived, but declined additional elaboration on the matter, deeming it unimportant at present. Instead, he turned to a lighter subject. "Do I have Nenetzin as my partner tonight?" he asked.

"I'll have her sent to you. You know, she is an admirer of yours, or rather it is more accurate to say she savors your renown for exploits in bed."

"I had no idea she did," the Texcocan grinned, very much flattered by that revelation.

"It's true enough. She's made no secret of it in her many conversations with my ladies."

"In that case, by all means send her to me; she is my favorite here and I shall endeavor to live up to her expectations."

"No doubt you will," Ahuitzotl dryly commented. He had no particular respect for the kind of reputation enjoyed by Nezahualpilli—his preference ran for conquests on the battlefield; those in bed were incidental in comparison. And he knew Nenetzin to be the palace trollop—to have her as an admirer was nothing to boast over. For an instant, he felt a compulsion to tell his friend of her alleged escapades, but then negated this impulse on the grounds that there was no point in casting derogatory slurs on members of the royal family, even if they merited it. Let the Texcocan have a fling with his disreputable niece; as for himself, he would end the day in far better company—with his beloved Pelaxilla.

XXVII

The horrendous killing resumed on the next day following a nearly similar procedure as before with captives lined out to as far as the causeways awaiting their turn on the block. It was the inhabitants of Tlacopan, Atzcapotzalco, Tlatilco, Chapultepec, Coyoacan, and Tacubaya—the principal cities flourishing along Lake Texcoco's western shores-who were required to witness the event on this day. They filtered into Tenochtitlan's central plaza at early dawn, many having entered the previous night and staying with relatives or friends, and soon stood as densely packed as the first day's local crowds when the lordly sacrificers ascended to their stations atop the temple.   The stench of yesterday's slaughter still clung about the upper platform and emitted a particularly foul odor from the mouths of the idols, reeking so fetidly that the priests who approached them held their breath so they would not be overcome by the putresence. But as fresh hot blood splattered over the altars and scrubbed masonry, the decaying smell was drowned out by the new flow which, in the crisp morning air, ran with abundance.

Ahuitzotl and his allied rulers cut out the hearts from many victims to begin this second day's ritual prior to being relieved by rapacious priests who avidly engaged their task with an equal zeal as exhibited on the previous day. With renewed vigor, as if rejuvenated by their night's respite, they undertook their grim duties in the same fast-paced method that had characterized the competition between the lords earlier. In seconds, a prisoner was spread on the block, stretched taut, cut open and his heart torn from him, and then thrown over the steps.

With the number of disposal crews doubled, the task of decapitating the bodies and dragging them to waiting barges kept apace the rate of the cutting. At least that was the case earlier in the day, but as it continued on, these workers, who remained on station without being relieved, tired under their ceaseless toil and fell behind. Again corpses began to accumulate in twisted heaps, lying in thick pools of blood creeping outward with each additional body plummeting from the platform, and by the day's end, another full night's work lay ahead with the dead piled up to a man's height beneath the stairways. And while this chore was progressing that evening, another banquet transpired in the palace setting the tone for these events: the excesses of the day followed by feasting to commemorate its ending–all designed to astound Ahuitzotl's visitors with the wealth and power under his command.

The third day followed the sequence of the second so closely in every respect that they might have been duplicates, and if the visiting dignitaries received the endless slaughter with any reservations, or became bored with its monotony, they gave no indication of it. Indeed, they seemed in unusually good spirits during their evening's gala when presented with the day's allotment of gifts as the magnanimous give-away that highlighted each fete had its effect in nullifying the ennui or horror of the day. Ahuitzotl knew this, applying every effort in regalling his guests with all the generosity and delights considered necessary to make their stay in Tenochtitlan a memorable one. By the time they departed, he reasoned, the entire affair will be firmly fixed in their minds–a permanent imprint of how the Mexica hosted them.

If the mood up to the third day had been one of impervious detachment on the part of the visitors, or a displayed pretension of it, by the time the final day came upon them, it changed considerably. As they watched the endless slaughter, a sober countenance now could be discerned on their faces and some of them even exhibited signs of abject fear as the sheer immensity of this carnage finally struck them with its full meaning. No longer discussing the affairs of their states and making light of the situation, they now sat grim-faced and quietly, puzzled over its meaning and fretting over what it might signify. The butchery was grossly overdone, and like all things overdone, it ultimately invoked a sense of revulsion in the observer.

The caustic stench of death now festered inescapably all about the Great Temple. The structure reeked of it in the hot sun; it spread from there into the square and even the city. Streams of blood ran everywhere and congealed into a thick fetid paste over the steps and sacrificial blocks; trails of it led to the idols and coated their mouths into which the thousands of hearts had been dumped; priests stood saturated in it, their hair matted with it, and they stank of its decay as it dried on them in smeared patches splattered over their skin and clothing.

Bewildered captives glared wild-eyed and frightened at seeing their lot heaped ignominiously in grotesque piles below the temple rotting in the heat. Although drugged into a semi-sensitive state, they retained some comprehension of their duty and nervously memorized the messages they had been instructed to deliver into the next world. But by this time, none could have believed that he would be heard-the singular importance of their words had been reduced to total insignificance by the enormity of their numbers. Confused, embittered, and fearful, many of them wept openly in their utter disillusionment as their glorious moment, their reason for being, was all but negated for them, drowned in an abyss of excess. Those of them still waiting slipped on the blood-soaked stairs and fell against one another, and they crawled on all fours up the last few steps and were seized by foul-smelling priests who dragged them onto the drenched altars. They could feel the hot viscosity of the congealing blood on their bare backs; the rancid stench seared their nostrils as they stared at the knife descending on them under the tiring weight of a bloodied hand. In this slimy and stinking gore, they met their end.

Vultures, hawks, and other flesh eating birds flocked in clouds above Tenochtitlan and descended on the chinampas where the corpses numbering in the thousands were rotting. Too many for burning, they had, for the last two days, just been deposited there until they rose in ugly heaps covering the floating plots entirely. some rolling into the lake waters where they remained partially submerged. This afforded a windfall for the carrion eaters; they hovered in thick clusters over the chinampas when the canoes came with more bodies, and then swooped down after this latest dump was completed, partaking in their gruesome meal as one solid squirming mass.

On that final day, the entire disposal system ollapsed. With all of the chinampas filled over capacity, the crews next used their available barges to hold the latest corpses until these too were filled; then they amassed them at the docking facilities, leaving them lying there in stacks until they could be later removed-when that would be, no one knew-and yet still more captives ascended the Great Temple. To the frantic anxiety-ridden squadrons tasked with disposing the bodies, this was an utterly despairing sight. Their chieftains informed supervisors of the inability to remove any more corpses who, in turn, told their overlords until word finally reached Tlohtzin, and he hastened to report it to the monarch. He found him sitting among his allied rulers and informed him of his need to confer with him in private. Ahuitzotl welcomed this distraction: the spectacle had become tedious.

"Yes, Tlohtzin," Ahuitzotl said when he came to a secluded corner by the stands, "What prompts your interruption?"

"A serious problem, Lord. The bodies are accumulating at the mooring grounds. They can no longer be taken to the chinampas."

"Are the crews insufficient? You must get more men."

"It's not the crews that are insufficient, but the facilities. All the chinampas used for depositing the bodies are filled-they could not be burned for lack of kindling. The carrion feeders are everywhere. We have to do something."

"What do you propose?" Ahuitzotl answered indignantly, displeased over being presented with such a problem.

"You must stop the sacrificing. Certainly we have more than satisfied Huitzilopochtli and Tlaloc by now. As it is, we will have to spend weeks to clean up this mess."

"When we're almost finished with the last of them? I advise you not to give me this kind of counsel."

"I recommend it for safety's sake. Many physicians see this as a major concern-decaying corpses pose a health problem."

"The gods will protect us. They would not inflict disasters upon us after we so abundantly honored them."

"I beseech you. Lord! You cannot know this-we face risks."

"No man can predict how the gods will behave, Tlohtzin, but if ever they had cause to be gratified by what we've done for them, this is certainly the case. They will show their appreciation by sparing us from any hazards arising out of this situation."

"That is crass arrogance! Now you presuppose how they should reward us."

"Take heed, Tlohtzin," Ahuitzotl sternly cautioned, "lest you allow your own arrogance to lead you into an ill-advised position. The sacrifices will end when the last captive has been dispatched-not before."

"I have done my duty in alerting you to the danger," Tlohtzin fumed. "If you will not listen to me, so be it, but remember—you were warned!"

Shaken by the surety in which Tlohtzin regarded this threat, Ahuitzotl glanced toward the temple to ascertain how much longer the sacrifices would go on; he was relieved to see the lines ending only a short length from the steps. "See?" he pointed out, "It's nearly over; there are only about a hundred left in each line."

"Yes, and that many more bodies lying exposed in the city."

"That is enough! Do not incite me to greater vexation than you have already succeeded in doing. I've made my decision, and if this does not meet your approval, I'll have you explaining your insubordination to the courts."

"You threaten to discipline me?" a shocked Tlohtzin replied.

"Do not test me; I warn you!"

Tlohtzin's face was contorted in bewilderment; never had the Revered Speaker actually threatened him with a courts-martial. And this for advising his lord of potential dangers! He deemed his castigation both incomprehensible and unreasonable, but recognized the limits of his discretions and did not persist in warnings that were being ignored. Instead, he angrily turned about and walked away.

Ahuitzotl watched Tlohtzin go with an unsettling perturbance; such a confrontation with a trusted friend was most unwanted and he appeared visibly strained by it. He disliked resorting to threats in order to attain compliance with his directives-it was quite out of character for him to do so-and he paused in his consternation over what drove him to this extreme measure. A troubled demeanor remained with him when he returned to his seat and spent the rest of the day with anxiousness awaiting the last of the victims being send into paradise.

The relief sensed by the spectators and guests was heartfelt when the sacrifices at last came to an end. In a ceremony never before equalled and in all probability never likely to be repeated, Tenochtitlan was bathed in blood and the horrific magnitude of it was irrevocably stamped with cold efficiency into the minds of everyone in Anahuac who had been there to see it. On all lips recounting this event was heard the name Ahuitzotl; he would forever be linked to this event and, as men are often wont to do when speaking about feats of extraordinary dimensions or impact, the numbers sacrificed would be magnified at each retelling. Ahuitzotl understood this; his fame rested firmy secure and the reputation of his city was all the more enhanced by it.

The feasting that final evening was more grandiose than on any previous night as a fitting climax to the inauguration with the allotment of gifts and prizes doubled in quantity and the entertainment lengthier and of more variety. Gratified lords dined on the most appetizing dishes the chefs could create. There was singing and dancing, and adept performances by acrobats, jugglers, wrestlers, and animal acts, even comic interludes offered by misshapen dwarfs. Ahuitzotl excelled in contributing to the congeniality and splendor surrounding this gala, efforts to which he was well suited as he possessed a natural talent for sociability; he mingled freely with his visitors, engaging them in pleasant conversations and enjoying their company. Absorbed in this revelry, he stayed with his fellow carousers until the evening was expended, when he was one of the last to retire.

On the following day, Ahuitzotl bade his many guests farewell. His allied visitors left during daylight while the enemy lords stole from the city in secret at night as they had entered, taken by canoes across Lake Texcoco to a designated receiving point from which to resume their journeys. They were provided with numerous slaves to carry their weighty treasures as part of their memorabalia for having attended this inauguration. In addition to these lords and their delegations, Ahuitzotl also rewarded the artisans, chefs, and the many attendants whose work contributed to the success of the celebrations.

After having said his goodbyes to the last of the foreign potentates, Ahuitzotl, accompanied by Cihuacoatl, was returning from the docking area where his visitors had departed and passed by the structure that had been honored in such unprecedented enormity Cleanup crews were busy removing the vestiges of the slaughter, and although corpses remained heaped beside the canal, they were cleared from around the temple precinct. As they headed in the direction of the royal palace, they passed by the tzompantli, the skull rack, and Ahuitzotl paused.

"This skull rack is not adequate for the numbers we slew," he said. "We must have a new ne, a much larger one, erected in its place. Begin your work on it as soon as possible, and in the interim period, set the new skulls upon temporary stakes next to the Great Temple."

"We will start on it tomorrow. I'll make sure twenty thousand more skulls are displayed on it when it's done."

"Make that twenty thousand and one."

"And one?"

"Have you forgotten Xaman Utec? Now that he has seen all his warriors honored, let us put him out of his misery. He shall meet his end with the painful knowledge that we have denied him entry to our paradise-he will never see his warriors again."

This was a cruel way in which to treat a former lord, thought Cihuacoatl, and it told him something of his master's nature. He was the kind of person who was magnanimous to his friends, but utterly unforgiving to his enemies: woe to the person who came into his disfavor, as Xaman Utec, to his misfortune, had learned.

Later that quiet evening, after the monarch and his minister had retired, Motecuhzoma walked with two soldiers through a dimly lit street in Tlatelolco to make his appointed meeting with the doomed Huaxtecan. They solemnly entered into the inner courtyard of the palace of Moquihiux, its last sovereign as an independent city before it was annexed to Tenochtitlan by Axayacatl, where they saw Xaman Utec lying emaciated within his wooden cage. Weakly, he crawled back to his enclosure's far corner when he spotted them coming, aware of the destiny decreed for him; fear was in his eyes. Without uttering a word, Motecuhzoma nodded to one of his warriors who then proceeded to the rear of the cage where Xaman Utec was huddled. Methodically, the soldier wrapped a cord around the Huaxtecan's scrawny neck and squeezed it tight. Xaman Utec squirmed and jerked violently; he gasped for air that was cut off from him as his eyes bulged from their sockets and his tongue stuck out of his frothing mouth. In a few minutes it was over and a lifeless body hung limply from the upright stakes, held there by the executioner's powerful arms until he let go of his grip and it dropped to the floor.

They flung the body over a shoulder and carried it to the docking area adjacent to the central square where many of the sacrificial victims remained in grim stacks. There they hacked off the head and lifted it by its hair into a reed basket; the body they tossed on the heap, horrid in its decapitated and emaciated state. Thus had Xaman Utec become the last victim of the dedication ceremony.

XXVIII

The stench of decaying flesh hung oppressively over Tenochtitlan for several more days as work towards its elimination resumed. Wood, dried reeds, and other kindling material were taken out to the chinampas in order to burn the rotting corpses, and for the laborers assigned to this disagreeable task, a revolting sight met them. The mounds of corpses had been horribly disfigured by countless carrion-eating birds which clung so tenaciously to their meals that even approaching crewmen in canoes failed to send them scurrying away. The odor was abominable-so foul that the workmen wrapped their noses with dampened strips of cloth in the hope this would prevent their smelling the decomposition. They had to physically scatter the obstinate birds when they stepped upon the chinampas to spread their kindling.

After covering the putrid heaps with their burning material, the workmen cast torches to them and set them ablaze. Thick black smoke rose to the sky as the fire soon consumed the fetid corpses, disintegrating them in its crackling combustion. Once these plots were depurated by the flames, work could proceed on removing those bodies left stacked about the moorage, and shortly thereupon these were oared out to take the place of the ones already reduced to ashes. Slowly, over the next few weeks, the city was being steadily restored to its former cleanliness, but the aftermath of the dedication ceremony had not yet run its full course.

First to succumb to sickness were the laborers who toiled at the disposal tasks. It came upon them unseeing and in stages, so that many of them did not associate it with their assignment initially. After they had completed a day's work, they began to feel feverish in their homes, and on the following morning, they were in pain and too weakened to get up, sweating profusely and burning in high temperatures. Frantic wives and relatives ran forth to fetch physicians for their ailing spouses and it soon became apparent, from the sheer number of requests for assistance which came to them, that they were faced with a crisis situation.

Ahuitzotl was lying in bed with Pelaxilla when he was aroused by a sudden furious pounding at his chamber door.

"Who is it?" he inquired.

"Your minister, Lord! I must speak to you."

Ahuitzotl quickly arose from his mats feeling some nervousness about what necessitated this kind of immediacy. He threw a cloak over him and proceeded for the door and, after flinging aside its drapery, was startled by the fear apparent in his minister's eyes. He met him in the corridor and closed the drapes behind him.

"Yes, Cihuacoatl? What is it?"

"The city is being ravaged by disease! Already the physicians say that hundreds are beyond their help, and they are alarmed by its rapid spreading."

A chill gripped Ahuitzotl as he recalled to warnings of Tlohtzin. "A disease you say? Is that not the work of the gods? What do the physicians say?"

"They are too preoccupied with their patients to relate its cause to me."

"We must find out. Call a meeting of our chief physicians-and the priests. If the gods are angry with us and mean to punish us, I must know why. I will meet you in the assembly hall as soon as I'm dressed."

As Cihuacoatl hurriedly departed to call on the persons to attend the session, Ahuitzotl re-entered his chamber and stood pale and shaken against its wall; he was trembling and the perspiration glistened on his forehead.

"Is something wrong?" Pelaxilla asked him when she noticed his anxious state. Ahuitzotl heightened her fears by not immediately answering "You will not tell me?" she fretted. "Can it be so serious that I am not to be informed of it?"

"How can it be that I have offended Huitzilopochtli?" he replied, his words directed more to himself than Pelaxilla.

"What is it?" she cried out, frightened by his refusal to divulge the cause of his distress.

"A disease is spreading through the city," he finally said. "Tlohtzin told me this might happen and I rebuked him for it."

"He told you?" Pelaxilla was puzzled. "Is he a magician? How could he know this before it happened?"

"He advised me to stop the sacrifices when our disposal units were unable to get rid of the bodies. I refused, believing Huitzilopochtli would protect us. It appears I erred."

"The exhibition was unprecedented; everyone speaks of it as having been excessive. To this day Tenochtitlan reeks of blood."

Ahuitzotl gave her an angry glance, but was in no mood to argue. He worried over what sort of negative impact this would have on his grand show. He flung a cotton tunic over his upper body and put on a breechcloth, then opened the doorway and called on one of his awakened valets to bring him his tilmantli, and while he waited on it, he slipped into his sandals and put on a headband. Pelaxilla sensed his concern.

"Is there anything you want me to do?" she asked.

"Keep yourself within the confines of this palace until the physicians or priests declare it is safe to walk the streets. Inform Tlalalca and the other ladies to do the same."

With that precautionary message, Ahuitzotl left for the front door where a servant had his tilmantli ready for him. He draped it over his shoulder and fastened it at one end with a practiced knot, then hurried off to the reception room. A number of advisors were already present when he entered, but the chief priests of Huitzilopochtli and Tlaloc had not yet arrived, and as he waited for them, Ahuitzotl paced the floor in his customary manner when troubled.

"Did you call for the astrologers?" he asked the minister.

"They will come with the priests," answered Cihuacoatl.

Their wait was of short duration; soon after Ahuitzotl's entry, his critically sought-after notables appeared. Also present were numerous other priests representing a multitude of deities as well as the city's most renowned physicians, and after the monarch took his seat, he addressed them soberly.

"I called you here to learn why the gods are angry with us after we have rendered them such honor. What explaination can there be for this sickness presently infesting our city? I want to know why this is happening and what we can do about it."

Some of the priests first heard of the epidemic at this moment and were clearly alarmed by this revelation. They peered at each other in confusion and spoke among themselves while searching for possible interpretations for this affliction. Ahuitzotl grew impatient with their babbling and dallying, and it became apparent to him that he would have to call on each individual by name if he was to have an answer. His eyes roved from person to person, then fixed on the chief physician, the ticitl.

"Tezotzin, my court phjysician," Ahuitzotl named him, "Have you been among the sick?"

"I have, Lord!"

"What is the nature of their malady?"

"It has the appearance of a breathing ailment. It's too early to assess all the effects, but the patients have a high fever and cough consistently. They perspire to excess, and the ones we believe can no longer be helped are spitting blood-these are near death, very weak—their eyes roll back on them as in the dying. None of the herbs we applied seem to work at this stage, but we need to allow more time to know this."

"What do you think is the cause of it?"

"We think it is connected somehow with the decaying corpses. We suspect the rotting flesh, especially when eaten by scavengers and further decomposed, exudes poisonous substances that are by some means transmitted to those exposed to it. Our suspicion is that it is inhaled, but we do not know how it spreads from one person to another-perhaps his own air then becomes poisonous and he breathes it on others. What we know for certain is that those working on the disposal crews were the first to contract this illness and have now, in turn, infected the members of their households."

"But if decaying corpses are indeed responsible, why doesn't this happen every time we have sacrifices?"

"I surmise it has to do with how quickly the bodies are disposed of. Our records mention such sicknesses have occurred in the past usually when a large number of dead were left lying around for many days, either on battlefields or destroyed cities. Those who wrote our sacred texts understood this when they recommended that we rid ourselves of the corpses by burning."

Ahuitzotl smarted over the possibility that his actions somehow may have produced their present misfortune, but also found his curiosity stimulated by what he heard. "You said the laborers infected members of their household," he said. "Have any others been afflicted with the sickness?"

"So far it is only in the homes of the laborers, Lord."

"If we were to keep them confined there, would this not keep the sickness restricted to that area?"

"It's a reasonable assumption."

"We must place guards around their houses and prevent their mingling with others and breathing on them. Food and drink can be placed at their doorsteps. But why should this be happening?" Ahuitzotl questioned the Tolpiltzin, head priest of Huitzilopochtli. "Huitzilopochtli instructed us to supply him with the blood of our war captives, and so we did. Where did we err?"

"It's as you say, Lord," the priest coldly emphasized, "but was it out of proper reverence for him and Tlaloc that you ordered this? Perhaps he is angry over your motivation for the sacrifice-your sincerity is known to him."

"Am I not Huitzilopochtli's most devoted servant?" Ahuitzotl scowled, not appreciating the Tolpiltzin's reply. "Have I not captured more warriors for him than anyone before me? And all that I have done, I did for the glory of his name. Not one campaign did I embark on without invoking the greatness of his divinity-you all bore witness to that. How could I have offended him?"

"Indeed that is so, and do not think that Huitzilopochtli has not been grateful, for he smiled on you when he granted you your many and impressive conquests. If he is angry with us now, I must conclude that it is due to our dedication ceremony. What else can it be?".

Ahuitzotl blanched when he heard the Tolpiltzin. He could not refute that the scope of the sacrifice was initiated on impulse-out of his envy for the memory of a dead man-rather than for any true regard or gratitude over what Huitzilopochtli had given him. Indeed, the conceptualization that he was doing this for the god's benefit came only as an afterthought to justify its enormity to his own conscience. And he could not hide from this-everyone present here knew it as well.

"If it's true we have displeased Huitzilopochtli, what can we do now to make amends?"

"I must confer with my associate priests on that, Lord. It's essential we speak with him to find out what he will demand of us. We shall eat of the divine ololiuhqui and teonanacatl plants to see what kind of visions will be unfolded to us."

"Inform me of what you discover as soon as possible. It is frightening to have the gods opposing you. You, astrologer! What do the stars say?"

The astrologer unfolded some of the sacred pamphlets he carried with him and studied their inscriptions with extreme absorption. He brought his hand to his chin in his serious study, never parting from the fixed gaze in which he scrutinized the documents. Ahuitzotl viewed his hesitation in nerve-wracking tenseness.

"Why this delay?" he asked, "Is it a dire picture you see?"

"The crisis will pass soon enough," commented the seer grimly, "but not before it will have left its scars on the city. There is a temporary setback denoted in the sacred glyphs concerning your reign, which I assume pertains to the present difficulties, but overall, the indications are that there will follow a period of copious activity, all of it favorable to us."

"Favorable you say?" Ahuitzotl nearly sighed in relief, these being the first words of encouragement he had heard since the day began. "Then we shall surmount this current hardship."

"We shall, Lord, but I must remind you it will not be without its pain and sorrows. Many will mourn their losses."

While this was unpleasant, Ahuitzotl was so assuaged by the astrologer's prediction of a succeeding period of greatness that he almost eagerly awaited it-temporary reversals were not so critical; the long range projections were what mattered. He left the meeting placated of his worries by prognostications he deemed singularly uplifting and was inspired by the fortunes that were in store for him.

The setback was far more serious than Ahuitzotl had dared envision. In successive days, the plague ran rampant through Tenochtitlan taking its toll among the inhabitants and leaving multitudes in anguish. None were immune from its ravages, and even in the royal palace, a number of personages suffered from it, primarily among the guards and servants, and a few of them succumbed to it, but most of the court was spared its lethal effect, including Pelaxilla and Tlalalca, to the sincere gratitude of the monarch. The seemingly randomness in which the disease struck its victims rendered it most mystifying to medicine men who tried their best to deal with it, giving somber credence to the words of angry priests who proclaimed that their gods, driven to offense, had invoked this disaster upon them. Ahuitzotl found their repeated explanations wanting, devoid of the realistic assessment he was seeking, for he had tried everything the chief clerics recommended to him-the fasting, auto-sacrifice, and endless orisons-and yet the sickness continued. Highly frustrated, he decided at one more attempt in seeking counsel and summoned for his court physician whom he trusted to a greater degree than any priest.

"How are things progressing, Tezotzin?" Ahuitzotl inquired.

"The sickness is still rife, but some of the drugs appear to be working. Not as many patients are dying, even in the advanced stages, as was the case earlier in the week."

"How many succumbed to it?"

"Perhaps as many as a thousand-I have no precise figures. Many more became afflicted with it, but are now recovering."

"How is it that some become sick while others do not? In my own palace I observed this. And why do some recover when others perish?"

"If I could answer that, Lord, I should be a god."

"The priests say the gods have selected those whom they spared because of their individual devotion and piousness. As one trained in medicine, is this a plausible explanation to you?"

"Why does my lord ask this of me? Do you want me to say that the priests are wrong? Am I to discount the workings of the gods who speak through them?"

"Then why have none of their recommendations worked? I have done all the oblations they asked me to do; I have fasted for days, spent my time in prayer, and have even cut my flesh to spill my blood in repentance, as they told me I must, but to no apparent avail. I did not call you in here to fill my ears with the same diatribe the priests have given me. I want an explanation from a man learned in the art of healing. What can you tell me?"

"As to why some recover and others die, the only answer I can give you is that it is dependent upon the individual make-up of the person affected. Some are strong while others are not, in will as well as body, and the strong manage to survive."

"There must be more to it. I have seen many strong affected who have, in fact, died. Why haven't you become sick? You've been around the afflicted more than anyone else."

"It is mysterious, Lord," Tezotzin replied after pausing to reflect on it. "Indeed I have no explanation for it-perhaps the priests are correct in what they say."

Ahuitzotl wanted a more definitive response, having already dismissed the priests' credibility, and he probed the physician for clues. "Do you take any special foods or certain drugs that protect you?"

"No, lord! My diet remains tediously the same-nothing that is different from anyone else's. As for drugs, I administer them to my patients, but have no need to take them myself."

"There's nothing you do differently?"

"Nothing, Lord! I examine my patients and when I'm done wash myself, as is the practice. It is nothing different."

"You wash yourself? That's all you do?"

"Yes, Lord!"

"And your patients? Do they also wash themselves?"

"They are with fever and have difficulty breathing. With such symptoms I would hesitate to recommend that they immerse themselves in water, although I admit the tamascal may be beneficial."

"The steam baths?"

"Yes, Lord. It's been long known there is therapeutic value in that, but we have not permitted the sick to use them fearing it would enervate them even more."

"Maybe we should. At least experiment with it on some of the sick to see what happens. We've always placed an emphasis on cleanliness-the gods have counseled us on this. It may help to clean out all the houses, and streets as well, also the clothing worn by the sick. Implement instructions to do that. You say that you've come upon a drug that helps the patients recover?"

"Yes, Lord. We found a plant which aids them in breathing; this appears to be a major step in their improvement."

"Good. You understand we must try all measures that come to us-even the priests should grant us that concession. They have greatly disappointed me in this crisis."

"Perhaps the gods were sparing in their counsel and meant for this to happen, Lord. It is not wise to belittle them."

Ahuitzotl hesitated, fearing he may have committed heresy and might add to it by saying more. "Go, Tezotzin," he presently said. "I will not take any unnecessary risks and will do what they ask of me."

Tezotzin departed leaving Ahuitzotl unsettled over whether he may again have offended the gods by speaking ill of their devotees. He was lacking confidence on how to approach them, for the priests claimed his arrogance led to this calamity, a notion which had severely shaken him. He concluded that the measures he mentioned to Tezotzin were not enough; he would personally speak to Huitzilopochtli. Resolved to make his restitution, Ahuitzotl donned his finely woven tilmantli and left his palace for the Great Temple.

When he came to the huge edifice, Ahuitzotl gazed uneasily up its steep steps which had been thoroughly scrubbed and bore no more trace of the enormus slaughter three weeks earlier. It stood eerily in its vacancy of occupants, as empty of life as the central plaza, for the plague kept everyone inside their homes, rendering it difficult to imagine that only a short time ago this place was teeming with thousands who witnessed to most amazing spectacle ever staged in Tenochtitlan. He began ascending the stairway, never glancing back as he climbed to the upper tier. On reaching it, he noticed that the altarstones had been removed, lending a spaciousness to the platform he failed to see earlier; its effect was to magnify the temple's immensity, and he felt significantly dwarfed under the mammoth twin shrines ahead of him.

Overcome with extreme tenseness, Ahuitzotl proceeded into the shrine where the idol of Huitzilopochtli was housed, grim and gruesome, reaching from floor to ceiling. Its sightless eyes faced toward the western horizon beyond the portals of the abode; the open mouth still was spotted with caked blood and emitted a putrid odor, and there remained stains of a pool of dried blood on the stone pedestal beneath it. The whole sculpture stood bathed in a gloomy red-like hue given off by its adjacent burning braziers. After halting but a few paces from the idol, Ahuitzotl raised both hands over his head in a sign of adoration and submission. Then he sank to his knees, humbling himself before his revered lord.

"Oh Mighty God!" Ahuitzotl began, "Great and Glorious Huitzilopochtli! How has it come about that I, your most devoted subject, have incurred your wrath? My entire life had been dedicated to your service; all that I have done, I did in honor of your name. The captives I took, I offered in sacrifice to your glory. I have done all that you have requested from us, your chosen ones. Why, then, have you brought the scourge upon us?."

He paused and bowed to the idol so that he would demonstrate his full submissiveness to it. Then he continued.

"There are those who say I have angered you by my lack of sincerity when dedicating this temple to you. Your own priests are among the accusers. They are wrong. I admit that I ordered the sacrifice of all our captives in a fit of anger because I resented my dead brother being given recognition for this magnificent house to you and your compatriot, Tlaloc, at a time when we were to grant you the highest honor. I may have been envious of him, but never have I faltered in my loyalty and devotion to you. All those we sacrificed were bold warriors honorably taken in battle; there were none among them to taint your heavenly presence. If I erred in my efforts to please you, then properly you should seek to punish me for this, but I implore you, let the punishment fall on me alone. I await your discipline, Great Lord."

He bowed again, expecting the worst to strike him, and when this was not forthcoming, he suspected that the god was holding his judgment in abeyance. He decided to offer one more appeal which might incline him towards favorable action.

"If you, in your beneficence, will grant us relief from this scourge, I vow to spread your glorious name to the farthest reaches of the world. Your name shall be known and feared by all the dwellers of the world, and they shall tremble in reverence when it is spoken. They shall offer their precious blood to you. It will be as you instructed us in the beginning."

Ahuitzotl lay in his prone position for awhile longer before eventually arising, keeping a wary eye on the idol as if still anticipating a response out of it. Satisfied he had done all he could, he then turned about and proceeded from the darkened shrine back across the sunbathed level of the upper platform. He halted when he came to the edge of the steps and surveyed a vast emptiness in the square below. In all its wideness, not one solitary figure was to be seen, a sight casting an eerie impression on Ahuitzotl as he climbed down. But he felt that a burdensome assignment had been lifted and was quite pleased with himself in having taken this extra precautionary strategem by making a personal appeal to Huitzilopochtli. Physicians may have their own remedies in attacking the disease, but a more prudent measure was to go to the source of the problem-to address the gods directly when faced with this kind of exingency.

In the days that followed, the plague ended. It had run its full course and died on its own accord, the sanitary practices of the people, with their frequent bathing and washing, contributing to its demise. Once the decaying corpses had been removed from where had accumulated and were properly disposed of by burning, and once the streets had been vigorously scrubbed and the last vistages of blood and gore cleansed from the masonry, and after the hygienic procedured recommended by Ahuitzotl had been put into effect, the fate of the epidemic was determined. With the conditions upon which it was fostered and spread destroyed, the disease vanished as mysteriously as it had come.

Atop the smaller, former temple of Huitzilopochtli which was situated directly east of the Great Temple and now functioned as the Coateocalli, the house of the minor deities of the Mexica and those of other nations which had been accepted into their pantheon, the physician Tezotzin lay prostrate before the idol of Toci, the Grandmother Goddess, patron deity of medicine and those practicing the art. He thanked the goddess profusely for having imparted the knowledge of that herbal concoction which he believed had enabled him and his fellow healers to bring the disease under control. There was no doubt the drug led to recovery, for after it had been administered where needed, it invariably resulted in an improvement of those infected and a subsequent disappearance of their symptoms. Tezotzin's gratitude was heartfelt; tears of joy streamed from his eyes as he acknowledged his deep indebtedness to the gracious goodwill of the Grandmother Goddess: she had saved Tenochtitlan.

Only a short distance away, inside the shrine of Huitzilopochtli atop the Great Temple, the Revered Speaker was also standing before an idol giving his profuse thanks. But to him, the interpretation for the end of the sickness was considerably different.

"You have heard me, Great Huitzilopochtli," Ahuitzotl cried out. "I am in your debt. My promise to you shall be fulfilled."

When Ahuitzotl emerged from the shrine to again gaze over the central square from the temple's upper tier, he saw a multitude of people mingling there in the conduct of their business as usual: life had returned to the city. There was a glow in his eyes, and for the first time in weeks, he smiled.

PART 3

THE EAGLE SOARS

"For those who are special warriors, the brave, the valiant, the impetuous, their name will be the Capturers as I order it and they are the ones who will be without fear for themselves. They will acquire the quilted mantle; the loincloth; the painted mantle. Quetzal feathers shall be their insignia; you will go to the source of the feathers and the jade and they shall be given to you and the people will fit you out with them. You will then go to those populations who have not known combat, who are unpracticed in war and who are unskilled, those who have settled together on the land, those who have dwelt a long time in one place and where things are flourishing and organized, places in flower, where want has been banished and where all things can be had for the taking by those who work at war."

—Huitzilopochtli's instructions
Cristobal de Castillo, "Historia *

* Gordon Brotherston, "Images of the New World", Thames & Hudson Ltd, London, 1979, p 201.

Seven months had passed since Ahuitzotl made his vow to Huitzilopochtli. He allowed for that length of time so that Tenochtitlan's populace might savor a return to normalcy after the plague had disrupted its calm, but he was not idle during this respite. Almost immediately following his solemn promise, a new situation confronted the monarch which had no precedent. News arrived in Tenochtitlan through the merchants that a major power to the south no longer desired future trading contacts with the Mexica. While this, in itself, posed no restrictions on the pochteca traversing their traditional routes, and did not place them at risk, their security being honored by mutual agreements, it nevertheless made their future activity in the area unprofitable, the exertion applied to the enterprise not worth the rewards gained.

The power in question was Teloloapan, a major city in the kingdom of Tlachco which lay halfway between Anahuac and the great western sea. Curious to learn of the actual motivation behind its uncustomary decision, Ahuitzotl dispatched messengers there to ascertain the truth. He had sent them over a month ago and was presently ready to receive them in the great hall, attended by his usual gathering of ministers, priests, and commanders. Summoned in by Cihuacoatl, they now obediently stood before the monarch.

"What have you discovered?" Ahuitzotl asked their spokesman.

"It seems that the lords of Teloloapan, at the instigation of its ruler, have decided to shut themselves off in their city and its environs, Great Lord. They have told us they no longer desire to maintain any kind of relations with other powers, friendly or hostile, and expect these to likewise ignore their existence. They claim that by adhering to such a policy, they shall have no more use of wars and will be able to avoid them."

"How brazen of them!" exclaimed Ahuitzotl. "With no wars, the gods would be in want of sustenance. They actually believe they can live in seclusion to the rest of the world? How did you perceive this? Are they sincere in their unusual proclamation?"

"Indeed yes, Lord. They claim that by disbanding all ties with us, they will receive a similar treatment in return. That, they maintain, will insure their security."

"It assures them nothing. No city can remove itself from the world around it, and especially, no city as rich and large as Teloloapan. But why do I tell you this? This is a concern for our council to dwell on. You have done your duty and will be rewarded for it. You may go."

After the messengers had departed, Ahuitzotl remained somewhat intrigued over the news related to him, never having been previously presented with such a case. "An audacious concept," he remarked, "but I don't believe we can afford them that luxury. A city entering upon self-imposed isolation does not guarantee safety for itself, nor for us—it's an obvious ill-conceived notion, however novel. Teloloapan would become easy prey for our enemies, particularly the Tarascans who border it. What assurances do we have this will not be its fate, thereby becoming a future threat against us?"

"The Tarascans may not want Teloloapan," said Cihuacoatl.

"I merely cited them to point out the nature of the problem. If not them, then someone else, but the fact that such a potentiality exists at all renders their position unacceptable."

"Then you propose bringing them under our domination."

To preclude someone else from placing them under theirs. But there is more. Does not Huitzilopochtli instruct us to subdue those people who do not practice at war? There are reasons for his words-we are called upon to sustain this world by nourishing the gods. It is a sacred duty."

"That is a distortion," the Topiltzin interjected.

"In what way?" Ahuitzotl scowled, vexed that he had been contradicted.

"Those were his instructions at a time when we were a small tribe, new to Anahuac, and mocked by our neighbors. They were meant to instill the martial spirit that enabled us to gain supremacy over our adversaries and to carve out our realm."

"It was wise counsel, then as now."

"We are no longer a small tribe, Lord-nor mocked by our neighbors. They now fear us and pay us homage."

"Not all, priest; Teloloapan does not. Do you suggest that our realm has reached its limits?"

This silenced the Topiltzin who blushed in his retreat.

"Now hear me," Ahuitzotl addressed the council. "Teloloapan is not the objective of the operation we plan, but merely a stepping stone. Still, the situation makes it convenient for us to initiate a strike on it-we have the justification-to supercede another power from laying claim over it. It is a drive to the western sea that I contemplate. Teloloapan is but one of many rich cities there for our taking–we also have Alahuiztla, Oztoma, Tlacotepec, Acapolco, to name a few. It's for the long-term purpose of securing all of our western and northern frontier from the Tarascan threat that we should undertake this expedition. Besides, our power and prestige is enhanced by having them oppose us rather than seclude themselves from us."

"You tell us that you have already decided on this venture," said one of the speakers. "Why do you need this council?"

"To obtain your concurrance and support. Would you prefer I begin this without your knowledge?"

"You are the Revered Speaker. Can we deny your intentions?"

"You have that right."

"A right turned into a meaningless option, because to exercise it would constitute opposition to Huitzilopochtli, or so you would interpret it."

"The interpretation is accurate. We do his holy work."

"Then your approval is assured. Can anyone object to it?"

This exchange confirmed what the tlatoani, the clan speakers, had long suspected: once they had appointed a Revered Speaker, almost all the power they could wield over him was lost. As their monarch, he had the 'divine right' and spoke as Huitzilopochtli's emissary on earth; challenges to this entailed risks. Other rulers might have been more inclined to heed the advice of the council, but with one as headstrong as Ahuitzotl, the situation was reversed and the council listened to him.

Only the chief priests managed to exercise a measure of control over Ahuitzotl. Although by office the Revered Speaker was also the supreme priest, by training and predisposition Ahuitzotl found himself at a disadvantage and was largely dependent on their guidance, a notion never sitting well with him. His duties as the chief priest of Huitzilopochtli before becoming ruler were, as Cihuacoatl once described it, perfunctory for him, a station assigned him to complement his royal heritage, and while he tackled these with significant zeal in patronizing his favorite deity, he learned, in the aftermath of the scourge following the inauguration rites, that there were risks in presuming the wishes of the gods and it became necessary for him to give greater consideration to the prognostications of his priests.

"How soon can we begin?" he asked the Tolpiltzin.

"You must wait at least two more weeks. The present time is unfavorable and portents misfortunes for us."

This was the sort of response frustrating to Ahuitzotl, typical of the priests, without adequate explanation for an inquisitive mind. If he were to ask why dangers were expected, they would give him a long harangue based on the positions and movements of specific stars. Not that he doubted its validity, but he had no desire to listen to their monotonous clarification: to heed their advice was necessary, but it did not have to be lengthy.

"Then we must wait," Ahuitzotl replied. "We can use the time to evaluate the operational aspects of this campaign. I intend to advance on Teloloapan in a variation of our usual practice. Each army will take a separate route and converge at a designated site-Tlachco in this case-before proceeding on our objective."

Murmuring arose among those present, a reaction expected by Ahuitzotl who had grown used to the usual bickering when he did not abide by conventional methods. He was also growing weary of it. "Always you are resistant to what I do," he berated them. "I have cause for what I propose, and as your warlord, I must take all matters into account and act accordingly."

"We do not oppose your move, Lord," one of the tlatoani spoke out, "but prefer to know your reasons."

"Our stock of supplies is depleted; we exhausted it in the dedication ceremony, and the sickness prevented us from replenishing it. Even though tributes succeeded partly in restoring some of it, it's not enough to feed an army. We cannot at present quarter the Acolhuas or anyone else."

His answer satisfied them as most had not been updated on the shortages. With an agreement obtained, Ahuitzotl terminated his conference, dismissing all its members except Tlohtzin with whom he wished to cover a few more points.

"You've studied the plans?" he forwarded.

"I have, Lord! I see nothing amiss in them, which is more than I can say of your reaction to the priests. I confess I am surprised that you so readily agreed to deferring this operation. It's not your habit to be so accommodating to them."

"I've learned the folly of speaking for the gods. You warned me on the peril presented by the decomposing corpses and I ignored your advice convinced that Huitzilopochtli was going to protect us. It was a hard lesson for me."

"You have changed."

"It came as a startling revelation that he could so directly influence our lives."

"Lord?" Tlohtzin thought this remark most peculiar.

"He brought the scourge to an end after hearing my vows. I promised him that I would spread his glory throughout the world if he ended it, and he did. It's one of my primary motivations for planning this drive to the sea."

"I thought you had your designs on that for a long time."

"True, but what I once thought as optional has now become an imperative condition upon me. I must approach this with greater dedication-this makes a major difference. What's your assessment of the separated moves to Tlachco?"

"A good plan, not only for the reasons you stated, but also because it should confound our enemies. If they learn we operate in a predictable manner, they can adjust their defenses to counteract this. It offsets their plans if we deviate from ours."

"I couldn't agree more. While we speak of plans, what duties shall we give our young upstart, Motecuhzoma? He gave a good account of himself against the Mixtecs, and I think it's time we offered him greater challenges-something more commensurate with his abilities."

"I propose we give him command of a division."

"But he commanded the Army of Tlatelolco, although at reduced strength, against Coyolapan. Isn't this a step down for him?"

"It is, Lord, but there is an impetuous side to him that has yet to be kept in check and properly nurtured. It's necessary that he obey orders from his superiors if he is to fully understand the command structure. He must gain a perception of all aspects of its function."

Ahuitzotl mused over this and of how he might have reacted under similar circumstances—certainly with disfavor towards a less than fully challenging responsibility. Motecuhzoma was the son of Axayacatl, a royal prince, and ordained for greatness; Ahuitzotl's duty was to adequately prepare the youth for the destiny predicted for him in the stars as related by the astrologers-a duty he viewed with some reservations.

"He's of a serious mold," Ahuitzotl replied, "not given to the sporting, carousing life. I don't think that's good for one so young and contrasts my own upbringing. But he has genius, and we would be remiss if we did not see it applied. Have him command the Tlatelolco complement again, but this time make it permanent."

After discussing a few more points, their conversation ended and Tlohtzin returned to his headquarters displeased over having his wishes countermanded. He groped over how he would break the news to the present commander that he was going to be replaced by the younger, less experienced, Motecuhzoma. Unlike Coyolapan, where the prince was placed temporarily in leadership over a single incursion, this was to be a lasting change. It would probably require a direct order; he was certain there would be compliance, but also deep resentment-such things cannot be done without entailing hard feelings. Motecuhzoma would again have to prove his 'genius'.

elaxilla was not at all pleased on hearing of another war being planned. Her relationship with Ahuitzotl was now one of sufficient familiarity that she felt no more constraints in demonstrating her anger to him, and it was in this mood that she confronted him.

"There is talk that you mean to launch a new expedition," she objected. "It's only been a year since your last one."

"Indeed?" Ahuitzotl retorted, "What is that to you?"

"What is that to me?" she raised her voice. "Why, it is a great deal to me. Am I to forever see you off on your ventures while remaining here to fret over your safe return? Why can't you assign these tasks to your subordinates?"

"It's my duty to be with my army on its divine missions-I've told you this repeatedly and always you contest it. I'm tiring of your unwillingness to accept my commitment to this; if it doesn't satisfy you, then I expect you to maintain your discontent in silence, but I will not be addressed in a surly manner."

Previously she might have been intimidated by his rebuff, but no more-she faught back. "What cause have you to censure me so cruelly?" she said. "It's because I care for you that I am upset by the news. You ought to have an appreciation for that!"

"I will not be reproached like that. I don't have to justify my actions to you, and will not be interrogated by you."

"So it has come to this," she moaned. "You have no more regard for me, else you would not berate me for having your welfare at heart. You no longer love me."

"Oh, stop it! You know that's not true."

"Do I? Has this castigation been an expression of it?"

Her distress quieted him; perhaps he had been too harsh in his censure. She reacted adversely to it, not that she could be blamed for this, for he was often more severe in his words than he intended. "Understand me," he was moved to explain, "when I say there are objectives I must fulfill. I am entrusted, indeed obligated, to preserve our gods and institutions; you are aware that war is an indispensable part of this requirement-the blood of captives sustains them and preserves this world for us. This in itself is sufficient to justify my devotion to its cause, but it has become much more for me. It's a matter of personal indebtedness, a promise I made to Huitzilopochtli, and nothing will deter me from keeping my sacred oath."

"Very well," she decried bitterly, "Do what you must, but do not expect me to keep your bed warm for you."

"You will deny me my pleasures?" Ahuitzotl replied in amazement.

"If my own considerations are so callously neglected by you, I will indeed do so."

In the past, he would have taken precautions against dismaying Pelaxilla, but now, having adjusted to her peculiarities, he did not deem such measures essential.

"If you don't stop this pouting, I shall spend my remaining nights here with Tlalalca. I'm not going to listen to the harangues of an impertinent woman."

"You wouldn't dare." a disbelieving Pelaxilla muttered.

"Watch me."

"So my fears are at last confirmed. It's not that I haven't suspected it; you have always favored her over me in spite of your pretensions to the opposite."

"I've exhausted myself in my efforts to please you, to prove my love for you, and still I must endure such unwarranted outbursts from you. If you won't believe it now, you never will. No, Pelaxilla, you are first in my heart, and have always been so, but you always doubt it. I'm fed up trying to convince you of it."

"Why would you even consider being with her if that's true?"

"Because I find your constant bickering irritating. I put up with enough of that from my ministers in my daily exchanges with them. I will not have my privacy likewise spoiled."

"And Tlalalca does all your bidding and is more responsive to your needs? Everyone in this palace talks about how you two always argue. You take it from her, Why not from me?"

"By thunder, I'll not endure this badgering! If it's her I go to, it is because you have driven me to it."

"Then go!" she screamed at him. "And don't think I will come crawling to you whenever your fancy strikes it. Let your empress be the sub-servile woman you desire, but I will not!"

"I'm going!" Ahuitzotl shouted back. "To escape your irascible presence-not because I want to!"

It seemed incredible to Ahuitzotl that he should be brought to such anger by his adored Pelaxilla, but she had assumed an arrogant posture he found intolerable. Who did she imagine herself to be that he, the Revered Speaker, should have to answer to her? The more he examined this, the more pronounced became his vexation, and he needed to release his pent up frustrations by speaking to someone. The empress would serve this purpose.

Fuming, Ahuitzotl came stomping into Tlalalca's chamber where she was reciting poetic compositions to Xoyo. The old woman's presence added to his irritation; she was always there when he wanted to be alone with Tlalalca. "Leave us!" Ahuitzotl told Xoyo. "I'll be my wife's attendant tonight."

Xoyo gazed anxiously at her lady, but Tlalalca reassured her by nodding her consent that she go. Reluctantly, Xoyo proceeded for the door.

"Must you speak to her like that?" Tlalalca protested after her servant had departed. "She has done nothing to merit such contempt from you."

"Her very presence is a source of objection to me. Whenever I want to be alone with you, or have a need to speak with you, I find myself inhibited by her constancy about you."

"If your intentions were made known to me, I could arrange it otherwise."

"I can't predict these things in advance," Ahuitzotl growled. "Can't you do anything for yourself?"

"Of course I can do things for myself!" Tlalalca lashed back angrily. "But she is a faithful companion for me since you will not come to me."

"I thought we had resolved that."

"Oh yes. I had forgotten. The two nights a week you allocate to me are supposed to be sufficient. This is not one of them, yet you want to be alone with me. That's unusual for you."

"I have my needs also, you know."

"Yes, but being with me has never been one of them. Let me guess what prompts your presence-you must be having difficulties with Pelaxilla."

Ahuitzotl momentarily paused, unsettled by her observation that his behavior was prone to such easy discernment. "Are my actions so predictable?" he asked.

"When one knows of them, yes."

"And you do?"

"I believe so. Have you ever come to me like this, especially during your last nights in Tenochtitlan before going on another one of your wars?"

"You know that too. My plans are known to everyone. Is nothing sacred?"

"You would do well to tighten your grip on the loose-tongued ministers you keep. They speak of your meetings to their wives who in turn relate it to us, but yes, everything you decide becomes common knowledge."

Her divulgement troubled Ahuitzotl. If his plans were indeed known to everybody in the court, then so they would be to enemy agents operating in the city. "Leave the disciplining of my ministers to me," he said. "I did not come here to discuss them with you."

"No, that is for certain; it's Pelaxilla you wish to discuss. Why come to me when you have problems with her? Am I supposed to ease your torment?"

"You could. As women, there are matters you know of each other that no man can adequately understand."

Tlalalca was mildly surprised by this admission; it denoted a sensitivity he occasionally demonstrated-but she was pained that Pelaxilla was the object of his concern rather than she.

"Why should I?"

"Because I am asking for your help."

His request unveiled the dilemma arising out of this complex relationship between the three parties. It was perhaps natural that Ahuitzotl should seek her counsel with this kind of problem-Tlalalca had never told him that she loved him, and every time she meant to, he immediately deprecated her attempts to convince him of its truth. Tlalalca studied the quandary she was in. She could help him conciliate his differences with Pelaxilla and by restoring their harmony keep him from herself, or she could reject his appeal for advice, thereby angering him and also keeping him at distance. Either way, she would come out the loser. As long as Pelaxilla remained at the court, she would never receive the degree of affection she sought from him. Resigned that she remained forever second to Pelaxilla in his heart, if indeed that, Tlalalca dutifully although sadly decided to adhere to his wishes.

"Very well," she said, "Tell me about your problem with her."

Ahuitzotl next related the course of his conversation with Pelaxilla as he remembered it, omitting nothing, not even her references to the empress, and in retelling the events he realized that it may have been he, not his beloved, who overreacted. "In truth, I respond adversely to being reproached by women-even the ones I love," he confessed in summarization. A Revered Speaker's word is final-she should not questioned this."

"You must learn to differentiate your private affairs from your official ones. Your status as Revered Speaker has little meaning to a woman in love with you."

"Am I not the Revered Speaker at all times?"

"Would that be desireable to you? To have all your private pleasures met because you were at all times perceived as ruler so everything done to you was in an official capacity-as a duty and obligation? If so, then how can you ever know those who truly love you from the flatterers?"

In those simple words, Tlalalca made the situation appear patently clear to him. "Then I was wrong," he said. "I allowed my temperament to rob me of my better judgment. But you must concede, she gave me ample provocation."

"And you gave her none? How blind you are. What she did was out of concern for your safety and her fears of being without you. Isn't that what started it all?"

"Yes, but she should not have become so angry with me."

"She wasn't angry with you, but upset, and not at you, but her situation-her helplessness in seeking a deferral in your plans. We are not disposed to sound judgment under such duress. You know this."

"Perhaps. Still, she should not have yelled at me."

"You love her, don't you?"

"Of course."

"Yet you yelled at her. Surely you did not mean to."

Ahuitzotl paused; he appreciated her ability to make the problem apparent to him and thought it fortunate that he came to her for advice. "Do you think she's still angry with me?" he asked.

"Quite the opposite. She is more likely weeping over her emotional outburst and deeply regrets it. If she remains angry, it is at herself."

"You believe this?"

"I know this. Why would she willingly offend the man she loves? It makes no sense."

"What do you think I should do?"

"Go back to her and apologize for having distressed her so; it will work wonders."

"Apologize?"

"Is it so contrary to your nature that you cannot bring yourself to it even when you admit having been wrong?"

"It's not like me-she will know it."

"You will discover that it will be well received."

Bolstered by Tlalalca's certainty, Ahuitzotl envisioned an appreciative Pelaxilla smothering him with kisses and words of gratitude; a grin came to him as he drowned himself in such fancies, but it readily vanished when he noticed the indignant glare on the empress. He could have sworn that she knew what he was thinking.

"I'll take your advice," he determined. "I'm thankful for your help-you've greatly uplifted my spirit. If you're wrong, however, I may be back."

He departed from the chamber leaving Tlalalca almost hopeful she might have erred. He did not find Pelaxilla in her room and suspected she may have gone to the guest room usually reserved for Nezahualpilli on his visits to Tenochtitlan. When he arrived there and entered, he saw her lying on the mats as Tlalalca had surmised-weeping. Nervously he neared her, then hesitated, uncertain over how to proceed. He watched her in quietness, deeply torn by her crying, until she realized she was not alone. She raised her tear-filled face from her clasped hands and saw him peering down at her.

"Go away," she whimpered, "You've made it apparent that I'm not worthy of your love."

"If that were so, I should not be here."

He sat down next to her and took her in his arms, but she recoiled at his touch, quivering with tenseness. "Don't," she murmured.

"Please, I want to," he replied, dismissing her protests, and then held her close to him.

"I didn't mean to get angry with you," her broken voice continued. "I'm so sorry."

"I know that. I was wrong to upbraid you when you were worried about me. I love you, Pelaxilla; no one could ever take your place for me, and if, in a moment of thoughtless frustration, I say things that are painful to you, I do it unwittingly. It would cause me untold grief if I were ever to hurt you."

She snuggled close into his arms, smiling through her tears. Ahuitzotl gently stroked the wet droplets from her cheeks and then clasped her tightly against his broad frame, comforted by her reassuring glances. He was again reminded of how much she meant to him and how deeply he was affected by her happiness, and when they retired that evening, after a long session of intense lovemaking, he reposed in relaxed contentment.

But in another chamber, Tlalalca was again to pass her lonely night with no hope of seeing the man she had also come to love. She was not pleased over the counsel she had given him and was kept awake by restless thoughts of how things might have gone better for her had she advised him differently. She could have pleaded with him to remain with her and forget about his mistress, or at least agreed with him that Pelaxilla deserved his castigation, or even attempted to place her in a bad light, but that would have been futile. What was she to do? After all, he asked for her help. She certainly would not have improved her standing with him had she refused her assistance, and he would have thought only of her rival if he had stayed with her to the dissatisfaction of both of them. No sleep awaited her this night as she was thinking again of the joys he was giving Pelaxilla-pleasures she so avidly craved for but were denied to her.

"Xochiquetzal," she moaned in her despair, believing the goddess might perhaps take pity on her, "Why are you so cruel to me?"

I t took the Army of Tenochtitlan and its separate Tlatelolco complement three days to march to their designated meeting point at Tlachco. Exuberance swept the ranks as eager warriors followed their warlord to what was expected to be another resounding triumph for them. Their confidence in Ahuitzotl's generalship was now absolute and much in evidence from the words heard on their lips, no longer mentioning 'if' they would conquer, but rather 'when'—a stark illustration of how his brief reign had transformed the morale of the soldiery. Their trust in the monarch was complete; their belief that he would lead them to victory total; their ardor supreme.

But if Ahuitzotl counted on a timely reunion of the armies of the Triple Alliance, he was met with disappointment. First came a message from Tlacopan's army relating that it would be delayed by a half day's march, despite having left Anahuac on the same morning and with no greater distance to travel. Then he learned that the Army of Acolhuacan was a full day's march behind schedule. While the journey was longer from Texcoco to Tlachco, which meant some delay had to be anticipated, an entire two days was more than reasonable; he thought Nezahualpilli would set out earlier.

"Not a good beginning," Ahuitzotl told Tlohtzin. "Warriors in want of battle cannot be held on a leash-it undermines morale."

"The admonitions of the priests prevented an earlier departure. You cannot change what is written in the stars."

"Sometimes I think they stand in the way of Huitzilopochtli's work," Ahuitzotl grumbled as he reluctantly ordered his captains to set up camp.

By midday, the standards of the Tepanec army were sighted nearing the encampment, and Ahuitzotl was eager to brief Chimalpopoca on his battle plan. Much to his astonishment, he was met by Colotl, the commanding officer of the force, rather than Tlacopan's lord. "What's this"" he declared, "Where is Chimalpopoca?"

"My messenger did not tell you?" replied Colotl, red-faced, "Lord Chimalpopoca has decided to forego this operation."

"What! For what reasons?"

"He cites his age, Lord, contending his body no longer responds well to the rigors of the trail and that this is the business of younger men. He could endure it when there were but one, perhaps two expeditions a year and they were in close proximity to Anahuac, but your campaigns are too far and too frequent for him, and they exhaust him too much."

This was not the first time that had been brought to Ahuitzotl's attention. He recalled how, during the Huaxtecan campaign, his aged ally complained of the strain these duties placed on him, and while Ahuitzotl was hesitant to accept the excuse as legitimate, he could not deter the ravages of time-even he would eventually succumb to it.

"If Chimalpopoca is unable to respond to the call of war," Ahuitzotl spoke harshly to Colotl, "He should inform me of it in advance."

"I shall advise him of that when we return, Lord."

"Leave that to me; it's not your place to make such suggestions. I relied on that old fox's guardianship of our right flank, despite of listening to his endless complaining. But come, Colotl, I have not properly welcomed you. We have many things to discuss."

As the evening wore on, Ahuitzotl begrudgingly reconciled himself with Chimalpopoca's absence, and if he could understand how the strenuous demands of long marches and fierce fighting affected an aging and weakening body, he still believed that a ruler ought to be transported in a litter in such a case. But under no circumstances should a monarch fail to accompany an army on its sacred function; Ahuitzotl firmly held to this principle and this, more than any other aspect of his ally's truancy, is what rankled him. When the chieftains sat in council to review their strategy for attacking Teloloapan and its neighboring cities, it became clear that he extended his irritation toward his objectives and appeared to bear an unusual hostility for Alahuiztla and Oztoma, something that struck Tlohtzin as strange.

"We know we war on Teloloapan," he said, "But why the others? Are they allies of Teloloapan?"

"They have. in fact, denounced Teloloapan, for they maintained peaceful relations with us and traded freely with us. But by this hostility, their own produce is now subject as tribute to us owing to our treaty agreements with Teloloapan. When we informed them of this, they replied that they would rather die than consent to rendering us tributes. Their lords were very abusive in relating this to our delegations, insulting them openly and calling them women. By this, they have solicited extending this conflict to their cities.

"That shouldn't change anything for us; at the council you said you wished this war with them."

"Our influence must prevail here," Ahuitzotl related. "This region marks a major defensive line against the expanding Tarascan power-these cities must serve us rather than Michoacan."

Their meeting ended later than usual. Because they still had to wait for the Acolhuas, there was no compelling reason to dismiss early for acquiring ample rest, so when it finally did cone to a close, this was mainly due to lack of further discussion material and its ensuing boredom.

On the following morning, a tired messenger ran through the camp for the Revered Speaker's command post; the embroidery on his breechcloth and headband identified him as an Acolhua. When he arrived at his destination, he was met by Ahuitzotl who was with his three major commanders Tlohtzin, Motecuhzoma, and Colotl.

"You bring us news from Nezahualpilli?" Ahuitzotl asked when he noticed the insignia.

"I do, Great Lord! My master instructed me to tell you that he regrets he cannot march with his army on this expedition, but he has placed its charge to Lord Acamatl, a most able commander, and he trusts that you will render him the same respect that he himself would receive. My lord states he is too old and enervated to participate, having recently recovered from an illness, and knows you will understand. He..."

"I have heard enough," Ahuitzotl shouted. "This is too much!"

He dismissed the frightened messenger who did not understand why he had offended his overlord and began to pace furiously back and forth with his hands clasped behind his back, as was his habit when incensed. "So Nezahualpilli also absents himself," Ahuitzotl fumed. "Too old and enervated? Why the man isn't any older than I am."

"He's not as strong as you, Lord," replied Tlohtzin.

"Did I ask you to defend him? Why are you compelled to oppose what I say? He is as healthy as I am! If he is indeed enervated of strength, it's because of all those women he has in his palace-he expends himself in his lust. I will not have this operation inhibited by his excessive lovemaking."

"Lord Acamatl is, by reputation, a most competent commander," Tlohtzin said, attempting to redeem his previous blunder and alleviate the monarch's rage, "as good a leader as Lord Nezahualpilli."

"That's not the point! Huitzilopochtli's work demands the wholehearted support of our rulers-an imperative duty to oversee it. I'm wasting my time repeating this. Have a messenger brought to me."

Tlohtzin directed a subordinate chieftain to fetch a courier; within minutes he stood before the intractable monarch.

"Tell Lord Acamatl to march straight for Oztoma," Ahuitzotl instructed the messenger, "our next destination after Teloloapan. We shall keep him abreast of our movements through use of continuous dispatches. I have endured enough setbacks for one day and refuse to be delayed further." He then sent the courier on his way with a flip of his hand.

"Am I to understand you will march on Teloloapan without the Acolhuas?" Tlohtzin inquired. "They will be here tomorrow. Does one more day of waiting merit a risk of straining our alliance?"

"It does. I'm in need to lend expression to my restrained energy-now! Teloloapan stands as an appropriate recipient for my requirement."

"By tomorrow your anger will have subsided."

"We march on Teloloapan tonight. We're but fifteen leagues from it and the road is good. That's how we'll defeat them without the Acolhuas; they'll be so startled to see us attacking at sunrise that they won't be able to effectively counter us."

As a seasoned veteran, Tlohtzin could appreciate the value of such a move, and if he was somewhat skeptical at first, he soon became enthusiastic over the prospect of a surprise dawn assault and gave his full support to the scheme.

The Mexica completed their night march under the strictest observance of enforced silence, and assembled into their battle stations while darkness still shrouded Teloloapan. Warriors took turns getting sleep while they awaited the dawn; throughout all this, talking was prohibited so that even the sharpest lookout from the city would not have managed to detect a sound which might have revealed their presence. Not until twilight slowly unveiled the countryside to the sentries who kept an eye on the city's approaches did they, to their horrid shock, discover an enemy force facing them in full battle array. Frantically, the guards shouted out an alarm to their chieftains who rushed to amass their units, but before these could be mustered into action, Ahuitzotl commenced with the order for his armies to advance.

The dismayed sentinels tried to make a stand in spite of the overwhelming odds against them and hoped by their effort they could stall the attackers long enough for their own forces to merge into a full body capable of launching a counterattack. Their measures came to naught; charging Mexica surrounded them and disarmed them before they could offer any substantial resistance, and they were turned over to the rope-handlers who bound them and took them into speedy captivity. With the guard force thus eliminated, the path stood cleared for the advancing warriors who ran at will through Teloloapan's streets, breaking down the doors of houses and slaying those occupants inside who resisted their efforts and objected to the pillaging.

Some local units succeeded in taking a defensive position near the city's center. From the beginning the situation was hopeless for them; small hastily assembled squadrons had no chance in repulsing a full-scale juggernaut bearing down on them, and while a number of their lot fell under the dreaded maquauhuitl, piercing the morning air with their agonizing death cries, most were taken captive. However, at the ruler's palace, a bodyguard detachment formed into a square, bent on making a final stand and prepared to die fighting to the last man in defense of their lord and his royal household; Ahuitzotl's warriors were the first to meet it. He directed them to hold off from their assault and within minutes the whole of his army ringed the palace as if kept at bay about a hundred paces from its quarry. Prevented from attacking, they jeered, whistled, and threw abusive gestures and declarations at the defenders until Ahuitzotl, having heard enough of their baiting, raised his hands and signaled for quiet so that he might speak to his foe. He stepped ahead of his phalanx of warriors and fearlessly walked up to the palace guards, stopping only a hand's width from the tips of their extended spears.

"Where is your lord?" he addressed them.

"I am here!" a voice shot back.

"Who speaks?"

"I am Techolatzin, ruler of Teloloapan. Say what you will; I am prepared to listen."

"Your city is in our hands. I advise you cease this absurd opposition as we would make short work of your pitiful force. Concede defeat and spare yourself further humiliation and unnecessary suffering."

"What will become of us?"

"The warriors we have earlier captured from your guard force-not many-will remain as such; a tribute will be imposed on your people; you will provide us with guides to lead us to Oztoma. As for yourself and the royal house, if you swear allegiance to your new masters, we will keep you in charge here. As long as you meet the tributes we ask and maintain your loyalty, you will suffer no more at our hands."

"Domination is a high price for desiring neutrality. We wished you no harm; all we wanted was to be left alone and not involve ourselves in the affairs of others."

"Do not dally in your decision. I am not typically disposed to the leniencies I have offered you. It is of no importance to me if I destroy your city and its inhabitants."

Techolatzin, requiring little persuasion about the hopelessness of his predicament, took the prudent course and directed his warriors to cast aside their arms. As it was still early in the morning when Teloloapan capitulated, Ahuitzotl insisted that Techolatzin host him and his chieftains to a hearty breakfast within his palace. While dining there, Ahuitzotl informed his host of the tribute requirements, covering item by item, as if he meant to have the poor monarch suffer from indigestion. Amused in seeing the pained expressions on Techolatzin's face, he read off a list of produce to be sent every eighty days to Tenochtitlan. But even the Revered Speaker's seemingly callous heart showed a degree of compassion and, in the end, he reduced the quantities by a considerable amount. His intent was not to bleed opponents to death: Anahuac's weight had to be felt, but it did not have to crush its victims.

Early on the following morning, Ahuitzotl assembled his armies for their advance on Oztoma. Techolatzin furnished him with a number of guides to lead the Mexica through the unfamiliar region and the movement was soon underway. It required a day's marching to arrive there, and Ahuitzotl set up his camp only a league from its outer edge where he was to wait on the Acolhuas. During this period, he sent envoys into the doomed city to make the customary appeals, but they were sent back indignantly with a confirmation that Oztoma preferred death to living under the Mexica yoke.

"If that is their wish," said Ahuitzotl, embarrassed by the rudeness in which he was rebuked, "we shall see that it's granted."

Two days had passed before Acamatl came with his Acolhuas, and by then, Ahuitzotl was beside himself with anger that he should be so detained. He had almost called for an attack, but was again held back by Tlohtzin and Colotl who argued that it weakend the interest of the alliance to have one of its armies excluded from the honors. Reluctantly, Ahuitzotl acceded to their pleas; he was still annoyed over Nezahualpilli's absence-he may have tolerated this from the aged Chimalpopoca, but not from his Texcocan counterpart-and when Acamatl finally presented himself to the monarch, it served as just another reminder that Nezahualpilli did not consider this campaign worthy of his endeavors.

"You have cost me a day's setback," Ahuitzotl icily greeted his ally. "Time for Oztoma to bolster its defenses against us."

"I see no cause to be treated in this surly fashion," Acamatl declared, reacting adversely to a reception he deemed undeserving of his rank and title. "I came as quickly as I could, and did not have the benefit of local guides. I am Lord Nezahualpilli's representative here and should be accorded the same respect as he."

Ahuitzotl at first resented being corrected by a subordinate chieftain and his immediate impulse was to reprimand Acamatl for his impertinence, but he recognized that his displeasure was with Nezahualpilli, not the commander, who was right in insisting that he be given appropriate treatment. "My error," he said. "You are quite proper in your demand. Indeed you are welcome, Acamatl."

To those around him, Ahuitzotl seemed quite amiable and even apologetic over his ill-mannered outburst, and they may have been puzzled by this as it was not in his nature to be thus disposed. And indeed they were justified in their suspicions, for within, the monarch was a raging inferno.

He was not about to be slighted, not by the Oztomans, not by Acamatl, and not by his peer, Nezahualpilli; he may overlook this temporarily for the sake of presenting a show of unity and cohesiveness, but he was not likely to forget it, and if he could not vent his fury against his fainthearted allies, he would do so against his enemy. While Teloloapan fared reasonably well under Ahuitzotl's conquest, Oztoma was to suffer the full consequences of his pent up rage; he unleashed a firestorm of violence on that beleaguered city on such a scale that even his staunchest supporters recoiled in horror. He meant to punish them severely for their unspeakable audacity, and determined no mercy would be forthcoming.

With his forces heavily outnumbering the defenders, Ahuitzotl initiated a three-pronged attack on the city in which each army of the Triple Alliance comprised its thrust. Ahuitzotl advanced on Oztoma from the south along its major roadway; Colotl approached from the east, and Acamatl from the west; they did not attack in a broad front as was usual, but rather in a massed spearhead, such as Zozoltin used against them in Toluca, a move that greatly impressed he Revered Speaker. To the Oztomans who left the improvised fortifications of their city to meet the enemy in the traditional forward lines, this centralized concentration of battalions spelled their doom. Unfamiliar with such tactics, and unable to counter them, their thinly spread ranks could not withstand the penetrations of the Mexica and they were rapidly overwhelmed. All three armies breached the Oztoman defenses simultaneously; they circled around the enemy's rear, entrapping them. No quarter was given and they were cut down where they stood, many fighting to the end, but most, lost in the confusion, became wedged between the Mexica advances and perished under the thrust of a thousand lances hurled into their tightly compressed packs. Before half the morning was spent, the Oztoman army lay in dreaded heaps before their city.

With the defending army now annihilated, Mexica warriors ran unchecked through the city dragging old men, women, and children from houses and setting the reed and stone structures to the torch. The frightened residents were then slain, except for the children who were destined to be carried back to Anahuac and distributed as rewards to the leaders. In the city's center, priests and lords were taken from their ransacked temples and palaces and assembled within the open plaza. They were then made to watch as the conquerors violated their women, many taking turns on a singular attractive one, until they tired of their sport and silenced the screams of their victims by stabbing or clubbing them. They then proceeded to systematically execute the terrified captives, decapitating them one by one until none were left alive. Only the boys and girls were spared; the remaining population was slaughtered in an unprecedented act of savagery heretofore not known even to the ferocious Mexica, and when the armies departed from Oztoma near day's end with their wailing young captives, the city was an utterly destroyed ruin with no life existing in its confines.

News of the massacre at Oztoma outpaced even the fast marching forces of Ahuitzotl, and when he arrived at his next objective, Alahuiztla, two days later, he found its inhabitants fearful but determined to take on the enemy in defense of their city. The envoys he sent to the local monarch were reminded of their brutality exhibited at Oztoma and rudely ousted from the palace. They returned with word that the Alahuiztlans would reject all offers made by the Revered Speaker whom they regarded as a cruel monster and stated so to the emissaries. Ahuitzotl was not that disturbed by this appellation; indeed he preferred it so he would not be constrained by custom into granting clemency to his adversaries.

"Let Oztoma stand as a permanent example of the risks in provoking my wrath," he told the legates. "Alahuiztla, having decided on the same course, shall suffer the same fate."

But Alahuiztla was resolved to fight, and when the Mexica armies met them in the attack, they were waiting for them. Ahuitzotl launched his offensive using the same tactics he applied at Oztoma, striking from three sides with his warriors massed in a spearhead, and while the defenders were caught equally off guard by the unfamiliar maneuver, they managed, through reserves held in depth, to hold their lines, even keeping the issue momentarily in doubt, inflicting significant casualties on their attackers.

Despite their courageous and fanatical opposition, the Alahuiztlans lost ground to their numerically superior aggressors who broke through the city's ramparts on all three sides and had only the reservists to contend with, the regular army having been destroyed or scattered. They battled from street to street, house to house, resolute in not being taken alive to suffer a fate like the Oztomans. All afternoon the battle raged as the

Mexica were forced to dislodge their adversaries from every structure they came upon, but steadily they neared Alahuiztla's central square, hemming in the defenders from every direction. Ahuitzotl sent Motecuhzoma to circle around the city's rear and approach it from its one remaining exit so that escape was impossible. Now completely surrounded, the Alahuiztlans took up a position at their main temple occupying the plaza where they stood poised for a final stand. Ahuitzotl, arriving early on the scene, held his army back until he was joined by those of Colotl and Acamatl. Soon the defending force starkly contrasted the enormous numbers assembled around it: it was the last remnant of a once powerful city.

Ahuitzotl did not waste his time offering terms of capitulation to them as he recognized its futility-they clearly meant to fight-and when the entire Mexica force had converged on the plaza, he signalled for the final assault. Completely overwhelmed, the Alahuiztlans died where they fell, unable to even make their stand costly for their attackers. At the temple's base, they were so tightly congested that they could not wield their weapons without striking their own warriors and were bashed down before they could inflict any damage. But those warriors fighting on the steps were fewer and able to swing their clubs wildly at their foes who had to climb up to engage them. They put up a heroic defense, hacking and slashing, crashing their shields upon their fierce assailants, and finally, in their death throes, clasping the closest enemy, clawing at his eyes and dragging him over the ledge of the platform.

Their end was inevitable. No handful of warriors, however bold, could hope to deter as large a body as Ahuitzotl had swarming upon them and within a short time, the struggle was over and they lay in contorted heaps beneath the temple where they had been flung from the tiers. With all resistance broken, the Mexica combed the city rounding up the remaining residents and herding them into its plaza. There they selected the leaders who were to join their Oztoman counterparts in captivity, leaving the rest to lament the losses suffered, but the city was spared the torch, its staunch defense having won it respect.

Despite the easy victories, Ahuitzotl still festered irritation over the absence of his allied monarchs and decided to terminate the campaign after taking Alahuiztla. He strengthened his gains over the region conquered, allowing his armies to ravage the countryside until the people at last gave their full concessions to him and accepted him as their master. He then took his time returning to Anahuac, for he was besieged with praises and acclamation by the subject cities that lay along the route back and he relished this homage paid to him. Everywhere he was received with great exultation, welcomed with gifts and flowers and precious gems and offered invitation to dine with the local ruler. It all made for a glorious march back: he was now proclaimed as the mightiest conqueror ever known-greater than even the revered Motecuhzoma Ilhuicamina.

On arrival in Tenochtitlan, ten days after having departed Alahuiztla, the Revered Speaker was greeted with the usual pomp and pageantry that followed a triumphant campaign. A multitude thronged the main avenues to accord him a fittingly noisy applause and Cihuacoatl rendered the customary welcome speech to the army before it was dismissed. The young captives were delivered the prescribed courtesies and treated to fine meals which included cocoa drinks normally reserved for dignitaries, and then were led to the different wards of the city to be housed in various guest quarters until their final disposition was determined. And as for Ahuitzotl, he immediately sent out messengers to Texcoco and Tlacopan with a directive that the lords of those cities meet him one week hence.

IV

Chimalpopoca and Nezahualpilli stood in the outer courtyard of the royal palace prior to making their entry. Both rulers, aware of why they had been called, expected to be criticized for their actions. "He means to upbraid us," Chimalpopoca said to his ally. "I have heard Colotl speak of it."

"Do not fear it." Nezahualpilli calmly replied. "If that is his purpose, then he'll have difficulty in getting me to follow his orders again. I will not be chastised like some undisciplined schoolboy. We are the Revered Speakers of our realms and are his equal; he must treat us accordingly."

"It is easier for you to say that; Texcoco is a greater distance from here-I am within his grasp. Tell me, friend, how is it you absented yourself from the campaign?"

"I felt myself wearied from all his enterprises. I'm missing out on the comforts of my court, the pleasure of my women and of composing poetry, among other things. I must be allowed time for myself, and also for my city if I am to rule effectively."

"You echo my sentiments to precision. What does the man want from us? There is more to life than waging endless wars."

They were startled to see the number of personages assembled within the hall when they entered. There was Cihuacoatl standing next to the throne in which the monarch was regally seated; in addition, they noticed Tlohtzin and Motecuhzoma among the commanders, as well as some of the principal ministers and counselors-even the chief priests were in attendance

"Can you believe this?" Chimalpopoca whispered with troubled alarm to Nezahualpilli, "He not only will berate us, but will make a public exhibition of it as well."

"I don't think so," Nezahualpilli concluded after surveying the audience. "Not even Ahuitzotl is that callous. Cast aside your fears. He has something else in mind."

These words comforted the daunted Chimalpopoca and he assumed the proud, haughty posturing of a lord as he approached the Revered Speaker. Ahuitzotl glared fiercely at both rulers when they came up to him, making his vexation manifest without uttering a sound, but when he began to speak, it was evident enough that his anger had abated-the gala receptions and laudation rendered him on his return journey had done its part in alleviating his wrath.

"It appears we made a mistake in the manner that we destroyed Oztoma," Ahuitzotl began. "Our actions have unwittingly weakened the frontier bordering Michoacan. I have you two to thank for this miscalculation-your truancy drove me to the foul deed, but no more on that. The damage has been done, and we must look for ways to remedy the situation. I called you here to address the entire matter of these endless insurrections, not only along our southern border, but throughout the realm. Our current practice of suppressing rebellions, taking hostages, punishing those responsible, and exacting tributes is not effective. As soon as we leave, or new lords take over, they again rise to confront us. There has to be a better way to resolve this nagging problem."

"The problem is one of having trusted and loyal defenders," Nezahualpilli replied, ignoring Ahuitzotl's negative dispersions and succeeding in his usual fashion on taking the center stage, "We are unable to attain these from the people we have subjugated."

"Exactly," said Ahuitzotl, impressed that his Texcocan peer was equally concerned over the issue. "We lack dependable sources, particularly in the west. Where can we get such support?"

"Certainly not from these foreign people who do not speak our language and whose customs differ, and indeed often contravene, ours. They do not think as we do and have other priorities. We must look to our people, or at least those who speak the Nahuatl tongue and hold our beliefs and practices, to get the support we seek."

"You read my thoughts, Nezahualpilli. I'm convinced that retaining local rulers in charge of their defeated cities has been counter-productive for us. They will never defend our interests or protect our borders, and would side with whoever offered them the greatest advantages. My suggestion is that we replace the ruling heirarchy of the cities we conquer with our own lords and that we impose our administration and authority over the inhabitants."

"The plan is frought with potential adversity, Lord. We must be careful on what practices we impose on them; there may be even greater alienation if it is not done properly. We cannot replace their officials altogether as we will depend on their own lords to interpret our wishes to their people. Ideally, we should ourselves learn their language and customs.

"Our schools could teach that if we make it a requirement-that's a long range perspective. A more immediate problem confronts us now. We must establish a dependable outpost in the vicinity of Oztoma to keep watch on the Tarascans. I propose that we colonize the area with our people. I'm thinking that we send four hundred people from each of the alliance cities, and another twelve hundred from our neighboring ones. This will make a sufficiently-sized community to protect our interests in the area."

"How does my lord intend to select those who will go?"

"Why, through conscription of course."

"You seek allegiance out of them and want them to defend our border. That will be better forthcoming from volunteers than from those forced to go."

"Who would want to leave Anahuac voluntarily? Is this not the best of all possible places?"

"It is, so we shall have to provide inducements for them. We could offer them rewards and invite them to undergo this task with promises of rich lands, teeming with produce and water. We will want to make it attractive for them."

"Do you think that many would leave?"

"I do, Lord. It will prove quite effective."

Ahuitzotl pondered on it for some time, as well as the odd predicament he saw himself in: it confirmed what he found so paradoxical in his dealings with the wily Texcocan-he originally sent for him to scold him for his refusal to participate in the recent campaign, and was now taking his advice.

"Personally, I don't think we'll get enough volunteers, but I shall give your idea a chance," he finally said. "We'll send out a call for them and see what sort of response we get. My ministers will work on the inducements. No doubt the priests have candidates selected–will these also be volunteers?"

"They will. Lord," answered the Tolpiltzin.

"What incentive will you offer them?"

"A higher position within the heirarchy, Lord, and a promise of faster promotion. We find this works well."

"So let it be. I want this plan to begin as soon as possible; we cannot afford leaving our frontier unprotected for long. Promulgate the necessary arrangements, Chihuacoatl, but for the present, this meeting is ended."

The minister struck the signal with his staff and those attending were about to depart when Ahuitzotl added one more comment. "Not you, Chimalpopoca, or you, Nezahualpilli. I wish to speak to you alone."

Chimalpopoca gave his colleague a tense glare; this was it, he thought: the moment he had dreaded since he received word that he was to come to the capital. Ahuitzotl waited patiently until the hall was cleared of everyone save those two before continuing. He arose out of his throne and slowly walked up to them until he stood so close to Chimalpopoca that he could hear his rapid inhalations.

"You say you are too old to do Huitzilopochtli's work," he said to the Tepanecan. "I believe we use the term malingering-a shirking of your duties as Revered Speaker. What do you say to that?"

"I say it is an erroneous interpretation of my duties, Lord," countered Chimalpopoca.

"Explain that to me."

"The requirement that a Revered Speaker personally attend each and every campaign is not now, nor has it ever been, mandatory of that office. Even the great Motecuhzoma only occasionally participated in his wars, leaving most of the work to his commanders. It's only since the reign of Axayacatl that rulers have led their own armies, and then, Tizoc did not at all times. My chieftains are fully capable. I have confidence in them and see no need to keep them under my constant surveillance."

To Chimalpopoca's relief, Ahuitzotl did not explode in a rage as he had anticipated; instead he seemed genuinely curious.

"You adhere to this principle in spite of my belief to the contrary?" asked Ahuitzotl.

"I was not aware such was your belief. That has never been expressed to me before your last campaign, Lord."

"I make it known to you now."

"If you direct me to personally attend your campaigns, Lord, I will do so, but it does not shake my belief about its necessity."

"I do desire it."

"Then I will go."

Chimalpopoca's answer favorably imparted on Ahuitzotl who preferred ready compliance with his directives, but when he closely scanned his aged colleague, noticing every indented wrinkle in his hardened, weatherworn face, he felt a touch of empathy for him. Perhaps his far reaching ventures were a bit too much for the old warrior-indeed even the younger soldiers complained of being driven too hard.

"No, Chimalpopoca," Ahuitzotl relented, "I will not insist that you go on every one of them, but I expect to be told of this in advance. I don't want to be surprised as in the last case."

Chimalpopoca nodded his assent, retaining a full knowledge that he was not altogether released from his obligations, for it would be the monarch's mood that dictated which of the campaigns he could absent himself from. But he was grateful his berating was not any worse and thought himself fortunate to escape with only this.

Ahuitzotl next turned to face Nezahualpilli who knew he would not get off so easily. "Chimalpopoca is justified in pleading old age as a cause for his absence," he said, "But I will not accept that from you. What will you plead in your defense?"

"Why should I plead any defense at all, Lord? Texcoco is a city of the Triple Alliance; it is not subordinate to Tenochtitlan, and neither is its ruler subordinate to Tenochtitlan's ruler."

"In name only, Nezahualpilli," Ahuitzotl told his confederate. "In practice, Tenochtitlan rules. What are your reasons?"

"I share Chimalpopoca's belief that it's unnecessary for me to go on every one of your frequent expeditions. No, Lord, I do not plead old age for my defense, but I will implore for my time to engage in other pursuits than ceaseless wars."

"Wars are too trivial for your pursuits?"

"I did not say that. I pray you do not misread my words."

"No doubt you speak of pursuing your fleshpots in Texcoco."

Nezahualpilli became offended in his indignation over having to justify his actions to a peer. "I make no denial of that," he said, "but I speak of other things-the pleasures of maintaining my gardens, of overseeing numerous building projects, and of scholarly endeavors. As of my women? Yes, I enjoy my time with them, most especially my Lady of Tula; she is a highly educated woman who appreciates my poetical works."

"Poetical works?"

"I happen to enjoy composing verses. It's a pity you do not engage in hobbies yourself, Lord; you would find it a rewarding experience."

"You would absent yourself from doing Huitzilopochtli's divine work for poetry?" Ahuitzotl scowled as if the notion was utterly absurd.

"It's a point I am making; the nature of the activity is immaterial!" Nezahualpilli shouted, losing patience over his being thus interrogated. "I meant to indicate to you there are other concerns I wish to do and, as ruler of Texcoco, will see to these."

"And if I object to it?"

"I will not be deterred from my other pursuits."

"You dare to oppose me?"

"I am a ruler, as you, and I shall determine my priorities as I see them. There has never been a mandatory condition that a monarch accompany his armies in the field and, with the exception of you and Axayacatl, few have done so. The gods have not been offended by this In fact, one can make a solid case that you neglect your ceremonial requisites with your constant campaigning and thereby run a greater risk of displeasing them than I do. I will not have you imposing this condition on me."

"I'll not impose this on you," Ahuitzotl shouted back, "but know that I consider it your avowed duty to march with your army."

"I do not!"

"By the gods! Has it come to this? I will not be treated in such contempt!"

"With all due respect, Lord, you have invited it. I would never venture to make your private affairs a matter of issue, nor should you dare to do so with mine."

"It becomes an issue when it obstructs my plans."

"Never have I permitted my personal affairs to interfere with your plans, and I resent this implication."

"Do not tempt me so, Nezahualpilli," Ahuitzotl warned, "or I shall do something I will surely regret. My tolerance is being severely tested by you."

"What will you do? Will you war on Texcoco? No one will follow you against your ally."

"You make a mistake by underestimating me."

"No! You make a mistake by regarding me as your inferior. Let the other lords tremble like cowards in your presence and grovel like sniveling dogs at your feet, but Nezahualpilli will not! I'm as great a lord as you and will not have you demeaning me in this manner!"

Chimalpopoca was frightened by this encounter; he had never witnessed anyone in such a heated exchange with the Revered Speaker and thought this a shocking display of irreverence. He strongly felt Nezahualpilli was doing himself grave injury, as Ahuitzotl was not a man to have against you, and he repeatedly motioned for the Texcocan to desist in his obstinacy but found his efforts ignored.

"I warned you about crossing me," Ahuitzotl snarled. "Take heed, or you will regret this insubordination."

"Do not threaten me, Lord!" Nezahualpilli angrily countered. "I'll not stand for it!"

This bold reproach quieted Ahuitzotl, and while he was still seething over what he perceived to be Nezahualpilli's disrespect for him, he managed to keep himself under control. But he eyed the Texcocan in his intense glare, and Nezahualpilli may have possessed second thoughts over having so angered his colleague, yet he was not one to permit himself to be manipulated or cowed by demonstrations of vehemence and would not have this confrontation unnerve him.

"You've made your position clear enough," declared Ahuitzotl, his irritation seemingly subsided. "If I slighted your lordliness, then I recant. I did not want this kind of altercation."

"Am I to consider that an apology?" replied Nezahualpilli.

Ahuitzotl gazed fiercely at the Texcocan while Chimalpopoca held his breath. There was so much tension in the hall that it appeared to hang over the lords like an impenetrable cloud.

"If you wish," Ahuitzotl finally said to the deep relief of the others. "I have no desire to question either your authority or prerogatives as ruler of Texcoco."

"I'm gratified to hear you say it, Lord, and will endeavor to meet your expectations. I do not want to have you opposing me. We are allies and ought to refrain from such quarrels–they make me most uncomfortable."

To Ahuitzotl, the words were tantamount to an admission by Nezahualpilli that he had erred and meant to atone for his breach of conduct, and he strove to do his part in abating the friction which had arisen between them. Like his Texcocan counterpart, he placed too high a value on their alliance to have its cohesiveness jeopardized by unwarranted disputes.

"It's because I honor your judgment that I would have you accompany your forces," Ahuitzotl said, "but I will not insist on it. You must rule Acolhua as you best see it. I failed in my diplomatic skills if I did not convey this to you."

"Then, for my part, this affair is ended," Nezahualpilli reconciled. "I'll make no more reference to it. Rest assured that Texcoco remains your faithful ally."

"And so Tlacopan, Lord!" added Chimalpopoca.

"Then all is well," Ahuitzotl proclaimed. "I'm satisfied. We shall meet again when our colonization party is ready to depart Anahuac. Until then, may you both fare well."

"And you, Lord." Chimalpopoca replied, happy to have this encounter over. Nezahualpilli nodded, similarly relieved, and they turned about and walked away from the Revered Speaker who sank into his throne exhausted by the ordeal.

All was not well, Ahuitzotl knew; his relationship with Nezahualpilli could not be construed in any other way except severely strained after their heated exchange. He understood men's behavior too well to accept that this dispute would be simply dismissed: it had been too intense and personal for that as sensitivities had been rubbed raw and hostilities engendered. He had censured his Texcocan colleague harshly and held no illusions that he would harbor a lasting resentment over it. The seeds of discord had been sown and it was Ahuitzotl who planted them; he deeply regretted his rashness and cursed his volatile temperment. Texcoco was important to him as an ally, and he could not operate without its assistance. No one knew this better than Ahuitzotl, and he now searched for ways in which he could reclaim Nezahualpilli's good graces and confidence. Somehow, he had to make amends to him.

V

Tlalalca sensed her lord was not his usual self that night; he was too quiet, and she knew his habit was not inclined towards the kind of stillness he exhibited. At first she concluded he was merely fatigued from an inordinately demanding day, but when he failed to respond to her erotic stimulations as they lay naked in bed, she suspected that the cause of his distress was a longing for Pelaxilla. So the horrible truth manifested itself, she feared; she could not even distract him from her during those few nights she shared with him. Unable to move him to any passion, and fretting that he found her undesirable even for the short time he spent with her, Tlalalca gave up trying and simply lay silently next to him. Still he said nothing and this became uncomfortable for her; she prepared to leave, rising from the bed to fetch her clothing.

"Where are you going?" Ahuitzotl finally spoke.

"To a guest chamber. It's quite apparent you have no wish to be with me tonight. If I bore you so much, have the courtesy to inform me rather than leaving me to languish over your brooding."

"You do not bore me."

"Well, I certainly haven't excited you any, or you have a most lethargic way of showing it. If you wish to be with Pelaxilla, say so. I know I cannot fill her place in your heart."

"I did not think of Pelaxilla."

"Oh? You assuredly are not thinking of me. If this is the response I solicit when you are thinking of me, I am lost."

"Please, remain with me. My mind is deeply troubled tonight-it does not concern you or Pelaxilla."

She was happy in her relief to hear this and became curious about the source of his turmoil. If its cause was neither Pelaxilla or herself, it had to be something connected with his duties, and she was quite touched over his admission that he needed her for consolation. "Can you tell me what it is?" she said as she returned to bed and snuggled up to him.

"I had a rather severe quarrel with Nezahualpilli this afternoon, one which has resulted in hard feelings between us. To make the story short, I blame myself for it. I did not accord him the courtesy I should have and fear I may even have insulted him."

"I thought he looked upset today."

"You saw him?"

"As he left the palace, I chanced to be coming in the opposite direction. He must have just come from your meeting."

"You say he was upset?"

"So it appeared to me. He gave me his usual cordial greeting and smiled when he saw me, but I could tell he was not in a good mood. He did not linger to speak with me as he normally does and he seemed to be lost in thought."

"Our altercation remained in his mind, as in mine. Do you know where he went?"

"To Axayacatl's palace."

"The guest quarters? He did not even take the room reserved for him in my palace."

Ahuitzotl grew concerned; this confirmed that Nezahualpilli had indeed taken their confrontation bitterly-it now seemed imperative to seek atonement and improve their faltering friendship.

"Nor did he ask to see Nenetzin," Tlalalca added. "That surely ascribes to his troubled demeanor. She complained all afternoon about being rejected by him."

"She can use an occasional rejection; it might teach her some humility and knock the illusions about her beauty out of her head. How my noble brother Axayacatl could have fostered such a conceited woman is a mystery to me."

"That's not fair to her. She does profess to love the man."

"I thought she loved all men. As long as there is something hanging from between the legs, she would be enraptured by it."

"Nezahualpilli is special to her."

"He was wise to reject her. If he knew of her escapades, he would not be so enamored with her."

"I think she really loves him."

"Only because she is intoxicated by his exulted rank. I have doubts if that woman even knows the meaning of the word love."

"Perhaps," acknowledged Tlalalca, "but you must remember Nezahualpilli is himself quite attached to her. She is his favorite in Tenochtitlan."

"And to think I always admired the man for his wisdom."

"Come now, you cannot blame him if Xochiquetzal has cast her spell over him. Besides, he does not know of her escapades."

"That amazes me. Nenetzin has not been entirely discreet in her affairs. Her adventures with the lords are the talk of the palace, and he has ears. If he is indeed interested in her, he's probably inquired about her. How could he not learn of them?"

"Would that make a difference to a man in love? Is he not blind to all her misdeeds, as the poets so often tell us? No matter how many people were to tell him of her escapades, he would still not believe them. Such is the power Xochiquetzal has over us."

"Can this be true of a man as learned as Nezahualpilli?"

"It's true of all men, and in particular it's so of learned men, for they foolishly assume that because of their knowledge, they are somehow immune to Xochiquetzal's spell. Even they cannot compete with the goddess, although they will never admit to this."

"You seem to know of such things."

"I have only to observe you. As entranced as you are with Pelaxilla, would you believe anything derogatory about her? Of course not. For the same reason, Nezahualpilli would not accept anything depreciative about Nenetzin."

"No one could love anyone as much as I love Pelaxilla."

Tlalalca was stung by his remark but did her best to keep from displaying any disappointment by pretending not to have taken any note of it. "It's Nezahualpilli's love I speak of," she replied. "If, with all those women he has, he still has eyes for Nenetzin, it must truly mean something."

"All those women he has will prove his undoing," Ahuitzotl was compelled to add. "But I admit you have something there. He evidently sees something in her that escapes the rest of us."

"She is an attractive woman and would be pleasing enough to any man."

"She's doing her best to convince herself of that."

"You are so obtuse," Tlalalca said, becoming flustered. "The point is that he's fond of her but has not requested to visit her tonight, contrary to his habit when here. So it's apparent that he is distraught. And she is hurt by this, and it's not like Nenetzin to be so despondent over a man."

Her words focused Ahuitzotl's attention back to his primary concern-how to appease his Texcocan ally and repair their damaged relationship. "Do you believe those two could be happy with each other?" he pondered.

"I can't see why not. It's evident there is a strong attraction between them. I have no doubt they are in love."

"You say this with such surety. I wish I felt as secure about it as you are. Somehow I find it extremely naive accepting that Nenetzin could truly love anyone, but perhaps I misjudge her. I should be more kindly disposed towards my niece."

"You should. She is as much a woman as I and Pelaxilla; she has feelings and can be hurt like the rest of us."

Tlalalca may have wished this to tell him something, but he was too preoccupied in deliberation to seriously regard it. "What would you say if I offered him the hand of Nenetzin in marriage?" Ahuitzotl presently said.

Tlalalca sat up in her excitement, letting the sheets fall to her waist exposing her appealing and firm breasts; a widened smile illuminated her face with a radiance that warmed him.

"I think it's wonderful! She will be overjoyed."

Ahuitzotl was skeptical. He needed assurances the marriage would be well received by Nezahualpilli-how Nenetzin reacted to it was inconsequential. He also was distracted by Tlalalca's bared breasts and his eyes continuously fell on them until she, feeling a slight embarrassment, covered herself again.

"Then you think this would please him," he said.

"Absolutely! I cannot imagine anything that would make him happier. He will be grateful to you."

"I sincerely hope you're right," replied Ahuitzotl, still unconvinced. "This union is of utmost importance to our cities-nothing can go amiss in it."

"What could go amiss?" questioned Tlalalca, puzzled over his reluctance. To her it appeared as a perfect match and she saw no grounds for possessing any hesitancy over it.

He did not answer her immediately as he was still much engrossed in his reservations. She patiently waited for his reply. "Would Nenetzin make a dutiful wife?" he finally asked with extreme soberness indicating the question weighed heavily on him.

"Of course. Why would you think otherwise?"

"Come now, we know of her, ah, tendencies. Once she's married, she must be wholly devoted to her husband and cannot go about seeking the companionship of other men as she is wont to do."

"If she loves him, she will be content to serve only him."

"Were it anyone else, I would be the first to agree with you on that, but with Nenetzin, there's cause to worry. I suppose it's a chance I'll have to take. If it pleases him to have her, this appears the proper method for me to cement my alliance with him. Much is at stake here."

"You shouldn't be so troubled over it. Nezahualpilli has so many wives; with all those women, he surely must have an understanding of their needs. He would have some tolerance if she transgressed in her obligations."

"You're wrong there. He has all these many women, but he imposes rigid standards on them. He is extremely possessive of them; as I hear it, none may touch them except himself. He is so adamant about this that he has ostracized one of his sons from any claim to the throne for having meddled with one of them. They are his private domain, and he guards his reserve jealously."

"Ostracized his own son?" Tlalalca was quite astounded by this. "Who can believe this of Nezahualpilli?"

"Now do you see my concern? How would Nenetzin behave under his kind of constraints?

She understood, taking the full gravity and implications this marriage represented into regard, but still held to her view that Ahuitzotl was overly severe in his judgment. She knew of Nenetzin's wayward inclinations but felt strongly that, once wed, she would be a compliant wife. In truth, she had always believed Nenetzin's lustful activity was due primarily to her not being married.

"You're not suggesting Nenetzin would have any adulterous relationships?" Tlalalca asked.

"With her, that's not outside the realm of possibilities."

"Really, Ahuitzotl," she rebuffed him tactfully. "Nenetzin has the sense to know what is expected of her-she would never do that."

"You can say that," he replied, both encouraged and amazed over her certainty, "knowing about her inordinate sexual appetite?"

"Once she is married, you will find her greatly changed."

Ahuitzotl valued Tlalalca's sagacity. She was a well-educated woman and possessed a keen mind that he admired; indeed, he preferred her to Pelaxilla when it came to engaging in provocative conversations. Bolstered by her obvious confidence in Nenetzin, he became convinced he had hit upon the correct solution in reinforcing his flagging association with Texcoco. Certain now over his course, he could barely repress his eagerness to inform Nezahualpilli, who was sure to appreciate having the daughter of Axayacatl as a member of his family as such a lineage was highly esteemed among the ruling circles.

Elated, Ahuitzotl was stimulated by Tlalalca's sensuousness and turned his attentions towards expending his enflamed fervor on her, and as he began his caresses by gingerly stroking his tongue over her soft flesh, she felt herself drowning in ecstacy. For her, this was supreme bliss, and she wished it could last.

A torrent of fanfare accompanied the announcement of an impending wedding between Nezahualpilli, Lord of Texcoco, and the Princess Chalchiuhnenetzin, daughter of Axayacatl. Ahuitzotl meant for this to be an occasion of special significance, unlike his own marriage to Tlalalca, and took painstaking care in its arrangement. There was far more at stake in this espousal than the mere merging of two royal clan members: it was to be a vehicle by which Tenochtitlan and Texcoco were forged into a closer union, of far-reaching and crucial value to the Revered Speaker who saw himself as the principal beneficiary of such a strengthened alliance. Every detail received his personal attention; nothing was left to chance: the affair had to be flawless.

When messengers first informed Nezahualpilli of the proposed marriage, he expressed some reluctance out of mistrust over Ahuitzotl's motivation in spite of his fondness for Nenetzin, harboring suspicions the monarch had designs that aimed at subordinating Texcoco to his own city. But when his watchdogs, the agents he kept in Tenochtitlan's court, notified him of the Revered Speaker's sincerity in trying to re-establish a harmonious association with Texcoco, he had a change of heart and eagerly looked forward to the arrival of his new bride. He greatly appreciated Ahuitzotl's gesture and wanted to do his own part in alleviating their discord. He thereupon requested that the ceremony take place in Texcoco, promising a regal welcome for his invited guests, as a sign of further reconciliation.

While Ahuitzotl was scanning the guest list issued from Texcoco's court with his minister, Cihuacoatl, Tlalalca was also doing her best to prepare the young would-be bride for the new life about to unfold for her. She called Nenetzin into her chamber so that she might give her some advice.

"It's a great honor to be selected as a wife for Lord Nezahualpilli," she told the princess who seemed strangely unmoved by it. "I'm sure you are fully aware of that. Many here who would readily exchange places with you."

"I know, my Lady," replied Nenetzin, "and I don't want you to think I'm unappreciative, but I must confess that I do not fancy myself to be but one of so many wives to him."

"I thought you loved him."

"Oh, I do, and because I do, I will insist that he give me greater deference, as befits a princess of the royal House of Tenochtitlan, than he gives his other wives."

"Indeed?" the disappointment was clearly discernible in Tlalalca's face. "What will you do if he falls short of your expectations?"

"I'll think of something, but I will not be neglected."

"My, aren't you the demanding one. And you're not even married yet. It would be well for you to think about how you might best serve Nezahualpilli instead of how he should best serve you.

Remember, there are responsibilities associated with this marriage. Lord Ahuitzotl is much concerned over our alliance with Texcoco, and he expects you to play a crucial part in sustaining it. There is more involved here than your mere self-interests: do not lose sight of that."

"I see. So this is essentially a political arrangement."

"It is, but not without its romantic side. We both know Nezahualpilli has long had his eyes on you. This speaks for itself and makes it desireable for both of you."

"Don't worry. I have no illusions about the reasons behind my marriage. But if it's true that he loves me, it should be no bother for him to treat me accordingly; by that I mean to render me the attention I am due."

"Really, Nenetzin," replied the empress exasperated. "I do wish you would not be so preoccupied with yourself."

"He has so many wives-forty of them I am told-to say nothing of his countless concubines. Am I to be numbered as one of that multitude without any special regard? Is it unreasonable for me to fear that I might be lost in that swarm?"

"No, I suppose not," conceded Tlalalca, "but if that is Nezahualpilli's will, then you must. Such is the condition of women."

"Hmmph. That is for the more submissive women. I do not count myself among them."

"This is very distressing to hear. Your attitude is not at all seemly."

"I am not as other women."

"No, indeed you are not. That is for certain. It might make things more amenable for everyone concerned if you were."

"It is my happiness I am concerned with. I'll not have Nezahualpilli treat me in the same way Lord Ahuitzotl treats you."

"What?" Tlalalca expressed utter astonishment. "What is that supposed to mean?"

"You are his wife, but everyone knows how he craves for Pelaxilla, and you must remain content to live with this. It certainly is not a relationship to be admired."

"Why, you are an impertinent little snob!" Tlalalca retorted angrily. "It's a condition I agreed to when he asked me to marry him and am duty-bound to fulfill. Do not pretend to know all that goes on between us; you will soon learn things are not always as they appear. What is important here is that I must perform my obligations as his wife, and I implore you to think of your own duty to Nezahualpilli once you are his wife. Do not play games once you are married, Nenetzin. You will fare badly for it."

"I shall do what is required of me."

"Only what is required? Nothing more?"

"Oh, much more-more than all his other wives together could do for him-but only if he gives me his full adoration."

"You cannot be his wife on your terms. If that is your intent, then I advise you to speak to Lord Ahuitzotl about releasing you from your marriage pledge. He may object to it, but I can make him see its necessity if you want me to intercede for you."

"Never! I do not wish to be released from any pledge. I want to marry Nezahualpilli."

"But, but..." Tlalalca was totally bewildered, "If you will not consent to be his wife under his conditions, why would you persist in going through with this?"

"You said he loved me. If that's so, he will do as I ask. I'll make him bend to my will in return for my affection."

"In return for...? I've never heard of such a thing! What a lofty opinion you have of yourself. It will indeed be a regrettable state of affairs if he does not share this notion."

"But he does. We are both agreed on that-else why should he want to marry me?"

"I daresay, you have a twisted conception of what marriage is all about. You will find it far different than you ever imagined it to be. Nezahualpilli is not a man to do a woman's bidding."

"Nor is Lord Ahuitzotl, yet Pelaxilla manages quite well in getting her way with him. He does almost everything she asks."

Tlalalca could not deny this, but she was disturbed that what she had thought was a discreet matter somehow appeared to be well known to Nenetzin. She herself was not aware that Ahuitzotl's association with Pelaxilla was so open and surmised its revelation to the court must have come from the mistress-evidently Pelaxilla was more loose-tongued than she had suspected.

"Theirs is not the typical romance," Tlalalca emphasized for Nenetzin's understanding. "There's an intensity in their relationship that is unusual even for lovers. Do not assume that Nezahualpilli will be similarly enamored by you."

"I think he already is."

"Do you? I doubt it."

"I don't."

She was a headstrong woman indeed, Tlalalca concluded, impervious to all the counsel given her and determined to have her say; she would have to learn the hard way by experiencing things for herself rather than through heeding the warnings of others. "It's apparent you are not inclined to listen to me," Tlalalca said. "I'll not detain you any more, but I want to strongly impress upon you the importance of this marriage. You must be an obedient and dutiful wife, and I sincerely hope, for your sake as well as ours, that you will."

"I already told you I would," Nenetzin coldly responded, then courteously bowed and departed the chamber, leaving Tlalalca with the gravest misgivings. For the empress, their exchange afforded her a perspective which could only be described as disappointing in the extreme, if not outright alarming, and she finally awakened to fully apprehend

Ahuitzotl's fears about this union. Like him, she now had worries about Nenetzin's value to the alliance.

Tlalalca was not singularly disgruntled. When Motecuhzoma heard of the proposed marriage, he immediately requested to see the Revered Speaker, the man he held responsible for having arranged it. Ahuitzotl reluctantly agreed to speak with his nephew; he was not in the habit of answering to subordinates, even if they were members of the royal family. Cihuacoatl led Motecuhzoma to his master and then left them to their privacy. Ahuitzotl looked the prince over carefully, curious over what prompted his urgency.

"You wanted to see me?" Ahuitzotl initiated the meeting. "Something significant I assume. You have never requested an audience with me before. Are you dissatisfied with your command?"

"My request has nothing to do with my duties, Lord. It relates to a personal matter."

"I do not hold official audiences over personal matters."

"Does this mean you will not hear me, Lord?"

"Since you have already contrived your entrance here, you may as well say what is troubling you."

"I've heard the announcement that Nenetzin is to marry Nezahualpilli and must voice my objection to this."

Ahuitzotl glared at him, taken aback by the man's audaciousness. At first he took offense that this brash young upstart had the unmitigated gall to question one of his decisions, but then his curiosity superceded his impulse to castigate the youth and he became interested in learning the reasons for Motecuhzoma's dissent.

"You object? Why?"

"She is my sister; I'm very fond of her and am greatly concerned about her welfare. I have come to assume a sort of protectorship over her."

"A protectorship? Is she aware of this burden you have imposed upon yourself and, more importantly, does she consent to it? I would be astounded if she did."

"I've never spoken to her about it, but it's something I felt obliged to do, whether she consented or not."

"Why? Nenetzin is in no need of a protectorship; from what I hear, she manages her affairs quite skillfully."

"She is a frail young woman who needs someone to look after her."

"Nenetzin frail? Are we speaking of the same woman?"

"She's not as she appears. The conduct you know her by is a mask to hide her fears."

"I'll not refute it. Aside from that, why should you oppose her marrying Nezahualpilli? She has led us to believe she loves the man, or have you also come to do her thinking for her and know otherwise."

"With all his wives, what good will one more do him? He will not give her the kind of consideration and affection she must have; she will be sure to feel ignored and unloved."

"I am mistaken. You not only do her thinking for her; you also do Lord Nezahualpilli's thinking for him. Very presumptuous of you-I dispute its validity."

"It's what I feel. I wanted to inform you of it."

"What you feel has no preponderance for me; I prefer something more substantial."

"The priests claim there is something to that; often this is how the gods impart their messages to us."

"In such matters, I will heed the evidence I have available. First, Motecuhzoma, you do not know what Nezahualpilli thinks or what he will do, nor do you know this of your sister. Second, no one chose you to be Nenetzin's spokesman-I'm certain if she knew of this she would disapprove. Unless you have her concurrence in this appeal to save her from a marriage we all believe she wants, you have no basis to speak on her behalf. I've decided this wedding is of benefit to Tenochtitlan in that it should lead to a strengthened political affiliation with Texcoco. It is for such reasons that marriages between royal houses are conceived. Now, if you have any solid grounds for challenging these points, say them, but do not tell me what you feel-I want justifications!"

"I cannot contest these things."

"Then you are wasting my time."

"If you could get some assurances from Nezahualpilli that he will treat her with due regard, I would be satisfied."

"That is preposterous! Rulers do not prescribe to each other how they should treat their wives. Affairs of states are complicated enough without delving into the realm of the bedroom."

"So you will do nothing?"

"I would never tell Nezahualpilli how to handle his women; that is none of my concern. Indeed, if you thought about it, you would see it's an utterly absurd request. Had you wives of your own, would you tolerate such an interference? Of course not. By what right do you presuppose such an imposition on him?"

"We are speaking of a relative; it is within our prerogatives to see that she is fairly treated."

"Such things cannot be done without casting ugly dispersions. If she requested this, I might agree with you, and even then with utmost reservations. No, Motecuhzoma, I shall not intrude upon Nezahualpilli's private life. The issue is closed."

"If any harm comes to Nenetzin, I shall forever hold that against Lord Nezahualpilli."

"How naive you young are. From what I hear among our ladies, it may be Nezahualpilli who might come to harm. I trust you will attend our reception honoring the announcement tonight, as well as the wedding itself in two months. You are one of the family."

"I will be there, Lord."

"Be cautioned, Motecuhzoma. I place the highest priority on this marriage and will not have it jeopardized. If you say anything at all that may be construed as derogatory toward its consummation, tonight or at any other time, you will invoke my wrath and suffer sorely for it. Is that clear to you?"

"You do me an injustice by suggesting I do not have the prudence to keep family matters confined to its members, Lord."

"Good. I'll have no reason to worry."

"None will even suspect what I have expressed to you, Lord."

This satisfied Ahuitzotl, and he felt relieved when he gave his nephew permission to leave. But if the monarch was placated, Motecuhzoma was not, and his displeasure was outlined vividly in his contorted face. He had achieved nothing by coming here; if anything, he succeeded in making a fool of himself by approaching his lord with an appeal based on mere emotions rather than a presentation of solid facts-a mistake with Ahuitzotl he would not repeat.

The gala that evening went as planned and turned out to be a joyous event for all parties present, except perhaps Motecuhzoma who still moped over his performance before the Revered Speaker in their earlier encounter. Lords from the royal houses of Tenochtitlan and Texcoco, including many notable guests from outside these families, dined on the delicious preparations of the chefs while being entertained by musicians and singers. Nezahualpilli sat with his future bride and was a happy man, thoroughly relishing the company of Nenetzin; anyone witnessing their mutual delight would have sworn they were a perfectly matched pair. Prevailing was a general agreement that this would be a fruitful and happy marriage and much rejoicing surrounded its initiation. Only one man doubted it: Motecuhzoma, staring with piercing cold eyes at the Texcocan, felt resentment over what he perceived as his feigned happiness. Alone among the attendants, he feared for his sister.

VII

Two weeks later, Chimalpopoca, Nezahualpilli, and Ahuitzotl met in the capital to give their farewells to the migrants who had volunteered to settle in Oztoma. The colonists were gathered in the central plaza for presentations of speeches and prizes by their overlords before embarking on the journey from their homelands.

"As usual, your advice proved sound," Ahuitzotl praised Nezahualpilli. "I never expected to get this many volunteers."

"There were even more, Lord; we had to turn our backs on many of them. Such was the attraction of the inducements we offered them."

"Who leads them?"

"Acamatl."

"Your chief commander?"

"In exchange for being appointed ruler of the settlement they will build. I did not think you would oppose his selection and took the liberty of granting him his request."

"But Acamatl has commanded your army numbering in thousands. Why should he be content to rule a mere colony of eighteen hundred? Isn't this a reversal of responsibilities?"

"In our eyes, yes. But Acamatl, often erroneously called a lord, is in fact one of those rare commoners who has risen through the ranks on his own merit. He realizes he has reached his pinnacle in Texcoco and hopes that by volunteering to lead these settlers, he will be made a noble and rear a royal family." Nezahualpilli was distracted by Ahuitzotl's smiling and paused over what brought it on. "You are amused, Lord. Do you find Acamatl's ambitions comical?"

"Quite the contrary, Nezahualpilli. I'm impressed by what you've told me; it indicates that Acamatl expects a long and prosperous future in his new community. He exhibits the optimism that is essential in making this attempt at colonization a success."

Amidst a dignified show of pageantry before a multitude of spectators, the rulers of the Triple Alliance took their turns upon a platform erected for this occasion to address the migrants. Ahuitzotl spoke first.

"Brave Travelers! Your journey has been well prepared for you. We have sent messengers to the lords of the cities you will pass through and have instructed them to receive you with all the courtesy and respect that I myself would be accorded. They shall provision you with food and lodging as you move to your new homeland. The mission you have consented to fulfill is of major importance to us and the future of our realm; glorious Huitzilopochtli himself has ordained us to undertake this project and you have honored him by accepting his call. Your purpose is to provide us with a stabilizing influence on our western frontier, to keep watch on the activities of the Tarascans who border you, and to grow the precious cocao plants that abound in the region. You will receive abundant rewards for your effort: rich lands rife in the produce we enjoy will be yours. Look to your leader, Lord Acamatl, for guidance and do as he directs and your prosperity will be assured. Good fortune to you and may the gods bestow their blessings upon you."

By officially addressing Acamatl as lord, Ahuitzotl in fact conferred this title upon him, an act instantly recognized and highly appreciated by the one-time commander. After the monarch finished his speech, Nezahualpilli took his place and added his own words to the party.

"I cannot say much more than Lord Ahuitzotl has already told you. I am honored that so many of you have willingly answered our call for this unique undertaking. It is not an easy thing to leave the land of your fathers and your grandfathers, where you yourselves have been born and lived your entire lives. We respect your having made this choice and applaud your courage in accepting these new challenges. Always remember the importance of your work; heed to the requirements of the gods; obey the instructions of your ruler, Lord Acamatl, and the priests. If you do these things, great wealth will be given to you and you will find your new settlement a rich and happy place to live. May the gods protect you!"

Following Nezahualpilli, Chimalpopoca paid his homage.

"Tlacopan honors you! All Anahuac honors you! Such is the significance of the work you have chosen to accept. You will be a permanent part of Anahuac in a strange land, but our gods will be pleased and will reward you generously for it with fertile harvests and a prosperous life. Fortify your settlement for protection, maintain your vigilance on our enemies in the west, and see to the gods and your leaders. We place great reliance on you in this venture, and our hearts will be with you even though a hundred leagues divide us."

At the conclusion of these speeches, the spectators loudly applauded the speakers as well as the bold adventurers. Then, as a chorus sang out songs of praise and sorrow over leaving their homeland, the rulers distributed clothing and jewelry to the migrants, thanking each of them personally for taking up the quest. Ahuitzotl placed a diadem around Acamatl's neck, the symbol of his authority.

"We shall miss you in the army, Acamatl," he said. "It is a loss to see an able commander leave his units."

"I believe I can serve my lord better by ruling over this colony," a grateful Acamatl replied.

"I am confident you will. Do you have the necessary craftsmen and administrators with you to help you manage a community?"

"I do, Lord."

"And the engineers-and priests?"

"Those too, Lord."

"Then I won't go into any more explanations; you know why we seek this settlement. Pay heed to the engineers. It is a new city you must build, and you'll have to depend heavily on their skills. They are well trained in their disciplines and will enable you to accomplish this."

After all the presents had been alloted and numerous porters provided to carry these, the farewell ceremony came to its close. The party was escorted from the city across its southern causeway to Coyoacan in the accompaniment of drummers, flutists, and singers. All in all, it had been a splendid departure observance and the volunteers honored must have felt highly gratified by it. Ahuitzotl stood looking after the procession until it diappeared beyond the serpent-headed wall and distant street; Nezahualpilli and Chimalpopoca stayed with him as protocol demanded. The Texcocan, his previous hard feelings eclipsed by the marriage proposal, suspected that Ahuitzotl possessed a secret desire to be with the colonization party.

"Is it sorrow you feel at their departing, Lord?" he asked.

"Not at all," answered Ahuitzotl without hesitation, a reminder to Nezahualpilli how easily he could be misread. "I am thinking that, should this prove a successful enterprise, it would portent major changes in our dealings with the conquered."

"You mean displacing defeated populations with our own as a matter of policy."

"I see potential in it. Obviously we could not replace all the people, but their leaders we can—by imposing our own heirarchy on them. The incessant uprisings we face when leaving conquered nations their autonomy can be solved through this."

"An attractive notion; however, we must recognize that many of these people may resent our presence even more than our tributes. This requires providing an adequate bodyguard for our rulers as well as our settlers. Oztoma's situation is unique-we cannot apply it to every case."

"You excel in shattering my visions, Nezahualpilli. I'm not given to dreams ordinarily, but I believe colonization will be the key to our future operations; if not during my reign, certainly for my successors."

"It is a propensity of mine to shatter illusions, Lord. So you envision conquests will mark our future."

"I have a number of campaigns in mind. I want to continue my march to the western sea-the first of many."

"I shall be ready."

"Then you plan to join me?"

"I will."

For Ahuitzotl, no more effective message than Nezahualpilli's words could have told him that their alliance was restored to its former harmony. Indeed, his ally seemed as eager as he himself to begin on this venture. The marriage proposal between their two royal houses had worked its charm, and Ahuitzotl quietly thanked Tlalalca for having given him the idea.

VIII

The wedding of Nezahualpilli and Chalchiuhnenetzin presented a magnificent showcase for Texcoco. Distinguished guests from all the principal cities in Anahuac came to participate in the celebration and render their congratulations and well-wishes to the bride and groom. Ahuitzotl thought this fanfare paradoxical, coming from a man with hundreds of concubines and wives, but perhaps Nezahualpilli was truly so stricken with his latest royal acquisition that it actually made a noteworthy difference. He hoped this was the case, even as he fought off recurring bouts of nagging skepticism.

Ahuitzotl had not been in Texcoco for several years and marvelled at all the construction that had taken place since his last visit. Like Tenochtitlan, this was a thriving and progressing city and in need of an elaborate conduit system which Nezahualpilli had constructed in sufficiency. The Texcocan's palace was larger and more magnificent than any Ahuitzotl had ever seen, with at least a hundred rooms. "I had no idea you lived in such surroundings," he enviously related to his host. "Your palace is nearly twice the size of any in Tenochtitlan, including the new one I'm building."

"It was built by my father, but I have greatly expanded it; however, this is not my major source of pride. My gardens are my greatest pleasure, mainly the one adjacent to the palace. It holds a thousand varieties of plants, many of my own creation."

"How does a man with so many women find the time to work a garden?"

"That is why," Nezahualpilli laughed. "I must find relief from their endless demands. I spend my days in the garden, and my nights with them."

"I surmise your days are more entertaining for you. Nothing is more dreary than to have too much of something."

"True, yet each of my wives and concubines is her own person and has something unique to offer-else I would not have her."

"That is good to hear. We were concerned about whether you could give Nenetzin the kind of attention she is used to receiving. You may find her more craving for your affection than your other wives. While I'm loathe to make such recommendations, I do suggest that you give her greater consideration than-than your plants."

"You can be sure I will."

"You ease my anxieties. Our young upstart, Motecuhzoma, will also be gratified in hearing that. He related misgivings over this marriage, and I had to admonish him for it."

"Indeed? Was he opposed to it?"

"He's always been extremely fond of his sister-almost to the point of being obsessive. To use his own words, he has assumed a protectorship over her, although she does not know this and would object, I'm sure. It's nothing more than a self-imposed burden."

"Let's hope that is all it is."

"There's nothing more," Ahuitzotl assured his colleague after noting his concern. "Nenetzin has made it clear to everyone in my court her eyes are only for you. It was for this reason that I suggested this marriage."

"A good decision, but I desired everyone'a approval on it. This wedding was to improve our relationship, not to engender hostilities."

"I would not fret over what Motecuhzoma thinks. He is but a youth-you need not take him seriously."

"I differ with you on that, and do not think he should be lightly dismissed. You've told me more than once you thought him too sober for you. Such men's minds are often active and there is turmoil underneath their sour facades."

"What can he do? Surely you don't fear him?"

"Fear him? No, that is not the correct word. Let's say I am not that comfortable with him. Just as I would be cautious of a reposed serpent into whose lair I have trod, so I would be wary of a man who does not enjoy any pleasures in life. Our young Motecuhzoma appears to be such a man."

"He's no threat to you. Your mistrust is groundless."

"Still, I would feel better if I had his blessings on this wedding, as I have yours. It portents misfortune to have someone opposing your marriage."

"You do astound me at times, Nezahualpilli. A powerful lord such as you, monarch of the Acolhuas, and you are daunted by the intimations of a mere youth whose devotion to his sister causes him to resent losing her. Is this the prowess that has made your name as feared and respected as any among us?"

Nezahualpilli became red-faced in his embarrassment, but he quickly recovered and smiled. "You've made your point," he said. "Foolish me-if we allow minor striplings to frighten us, what hope is there for fulfilling your other grand schemes?"

"None."

"Then let us dismiss our upstart for what he is: an impudent young man for denying me my happiness. He must be taught his courtesies. Come, let me give you a tour of my garden."

The garden was the first of many facilities Nezahualpilli was to show Ahuitzotl that afternoon, although by all indications, he beamed prouder of it than any of the others. Ahuitzotl, only mildly interested in things botanical, tried to maintain his feigned attention out of civility to his host, but the Texcocan soon recognized that this was tiring his guest and decided to move on to a project he knew would stimulate his imagination-the construction of an aqueduct into the city from nearby spring waters. This greatly enthused Ahuitzotl who envisioned a similar undertaking for Tenochtitlan.

"You designed this yourself?" Ahuitzotl asked, impressed by what he saw.

"Yes, with the assistance of my engineers. Remember, I have had schooling in the art."

"Your reputation as a master builder extends throughout Anahuac. I must say this certainly attests to that."

"There are advantages in knowing about the principles of construction as ruler. Engineers are prone to do things their own way and not according to how you want it done. I find some of my hardest fought battles are with them."

"I'm familiar with what you say. I lack your training and am often at the mercy of what they tell me. Too frequently I'm forced to do what they want although I'm not pleased with their ideas."

"They know what they're doing, but are usually resistant to changing their techniques, holding dearly on to these because they are time-tested and have proven their worth. Still, it's dangerous to dispute them if you don't know what you are doing yourself. I understand your dilemma. I've always thought it beneficial to know about what they speak."

Ahuitzotl was envious of Nezahualpilli in this regard, as he entertained visions of being a great builder. Big engineering feats enthralled him and he fancied himself a good designer despite his lack of formal training in the art, and especially, he dreamed of constructing a second aqueduct for Tenochtitlan, the major accomplishment of his reign and his foremost contribution to its citizenry. He was favorably impressed with Nezahualpilli's remark that one of the hardest battles had to be waged with engineers, having already experienced such a struggle in proposing the design for his new palace. He would remember the Texcocan's words.

The wedding ceremony itself was held in the traditional manner, with the tying together of tilmantlis worn by bride and groom and listening to seemingly endless speeches and well-wishes. The sacrament was rendered a more dignified posture by singers ringing out their choruses and the large number of guests in attendance. But the feasting afterwards was what everyone looked forward to, and Nezahualpilli saw to it that the occasion would be memorable. He strove for a grandiose exhibition of his hospitality, sparing no effort in delighting his notable visitors and making them feel suitably comfortable in their present surroundings.

Lords were seated in benign companionship with lovely auianime provided for them by Nezahualpilli-their own wives rarely accompanied them on journeys beyond their cities-in the largest hall of their host's magnificent abode. At its head sat Nezahualpilli with his new bride, Ahuitzotl with one of the Texcocan's personal favorites, the Lady of Tula, and Chimalpopoca with his chosen escort. Seated nearest to them were members of the both royal houses, with each prince and princess placed alternately so that the families were well interspersed; Motecuhzoma was no more than a few paces from his host. The remaining guests filled out the rest of the facility and all were served their dinners, in addition to cocoa drinks and the intoxicating pulque reserved only for such occasions of rare joy, as acrobats, jugglers, and musicians offered pleasing diversions.

While they thus demolished their exquisitely prepared meals, Ahuitzotl's escort overcame her initial inhibitions, evoked by the awe she felt at being seated beside such a reputed conqueror, and she solicited a conversation with him. "At last I am privileged to see the great Lord Ahuitzotl," began the Lady of Tula. "Your fame has reached far; it's all that is heard in the court these days."

"So has yours," answered Ahuitzotl. "You are Nezahualpilli's greatest passion."

"Is that good or bad?"

"For me, it's an obstacle-you keep him from my campaigns."

"Only Nezahualpilli can keep himself from them, Lord. I make no demands on him to stay with me."

"You don't have to; your mere presence here inclines him to it. Nezahualpilli enjoys his scholarly pursuits, as well as his sensual pleasures, and you fulfill both these objectives for him-and quite well I should add."

"I cannot tell if I am being complimented or berated."

"You are being complimented."

"Yet you blame me for keeping him from your activities."

"True, but with his new bride, I believe my problem will be solved. His distractions should be divided more equitably, for Nenetzin is quite scholarly herself. Without one of you to dominate his private life, perhaps he'll think more of his lordly duties."

Ahuitzotl surveyed his partner carefully to see if she was upset by the prospect he unfolded: she gave no sign of this.

"Nenetzin poses no threat to me," she replied confidently. "My relationship with Lord Nezahualpilli is quite special."

She was a beautiful woman, Ahuitzotl noted, and he could see how Nezahualpilli would have preferred her to his wives. Although being the Texcocan's favorite concubine, she could never be his wife because she was the daughter of a local merchant and of no noble descend. Yet she was renowned for her erudition and was said to be equal in intellect to him as well as any of his sages. She exerted an inordinate influence over Nezahualpilli; some even maintained she dominated much of his policy decisions, and rumor had it that he would grant her any wish. Ahuitzotl almost regretted that with Nenetzin a wedge was driven between their harmonious association.

"That remains to be seen," said Ahuitzotl. "One thing is certain: Nenetzin will not stand by and be ignored by her husband. She will insist on his devotion to her."

This time Ahuitzotl detected a visible change in her countenance, even though she presented a composed exterior and continued with her dinner as if nothing ruffled her. Yet she gazed repeatedly toward her lord and appeared somewhat disturbed over his evident delight over his new bride with whom he was so enamored that he did not once return her glances, something he had never failed in doing before. Ahuitzotl missed none of it and was reminded of his difficulties with Pelaxilla and Tlalalca. Like his own sweetheart, the Lady of Tula seemed to fear she would be neglected.

As the gala proceeded late into the evening, Nezahualpilli continued to be enraptured with his latest wife, and increasingly the Lady of Tula became distressed over the spectacle until she was unable to endure it further and requested that Ahuitzotl dismiss her from her social obligations. "It is a painful thing to see," she told him in a quivering tone, her eyes glazy. "Until today, even if I knew I could never be his wife, I was assured he loved me. This evening has severely shaken my faith in that."

Ahuitzotl connected this with Tlalalca and was struck with an unusual sympathy for her. "I understand," he said.

"You will not be angry with me for my discourteous conduct?"

"Of course not."

She thanked him and hurriedly departed. Ahuitzotl looked after her until she disappeared through the door; this was the first time he had seen or spoken with the famed Lady of Tula and he now realized why she was so admired by his colleague. Had she resided among his own ladies in Tenochtitlan, he likewise would have regarded her as one of his favorites.

The Lady of Tula was not the only one upset: Motecuhzoma also focused enviously on his host and found himself resenting the apparent pleasures he was deriving from Nenetzin's company. He knew it was unreasonable for him to react in this fashion, but could not control the emotions he felt. Perhaps he was angered because Nezahualpilli was proving his prior suspicions erroneous by being the ideal husband to Nenetzin and affording her all the love and devotion that was in his capacity to give. Or maybe he still yearned for his guardianship over his sister and deplored having that function lost to her husband. He may have actually loved her himself and was overcome with the horrid pangs of jealousy that lovers feel when they are not similarly the object of their adored one's devotion. But whatever the reasons, the hostility was there, and it prevented him from joining the other well-wishers in their exultation. In this fashion transpired the wedding ceremony of Nezahualpilli and Chalchiuhnenetzin, and for more than one person participating in the celebration, it did not portent happiness.

IX

huitzotl was delayed longer than he had anticipated in his planned drive to the sea. It had been six months since the royal wedding and still he was not ready to begin his advance. Much of this postponement centered around the nature of the operation; he aimed at moving north along the coast to cover the entire western flank of Michoacan, the Tarascan nation, a distance of several hundred leagues, and all of it in unknown regions. The logistical demands of sending a large-scale army into areas heretofore unchartered posed a major encumbrance, for unlike his previous campaigns, where he could depend on local allies or kingdoms friendly to the Mexica to furnish its supplies, there would be no such provisioning available on this operation. Consequently, Ahuitzotl was waiting for information from merchants and other agents he had dispatched into these regions; many never returned while the rest of them seemed to take forever in arriving back in Tenochtitlan. By the time the first reports at last reached him, the news was discouraging and necessitated further delays as alternate plans had to be promulgated to meet the supply problem.

Although Ahuitzotl had long expressed an interest in seeing the great western sea, this in itself would not have justified the sort of expedition he envisioned and constituted only a minor aspect of his true objective. His real purpose for undertaking this quest was considerably bolder and far-sighted. He meant to outflank the whole of Michoacan and cut off its supply links with the coastal kingdoms, a design aimed at nothing less than isolating the Tarascans from all actual and potential allies so that they would stand alone against an eventual conflict with Anahuac which Ahuitzotl believed was inevitable. The expedition was therefore conceived as the opening phase of a subsequent long-ranged plan to conquer the undefeated Tarascans. To accomplish this end, he had to secure the coastal realms under Mexica influence and lock them into a trading and tribute relationship with Anahuac. Such a design entailed an enormous risk-Ahuitzotl was baiting the Tarascans with severe provocations.

His audacious conception led Ahuitzotl into thinking he required a large numbered force as the Mexica stood a good chance of being met by the Tarascans who would understand the aims of his operation and seek to counter it. However the foreseen logistical problems worked against the use of such legions; only a smaller army could sustain itself by supplementing its rations with the game and produce of the region. At length Ahuitzotl acceded to the unique peculiarities imposed, sacrificing the size desired to impress his adversaries-a feature of his operations he exploited to the maximum-and the conclusion was drawn that a complement of only ten thousand warriors would comprise the expeditionary force, not large by recent standards.

After the size and composition of the force had been decided on, all that remained was for the priests to designate the appropriate date. They proceeded assiduously with their tasks, consulting with the stars, drawing up charts and making their calculations, and when they at last informed the Revered Speaker of the propitious time, the departure date was fixed. Messengers announced the activation of those units honored to participate in this venture; no sooner was word received when the armies were on its move, leaving each alliance city in three seperate columns to converge at Oztoma, their designated assembly point. Ahuitztl led Tenochtitlan's division with Tlohtzin and Motecuhzoma his direct subordinates; Nezahualpilli headed the Acolhuas, and Colotl the Tepanecs; Chimalpopoca was excused because the smaller army did not require his presence.

In five days, they reached Oztoma. The city was now inhabited by those Mexica settlers who left Anahuac eleven months ago and its ruler, Acamatl, was kept abreast of the delays and movements of the expeditionary force through couriers sent by Ahuitzotl so that he could arrange a proper reception when the army finally arrived. His people cheered as the expected warriors made their entry and treated them with sweetened cocoa beverages while showering them with an assortment of colorful flowers. Acamatl invited Ahuitzotl and his leading commanders to a feast in the refurbished palace of Oztoma's former ruler, and if the reception was austere in its presentation, Ahuitzotl attributed this more to his host's military background than a lack of sincerity; he would learn the ways of courtly protocol in time.

"What can you tell me about the Tarascans?" Ahuitzotl asked Acamatl, using the occasion to obtain information on his enemy.

"They know we are here, and we suspect many of the merchants and farmers who bring our produce in are their agents. We expelled the ones who asked too many questions. I'm convinced they know the purpose of our settlement, but have not been inclined to oppose us. It's a peculiar thing about them-they're seemingly uninterested in what goes on beyond their borders."

"If that was the case, they would not be sending their agents here. Do not let your guard down. They could be looking for just that before making any moves. What's your own survey of them?"

"As best as we can determine, they are committed to waging defensive battles. They have no forward supply distribution points or storage facilities outside of their borders, nor do they task their neighbors to provide these for them. They could not engage in sustained offensive operations, having no capacity to feed their armies."

"They face the same problems we do on this expedition, only they're much closer to their home base and should be able to organize supply chains if they wanted to confront us."

"I'm not sure they have adequately trained themselves for such a purpose, Lord. Their wars have been defensive for so long that, we believe, they simply are unable to induce their warriors to fight a war of aggression."

"A remarkable assessment, but is it accurate?"

"Their warriors are not motivated by demands from the gods as ours. They require justifications for moving across their borders and do not approach such ventures with the same zeal that we do. In defense of their homeland, however, they are formidable. They make abundant use of their victory over Axayacatl, glorifying it and speaking of it as if it had occurred but yesterday, boasting that all invaders will suffer the same fate."

"We haven't forgotten it either-and a day of reckoning is in the making. If what you say is true, you've served me better than you realize."

Ahuitzotl was pleased over what Acamatl had told him, for it alleviated his worries about taking an inadequate force on an enterprise of such daring intentions. He next turned his attention on the secondary objectives toward which his expedition was directed. "Have you sent any merchants to the coast?" he asked.

"No, Lord, but we've received some of them from there."

"What sort of wares do they bring?"

"Mostly produce. The major crop in that region is cotton, and they supply us with abundant quantities of it. They also bring many variations of pepper, nuts, and cocoa beans."

"What of metal-ware? Or jewelry?"

"We've received none of these things from their merchants."

"Surely you are wrong. Reports have spoken of wealth in these coastal cities."

"I've heard no such reports, Lord. Judging from their appearance, I do not believe there is much wealth there.

"How about stoneware? Have they brought you any jade?"

"Some. but poor in quality. We did not bargain for it."

"I'm reluctant to ask you more; I fear you will shatter all my hopes. Is there nothing in these regions we prize?"

"You mean aside from cotton?"

"I don't mean to undermine the importance of cotton," Ahuitzotl replied with a touch of sarcasm, "but it's hardly a commodity one conquers a region over. Many places grow cotton; we are in no shortage of it."

"They have plumages that we value there, Lord. They make fine feathers from a variety of birds which thrive in the region, including parrots and the sacred quetzal."

"At least that's something. You had me believing that this entire venture would prove unprofitable for us."

If he did not say it directly, Ahuitzotl was nevertheless considerably disillusioned over their brief interchange, and to avoid suffering additional setbacks in his held suppositions, he spent the remaining time with Acamatl discussing numerous projects being planned for his settlement. The damage had been done, however, and the monarch feared his enthusiasm over this enterprise may have waned. Possibly Acamatl might be in error, but if there were riches to be had on the coast, one would have at least expected samples of it in the trades. Perhaps these shore people were very possessive of their treasures.

The Acolhuas arrived on the following afternoon and again Acamatl hosted a reception for them and seemed especially delighted at seeing his former lord. More feasting was held in the palace where, in the course of the usual dinner conversation, Ahuitzotl addressed his planned advance with Nezahualpilli and Colotl.

"We'll proceed directly south from here, traversing the western edge of Yopetzinco, for Acapolco. From there, we'll move north along the coast as far as Zacatula to secure this region for ourselves. These people have enjoyed their autonomy long enough; it's time they learned there are masters to be served. In doing so, we deprive the Tarascans of their coastal contacts."

"This is well and good," commented Nezahualpilli, "but you said traverse Yopetzinco. You will not subjugate the Yopis?"

"They pose no threat and have nothing of value to interest us. From the information we have on them, they are an impoverished lot. What tributes could we collect from them?"

"They are ripe pickings for sacrifices," Colotl replied.

"We defile the gods with such unworthy offerings. Besides, with our reduced force, we must use it for battles which will reap rewards for us. I have no wish to squander it on attacks upon an unimportant people."

Ahuitzotl's position was well founded. No nation had ever expressed an attraction towards conquering the Yopis who were a relatively primitive people and could not be expected to provide any useful services or products. Unique among all the nations circling Anahuac, Yopetzinco retained its independence simply because it was deemed too undesirable for the taking.

After completing their talks on the specifics of the mission, they next turned to lighter themes, and although Ahuitzotl generally avoided private topics even on such occasions, he possessed a curiosity about Nezahualpilli's relationship with Nenetzin. "So how goes it with your new wife?" he asked.

"Very well," replied Nezahualpilli, grinning from ear to ear. "She is remarkably skilled in lovemaking. In fact, to be perfectly candid, she's the best bed partner I've ever known."

She ought to be, Ahuitzotl was thinking; all her romantic escapades should have taught her something in that regard. "We feared she might be too demanding," Ahuitzotl said. "It gave me some reluctance to offer her to you."

"Too demanding?" Nezahualpilli thought this almost hilarious, "Why, she's not at all."

"She isn't?"

"Certainly not. Indeed she's a most dutiful wife; she's not raised any objections to the times I spent with my other wives, or my Lady of Tula."

This astounded Ahuitzotl to such a degree that he thought the Texcocan was talking about someone else.   "Amazing!" he said. "It's not like her; maybe Tlalalca was right."

"About what?"

"She said that marriage would change Nenetzin, but I didn't believe it."

"Change her? In what way?"

Ahuitzotl had momentarily overlooked that Nezahualpilli may have been unaware of Nenetzin's amorous capers in Tenochtitlan's court and had now unwittingly aroused his colleague's suspicions. "Nenetzin is used to having things her way," he hastily responded to suppress Nezahualpilli's curiosity. "I thought her a spoiled child unable to adapt to the obligations of a wife."

"I can assure you she has," Nezahualpilli beamed as if he merited some personal credit for it. "But why not? She certainly has nothing to complain about. I have dozens of menials to see to her needs. You must know how to deal with women; you cannot allow them to lead you."

"I'm not sure how you do it. I have enough problems with the few I keep for myself—in fact, all my frustrations evolve around just two of them. They are more than enough for me."

"That's precisely your problem; you concentrate on just two of them. If you were to diffuse your energies over many of them, no single one could give you much grief."

"The fault is mine. Those two are all that interest me."

"A ruler interested in but two women? That is unheard of. You are obviously too seriously involved with them. My advice is to branch out-pay more attention to your other women."

"The others do nothing for me."

"Yes, and those two know it and will exact all they can out of you. You make a mistake if you try to please them."

"I've often thought that myself."

"Properly so. Once they know you are captivated by their charms, you are at their mercy, and they will push it to the hilt. Believe me, it's better to ignore their pleas for affection than to have them know you will adhere to their every whim."

"If this is how you treat Nenetzin, I would caution you on it. I don't think she'll stand for being ignored."

"I treat her as I do all my wives. She'll not see me submitting like a common slave to her fancies. Am I not her master?"

Ahuitzotl eyed him warily without saying more, but his mind was not at ease. If Nenetzin placed no demands on her husband, as he so freely admitted, it could only mean one thing—she had found some interesting diversion. He was surprised that this should happen so soon in their marriage, and while he knew he could be mistaken, he thought this highly unlikely. He feared his original estimations were being proved accurate, and that did not show promise for the alliance.

Their feasting ended early as the Revered Speaker made his intentions known he would begin his march early in the morning. Acamatl may have wished for them staying longer but prudently refrained from mentioning it. Already he detected a feeling of apartness among his people; he would not have imagined it possible, yet in the short time they had lived among themselves, although many might have disputed it and strongly acknowledged their loyalty to Anahuac, they were already transformed into a distinctive group. So whereas his subjects seemingly preferred that Ahuitzotl chose to leave, he himself wanted his old companions to remain awhile longer: the old comradeship was still there.

At dawn, Ahuitzotl eagerly embraced his long sought drive to the coast, and if Acamatl had disillusioned him earlier, now that the march was about to commence, he felt his enthusiasm rekindled. He was born for such adventures; the excitement of entering previously unknown and unconquered regions was like a narcotic for him, leaving him euphoric and craving for more. He honored his host by assembling his warriors in Oztoma's plaza to participate in a farewell ceremony requested by Acamatl. It offered a moment of glory for the former Texcocan who, through his short but moving oration, relived the days when he commanded the Acolhua army. "You shall always be welcome in our settlement," he said in ending his speech, "and we wish in out hearts that you will see us again."

With Acamatl's address concluded, his settlers applauded the warriors as they marched out of the city. Some of the more exuberant among them ran up to the soldiers and placed flowers in their headbands, but most stood by cheering as they watched their former comrades heading for the distant forest. For the longest time, Acamatl looked after them torn with conflicting emotions; at this moment he may have wished to be with them and deeply regretted his decision to give up his command. Even after they had disappeared beyond the far-off hills, he continued to stand there gazing fixedly out to the spot where he last saw them. There were tears in his eyes.

X

ugged terrain predominated Ahuitzotl's approach to the sea, making his movement slower than he had considered. He proceeded in a southerly direction from Oztoma keeping his army divided by a half day's march from the combined Acolhua and Tepanec contingent, but his trail zig-zagged up and down through repeated mountain ridges and deep valleys and often there was uncertainty if they were on the correct approach. They bypassed the region generally held as comprising Yopetzinco taking care not to be detained by warriors marauding the Yopi villages or being lured into trading prospects. The few villages they passed through left Ahuitzotl with feelings of repugnance, their backwardness authenticated by the squalor in which the inhabitants lived. They lacked even the must rudimentary sanitation facilities or water systems and Ahuitzotl could not hide his personal disdain over their hygienic habits; he thought they smelled horribly and questioned if they ever bathed.

"Who would want to deal with them?" he said to Tlohtzin. "It would discredit us and outright embarrass the gods to subjugate this miserable lot."

Acamatl's words haunted Ahuitzotl as he observed the humble communities of the Yopis, each successive one appearing worse than the last one. What if it came about that they would find nothing of value for their exertion, perhaps not even a worthy opponent to offer them battle-how would this be received by his warriors? He saw the aversion in their faces as they combed the villages, discerning that the Yopis were a contemptible prize for them—to view them as captives or sacred offerings was almost insulting.

The road to the coast, if that is what the narrow pathway deserved to be called, passed over craggy peaks and through deep-cut ravines forcing the army to move in columns of only one or two men abreast. Traversing inhospitable, insect-ridden forests and rugged defiles made the trek exceedingly miserable under a scorching sun and led to cramped muscles and sores as feet tramped over the roughened surface. Discomfited by humid temperatures in the lower valleys, with flies and mosquitoes pestering them unmercifully while they ate and slept in their camps, the Mexica kept up on the tortuous trail prodded onward by their warlord. So it went on until midway into the fifth day, by which time the warriors were drenched in sweat and yearned for clear waters to bathe in, when a refreshing breeze fluttered upon them, cooling them, after they crossed over the final pass. Between the trees ahead of them, they saw a vast, endless stretch of blue ocean: for the men of Anahuac, it comprised a grand spectacle.

"Look at it!" exclaimed Tlohtzin. "It's as huge as the great eastern sea! And we are the first in Anahuac to gaze upon it."

Looming majestically before them, more expansive from the elevation where they observed it than anything they could have imagined, Ahuitzotl thought it one of the most breathtaking sights he ever beheld, and for the longest time he stared spellbound by its enormity. "We're still ten, perhaps twelve leagues from the shore," he presently said. "It will take us most of the day to get there."

"But we have the sea in sight, Lord." replied Motecuhzoma. "How much better than to be faced with more of those unending ridges we crossed."

"Also the heat is more tolerable. Hopefully our advance party has found an inlet where we might wash ourselves-I smell like a Yopi."

Inspired at seeing their first destination within reach, the Mexica covered the distance to the shoreline faster than Ahuitzotl had predicted, arriving there before the afternoon was spent. An improved trail leading to Acapolco skirted adjacent to the sandy beaches and soon the entire army was extended along it with its warriors rejoicing in the cool winds coming off the ocean and awed by waves crashing thunderously on the strands. None of them had ever seen such a sight, most wondrous and impressive, and making the waters of Pantitlan seem insignificant in comparison.

Turning north, the army rounded contours of hills sloping to the shores following the markers left by its advance squadron which told the soldiers that their campsite was near. As they suspected, they were shortly met by the first guides who were to direct them to it; in the distance, they noticed some stone structures gleaming brilliantly white against the contrasting deepened green of the wooded hills behind them.

"It is Acapolco, Lord!" declared the guide, "Approximatly six leagues from here."

Ahuitzotl strained to make out the city's distinguishable features and saw no large temples rising into the sky or any building that could match those of Anahuac cities in size or grandeur. In fact, the entire community had an austere look about it and bore no resemblance to the magnificent cities he had been used to seeing heretofore. Yet he was still some distance from it, he said to himself; perhaps up closer it would be more impressive.

They were led to a beautiful river-fed lagoon surrounded by swaying palms and dense undergrowth that gave the campsite a wonderful secluded distinction. They heard the melodic twittering of birds above the rustling of a wind and the trickling of running water: it made for an idyllic spot-only home itself might have been more inviting. In very little time, they enjoyed the amenities this pleasure garden offered; after seeing to the usual activity entailed in setting up an encampment–posting sentinels to form a defense perimeter, establishing a command center, spotting their sleeping areas, among other things-most of the warriors plunged into the cool waters, relishing its freshness, and scrubbing off the accumulated dirtiness of five days on the move. Others had to wait their turn, being first tasked to hunt game for the evening meal in the nearby forests.

Ahuitzotl doubled his guards for the night to preclude any possibility of a surprise raid by the Acapolcans. In addition, he kept the area between the city and campsite well patrolled with orders to engage any enemy scouts and prevent them from returning to their base. Later that evening, as the sun was sinking spectacularly into the distant ocean in a giant red ball, the second half of the expeditionary force arrived and was escorted to the bivouac area. Ahuitzotl called on his typical briefing after allowing the late comers to freshen up during which he imparted his observations and reviewed tomorrow's strategy with them. By the time the conference was concluded, not one of its participants questioned that an easy victory awaited them.

At early dawn, the Mexica advanced on Acapolco divided into two columns, one moving on the primary road leading to the city, the other along the beach. By the time the sun broke over the mountains to shed its brilliance over the scene, they stood within shouting distance of their objective and faced a small host hastily assembled in a two-hundred paced front and blocking the roadway. It numbered only half the strength of Ahuitzotl's force and at this point was apparently unaware of a second column approaching it from the shore. Only after Ahuitzotl had massed his units into an attack posture and signaled the other column, and received a responsive call from Nezahualpilli's trumpets, did the defenders realize that they opposed another equally large army on their flank.

The Acapolcans, wholly demoralized when they spotted this additional Army, fell into frightened confusion; many of them bolted from their formation, throwing aside their shields and spears, and fled into the forests. Clearly they had no stomach for fighting and cries of disorder arose everywhere as commanders had troubles keeping their units in position. Their anxieties were heightened by the manner in which the Mexica neared them, marching to the cadence of drums and awesome in their battle array with the plumes of their helmets extending above their heads to make them appear as physical giants. Death approached them, stepping to the beat of its thunderous percussions and pounding out its dreadful song, and they trembled as they watched it coming.

When Ahuitzotl sent his emissaries forth to propose the traditional plea for surrender prior to commencing hostilities, it came as no surprise to him that the local ruler readily acceded to all his demands and capitulated without initiating any opposition. Through an interpreter, the monarch informed the envoys of his decision.

"We are not a martial people," he said, "and do not have a well-trained army. We cannot resist you, and your lord's conquests are known to us. We have heard of the cruel method in which he destroyed Oztoma. Inform your lord that we place our lives in his hands and appeal to his sense of honor to treat us with respect and decency. It is all we can do."

After the envoys conveyed these words to Ahuitzotl, he sent messengers to Nezahualpilli and Colotl notifying them that the enemy had conceded defeat. Although achieving a bloodless conquest, this was not altogether appreciated by the warriors as it robbed them of opportunities to engage in plunder and, even more importantly, deprived them of the distinction in taking captives. Their grumbling was not unnoticed by Ahuitzotl; he would once more have to remind his chieftains on the purpose of their mission.

While Ahuitzotl and his major commanders were hosted in the palace-an exceedingly humble facility from their perspective-by the local ruler, the townspeople were tasked to provide for the needs of the soldiers, short of disrespectful demands; they fed them warm meals and gave them cocoa to drink, and as this was their first decent dining since having departed Oztoma, it helped in alleviating their frustrations. Meanwhile, in dining with the lords of Acapolco, Ahuitzotl defined his tributes and other exactions to them. He received a detailed account on the amount of produce generated locally in a six-month period and, based on the quantities cited, specified the proportions to be allocated to Anahuac. He showed significant generosity in spite of his disillusionment over the lack of riches identified on the lists read to him; his priority was to secure these people as neutrals against the Tarascans, not to alienate them through excessive burdens.

His other major demand, requiring Acapolco to cease its trading with Michoacan and instead establish such intercourse with the cities of Anahuac, was readily accepted, much to his surprise. To all appearances the extend of this commerce was minimal and the conditions extracted afforded no undue hardships on the local merchants. While no ruler favored paying any amount of tribute to a foreign power or having stipulations imposed on his autonomy, the Acapolcan king realized he had been treated better than most conquered lords and regally entertained his 'guest' in a show of appreciation. The feasting, however, was interrupted by some priests who accompanied this expedition; they sought an audience with the Revered Speaker and hastened to send him word of it. Ahuitzotl bade them to speak.

"Has my lord forgotten?" their leader asked. "We must give thanks to Huitzilopochtli for granting us this victory."

An interpreter kept the Acapolcan lords abreast of this discussion; their disposition turned sober.

"What does he demand of us?" Ahuitzotl replied.

"Sacrifice. He requires the blood of captives."

"I know that!" Ahuitzotl retorted with some bitterness that their timing had disrupted the congeniality of the feast. "What I meant to say was how many does he need?"

"He has given you a bloodless conquest, Lord. How many is that worth to you?"

The question placed Ahuitzotl in an embarrassing situation. He was aware the Acapolcans were being informed of the conversation and that, if he did not handle this correctly, he could spoil the harmony just established. Faced with having to tell the Acapolcans he needed to slay some of their kind, a condition he did not specify to secure their concessions, this reflected adversely on his probity. Yet Huitzilopochtli had to be satiated and he was unable to evade the issue. Ordinarily, he would have no qualms about calling for these sacrifices, but in this case he seriously questioned the worthiness of captives not taken in actual fighting as palatable offerings. The Acapolcan lord was at his mercy and in no position to contest whatever number he specified. But his integrity was placed in question here, and among rulers, one's word to another remained sacrosanct."

"Take five of them," Ahuitzotl declared, "That will serve as an adequate representation."

"Five?" gasped the chief priest, his incredulity strained beyond belief. "That is all this triumph is worth to you?"

"You've placed me in an awkward position, priest," Ahuitzotl growled. "You require me to impose a stipulation not mentioned in the surrender terms. I can't be excessive in my demand-it would be a breach of honor. I advise you to reflect on this."

"It is the divine Huitzilopochtli that concerns us, Lord; not the wishes of earthly rulers. He will not appreciate this meager offering."

"I can satisfy him better by the methods I employ to achieve my purposes. It is bold warriors taken in dignified battle he desires; we do him no honors by these offerings."

The priest did not contest this; Ahuitzotl had won his case, although he did not wish to insult the Acapolcans with this smear on their bravery. He frequently found his earthly objectives at odds with his religiousness and felt as though he was doing a balancing act between the two in order to attain his goals. Fortunately the priests seemed to understand and prudently refrained from pressing their demands. They quietly stole from the palace leaving their master to explain himself to the Acapolcans.

The next morning, in a solemn ceremony conducted before the assembled Mexica, five captives were lined up in front of a sacrificial block placed centrally in the plaza. They had been randomly selected, Ahuitzotl rejecting the pleas of his helpless ruler to appoint them, although he chose them from the lower ranks so as not to further jeopardize his gains by inadvertently dispatching a worthy notable. The local population was made to witness the proceedings, mainly as a security precaution than out of any expectation of getting them to embrace Mexica gods. With all of them present in the plaza, the probability of an ambush was diminished as its victims would be the Acapolcans themselves. The five chosen as offerings demonstrated an extreme reluctance to be so honored and had to be forcefully dragged from the rest of the prisoners; clearly their beliefs ran counter to those of the Mexica and they possessed no hope of entering the East Paradise of the Sun after being slain on the altar. Even as the priests instructed them on the messages they were to deliver to Huitzilopochtli, they openly rebelled, cursing and spitting at their mentors and refusing to heed their dictates; only after they had been thoroughly drugged by potions which the priests always carried with them did they submit to the counseling given them. They now stood lethargically in line, sedated and only dimly comprehending what was going on–the priests took no chances in having this ceremony go awry.

No sooner had the chief priest finished his oblations, when, without a moment's hesitation, his subordinates reached for their first victim and flung him roughly upon the stone. Ahuitzotl moved up to it, lifted his flint knife into the air and circled it above his head until he covered every direction into the plaza. Then he plunged it with great force into the tautly stretched chest, opening a deep gash; he reached into it and tore out the heart. Blood spewed over the body and stone as Ahuitzotl raised up the pulsating organ for all to see before handing it to a robed votary who placed it in a bowl. Next, Nezahualpilli took his turn and dispatched the second victim with equal skill and then the head priest took care of the remaining three. Throughout it all, a shame-faced Acapolcan monarch closed his eyes and turned his head, unwilling to observe the gory event. For Ahuitzotl, the rites were essential, but they blemished his desired cordiality with Acapolca, and he may have harbored the unthinkable notion that Huitzilopochtli's demands were counterproductive to his own objectives.

On the morning of Ahuitzotl's departure, a small ceremony was held by the Acapolcan lords even though its sincerity was suspect to him. It amounted to a feigned show of allegiance, doing what they believed pleased their conquerors. Prior to setting out, Ahuitzotl was briefed on the other cities lying along the coast-the major ones were Coyucac, Xoloxiuhyah, Petlalah, Xihuacan, Itztapan, Apahcallecan, and Zacatula, his final destination. The nearest one, Coyucac, was a three day march from Acapolco; the rest of them were but a single day's journey from each other. He received all significant details known about these centers, including the names of their rulers, the size and composition of their armies, if they had one, their principle products, and other information which might prove valuable to him. Armed with this intelligence, Ahuitzotl led his units from the city; as before, he divided his force by a half-day's interval, and when the last of the Mexica left Acapolco's plaza, its ruler spat on the ground to emphasize his contempt.

They advanced in a northwesterly direction skirting the contours of the shoreline and staying on the primary route. The trail was in better condition along the coast, being more frequently traversed by merchants, thus making for a more pleasant journey as there was no requirement to cross over mountainous passes or trek through dense, humid forests, and the temperature, although hot at sea level, was endurable as a result of steady breezes coming off the ocean. Also they passed by frequent run-offs flowing from the coastal ranges to the sea which afforded them continuous drinking water. They selected campgrounds adjacent to these streams, providing them with ample opportunity to bathe, as was their habit in Anahuac.

Militarily speaking, the coastal realms were weak; the armies commanded by their rulers were called into being to counter existing emergencies. All their training and disposition was dictated by defensive doctrines and they had no offensive capability, showing neither an inclination for extended aggression nor having taken steps for arrangements that permitted sustained operations over any meaningful distances. This told Ahuitzotl that they might willingly accede to him as Acapolco had done, without a fight, which for him was undesireable-no glorious combat by which his warriors could distinguish themselves was in the offing. Worse, he could not assuage them with promises of booty because their ethical standards prohibited looting cities which had yielded to them, and it also became abundantly clear there was no wealth to be had here. The entire expedition was going against his expectations.

As surmised, Coyucac surrendered without lifting any arms on the Mexica. The lord of the city had been notified of what transpired in Acapolco and when he saw the host approaching, he immediately opened his city to the conqueror, sending word that he could not, nor wanted to, do battle with him. Instead, he regalled Ahuitzotl and his chieftains with the best treatment that his meager resources allowed, inviting them to feasting in his modest abode with promises of exotic seafoods and entertainment.

"What can I do?" grumbled Ahuitzotl to Tlohtzin. "There's no honor in warring on a people who will not fight. Can I treat the lords of Coyucac with less regard than those of Acapolco?"

"You don't have to explain it to me, Lord. It's the warriors who will not understand and must be placated."

"I emphasize it: to secure these kingdoms as strongholds, we cannot treat their people indignantly. Besides, our warriors would not debase themselves by slaying men who will not face them."

Ahuitzotl accepted Coyucac's surrender and remained there for the next three days while learning of its productivity and coming to an agreement on the terms to be assessed against it. As in Acapolco, five local warriors were offered in sacrifice to Huitzilopochtli before the Mexica departed.

The situation repeated itself with tedious regularity in the cities of Xoloxiuhyah, Petlalah, Xihuacan, Itztapan, and Apahcallecan. Ahuitzotl found it incredulous that his five thousand warriors, without counting Nezahualpilli's or Colotl's auxiliaries, so intimated these inhabitants that they refused to offer any resistance whatsoever to their subjugation. He now understood why the Tarascans disdained from expanding their influence into this area; they must have known there was nothing worth taking or battling over here. Only his belief that this venture deterred these people from becoming potential allies for Michoacan induced him to press ahead in spite of his wholesome disgust over their passivity. He now had a novel and serious problem to contend with: how to pacify the mounting irritation felt by his warriors. With each surrender, their grumblings became more pronounced and the chieftains expressed actual fears that they would soon be unable to control them.

If Ahuitzotl cherished any hopes that Zacatula, the last and largest of the targeted cities, would be the one to fight for preserving its sovereignty thereby giving salvation to his plight, these were eclipsed when he met its lords resolved to likewise accept his terms as soon as he came to them. He was now hampered, as he deduced from what these nobles told him, by the reputation of his many 'conquests' which preceded his advance and daunted his adversaries into capitulating even if they possessed the capability to mount an opposition. Although the largest of the coastal cities, Zacatula was as unimpressive as the rest of them, and when it also permitted itself to be taken without as much as an effort applied to its defense, Ahuitzotl feared that one more such bloodless score, while yet a triumph, would lead to open rebellion among his soldiers who were no longer motivated to extend this campaign.

Still Ahuitzotl was determined to succeed in this venture and proceeded farther north, and he even crossed the river bordering Zacatula's realm. But when his scouts reported the absence of any significant urban centers beyond it, his disillusionment stood complete: he decided he had enough.

"It's pointless to go on," he said to Nezahualpilli in his dejection. "There's nothing to be gained. We waste our time."

"You've brought the coastal region under our sphere. That is at least something."

"With the amount of opposition we faced, anyone could have done the same. I see no reason to be congratulated for it."

"We accomplished what we set out to do."

"Yes, but at what price. If one more city surrenders to me, I shall have a mutiny on my hands. Certainly our warriors have not been well rewarded, and I think at this stage even coming back empty-handed will be more satisfying to them than persisting in this unprofitable enterprise."

"Agreed. The discontent I hear out of my ranks is outright frightening-even to me."

"Then it's settled," Ahuitzotl concluded with scorn. "We will return to Anahuac."

XI

A huitzotl chose another route back from Zacatula, following the inland trail which paralleled a river into the high country. They spent an uneventful two weeks trekking back to Oztoma where Acamatl again took pleasure in hosting his former comrades and marvelling at their description of Tonatiuh sinking in his fiery hue into the western sea, decidedly the most impressionable feature of their total experience. After resting there for a number of days, they then finished the last leg of their journey and arrived in Tenochtitlan after an absence of nearly three months; their joy in seeing its beauty after the dismal coastal cities was readily declared in their elation.

While this expedition may have been a major disappointment for Ahuitzotl, to his people in the capital, it amounted to another resounding success story for their mighty warlord and they were out in droves to greet him accordingly. Throughout the campaign, the monarch had sent back messengers after each city fell under his control, and their reports dazzled everyone with the exotic sounding names of one city after another which their monarch had taken. So tumultuous was the acclamation granted the returning army that its warriors, caught up in euphoric exuberance over the exultation accorded them, forgot about their earlier frustrations over the fruitlessness of this undertaking and now fully savored the glory imparted on them. They felt as conquering heroes returned in triumph and, at this moment, not one among them regretted having participated in their venture.

Cihuacoatl met the army in the great square and gave a rousing welcome speech as befitted the occasion in which he praised its accomplishments, and when he was finished, servants poured the warriors cocoa drinks in recognition of their worthy deeds. When this fanfare was concluded and the soldiers were dismissed, Ahuitzotl and the minister headed for the royal palace to discuss events of importance which had occurred during the emperor's absence.

"I am mystified, Lord, that you seized so many cities, yet I see no captives to show for it?" asked Cihuacoatl, his curiosity getting the best of him.

"We acquired no captives because none of these coastal people did battle with us," Ahuitzotl scowled. "Those accomplishments you lauded my army for in your stirring speech were in actuality unopposed surrenders, most annoying for me, even giving me concerns that our warriors might rebel. I have no desire to dwell on it. What's new around here?"

"Trouble is brewing on our southern frontier, Lord. A full scale was has broken out between the Mixtecs and Zapotecs. As a consequence, both powers have made use of the situation to attack our merchants, kill them and steal their goods, and lay the blame on each other. I don't know what they hope to achieve by this marauding-I suspect each side wants us to get involved on its behalf to destroy the other. It's a tricky business; we don't know who's the guilty party or who we should hold responsible for this."

"Both are guilty. Isn't that what you said earlier?"

"So it is," affirmed Cihuacoatl. "I shall rephrase it. The question is-who shall we favor?"

"For the present, none. We will decide on that once more information becomes available. How many of our merchants have been attacked?"

"Nearly all of them operating there, Lord. Our trade has come to a virtual stop."

"Then the problem is more serious than I first supposed."

And so it was; Ahuitzotl was grimly aware of the seriousness of this situation. For years, the finest products in Anahuac were obtained from the southern kingdoms under terms that were unfavorable for them. Whereas their gold, precious stones, fabrics, pottery, and rich feathers were highly prized in the realm, the Mexica's own merchandise was not particularly appealing as an exchange commodity. A few items, such as certain weaponry, may have been of better quality, but by and large, nearly all the goods Anahuac had to offer were of inferior craftsmanship and poorer grade than could be produced there. Only the threat of military intervention in protecting the trading routes and Mexica possessions coerced these southern rulers and merchants to accept this less than desirable relationship. Anahuac profited greatly from the situation; a cut-off of this trade not only deprived it of its most valuable commodities, but more importantly, jeopardized the disadvantageous barter which the Mexica had for so long enjoyed, particularly if the cessation were to persist over a lengthy period. It portented grave consequences for the realm and could not be ignored for long.

"You did right in bringing this to my attention," Ahuitzotl told his minister. "At present, however, I'm not prepared to hear anything unfavorable. I shall call on you–perhaps tomorrow-to discuss this matter."

Cihuacoatl compliantly left the Revered Speaker to his own affairs, and certainly Ahuitzotl had other, more agreeable things on his mind. After such a long absence, Pelaxilla dominated all his thinking and he could scarcely wait to see her. He hustled into his quarters and instructed his attendants to arrange for the bathwater and to bring his mistress to him. His wishes were expeditiously carried out and he soon embraced her loveliness amid his joyous eagerness. They bathed together, scrubbing each other's bodies and, stimulated by their nakedness, delighted in the caressing of their flesh with longing hands. Having undergone weeks of abstinence, Ahuitzotl was aroused to such ardor that he was unable to restrain his cravings. He grabbed her in his arms and carried her from the cistern, proceeding for the adjoining bedroom.

"Again?" Pelaxilla teased, "At least let us dry ourselves."

"What does it matter? We'll just move into another chamber when we are finished."

"But they're all occupied."

"We'll throw them out! Do you object?"

"You don't see me fighting it, do you?"

Laughing, Ahuitzotl set her wet body on the mats and smothered it with his own hot flesh; he kissed her ravenously, covering every portion of her quivering body with his probing tongue. Then, with eager assistance from her willing hands, his phallus found her warm enclosure and settled into a snug fit. Heatedly, his motions rose in the delectable excitement that carried him to the climax in which he expended himself in a pleasureable rhythm of ecstacy. When it was over, he felt as if all his energy had been sapped from him, and he gasped for air that seemed inadequate in restoring his exhaustive body. His desires thus gratified, he lay on the soggy sheets, oblivious to its dampness, with Pelaxilla happily snuggled next to him.

"I can never get enough of you," she sighed in contentment. "We're getting so good at this. You really know the moves that thrill me."

"There's satisfaction in being told how great I am," grinned Ahuitzotl, "and realize I'm not the only person who knows it."

"You are so conceited," Pelaxilla laughed.

"I'll not deny it. But come, let's find a dry bed. Do you have anyone you wish to offend? We'll go into her chamber and oust her from it."

"How about Tlalalca's?" Pelaxilla responded teasingly.

Ahuitzotl's smile vanished as her remark triggered a serious demeanor in him; he glimpsed hard at Pelaxilla, his displeasure seen in his icy eyes.

"I was only joking," Pelaxilla tried to retract her statement when she saw its effect on him. "You needn't be so earnest about it."

"Tlalalca is the empress," he reproached her, "and must be accorded the courtesy and respect that title bestows. I do not want subordinates speaking ill of her."

"Did I speak ill of her?" she countered, taking offense.

"You implied it."

Pelaxilla was taken aback by his guardianship over his wife; she did not appreciate such an overreaction to a casual remark she made without any intent towards malice. "You don't have to present yourself as her champion to me," she retorted. "Just because she is with child does not mean that she should be now perceived as a goddess in your eyes. She is still the same Tlalalca."

"What did you say? Tlalalca is with child?"

His astonishment amazed her; she was certain Cihuacoatl would have told him of it when the physicians first learned about it. "You didn't know?" she gulped.

"No. No one has told me."

This disturbed Pelaxilla; if he had assumed his protective posture over the empress without having known of her pregnancy, it must have been due to a change of heart. Could it be that he had finally come to love Tlalalca?

"It's hard to believe," she said, seeking a confirmation of her worries. "The entire court has known it for over a month. Surely you must have received a message on it."

"I did not, and I will certainly castigate my minister for the oversight. I would have wanted to hear about this even while on my expedition."

"And you were not told when you returned?"

"I've already said I wasn't. Why do you question it?"

Her former fears were rekindling themselves, and she felt a pang of chill shooting through her at the awareness that he may now favor the empress over herself. "I thought the reason for reprimanding me was out of knowledge she bore your child," said Pelaxilla. "Now I discover you defended her in spite of that."

"I cautioned you to correct your disrespect for the empress; whoever holds that title is immaterial."

"You never found it necessary to berate me for that before."

"I haven't heard you express that kind of irreverence to the empress before."

"I'm sorry I ever mentioned it," Pelaxilla replied, not believing what he had just said, but also having no desire to anger Ahuitzotl over the point. "Let's just stay here. Your servants can replace the mats for us."

"I can't stay with you now. I must see Tlalalca."

"Why?" Pelaxilla reacted with disdain. "You always stay with me on your first nights back in Tenochtitlan."

"True, but how can I ignore my wife when she's carrying my child? She would have expected me to be informed of it, as you did, and now that I know, I can't just disregard it."

"What does it matter? You already have a number of children from others-why is this so different?"

"It isn't to me, but it is important to Tlalalca, as it would be to you if you carried a child; she will be hurt if I did not share in her happiness over this. I don't want to intentionally hurt her."

"You can go to her tomorrow."

"How would I explain that I chose to defer seeing her after learning she is with child? Tlalalca does not merit my continuous neglect, and certainly not in her present condition. She also has feelings you know."

Pelaxilla's disappointment was plain enough, but she knew Ahuitzotl meant well and had to do what was proper; she could not deny his argument-Tlalalca deserved his attention on this of all days.

"I understand," she conceded. "I will not insist on keeping you here."

"I'm grateful for that, Pelaxilla. Believe me, I'ld rather spend the night with you, but I must show some regard for my wife."

"When will I see you again?"

"Tomorrow. I will not abstain from my true love any longer than is necessary."

She nodded her consent with a smile, pleased at his answer.

Mixed emotions beset Ahuitzotl as he proceeded for Tlalalca's chamber. He was relieved Pelaxilla was not unduly upset with him and at the same time felt that he had not been altogether honest with her, for in actuality he yearned to see Tlalalca. Not that his love for Pelaxilla had waned. Far from it-she enflamed his passions to greater heights than anyone else was able to do, but therein lay much of the problem. In this respect, his association with the empress had become more harmonious; with Pelaxilla his feelings were marked with intensity and he was often seized with compulsions over trying to please her. These emotional peaks were absent in his relationship with Tlalalca and, as a consequence, he found her company more congenial. It troubled him that such was his deportment, but he did not know how to remedy the situation. The fault, he believed, was his.

Contrary to what he told Pelaxilla, Ahuitzotl was quite thrilled over his wife's condition, for although he had fostered several children by his mistresses, Tlalalca's case was very special. As a member of the Tepanec clan, she was of the royal lineage, claiming an ascendency to an ancient Toltec nobility whose progenitor was Tonatiuh himself, and that was held in mystical awe by priests preoccupied with such matters. A son born to her was a descendant of the Sun-a legitimate claimnant to the throne for the House of Tenochtitlan; such a birth portented great signification for the realm.

When he entered Tlalalca's chamber, after knocking and respectfully waiting until she bade him in, Ahuitzotl found her seated next to the faithful Xoyo reciting some poetry to her. A gleam flashed in her eyes when she saw him. As usual, he was distracted by Xoyo's presence, but Tlalalca detected this and motioned for her servant to leave, and the old woman immediately complied.

"Is it true?" he asked.

"About the child? See for yourself."

She stood up and pressed her loosely draped garment against her lean body; already Ahuitzotl could see the slightly bulging abdomen and the sight brought a sparkle to his eyes. Rarely had she seen him exude such radiance, and she was helplessly captivated in its spell as it wrapped her with warmth.

"I only learned of it a moment ago when Pelaxilla told me."

"And you left her to be with me?" she felt somehow that was meaningful.

"I wanted to be sure."

"Yes, I should have known. Will I ever see the day when you come to me first without requiring special inducement?"

He answered her with a smile as his eyes twinkled, continuing to emit that warm glow that seemed to penetrate Tlalalca to her inner depths and magically draw her to him. She must have been left puzzled by this, living in hope as she did; it came as a sign which gave her such encouragement her wishes might eventually be fulfilled that she was greatly uplifted by it. She sensed that day was at hand and her joy was immense. In awe, she marveled at the workings of Xochiquetzal.

XII

Ahuitzotl summoned for his minister early the next morning to study the situation on the southern frontier, deeming the problem threatening enough to warrant his immediate attention. Also he would use the occasion to inform Cihuacoatl that his omission in relating Tlalalca's pregnancy was not exactly appreciated. Cihuacoatl suspected that he faced censure for this, a conclusion he drew when he received word his master wanted to see him so early that day, and he sensed himself becoming taut when he entered the reception hall. There he saw the monarch standing next to his throne, another bad sign-he always stood when he was irritated.

"My lord called for me?" Cihuacoatl spoke first, forgetting about the appropriate etiquette in his nervousness.

Ahuitzotl scrutinized the minister's face, noticing its worrisome features; this made him hesitant to ensue his castigation. He decided he would tone down his beratement. "You did not tell me Tlalalca was with child," he said. "Did the news seem so trivial to you that you thought is unnecessary to relate it to me?"

"I confess to not informing you of it, Lord, but not for those reasons. I thought it might cause you to cut short your campaign before you attained all your objectives-that you might not actually have appreciated it."

"You think too much about what I will be thinking. You ought to know, above all people, I do not allow anything to distract me from my purpose. Yet I can see how you could draw that conclusion, but why didn't you tell me when I arrived here yesterday? Had you forgotten it?"

"I hadn't forgotten, Lord, but rather thought that, as you were already here, you would have preferred to hear it from the empress directly."

"Unfortunatly I went to my mistress Pelaxilla instead of the empress," Ahuitzotl related, grinning as he was struck by its humorous side. "I learned of it from her."

"My apologies, Lord."

"As it turned out, I did see her. But suppose Pelaxilla had never mentioned it-I would not have gone to Tlalalca, leaving her to believe her bearing my child was unimportant to me. I could be walking these halls today without knowledge of it. Think of it. Me, the Revered Speaker-the only person in the palace not to know his wife is pregnant."

"It was heedless of me, Lord, My intent was to please you."

"How odd the ways of the court are. The things I want kept a secret are known to all, while those believed to be common knowledge are not. But enough said on that. Your reports on the events along our southern frontier have disturbed me-I want to discuss it with you. I need to know what information we have available."

Cihuacoatl was delighted that the subject had changed; affairs of states are what he enjoyed talking about the most. "The reports are imprecise, Lord," he said. "I can only give you some of the observations we made while you were on the coast as we saw the situation developing."

"Then begin with these."

"Do you remember the Zapotecan lord, Cocijoeza? He was here for the Great Temple's inauguration."

"Only vaguely. Refresh my memory!"

"He was the lord who moved his capital from his old city, Zaachila, to Tehuantepec to escape the Mixtec expansion; the one who said he was indebted to you for your victory over the Mixtecs at Coyolapan because it inspired his own people to renew their wars with them and do the same."

It all came back to him now; he recollected how he had resented having another monarch reap profits from his own conquests, but more than that, he recalled the Zapotecan himself and how he disliked him-a heavily set man whose ugliness repelled him.

"Ah yes, I remember. He told us that he would try to expel the Mixtecs from his lands. His ambition was to resurrect the former glory of his kingdom. I warned him not to allow his wars to interfere with our trades."

"So you did, Lord."

"Then he has chosen to ignore my advice. You said that the Zapotecs as well as the Mixtecs prey on our merchants."

"Such has been reported by the survivors."

Ahuitzotl paced the floor with his hands clasped behind his back as he deliberated on the problem. "Would you say, in all your experience," he went on, "that such raids are accomplished by the sanctions of the local rulers, if not their outright direction?"

"That is my conclusion, Lord; certainly they could not be carried on without their knowledge, for their own trading is affected by it. Since the practice has not ceased-in fact it has increased-they must be condoning it."

"So we can assume that Cocijoeza is fully aware of these activities and has not seen fit to put a stop to them in spite of my warnings."

"I agree with the assessment; he may even have ordered them."

"To have us blame the Mixtecs. It makes sense. Obviously he would have an easier time destroying them if we also attacked them from the north. But the Mixtecs do the same. It's evident we must punish them both, although the Mixtecs engage in this without our specific admonitions."

"Which makes the Zapotecan's crime all the greater."

"True. Cocijoeza has willingly taken it upon himself to risk incurring our anger. He flaunts us with provocations."

"What do you propose we do, Lord-send an invasionary force?"

"Not yet. It's too soon after our coastal venture-Nezahualpilli will be arriving in Texcoco only today. As of present, send a party of emissaries to both the Mixtecs and Zapotecs to inform their lords of our displeasure and that we will not stand idly by to see our profitable trades coming to an end because of their regional war. I want the demands on these lords so hard that they'll have to refuse them-so I can have my excuse for destroying them."

"But you already have that excuse, Lord. The killing of merchants is, and always has been, prohibited by mutual agreement-it is a cause for war. The condition is understood by everyone."

"An invasion south will span over greater distances and require more of our warriors than any we have ever attempted. I want our warriors sufficiently incensed to willingly make the trek, and what better motivation than to have our attempts at conciliation spurned by the enemy?"

"I should think the riches of these kingdoms would be enough incentive."

"It certainly helps, especially after our last ininspiring undertaking, but to have our honor besmearched, that will drive them to fury."

"What kind of demands shall we insist on?"

"There are a number of ways we can do this. First, we insist that they provide armed escorts for all our merchants operating in their area; this will be difficult for them since their energies are directed towards their wars. Next, we complete a list of the total quantities of produce lost to us through the cessation of our trades and demand full restitution for these losses in a very brief time span-one that will severely strain their capacities to meet. Then, and this will be the most unacceptable, we demand a lifetime compensatory payment from them to be given to the widows and orphans of the merchants they have slain. Each of these conditions is in itself difficult to meet-together, they are impossible."

Cihuacoatl stood awestruck. Once again he was astounded by his master's genius for manipulating a situation towards a planned outcome and it stood for him as another reminder that this was most definitely a man to have on your side, and never against you.

"That should suffice for starters," Ahuitzotl summed up. "You may be able to add a point or two to spice it up even more."

"I'll think on it, but it will be difficult to top your suggestions."

"Do whatever you must to make our terms quite unacceptable for them-that's the main thing."

"I shall instruct the emissaries forthwith and send them on their way," beamed Cihuacoatl, regarding this meeting's outcome satisfying beyond his wildest dreams.

After dismissing his minister, Ahuitzotl remained alone in the hall to ponder over his decision. He might have been more empathetic to Cocijoeza's attempts at reclaiming his lost territories had it not been for his personal dislike for him which was heightened by the man's failure to abide by his warnings. While true that Cocijoeza had honored him in attending the Great Temple's dedication, Ahuitzotl retained an underlying suspicion that this was due more to learning about Mexica battle techniques which he might himself apply against the Mixtecs than out of any sincerity. Because he was present at the ceremony made his refusal to heed his host's precautions that much more offensive to Ahuitzotl, for it told him that, in spite of having witnessed the greatness and supremacy of the Mexica power, Cocijoeza seemingly was unimpressed by it. The purpose behind the mightiest spectacle ever staged was utterly lost on or ignored by the

Zapotecan lord. This, more than anything else, is what galled Ahuitzotl, and the longer he reflected on it, the greater increased his rancor.

Everything the Mexica did, every action planned, initiated, and executed, for an individual as well as the state, every word or thought expressed, was out of an awareness that the gods bore witness to it. Any insult hurled upon the Revered Speaker, such as a failure to adhere to his exhortations, was being observed by the deities he was sworn to defend and sustain and, if no actions were initiated towards its rectification, constituted a slur on them as well. More than mere personal satisfaction demanded punishment for those who opposed the Mexica in word and deed, more than the requirement for retribution was conferred upon the rulers of Anahuac–it amounted to an imperative obligation imposed by insistent gods.

XIII

Ceremonial duties kept Ahuitzotl constantly occupied during the weeks in which he waited for the return of the emissaries sent to the southern kingdoms. He was not only the Revered Speaker, ruler of the nation, but its commander-in-chief and supreme priest as well. Even though each of the priestly cults had its own particular superiors and the state's religious institution was administered by two priests of equal rank, the Teotecuhtli, Divine Lord, and the Heuyteopixque, High Priest, it was the Revered Speaker who predominated over them all and the man appointed to hold that office was usually highly trained in the priestly profession in addition to the martial arts.

For Ahuitzotl, whose proclivity ran clearly towards the military side of his duties, this posed an awkward dilemma as he was expected to initiate, if not actually supervise, rituals whose details he had forgotten or often never understood well to begin with. Unlike previous monarchs who had divided their interests and time more equitably between the military and religious necessities of the state, Ahuitzotl was almost totally devoted to the martial requirements. His frequent campaigning and expeditions into distant regions, coupled with his personal conviction that a warlord should at all times be with his warriors, kept him away from the capital for lengthier periods than was typical of his predecessors. If he harbored a private passion aside from things military, it directed itself towards great construction and engineering feats, and this predilection contributed in removing him yet further from a religious emphasis.

This is not to say that Ahuitzotl did not fear the gods; far from it-he was ever conscious of their presence and took their requirements into regard, as any monarch would have. Where he differed was that he chose to make the nation's patron God, Huitzilopochtli, his supreme deity and believed that by honoring him he in turn rendered appropriate homage to the other gods and goddesses. Few doubted that Ahuitzotl was their tribal god's most devoted servant, as he was fond of saying, but many questioned whether he imparted enough attention to the remaining divinities. But there were so many of them, and the pantheon was becoming ever larger with the inclusion of more and more deities from the conquered nations, that Ahuitzotl reasoned only full-time priests, dedicated to their duties, could possibly keep track of them all and meet their individual demands.

As a consequence, Ahuitzotl relied heavily on the counsel of a staff he kept on hand to keep him abreast of the many rituals. Although these repeated themselves, and he would never have overlooked the festivals of the principal gods, he nevertheless wanted to be apprised of particular ceremonial demands whenever the feasting periods occurred. For Ahuitzotl, this was the sensible way to conduct the business-he could not be expected to know all the complex elaborations and intricacies of each rite for such a multitude of deities. But for the specific priests of each individual cult, he came dangerously close to offending them through what was adjudged his demeaning omissions and neglect. Many grumbled over his irreverence, and they viewed with jealousy the attention he gave Huitzilopochtli at the expense of their own sacred masters.

Cihuacoatl was keenly aware of this problem and expended a considerable amount of his time explaining to the monarch that he was treading a perilous course by not showing more public respect for the other priests and the deities they served. He feared these zealots would invoke the vengeance of their gods upon Ahuitzotl, if these gods were not already disposed to such action. He had concerns about this even before Ahuitzotl was appointed as monarch, thinking that he exhibited a tendency to downplay the importance of the lesser gods. He was a paradoxical figure to Cihuacoatl, being their greatest conqueror and most dynamic ruler, and yet he kept his realm in the grips of fear with his habitual disregard for certain religious requisites. Many openly declared that he toyed with the gods, and this portented dangers.

"You must make proper concessions to the priests," Cihuacoatl cautioned his master. "To them, their rites are as as important as Huitzilopochtli's. You cannot slight them."

"Slight them?" retorted Ahuitzotl. "What are you speaking of? Have I ever neglected to initiate their ceremonies?"

"No, Lord, you have not."

"So what is the nature of their incessant complaining about my not granting them sufficient time? I spent last week presiding over the feasts to the goddess Coatlicue, and two weeks before, I was several days in attendance honoring the Tlaloque."

"You bungled your orisons to Coatlicue. Her priests were incensed over your lackluster performance."

"They should not have required me to say their prayers for them. All the other priests recite their own chants."

"That is exactly my point, Lord. The manner in which you approach your ceremonial duties infuriates them. If you truly feared Coatlicue, you would never have misspoken the prayers to her."

"The goddess will, in her wisdom, understand, which is more than I can say for her priests."

"Again you verify my point. You endanger us by alienating the priests against you. They speak to the gods and can invoke enormous powers."

"I have brought them more captives than anyone else. It's my expectation they should be thanking me rather than endlessly pronouncing their objections."

"Certainly you've brought us ample captives, Lord. But where have they mostly gone? Almost all were offered to Huitzilopochtli and Tlaloc. How many were left for Mictlancihuatl, Tlaltecuhtli, and all the others? Indeed, Lord, despite the glory you have brought us, there is a valid basis to the claim that you imperil us."

"If I please Huitzilopochtli, I also please the others."

"That's not what the priests tell us."

"They contradict their own teachings to us-in order to elevate their importance, I suspect."

"Such talk is blasphemous!" exclaimed Cihuacoatl, much alarmed that his warnings fell on seemingly deaf ears. "This kind of thinking makes me fear for you. The lesser gods you minimize will one day conspire against you and bring you to ruin. Even great Huitzilopochtli will eventually tire of seeing his compatriot gods diminished by a mere mortal. I ask that you take due care."

Ahuitzotl was not left entirely free of any worries over the minister's admonition. He remembered how helpless he had been in the wake of the plague ensuing out of the Great Temple's dedication rites when he believed his patron god would protect him. There was a danger in rendering one's own definition to the designs of the gods; Cihuacoatl was correct in reminding him of this.

"If it's true I have been remiss in this connection," Ahuitzotl said, "I shall attempt to rectify my dereliction."

"It is imperative that you do, Lord."

The response aroused a flash of anger in Ahuitzotl who was not used to such authoritative counsel, but he quickly dispelled his annoyance, taking the well-meaning intentions of his minister into regard. "Let us be off to Xiuhtecuhtli's temple," he said. "His priests require our attendance."

"Then you haven't forgotten."

"I never forget our principal deities, Cihuacoatl, contrary to what you think. It is Izcalli and the Lord of Time must be served. His priests will not find my attention wanting. I promise you that."

Izcalli, the Reawakening, eighteenth and last month of the year, called for the annual fire observance-said to be the first rite created by the gods-in which a rejuvenation of the cyclical time period was symbolized. To the venerable old God of Fire, Xiuhtecuhtli, Lord of Time, the month was dedicated, and his oblations emphasized the turn of the year through a rekindling of the sacred fire. Although not that demanding of victims-only four captives and a woman-his ritual was gruesome to behold and quite distasteful to perform as it required cutting the hearts out of roasted victims. Ahuitzotl never liked the stench of burning flesh and balked at the thought of having to touch the seared bodies; if he obediently initiated these rites in the past, it was nonetheless accomplished with feelings of revulsion-and this from a cutter as ferocious as himself.

When Ahuitzotl and his minister arrived, chanting priests and their cult members were solemnly seated in a circle within the temple's forward chamber; Xiuhtecuhtli's idol was kept out of sight in the rear chamber. In the middle of this circle rested the Teotlicuilli, the Divine Hearth, bordered by stones, which had been fed continuously with oakwood for over a day so that it glowed furiously with live embers heating the room to uncomfortable levels.

"Do you see the price we must pay for our indulgence?" Ahuitzotl said to the minister as sweat poured from him. "This is a living inferno."

"I pray Xiuhtecuhtli did not hear you," Cihuacoatl decried. "He would surely be offended."

The woman to be sacrificed, adorned in splendid array, sat by the doorway separating the two chambers; her male counterparts were to be slain before her instead of the idol which could not be seen by anyone except the high priests. An altar stood between her and the Divine Hearth, with the interior darkness reflecting a fiery hue from its burning embers, making it easy to see how such an atmosphere, numinous in its eeriness, could invoke the awesome powers of Xiuhtecuhtli, God of Fire.

The ritual began when a partially naked priest emerged from the rear chamber as his cultists hummed in deep moans, and when he came to the hearth, he raised both hands, bringing the intones to a halt. Then, after some pause, the priest sounded out a prayer. This completed, the first of the chosen offerings was escorted in from the outer platform; he was completely naked and when he was taken to the head priest, one of the lesser votaries threw yuahtli powder into his face. Upon inhaling it, his senses became numbed; he was about to collapse when four other priests reached for him, each grabbing a limb. They swung the dazed captive three times to and fro, and on the fourth fling let him fall into the live coals. The Divine Hearth was the width of a man's body so that he fitted neatly into it while permitting the priests to hang on to his extremities. Before he was dead, he was quickly pulled back out.

Half roasted, the prisoner was next carried to the stone where Ahuitzotl was standing with his knife ready. He stared at the charred body quivering in its death throes, both fascinated and repulsed by the caustic smell; in spite of still being alive, not a sound emanated form the victim. Quickly, Ahuitzotl plunged his knife into the crisped chest and tore out the heart–his hand felt burned from having touched the seared flesh. He placed the pulsating organ on a plate held forth by a subordinate and the body was ignobly dumped on the floor directly in front of the woman.

With their first captive thus dispatched, the priests came in leading the second one to his destiny and repeated the process over again-Ahuitzotl also slew him. Cihuacoatl then killed the third victim and the chief priest saw to the remaining one. Their corpses were placed adjacent to each other to form a dais for the woman who was next roughly siezed and thrown upon the still heated flesh. As soon as she landed on them, a priest leaped over her, yanked her head back by the hair, and slit her throat from ear to ear while a compatriot collected the gushing blood in a bowl. When filled, the recepticle was handed to the chief priest who then walked up to the Divine Hearth and sprinkled its sacred contents on the fire, leaving some of it to take to the idol and smear its face with the life giving fluid. The body of the woman was left lying straddled on top of the dais of slain prisoners.

After the fire sacrifices were concluded, one of the priests swept up the embers and ashes displaced from the Divine Hearth in pulling out the victims and deposited these meticulously back into a brazier. Next, all the priests came forward and placed a folded mantle, a breechcloth, and a belt beside the hearth. Atop these, the chief priest set a small image of the fire god. This done, each of their lot sat down and stripped off his garments, and then took two incense torches and lighted them in the fire. Their torches were coated with a waxy resin which, when melted by the heat, was allowed to run over the hands, torso, and legs, roasting these portions of his body in fiery penitence to Xiuhtecuhtli; not a whimper was heard out of any of them. After the torches had expired, they were thrown into the hearth, along with the material which had smeared the bodies of the atoners; incense was added to the fire which, together with the melted resin, gave off a thick cloud of smoke and pungent odor. While the divine Hearth was thus smoldering from the material cast into it, the cultists proceeded to dance around it, sweltering in its heat and chanting their sacred hymns of fire and sacrifice.

Ahuitzotl and Cihuacoatl left them when their dancing began, having completed their part in the ritual; their clothes retained the stench of smoke and incense as they headed back to the palace.

"It has its importance," Ahuitzotl remarked with acerbity, "but you must admit, compared with other observances, this one certainly leaves its mark on you. I shall have to bathe for hours to rid myself of this foul smell which clings to me,"

"It's a small price to pay for Xiuhtecuhtli," Cihuacoatl replied soberly. "He assures us the continuance of fire."

"I do not contest our gratitude to him."

"But you complain of the inconvenience it presents to you, and you do this oblivious to the repercussions your blasphemous conduct may inflict upon us. As always, Lord, you have a way of demeaning what is a most solemn ceremony."

Cihuacoatl stared coldly at his master; inadvertantly he had once again slighted another sacred rite and the minister wondered how much longer the gods would tolerate such mockery. Saying nothing more, he kept in step with the monarch as they strode across the central square in the direction of the royal residence, but his displeasure was apparent enough in the scowl exhibited on his face.

XIV

Weeks of waiting turned into months, and still there was no word from the emissaries sent to the southern realms. Ahuitzotl, never known for having much patience, was becoming increasingly agitated over this lack of communication and the continued cessation of trades with that region. His anger might have manifested itself more potently had it not been for the diversion offered by Tlalalca's pregnancy and his intermittent engagement in the numerous festivals marking each month. Her time was now nearing and this absorbed much of his attention as he eagerly anticipated a son who would be recognized a rightful heir to the kingship-none of his other children met that qualification as they had no direct claim to the royal line.

For Tlalalca, these weeks preceding the birth were some of the happiest of her life. Showered with compliments and attentiveness from the court ladies and servants, and visited almost daily by her husband who gave her no sign of the frustrations the Mixtec-Zapotec affair was causing him because he felt her condition should spare her from duress, this was a time when everyone's focus was on her well-being. She was the center of attraction and talk of the court and could certainly not be blamed if she believed herself especially favored by Xochiquetzal and Toci, the Grandmother Goddess, patroness of the midwives who would assist in the birth.

Not everyone in the palace was pleased with the situation. Pelaxilla, finding herself ignored by the abundant affection heaped upon her rival, was overcome with dreadful pangs of jealousy; she wanted desperately to carry her own child by Ahuitzotl but knew this was not the same thing. No child of hers could receive the adulations that a woman of the Tepanec family invoked-it would be but one of so-many offsprings Ahuitzotl had already fostered. This hurt Pelaxilla almost as deeply as not bearing a child, for she feared she might be barren, a prospect of horrifying dimensions for a Mexica woman. As in every martial society, enormous emphasis was placed on a woman's ability to bear children-it embodied a paramount social function bordering on a sacred obligation. A woman unable to conceive was a failure in a system that required procreation for conducting the divine role imparted upon it to sustain the world: she was useless in such an order.

If Pelaxilla worried excessively about her inabilities, Ahuitzotl did not. Although he spent a significant amount of his time with the empress in the later stages of her pregnancy, he applied ample effort to assure that his mistress was not left without his attentions and did not alter his scheduled nights with her even if Tlalalca might have preferred this. But to Pelaxilla, this was not perceived with the comfort Ahuitzotl may have wished; she felt overshadowed by the adoration everyone accorded Tlalalca and considered his attempts largely feigned. It should perhaps have been expected that the time of Tlalalca's greatest happiness was correspondingly the most depressing period for Pelaxilla.

Ahuitzotl tried to make sense out of the situation as best as he could, but was often bewildered by her morose moods, especially when he had come to her as she so dearly wished. This made his nights with her less than desirable and, after successive repetition, gave him cause to question whether her love for him was waning-a frightening notion.

"Are you so displeased with me," he said in exasperation when she was in one of her darker moods, "that you can no longer abide my company?"

"Why do you say that?" Pelaxilla replied.

"You give me ample reason to think it. You haven't been the best of companions as of late."

"And whose fault is that?" she snapped.

"What's that supposed to mean?" Ahuitzotl countered, reacting angrily to her derision while, at the same time, perplexed over her insinuations.

"All day long I hear the court speaking of Tlalalca-the endless praises and well-wishes. You yourself have gone to extraordinary lengths to extol her virtues along with the others. So she is with child! What's so special about that? Countless women bear children on any given day. Why exalt this to the high heavens?"

"You trouble yourself over nothing. I haven't allowed her condition to keep me from you."

His words embarrassed her. She loathed herself for the envy she bore the empress, believing her conduct unbecoming, and it unpset her that she could not share in what was an obvious happy occasion for him. Emotionally bound up in his declared 'arrangement' with Tlalalca, she could not look upon it with the cool detachment he seemed able to do.

"You do not have to feel obligated to please me," she said. "I know you would rather be with her now."

Ahuitzotl discerned that her open distress had nothing to do with any diminished love for him, and was much relieved by this. His own assurances reinforced, he strove to allay Pelaxilla's despair. "You're wrong," he said. "I come to you because I want to, but your sour disposition is not conducive to my remaining here with you."

"The whole court speaks of how enthralled you are with Tlalalaca. You don't have to deceive me."

"I'm thrilled over her bearing my child. My feelings for her are not changed."

"Oh, really. What proof have I of that?"

"Proof? What's this talk about proof? I'm here with you because I love you. Isn't that sufficient for you?"

"It is not."

"Indeed? Then perhaps you should enlighten me on what else I can do; apparently my presence is inadequate."

"I want you to be honest with me."

Ahuitzotl could sense his temperature rising. He wearied of constantly bolstering her flagging confidence about his sincerity. Kingdoms accepted his words, yet they were not enough for her. "I've never lied to you and very much resent your questioning my honesty," he said. "I'll not stay here to be insulted."

"Do not let me keep you from her. It's what you wanted all along anyway."

He gave her a leery glance before departing. He disliked seeing her in such straits, but also disdained from her company if she was bent on offending him. He would come back when she was in a more conciliatory mood. "I'm going," he said, strongly emphasizing his determination, "and not to Tlalalca, but rather one of my other mistresses. If you seek proof of that, you have only to ask her."

He turned and exited without giving her a chance to retract her hasty protestation which she now regretted. In tears and overwhelmed with self-loathing, Pelaxilla slumped her face down on her sheets which, had it not been for her unreasonable fears, would have felt the warmth of his body this night.

The midwife, tasked with delivering the baby, acted as a priestess and performed the natal rites. When it came time for Tlalalca to give birth, the midwife had already remained in the palace for a number of days and was aided in all her comforts and duties by the ever faithful Xoyo. It happened on the sixth month of the new eighteen month year, Etzalcualiztli, dedicated to the Rain God, Tlaloc, and on the fifteenth day, Cuauhtli, the Eagle, when Tlalalca went into labor and was moved to her chamber by Xoyo and the midwife. The pains came upon her severely and with suddenness, and Ahuitzotl, never around during the births of his previous children, was gripped with apprehensions that Tlalalca's recurring screams somehow meant the baby's life was threatened. He paced the floor anxiously through most of the day. By evening, when the sun was setting in blazing redness, the child was born-a son! The midwife cut the umbilical cord and spoke to the child after its arrival.

"Precious one, come alone into a world that is full of hardship and suffering, struggle and weariness, oppressive heat and bitter cold, and the cruel wind. Know that this is not your home—because you are a warrior, this house into which you were born is but a temporary nest for you. You were given life so that you may provide for the sun—to give it the blood of our enemies. We will provide for you, but your inheritance, your place, is in the House of the Sun."

She then washed the child while praying to Chalchiuhtlicue, the Water Goddess.

"Oh Goddess! May your water flush away all imperfections so that this heart and life may be pure, for we place this child into your keeping. May it please you to receive it!"

"It is a fine son you have, Lord," Xoyo in the meantime told the waiting Ahuitzotl.

"A son," his eyes were glowing. "And Tlalalca?"

"A proud mother, and doing well."

News of the birth was quickly sent to notables throughout the realm. This initiated a series of ceremonies which began with usual congratulatory rhetoric and was to end in the naming of the baby. Family members from both clans came to give their many special regards for the infant; they thanked the midwife profusely, giving her presents for her highly appreciated services. Chosen orators among them spoke out their lengthy dissertations, repetitive and embellished with laudation, most of it devoted to complimenting the father and aimed at pleasing him.

"A noble son you have sired—very much your image," they commented frequently.

The next phase of their ceremony called for the prognostications of a Soothsayer who was also a magician and learned in the sacred texts. He was informed on the exact moment of birth by the midwife and proceeded to consult his book of fates, the Tonalamatl, to declare the sign of the day and determine its fortune: the depictions were good.

"There is greatness in store for him," announced the seer. "He will be the commander of armies and will shine in battle. His name will be revered by the people and he will attain glory transcending his death."

Ahuitzotl could not have been more pleased.

Naming the child involved a two-part ceremony-the first was a formal baptism, the second the actual presentation of the name-and again it fell on the midwife to conduct these observances and usually assign a name, but with powerful nobles who sought commanding titles for their sons, a decision of such importance was not left to her mere fancies. Special powers were attached to names; the bearer was believed to reflect the personality of its description. Above all, a name had to be borne proudly and invoke respect, and if possible, particularly among the lords, lend itself well to pictographic representation. Ahuitzotl already had a name in mind for his son; he would inform the midwife of it on the announcement day.

The ritual washing began with royal family member assembled in the palace courtyard. The midwife was given a full water jar which she set next to her and then the child. After again speaking to it, she placed some water droplets into its mouth gently using her finger. "Partake of this water," she said to the child, "for it is with this life-giving water that you will preside upon the earth." She then rubbed the baby's chest with her moistened hands saying, "With this fresh water–so precious, so pure-you will be cleansed. It washes your heart and rinses away all weaknesses."

Next, she sprinkled some droplets on his head and said, "Let this sacred water come into your body and may it dwell there, this life-giving water." Finally, she bathed the baby's entire body and addressed the evil spirit being washed away from the skin, "You, go away! You who would harm this child, be gone! This child is now newly born by our mother Chalchiuhtlicue." During all of this, the baby seemed uniquely fascinated and did not cry out, to the joy of its proud parents.

Lastly, the midwife lifted her charge four times into the air toward the sun, entreating that the child become a bold warrior. "Let him be destined to enter your palace where the valiant, those who die in battle, reside. May he come to your glorious house."

This done, the time to officially announce the child's name had arrived. All members present eagerly awaited this tension filled moment; none among them knew what appellation the midwife would give it-except for Ahuitzotl who had informed her of his desires before the ceremonies commenced.

"Because you are a progeny of the Sun, the inheritor of the domain, whose symbol is the Eagle, because all the signs were present at your arrival, for you were born on the day Cuauhtli at a time when Tonatiuh descended from the western sky, you will be given a name to describe that portentous event. You shall be known as Cuauhtemoc."

Tlalalca beamed, and the family members heartily approved. When the ceremony was over, Ahuitzotl hosted his guests to a banquet in which the older men and women, having survived the rigors of a hard life and duly merited its fruitfulness, were afforded the pleasures of the intoxicating drink, octli. Throughout this festivity was mentioned the name of the monarch's son. He was Cuauhtemoc, Descending Eagle, and he was destined for greatness.

XV

A full year passed since Ahuitzotl sent his legates to the Mixtecs and Zapotecs, and still they had not returned. Even though the time had elapsed quickly, with each month's ceremonial requirements entailing his presence and he himself being heavily absorbed in the construction of his new palace now underway, the unresolved matter of the southern frontier was beyond deferment. The trading once so lucrative for Anahuac remained closed and many lords openly complained of being deprived the wanted commodities produced in these favored kingdoms. And always Ahuitzotl thought of the contempt in which Cocijoeza held his warnings-admonitions issued personally to him when he was in Tenochtitlan-and he fumed.

His patience expended and under pressures to remedy the adversive barter affecting the realm, Ahuitzotl called for a council of his primary advisors in order to discuss the situation and propose some action.

"Something has happened to them," Ahuitzotl declared from his throne. "It should not be taking them this long."

"Tehuantepec is a great distance, Lord," Cihuacoatl reminded his master, "and much of it is over difficult terrain."

"Not that far. Not for royal emissaries who are provided sanctity along the roadways."

"They may have been detained by the lords they visited; rulers frequently take their time in giving responses to our envoys. It is the fashion."

"They were instructed on the urgency of their mission, were they not?"

"So they were, Lord."

"Did these instructions specify for them to send messengers if they were unduly delayed?"

"They did, Lord."

"But we have received no messages, have we?"

"No, Lord."

"Then how can you maintain nothing has happened to them when all the evidence points to the contrary?"

"Messengers do not enjoy the same protection accorded the envoys, Lord. Possibly they met with four play."

Ahuitzotl eyed the minister with disdain, finding his position untenable in the face of all the indications. "What of our operatives in the region?" he went on. "Have they reported seeing the emissaries?"

"The last reports we received mentioned that they had departed Mixtlan and proceeded for Tehuantepec."

"To the Zapotec capital."

"Yes, Lord. I checked only this morning with Lord Huactli to see if any additional sightings had been made of them and..."

"Yes?"

"I was told that none of the merchants sent there have returned to us."

A long silence fell upon the meeting's attendants; they glanced disbelievingly at Cuhuacoatl who must have felt extremely foolish at the moment.

"Let me understand you," Ahuitzotl confronted his minister. "We have received no word from our emissaries in a year; no pochteca have returned from Tehauntepec where they were last sighted; no messengers have come to us from them, and, in spite of all this, you can still say to me that you believe nothing has happened to them?"

"It is an affront to the gods to bring harm to envoys. Who would risk it?"

"It appears Cocijoeza would. I never liked the man. From the beginning he seemed the devious sort to me. We have no proof, that I grant you, but there is certainly enough evidence to give credibility to our suspicions. Is there anyone here not convinced of this?"

None disagreed.

"Then our course is plain to see," concluded Ahuitzotl. "I propose we call for a war council to approve an invasion of Mixteca and Zapoteca."

The assembly sounded out its general consent; only Cihuacoatl gave an impression of dissent, and Ahuitzotl was not enthused over it. "Do you object, minister?"

"I would offer that we wait awhile longer, Lord-until we're certain."

"And how much longer might that be? Another week maybe? A month? I submit we have already waited longer than we should."

Cihuacoatl recognized that his stand was indefensible, and also that he was coming close to irritating his master with his obstinacy. In principle, he was not that far removed from them, but by training and inclination, he leaned towards an adherence to conducting the affairs among kingdoms in accordance to the compacts secured from them, provisions demanding of proof and not subject to mere conjectures. Reluctantly, he acquiesced to the wishes of the others.

"Good," proclaimed Ahuitzotl. "We are now resolved that this issue must be decided by force of arms. Send word to our allies to meet here so we can obtain their concurrance and mutual support."

With their decision reached, the meeting was terminated and its members departed in obvious delight; all of them knew of the richness abounding in these southern empires and evinced their strong expectations out of such an incursion. Moreover, a year of inactivity was clearly detrimental to the realm's well-being; the sinews of the nation required flexing, especially for its majority warriors who had not participated in their ruler's expedition to the sea, and while the gods were yet nurtured with life-giving blood, this now came from slaves and criminals, the availability of war captives having been exhausted. Even this supply was dwindling, and they were near calling for the Xochiyaoyotl, the War of the Flowers, an institution arranged by treaty with their powerful enemy neighbors, namely the Tlaxcalans, whereby battles were fought between them for the sole purpose of acquiring prisoners for sacrifice. Ahuitzotl held such wars in derision, preferring legitimate conquests to these staged affairs, thereby rendering him ripe for an actual undertaking against whatever antagonist he could find. Any pretext, however slight, would have sufficed to dispose him toward implementing such measures, and in the present case, he had the appropriate justifications. His long envisioned confrontation with the Zapotec lord, Cocijoeza, whom he never saw in any other light except as a rival, was one step closer to being realized, and he looked with eagerness to the day when he would meet his adversary face-to-face.

Others in the royal palace were not as anxious to see that day arrive as was Ahuitzotl. Tlalalca demurred, not because she questioned the necessity for the impending campaign, but she knew this would be a lengthy one-much longer than any of his previous expeditions. She discerned well enough that it was not within her powers to dissuade Ahuitzotl from his purpose; having acquired an understanding of the duties inherent in the kingship over her many years as empress, Tlalalca accepted the station of women in the social order and fully recognized that her objections were improper.

But Pelaxilla did not. When Ahuitzotl informed her of his proposed operation, she was outspoken in her criticism of his leaving for such a long time and made her disappointment known to him. "Six months!" she protested. "You will be gone for an entire six months?"

"I'm being optimistic. It could easily take longer; we must cover enormous distances."

"What I fail to comprehend is why you personally have to go on all these ventures of yours. You could easily delegate such duties to your chieftains as other rulers do."

"Because Huitzilopochtli himself beckons me to do his divine work. I do not shrink from the responsibilites thrust upon me—to the contrary, I embrace them."

"An intelligent man knows how to make good use of his subordinates. Is it because you lack confidence in your commanders that you must oversee their work yourself?"

Ahuitzotl disliked her taunting but realized that she needed to vent her pent-up frustrations on someone; this motivated him to answer her even though ordinarily he would have rejected such an interrogation out of hand. "I trust Tlohtzin implicitly," he said. "And Motecuhzoma also is proving himself a most capable commander."

"So let them lead this operation and stay here with me."

"Don't be daft, woman! With all of Tenochtitlan's warriors on the march, what would I do here by myself?"

"There are others who will be here with you—the builders who work on your new palace, as an example. You could supervise them."

"It's useless for you to persist in this, Pelaxilla. This is no ordinary expedition we embark on. We are taking on the richest and most powerful realms known to us—some say they are as great as our own. Do you think I would miss out on something like that? Nothing could keep me from an operation of this scope and purpose."

"You men. Always going on these endless wars while leaving us to worry over you. It's as if we did not matter to you at all."

"Refute it all you like, and it makes no difference. Such is the order of things as the gods have ordained it-your standing in contravention to this will not alter anything."

Pelaxilla knew this, of course, just as she knew the impossibility of keeping him here for her sake; Ahuitzotl was the warrior king personified-for him to sit idly at home while his army carried the standards of their divisions to the farthest reaches of the world was unthinkable. Other rulers might have been deterred by the rigors of such a journey, but never Ahuitzotl.

"What powers can I call upon to keep you here?" she moaned.

"You must not think of this as any failure on your part. It is the gods you compete with, and they will always win."

"Is not our love the handiwork of the goddess Xochiquetzal? Am I to deny her will?"

"The will of Huitzilopochtli is stronger. I wish you would remember that-so we can be spared these insufferable arguments."

Her cause was lost from the outset and she should have known better. Perhaps it was just as well that Ahuitzotl had not married her, Pelaxilla thought; he would have found her persistance irritating and, in all likelihood, divorced her as a result. In the end, Pelaxilla, as Tlalalca earlier, was reconciled to the notion that Ahuitzotl was his own master-no woman's love would control him.

XVI

The war council which convened two days later unanimously approved the plan to send an invasionary force to conquer both the Mixtecs and Zapotecs. No sooner was this decision announced when Ahuitzotl instructed his commanders to implement full-scale preparations for the deployment. Conceived as the most ambitious undertaking of his reign, this operation entailed the services of all resources available to the Mexica; intelligence was analyzed for the latest changes; all routes, landmarks, valleys and mountain passes were identified; storage facilities were established with local rulers tasked to furnish the quantities of produce required; weapons and supplies were amassed; priests and astrologers were consulted to declare their prognostications and set the time in which to begin the march; couriers were dispatched regularly to coordinate the proposed movements and availability of adequate provisions at the specified supply points.

Two weeks after the council had sat in session, Ahuitzotl sent forth the advance parties to cover the different routes planned for the invasion armies. And on the following day, a gathering of priests prepared for their departure, accumulating their idols for transport in their litters. In military matters, Ahuitzotl assumed his role as the supreme priest to give them their directions, but may have ingratiated himself little with his admonitions that he meant to have victories.

"Do what you have to," he advised them, "but I will not be deprived of conquests. I depend on you to convey that message to the gods."

"What kind of talk is that?" the party's leading priest decried. "You cannot dictate to the gods who is to win the battle-they will decide this for themselves."

"Their decision is based upon the nature of the oblations you give them. See to it that I am not disappointed."

His declaration made for an edgy group of priests departing the capital. Obviously they would do their part to win the favor of gods, but the Revered Speaker's warnings hung like a dark cloud over them and they worried how he would react if his stipulations were not fulfilled. Suppose the gods failed them? How would they face him then?

Satisfied that all preparations had been implemented, Ahuitzotl issued orders to sound the war drum and call his squadrons to assembly. Its deep booms rang out across the city and was audible in every quarter and ward. Eager for plundering reputedly rich cities, the call-up was met with hearty enthusiasm and no warrior was wanting in his zeal towards participating in this venture. It represented the most complete muster to arms ever witnessed, with every able-bodied male in the city enjoined to accompany his unit. The supply contingent, which had spent days gathering up enormous quantities of stores indispensible for the march, was nearly as large as the army itself and was also assembled to hear Ahuitzotl's speech commemorating the onset of so bold an undertaking. Chimalpopoca was present, although his Tepanecs and their allies would not begin their trek until the following two days. Despite the expanses this expedition planned to cover, Tlacopan's lord was sufficiently caught up in the euphoria surrounding this adventure that he decided to lead his army as in the past; Ahuitzotl was pleased to have his old colleague with him.

As usual, a tumultuous greeting met Ahuitzotl when he emerged from his palace to take his place on the dais set up for him so he could address his soldiers. Spirits soared; every participant anticipated a rich return from this operation, and with their undefeated warlord at the helm, known victory was assured. Cihuacoatl marveled as he watched the procession from the doors of the palace-no ruler had ever so inculcated his warriors with the certainty of triumph; its effect was contagious as the minister felt himself captivated in the excitement of the occasion and ached to be with them. Unfortunately his duties kept him in Tenochtitlan, for the festival days with their demands of sacrifices could not be ignored even for this. A small number of priests, laborers, administrators and other officials, craftsmen, also a reduced guard force, remained to see to these tasks. Additionally, Ahuitzotl left Cihuacoatl with some instructions on supervising the engineers and artisans involved in the work of his new residence. The project was proceeding rapidly and the monarch expected to move into the building shortly after his return.

"See to Tlalalca and the child," he added as an afterthought before speaking to his warriors.

In as evocative a speech as ever delivered, Ahuitzotl promised them a large share of the plunder which would be taken, exactly what they wanted to hear, but also reminded them of the nature of their business and that they should not elevate their own greed to the level of their greater purpose, fulfilling the needs of their deities. "Always remember," he advised them, "We do Huitzilopochtli's divine work and he has already chosen those among us who are to join him in paradise-an honor beyond measure and our reason for being. To those of you not chosen, in many ways less fortunate, you will see the forging of the mightiest empire ever seen."

Next, Ahuitzotl made a direct appeal to Huitzilopochtli with a message not heard from him for a long time. "O' Lord of Battles! Emminent Host! Let those noble warriors who perish be received in the house of the sun with love and honor, to reside with those who have preceded them so that they might together serve our lord, the Sun. We beseech you, Mighty Lord, to care for those who perish for your glory."

He finished to a thunderous ovation, but to Cihuacoatl his address seemed baffling. "How strange," he said to Chimalpopoca who stood beside him. "More like his speeches of old, when he was Huitzilopochtli's high priest, than he's given as Revered Speaker. One suspects he's not as positive of winning this campaign as the others-he does not want to take unnecessary risks and moves to have them minimized."

"Are the Mixtecs and Zapotecs so powerful that he should be that wary of them?" asked Chimalpopoca.

"Individually no, but he fears they may form a coalition against us-that is a formidable power to reckon with."

"Align themselves against us? But they are enemies!"

"It's happened before. Even traditional enemies will unite to defeat a common invader. Neither the Mixtecs nor the Zapotecs have any illusions as to our intent."

Following Ahuitzotl's speech, the army set forth from Tenochtitlan, unit after unit leaving from the central square under the command of its respective chieftain. Ahuitzotl took his position amid his Eagle and

Jaguar knights near the army's center as it headed in the direction of the southern causeway which branched off to Ixtapalapa. The remaining populace, consisting almost entirely of women and children and older men no longer able to take part in wars, lined the avenue to see its warriors depart, cheering them and showering them with flowers, while the soldiers themselves sang martial songs in their jubilation. No campaign in anyone's memory ever got off to a more enthusiatic start.

From the upper terrace of the palace, ladies of Ahuitzotl's court watched the proceedings below them as the army began to move out; by the time the last unit passed the plaza's southern gate, most had become bored with the spectacle and went about their usual activity. But two women remained long after the square had emptied and continued their gaze toward the distant causeway seeing the trailing elements of the army fade into the horizon. One was Tlalalca, staring blankly after them but apparently seeing nothing as she was lost in her deliberation; not until she was about to return to her chamber, after having stood there for nearly half the morning, did she notice that she was not by herself. Only a few paces from her was Pelaxilla leaning against the stone walls as if she needed their support to keep from falling. Tears streamed from her eyes, but she wept in silence.

Tlalalca was moved to great pity when she saw Pelaxilla so distressed, yet she was reluctant to approach her at first, unsure if her presence meant an unwelcome intrusion, and simply observed her for some moments, until at last, overcome with a sudden compulsion to offer help, she could no longer restrain herself. She walked over to her.

"Dear Pelaxilla," Tlalalca began, "You must not take this so hard. He shall return to us."

Pelaxilla turned her head and glared at Tlalalca, and all her resentment towards the empress vanished at that instant when she saw Tlalalca's own sorrow etched in her face—the empress shed no tears, but the heartache was as visible as if she had. Breaking out in sobs, Pelaxilla was torn with remorse over her unfair treatment of the empress; she leaned her head into Tlalalca's shoulder weeping uncontrollably.

"Please forgive me," Pelaxilla cried. "I have said so many unkind things about you to him."

Tlalalca was so touched by her lamentation that she could scarcely hold back her own tears, but she maintained her composure and tried her best to console the forlorn mistress whom she once again adored.

"You did not mean it," Tlalalca comforted her. "Xochiquetzal contrives these affairs and twists our thoughts so that we say things we do not really wish. I know how deeply you love him and it's natural that you should want him for yourself."

"Six months will pass before we shall see him again. How can I endure my loneliness?"

"You will manage, Pelaxilla. We all do," Tlalalca answered, and then added with sadness, "We have to, because there are simply no alternatives given to us."

Pelaxilla lifted her head and, with tears still trickling down her cheeks, gazed at the empress. "He told me that I compete with the gods for his attention," she said, "and would always lose in such a contest."

"He said that?" Tlalalca expressed her dismay. "Lord Ahuitzotl can be so ill-mannered at times; it's as if he was oblivious to how upsetting his remarks can be."

"But he believes this."

"I think you perceive it wrongly, Pelaxilla. We both know how he truly loves you. He wanted you to understand that he has his requisites as Revered Speaker-duties to the realm, the gods and their priests, the military-and many of the things he does because he has to, not because he wants to."

"You are kind, my lady," Pelaxilla said, finding some relief from her depression. "How can you say good things about him when he is so coldhearted to you?"

"True, I have a sad relationship with him, but the fault for this is not his; he has been quite consistent in his devotion whereas I have not. He has always loved you, as he still does, but I loathed him at first. I hated him because I once thought he meant to harm Tizoc, and when Tizoc died, I blamed him for it and persisted in my anger against him. But then something happened-I have no explanation for it and can only attribute it to the workings of Xochiquetzal-and I began to see him differently. Indeed, I have come to also love him, and that has been my ever present torment. He loves you, Pelaxilla, and it is I who must remain the outsider in this affair. I suppose it's an appropriate punishment for me, but it has been truly painful."

Pelaxilla felt heartfelt sympathy for the empress, at last comprehending her sorrows and more than that, acquiring an admiration for the quiet dignity in which Tlalalca bore her suffering, seeing a serenity in this which surpassed her own vituperative outbursts. She realized why Ahuitzotl concerned himself with trying to spare her undue grief and felt shame over her repetitive efforts to keep him from her.

"How oddly things work out," Tlalalca went on. "I came here to bring comfort to you and instead find myself relieved by having spoken with you. I do hope I brought some solace to you as I intended."

"You have, my lady," Pelaxilla answered, giving her a wide smile, "more than you know."

Her smile deeply touched Tlalalca, and it recalled for her the days when Pelaxilla was her courtly favorite and elevated her life with her cheerfulness-days long absent from her when she loved the mistress as a daughter. How rare it had been since Pelaxilla so tenderly beamed at her. Warmed by her radiance, a happiness came over Tlalalca, and she knew Pelaxilla's hostility for her had been forever dispelled.

"I shall retire now," Tlalalca said as she gingerly released Pelaxilla's hold. "Do not linger here by yourself too long, dear; it's not a good thing to face despondency alone."

"Only a while longer, my lady," Pelaxilla answered and then gave Tlalalca pause when she added, "I'm so thankful you spoke to me."

"We shall have more to say to each other," Tlalalca gleamed. "I feel as though we have become acquainted anew and will again enjoy our company."

They glanced into each other's eyes and gave approving smiles that told them far more than anything further said. In their own way, they had come to terms with each other and reconciled all of their differences that had marked their past few years without a trace of ill-feeling remaining between them. It had been an encounter which rewarded them both immensely and imparted on them a recognition that their relationship was permanently changed as a result-and it was for the better.

XVII

Ahuitzotl's force took the high road from Anahuac to its first connecting point, Tochtepec, leaving the valley through the saddle–the Eagle Pass-between the twin peaks of Iztaccihuatl and Popocatepetl and traversing the southern flank of Tlaxcala, land of the Mexica's most tenacious long-standing enemy. It advanced divided into the same two components marking all their large-scale operations, without including the huge quartermaster element which comprised a virtual third army in itself, and these were separated by a day's marching interval. The first group, overall led by Ahuitzotl, but nominally under the immediate command of Tlohtzin was the Army of Tenochtitlan; the second was its Tlatelolco component, headed by Motecuhzoma. Another day removed these from the cumbersome supply section which included scores of women who served as cooks, nurses, launderers, and other useful functionaries.

The Army of Tepaneca, led by the aged but indefatigable Chimalpopoca, traveled the southern route around the shores of Lake Texcoco, past the south face of Popocatepetl, and through Tlappan, previously conquered and now a subject state. North of Iztaccihuatl, the Army of Acolhuacan set forth under Nezahualpilli; its chosen route would converge with the one taken by Ahuitzotl in circumventing Tlaxcala. Ahuitzotl had sought permission for the Acolhuas to enter through Tlaxcala but had this rejected by its lords who were not about to assist the Mexica in the expansion of their domain. As a result, Nezahualpilli had to take the same trail covered by Ahuitzotl but a day's journey behind his logistical unit. This might have strained the resources available along their passage, but through a prior arrangement, plans had been coordinated whereby Ahuitzotl's supply section would leave the provisions required for the Acolhuas should such a step be necessary.

All together, an awesome juggernaut moved against the Mixtecs. In numbers it totaled nearly eighty thousand warriors, and this did not include its huge supporting contingents trailing the main armies. Villages had been literally depleted of their entire male populations, leaving only women, children, and a few old men behind-so complete had been the call-up. Never had so large a force embarked on conquest from Anahuac, and to no-one's recollection was one ever sent forth with a more ambitious purpose, and no warlord ever commanded a mightier host than Ahuitzotl at present.

Ahuitzotl's first major stopover was at Cholula, a friendly power, where he was regaled by its ruler and invited to partake in a feast in his royal palace. Cholula was one of the centers designated for replenishment of food supplies; its storage facilities were extensive and filled to capacity and it had been allocated to provide specified quantities of provisions as had several other key cities along the way to Tochtepec. This bore no major inconvenience to the city as the Mexica had, at this stage of their expedition, not overly drawn on their own resources. Relations were kept amiable as a result and neither host nor visitor infringed on each other's welcome.

It took another week of marching before the Mexica entered the Valley of Oaxaca and Ahuitzotl was met with great enthusiasm by the local inhabitants of the first few cities he came upon. He was able to piece together the diverse reports obtained through his inquiries with the various monarchs and in this fashion acquired sufficient intelligence about the Mixtecs to learn of their strength and capacities. He learned that the wars between the Mixtecs and Zapotecs were differently fought from how he conceived them, being waged not in pitched battles but rather in small hit-and-run skirmishes with neither side gaining or holding on to any terrain. The upshot of this was that he could be expected to face the bulk of the Mixtec army intact–estimated at about sixty thousand strong-not that formidable if he confronted it alone, but quite problematic for him if it were combined with an equally large Zapotecan host.

Three days later, Ahuitzotl arrived at Tochtepec, one of the principal Mixtec cities in the valley, and directed his chieftains to establish their base camp within site of it from where he would wait on his remaining armies. From here Ahuitzotl meant to initiate his attack on Mixtlan, the enemy capital, only a two day trek away. The lords of Tochtepec viewed the movement and were anxiously anticipating reinforcements from Mixtlan. They had believed their support would arrive before the Mexica, but as it did not, were now faced with a serious dilemma over whether to try and hold the invader off until help came or to capitulate.

Their decision was to make a stand, and when Ahuitzotl sent the customary legates to them on the following morning, they rebuffed them with messages that Tochtepec was not about to submit to the Mexica. Although eager for battle, Ahuitzotl prudently decided to defer an engagement until Motecuhzoma arrived with his Tlatelolco divisions, expected this very day, as he did not want to deprive its warriors a share of the combat. After his bloodless campaign to the sea and the stagnant period following it, Ahuitzotl believed that he owed them a good fight.

By noon, Motecuhzoma made his appearance and was accordingly briefed by the monarch on the planned attack, scheduled to commence at dawn tomorrow. In general, the youthful commander was in agreement but expressed some concerns over extending this opportunity to their allies who had been equally inactive for a similar length of time. "Shouldn't we wait for Chimalpopoca at least?" he asked.

"No," determined Ahuitzotl. "We have enough warriors to take the city. There'll be ample occasion for him to do battle later."

The lords of Tochtepec became much alarmed when they saw the second army arrive, determining they stood little chance of holding off such numbers. They hastily met in council, agreeing to countermand their earlier position; however when they sent out their envoys to inform Ahuitzotl of this, only to have them return with word that he refused to see them, they knew they faced grave consequences. In desperation, they dispatched their speediest runners to Mixtlan with urgent pleas for immediate reinforcements which they hoped would come prior to the battle's onset. Ahuitzotl's scouts reported sighting their messengers, but he was unconcerned. Even if the Mixtecs were to march forth now, which he deemed unlikely, it would still take them two days to arrive and by then it would be too late.

By the time Tonatiuh revealed himself over the eastern ranges, gracing the bedewed valley in warmth, Ahuitzotl had already formed his units into an attacking posture. Armed rows of poised warriors greeted Tochtepec's nervous defenders who hurriedly swarmed to take up their arms and assembled chaotically into their battle stations. In actuality, they had enough time, as the Mexica were kept from their advance by the ritual fires and had to wait for priests to scatter the embers along their ranks, and could have spared themselves the poor spectacle they presented in their extreme consternation-a display immediately picked up by Ahuitzotl's discerning eye as indicative of a woeful weakness and imbuing him with a surety of speedy conquest.

In time, and undoubtedly too soon for the defenders, the fires flickered out and the embers were strewn about, and shortly thereafter, the head priest sounded his trumpet. Ensuing commands echoed by chieftains spurred the Mexica lines into action, walking at a steady advance initially, then accelerating to a steady trot and finally rushing at full speed headlong on their fear-ridden opponents. Ahuitzotl devised no special tactical plan for taking Tochtepec and relied on conventional methods; his warriors attacked on a broad front straight for the enemy and were expected to make a breakthrough with their overwhelming numbers. Partly, this was because he wanted his soldiers to experience the exhilaration of physical combat, and this was best accomplished in a slugging match resulting out of two adversaries clashing head-on. Also he was so sure of victory that he felt no compelling reason to resort to deception.

His assessment proved correct. The zeal in which the Mexica assaulted the defenders created such terror amid their ranks that they panicked and fled from their stations, some to be beaten back in line by furious commanders. Ahuitzotl's warriors crashed into the Tochtepecans with such demonic fury that nothing could have withstood them, and shortly after contact, the opposition's lines crumbled, crushed under the waves of frenzied, rampaging hordes. Within minutes, all effective resistance was broken and the warriors were in the streets.

"Their army is dispersed," Tlohtzin informed Ahuitzotl, "and our soldiers are pillaging the city. Shall I issue a orders to restrain them?"

"Let them have their day," Ahuitzotl said after a pause, not altogether committed to the notion, "It's been a long time since we last gave them a free hand of things."

Unbridled, Mexica belligerents ran wildly through Tochtepec, raping, killing, and looting. Residences they put to the torch after taking what they could from within, and in the temples they massacred the priests who huddled about their idols vainly crying out for the gods to protect them, then set fire to all material that would burn inside the shrines.

Those male inhabitants of military age who did not get away-not very many-were herded into the city's plaza and summarily executed. Ahuitzotl kept the ruler alive long enough to witness the carnage and then had him decapitated.

This was a cruel fate for Tochtepec, and Ahuitzotl viewed the activity with a somewhat disturbed detachment, not as convinced of its value as a tool for subjugation as he had once been. Overall, he disliked the lack of control pillaging and rampaging presented, invariably leading to a disruptive breakdown of order and discipline that was repugnant to him. Both Toluca and Oztoma had patently demonstrated the pitfalls of carrying such measures too far. He meant for it to infuse a shock effect on Mixtlan's monarch as part of his strategy to instill terror among the Mixtecs so that they would tremble in fear at his mere coming. By destroying one or two cities in such a fashion, Ahuitzotl reasoned that he could win ten or more cities without major opposition and achieve his objectives with overall less exertion. Besides, he did not come to here to be the benevolent conqueror but to inflict punishment, which necessitated that the enemy was to understand the full weight of his powers.

At the outskirts of Tochtepec's smoldering ruin, Ahuitzotl remained in his encampment for the next three days until the total complement of his allies arrived. At his orders, the storage silos and granaries were kept intact so that their contents could be used to feed his large army and still provide for the forces yet to come in addition to replenishing their depleted stocks. First to arrive was Chimalpopoca and his Tepanecs, to be followed the next day by Nezahualpilli's Acolhuas. Finally, on the third day, the last of their supply contingents arrived, and with all their units merged, Ahuitzotl met with their chieftains to discuss his designs against the next targeted city, the capital, Mixtlan.

"I expect a hard faught battle," he told them. "With their force at sixty thousand, it will take our composite strength to defeat an army of that size in defense of its own realm."

"At least, we'll take part in it," Nezahualpilli commented cynically.

"Tochtepec was but a mere exercise, "Ahuitzotl scowled, the sarcasm not lost on him, "unworthy of our combined efforts. As it was, most of them ran from the sight of us."

"Undoubtedly, Lord; I merely complain because I seem to always be the last army in the march order."

"You won't be at Mixtlan. It's two days from here and we can carry our rations with us for that short trek. We'll all leave here tomorrow so we arrive at the same time-at full strength."

A general plan was drawn up to approach the city along three separate routes so they would converge in their usual battle configuration, that is, with the Acolhuas on the left and the Tepanecs on the right, and the armies of Tenochtitlan and Tlatelolco in the center. They were to unite on the plain extending beyond the Mixtlan's northern edge and, after a full day's resting, commence their assault on it.

But Ahuitzotl could never have guessed what was to greet him him at Mixtlan, for when he came upon it, he was to find it virtually abandoned. All of its male population was gone; only women, children, the aged and crippled, and, oddly enough, a local minister, remained there to gaze with seeming indifference at the Mexica's entrance. At first, Ahuitzotl suspected a trap had been set for him, but after his patrols thoroughly combed through the adjacent hills and forests, it became apparent he would meet no opposition here. Frustrated, he had the official brought before him for an explanation.

"Where is your army?" Ahuitzotl demanded, "And your king?"

"Gone, Great Lord." he answered nervously.

"I can plainly enough see they are gone, fool! Gone where?"

"To Xaltepec, Lord."

"Xaltepec? That's south of here, isn't it?"

"Yes, Lord, a week's journey from Mixtlan."

"Why does your lord go there? Did he see my approach and seek to escape from it?"

The minister demonstrated a reluctance to let Ahuitzotl know. Incensed, he called for Tlohtzin to fetch forth the man's wife and children. They were promptly assembled in front of the gathering, fear visibly read in their faces.

"Do not play games with me," Ahuitzotl cautioned. "If you do not tell me everything I wish to know, I shall have my warriors cut off the heads of your family members before your eyes. Is this clear?"

The minister nodded, too paralyzed in his fright to speak.

"Now, why does your lord go there?" Ahuitzotl asked again.

"My master, Tezacoalco, was prompted to go there after hearing of your destruction of Tochtepec. He seeks to meet with his enemy, Cocijoeza, the Zapotec ruler, at Xaltepec with the hope of concluding a truce with him. No, not a truce, but rather an alliance, so that together they will be able to concentrate their energies into defeating you."

"An alliance. With his life-long enemy?"

"Yes, Lord. He believes that if united with the Zapotecs, he will have the capability to destroy you."

"I had not excluded the possibility, but believed it remote. For kingdoms who have warred on each other for generations to combine forces against us-that is an act of desperation."

The idea seemed quite incomprehensible to Ahuitzotl; he pondered if the Mexica would ever allign themselves with Tlaxcala to counter a foreign enemy and concluded it unthinable, even under such dire circumstances. He turned his attention back to the official. "When did Tezacoalco leave for Xaltepec?" he asked.

"Five days ago-as soon as he learned about what happend at Tochtepec."

"How far is Xaltepec from Tehuantepec?"

"I would say about a two week's march, Lord."

"It will take some time for the two rulers to have their conference," Ahuitzotl said to Tlohtzin, "assuming that Tezacoalco must first make overtures to Cocijoeza in proposing his alliance and then allow him time to deliberate over it. Such a pact, contravening generations of their conduct, will not be readily accepted. We could arrive at Xaltepec before the Zapotecs do. If so, we can still first destroy the Mixtecs and then turn on the Zapotecs."

"And if we do not, Lord?"

"Then we shall have what might well be the greatest battle ever waged," Ahuitzotl concluded and again addressed the minister. "How many warriors does Tezacoalco have?"

"Sixty thousand, perhaps more."

"And Cocijoeza?"

"About the same, Lord!"

"United they pose a danger for us, Tlohtzin. We must move quickly to prevent their joining forces. Send word to Nezahualpilli and Chimalpopoca to continue their march–to Xaltepec."

"What about Mixtlan? Do you want to destroy it, as we did Tochtepec?"

Ahuitzotl looked at the frightened Mixtec minister while considering the fate of his city as if a god in whose hands rested the lives of its citizens. An anxiousness delineated the official's face revealing his awareness of the decision being contemplated.

"No," Ahuitzotl finally answered. "There's no time."

With such whimsical judgment, Mixtlan was spared destruction.

XVIII

Xaltepec stood on an elevated bluff overlooking the fertile green valley below which afforded its residents a clear field of observation, especially of the northern approaches by which the Mexica came. Ahuitzotl's scouts alerted him to this situation and also of the Mixtecs gathered in full strength and prepared to do battle at the site. Anxiety plagued the monarch as he advanced on his objective, for his entire army was strung out for miles along the narrow confines of a defile, presenting a vulnerability to ambush and precluding good interior communication for coordinating movements and battle orders. This was the ideal time for Tezacoalco to attack, he thought; while his force was thus constricted and unable to effectively counter any opposition. Still, he decided to continue his march, using prudent caution, and concluding that his antagonist would rely on conventional doctrine in waging battle and permit the Mexica to amass for attack so that the gods could determine the outcome.

Although Ahuitzotl proceeded carefully, making full use of patrols to guard his flanks, he was astonished to discover that he had actually caught the Mixtecs by surprise and managed to assemble his total force into a concentrated body capable of providing for a reasonable defense should he be confronted now.

"Tezacoalco has lost a prime opportunity to engage us," he told Tlohtzin. "He shall never have another one."

"He still outnumbers us and would be wise to make use of it; once Chimalpopoca and Nezahualpilli join us, it's over for him."

"It's too late for him now. He must initiate an attack to dislodge us from here, and we are too many for that. Huitzilopochtli has truly graced us."

Whether Tezacoalco shared Ahuitzotl's assessment of their situation he could not have known. What was apparent was that his deferring a confrontation with the Mexica allowed Ahuitzotl to bolster his security measures as he waited for the arrival of his allies. He dispatched long range patrols to keep watch on the southern road leading to Tehuantepec from where he expected the Zapotec reinforcements. Their mission was to give early warnings if they sighted this advance, and as long as Ahuitzotl received no word of it, he could maintain a defensive posture until he achieved maximum strength; otherwise he would be forced to take the initiative and defeat the Mixtecs before their allies could unite with them.

For two days Ahuitzotl remained on his fixed position until the armies of Acolhuacan and Tepaneca came to give him the capability to commence an attack and storm Xaltepec. Yet he heard nothing on the Zapotecs; he was kept informed daily by messengers from his patrols—even negative reports were sent so that he knew the information was current. Tezacoalco's failure to seize upon his advantage convinced Ahuitzotl that he was banking all his hopes on Zapotecan support which the Revered Speaker now believed would never come.

"He waits vainly for Cocijoeza," Ahuitzotl said to Nezahualpilli. "It appears the Zapotecan is too indecisive to commit himself to his life-long enemy's aid."

"I'ld like to know his reasons for such a reluctance; his best chance in holding us off, and preventing us from reaching Tehuantepec is in uniting with Tezacoalco here."

"He presumes that this will be a costly encounter for us, as well as the Mixtecs, so that the advantage is his regardless of the outcome. His old enemy we will have destroyed for him, while having our own strength so reduced in the process that we cannot take on his Zapotecs. It is quite logical; Cocijoeza is a shrewd man."

"He may be right," declared Nezahualpilli soberly. "Xaltepec is almost a fortress. How do you propose to take it."

"We must somehow induce the Mixtecs to fight us on the field. Once we've destroyed their army, we ought to be able to take the city without difficulty.

"Granted, if you can get Tezacoalco to do that. So far, he has shown no inclination for it."

"We'll create a diversion. I have one in mind. Tezacoalco eagerly expects to be reinforced by Cocijoeza; we shall delude him into believing the Zapotecs are coming to his rescue."

"Let me guess how. You will send part of our army against a nonexistent Zapotec force to prevent it from joining the Mixtecs. A devious scheme, but quite typical of you."

"I'll send you and Chimalpopoca's Tepanecs on the south road-you will have to skirt the far edges of the valley to bypass the Mixtec camps, but yet make certain they see you depart. We'll circulate rumors that you are on your way to intercept Cocijoeza's advance. A convincing show of this should bring Tezacoalco off his hilltop."

"And if he does not?"

"I'll give him one day after you leave-keep your army in waiting about a half day's distance from here and be prepared to return on call. If by then he still does not make a move, I will take the offensive and force his hand."

As luck would have it, Ahuitzotl received word later that evening while he held his conference to explain his plan that a Mixtec messenger had been captured-he was to report to his lord that Cocijoeza proposed to meet with Tezacoalco at Tototepec rather than Xaltepec, a midway point between the two cities. For Ahuitzotl, it came at such an opportune moment that he believed this the work of providence: the gods meant for him to win this battle. "What a stroke of fortune!" he rejoiced. "This confirms that Cocijoeza will not sent his forces to Xaltepec. We won't have to worry about the Zapotecs."

Clamorous activity abounded in the Mexica encampment on the following morning. Trumpets blared, drums thundered, and a thousand voices shouted out commands up and down the Acolhua and Tepanec ranks as they prepared to move forth. Unit by unit, with each one's insignia standard denoting its position in formation, the armies assembled into their march order. All commanders spoke of their need to intercept an approaching Zapotec force; the warriors, unaware this was a ruse, believed it. The patrols, couriers, soldiers, and priests withheld no restraint in mentioning the threat facing them. Ahuitzotl even arranged to have some of his messengers captured by Mixtec patrols in order to make a pursuasive display of his maneuver.

Tezacoalco, who must have observed the activity from atop his lookout, probably guessed why the army was being divided and moving out. What other explanation could there be for them leaving before having offered battle with the Mixtecs? But if he still vacillated during most of the day, when word was sent to him that a Mexica courier had been taken who bore messages confirming that Cocijoeza was advancing to Xaltepec, the last shred of doubt was removed from his mind. He was now at equal, if not actually greater, strength than the enemy force which remained and thought it shameful to have his coalition ally meet the Mexica in battle while he sat idly by. Accordingly, he informed his chieftains that the time was ripe for taking on Ahuitzotl: they would attack in the morning.

Ahuitzotl, unaware of Tezacoalco's decision, patiently stood by through the rest of the day for some indications that the Mixtecs would confront him. "We will launch an assault on their camps at dawn," he told his commanders. "I have waited long enough."

To Ahuitzotl's satisfaction, he found a huge Mixtec army readily assembled in its battle configuration beneath Xaltepec's northern slope the next morning. It stood formed into a huge arc with about twenty ranks of warriors in depth which extended across the total width of the valley-a sensible grouping, Ahuitzotl thought as, it permitted good interior control and communication.

"How many?" Ahuitzotl asked Tlohtzin.

"As was rumored I would say-at least sixty thousand."

"A numerical edge, but we should be able to keep them at bay until our allies return. Have you sent the messengers?"

"They're on their way, Lord."

"Then let us begin the rites. There's no point in deferring this any further."

Ahuitzotl's army entered the open field lined up in its usual broad front of ten ranks deep; behind a gap approximating fifty paces stood a second line of the same depth, whereas near the center, where Ahuitzotl remained with his Eagle knights, the warriors stood at greater density-the monarch intended for them to initiate the action. Soberly, the Mixtecs watched the Mexica nearing them, and when the two armies closed to within half a league from each other, the warriors halted and remained in place while priests on both sides erected their sacred fires amid loud incantations and oblations. Both sides called upon their chosen deities to grant them a victorious outcome, and when they were finished, a cacophony of trumpets and drums stirred the lines into motion.

Each army advanced at a steady pace. Soon the Mixtec lines thinned as they progressed, with the number of gaps between their ranks widening, but the Mexica, more disciplined, retained their formation and moved ahead as one solid body with each warrior's shield abutting agains the other's. Closer they came, and when the distance between them narrowed to only a hundred some paces, the Mexica forward wall of warriors halted and knelt down in nearly perfect unison to permit two ranks of standing archers an unobstructed release of their deadly missiles-the same tactic applied at Xiuhcoac on the Huaxtecs-Ahuitzotl never forgot a maneuver that proved successful.

For one brief instant, a hail of obsidian-tipped arrows bore down on the Mixtec front line; some of its warriors managed to protect their vitals with their shields, but others were struck down, blood spurting from terrible wounds as they cursed or screamed in pain. The archers had accomplished what they set out to do, for the Mixtec ranks, in trying to avoid the volley, were disrupted. Their order broken, no longer advancing as a cohesive front, they instead were now disarrayed in individual clusters. Immediately, even as their projectiles pounded the enemy creating confusion, the Mexica charged ahead with unbridled raging fury, shrieking out their battle cries. Coming within twenty paces of the stalled Mixtec rows, they hurled their spears into it with devastating effectiveness, and the harried opposition, having just evaded the darts, now faced a torrent of lances crashing into their shields and cotton armor and penetrating both. Before they could sufficiently recover, the Mexica met them, colliding in one continuous clash until the whole of their force was locked in combat. Within the first few minutes of battle, the numerical superiority of the Mixtecs was destroyed.

Ahuitzotl led his Eagles straight for the Mixtec center where he thought Tezacoalco had stationed himself; they charged with such maddened ferocity that no unit could have withstood them, and those enemy soldiers daring enough to confront them were hacked down and dropped dying and bleeding under trampling feet. Before Ahuitzotl reached his target, however, he heard the piercing blare of a trumpet; it emanated from the Mixtec side and called for their force to fall back. When he was informed of its meaning, he issued his own orders above the din.

"Press them hard! Make their retreat costly for them!"

His orders were hastily transmitted to the units fighting all along the field and chieftains responded by urging their soldiers onward so that the pressured Mixtecs, in trying to react to their call, were unable to execute their directive without actually bolting from the scene; if they turned their backs on their attackers, they were sure to be struck down. Slowly, while desperately fighting off the Mexica who maintained an incessant squeeze on them, the defenders managed to retire leaving their wounded and dying where they fell. When they reached the foot of Xaltepec's hill, their reserves moved out to give them added protection; Anahuac warriors sprang on them, furiously hammering at their buttressed lines, but failed to breach them.

"Sound a withdrawal!" Ahuitzotl shouted. "We must regroup!"

A distinct trumpet call signaled the units into a reversal; throughout the line they began to disengage themselves, to the relief of their shaken opponents, and as they retired, they picked up their wounded and a number of enemy captives. Soon, the same distance which had divided the antagonists at the day's onset again separated them, only that the field between them lay strewn with dead and dying warriors, a vast majority of them Mixtecs.

Ahuitzotl and Tlohtzin studied the situation presented to them after completing their deployment. The enemy was now thickly clustered in a semi-circle stand below the city's northern slope apparently waiting for Ahuitzotl's next move. They had lost close to a quarter of their force in their ill-fated assault and displayed an uncertainty over how to proceed, having been severely stung for their earlier aggressiveness.

"They're tightly massed," Ahuitzotl said, "and won't advance anymore. It's up to us to break their ranks."

"That will not be easy, as concentrated as they are," replied Tlohtzin.

"The hill prevents Nezahualpilli and Chimalpopoca from an effective attack on the Mixtec rear. We must somehow split them so each half of their force is spread along its sides making it vulnerable to our reinforcements. Signal our units into a wedge behind a screen of warriors. As soon as they're ready, we'll resume our attack."

Within minutes their maneuvering was completed and Ahuitzotl directed the assault to proceed. To the sound of drumbeats, Mexica squadrons again advanced toward the waiting Mixtecs while side-stepping the casualties of their previous encounter still lying about. At ground level, the wedge formation was hidden behind several rows of warriors on line, but from atop the hill it was clearly visible and astonished its observers. Frantically, the lookouts dispatched a messenger to their force below, but at this point, the warning came too late to counter the move-to shift units now in the wake of the Mexica assault invited utter confusion and perhaps even panic. Tezacoalco must have sensed his end was near when he received this warning and found himself unable to react to it. His gods had forsaken him.

An instant later, the center of the Mexica line opened up to make way for the horde of shouting, wild-eyed warriors rushing full speed at the enemy in their formidable wedge. Before the stunned Mixtecs could counteract it, the shielded Anahuac squadrons crashed like a sledge into the wall of defenders. Ahuitzotl himself strode forth in the middle of the formation with his Eagles and Jaguars, and with the fiercest, most valiant, and finest trained soldiers comprising the wedge, it personified an approaching death and the outer Mixtec lines crumbled under the intensity of the attack. The ferocious Mexica hacked and sliced into their opposition and appeared as though they would make short work of it; they aimed directly for the enemy center.

"Find me Tezacoalco!" Ahuitzotl roared out. "The first warrior to take him will be richly rewarded."

But success was not to come that easy. At first, having caught the Mixtecs off guard, the wedge penetrated their ranks readily enough, but then, after they had recovered from their initial shock, resistance stiffened. The Mexica were slowed down, but not stopped, and gradually, through bashing out every step gained and at the cost of a fallen warrior, they managed to split the Mixtecs into two groups. Then, as if the defenders had suddenly awakened to the danger of their situation, Ahuitzotl's squadrons found themselves met with a fanatic determination to reunite the divided army; their adversaries slammed at them from both sides with maniacal fury. Tezacoalco called his reserves from the city into the melee; they came charging down the hill like a pack of maddened dogs and, in a startling reversal of earlier events, it was now the Mexica who were in severe straits and fighting for their lives.

In that bleak circumstance, when Ahuitzotl's force was about to be overwhelmed, numerous trumpet calls echoed across the battle field above the clamor of clashing arms.

"It's Chimalpopoca and Nezahualpilli!" Tlohtzin shouted out in great relief.

"A timely arrival," Ahuitzotl added. "Now let Tezacoalco feel the full weight of our arms."

The Acolhuas came charging along the western slope of the hill while their Tepanec counterparts ran up its eastern flank; both impacted on the Mixtecs with equal voraciousness. Yearning for a hard struggle too long denied to them, they meant to show their comrades-in-arms of Tenochtitlan what they were capable of doing.

Hammered between Ahuitzotl's wedge, which still stood intact in spite of the beating it sustained, and the attacking Acolhuas and Tepanecs, the Mixtecs saw all hopes of victory vanish. But they were not about to cede over their kingdom by merely running from the field; they held their ground everywhere, putting up a frenetic effort to make their capture as costly as possible for the aggressors. With equal pugnaciousness, Mexica warriors tore viciously into the defenders, thrusting spears into their compacted units and crashing into them with shields and clubs. A most horrible and bloody slaughter ensued; the Mixtecs reeled under the fearsome assault, but for every one of them struck down, an attacker paid the price with his own blood and together they collapsed in gruesome contorted heaps.

Eventually, the greater Mexica numbers began to assert themselves over their trapped opposition. For every agressor slain, two more took his place, but every defender lost left his unit that much weaker. Just then, with an enormous concentration of effort, a sizable segment of the Mixtecs made a lunge for the forests bordering the valley by hacking a path through a more thinly scattered section of the Mexica lines. Ahuitzotl spotted them from where he stood. "They're getting away!" he barked. "They must not escape!"

"Stop them!" Tlohtzin shouted.

Both were too far away to put a halt to the flight, and all the units around them remained engaged in fighting which impeded any attempt to reach the fleeing Mixtecs. Ahuitzotl was furious; he called on his Eagles to rush at them, but as they did so, they were intercepted by elements of defenders who rushed up to forstall them. They died in this heroic endeavor but succeeded in preventing the Mexica from stopping the escape, and all Ahuitzotl could do was watch as the enemy disappeared in the tree-line.

The Revered Speaker raged, and his vehemence was vented out upon the unfortunate Mixtecs remaining on the battlefield. Mexica squadrons surrounded the surviving elements and hacked them to pieces allowing them no opportunity to yield to their conqueror. Those Mixtecs who threw aside their weapons and dropped to their knees as a sign of submission had their skulls split open by the maquauhuitl with the same lack of regard as those who persisted in fighting until they perished. Only a handful of survivors were left on the field, and these were promptly dragged before Ahuitzotl.

"Where is Tezacoalco?" Ahuitzotl shouted at them, still an angry beast.

They did not know, they related, at which point Ahuitzotl directed his chieftains to escort them across the battleground to see if they could identify their master among the casualties, after which they were again brought to him.

"Well?" Ahuitzotl fumed. "Did you find him?"

They spoke rapidly through an interpreter who gave the monarch a solemn glance.

"They say he is not among the dead or wounded, Lord!"

"I thought so," snarled Ahuitzotl. "Tezacoalco has escaped."

He presented a frightening spectacle to his colleagues when enraged; both Chimalpopoca and Nezahualpilli felt uneasy, fearing the unexpected. "What sort of ruler abandons his army?" Ahuitzotl went on. "Have you ever seen anything so dishonorable?"

"What have we to fear from him?" said Nezahualpilli. "His army is destroyed. Even if he joins the Zapotecs, he has nothing to offer them. He can be no more threat to us."

"As long as he is around, he exists as a rallying point for his people, or whatever remnant of his army he has left. It may not be a significantly large force he can come up with, but it is still more than Cocijoeza alone could bring against us."

"We can't do much about it now. Let us see to our dead and wounded."

Ahuitzotl gazed over the field blanketed with fallen warriors; he nodded his concurrance.

"What shall we do with them?" Tlohtzin asked about their captives.

"Turn them over to the priests!" Ahuitzotl declared. "They must have their sacrifices."

By the time all their dead were amassed and deposited upon the many funeral pyres, dusk had enveloped the valley and deterred Ahuitzotl from sacking Xaltepec. Its inhabitants now literally became trapped within their own city as the Mexica established their camp around the entire base of the hill and maintained a night long vigilance for anyone daring enough to attempt an escape from it. Frightened and weeping, they dreaded the coming of dawn.

They had ample reasons for their fears; Ahuitzotl remained embittered over Tezacoalco slipping from his grasp the next morning and meant to make Xaltepec an example of his wrath. He issued orders for his commanders to devastate the city and observed from below with Chimalpopoca and Nezahualpilli while the warriors, led by Tlohtzin and Motecuhzoma, stormed it. Spurred on by their free reign of the spoils, Anahuac soldiers assaulted Xaltepec from all sides and, in an orgy of fire and blood, massacred its inhabitants and set its structures to the torch.

XIX

A week after they had sacked Xaltepec, the Mexica came to Itzcuintepec, another major city along the route to Tehuantepec. It avoided the cold and ruthless slaughter of Xaltepec, for news of Ahuitzotl's approach was now enough to send the local population of villages and cities into panic. The Revered Speaker capitalized on this by sending messengers ahead to drop word to the regional rulers that he was coming; this was sufficient to instill such abject fear in his opponents that they capitulated without making any attempt to do battle. In this way, almost the whole of the Mixtec nation fell to him.

At Tototepec, however, Ahuitzotl for the first time met the Zapotecs who had combined one of their armies with the Mixtec defenders. Prior to engaging them in combat, he and Tlohtzin chanced to see a large eagle flying over the city. Circling repeatedly in its flight, the bird suddenly dove with startling speed towards the earth, apparently having spotted its prey, but when it rose again, it carried no quarry between its talon. To Ahuitzotl this was not only an impressive sight, but also filled with mystical connections, and he called on his head priest to explain its meaning. "What does this portent?" he asked after having related what he had seen.

The priest appeared visibly disturbed and hesitated before answering but knew he could not refrain from informing his lord of the omen's signification. "The eagle is the aggressor," he presently said, "as we are, and attacks its prey, which is the city of our enemy, but us unable to fly away with anything. It is an indication that although we may continue to attack our foes, we will ultimately return to Anahuac empty-handed, or at least short of our intentions The prognostication is decidedly unfavorable."

"Is your estimation about this reasonably precise," Ahuitzotl asked with some concern, not appreciating what he heard, "or is this but one of several plausible interpretations you offer?"

"No mortal can know for certain, Lord."

Ahuitzotl chose to disregard the priest's translation as he could ill afford to be influenced by what he deemed adversive signs-they disrupted the morale of his warriors.

The day's events were to prove the prediction false; Ahuitzotl scored a stunning victory over the combined Mixtec and Zapotec forces and sent them fleeing from the field leaving a notable number of casualties. It amounted to his most complete success so far, with the Mexica handily eliminating their opposition from the city and then looting it, taking from its occupants and residences many items of value. Afterward, Ahuitzotl savored a feast in its royal palace to celebrate his easy triumph and, in his elation, spared the local lords and populace from any punishment for having confronted him.

At early dawn, the more serious aspects of their duties resumed as the Mexica broke camp to prepare for their trek to the sea where Tehauntepec was situated. In getting there, they had to traverse some of the most rugged and uncompromising terrain of their entire journey and their progress was slowed considerably as a result, requiring them a week to close within a day's march of the Zapotec capital. At this point, Ahuitzotl received information of some importance from his scouts who preceded his main column and kept him abreast of the enemy's activity.

"Cocijoeza has left his capital," the ranking patrol member reported, "and is moving to Giengola where he expects to face us."

"Where is Giengola?"

"Approximately ten leagues north of Tehuantepec-that much closer to you, Lord."

"If he means to deter us from his city by this move, he is mistaken."

"Giengola offers a better defensible position for him, Lord. It stands upon a high cliff overlooking the surrounding area. The terrain is rocky there and hides many ravines and caves which he can use to his advantage."

"I assume he leads his force. Does it equal ours?"

"Nearly so. We estimated it at sixty thousand, but he also is augmented by a Mixtec army numbering another fifteen thousand, and it is led by their lord, Tezacoalco."

"So we are to meet again," Ahuitzotl mused. "This time he won't get away from me."

Actually Ahuitzotl found these reports more disturbing that he allowed his chieftains to believe. The enemy was at significantly greater strength than he had hoped, and he had an intuition that Cocijoeza would somehow prove a more formidable antagonist than Tezacoalco. He did not favor his adversary having an edge in battling on rocky and treacherous grounds familiar to him while he would be forced into dislodging him from creviced terrain. Moreover, he had learned that Cocijoeza expressed an inordinate amount of interest in Mexica battle techniques when he came to Tenochtitlan for the inauguration of the Great Temple; this was enough reason to regard the Zapotec monarch with some degree of caution.

Ahuitzotl came upon Giengola in the afternoon of the ninth day after having departed Tototepec, and was overcome with utter astonishment when he first viewed it and scanned the defenses Cocijoeza had established for his army there. For one thing, Giengola was not a city as he had supposed, but a royal retreat resting atop such a prominently impressive terrain feature that it merited being mentioned by a proper place-name. In fact an enormous escarpment which rose several hundred feet almost vertically from the valley floor, its cliffs were honeycombed with sharp ridges, rocky outcrops, caverns, and gorges. It held tremendous advantages for its defenders, and conversely, presented an attacker with immense obstacles. He saw the Zapotecs looking down on him from atop their promontory.

"We must teach our scouts to be more accurate in describing what they see," Ahuitzotl said to Tlohtzin. "This rock is several leagues long and at least a league wide-a veritable bastion."

"We can't dislodge Cocijoeza from there."

"That would be suicidal. No, if we are to defeat him, we must accomplish it on the ground. He's going to have to come off that rock to face us, else we can cut off his supplies and starve him out. Cocjioeza is aware of that."

Ahuitzotl directed his armies to establish their camp about two leagues from the escarpment in an area adequately concealed from observation by forests and at the valley's end where it narrowed into a canyon at the foot of a hilly ridge. He could see Giengola from there and tasked a squadron of guards to keep watch on his enemy's stronghold. Later that evening, after darkness had settled on them, he held his usual conference with his chieftains to determine how they might embattle their opponents if indeed they offered an attack in the morning as expected.

"At present, they are more than double our numbers," Ahuitzotl imparted on his subordinates seated about the bonfire, "and I believe that their ruler, Cocijoeza, knows this."

"This suggests that we should take up a defensive position and require them to attack us," said Motecuhzoma. "We can then retreat into the mountains until our allies join us."

"It may come to that, but for now I prefer if we initiated the action, mitigating their numerical edge through some deceptive maneuvers. If we sting Cocijoeza early, he will become cautious-that will help us in the long run."

"We must come up with something different," added Tlohtzin. "Tezacoalco would have told him about what we did at Xal.." At that instant a loud clamor suddenly erupted from the camp's outer perimeter. They heard several warriors shouting, followed by horrid screams. A trumpet call resonated through the darkness, and its sharp blare was clear to everyone.

"It's an attack!" Ahuitzotl shouted as he jumped to his feet. "By the gods!"

"To arms!" Tlohtzin directed. "Commanders! Return to your units-prepare to counter it!"

All about the camp, warriors scrambled to pick up their armaments; commanders bellowed out various orders after rejoining their squadrons and brought the army into a semblance of cohesion. The fires were doused to permit visibility in the dark. Ahuitzotl led a group of his Eagle knights to the forest's edge from where the sound of clashing weapons emanated.

"There they are!" he announced when he spotted some blackened outlines of soldiers ahead of him.

His Eagles rushed at the enemy and suddenly were overwhelmed in fearsome closed-in fighting as several more assailants came out of the brushes than at first thought. They became locked in savage combat, swinging their maquauhuitl at the shadowy figures enveloping them, unable to see where they would strike them, but guided by their movements and hearing a painful cry when the weapon found its mark.

Throughout the perimeter, warriors fell entangled with unrecognizable forms which sprang up everywhere about them, and the darkness was pierced with a clashing of parrying and colliding weapons, impacting shields, snapping twigs and rustling foliage, and echoing cries from the wounded accompanied by shouts of triumph. No one could tell how many were engaged, but at night, with sounds greatly magnified, it seemed as if the entire camp was embattled. Warriors who could not see their attackers moved toward where the noise of battle directing them and joined their comrades in fending off the assailants.

Then, almost as abruptly as it had begun, the conflict ended. Groups of attackers, never seen distinctly throughout the melee, ran into the shadow of the escarpment from where they had come, and an eerie silence encompassed the camp only to be broken here and there by the pitiful wails of severely wounded soldiers calling out for help. In blackness, warriors groped painstakingly for their injured or dying comrades, led to them by the moans they emitted; it had a horrifying aspect to it, with the stillness of night intensifying the sounds and giving an overall impression of frightening losses.

Ahuitzotl came back to his command post both shaken and angry over the treacherous attack. "Cocijoeza will pay dearly for this," he swore.

Soon Tlohtzin and Motecuhzoma rejoined their master, as did the other major commanders; the fire was relit and their meeting resumed.

"How many casualties did we sustain?" Ahuitzotl asked.

"At latest count-and we're still searching for more-about four hundred, including one hundred thirty dead," Tlohtzin replied.

"We should not have been caught off guard like that. Our losses speak for our lack of alertness. What is the enemy count?"

"One hundred and four that we've found."

"Never since I have been Revered Speaker have we suffered more losses than the enemy. This confirms what I suspected, that Cocijoeza will be a resourceful antagonist. Make certain our warriors are alert to this at all times."

"After tonight, they won't have to be reminded, Lord."

They dwelled on their battle plan late into the night unable to decide on what course of action to pursue tomorrow, and Ahuitzotl deemed it prudent to study Cocijoeza's formation of units before determining how to arrange for his own countermeasures. He was inclined to hide his archers behind his forward ranks as at Xaltepec, but wanted the flexibility to make hasty adjustments if he thought this necessary. "What is important," he advised his chieftains, "is that you be able to respond readily to any changes I order tomorrow. Your warriors must recognize that although it may seem unusual for them, it has its purpose and requires speedy compliance."

With that precautionary advice, Ahuitzotl ended his meeting and stayed alone by the fire to reflect over how Cocijoeza might conceive to do battle with him. He was frustrated by his inability to come up with any inspiring plan in which to counter his foe. He suspected that Cocijoeza would commence the action because he at present significantly outnumbered the Mexica, and the most prospective method Ahuitzotl could think of in thwarting his plans was to seize the initiative himself. Yet, such a move entailed serious risks and ran counter to the basic doctrines that an offensive power always have a numerical superiority over its opposition. But the more he dwelled on this, the more he deemed the idea as having merit. His warriors were humiliated tonight, and would seek to compensate for it in the morning–of this he was certain.

Early at dawn, conch trumpets alerted Ahuitzotl's armies to take up their battle stations. As anticipated, Cocijoeza had decided to move against the Mexica; he brought the bulk of his army down from his rocky bastion and assembled it into a wide, solid phalanx of about twenty rows deep. Ahuitzotl, in the meantime, kept his force behind the tree-line, using it for a natural barrier and cover as the forests provided some concealment in revealing his actual numbers. But in back of his front lines, he again formed many of his units into an attacking mode, capitalizing on Zozoltin's wedge as his primary instrument for penetration and shock effect. He intended to launch his assault shortly after the enemy commenced its advance under an illusion that the Mexica would wage a defensive battle.

Cocijoeza evidently distrusted what Ahuitzotl would do, for he kept his warriors at their stations, apparently in the belief that the Mexica would form up opposite his Zapotecans and also make an attack.

"He's leery of us," Ahuitzotl noted. "He expects us to move against him."

"How long will he wait?" replied Tlohtzin.

"Until he becomes convinced, or his advisors lead him to believe, that we will not take the initiative."

"What if he does not advance on us?"

"That is his misfortune. We can wait all day without fighting-tomorrow Chimalpopoca joins us and we will be at greater parity, and Cocijoeza will have lost his prime opportunity."

They espied the enemy monarch consulting with a number of his chieftains as if trying to extract some sort of agreement out of them on how to proceed; there was a conspicuous movement of individuals adorned in splendid costumes-an indication that they were high ranking leaders. After a lengthy meeting, they moved back to their positions, and soon thereupon drumbeats and shouting prodded their lines into an advance. Covering the total width of the Mexica front with their phalanx, they advanced with each soldier's shield abutting the other's while Ahuitzotl and Tlohtzin strained to assess their composition.

"Do you see any archers?" Tlohtzin asked, thinking it implausible that he failed to notice them.

"None."

"Surely Tezacoalco must have explained our use of them. I can't believe such advice would fall on deaf ears."

"Let's put him to the test," answered Ahuitzotl, equally mystified. "Feign an attack on them making use of our own archers to see how he reacts."

Commands forged the Mexica army into its assault line and when the trumpets resounded, its warriors started their advancement bent on confronting the opposition head-on. When the gap separating the two armies narrowed to only a hundred-some paces, the leading soldiers in both armies turned aside, nearly simultaneously, to expose hidden bowmen–Cocijoeza had indeed listened to his Mixtec ally. After firing a volley, the archers ran for cover behind their shielded comrades as they saw the opposite flight of missiles coming. They had neutralized each other's effectiveness, doing minimal damage, and the battle assumed its next phase.

Cocijoeza focused on a concentrated drive for the Mexica center, having massed several of his units in a densely packed square that outpaced his other squadrons which proceeded at a steady gait. Ahuitzotl, on seeing this, after having at first ordered his wedge to drive for a frontal penetration of the Zapotec lines, directed it to veer off and strike Cocijoeza's square along its lateral edge. In a sickening crunch, warriors and weapons of the two forces met in collision, and the Mexica were to learn first-hand of their adversary's cunning in using a square rather than a wedge which might have seemed more suited for an attack. Whereas Ahuitzotl's formation managed to penetrate the outer wall of the square, it soon became evident that keeping up the momentum was going to prove extremely arduous. The square, solid and strong, had the advantage of affording Cocijoeza equal protection on all sides with its tightly massed warriors spread evenly throughout and thereby posed a major obstruction to an attacker trying to cut into it.

Furiously, Ahuitzotl and his Eagles and Jaguar squadrons fell on the sturdy rows which bent but did not collapse. They cut down one opponent after another, wielding their maquauhuitl in powerful strokes and inflicting horrid damage but found that their progress was virtually halted and could not make further inroads. In the meantime, the enemy's remaining lines had made contact with the Mexica and the whole of both forces was deadlocked in violent combat.

Tlohtzin, commanding that portion of Tenochtitlan's army not committed to Ahuitzotl's wedge on the right, was intent on augmenting his master as soon as he reduced his opposition. But the Zapotecan lines, consisting of as many as twenty ranks deep, presented a near impenetrable barrier against his murderous onslaught; they held their own and, while not progressing further, neither did they falter. He was unable to gain any headway as the whole right section, a cauldron of heated action, remained fixed in place, its combatants yielding no ground to each other.

On the left, Motecuhzoma fared somewhat better at first in leading his Tlatelolco divisions, making an early breakthrough in the Mixtec lines facing him. His squadrons carved out a pathway, using long spears hurled at close range into their opposition to disrupt its cohesion and then crashing into it with their shields as a battering ram. They hacked wildly at the Mixtecs, the lethal clubs splattering brains as they crashed into the protective headwear, pushing forward in their fury and determination to crush the resistance. But the drive was short-lived. As Motecuhzoma turned right to lend support to Ahuitzotl's stalled assault by attacking Cocijoeza's square from its opposite side, he was unexpectedly met by several Zapotec reserve squadrons which had been signaled into the fray. Hammered by the fresh attacking squadrons, he was halted in his advance and had to call on back-up support to keep from losing the ground gained earlier.

As the battle progressed, more and more units were directed into it when exhausted commanders on both sides called on their reserve squadrons to relieve the primary combatants. Soon every available unit was committed to its fury, leaving little room for maneuvering, a situation which disrupted the plans of both rulers who were inclined earlier in the day to resort to deployments for attaining a victory. The entire struggle transformed itself into one gigantic slugging match that in effect matched the greater discipline of the Mexica against the greater numbers of the Zapotecs and Mixtecs. Throughout the day the battle raged, its ferocity unabated. When warriors of one unit became too exhausted to continue fighting, they were replaced by fresh ones which had sat out and rested; these in turn were later substituted by the same ones they had relieved. In such a rotation, every squadron participated in the battle during the course of the day with no lengthy respite for any of them. Neither side gained the upper hand and, by the time the afternoon was spent, both powers were still stalemated when finally distant trumpeters annouced the arrival of the Army of Tepaneca.

Cocijoeza, on hearing the blares, issued orders for his army to withdraw. His retreat was executed in an orderly fashion, without any breaking of ranks, and helped greatly by Ahuitzotl's inability to launch a pursuit because of the high casualties and enervation among his Mexica. Accordingly, the Zapotecs and their ally retreated behind the protection of their formidable natural barrier, hastily disengaging themselves from the fighting, and by the time Chimalpopoca came upon the scene, the enemy had completed a full retirement depriving the Tepanecs a share of today's action.

It had been a brutal day-the costliest one in Ahuitzotl's reign-with a multitude of warriors joining their gods in paradise. The funeral pyres that night were extensive and there ensued great lamentation, much of it expressed for the survivors who, in all likelihood, were doomed to undergo another such day-the dead were now amid blissful and serene surroundings. Chimalpopoca regretted not having made an earlier appearance-his Tepanecs had missed out in an awesome engagement. As Ahuitzotl observed the many pyres burning, Tlohtzin answered his inquiry on the casualties they had sustained.

"We counted nearly four thousand dead and another six thousand wounded, Lord. In addition, we lost approximately a thousand as captives."

The numbers appalled Ahuitzotl; he should have appreciated what the gods had invoked, but his practical nature made him think only about how he was to continue his campaign without them.

"And the enemy?"

"We estimate their dead at five thousand, with as many wounded as we had, but we only captured four hundred of them."

"So the battle can be considered a draw."

"A draw? Oh no, Lord. It must be deemed a victory for us, and a great one at that. They heavily outnumbered us, yet we fought them to a standstill."

"A victory then, but certainly a dearly bought one."

"But more so for Cocijoeza, Lord."

Tlohtzin was correct, but the Revered Speaker was still too dazed to properly assess his losses in relation to his gains. What he knew was that this had been the bloodiest fought battle ever, and that he did not feel as though he had won it, and if this was an indication of what could be exacted from the Zapotecs and their ally, he faced trying times.

XX

If Ahuitzotl had been badly shaken by his casualties on this first major encounter with the Zapotec host, Cocijoeza's shock must have been even greater; he revealed this by an unwillingness to consider a move against the Mexica on the following day, thereby forsaking a situation which still greatly favored him tactically. It would have been opportune for him to attack as the Acolhuas had not yet joined Ahuitzotl's force and his opponent remained at a numerical handicap.

"See?" Tlohtzin rejoiced after the Mexica had assumed their battle order. "Cocijoeza is afraid to move. What better evidence than this that yesterday's carnage ended in our favor."

"Maybe he's lost his nerve," replied Ahuitzotl soberly. "Just the same, I welcome the opportunity to rest today, as do the warriors, I'll wager."

"Shall I dismiss them?"

"Yes, but keep a guard force on alert so we do not fall for one of Cocijoeza's ruses."

This done, a portion of their time was devoted to sacrificing some of the prisoners taken in yesterday's battle. The priests set up a techcatl amid a circle of warriors when a number of captives were brought forth. Ahuitzotl began the rites when he plunged his knife into the heaving chest of the first one thrown upon the block and tore out the beating heart. Tezcatlipoca, as well as Huitzilopochtli, had to be honored this day. After having undergone such an unprecedented slaughter, it did not suffice to render homage to only the war god—it necessitated appeals to the Creator himself, the Emminent One, Tezcatlipoca!

Cocijoeza made no move that entire day, nor did he show himself on the succeeding day, and this baffled Ahuitzotl as there appeared to be no adequate explanation for these seemingly self-defeating delays.

"Is he getting reinforcements?" Ahuitzotl asked Tlohtzin. "Nezahualpilli joins us today; yet he seems unconcerned about it. We have all the approaches to Giengola patrolled, don't we?"

"The roads are under our constant surveillance, Lord, and we've had no sightings reported."

"This is strange. Does he really think I would expend my warriors in trying to dislodge him from his rock? Surely he must know we can just leave him here and take Tehuantepec."

"Perhaps he wants to surrender but requires a consensus from his council, which is reluctant to grant him one."

"Cocijoeza is too wily for that. He's up to something, although why he would wait until we are fully united is odd. Yet I have no doubt that he presently believes he controls the situation."

Ahuitzotl felt reasonably assured he was prepared to counter any move Cocijoeza might attempt, but remained bewildered why the Zapotecan would allow such an opportune moment to slip from his hands. He sensed the answer lay in reinforcements; his adversary apparently planned on receiving them-but how?

Later that afternoon, Nezahualpilli arrived. Ahuitzotl, always gratified at seeing his Texcocan ally, updated him on all that had transpired in the last two days and of his plan to leave Cocijoeza isolated upon his rock if the Zapotecan refused to do battle. Nezahualpilli found the plan wanting.

"You overlook an important detail," he told Ahuitzotl. "If you take Tehuantepec without defeating Cocijoeza, what will you do when the time comes for us to leave the city?"

"There won't be a city; we'll have it burned to the ground."

"What will that accomplish? Certainly it exacts some punishment on the Zapotecs, but have we secured our purpose here? As soon as we leave, Cocijoeza will return to his city, rebuild it, and then continue to disrupt our trades as before. We will have achieved nothing by coming here."

"Suppose we left a garrison there to protect our interests?"

"It would have to be a large one indeed if it is to hold off the entire Zapotec army Cocijoeza still has with him."

Nezahualpilli made his point patently clear, and Ahuitzotl was somewhat vexed at having failed to consider such a crucial factor himself: it at once confirmed why he needed the Texcocan fox with him on these campaigns. "Why did none of my advisors tell me this?" he growled. "I cannot think of everything."

"The apparent is often the most elusive to come to one's mind."

"The apparent has eluded all their collective minds it seems. Have you seen the fortress Cocijoeza has selected for his defenses?"

"I have. It stands like a monolith over our camp."

"I mean, have you seen it up close-with all it's caves and ravines? It portents a disastrous undertaking to dislodge an enemy from there."

Nezahualpilli stood up to get a better view of the features Ahuitzotl spoke of; he studied the escarpment carefully, noting all its ruggedness, the ridges and crevices, the defiles and repeated canyon walls and caves, more than he could count, which afforded excellent cover and concealment for its defenders. There was no exaggeration that it posed a stupendous obstacle if the Mexica were to extract the Zapotec army from its position. "It may require a long siege," said the Texcocan, "but we could eventually starve them out."

"That could take weeks, perhaps months, and I have our own supplies to consider. Also, the eastern and southern face slopes directly into the jungles-we would find it difficult to emplace our forces in that growth. Better that we induce Cocijoeza into battling us on the ground."

"Agreed, but given his reluctance, how will you do that, especially now that we are at equal, if not greater, strength?"

"Maybe we can smoke him out-there has to be a way."

To Ahuitzotl's amazement, Cocijoeza managed to reinforce his army to where it equaled the Mexica in numbers. His units had infiltrated through the forests familiar to them in single files, mostly at night, but also in daylight having eluded the numerous Anahuac patrols scouting the area. These movements might have continued unnoticed had not one of the patrols made contact with an enemy column as it snaked through a wooded trail. It happened to be a Mixtec detachment and, upon spotting the patrol, tried to capture its members so word of its movement would remain a secret. In giving chase, one of the Mixtecs who had become separated from his companions was captured by the Mexica who then evaded being caught. Through this prisoner, Ahuitzotl learned about the infiltration and that it had been taking place or three days and nights, and that an estimated twenty-five thousand warriors had united with the Zapotecs at Giengola.

Alarmed, Ahuitzotl next ordered his warriors to clear the forests with fire, a measure he knew as too late for any significant deterrence-the best he could hope to achieve at this stage was to prevent food supplies from reaching Cocijoeza.

"He could have escaped," said Nezahualpilli, viewing the episode more optimistically, "But instead chose to reinforce his army. This means he will offer us another battle."

As soon as he related this, trumpets blared from the direction of the rock. "Look!" Nezahualpilli pointed there, "Cocijoeza comes with his army now!"

Ahuitzotl stared disbelievingly at the enemy force being assembled as units merged from behind Giengola's crags. "I don't like this," he scowled. "He plans some trickery."

Responding to the challenge, Ahuitzotl hastily called his own force into its battle alignment; Nezahualpilli proceeded to do the same with his Acolhuas, as did Chimalpopoca with his Tepanecs. The enemy did not permit them time to partake in the ritual necessities demanded before engaging in combat; as soon as both armies were assembled, the battle commenced.

Cocijoeza initiated the attack-a move which surprised Ahuitzotl who was about to order his advance-with a massed assault on the Mexica right manned by Chimalpopoca's Tepanecs. His Zapotecs mounted their charge configured in a square as before, howling madly as they rushed head-long into the astonished Tepanecs, crushing through their lines behind the weight of their numbers.

"He drives on our right!" Tlohtzin shouted to Ahuitzotl.

"Yes-the question is, can Chimalpopoca hold them off?"

"I think not. They've pierced his ranks; in a moment, they will be on Chimalpopoca himself."

"We must come to his aid," Ahuitzotl quickly decided. "Turn our center towards him!"

A succession of commands, repeated by chieftains at every echelon, set into motion the task of diverting the bulk of the army's center to move against the Zapotecs on its right; Ahuitzotl personally led this attack. They came not a moment to soon, for Chimalpopoca, amid his Eagles and Jaguars, was fighting off a daring host bent on capturing him, and he found his ability to hold the position assigned him severely taxed.

Nezahualpilli, far to the left of the field, grew tense when he saw Ahuitzotl's squadrons adjacent to him pulling away to relieve the pressured right. A wide gap opened up between his army and those of Tenochtitlan and Tlatelolco, and he sensed something was wrong. His apprehensions were suddenly realized when he heard the shouts of thousands of enemy warriors bearing down on his exposed left. So ferocious was their charge that the Acolhuas wavered in their advance; in an instant, the two forces collided, the crashing of their arms resounding across the field. Jubilant cries arose from the Zapotecs who fully meant to rout the alarmed Acolhuas under their momentum. Nezahualpilli frantically shouted words of encouragement to his soldiers, entreating them to withstand the onslaught.

"Stand fast!" he roared. "Do not let them penetrate your ranks!"

Nezahualpilli was bidding for time; he knew if he could stall the Zapotec drive for only a few minutes, Ahuitzotl would notice his predicament and send a relief column, but it presented an awesome imposition. Zapotec warriors hacked out their bold advance through stubborn Acolhua lines, bashing down the fierce resistance they encountered with relentless fury, and the dead fell in gruesome heaps, slowing their progression as they had to circumvent the bodies of their comrades. Nezahualpilli was embattled in the thick of it, himself surrounded by the Zapotec wolves. He struck down the first one to reach him, smashing both the soldier's helmet and skull with a single broad sweep of his warclub; then he evaded the blow of another, stopping it with his wide shield–him he dispatched by embedding the obsidian blades of his weapon into the abdomen. A third warrior sprang upon the Texcocan, but he was speared in the chest by one of the Eagle knights assigned to protect his master. Yet more Zapotecans rushed into the bloody melee; the Acolhua opposition was ferocious, but they began to fall one after another piling up in twisted, mangled heaps of bodies.

In the meantime, after Ahuitzotl had rushed ahead to assist Chimalpopoca, the Zapotecs reacted to his assault by immediately withdrawing, offering only a token resistance. Ahuitzotl instantly recognized that something was amiss-the rescue was entirely too easy. Against his own warnings, he had been deceived. He glanced down to the opposite end of the field and saw the Acolhuas in their threatened circumstance, fiercely engaged with the enemy–his countenance one of utter shock. "Cocijoeza feigned this attack," he informed Tlohtzin angrily. "It's Nezahualpilli we must assist. Give your chieftains the order!"

New commands echoed through the Mexica ranks; bewildered, the warriors completed an about face and raced toward their left where they could see their allies in dire straits. Critical moments were lost in the issue and reissue of directives and in reacting to them-moments in which many more Acolhuas met their gods in paradise.

When the Zapotec commanders saw Ahuitzotl's support nearing, they hastily sounded a call to retire back to their rocky sanctuary. Even before the first of the warriors could make contact with them, the enemy was in full flight for their defenses. Nezahualpilli had been rescued from certain harm or capture, but the soldiers of Tenochtitlan achieved no glory on this day. Moving first to the right to attack the enemy, then to the left, they offered no appreciable contribution to either side, and in the interim period, nearly a quarter of the Acolhua army was left as casualties. The gods did not favor them today.

"A cunning enemy," Nezahualpilli was capable of saying after his timely deliverance. "He set a trap for us and we became ensnared in it."

Ahuitzotl's eyes blazed. Never before defeated on the battlefield, he could not deny that he had been outfoxed by his antagonist. "He's had his moment of glory," he snarled. "Let him savor his triumph. There shall be no more such days for him."

The belligerents again met in a brief encounter the next day, and then once more on the following day, and each time the Mexica were about to entrap and overwhelm their opposition, Cocijoeza ordered his army into retreat behind his impenetrable natural bulwark, thoroughly irritating to Ahuitzotl.

"His methods are becoming clear," he told his commanders. "He feigns an attack in one place, strikes in another to inflict as many casualties as he can, and then makes a speedy withdrawal behind his defenses before we can do significant damage to him. He hopes, in this way, that he can wear us out."

"He shall wear himself out first, Lord," Tlohtzin said. "In his last two attacks his losses exceeded ours."

"Yes, but we're running low on supplies. We have only enough rations for two weeks or so, and what we forage by raiding nearby villages does not meet our needs. If we do not score a major breakthrough soon, we will face major adversities on our return trek to Anahuac."

"How is Cocijoeza able to feed his army?" Nezahualpilli interjected. "Surely he faces the same problem."

"We've cut off all the roads and trails leading to Giengola, but the jungle paths are difficult to patrol-even the areas we've burned are extensive to cover, especially at night. Somehow his suppliers are able to elude us and slip through."

"It takes enormous quantities to sustain his large army. I question if a few supply units slipping by our patrols are sufficient for this."

"Somehow he does it. The point is we must achieve a decisive blow to him, and soon. We have no capacity to conduct a siege."

There was no activity that following morning, nor during the next seven succeeding days, and Ahuitzotl was left to storm about his command post as he was getting nowhere while his provisions continued to dwindle. On the ninth day, however, Cocijoeza once more sent his army forth from his stronghold; he apparently understood his entrenched foe's predicament and intended, through these planned piecemeal efforts, to keep the Mexica's appetite whetted with an anticipation of victory while in the process depleting the available storages upon which their eventual success rested.

This time it was Ahuitzotl who set the trap. When Cocijoeza drove for the Mexica center, Nezahualpilli and Chimalpopoca, in an extreme departure from any previously applied tactical maneuver, instead of coming to reinforce it, advanced in a wide half-circle around the Zapotec host and tried to envelop it between each flank. But the wily Cocijoeza recognized the situation about to unfold on him and sounded a retreat prior to making contact with the center. Ahuitzotl flew into a rage when he saw his antagonist eluding the ploy; he looked about him for the nearest chieftain in his vicinity.

"Motecuhzoma!" Ahuitzotl shouted when he spotted the young commander. "Take your warriors and pursue them!"

Motecuhzoma was momentarily dumbstruck as this directive was tantamount to negotiating an assault against the rock. "Do you mean, Lord," he said, "that I am to attack Giengola?"

"Yes! It's time we tested their defenses, but be wary of any pitfalls."

Motecuhzoma, although viewing the order as capriciously issued, hastily complied and led a number of squadrons in pursuit of the fleeing enemy. The Mexica ran hotly after them, catching up with the stragglers and cutting them down from behind as they raced for their sanctuary. The Zapotecs proceeded through a narrow defile which extended parallel to the rock between two ridges; Motecuhzoma, in his eagerness to impress the monarch, overlooked the potential hazard and directed his units to follow them. They snaked along a gorge in chasing their prey.

Suddenly a thousand archers from both sides of the cliffs released their deadly arrows upon the advancing Mexica below. Before Motecuhzoma's warriors could lift their shields over their esposed heads to protect themselves from the frightful rain, hundreds of them were struck by the missiles and fell to the ground, bleeding and screaming in pain. The enemy followed their volley with charging warriors who descended upon the confined Mexica from all sides.

"There are too many!" Motecuhzoma shouted. "Fall back! We must get out of here!"

With his units stretched out as a long column within the ravine, only the forward elements heard this command, and when these turned around to comply, they collided with the trailing soldiers who were still advancing. Disorder and confusion reigned as they bumped into each other and became dangerously compressed; by the time they all moved in the same direction-back toward their own lines-the enemy blocked off the entrance to the gorge with a phalanx of warriors trapping the Mexica within it. Hemmed in, attacked from both front and rear and from above, Motecuhzoma's sqaudrons faught with the determined fanaticism of doomed men; one enemy warrior after another who rushed upon them was hacked under, but more came, springing out from hidden crevices and tearing into their trapped quarry. Motecuhzoma saw that if he could not break out, his soldiers faced annihilation.

"Make a charge for the entrance!" he frantically ordered. "As one, rush on it! It's our only chance!"

Gathering the momentum of a battering ram in their race for the entrance of the ravine, his frenzied warriors crashed into the blocking enemy squads, slashing furiously at them as they went, and nearly forging out a path. But additional soldiers leaped on them from the heights causing them to fall so that they could be dragged off. One soldier jumped on Motecuhzoma, who fell to the ground under the weight; he smashed his maquauhuitl into the Zapotecan's face, killing him instantly. Another took his place and grabbed the prince from behind; Motecuhzoma threw him over his shoulder but before he could strike him with his club, two more warriors took hold of him. With three of them grasping him, he was again knocked off his feet and then carried away. Half of the corps was able to break out, carving its way through the rapacious pack of Zapotecans who held the passage. They were met by Ahuitzotl who led a relief force toward the ravine to assist them in getting away, but almost two thousand of them were left within the gorge.

"Motecuhzoma!" Ahuitzotl shouted when he did not see the commander among the rescued. "Where is Motecuhzoma?"

"Back there, Lord," a chieftain answered.

Cold fear gripped the monarch; he had not expected the attack to lead to disaster. "Is he...?"

"I saw him dragged off, Lord. He was taken alive."

Ahuitzotl stood horrified; even though there was much honor attached to being captured, and thus sacrificed to the gods, he did not appreciate his enemy having acquired so notable a personage for such an offering. He could not mount a rescue attempt-the enemy position was clearly too strong-and so, with heartfelt bitterness, he ordered his units to fall back to the camp.

"You erred in sending him against such a bulwark," Nezahualpilli told the Revered Speaker that night after having learned of Motecuhzoma's capture.

"I thought he could catch the enemy off guard with a heated pursuit," Ahuitzotl replied sullenly. "I never imagined that he would allow himself to be lured into the ravine."

"Then his own impetuous action led him to it." concluded Nezahualpilli.

"What a prize for Cocijoeza. His Zapotecan gods will be highly rewarded tonight."

"He will recognize him as a high noble by his dress and bearing, and will decide his fate accordingly."

"That is my fear."

"Cocijoeza is too prudent a man to turn Motecuhzoma over to his priests. He understands a royal prince is more valuable to him alive. He will want to use him for bargaining purposes."

"We shall know in the morning, I expect." said Ahuitzotl, encouraged by his colleague's deductions. "If what you say is true, Cocijoeza will send us an emissary to present his case."

"Would you end this campaign if that was his demand?"

Ahuitzotl pondered it momentarily, and then gave his Texcocan ally an emphatic "No!"

Zapotec trumpets rang out early the next morning, alerting the Mexica to resume their battle formations. But after they had taken up their prescribed positions, they saw no enemy facing them; even though the Zapotecs had sounded the call to arms, no army came forth from Giengola to confront its opposition. Ahuitzotl shared his bewilderment with Tlohtzin. "What does it mean?" Tlohtzin asked.

Ahuitzotl, too dumbfounded to answer, surveyed the enemy's rocky bastion extensively but saw no trace of Zapotec units beneath it. Then, from the same opening of the ravine through which the Mexica had pursued the enemy yesterday, a singular figure emerged and walked toward the poised army. When he drew nearer, he was identified by everyone.

"Motecuhzoma?" Ahuitzotl mumbled, utterly perplexed.

"It is him," Tlohtzin affirmed.

The young commander headed straight for Ahuitzotl in his characteristic proud, slow gait, tall and erect, and when he stood directly in front of the Revered Speaker, who appeared still entranced in his befuddlement, he smiled. Ahuitzotl remained stonefaced, not knowing what to make of the situation.

"You don't seem pleased to see me, uncle," Motecuhzoma said.

"Evidently you did not enter the House of the Sun," replied Ahuitzotl. "How is it Cocijoeza released you?"

"To inform you of things you might be interested in."

"I am interested in Cocijoeza's surrender."

"He speaks of other things, Lord."

"Go on."

"First, concerning the emissaries you sent to Tehuantepec, Cocijoeza says he has them under palace confinement, but that they have not otherwise been harmed, except for the indignity they may have suffered."

"Why does he want you to tell me this? Does he think this exonerates him from having violated the standing agreements existing among kingdoms?"

"He leaves that up to you, Lord, but has said he would free them upon your departure from his lands."

"What reason have I to leave here before my work is done?"

"He has also promised to resume trades with our pochteca; he means to do whatever is necessary to end the hostility which has arisen between his people and ours."

"That's not sufficient."

"He says he will be able to hold out longer than we can if you are bent on pursuing your present course. He is correct–I have seen first hand how he is able to do that."

"So tell us," Ahuitzotl demanded.

"You wanted to know how Cocijoeza is able to feed his army. He showed me a pile of human bones and told me that he could stay on his hill forever as he has a plentiful supply of meat."

"What!"

"Yes, Lord! Cocijoeza is keeping his army fed by eating our captured warriors."

Ahuitzotl was stunned; he glanced at Tlohtzin who was equally astonished. While one thing to eat human flesh as a means of communion with the gods and in connection with ritual practices, to eat it as a steady meal, unrelated to any religious signification, was a shocking novelty, very much out of the ordinary–even unthinkable.

"How much of this-this meat does he have on hand?" asked Ahuitzotl, his face still ashen in his paralysis.

"He has over three thousand of our warriors captive; a dozen or so are devoured each day."

"We must call for a council," Ahuitzotl announced to Tlohtzin. "Inform the commanders."

Shortly thereafter, the chieftains were gathered about the command post and Ahuitzotl related to them what Motecuhzoma had reported. Murmers arose from these battle-hardened veterans when the inglorious fate of their comrades was revealed to them. For a captive to be offered as food to the gods was the greatest honor, but to serve as food for the living without proper sacrifice was criminal–an outrage against all accepted standards. They mumbled over its indignity until Ahuitzotl put a stop to it.

"I did not call this meeting to discuss the fate of our comrades," he declared, "but to decide on what action we ought to take now. Cocijoeza has promised to restore our trades, which stood as our primary cause for this operation, and to release our emissaries if we leave. So it can be said that, even though we did not defeat him, we attained our objectives to some degree; I see no disgrace in our returning to Anahuac under that circumstance."

His statement provoked considerable grumbling among them, making it clear the decision was not popular.

"And our brothers taken by the Zapotecs?" Chimalpopoca asked. "Will they not be avenged by us?"

"In being taken captive, they adhere to a destiny ordained by the gods," Ahuitzotl said. "Their fate has been predetermined."

"But you said that the Zapotecs do not sacrifice them, Lord. If so, then their deaths do nothing to enhance the blessings of the gods on anyone-it is but cruel murder. Murder demands punishment."

"We can do nothing for them. The gods had some purpose in allowing for their captivity. Perhaps Cocijoeza will release them once we've departed, or properly sacrifice them, although he is under no obligation to do so. That's not our immediate problem. Our food supplies are expended. We do not have enough rations on hand for the march back, and obviously can't stay here any longer, unless you want to start eating the Zapotecs we've captured."

The shocked expressions in their faces made it evident this idea was also highly disfavored.

"In that case, we are in trouble, Lord," Tlohtzin said. "Tototepec is a week's march from here and we already know the local villagers do not have the provisions we need."

"There's one place that does—Tehuantepec."

"Perhaps you should explain yourself, Lord," requested Nezahualpilli. "Won't this cause Cocijoeza to refute his stated terms? Why would he permit us to plunder his city?"

"You have pinpointed the problem, Nezahualpilli. We have no choice if we are to provision our forces-this is where you all must do your part. There can be no sacking of the city! You will prohibit any killing or looting, or destruction of property. We shall send word to Cocijoeza on what we propose to do; he will understand why we must do this and permit it if we show respect for his people and city. He cannot stop us, emplaced in Giengola as he is, and for him to interfere will place his army in jeopardy. In this respect we hold a certain leverage over him and can offer conditions of mutual benefit. I see no other way for us. If any of you have a better plan, let him speak of it. I am prepared to listen."

A number of chieftains muttered among themselves as they gave the matter their sober consideration, but when the discussions finally ended, nobody could come up with an acceptable alternative. Few problems were as critical as that of supplying armies in the field.

"Then it's decided," Ahuitzotl said after hearing no counter proposal. "We shall move on Tehuantepec."

At dawn, Ahuitzotl sent envoys to Cocijoeza to explain what he meant to do in Tehuantepec. Half of his force remained at the encampment to engage in battle if the Zapotec monarch opposed this plan while the Revered Speaker took the rest to the enemy capital in order to obtain his essentials there.

In spite of Ahuitzotl's stern admonishment about looting, some misconduct nevertheless took place when the Mexica entered Tehuantepec. To a degree, the inhabitants contributed to these infractions by offering resistance, mainly by the palace guard unit which Cocijoeza had left behind when he moved his army to Giengola. But mostly, this was due to an increasing resentment felt by the warriors that limitations were imposed on what they regarded as their right. Many maintained that the Revered Speaker, who promised them spoils, was now backing away from his word. When Ahuitzotl was informed that some of the soldiers were breaking into houses and harassing their occupants, he exploded in rage and called forth his chief commanders to berate them for their failure to enforce his instructions.

"I want all sacking stopped!" he emphatically warned them. "Make sure that your warriors comply."

"They believe you promised them booty, Lord, and question our orders forcing a contrary condition on them," a chieftain said.

"They question your orders?"

"They threaten that they will never again march so far if they are not allowed to share in the fruits of victory."

"Are you saying we face a mutiny?"

"No mutiny, Lord, but much resentment."

"They must recognize that there are cases when it is more advantageous for us to treat a local population with some measure of clemency and respect. However, I did promise them booty and their complaints are valid. Inform them that whatever concessions and prizes we obtain from here will be distributed among all of them: that I guarantee them."

The ploy worked and their pillaging was quickly ended, and in response, the lords who remained in Tehuantepec showed their gratitude by offering up an ample quantity of gifts to Ahuitzotl. True to his word, he divided these among his soldiers, keeping nothing back from them. He thus courted the favors of his army as well as won over the appreciation of the city's residents who had heard of his treatment of several Mixtec cities and feared the worst when they first saw the Mexica coming.

Ahuitzotl directed the granaries and storage houses reduced of their produce in order to secure what provisions his armies required for their return journey to Anahuac. When all the litters were filled and each warrior carried his portion of rations, he returned to Giengola, taking the emissaries who were found safe in the palace with him. The entire operation lasted a week. Back in Giengola, Ahuitzotl learned that Cocijoeza made no opposing movements while he had been at Tehuantepec, and he interpreted this as a tacit approval of his plan on the part of his adversary.

"He could have made things extremely hot for you," Ahuitzotl informed Tlohtzin who had commanded the units left to maintain a watch on the Zapotecs. "He must have outnumbered you here at least two to one. We are justified in believing this an agreement to what we proposed."

"He has not released any captives, Lord."

"Nor will he, I suspect. Their fate is already determined, as that of the Zapotec prisoners in our possession-they shall be sent to the gods."

Not inclined to remain a day longer in the vicinity of Giengola, which now only served to remind Ahuitzotl of his ultimate failure in achieving his actual objectives, he accordingly set his departure time for two days later and, after the provisions had been equitably alloted, the first of the armies set out on its long trek home. With due haste, having set his goals in new directions, Ahuitzotl led his divisions ahead and in this inglorious fashion came to a close the most far-reaching of Mexica campaigns.

XXI

News that the allied armies were on their way back to Anahuac reached Tenochtitlan through the messengers Ahuitzotl sent at periodic intervals and were received by Cihuacoatl with significant delight. As Vice-Ruler, he had smoothly guided the city's administrative and religious functions, with all the requisites these duties imposed, but he wearied of them and, in particular, he longed for a master to report to. By training and inclination, he was servant loyal and obedient, and found his greatest satisfaction in a role as advisor, counseling others, whom he felt were better suited and abler than himself, to determine the appropriate actions and policy decisions. A different kind of capability was required in directing men, skills the minister believed he did not possess, and he discovered that having ruled over the city for the lengthy time that the Revered Speaker's current expedition entailed, had strained him considerably more than he was used to, leading him to suffer frequent bouts of indigestion which he was peculiarly vulnerable to. While true that the city was almost entirely depleted of its manhood, the bulk of which had been committed to the campaign, and this left only a small minority to work on a few special projects under constructions in addition to the priesthood that performed the sacred rituals, this in itself did not ease the minister's burden. He frequently was at odds with them over their assignments, a result he attributed to his lack of engaging personality and diplomatic finesse. Nobody in Tenochtitlan was more eager to see the return of Ahuitzotl than Cihuacoatl.

At some point after having received another messenger, Cihuacoatl decided that he should perhaps relate the good news to the empress Tlalalca so that he might not be caught in a situation where a remission of courtly events escaped his attention leading to his subsequent mortification, as had been the case following the coastal operation. He concluded that a visit to the palace inner courtyard, where Tlalalca was known to spend much of her leisure time, was in order and proceeded to go there. Upon arriving, he was greeted by a younger lady whom he had seen from time to time about the premises but never actually had met.

"I am your Chief Minister," Cihuacoatl introduced himself. "And who might you be, my dear?"

"I am Pelaxilla," she replied.

"Pelaxilla!" exclaimed Cihuacoatl. So at last he stood face-to-face with the notorious mistress, the seductive temptress who was most responsible for his master's private turmoils, who so enflamed his passions that he neglected state obligations over her, the tormentor of his personal life. Certainly she had appealing features, and the minister could understand how men could be led astray by her charms, but, overall, his impression of her was in the negative, regarding her as a manipulative concubine disruptive to the Revered Speaker's well-being.

Pelaxilla, for her part, while initially taken aback by the emphatic way in which Cihuacoal had stated her name, had only a vague recollection of the minister, remembering him mainly for his leering over the palace women and her detraction of him for this to Nenetzin. But that was years ago, and she had never actually encountered him directly or spoken to him before.

They gazed at each other in a momentary pause, both seemingly surprised over having so suddenly met, yet sensing that a familiarity had long existed between them.

"I have news for the empress," Cihuacoatl then said. "May I see her?"

"If the minister will follow me," replied Pelaxilla. "She is in the garden."

Pelaxilla led the minister to the slab near the garden's entrance where Tlalalca was sitting holding her son while Xoyo was reciting poetic verses to her in a seemingly idyllic setting.

"My lady," Pelaxilla said when coming upon the scene. "Our Lord Minister is here to see you."

Tlalalca turned about to greet Cihuacoatl with a wide beaming smile that warmed his heart. He held a deep affection for the empress, believing that they shared a mutual bond in their long affiliation with each other, especially in the aftermath of Tizoc's death when she was most vulnerable and he saw to her needs and comfort. His own execution in that matter he no longer cared to think about.

"Xoyo, take Cuauhtemoc to his chamber," Tlalaca directed her servant as she handed the baby to her and then addressed Cihuacoatl. "Lord Minister. You do not come here often. Do you bring us news of Lord Ahuitzotl?"

"I do, my Lady," said Cihuacoatl, seating himself on an opposite bench.

Tlalalca and Pelaxilla looked toward each other; they sensed a momentary tenseness, both fearing that their former rivalry might again reassert itself now that Ahuitztotl would be back in their lives, but the apprehensiveness was short-lived as their glances turned into mutual affectionate glows. Bolstered by the silent reassurance, Pelaxilla was about to make her departure conforming to the minister's request in meeting with but the empress.

"Stay with me, Pelaxilla," Tlalalca requested. "News of Lord Ahuitzotl will be of interest to both of us."

For Pelaxilla, this was best expression of their friendship that could have possibly been given; she seated herself next to the empress happy that she should be included in matters of official importance previously never confided in her.

"I trust the news is favorable," continued Tlalalca as she again turned to the minister.

"It is, my Lady," Cihuacoatl said, viewing Tlalalca's overture towards Pelaxilla with cynical skeptism, but choosing to go on. "The latest messenger was sent from the vicinity of Cholula. Lord Ahuitzotl is on his way back and should be arriving here within a week. He has concluded his operation—all victories for us. The declared objectives of his mission have been accomplished. I am at present proceeding on the arrangements to welcome his return."

Again Tlalalca and Pelaxilla exchanged glances, but this time their eyes reinforced an eagerness to have their lord return to them.

"My real reason for coming here," Cihuacoatl went on, "was to learn if any important changes have taken place within this palace that I should know about. You will recall my embarrassment after his last campaign when I failed to tell him about your pregnancy."

While he spoke, he continually looked over Pelaxilla, as he grabbled in his mind how it was possible for this rather diminutive woman to acquire such an ascendancy over his master. He was intrigued by what means she managed to accomplish her designs, for that is how he interpreted it, unable to apprehend neither its infancy nor duration.

"I was told about the indignity you underwent," Tlalalca laughed as she said this.

"So you understand. It's not that I mean to pry."

"There's no pregnancy in the offering this time, Lord Minister. Our master's frequent campaigning obviously preclude this from happening."

"There is nothing else worthwhile commenting on?" Cihuacoatl inquired. "You know, in case he asks me."

Tlalalca turned to Pelaxilla as if seeking a confirmation about whether their blossoming friendship merited the minister's attention; their resolved jealousies seemed a natural enough progression they had undergone that it did not appear to warrant any special explanation. Pelaxilla's look indicated to the empress that she shared this conclusion

"Only if he asks you," Tlalalca then went on, "You may inform him that Pelaxilla and I will no longer compete for his affection. We have become close friends since the time he left Tenochtitlan and no longer desire that anything infringe upon this." She then gazed at Pelaxilla who smiled approvingly over the response.

Cihuacoatl did not entirely believe it, despite the amiability liberally demonstrated by the two women, so contradictory was its revelation to all his previous assessments of their situation. Yet it was something, and if an aura of triviality surrounded it, at least it furnished him with a change from what had been. And indeed, as this was a favorable development, the Revered Speaker may actually find such a disclosure to his liking. His visit here had reaped a suitable reward for him, so when the minister rose to make his departure he was amply satisfied over his exertions. "I shall leave you two to your amity," he said. "Who among us would not prefer a more harmonious relationship within his own house?"

With that, he exited the garden, leaving Tlalalca and Pelaxilla to gaze after him.

"I do not like him," Pelaxilla was moved to say after the minister had gone. "He ogles at me with his lecherous eyes and makes me feel as though I were a whore."

"You misread him, dear," said Tlalalca. "Do not let it trouble you."

"But it does, my Lady. It's as though I stood naked in front of him. I swear he can see through my clothes."

"Really, Pelaxilla," Tlalalca said amid her chuckling. "You do have a vivid imagination. I had no idea you were so sensitive about this. Besides, even he were to see you all stretched out, lying deliciously naked underneath him, it's unlikely he could do anything about it."

A burst of laughter sprang from Pelaxila, and then both of them broke into continuous hearty giggles until Tlalalca, overcome with contriteness over having unmindfully maligned Cihuacoatl, whom she actually held in high regard, felt compelled to make amends. "You should be more kindly disposed towards our Lord Minister," she told Pelaxilla. "True, his demeanor is generally cold and calculating, but he is a man of influence, loyal and dedicated to his duties. It is wise to have him on your side."

"I know this, my Lady," Pelaxilla said, still drawn to snickering as Tlalalca's earlier comment lingered in her mind. "To be honest, I don't think he is overly fond of me either—we appear to have that much in common."

"I sensed the same thing, and am mystified why that should be so. I am guessing here, but perhaps Lord Ahuitzotl has allowed his personal frustrations over our demands on him to affect his official duties. Our Lord Minister, ever preoccupied with the requisites of office, apparently holds you accountable for this. I do hope I am wrong."

Until this moment, Pelaxilla had never considered how her relationship with Ahuitzotl, which she knew frequently left him storming from her presence in extreme agitation, might have in actuality influenced his performance of duties in undesireable ways. Perhaps she had been excessively demanding in her cravings for his affection, a circumstance that she now viewed as very self-centered. She blushed in her recognition that Cihuacoalt may be justified in viewing her as detrimental to Ahuitzotl's effectiveness as a monarch.

Tlalalca seemed to be aware of the notions that Pelaxilla entertained; she was deeply touched by her exhibited embarrassment, finding a poignancy in its demonstrated self-realization, and this gave her temporary pause before determining she should give expression to her thoughts. "I think neither of us wishes a return to our former wretched condition," she told Pelaxilla. "I will not allow myself to again be dominated by emotions that leave me in a perpetual state of anxiety. I should like to believe that we both have transcended that sort of insidious behavior."

Pelaxilla was not as secure in her strength of convictions as Tlalalca seemed to be. Now that Ahuitzotl was about to enter their lives again she momentarily delved on whether their friendship was held up by fragile threads or would endure. She truly adored Tlalalca, and a strong bond had developed between them, an affiliation previously missing during Ahuitzotl's presence; she convinced herself that this major difference would supercede any future alienation. She nodded her agreement to Tlalalca's assessment.

"Can you believe it?" Pelaxilla then said. "Lord Ahuitzotl is almost here. I have missed him so!"

"I'm sure he feels the same about you," replied Tlalalca. "Quite natural for lovers."

"When he comes to my chamber upon his return, I will make him forget the rigors of his long journey."

Tlalalca thought about this for a moment, a sudden reservation having possessed her, and she hesitated over how she should proceed on the matter. "What will you do," she asked, "if he does not come to your chamber first?"

Pelaxilla paused, but then readily discounted its possibility. "He will most assuredly come to me," she answered. "He always has."

"This time I'm not so sure. It's not that he would not want to be with you, my dear, but he may place a greater priority on seeing someone else."

"If he sees you, my Lady," Pelaxilla replied, trying not to let that prospect alarm her, "I shall try to be understanding. As you, I'm resolved never to let my previous fears haunt me again."

"Not me, Pelaxilla, but his son, Cuauhtemoc."

Pelaxilla had not counted on the likelihood of that happening, having in fact forgotten about his son altogether, yet she could not deny that Ahuitzotl might well be motivated toward that purpose. "I didn't think about that," she said, and then added in downcast resignation, "This means he would come to your quarters first to learn how Cuauhtemoc is doing."

"Yes, and, once there, may feel obliged to just stay. Oh, Pelaxilla," Tlalalca spoke out, her voice trembling, "You have become my dearest friend, and I want the best for you. Should this happen-I pray it will not-I shall encourage him to come to you."

Pelaxilla thought about this, concluding that she should not place that kind of inposition on Tlalalca. Not only did it seem exceedingly selfish of her, but it also undermined the deep affection she had acquired for her Lady, a friendship she also highly valued and was not about to place at risk, not over an issue as inconsequential as this. At long last, she came to realize that she was happier residing in a harmonious relationship with Tlalalca than with whatever sensual gratification she might derive from Ahuitzotl.

"No, my Lady," Pelaxilla replied. "If he decides to stay with you, do not distract him from his intentions. I shall have ample time with him in subsequent days."

Tlalalca gave Pelaxilla an endearing glance, appreciating the essence of the considerable leap ahead her decision represented. "Promise me, Pelaxilla," she said, "that you will not allow yourself to be hurt if this occurs. My love for you will lead me to grief otherwise."

"Do not worry about me," Pelaxilla replied without hesitation, a broad smile brightening her face. "Nothing more can displace the affection I now have for you. I truly cherish it."

Tlalalca was deeply moved by this affirmation, acknowledging her approval with a small bow of her head. No longer the self-involved, solicitious, or impulsive woman she had been, Pelaxilla had acquired a degree of sophistication in the recent months she spent in frequent companionship with the empress which bespoke of real understanding, gaining an insight into the things that really mattered, and being able to differentiate these from the inimical actions that she felt had characterized her past. In her introspection, which occupied more and more of her time, she often found herself ashamed over her earlier conduct, especially the envy and jealousy she held for Tlalalca, filling her with guilt and humiliation, to the point of outright embarrassment. Through getting to know her Lady on a personal level, with the sharing of feelings and attitudes, of hopes and fears, and its ensuing emotional attachment, she blossomed in her regard and admiration for Tlalalca, even caring about her happiness. Pelaxilla need not have worried about whether their friendship would endure. The bonds that had been forged between them were strong; both deeply concerned themselves about each other's welfare. Tlalalca knew all this, and she was pleased.

XXII

aking into account Tenochtitlan's depleted manhood, a remarkably stellar acclamation greeted Ahuitzotl upon his entry into Tenochtitlan. The applause rendered him was ear-shattering; reeds and flowers were strewn abundantly over the avenues on which the warriors marched; braziers were lit along the entire route; trumpets resounded; the total population, almost all women and old men, turned out to cheer the mightiest conqueror it had ever known. Drinks of cocoa were offered to the soldiers and multitude of captives the Revered Speaker had brought back with him-enough to meet the ceremonial demands of many seasons. Cihuacoatl, always pleased when greatness befell upon the realm, could scarcely contain his immense joy when he met his sovereign after he had relinguished the dismissal of the army to subordinates following the reception orations. "What glory you have brought us!" he beamed. "Our standing in Anahuac, indeed the world, has never been higher. We are looked upon in awe."

"There were setbacks," Ahuitzotl said as he gave his minister a dubious glance, "but I won't mar this occasion with these. As you undoubtedly saw, our losses were considerable. I shall call you in the morning to discuss it-do not dwell on the dispersions I have cast on this venture until you learn its details."

An urge to see his son superseded Ahuitzotl's usual cravings for his mistress. He instead hurried to Tlalalca's chamber where he found her in the usual accompaniment of Xoyo; for once, he did not object to the old woman's presence. The empress beamed with excitement when she saw him enter.

"Where is Cuauhtemoc?" he asked.

"In his bed asleep," answered Tlalalca cheerfully. "He gives his father a noteworthy reception."

Tlalalca thereupon led him to an adjoining chamber where the baby was soundly dozing upon layers of small mats. He was lying on his stomach with his head turned just enough to one side to permit Ahuitzotl a glimpse of his face.

"He's a year and two months now," Tlalalca said. "He will not know you."

Ahuitzotl's eyes sparkled on seeing his son.

"He has your facial features," Tlalalca glowed. "Your nose and sparkling eyes; a handsome prince will grace your new palace."

"Ah yes, the new palace. When will we be able to move in?"

"The head builder says in eight months."

"Ah, Cihuacoatl has done his duty and kept on them," Ahuitzotl replied, then turned his attention back to his son, "You say he resembles me? I could not tell when I left."

"Very much so. Everyone who has seen him has said as much."

Ahuitzotl smiled, feeling immense pride in her observation. Then his eyes focused on the empress, and when he saw her enraptured in warmth as she viewed her son, she seemed more alluringly attractive to him than he had ever previously thought. He tried to distract his desires for her by thinking of Pelaxilla, but his mind brought him back to Tlalalca. To his own amazement, his greatest longing at this time was to spend it alone with his wife.

"Come," he said to her, "and join me in my bath. I want to enjoy your company."

Tlalalca's heartbeat accelerated. He had never asked for her when he returned from his expeditions; always it had been for Pelaxilla. "Remain here to watch our son," she directed Xoyo. "I will be in my lord's quarters."

Ahuitzotl's attendants had dutifully prepared his bathing arrangements, filling the cistern with warm water and setting aside cakes of soap and towels. This was done out of habit when news of their master's arrival reached them, and Ahuitzotl appreciated seeing his private chamber neatly set up and vacated when he and Tlalalca walked in. No sooner had they entered when Ahuitzotl, in his thoroughly aroused state, ripped the garments from his stunned wife and did not stop until she stood completely naked before him.

"Was that necessary?" she quipped.

"You ask this of a man who has abstained from sensual pleasures for months?" It was."

"Subtlety has never been one of your strong points. If you had simply asked me to undress, I would have surely done so."

"The drama is heightened by using a blunt approach. Excuse my impatience-it's been so long since I was last in the presence of a ravishing beauty."

"Ravishing beauty? This campaign must have been harder on you than I dared believe."

"Yes, and now I mean to make up for all that suffering," Ahuitzotl grinned.

"Then who am I to deny you that pleasure?"

He tore off his own clothing and lifted her up to him; together they stepped into the cistern where they took turns scrubbing lather over each other and then rinsing themselves, assuring their careless hands made the appropriate contacts. This merriment was resumed after they had finished bathing and wiped their bodies dry with towels. Next, Ahuitzotl carried Tlalalca to the adjacent bedroom where their lovemaking assumed more serious aspects, and when it was all over, he relaxed in what he considered his most blissful state-with a desireable woman nestled up to him as he lay comfortably on the mats.

"There's nothing quite like it," he sighed, "and you're one of the best a man can have."

"Are you certain your eyesight is not impaired? It is I, Tlalalca, you are with–not Pelaxilla."

"I shall be with her tomorrow night, but no, I wanted your companionship today."

"She expects you to be with her on the night of your return from your ventures."

"She must not take me for granted. I do as I please."

"I think you will find her a changed woman."

"Oh? How so?"

"She and I have come to an understanding after you had gone. You'll see she is no longer jealous of me and will not compete for your attention as she used to. We have, in fact, become very good friends.

To Tlalalca's puzzlement, he did not seem particularly enthusiastic over what she just told him; she had considered an opposite reaction. Typically, she miscalculated his reactions again, and she ought to have known by now that Ahuitzotl's responses rarely conformed to her expectations. "You don't seem that happy about it," she said. "I thought this would be more appreciated."

"If what you say is true, then she would not be dismayed at my being with you, would she?"

"Not anymore," she replied.

He lay back somewhat perturbed by his thoughts, not as content about the situation as he should have been. In many ways, Pelaxilla's anxieties over Tlalalca's encroachments with him stood out as a constant affirmation of the intense love she bore for him, something he savored even if it did cause him many troublesome moments. With this striving for his assurances absent, he wondered by what means he would now be able to tell. His obsessive reflection caused him to undergo a restless night and, while Tlalalca slept in peaceful comfort snuggled beside the warmth of his body, he spent most of the time awake. Such is the power of inurement.

Early in the morning, they were awakened from their slumber by the crying Cuauhtemoc whom Xoyo had carried to their chamber. Tlalalca hurriedly arose from the bed and took the child from her servant and bade her to wait outside until she joined her.

"My little one," she said as she swooped him playfully up and down in her arms, "What distresses you so?"

"He has the voice of a jaguar," Ahuitzotl boasted. "See how lordly he roars."

Tlalalca brought the baby to him and handed it over as she said, "Here, hold your son."

Ahuitzotl's face reddened. He had never held a baby in his arms and felt unsure if his powerful grip would not crush it–this was not like holding a maquauhuitl. The baby's crying ceased when the monarch's strong arms took it from Tlalalca as it seemed overcome with a curiosity that surmounted whatever discomfort led to its earlier wailing. Ahuitzotl at first felt quite uneasy about carrying the baby, but after he realized it was not as fragile as he had feared, he lifted it high over his head and avidly proclaimed his joy.

"What a noble son I have!" he exclaimed in a wide smile.

The baby gazed at him with rounded black eyes that sparkled like stars, but then, as if suddenly frightened, burst out crying again. Tlalalca came over to take him from his perplexed father.

"He's hungry," she said, "I shall have to feed him."

"That's all it is?"

"Of course," she answered as she exposed her right breast to the infant whose small mouth found the nipple and attached on to it. "See? He's too busy now to think of shedding tears."

Ahuitzotl watched in wonderment for a length of time until he satisfied his inquisitiveness over such delicacies. "I shall leave you to your task," he said. "I must see to today's business."

"And tonight?"

"I shall be with Pelaxilla."

"That is good. She so misses you."

He rendered her an askance look; things had indeed changed between them, he thought. Then he left.

Ahuitzotl spent most of the day with his minister discussing items of importance and significant events which had elapsed in Anahuac during his long absence. For once, he was told that the frontiers remained calm; he had come to expect the usual troubles that seemed to perpetually manifest themselves whenever he was engaged in any extended operation.

"As long as you rule in Anahuac, no one will dare rise against us," Cihuacoatl informed his master with delight. "They fear you-your method of putting down insurrections has been effective."

"Not entirely."

"Surely you are wrong, Lord. Where have they failed you?"

"I have failed on my last expedition."

"How can that be? All the cities you have taken-more than any previous Revered Speaker-and you have subjugated the Mixtecs and the Zapotecs, both powerful foes. Who else can speak of such accomplishments?"

"You don't understand. You were not there. We did not defeat Cocijoeza, but rather ended the hostilities with a truce. A truce-not a surrender. His army remains intact; his city is under his control-we did not subjugate the Zapotecs."

"But, as I've heard it, the lords of Tehuantepec rewarded you handsomely for sparing their city and agreed to pay us tributes."

"A token gesture-to keep us from infringing on their autonomy. They could terminate it at any time should Cocijoeza be of mind to. We exercise no authority over them."

"Yet the trades are resumed, and our emissaries were safely returned to us. Our punishment has been meted out. Agreed, this may not be the same as a conquest, but our influence has been felt in the region and they will not cross us again. That is not a failure."

Ahuitzotl did not answer immediately but rather stared blankly at the floor as if in a trance. When he presently spoke again, he breathed heavily as he snorted out his vehemence.

"I will have no foreign ruler boasting of how he held his own against me. As things stand now, Cocijoeza is able to do just that. By the gods! You do not know how that galls me!"

A revulsion gripped Cihuacoatl as the true nature of the problem revealed itself. The Revered Speaker's vanity which was at issue here; the affair was completely personal, and demanded rectification. It mattered not that state objectives had been achieved, discords settled, and a favorable trading compact restored–these were trivial to the need for raw vengeance. The vindiction of a private injury supplanted the relevance of a kingdom.

"What will you do?" the minister asked with some disdain.

Ahuitzotl continued to look entranced, then muttered slowly, "I don't know yet, but one thing is certain..." He paused.

"Yes, Lord?"

"My affair with Cocijoeza is not ended-not by any means. In truth, it is only beginning, for I shall not rest until the day he begs on his knees for my mercy."

"I see." said Cihuacoatl with a conclusionary emphasis, still unable to suppress his distaste over his master's seeming pettiness.

They expended their afternoon inspecting the new palace which was in its finishing stages of contruction. Somewhat larger than the present residence, its unique feature was that a section of it straddled the canal bordering the central plaza's northern edge, held in place by numerous stone and wooden posts, an innovation in architecture suggested by Ahuitzotl of which he felt significant pride. The monarch's own second tier private chamber spanned the channel, and he spoke of the novelty of arising at dawn to a view of Tonatiuh's rays reflecting off the waters. Its great halls, for dining and receptions, stood at ground level on the side facing the square, while the quarters of the household servants were located on the ground floor anchored north of the canal. The second level was devoted in its entirety to the royal residence, with a narrow open corridor connecting the servant quarters to the main court. The spacious garden behind the present palace abutted on the lateral edge of the new one, increasing its total area by nearly half its size.

"Magnificent!" Ahuitzotl proclaimed. "A structure to match my worthy deeds. I shall enjoy residing within these walls."

"You're not worried about the span's width over the canal?"

"Should I be?"

"Lord, I'm no engineer, but to my eye, there's a precarious look to it. There was great difficulty in its construction; a number of laborers perished working on the span-they fell into the canal and were struck by stones that tumbled in after them."

"I didn't know this, but no matter; the span is completed, its strength is reinforced by the weight distribution of the masonry resting above it. So the engineers have told me."

"I assume they know of what they speak."

"They are well educated in their discipline, but that's not to say they are responsive to new ideas. I had my problems in convincing them of how I wanted this palace built."

"Then the design is yours?"

"I thought you knew. Yes, indeed it is, and I must say it's as grand as I envisioned it."

Cihuacoatl gave his lord a skeptical glance. He did not share the same enthusiasm over this unconventionally built structure but detected Ahuitzotl's obvious delight in it and was not about to cast dispersions on it. Having thus engaged the day on their inspection, they returned to the present royal palace where the monarch dismissed his minister for the evening, satisfied that he had obtained all the current information available.

Later that night, after he had dined with his family, Ahuitzotl went to his private quarters and directed one of his valets to fetch Pelaxilla. Not long thereafter she entered and stood facing him, and when he saw her, he was captivated by her singular loveliness. Each time he saw her, she seemed more beautiful than the time before, and he knew why he so desired her. He could feel his pulsating heart in his throat.

"I missed you last night," she said, her eyes gleaming.

"I wanted to see my son, and once in the presence of Tlalalca, felt it proper to stay with her."

"Tlalalca told me earlier today. She believed all along that your first inclination upon returning here would be to see Cuauhtemoc. You were right to do so-I understand."

"You're not angry then, or dismayed?"

"No. I've learned many things while you were away."

"About the empress?"

"She is so goodhearted, and I was horribly wrong in my unfeeling attitude towards her. I'm very much ashamed of myself whenever I think of how awfully I behaved."

"This sentiment is not like you."

"I never really knew her before. Perhaps because we have now become good friends and I learned about her own difficulties and needs. I've come to truly admire her, mostly for the dignified manner in which she has maintained herself in spite of being deeply hurt-by me as well as you. She never displayed any malice for me or spoke ill of me even though knowing it's me you love. That's not easy for a woman."

"She was aware of that from the beginning; she was not opposed to our arrangment."

"Yes, but it has been very painful for her."

"Why?"

"Because..." Pelaxilla paused; she could not believe how he could be so callous and fail to see the signs which bespoke of Tlalalca's tenderness for him. "Because she is also much in love with you, yet knows you will never in your heart belong to her."

"I think you are mistaken. Tlalalca does not love me."

"How do you know?"

Ahuitzotl drew a blank as he sought to answer her; he had ignored all her significations with admitted insensitivity and was not at all certain. "She's never said this to me," he presently said.

"You cannot see it in her eyes?"

"I haven't given it much thought," he lied, the crooked smile coming to him speaking of more than a mere passing delight in the notion. "At any rate, I didn't have you come here to speak about Tlalalca. Let's enjoy our company without distractions." And with that, he led her to his bedchamber where he next drowned himself in the ecstatic sensual pleasures that only Pelaxilla could give.

XXIII

The months passed, and with each day that elapsed, Ahuitzotl brooded increasingly over his inability to bring the Zapotec ruler, Cocijoeza, under his heel. He became obsessed with the belief that his adversary contemptuously boasted of having accomplished what no living monarch had ever achieved-fought the Revered Speaker to a standstill, which could only be accepted as a victory for him. The more he reflected on it, the greater he magnified his imagined conceptions of Cocijoeza's self-adulation over his triumph, and the more he fumed over it. He existed as a man possessed, his anger mounting and giving him no respite from fantasized indignation-day after day, and into his nights, his mind was preoccupied in this abyss of self-loathing and seething rage.

Soon enough his behavior changed as a result of these obsessions and this affected his relationship with those nearest to him. He could no longer carry a conversation with them without making some reference to his resentment over the Zapotecan. Many found his disposition too bitter and were much discomfited in his presence, and even Pelaxilla thought it unpleasant to be with him lately and felt her communication strained. This did not concern him as it once might have as only one thought dominated him: how to avenge the humiliation inflicted by Cocijoeza.

During this time he relocated his residence into the new palace, but even this was not enough to divert his attention from his sullen brooding, and the view from his bedchamber over the water, once so eagerly awaited, now fell on unimpressed eyes which could only see the imaginary afflictions he would mete on his enemy. In addition, his ceremonial duties suffered as a consequence and he increasingly failed to remember the appropriate intones, their memorization interfering with his obsession, as well as many other procedural requirements, to the irritation of the priests. Cihuacoatl became alarmed over his master's remissions.

"You must do something," he cautioned the monarch, nearly on the verge of an angry outburst. "You cannot continue in this manner without alienating all those who depend on you to properly perform our sacred rites. You will offend even the gods."

Ahuitzotl's hostility patently revealed itself in his blazing eyes when he turned to the minister. "Offend the gods, you say?" he responded, "Indeed you are correct. I offend them because I refrain from waging war against this vile Cocijoeza. For too long I have sat around idly when I should be planning his destruction."

"Then why don't you do so?"

"It's not as easy as that. I must first devise a scheme to keep him from occupying his bastion at Giengola-to face him there again is tantamount to self-defeat. I must learn of the pathways and means by which he supplies his army should he go there."

"Our pochteca operate back in that region. Let them find out for you."

"Cocijoeza distrusts them and would never confide such details to them. They are useless to me in this regard. I must think of another way."

"Do that, Lord. In the meantime, I strongly urge that you put this matter aside and pay proper heed to your official duties. You have poisoned yourself with this ceaseless preoccupation and the ceremonial functions have suffered accordingly."

"Have they?"

"My lord, you failed to appear for the rites to our goddess Tlazolteotl yesterday. Her votaries were not at all impressed. There have been others too; the grumbling grows more prevalent-many openly proclaim you do not have respect for their functions."

Ahuitzotl was genuinely shaken over hearing this, not having realized that his obsession had so impaired him. "Perhaps you're right, Cihuacoatl," he said, "My mind has indeed become poisoned. I shall take your advice and give my duties necessary consideration, although strenuous for me-this Cocijoeza haunts me!"

"And will persist in doing so, Lord, until you have put this matter to rest. Pardon my insolence if I maintain grave doubts about your ability to do as you say-you will not be able to conduct your tasks correctly until you settle your score with Cocijoeza."

"This leaves but one path open for me."

"Yes, Lord. You must launch another campaign, and this time you must destroy him."

Ahuitzotl knew this, but also that he would never succeed in attaining a victory unless he learned of his enemy's defenses and, in particular, of his supply network at Giengola. The problem therefore remained unresolved for him and its persistence continued to gnaw at him.

That evening, after finishing his meal, Ahuitzotl retired to Tlalalca's chamber where he meant to spend the night. As he was about to initiate his usual lovemaking, he was taken aback when she recoiled at his touch. "What's wrong?" he reacted bitterly.

Tlalalca was herself startled at what she perceived as an involuntary response against his advances, never believing this possible, and could not find the words to describe her behavior. She did not answer him.

"You have nothing to say?" Ahuitzotl went on. "Have I suddenly become an unspeakable fiend to you?"

"No, but you have changed as of late," Tlalalca replied.

"Indeed. Cihuacoatl said much of the same thing to me this afternoon. In what way have I changed?"

"There is a frightening countenance about you-you gaze into the distance when I speak to you and often do not hear what I say. Your disposition has been extremely sour and makes those around you feel uncomfortable, but you do not speak of the cause of your affliction, which fills me with apprehensions about myself."

"About yourself?"

"Yes, because I don't know if I'm the cause of your distress."

Ahuitzotl was troubled over Tlalaca's revelation. "It has nothing to do with you," he said.

"No? You mope when in my presence. The inference seems plain enough to me."

One look into her anxiety-ridden eyes and Ahuitzotl understood that he had been wrong in keeping his festering frustrations within himself; he decided to reveal them to her. Accordingly, he gave her a lengthy explanation of the ever increasing dissatisfaction and resentment he felt over his truce with the Zapotecs, of the humiliation this represented for him, and of his inability in resolving this conflict. Tlalalca listened attentively and, in its unfolding, lost much of her fear of him as the situation became comprehensible to her and was, at the same time, relieved that she had not been somehow responsible for his changed character.

"I've told you everything now," Ahuitzotl stated when he was finished with his elucidation, "so you know you have nothing to fear from me. Nothing is directed towards you; all my anger is against Cocijoeza."

"Had you said so earlier, I'ld have been a better companion for you."

"Not until you shrank back in dread a moment ago did it dawn on me what I was doing to everyone. It shocked me. Worse, I'm not sure if I can restrain my hostility for Cocijoeza and fear my relationships may continue to be harmed on account of this."

"You must do as Cihuacoatl has advised and decide this issue once and for all."

"I know that; you do not have to lecture me on it."

"You needn't get angry with me," Tlalalca retorted, her confidence fully restored. "I want to help you."

"You?" he reacted with surprise. "How can you help me?"

"You said that your primary reluctance in undergoing a second expedition against Cocijoeza is the fear that he may again confront you at-what was it, Giengola?"

"Yes."

"You want to learn of his defenses and pathways, and how he sustains his army there, but realize he will never reveal this to your spies. If you cannot obtain this information through ordinary means, you must resort to some kind of deception to get it."

"Nothing seems workable."

"Have you thought of using a woman?"

"What?"

"A woman. Use a woman to get the information you require."

Ahuitzotl's response was clearly in the negative. He deemed it utterly absurd to involve a woman in what was so obviously a warrior's game-the idea was almost insulting. "Do you know what you're saying," he scowled. "You imply that a woman will succeed in an effort requiring my craftiest men. I should have known better than to speak to you about these things."

She simply gazed at him and said nothing, and this hesitancy led him to ponder the notion some more.

"Are you suggesting that Cocijoeza would reveal things to a woman that he would never confide in a man?" Ahuitzotl asked.

"If she is attractive enough to strike his fancy."

"Ridiculous. No ruler discusses his tactical plans with women."

"If he should fall in love with this woman, and she expresses an interest in such affairs, he will tell her everything she wishes to know."

"Fall in love?"

"That will be the prime ingredient."

This had never occurred to him, and now that the idea was introduced, he could see some merit in it and sought to fully explore its potential. "I don't see how it's possible to predict if someone will fall in love with a particular person," he said, "but I admit, were that to happen, your proposal would have distinct possibilities."

"You must send him someone exceedingly attractive so that he cannot help but be enamored with her. Also, if you show appropriate honors to Xochiquetzal, the goddess will accede to your desires and make this happen."

Her proposal no longer seemes as preposterous as he first envisioned it, and the more he dwelled on it, the better he liked it-at the least it offered a concrete approach to his predicament. Until this moment, he had wandered aimlessly among a myriad of suggestions of which each had major flaws and stood little chance of succeeding. But here was something decidedly different and, best of all, entailed a probability of success.

"Could it actually work?" he pondered aloud.

"Men are slaves to women they love, and Xochiquetzal's powers are strong. Yes, I believe it could work."

His eyes glittered, and he smirked. He should have discussed this with Tlalalca earlier and spared himself these weeks of frustration. "I like it," Ahuitzotl beamed. "It has a chance–all will depend on the kind of woman we send to him."

"She will have to be very beautiful and personable. You may have to search the whole of our realm to find her."

Ahuitzotl mused over the proposal at length, deeply immersed in his concentration. His eyes glared intensely into the blank wall ahead of him as though it presented an imprint of his cerebrations. "Ah, for once you are wrong," he finally replied. "We cannot just send any stranger to

Cocijoeza. We must be completely assured of her devotion to us so that she'll be certain to do all we ask of her".

"You mean you'll send him one of the ladies in your court?"

"One who is most beautiful and charming, and whose loyalty, not only to the court, but to me personally, is unquestioned."

"Is there such a lady here?"

"Only one."

Tlalalca was puzzled; she did not know Ahuitzotl had any interest in his other mistresses. "Who is that?" she said, eager in hearing his reply.

"Pelaxilla."

Tlalalca was stunned. She could not believe what she heard; that a man would send away the woman he loved more than anyone else was unimaginable. "Pelaxilla!" she gasped. "You would consider sending Pelaxilla to him?"

"Don't look so startled. It's imperative, if this is to succeed, that I send him someone I can trust implicitly. Who better than Pelaxilla?"

"But-but she loves you so. And you love her," Tlalalca remained dazed in her extreme astonishment. "How could you stand being apart from her?"

"It wouldn't be for long-a year at the most," he answered with confident ease. "Don't you see? Pelaxilla I can trust! It's precisely because she so loves me that I know she will do everything I ask. She is perfect for this."

"It's a perilous journey, and you have no way of knowing how this Cocijoeza will receive or treat her. How can you risk sending your greatest love on such a task?"

"She'll be well treated, I have no fear of that. As for the journey, she will be well protected by my boldest knights and comfortably transported in a litter, with ample menials accompanying her."

Tlalalca thought it incomprehensible that she feared more for Pelaxilla's safety than did Ahuitzotl. "I beg that you not send her," she pleaded in near desperation. "Surely there are others who could please the Zapotecan."

"You beg to have Pelaxilla remain here? I always believed you regarded her a rival and would be gratified to have her absent for awhile."

"You are wrong on that," she corrected him. "I'm very fond of her and do not want her facing possible dangers. Truthfully, I'm profoundly shocked that you should even consider her for this."

"Thank yourself for that; you gave me the idea."

"I gave...!" Tlalalca lashed out angrily at him, "Never that you should send Pelaxilla! You profess to love her? What manner of love is this that makes you want to send her to such a far-off region with no assurances you may ever see her again?"

"Never see her again? You fail to grasp my purpose in sending her to him. She will help me to destroy him and then we will be reunited, and believe me, once she sees his ugliness, she'll be as determined as I am to see that day arrive. You make too much of this; the journey is safe enough-she may even enjoy it."

"I know of no woman who would want to be parted from her lover, even if temporarily. Had I known you considered Pelaxilla for this, I would never have mentioned anything to you."

"Enough of that!" his disposition turned sour again. "I have no choice. This is a grave business where I can leave as little to chance as possible. I must be assured of success."

"She will never permit herself to be sent there."

"Yes she will-because I ask her to. Such is the power of Xochiquetzal, as you often say."

Tlalalca knew that nothing she could add was likely to deter him from his expressed purpose and she was extremely angry at herself for having offered her proposal. Fear of losing her dearest friend now dominated her; she almost wept in her exasperation that she could not dissuade him from its implementation. She loved Pelaxilla, and she was truly afraid for her.

"Please, I beg you," Tlalalca repeated, "Do not send Pelaxilla."

"Stop it!" he rebuffed her. "Your exhortations are useless. I will see this through."

"What hatred you must feel for this Zapotecan," she decried, "that you would risk sending your most beloved mistress to help you destroy him."

"I do. I make no pretensions about it."

"How can hatred take precedence over your love for her?"

Ahuitzotl ignored her question and instead cautioned Tlalalca in a most stern voice. "Do not involve yourself in this affair," he advised, "and say nothing to Pelaxilla on this. I myself will speak to her about it. Do you understand?"

She sadly nodded her consent but could not hide her disdain over the entire matter. Consequently, although she acquiesced to his wishes and sensual demands that night as was obligatory from a wife, her demeanor and actions made it apparent that she received no pleasure from his company. Ahuitzotl realized this but dismissed it from his mind and tormented her by prolonging his erotic activity and insisting all the more on her affections, much to her duress.

Ahuitzotl may have appeared firmly committed to his plan to Tlalalca, but throughout the next day he vaccilated between his determination to destroy Cocijoeza and his fears of being separated from Pelaxilla, and he often felt a compulsion to abandon the notion, believing it would be too painful for him to do without her. But then he checked his reservations as a sign of weakness and was once more possessed by overwhelming urges to wreak his vengeance on the Zapotecan. He reinforced his convictions by repeatedly telling himself that their separation would be of short duration and this worked towards making its proposition tolerable. He was beset in such a fluctuating state when he met Pelaxilla the next evening to inform her of his intentions.

He related the total sequence of events which had elapsed between the Mexica and Zapotecs and, in particular, between himself and Cocijoeza. She listened with interest, at first perplexed why she was being subjected to this narration, and then growing increasingly suspicious over it. When at last he came to the crux of the presentation, she turned pale in her utter shock as his design was revealed to her. She could not hold back her tears of despair and anger.

"No! No! No!" she wept in her tribulation. "You are so cruel! How could you ever think of doing this to me?"

Ahuitzotl was startled by her resistance and believed he had failed in conveying the importance of this to her. "Your reaction is most distressing," he said. "I wanted you to do this for me because you're the only one I can trust in this."

"I always thought you loved me. If you really loved me, you could never have considered such a thing."

"Do you think this is easy for me? All day I have been in torment about the wisdom of this, fearing the prospect of being without you, agonizing over the distance that will divide us, over how you will be received by Cocijoeza. But I know you love me and will do this for me. You will be loyal to me and will not be tempted by Cocijoeza to abandon your purpose. You alone I trust-anyone else I would have serious reservations about."

She was not consoled by this, concentrating only on her fears over being separated from him. "How can I live without you?" she fretted. "I shall be miserable in Cocijoeza's court. He will be sure to notice this."

"I am depending on you to perform your duties in a convincing fashion."

She perceived his determination and knew she would get nowhere with her present approach; she next tried to enflame his jealousy.

"You want this vile Zapotecan touching me? If I am to perform my duties in a convincing fashion, then I presume I'm to satisfy him in bed."

A torrent of hot flashes swept across Ahuitzotl's face and his breathing deepened; he viewed this prospect with utmost repugnance and almost changed his mind at that moment, but then his burning to avenge the humiliation incurred by Cocijoeza resurfaced to again possess him. "Do not speak to me about that," he exorted her. "Do what is necessary but no more, and I beg you, do not tell me of such matters-ever!"

"I see. You want me to be a gift to the Zapotecan but refuse to accept what that entails. I can assure you I will not be wanting in the attentions I will give him. I will definitely give him a convincing performance. So think about that before you decide to send me to him!"

"Stop this, Pelaxilla! I take no pleasure in what I ask of you. It's very painful for me. I entreat that you help me in this."

His pleading came with such sincerity that she was inclined to accede to his wishes. Yet the thought of her separation from him horrified her to such an extend that she was unable to keep her tears from streaming down her cheeks even as she reluctantly consigned herself to her fate. Ahuitzotl was severely jolted by her weeping, and he felt pangs of regret tearing at him over having mentioned his plan to her, yet he remained steadfast in his motivation towards revenge.

"Please say you will do this for me," he entreated her. "I shall be forever grateful to you."

She looked at him through her wet eyes and her pained expression filled Ahuitzotl with shame and remorse; he again was seized with a compulsion to reject the scheme but, as always, the hostility he held for Cocijoeza came to the forefront and heightened his resolve to see this matter concluded. "Think of it as a grand adventure-and of our joyous reunion next year," he tried to comfort her. "We shall both be so happy; our separation will make that moment immeasurably wonderful for us."

She could think of nothing further to keep him from his course, and saw herself in an absolutely hopeless situation, mired in her helplessness, unable to find release from its coercive grip. She glanced into his eyes, detecting the strain this decision was causing him, and her impulse was to relieve his anxiety and give her consent; however, she could not bring herself to make that unwanted concession.

"I'm sorry," she whimpered, "but I cannot submit voluntarily to this. If you mean to go ahead with your wicked scheme, then you must order me to go-I will never consent willingly to being sent away from Tenochtitlan."

"Spare me that, Pelaxilla," he pleaded. "If you love me, say you will do this for me."

"No!" she continued her sobbing. "You now make it appear as though I am the heartless one for opposing your plan. How can you do this to me and still say that you love me?"

"I had hoped you would do me the favor I asked," he said after a lengthy pause. "Evidently I was wrong. Very well, Pelaxilla, if you are not inclined to help me willingly, then, as your Revered Speaker I direct you to carry out the mission I have assigned to you. Will this satisfy you?"

In a peculiar sort of way he had made her seem the villain in this sordid affair and she suffered from guilt feelings over having displayed an aversion towards doing his bidding—so much so that she actually felt obliged to recant her position and make amends. "It sounds so formal," she remarked. "as if we were strangers. Forgive my resisting you, Ahuitzotl. I shall do as you ask."

He gazed squarely into her tear-filled eyes and placed his hands on her shoulders; then a sparkle revealed itself as his frown turned to a faint smile. He drew her against him in his satisfaction while she suppressed her anguish as he held her close to him.

"Ah, Pelaxilla," he sighed, "This means a lot to me. You have ended my depression by speaking these words."

She said nothing and remained quite fear-stricken as she contemplated that the one world she had known for so many years was about to end for her. Despite all his assurances that their departure was but temporary, she only saw it as final. Her intimidation was accentuated when she thought of the horrible deprivation that losing Tlalalca's companionship would cause her; as her only true confidant in things personal, being able to relate deep felt sentiments and share in pleasureable conversations, her association with the empress was now profoundly meaningful to her and she no longer thought she could enjoy life without it. Most of all she dreaded her separation from Ahuitzotl-its mere prospect filled her with abject terror-and she seriously questioned how she was to survive this, the cruelest of fates.

Her initial fears subsided somewhat in the succeeding weeks as Ahuitzotl remained constantly with her, satisfying her with sensual pleasures at night and tutoring her during the day on what she should look for and report to him while in Tehuantepec. He carefully instructed her on all aspects of Zapotec military procedures and of the logistical operations that she was to closely observe. Interestingly enough, the more material he covered, the greater was aroused her curiosity about the man she was to spy on and eventually betray. What sort of person was this Cocijoeza that he should inculcate such a demand for revenge upon the mightiest monarch in the world? Nations trembled at the mere mention of the Revered Speaker being on the move against them, intimated by his reputation and proficiency in war, bowing to his will, but evidently not this Zapotecan. That he was quite unsightly she had been told enough times by Ahuitzotl, but that did not seem to tell the entire story; his ability to match the Mexica host on the battlefield bespoke of an extraordinary accomplishment, remarkable in itself, and suggested that the man had capabilities. Indeed, there was an element of excitement abounding this affair which fascinated her, and she soon discovered, to her own bemusement, that her trepidation was being gradually superseded by an inquisitive eagerness.

In addition, Pelaxilla felt increasingly confident about her separation lasting a short duration as all subjects Ahuitzotl appraised on her reinforced a belief that he meant to come for her before long. Everything taught her was directed towards a conclusion committed to Ahuitzotl's purpose in reclaiming her. This lent a challenging aspect to her assignment which she considered quite stimulating, primarily because she knew it to be but temporary. Secure in this knowledge, she became an avid student in learning all there was to know about reconnaissance work.

She was given as complete a background as was possible on the Zapotecs; their customs, religious practices, dress, arts, music, cuisine, even the idioms of their way in speaking Nahuatl which varied from Anahuac, were taught to her. Ahuitzotl combed through the scores of Zapotec captives in order to gather up those scholared in these disciplines who could provide Pelaxilla the lessons she needed, and in return for these services, he would free them to escort her-they knew nothing of her true mission-along with several Mexica servants, to Tehuantepec as a goodwill gesture to Cocijoeza. Unlike the Eagle knights tasked to furnish her armed guard, these attendants were to remain with Pelaxilla at the Zapotec capital. Ahuitzotl felt the congeniality offered by her servants would prevent Pelaxilla from suffering undue pangs of depression and also help pass the time more agreeably until he came for her. This had its desired effect, greatly alleviating her anxieties over facing an unknown future in a faraway land.

During this time, Pelaxilla also maintained her close association with Tlalalca. At first their meetings were teary-eyed affairs with both women in deep despondency over what fate had decreed for them, which the empress always seemed to take much harder, perhaps because of her involvement in the plan's conception, and Pelaxilla found herself in the odd position of trying to ease Tlalalca's gloominess when it was she who was being sent away. However, as the days passed, and Pelaxilla began to reveal an increasing interest in the role imparted on her, with its corresponding relaxation of her tensions and a firing of her enthusiasm, Tlalalca's also benefited from this, finding that her own unhappiness was similarly being gradually dispelled. With their burdens thus eased, in great measure the result of Pelaxilla's optimistic depiction of the separation as only temporary, their exchanges again became more lighthearted, abounding in sufficient cheerfulness and pleasantry despite of masking an underlying sense of loss both women knew they faced.

After weeks of tutelage and in preparation for the duties entrusted to her, the day at last arrived when Pelaxilla's journey was to begin. Long before this, Ahuitzotl had sent messengers to Cocijoeza's court to relate his gift to the Zapotec monarch so that their friendship might be cemented into an alliance thereby protecting Mexica interests in the southern regions. He went so far as to pass Pelaxilla off as a royal princess connected by blood to the Tepanec clan in order to give special signification to his present. Cocijoeza had given a reply that he was deeply honored by this gesture and meant to do everything in his power to make their symbolic connection a lasting one. All the preliminary measures had thereby been taken to insure a dignified and warm reception for Pelaxilla. This was all done over the persistant objections of Tlalalca who kept up her attempts to sway Ahuitzotl from his design, but her efforts were of no avail.

Admittedly, Ahuitzotl looked to this day with notable mixed emotions, alternating between moods of eagerness that the first phase of his planned destruction of Cocijoeza was at last beginning and acute apprehensions over the risks he was exposing Pelaxilla to and whether he would be able to endure her absence. As he walked alongside her from his palace into the square where the litter bearers and detail of warriors and Zapotecs were waiting, he appeared considerably more nervous than she herself who, by contrast, had been now imbued with an adverturesome spirit over her mission and was brimming with excitement.

"Maintain periodic contact with our pochteca in the area," he counseled her, "with necessary discretion, of course. It's through them that I will send my messages to you and expect to hear from you. If you yourself have no access to them from your court, then send the information through the servants I leave with you."

"I understand. So when will you resume your war with Cocijoeza?"

"I'll let you know of the time; much of it will depend on what I learn from you and..." he paused.

"Yes? And?"

"And how long I can endure your absence."

His was not a good comment to have mentioned at this time, for it brought back to Pelaxilla her deepest dread over their separation; a cold chill shot through her as she was again struck by the stark reality that this was the day she would actually leave him. She glared at him, and he could clearly discern the anguish reflected in her eyes, a visage impacting heavily on him.

"Then perhaps I shall not have a long wait," she replied in a broken voice, her eyes moistening.

"This is very painful for me," he affirmed, feeling a lump in his throat. "I press ahead only because I can see no other way. You do undertand this, don't you?"

"I want to but it isn't easy. My inclination is, even now, to scream out do not do this!"

"When all this is over, and we shall find ourselves together again, we'll delight in recalling these as eventful times in our lives. Look forward to that, as I will, and it should go easier for both of us."

"I'll try," she said as she muffled her sobs.

By now they stood amid the entourage chosen to accompany Pelaxilla on the journey. A canopied litter was lowered for her, as for her handmaidens, who would all be carried by the Zapotecans. Before entering, Pelaxilla reached for Ahuitzotl with one more longing glance that begged for a reprieve from her abhorrent assignment. He touched her shoulders with both his hands, wanting to embrace and kiss her but prevented from doing so by convention. There was no need for him to make his intentions known, for his weak smile told Pelaxilla amply of his anguish and sorrow. He beamed nervously in an awkward attempt to cheer her up.

"Our reunion will be a most happy occasion," he promised her, as well as himself. "Until that joyous time, may the gods protect you."

She abandoned all proper etiquette and rushed for him, clasping her body tightly against him to savor his warmth once more. Then, just as quickly, she released herself from his trembling arms and stepped into the canopied litter. Immediately the bearers lifted it upon their shoulders and waited obediantly for their master to grant his concent that they go. Ahuitzotl, fearing that any further delay would badly shake his resolve and lead him to abort his long planned mission, nodded for them to move out. As they began their march across the plaza, Pelaxilla once again turned her head around and gazed longingly at Ahuitzotl, her tears running like small rivulets down her cheeks to focus on her depression even if failing to detract from her loveliness. Then she faced forward and never again looked back as her entourage slowly diminished into the distance.

Ahuitzotl continued to stand alone in the square long after the ensemble had disappeared. Now that she was gone, the full weight of its meaning struck him—with cruel severity and pitiless regard. A loneliness unlike anything he had ever previously experienced engulfed him, overwhelming all other emotions, and leaving him gripped with a horrid sensation of utmost despondency in its awareness. He had deprived himself of his life's greatest source of happiness. Pelaxilla was gone-and it was unbelievably painful.

"Forgive me, Pelaxilla," he muttered aloud, breaking on the verge of a wailful outburst. "Forgive what this-this hatred has caused me to do."

From an upper window of the palace, Tlalalca, who had also observed the procession leave Tenochtitlan, stood grief-stricken over Pelaxilla's departure. Her sorrow was heartfelt, deep and personal, that comes from a terrible loss. She had, over so many years now, been intrinsically connected with Pelaxilla in her court relationships, so that the mistress was an integral part of her life, in both its emotional highs and lows, exerting an everlasting imprint in her memories. And in the recent months she had developed a deep affection for Pelaxilla, fondly cherishing her presence as a companion whose qualities she admired and felt she needed to brighten up her days. She tightened her grip on the shawl around her neck as she sensed a cold chill enveloping her, leaving her with a pronounced foreboding that she was never to see her adored friend again. In a stoical resignation that was quite typical of her, she lingered in quietness, but there were tears in her eyes as she softly wept in what passed as one of the saddest days in her life.

PART 4

RETRIBUTION

"Recognize, most mighty lord, that you have offended and sinned against the gods and for this cause, the Lord of Creation now permits that this city should be destroyed and depopulated. How will it appear in the eyes of the enemies that surround us, when Tenochtitlan is emptied of its citizens and you and your lords are compelled to flee, as an eternal vengeance upon you and upon them? What will they say, save that what your ancestors did build with so much sweat and labor, you have brought to ruin in forty days?"

—Nazahualpilli of Texcoco *

* Nigel Davies, "The Aztecs', University of Oklahoma Press, 1973, p 195

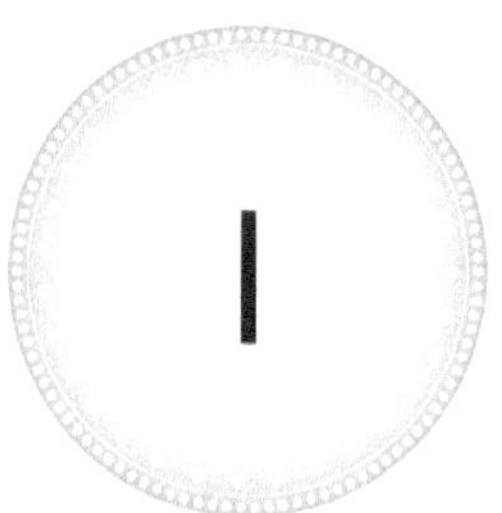

I

Months passed since Pelaxilla had departed from Tenochtitlan. Torn by the separation, Ahuitzotl absorbed himself in his recurring ceremonial duties by presiding over many of the rites he previously often neglected and over the royal game, tlachtli, in order to ease his sense of loss. Tlalalca tried vainly to compensate for Pelaxilla's absence by catering to all his wishes and trying to comfort him as best as she could, and even though he now spent most of his nights with her, his depression did little to make them enjoyable for her and they spoke few words to each other.

If loneliness characterized Ahuitzotl's mood at first, this changed as the weeks elapsed and he as yet received no messages from Pelaxilla. Worried initially, and then becoming increasingly vexed, Ahuitzotl could hardly control his mounting irritation over the situation.

"What could be wrong?" he muttered as he paced the chamber in front of Tlalalca. "Why is she doing this to me?"

"Perhaps Cocijoeza was not pleased with her and has relegated her to a minor place in his court, isolating her from him," replied Tlalalca.

"Impossible! Our pochteca have sighted them in the royal palace and say he is quite taken in by her. They're said to be with each other frequently-she has abundant opportunity to secure the information I seek from him, so why does she hesitate to notify our agents of it?"

"Maybe she's under close surveillance and cannot make contact with them."

"Even if so, you would think by now she could have managed to get some word to us. No, that's not it."

"Then what could it be?"

"She's angry with me for having sent her to Tehuantepec and is punishing me for it by her silence. It's a most cruel revenge, but that must be it."

"If she loves you so, she would never willingly upset you."

"Nor, in that case, would she delay our reunion. I've said that to myself repeatedly to explain this. It makes no sense."

"You said they are often seen in each other's company?"

"Yes. Cocijoeza even sent a messenger to relate his satisfaction with-with the gift I sent him. What do you make of that?"

Tlalalca had her ideas about it, but was horror-struck over the notions she possessed and dared not tell him. He, in turn, became discomfited by her quietness. He must have suspected it himself, she thought, and whatever she related would only affirm what he already sensed.

"Well?" he prodded her.

"There is another possibility," Tlalalca reluctantly said. "You will not like it."

"Nothing you can tell me has not been thought of myself."

"There is a chance, however remote, that she may have grown fond of this Cocijoeza and has no desire to betray him."

Ahuitzotl had indeed thought of this, but not until he heard it stated from Tlalalca did its full potentiality weigh upon him. He was stung; hot flashes enveloped him and his heart palpitated at a frightening pace. "By doing that," he fumed, "she betrays me."

Tlalalca thought that self-evident, but understood his denying this to himself-it was simply too horrible to contemplate. "It's only conjecture," she responded. "We have no way of knowing and ought to refrain from drawing conclusions which may not be valid."

"You're right," he readily acceded. "Pelaxilla would never forsake her love for me for such a despicable individual as this Zapotecan ruler-his ugliness alone would stand as a deterrent to that. No! Never!"

But he was not at all assured of his conjecture, and its mere prospect, its slightest probability, was enough to shake him to the core and he trembled as he stood beside Tlalalca, and there was a look of abject terror in his eyes. He felt his problem compounded by the enormous distance separating him from Pelaxilla; there was no way to speak to her and dissuade her from any curse Xochiquetzal may have inflicted on her. "I should never have sent her to him," he mumbled. "These fears tearing at me are making things intolerable for me."

"You were advised against it," she reminded him. "You have only yourself to blame for this."

"I know that!" he shouted at her, highly incensed. "I do not need you to shove it my face!"

Tlalalca reacted with alarm, shocked at the seeming vehemence emphasized in the inflection of his words. "I'm sorry," she answered. "Admittedly my remark was in poor taste. I know the horror you are experiencing and truly wish I could do something to ease your torment."

"You can-by maintaining your silence!"

With that, he stormed from the chamber and headed for the reception hall where Cihuacoatl was waiting to render him the latest reports on state affairs. He was clearly in a poor frame of mind when he entered; the minister knew he would have to be cautious.

"Any word from Tehuantepec?" Ahuitzotl asked him immediately after spotting him.

"None, Lord."

"Why is there never any word from there?" Ahuitzotl roared at Cihuacoatl, causing him to quiver in fright, but also angering him over what he saw as an unfair treatment.

"Do not vent your hostility towards Cocijoeza out on me!" the minister snapped back, his booming voice making Ahuitzotl's hair stand on end. "What would you have me do? Fabricate messages from Tehuantepec?"

Ahuitzotl frowned as he paced the floor; he did not like apologizing to anyone, even when he knew he was in error, regarding it as demeaning to his title. "Forget it," he declared, calming somewhat. "So there's nothing from Tehuantepec. What else do you have for me?"

"The Acolhuas are fighting a Flower War with Huexotzinco and Tlaxcala. Nezahualpilli himself is leading his warriors."

"What for? We have ample captives on hand from our Mixtec-Zapotecan campaign."

"I believe he has an ulterior motive, Lord."

"Apparently. He knows well enough I disapprove of expending our warriors in these staged battles. They can be better utilized on legitimate conquests. I'm not clear on his motive-he is like his father Nezahualcoyotl in many respects and is not given to having many sacrifices."

"But he allows for some; his father attempted to banish them altogether from his city."

"An absurd thing to do too. He was relying on the rest of us to keep the sun in existence for him. I have no respect for that. Thankfully Nezahualpilli carries some share of the burden. But why now when we have enough captives? What is this ulterior motive you speak of?"

"There are rumors from his court which will not be kindly received by my lord. They concern your niece, Chalchiuhnenetzin."

"Nenetzin?"

"The talk is that she is engaging in-how do I say it?-in extramarital romances, and her activities have come to Nezahualpilli's attention."

"You mean adultery?"

"Yes, Lord."

"Adultery is a crime punishable by death."

"Yes, and it is said that she has conducted these affairs since arriving in Texcoco. The business grows more sordid, Lord. They say, when she tired of her lovers, she had them slain and made statues of their likeness which she placed in her chambers. Nezahualpilli became suspicious of their increasing numbers, but she convinced him that they were her gods."

"Nezahualpilli believed that? And he is renowned for his wisdom?"

"Being enamored with her, he undoubtedly accepted her word against his better judgment. It seems he recognized a much-prized jewel which he had given her being worn by one of his lords and now distrusts her and wishes to catch her in the act-hence this war."

"To make her think he is involved in distant campaign so she feels free to do as is her inclination. Somehow I had a feeling my plans with her would go awry. Her habits were known to us. I was naive to believe Nezahualpilli could change them."

"If you felt that way, why did you send her to him?"

"At the time I thought it necessary to patch up my faltering alliance with Texcoco. Tlalalca and I both were convinced that she would do her part in strengthening our ties with Nezahualpilli; after all, she supposedly loved him. Who can believe a lover to commit adultry? What will he do if he finds her with someone?"

"What any ruler would do, Lord-condemm her to death. It is the law."

This posed a troublesome prospect for Ahuitzotl who knew that such action could generate considerable enmity between the two royal houses, especially if it was consummated without judicious regard for the formalities applying to the ruling elites. "This will not bode well for our alliance," he said.

"It certainly won't help it any, but if Nezahualpilli behaves prudently, the setback should only be temporary."

"Would it be appropriate to caution him on that?"

"Not yet, Lord; what we have discussed is only rumor. Once the facts are substantiated, it will benefit us to keep this affair subdued so as not to offend anyone."

"I will accede to your judgment. Keep me updated on this. It has grave overtones."

"Nezahualpilli will do that himself if he discovers the truth behind what has been rumored, Lord."

Ahuitzotl grimaced; Nezahualpilli could be counted on holding something like this against him if his suspicions proved accurate, for it entailed a deep personal humiliation for the Texcocan. For a monarch to be cheated on by his wife placed his sexual prowess into question, and Nezahualpilli was peculiarly sensitive to that.

"What else do you have?" Ahuitzotl inquired. "I trust it will be more pleasant than what you've said so far."

"There are no significant problems on the frontiers, and the subjugated cities have not failed in submitting their tributes to us. But of your plan to harness the springs of Coyoacan, Tzutzumatzin, Lord of Coyoacan, opposes this, maintaining the waters are dangerous to control."

"Who does Tzutzumatzin think he is that he questions the words of my foremost engineers on a project as critical as this?"

"He claims they are saying these things merely to please you and do not understand the nature of this spring."

"And he is arrogant enough to assume that he does. Our population is ever increasing. We need fresh water for drinking and washing, and to augment our food production—our chinampas must be expanded to grow the additional grain we need. Our present water supply is inadequate, as we all know, yet Tzutzumatzin sits in his small city and refuses to share the abundant water he has. I will not have his recalcitrance jeopardizing Tenochtitlan's future growth."

"My lord, he has not denied us his water, but simply warns us that it is perilous to divert its flow to Tenochtitlan. He asserts there are no natural outlets here; the water level will rise if it runs into the city unchecked."

"Does he expect us to transport his water across the lake in pottery? How efficient is that? I don't need him to tell me of Tenochtitlan's problems. I mean to build my aquaduct; I will not have my plans thwarted by the ravings of a rank amateur who does not know of what he speaks."

"You do him an injustice, Lord. Tzutzumatzin is well-learned in the construction arts and knows what he's saying."

"Why are you his advocate? Are my engineers wrong?"

Cihuacoatl felt great insecurity over offending his master and had to think quickly to avoid a confrontation. He dreaded seeing Ahuitzotl in anger, fearing that, like an uncontrolled beast, his actions could not be predicted. "Certainly not, Lord," he said. "I know little of these things. I would not be so presumptuous as to claim an aquaduct could not be built from Coyoacan."

"Understand, Cihuacoatl, that this is more than a mere exercise for me. This is a project comparable to the Great Temple in scope and conception-the major achievement of my reign. I do not initiate such an enterprise without full comprehension of what it entails or a thorough consultation of my most skilled builders. They have advised me of its feasibility. That's why I will not have Tzutzumatzin stand in my way."

"I see. Do you have any words you wish me to impart on him?"

"Tell him that we take proper note of his precautions over harnessing Coyoacan's springs, but find it imperative to do just that in order to solve Tenochtitlan's growing needs. We expect his fullest cooperation in seeing this project implemented."

"Perhaps I should go through Chimalpopoca on this. Coyoacan is under Tlacopan's jurisdiction, and Tztzumatzin is a close kinsman of his."

"That is advisable. Even though this project is still a year from being initiated, it will be beneficial if everyone understands our position regarding it. I do not want this plan opposed. Make certain Tzutzumatzin is clear on that."

"I shall inform him this very day, Lord," the minister affirmed, eager to please his master.

Ahuitzotl derived momentary satisfaction in witnessing the minister's hasty compliance with his directive as it exemplified the method in which he liked things done-with a sense of immediacy. But by the time he was briefed on the ceremonial demands facing him this week, after which he terminated his meeting, he returned to his chamber greatly agitated that nothing seemed to work well for him as of late. Everything Cihuacoatl told him this day was of an adversive nature, as if he did not have enough anxieties over Pelaxilla; now it seemed as if all his difficulties were suddenly aggravated a hundredfold. He recalled the words Cihuacoatl once conveyed to him-that those gods whom he minimized in importance would one day unite in their mutual discontent and conspire to bring him down. How real this threat presently appeared to him.

A n Acolhua courier nearly dropped from exhaustion when he entered the capital across its southern causeway from Ixtapalapa. He was the last of a number of runners who relayed an important message from Texcoco's court as fast as it could be carried. He transferred his words to Cihuacoatl at the royal reception hall where he often held his affairs, and the minister paled when he heard them.

"Give notice to the Revered Speaker," he soberly instructed one of the guards, "that I have an urgent need to hold an audience with him."

The guard sped to his master's quarters and encountered him just as he had finished his meal; he related Cihuacoatl's request.

"What has brought on this urgency?" Ahuitzotl asked.

"A messenger from Texcoco, Lord."

Instinctively Ahuitzotl sensed what the message entailed; he hurried to the hall where he took note of his minister's sober disposition. "What is the word?" he said on entering.

"It's about Chalchiunenetzin," said Cihuacoatl. "Lord Nezahualpilli means to execute her publicly for her crimes against him."

"What!"

"He has set the date and is inviting all of his subject lords, giving them instructions to bring their wives and daughters so that they learn first-hand what fate awaits them should they contemplate a similar crime."

"The charges have been substantiated?"

"She was found in a compromising position with each of three local lords who will likewise be executed. Nezahualpilli referred this matter to judges who set up a commission to make inquiries into the affair. They questioned everyone concerned-the palace servants, concubines, the purveyors who made the statues upon the queen's request, even the slaves. Nothing was overlooked. Its findings were conclusive."

"That stupid woman! To think she would dare to humiliate a monarch like that. I should have known better than to believe she could keep her depravity confined to one individual."

"He wants the lesson to be lost on no-one; that's why he has invited all the royal families to be there. He has even gone so far as to declare a truce with his enemies so that they also might sent representatives to witness the executions. He means to have his revenge by making a grand exhibition of it."

"That is a gross overreaction, and not worthy of his titled station. Our custom when nobles are guilty of crimes is to have them taken secretly at night for execution."

"That has been the practice, Lord, but it is not proscribed, and there's no requirement to adhere to it."

"It would be in good taste. I see no virtue in announcing the crimes committed by nobles to the world. Nezahualpilli ought to have greater regard for this."

"It has become personal for him, Lord. He is outraged over having been so foully deceived by his queen for this long."

"The crime is heinous, to be sure, and no-one will dispute his right to have justice exacted upon its perpetrators, but someone needs to remind him that Nenetzin is of the royal family and should be accorded a certain degree of propriety in her death. I see nothing dignified in making a public display of her punishment."

"That's not all, Lord. Nezahualpilli asks that we furnish the queen's executioner."

"That is outrageous!"

"He means, by that demand, to have us publicly acknowledge the grievance against him and our support for his measures."

"He goes too far!" Ahuitzotl growled. "Indeed, the entire conduct of this business goes too far. I want a message sent to him."

"Yes, Lord?"

"First, tell him that we expect him to render the members of our royal household the respect that is due them. I have no wish to protest the findings of his commission and recognize his passion to do things according to law, but there are discreet practices that we, as lords, should maintain for ourselves in order to secure our positions their official sanctity. With this in mind, I urge that he reconsider his intent to make a demeaning exhibition of Nenetzin's punishment. Indeed, if he persists in his present course, it will not fare well for the alliance. Emphasize that! Secondly, I will not even consider sending him an executioner–the matter is his to deal with. What would he have us do? Be a party to the vulgarity of her exposure? I am insulted that he should even suggest this."

Ahuitzotl paused for a moment; he wanted to pour out all his indignation and anger towards Nezahualpilli's proposed action, but also knew this was not possible without hurling personal abuses against him. For once, he resented the niceties of protocol. "If I told him exactly what I think," he continued, "I would guarantee a permanent breakup of the alliance. To think he would send out invitations to his enemies to see Nenetzin garroted. What sort of man could do that?"

"One whose degradation has made him mad with rage."

Ahuitzotl viewed his minister with a reflective glance; he was able to comprehend emotions which could drive a man to such extreme measures, but he deplored the lack of consideration for more important factors that such rage overlooked. He also knew that he himself was not exempt from such behavior. He had his own fits of irritation over Pelaxilla's unexplained silence and pondered if he might react differently if she betrayed him. The thought stung him, and he quickly diverted his attention from it.

"Send this message today so he may have time to think on it, and tell him that I await a reply regarding my appeal. Before you go, has word of this reached anyone else?"

"On your niece's activities, I would say yes, but on the findings of the commission and the established execution date, not yet. But if Nezahualpilli has sent out invitations and ordered that his lords require their families to attend, you can be certain before this day is spent the news will be spreading throughout our realm like the wind. Everyone will know."

"Great damage has then already been done, and I question if Nezahualpilli can reverse the conditions he has generated. Nevertheless, make certain he gets my message today. I shall have to prepare myself for Motecuhzoma; he will be incensed when he hears of what is in store for his sister."

"Shall I deny him entrance to your palace if I observe him in an angry mood?"

"No. I'll have to face him eventually on it anyway and he is, after all, a member of the royal house. Still, I confess I do not look forward to that encounter."

After Cihuacoatl left to fetch a messenger, Ahuitzotl went back to his private quarters and informed Tlalalca of what he had learned. Her reaction was one of stunned amazement, and when she at last managed to speak, she was not without guilt as she felt herself in part culpable for what had happened.

"I was wrong to contradict you," she lamented. "I knew of the things you worried about, but denied them to myself."

Ahuitzotl did not help her any by agreeing with that assessment. "That's my problem," he scowled, "I'm always correct in my judgments but I allow others to mislead me into doing things against my intentions."

Tlalalca resented his lack of support; she believed that her reason for approving the marriage between Nenetzin and Nezahualpilli was honorably based-that true love would surmount any habitual practices. "I see," she replied caustically, "I am being reprimanded for my misjudgment."

"Not reprimanded, but informed that you were in error."

"You needn't be so smug about it. Am I to conclude from your remark that you have never made a mistake yourself?"

"You may conclude from it what you like, but I have you to thank for this predicament."

"So it's all my fault now, and you abrogate yourself of a responsibility in this. If you must have your scapegoat for an erroneous decision on your part, very well then, I shall bear that burden, but do not hold me accountable for Nenetzin's behavior. I am no more responsible for that than you are."

Her words checked Ahuitzotl's obtuseness as he realized she was correct and his censure of her unreasonable. "I'm greatly upset by the news, and this has led me to make unfair comments," he conceded. "I was wrong to blame you for this, Tlalalca. I know you meant well at the time. You're quite right in saying I cannot abrogate my own involvement in this."

"I accept your apology, Ahuitzotl. I understand your disappointment, but you inflict ruinous damage to yourself and others by these hasty accusations. It would be well to think about what you say before hurting people with it."

"Do not counsel me!" he snapped harshly at her. "I have had enough of your advice!"

She recoiled in shock and dismay as her efforts to ease the tensions between them fell on deaf ears. Her look of anguish left an impression on Ahuitzotl.

"Please," he continued, the sharpness gone from his voice, "I want no more advice. Let me deal with this in my own way."

"As you say. I will not stand in your way, but I do at times fear for you."

"Fear for me? What do you mean?"

"What will you do if you never again hear from Pelaxilla? It was solely your decision to send her to Tehuantepec. How will you face that prospect?"

Hot and cold flashes swept over him. He was not prepared to confront that possibility in spite of its horrid likelihood striking him with recurring frequency lately. He rejected it outright, refusing to believe it could ever happen, but he could not dispel the tormenting doubts which hounded him.

"I'll hear from her," he declared as if insisting that she agree with him. "If I have to, I will send all the armies in Anahuac to return her to me."

She said nothing further, believing her words would only lead to more difficulty, and instead gave him a strange, yet longing gaze which remained transfixed in his mind after he left the chamber to seek solace in his private study where he stayed for the duration of the night.

Around noon the following day, the reply which Ahuitzotl and Cihuacoatl nervously awaited came. Guards led the messenger before the monarch, who was seated in his throne, and left him standing there to allow for the appropriate discretion.

"You bring word from Lord Nezahualpilli?" Ahuitzotl asked the panting young man.

"Yes, Great Lord," his voice rang out through his intermittent heavy breathing. "My lord, Nezahualpilli, has instructed me to say this: There can be no mitigation for the seriousness of the offense Chalchiunenetzin committed against my person and the royal house of Texcoco. In probing deeper into this matter, I discovered that she had habitually engaged in the notorious behavior of which she has been found guilty and condemned to death, even while she still resided in Tenochtitlan, and that this was of common knowledge in your court. This brings into suspect your motivation for sending her to me. Can it be that you meant to humiliate me and my noble family by tainting our worthy name with that shameful woman's conduct? I choose to believe otherwise, accepting that your intentions were honorable, but do not deter me from my declared purpose. She will be executed, along with her three paramours, in the manner dictated by our laws, by garroting and in public. A seat is reserved for your attendance."

Ahuitzotl sat too dazed for words. He dismissed the courier with a backward wave of his hand and, even after he had departed, the quietness hung oppressively over the minister who nervously expected a momentous outburst of unchecked fury. When Ahuitzotl finally spoke out, his voice was surprisingly subdued. "So we now know upon what Nezahualpilli places the greater value," he said slowly, "and it is not the alliance."

"He's made his assessment of the situation. Will the alliance terminate if he proceeds with the executions?"

"It may not end, but it will not be as it has been, and Texcoco will fare the worse for it."

"How so, Lord?"

"We shall increasingly formulate the policies and dictates of the realm here in Tenochtitlan to the exclusion of consulting Texcoco. The decisions to wage war, to enact laws, to appoint rulers of cities in and around Anahuac, to make treaties and compacts with foreign states, to administer justice, trades, ceremonies-all of these things will be initiated and executed in Tenochtitlan. Nezahualpilli shall pay the full price for having rejected my advice. I shall, in the end, see his Acolhuas reduced to a mere vassal status with the loss of power and prestige that entails."

"You impose a harsch condition, Lord, but is this wise? Nezahualpilli is merely intent on clearing the soiled honor of his royal name and the personal embarrassment he has suffered."   "He's defied my wishes. I asked for nothing more than an exercise of prudence on his part."

Cihuacoatl was about to answer when suddenly distracted by shouting near the entrance of the hall, and Ahuitzotl, highly annoyed over the interruption, called for a guard to offer an explanation.

"What's all that commotion out there?" he asked.

"It is Prince Motecuhzoma, Lord," the guard stammered, shaking with fright. "He means to disrupt your meeting and will not accept our denial of access to him as we are instructed to do."

"The audacity of that upstart! You were correct in the conduct of your duties, guard, and I shall sternly inform him of this, but let him come in. I know why he is here."

The guard proceeded for the door and shortly thereupon Motecuhzoma came stomping into the hall in obvious agitation. His face was contorted with rage, and he walked straight for Ahuitzotl who watched his approach with a scowl. He halted on reaching the monarch and paused momentarily; Ahuitzotl did not speak but rather looked him over in an angry glare.

"Does my uncle know what people are saying?" Motecuhzoma impatiently blurted out.

"Hold your tongue!" Ahuitzotl lashed out at him, unsettling him severely. "Upon whose authority do you intrude on my private conferences?"

Motecuhzoma stood open-mouthed, not realizing his breach of conduct until this moment. "By the gods!" he cried out in alarm, "I have erred!"

Instinctively he sank to his knees as a sign of repentance; his reaction was so spontaneous that neither Ahuitzotl nor Cihuacoatl doubted his sincerity.

"More than once," Ahuitzotl announced. "True, I am your uncle, but you will not address me as such-ever! To you I am your sovereign lord and that is the title you will confer upon me when speaking to me."

"I was beside myself with anger and grief. I did not know what I was doing, Lord. I humbly ask your pardon for my unseemly behavior."

"Stand up, Motecuhzoma!" Ahuitzotl ordered. "I do not appreciate members of the royal family lying submissively at my feet like sniveling dogs."

Motecuhzoma readily complied and arose, but he still could not look his master in the eye.

"That's better," Ahuitzotl said, the bite gone from his voice. "I excuse your intransigence because I know its cause. I was expecting to hear from you, although not this soon. Undesireable news does indeed spread like a whirlwind."

"You know?" Motecuhzoma now stared at him in utter amazement. "You know about Nenetzin?"

"Of course I know. Do you think your Revered Speaker lives in a void?"

"Excuse me, Lord; my astonishment is not over your knowledge of it, but rather why nothing is being done about it."

"Indeed. What would you have me do?"

The question threw Motecuhzoma into confusion; he thought it a paramount duty for a monarch to come to the defense of the royal family and was puzzled by Ahuitzotl's seeming lack of concern.

"Why, I should think you would direct Nezahualpilli to put a stop to the execution. Or perhaps send a rescue party out to save my sister, or...or..."

"Or maybe send my armies against Texcoco?"

"Yes! Anything to prevent him from carrying out his treacherous plan."

"What a fool you are. But I suppose it's understandable when you base your actions on rumors you hear. Where is the evidence of this training you received at Calixtlahuaca? Have you heard the results of the commission that Nezahualpilli set up to inquire into the charges Nenetzin was accused of?"

"I am aware of the charges against her, Lord."

"The charges have been substantiated, Motecuhzoma. Do you dispute the findings of the commission?"

"Ah...er..no! I suppose not."

"Do you dispute the law which prescribes death for anyone guilty of the crimes she is charged with?"

"I do not, Lord."

"Then how do you propose I put a stop to Nenetzin's execution when our laws decree that she is to die?"

"Well, I...ah...er...?"

"I cannot stop Nezahualpilli from carrying out the sentence of the judges in this case. I cannot even object to the manner in which she is executed, for that too is prescribed by law. All I can do is request that Nezahualpilli confer the punishment with regard for the royal House of Tenochtitlan, that is, with some degree of dignity which would not shame us, and this I have done."

Motecuhzoma was astounded by this, thinking a monarch could make his own law when the situation warranted it-and this was obviously a special case. "Am I to believe, Lord," he said, "that you will do nothing to save Nenetzin?"

"To save her?"

"By the gods!" Motecuhzoma cried out in his shock and irritation, "Is the notion so preposterous?"

"You will not raise your voice in anger against me, young man!" Ahuitzotl cautioned him. "Why should I want to save her?"

"This is incredulous! I should think it your manifest duty! Because she is your niece and my sister!"

"And what has that to do with it? Is that supposed to grant her license to do as she pleases irrespective of the provisions of our laws?"

"I do not suggest that, Lord!"

"What do you suggest?"

"I don't know!" Motecuhzoma trembled in his frustration. "Bargain for her life! Make concessions! Offer Nezahualpilli a fair exchange for her-do something! She is, after all, a member of our royal house."

"Indeed she is!" Ahuitzotl roared out. "Indeed she is! The little slut should have thought about that and the obligations that incurred. Do you think she even remotely considered it? No! Instead she participated in lewd conduct which could only bring shame upon our house. I sent her to Nezahualpilli to strengthen my alliance with Texcoco and now find it utterly imperilled because of her depravity. She has effectively ruined all I sought to accomplish-a common whore might have done a better job of it, but I doubt it. Do not defend her crimes to me, Motecuhzoma. I never questioned Nezahualpilli's right to mete out the punishment she has inflicted upon herself."

So virulent was Ahuitzotl's outburst that he sank exhausted into his throne and gasped for breath upon its completion. Neither Motecuhzoma nor Cihuacoatl dared say anything after such a harangue and stood spellbound and speechless staring at each other. Finally Motecuhzoma risked breaking the silence. "I didn't know you so disliked her," he muttered.

"Nor did I," countered Ahuitzotl, "until I learned of her despicable conduct."

"She is but a weak woman victimized by her foolish physical needs, and to be in Nezahualpilli's court with his numerous wives and concubines-how could he possibly have satisfied her cravings?"

"That did not trouble her when she agreed to marrying him. She knew what she was getting into."

"Had she refused, would this have prevented you from sending her there?"

"It's a moot question-she wanted to go."

Resigned that his efforts were not going to produce any results for him, Motecuhzoma felt awkward remaining in the hall and was desperate to leave as there were now long spells of silence in his conversation with Ahuitzotl which greatly discomfited him. But the monarch refused to dismiss him, even though he spoke little to him.

"You will do nothing then?" Motecuhzoma strained to say.

"She is beyond help," Ahuitzotl slowly replied, studying Motecuhzoma's face with care. "The nature of her crimes has determined her fate. Even as Revered Speaker I cannot interfere with the sentence pronounced by the judges."

The prince's despair was apparent, and he closed his eyes and quivered in his anger and helplessness. "So be it then," Motecuhzoma at last assented, tears coming to him.

He was a sorrowful figure, standing there distraught and unable to decide where he should turn next or what more he could say. Ahuitzotl was suffiently moved by the pitiful spectacle to allow his nephew to leave without castigating him on the rules of courtesy which he had so consistently neglected throughout their discourse. Before walking away, Motecuhzoma asked one more question.

"Nezahualpilli, I hear, has invited all the lords to witness Nenetzin's execution. Will you attend?"

"I will not. Nor will I permit anyone else in Tenochtitlan to attend."

"I see," Motecuhzoma uttered in a low pitch, then added, "I will never forgive Nezahualpilli for this! One day, he shall feel the full weight of my revenge."

Ahuitzotl assessed his nephew's somber countenance for a brief moment, then spoke to correct his faulty thinking. "He shall regret the public manner in which he has chosen to execute Nenetzin, but it is I, not you, who will take the appropriate measures in seeing to that. Always remember, Nezahualpilli has committed no crime and has initiated no move in which he did not have the full backing of the law. So whatever vengeance you envision for him, keep that in mind."

Motecuhzoma had a look of scorn, making it clear Ahuitzotl's advice was lost on him, as he gave a short bow and hastily turned about to exit the hall.

"An angry man," Ahuitzotl mentioned to his minister after the prince had departed. "He will not let the matter rest."

"Why didn't you tell him of the procedures you will impose on Texcoco for Nezahualpilli's failure to heed your warnings?"

"I'm not certain of what I will do yet–they were but options. Besides, Motecuhzoma was not interested in what I would do to Nezahualpilli, only in what I would do to help Nenetzin and..."

"Yes, Lord?"

"The woman is doomed. Nothing can absolve her of her crimes or save her from the fate she has brought upon herself. But see to it that my instructions are obeyed-no lord in Tenochtitlan is to attend the execution. I cannot allow Nezahualpilli to believe that we sanction his punishment after we urged him not to carry it out in public. Let me know when it's done."

Bitterly, Ahuitzotl rose from the throne, his seat of power that somehow seemed diminished of the mystical awe it should project, and returned to his dark chamber. He sensed his powers weakening as he had alienated members of his own family while at the same time being unable to coerce his colleague in Texcoco. His beloved Pelaxilla ignored him, his relatives berated him, his subject and allied rulers defied him, and his wife feared him. What more could go wrong for him?

Nezahualpilli's rage knew no bounds and he ignored all of Ahuitzotl's subsequent pleas and warnings not to proceed with a public execution of his empress or the Texcocan lords. He saw the wisdom of this request in his more lucid moments, but once the machinery of the procedures had been set into motion, found himself unable to reverse the process even if he actually might have wanted to. Reports made their way to Ahuitzotl saying how the Texcocan lord shunned all guests and moped alone in his palatial residence. His moods fluctuated between fits of rampaging fury and moments of deepest misgivings over having embarked on his present course. At one point, he even issued a directive to cancel the executions, only to change his mind shortly thereafter when he realized his invited potentates were already underway to his city.

A report on the execution itself reached Ahuitzotl by way of his steady old Tepanecan ally, Chimalpopoca. Although Tlacopan's ruler had abstained from attending out of respect for the Revered Speaker's wishes, he learned of its details from his cousin ruler of Azcapotzalco who was one of the invited guests. He gave Ahuitzotl a full account of the events as it was described to him, omitting nothing.

The site of the execution was a small ceremonial platform centered in Texcoco's main plaza equidistant between Nezahualpilli's magnificent palace and the Temple of Quetzalcoatl, the city's patron god. Bleachers had been erected around the platform for the lords and their families, with special seating for the representatives of the enemy states who, as during the inauguration of the Great Temple years earlier, were hidden from the public eye by canopies and screens woven of cotton. The foreign lords entered Texcoco in the customary fashion—at night escorted by guardians sworn to secrecy—and were hosted by the Texcocan monarch in one of his palace adjuncts maintained for their stay; a covered walkway led from there to the improvised arena.

Ahuitzotl winced when he was told how there was no space available after all the invited had taken their place in the stands. In addition, hundreds of local residents crowded into the open corner areas so that no spot offering a view was left vacated. Such was the interest aroused by the execution of the queen that Nezahualpilli did not have enough room in Texcoco for his visitors and had to set up temporary shelters for them-clearly this kind of spectacle equaled the best of the ritual sacrifices. Yet the occasion was a sober one, with the gravest of overtones, and, although none present would have denied an interest in it, the atmosphere was tensely charged and did not allow for any joviality or expressions of approval or elations. Its purpose was meant to be a stern lesson on Nezahualpilli's demand for adherance to the law.

Ahuitzotl tried to find out about Nenetzin's frame of mind as the time of her execution drew near. Even at a time such as this, he concerned himself with the dignified countenance he expected out of members of his royal house. The sight of a pleading, whimpering, and frightened woman who needed to be bolstered with continuous encouragement, and perhaps even drugs, would have been appalling to him. Somehow that is what he believed from Nenetzin-a woman who had wholly disgraced his family with her lascivious conduct in life would now dishonor it with incessant wailing in death. The picture of Nenetzin being dragged screaming to her fateful destiny haunted Ahuitzotl-it constituted the final deprecation.

The beat of a single drum announced the start of the procedures. A gap opened amid the throng through which passed the procession, headed by a gaudily beclad priest, and followed by Nezahualpilli who held his head low and seemed to just gaze blankly at the priest's feet. Then, under a guard escort, came the condemned, led by Nenetzin. Chimalpopoca mentioned that she appeared much startled by the huge audience; her eyes had a glassy sheen to them when she first glanced about her but she then lowered them and glared only at the ground to avoid the spectators. Her body was draped in a plain, white cotton frock that extended to her ankles, and she was bare-footed. At one point she nearly fainted and was helped back to an erect stance by one of the guards beside her. Her face was pale and her hair hung straight down; all ornaments, make-up, and articles of beautification were removed. Her lips were closed with a downward arc to give her a sorrowful demeanor that evoked pity from the crowd.

After the queen came the three paramours also sentenced to die, and as with her, all signs of their lordly heritage had been removed from them and they wore only a cotton loincloth and walked in bare feet. Two of them were red-faced. They were the sons of Texcoco's leading nobles and were ashamed of the disgrace and humiliation they had brought upon their families and hung their heads low. The third, a son of a subject ruler in one of the outlying cities, maintained a regal bearing, holding his head upright and advancing in a lordly gait. Perhaps he knew that his father had been required to attend and meant, through this final act of grace, to purge his family of the dishonor he brought to it.

Behind the condemned came the executioners-four of them, one assigned to each of the criminals. A mask hid their faces and in one hand they carried a rope for the strangulation and in the other a wooden peg around which they would twist the cord for tightening. These in turn were trailed by dozens of palace servants who bore the statues of Nenetzin's previous lovers in addition to all the queen's personal belongings, clothing and articles, which were to be burned after the executions.

Such was the procession which ambled into the plaza. When it reached the platform, the priest and Nezahualpilli ascended upon it while the guards kept the remaining group huddled below it. The priest spoke first, giving official sanctity to the event and reminding everyone that such things were preordained and it was a person's duty to proceed accordingly to conclude the machinations of the gods; the fate now in store for the sinners had been their destiny—an inescapable and unavoidable consequence of the lives they had led.

After the priest concluded his narration, Nezahualpilli stepped forward and spoke of the nature of the crimes perpetrated by the condemned and of its subsequent disclosure by a commission set up by him to probe into it. He went into a long discourse on the evils of adulterous conduct-Chimalpopoca could not relate the Texcocan's exact words to Ahuitzotl-and why he had insisted that the nobles invited to witness the punishment bring along their wives and daughters so they might learn first-hand about the fate in store for anyone foolish enough to dare similar misconduct. He intended for this event to be of lasting value to them through this emphasis on the disgrace which the condemned had brought upon their households and how their memory should be forever erased from their families' thoughts.

Ahuitzotl asked Chimalpopoca if Nezahualpilli had mentioned any of the families by name and was relieved to hear that he had not. However, in the case of the queen, he did not have to, Chimalpopoca reminded the monarch, as it was well known that she was from the Royal House of Tenochtitlan. Ahuitzotl frowned and entreated his colleague to continue the story.

After completing his speech, Nezahualpilli called upon the first of the condemned to be slain. He was the proud prince who did his utmost to maintain a dignified comportment throughout the proceedings; two guards led him up the platform to its center. There, his hands were bound behind his back and he was directed to drop to his knees as the first executioner, who had followed him, knotted his cord about the wooden peg leaving a loop wide enough to place over the prince's head. While the executioner waited to receive the signal from Nezahualpilli, the condemned man still held his head upright and glared into the stands ahead of him, although Chimalpopoca did not believe that he saw anything. Nezahualpilli then nodded.

Immediately, the executioner dropped his noose down over the prince's head and pressed it against his neck. With practiced rapidity, he rotated the peg around the cord, twisting it tight until it strained against the throat, bulging out veins. A choking, rasping groan, accompanied by heaves of gasping, emanated forth from the dying man; his body shook with convulsions as it fought against its cut off air. Then his eyes rolled back, his tongue protruded thick and heavy from his mouth, and his head reddened to a deep hue. His breathing ceased, but the executioner continued to strain at turning the stick until he could feel the victim's full body weight aching to fall forward when he released his hold and let it crash onto the platform base, where it landed with a loud thump.

The executioner next ordered four of the servant to carry the body from the platform to an adjacent wooden stack where it was to be burned later as befitted members of the nobility. By this fire, a sort of cleansing was to result which removed the taint of their criminal activity in the afterlife. The body, with the instrument of death still tautly wrung about its neck, was heaped on top of the pyre to await the remaining victims that would soon be placed alongside it.

Nezahualpilli next motioned for another of the lords to be slain, making it plain that he meant for the queen to be dispatched last. It may have been mere showmanship, since the greatest interest and lesson to be imparted rested with her, or perhaps Nezahualpilli wanted to instill or prolong a sense of fear in her by having her watch her accomplices precede her in death. He held her primarily responsible for enticing the others into their treacherous conduct; she could shake in her fright while awaiting her turn, and he would study her to see if it had the desired effect. Even as the cord was wrapped around the next man's neck, he still bowed his head in shamed embarrassment and could not bear to look upon his audience. He died writhing in the same painful spasms as the prince who had preceded him and his body was set on the pyre adjacent to its gruesome companion.

Within minutes, the third of the condemned lay dead at the feet of his executioner and was being lifted up by more servants and cast upon the pyre. Nenetzin trembled at the deaths of her former lovers and averted her eyes from their throes. Her body was quivering involuntarily when Nezahualpilli next stared at her—a hostile gaze with no evidence of sorrow or regret in it-and must have wondered whether she could maintain her composure and walk up the platform. Then Nezahualpilli gave his signal; there was a look of horror in the queen's eyes as her executioner prodded her into motion by pushing his hand into her shoulder. Pale and shaking, she slowly climbed up on the platform.

When she was properly situated, the executioner told her to get on her knees; her cotton frock was seen fluttering as she lowered herself, revealing her terrible trembling. Her fear-filled eyes glanced into the spectator area where she saw the lords, ladies, and their daughters gazing solemnly at her. She sank her head in contrition as her executioner dropped his looped cord over her, and when it rested on her shoulders, he began to twist it taut with his rotation. Nenetzin's head was yanked back when the cord compressed her flesh and offered resistance to the strangulation. The veins bulged forth from her neck and forehead; her tongue began to protrude as she gasped for air; spittle oozed from her mouth, and her white frock dampened as she wet herself. The executioner kept on twisting the cord until her eyes rolled back into their sockets and he began to feel her weight under his arms. When at last he let go of his hold, she plopped heavily to the wooden floor, her head striking it with a dull thud.

Nenetzin's body was set on the pyre next to the other three. The wooden statues of her previous victims were positioned along the sides to form a wall around the stack; the queen's remaining items were flung to the top until they covered the corpses. This completed, Nezahualpilli took a torch and walked to the mound; he set its brushes on fire at measured intervals and before long roaring flames crackled and shot skyward giving off gray clouds of smoke amid a caustic smell of burning flesh. Nezahualpilli had avenged his injury, but he seemed ungratified by it.

Perhaps not until this moment did Nezahualpilli grasp the damage he had done to himself over this sordid affair. The absence of the Revered Speaker and leading lords of Tenochtitlan was quite conspicuous and weighed heavily on him as the time of execution drew nearer, standing out as a somber reminder about the wisdom of his action, and now that it was over, he may have been struck by the hollowness of his justice. Although he would not have admitted that Ahuitzotl may have been correct in proposing the condemned by executed in secrecy, he clearly was not pleased and there remained a disturbing demeanor about him as he imparted his final cautionary advice on his hushed audience before leaving. He did not present himself at the feast held for his guests in the palace following the day's event.

Such was the execution of Chalchiunenetzin, daughter of Axayacatl, and niece to Ahuitzotl, as related to the Revered Speaker by Chimalpopoca. In addition to Ahuitzotl, Cihuacoatl and Motecuhzoma bore witness to the account, listening to its final grim details in the same numbed silence as the monarch. For each of them, the described event engendered a permanent change of attitude towards an allied city and ruler once held in esteem, infusing an irreversible tarnish on the harmony that had once existed between them. Not one of them saw any modicum of honor in what had happened, resenting the ignominy represented by the spectacle, and at least one of them, Motecuhzoma, swore as he left that he would one day exact his vengeance on Nezahualpilli.

IV

Ahuitzotl's anger towards Nezahualpilli was overshadowed in time, mainly because he again became obsessed with his failure to hear from Pelaxilla. It now dawned on him that she would not take the initiative to furnish the details she was to secure for him-for whatever reason he did not know-and he decided the time had come for his pochteca to be sent to the Zapotec capital to seek her out and discover the actual truth behind her remissions. While he waited for their return, events arose which provided him with a motive for planning another invasion into the southern frontier. Cihuacoatl brought these to the Revered Speaker's attention one morning after receiving a number of dispatches originating from that region.

"There are some disturbing reports coming from Tehuantepec, Lord," the minister began.

"From Tehuantepec? Reports on Pelaxilla?"

"Of another nature-one more germane to the administration and well-being of the realm."

"I'ld have preferred the former," Ahuitzotl replied in disappointment. "What is it–another problem with our trading?"

"Yes, Lord. Not only our trading, but our prestige as well. It appears that Tehuantepec has found its resources insufficient to pay the tributes we agreed upon."

"A wealthy kingdom as that? Preposterous. The tributes consigned to them were by mutual consent and quite meager."

"It seems some internal strife, along with unusually inclement weather conditions, have limited their ability to meet the terms agreed upon. As a consequence, they sent their own merchants to open up trades with a region known as Soconusco, farther to the south. Their merchants were abused and mocked for being lackeys to us; they were ridiculed for their status as a tribute state and called women-and fools for doing your bidding.

The reports say this castigation has so adversely affected the Zapotecs that they now question the conditions they agreed to."

Ahuitzotl was himself smarting by the report as stated, but also highly suspicious of its legitimacy. "Has this been verified," he said, "or is it a fabrication on the part of the Zapotecs?"

"Why do you question it, Lord?"

"I challenge anything coming out of Cocijoeza's court. It may be a ploy to get out of his agreements with us."

"Not in this case, Lord. Our own pochteca who went with the Zapotec merchants to Soconusco confirm it."

"Was any trading conducted?"

"No, Lord. They were sent back empty-handed as well as humiliated. They were told that Soconusco will never see its products sent as tribute to us."

"Very arrogant of them. What will Cocijoeza do about it?"

"As yet, we don't know. We suspect he will ask you to help him launch an invasion into Soconusco to teach these people humility-and to exact tributes from them."

"He can't do this on his own?"

"I don't think so. He perceives the insult as being directed against you rather than himself-intentionally, I believe. The situation promises him a challenging prospect."

"I can see how. If we do not respond to his request, it furnishes him with a pretext to default on his own payments. He will conclude that we no longer have the resolve to undergo another such distant campaigns. If we do assist him, he'll be able to conquer a people he has probably long had his designs on. In either case, he can enrich himself at our expense-a convenient arrangement for him which makes me curious if it was not contrived."

"Quite so, Lord. The situation is problematic for us."

"Where is Soconusco?"

"Far to the south of Tehauntepec, Lord. Far indeed-half as far as the Zapotecan capital is from Anahuac."

Ahuitzotl's interest was aroused; remote and distant realms held a mythic sort of fascination for him, especially if they promised wealth-and evidently Soconusco did, else Cocijoeza would not seek to go there. "Interesting. How far do these kingdoms extend in the south?" he wondered.

"A good question, Lord. I myself was amazed to learn of Soconusco, but the pochteca have brought us back reports of rich nations existing even beyond there."

"Have they seen them?"

"No, but they have made contact with merchants who came from these realms and they give a fabulous account of them, describing them as richly attired, with fine plumes and many ornaments, and dealing in products that are highly prized. They excel in adornments of gold and jade and other precious stones-all of it said to be of superb craftsmanship."

"So we are not speaking of your average kingdoms, but of ones worthy of our pursuit. We would derive major benefits be expanding our trade into that region."

"Such are the indications, Lord."

"Either that, or by extracting tributes from them," Ahuitzotl added as an afterthought, making it clear he would not balk at extending his conquests into even the most far-off places if there existed sufficient rewards meriting such efforts-the enormity of the distance traversed was of no consequence.

"Back to the issue at hand, Lord," Cihuacoatl said, seeking guidance on how to proceed, "Is there any message you wish to convey to Tehuantepec in regards to these reports?"

Ahuitzotl pondered on it and concluded that at present he would leave the matter in Cocijoeza's hands, not that he expected the Zapotecan to resolve the problem, but he did not trust him, regarding him as an adversary rather than an ally, a view all the more pronounced now that he had Pelaxilla with him. Also he lacked sufficient information on which to base an expeditionary force leading to the subjugation of Soconusco.

"Let us await developments until Cocijoeza officially requests our assistance. What I want done now-make certain Lord Huactli gives it his full attention.-is for our pochteca to conduct a thorough study of the that area, including Soconusco itself. I want nothing overlooked; we must know details on the terrain, vegetation, routes, rivers, cities and peoples; the strength of their armies; the weapons and tactics they employ; the supply methods used to equip and feed their forces; their compacts with each other-everything they have been taught to investigate. Even maps and diagrams."

"I shall instruct him on this today, Lord."

"The reports must come to us as soon as possible. We know nothing of this region, and if I'm to carry out any plans, I must have familiarity with it. Also, I have no desire to be at Cocijoeza's reliance for such information. It restricts the options I want available to me."

With that, Ahuitzotl dismissed his minister and returned to his private quarters overlooking the canal. He found the empress there with her servant, Xoyo, and was annoyed by this; Tlalalca was now well ebough acquainted with his mannerism to discern what bothered him. "Leave us, Xoyo," she directed. "See to Cuauhtemoc until I call for you."

The old woman readily complied, leaving Tlalalca alone with Ahuitzotl, and if at first neither of them spoke, she nevertheless knew what troubled him. "Still no word from Pelaxilla?" she asked.

The question set his nerves on edge. "Nothing," he muttered.

"I can't understand it anymore," Tlalalca went on. "What can she hope to gain by playing this absurd game?"

"I've told you she is bent on punishing me. It's her way of getting back at me for having sent her to Cocijoeza."

"Even if she meant to that earlier, and I do not exclude its possibility, by now I would have expected her to have a change of heart. She is pressing her luck. This will not fare well for her when you reclaim her."

"That little lady has done her best to provoke my anger and I'll see that she atones for it. I still can't believe she's doing this."

"Are you sure she has a choice?"

"I will soon know. I've given instructions for certain of our merchants to initiate contact with her and find out why she ignores me. It's especially important for me to get the information I require on the Zapotecs now."

"Why is it so important now?"

Ahuitzotl hesitated; he habitually kept such talk confined to those officials who had a part in implementing the plans connected with such affairs. His years of being associated with palace intriques taught him to distrust imparting vital information on those not meant to hear it. But in this case, he felt a need to speak.

"There are movements afoot which make it opportune for us to consider another expedition to Zapoteca. We're presently keeping these developments under observation and are waiting for the right time.

The information that Pelaxilla was supposed to get for me would be valuable now."

"You say opportune-am I wrong in concluding that you wish it to be so?"

"It offers a pretext to go after Pelaxilla. If she will not contact me, then I will come to her."

"You would wage a war over her?"

"I will do what is necessary to get her back, but why are you startled? She was sent to Tehuantepec to obtain the information enabling me to ultimately destroy Cocijoeza, The eventual continuation of my war with him was never in doubt."

"You seem eager for it."

"Thank Pelaxilla for that. Her omission to maintain contact with me has greatly heightened my determination to discover its cause. Indeed, I admit I fear losing her, and will do everything in my power to prevent this."

"Lose her?"

"What else can I believe? Why does she torment me like his? Not a single word in nearly a year, and the reports that she is seen frequently in Cocijoeza's company. Is it possible she's fallen for that repulsive fat man? It cannot be!"

His anxieties were understandable to Tlalalca, and she wished somehow she could alley his deepest fears, but no answers came to her. She could see his festering concern–the frustration was eating on him, and she hoped desperately that some word, any word at all, would come from Pelaxilla so Ahuitzotl might have his peace. "She loves you so," Tlalalca tried to assuage him. "I refuse to believe she does this out of spite. I do fear Cocijoeza may have confined her to the limits of his palace. There must be a reason why she is unable to communicate with us."

"For this long?"

"Pelaxilla is still a child in many respects. Perhaps she is afraid to risk it."

"What you say has frightening ramifications. Why, that makes her useless to me as far as my purpose for having sent her to Cocijoeza. Everything would have been for naught."

"You placed an enormous burden on her, and she may find it most difficult to do. It takes more than a few weeks of training to make an informant out of someone not used in dealing in treachery. I am sure that Pelaxilla has her own frustrations in trying to meet your demands and deceive Cocijoeza at the same time."

Ahuitzotl was unclear on how to respond to her observation; it seemed to him that Tlalalca was the one who was ignorant about Pelaxilla. He recalled how Pelaxilla once prodded him into expediting Tizoc's fall-certainly she was no stranger to nefarious conduct. But he was comforted by Tlalalca's optimism and appreciated her concern over his problem.

That night, for the first time in weeks, Ahuitzotl truly relished his love-making with Tlalalca and accorded her his undivided attention. For the empress, it amounted to one of those rare occasions in which she was able to drown herself in pleasureable bliss and forget about everything else-occasions she found wanting as of late and wished would present themselves more often.

V

More weeks passed, and still Ahuitzotl heard nothing from Pelaxilla. The first of those pochteca who had been specifically tasked to make contact with her had now returned to Tenochtitlan and their reports drove him to frenzied agitation.

"What do you mean she would not see you?" Ahuitzotl stormed when he had them before him in the reception hall. "Did you tell her that you bring word from me, the Revered Speaker?"

"We did, Lord." their leader replied, "and she shunned us and would not listen to anything we had to say. Indeed, she wanted to be rid of us and called on her guards to send us away."

"What?" Ahuitzotl was alarmed. "Did you check to see if she herself was under guard?"

"I saw none, Lord-not until she called for them."

"But...but how can that be? Did she say anything at all to you?"

"She said things were no longer as they had been, and that you should not expect them to return to their former conditions."

"She said that!"

"Yes, Lord! I did not understand its meaning."

Ahuitzotl did, and it sent a chill through him. His greatest fears were realized in that statement-it meant she no longer loved him and was truly lost to him. Nothing could have shaken him more. Every nerve tensed; his heartbeat tripled; his face burned. All of his additional attempts to discover more on Pelaxilla turned out negative, and he finally dismissed the merchants when he recognized its futility; he was in no mood to be seen by anyone this day. He did not know who to turn to, who could help in in his extreme anxiety. What he desperately needed was to be with Pelaxilla, to speak with her, but that was not possible. He would have to endure his torment alone-at least, for a while longer.

A few days later, another messenger appeared at the royal palace carrying a sealed parchment. Cihuacoatl took it and rushed to see the Revered speaker; he hoped it was the news his master had so long sought. He found Ahuitzotl brooding in his throne.

"A dispatch, Lord." the minister declared as he handed the parchment over. "It is from Cocijoeza's court."

"You say it's from Tehuantepec?" Ahuitzotl said, scarcely believing it.

"It bears his royal seal."

Ahuitzotl's fingers fumbled over the cover as he shook with excitement. He tore open the folded pamphlet and read its contents, depicted in Nahuatl glyphs, perhaps under Pelaxilla's very guidance. His face turned ashen as he read it; his knees became wobbly and he felt a weakness coming over him; he slumped into his throne stunned. His eyes were glazed and he placed his open hand over his mouth as if to suppress an agonizing outburst.

Cihuacoatl viewed the monarch's countenance with apprehension. The news was not good, he knew; he should have read the dispatch first. "What is it, Lord?" he dared to ask. "You do not look well."

Ahuitzotl gazed blankly at the opposite wall still too dazed to answer, and the resultant tension was so overpowering that the minister felt an impulse to run away.

"It's from Cocijoeza," Ahuitzotl finally replied, his voice broken and faint. "He informs me that he will take Pelaxilla as his wife."

The minister now also paled; this was the last thing he wanted to hear-he feared his master's full wrath would fall upon him.

"The marriage ceremony is to take place this week," Ahuitzotl went on with great difficulty, each word coming out slowly between deep gasps.

There followed a long period of quiet, but Cihuacoatl's nerves were taut and he would have found words, even if expressed in anger, more soothing. "What now?" he asked.

"I don't know. Obviously I can't stop him."

"Why does he write to inform you of this?"

"He thinks I should be pleased by the news as it brings his royal house and ours closer together. He not only thinks Pelaxilla is of the royal family but that we have an alliance with him."

"What else can he believe, Lord? That is why, in his eyes, you sent him Pelaxilla."

"You suggest she has not told him of the real reason she was sent to him. She must have."

"Would he send this message to you if he did?"

"Yes. To taunt me with it. To boast of how he achieved yet another triumph over me."

"I don't think so, Lord. The message has all the qualities of naivety about it. He writes as a matter of courtesy to inform you that your idea of sending him Pelaxilla was a good one and will contribute to improved relations between us."

"Improved relations? When he pays us tributes?"

"Perhaps he has hopes of having these reduced or terminated. That may be the true motivation behind his message. I am quite convinced his intentions in sending it are honorable."

Cihuacoatl's words offered a ray of hope for Ahuitzotl and he grasped at it in his desperation to believe Pelaxilla was still true to him and that this marriage was but an interim step she took in order to further secure the Zapotecan's confidence. She had to do this if Cocijoeza proposed it in order to eventually obtain a full disclosure of his secrets. That was it. She had no choice but to go along with him. But he needed to be sure. The reports negated what he wanted to hear and, in spite of the encouragement he gave himself to the contrary, came across as quite convincing. His mind fluctuated from one extreme to the other-if only he could see her and talk to her.

"Will you send a reply to this?" Cihuacoatl asked.

Ahuitzotl pondered long on that: if his deception over Cocijoeza was to continue, he had no choice but to give this marriage his blessings. Uncertain about what was actually happening, he concluded this union would have no affect on his true purpose-the unthinkable was that Pelaxilla would reject him for a disagreeable fat man.

"Yes," he presently answered. "Send a messenger indicating our approval. Make it sound good so it appears we are optimistic over our furture relations which this marriage should enhance."

"I shall give him our encouragement, Lord."

Inside, Ahuitzotl was afflicted with nervous uncertainty, and his mind aggresively probed for ways in which he could expedite Cocijoeza's eventual demise. "Arrange for a meeting tomorrow with Tlohtzin and the commanders," he said. "Also have the priests there. We need to discuss the feasibility of a military operation against Soconusco."

A restless night followed for Ahuitzotl as his impatience for tomorrow's conference kept him from sleep and in his mind he imagined over and over how he would torment Cocijoeza. He even dared to possess thoughts about punishing Pelaxilla for all the suffering she was causing him, especially now that she acquiesced to marrying his enemy, and repeatedly condemned himself for this situation he had in part created. He tried, as best as he could, to assure himself she had no options in the matter and actually looked forward to the day he would come for her. But why her silence? And why her devastating words to the merchants?

Tlalalca was also unable to sleep, aware of Ahuitzotl's restlessness. He had told her about the message received earlier and she spent much of the evening consoling him by saying he had placed Pelaxilla in a position where she could hardly have refused Cocijoeza his request. The effort exhausted her and, rather than persisting with it, she preferred to pretend she was asleep. She did not know if she succeeded in this, but thought it easier for her to feign sleep than go on reassuring his flagging convictions. For both of them, this was to be another of the unsatisfying nights that became more and more frequent over the last few months.

Early the next day, the commanders and priests Ahuitzotl called for were met in the palace hall when he and Cihuacoatl entered. He took his seat in the jaguar-skin throne and looked out over the assemblage noticing Tlohtzin and Motecuhzoma among the commanders and the chief priests of Huitzilopochtli, Tlaloc, Tezcatlipoca, and Quetzalcoatl. He wasted no time and immediately began to address them.

"You are summoned to consider the possibility of an expedition to remote Soconusco. Our problem is that Soconusco has insulted the Zapotecans for their status as a tribute kingdom to us and refuses to maintain trade relations with Tehuantepec, commerce that Zapoteca considers essential in order for them to meet their own payments to us. The issue facing us is if we can permit this situation-the implications are significant. If we do nothing, Tehuantepec is sure to use the occasion to default on its tributes, concluding we are not of mind to venture to their distant region a second time to enforce this. But if we allow them to escape their payments, using Soconusco as their excuse for not doing so, others will learn of it and follow Tehunatepec's example. You can be certain they are watching these developments with keen interest. Even more important, this could again lead to a cessation of the trades we know are more advantageous to us than to them."

"Is this a council of war, Lord?" inquired Tlohtzin. "If so, why are the rulers of Texcoco and Tlacopan absent?"

"Not a council of war, but a conference to determine the feasibility of waging war at this time and, if not, how soon. Have the pochteca brought back any information on Soconusco?"

"Some have, Lord. We have a good conception of the terrain and its key landmarks, including the trails leading there. It is rugged, similar to what we were in when we marched from Tototepec to Tehuantepec, and the heat is oppressive. The forests are dense with great distances between the towns and cities. According to the reports, none of these cities maintain extensive storage facilities for food supplies. A large army in that region will have to carry most of its rations with it."

"The forests should be teeming with game to supplement our requirements, but I concede a larger army might have problems in this regard. What else?"

"We would like a better idea in what cities the few granaries available are located so we can determine our approach routes. The reports are vague in some areas. Also, it would be helpful to know how the local inhabitants will receive us. We know virtually nothing on what sort of influence Soconusco excercises over them."

"In absence of this information, we must assume they will display a strong allegiance to their overlords and would offer us resistance. If this assessment is correct, how large a force do you estimate necessary to march on, and take, Soconusco, providing the Zapotecs assist us in the operation?"

"If they were to augment us with half our strength, I would say no less than forty thousand."

"If it must be that many, do you believe we have sufficient information to initiate an expedition of that size immediately?"

"Yes, Lord! What is lacking, we can obtain along the way."

"You have answered what I wanted to know, Tlohtzin; I'ld have drawn the same conclusion. I shall see you at the headquarters to review plans for its implementation. As for a propitious time to begin this undertaking, what say you priests?"

"The present time is propitious enough, Lord; we are in the middle of the planting season-the corn grows well!-and we honor our mother of corn during this month. Indeed, it will continue to be a good time throughout the eight month, Hueytecuilhuitl, when the corn is ripe. With proper reverence rendered, the gods will provide for us."

"Can they be appropriately served by the priests who remain behind in Tenochtitlan and the other cities for the length of time this expedition may last?"

"Yes, Lord, but we seek a clarification as to the intend of this expedition you contemplate."

"What kind of clarification?"

"You have made no mention of undertaking this venture to meet the needs of the gods; we want to know whether you embark upon it for their well-being or only for the interests of the merchants as it presently appears to us."

Ahuitzotl blanched; he thought the fact that he deemed such an action necessary should have sufficed to convince anyone of its proper justification. "I did not mention it," he scowled, "because I believed it understood. Are not all our expeditions conducted with the ultimate purpose of honoring and serving the gods?"

"So they are, Lord. Yet it is better to give voice to their inclusion so they know we do not slight them."

"I do not find it essential to state the obvious."

"It would benefit you to do so, Lord. The gods must know they have no secondary importance when such enterprises are conceived by men. How will you propitiate them by this expedition?"

"As always, priest, through the sacrifices of the captives we take."

"And for this you will march all the way to-to this place, Soconusco? There are ample captives for the taking in closer proximity to us."

The priest had now exceeding his authority, Ahuitzotl concluded, and he resented his meddling into matters outside of his sphere of influence. "What is the point of this inquiry, priest?" he demanded to know. "Do you dispute the cause under which we plan this operation?"

"Not so, Lord. I merely seek to make it clear that the interests of the gods are a first priority for considering this expedition."

"I do not need you to tell me that!" Ahuitzotl bellowed out, rising out of his throne in his annoyance. The priest recoiled in astonishment, as did everyone present–the railing was unprecedented against those entrusted to the care of the gods. The assembly watched its leader with apprehensive concern. "Have I not been Huitzilopochtli's most devoted servant?" Ahuitzotl raged on. "Did I not promise him that I would extend his glory to the farthest reaches of the world? And did he not instruct us to do just that? Everything I do is done with the full understanding it is to please Huitzilopochtli. If I fail, in my eagerness to fulfill our divine mission, to mention this, I do not expect to be reprimanded for it by some infernal priest!"

The assemblage stood aghast, numbed into silence, catching its breath, in abhorrence over the demeaning description of the high priest–most of all his fellow votaries. Cihuacoatl, as shocked as anyone, quickly wished to undo the damage. "I pray you recant, Lord," he whispered to his master. "You committed a serious offense against the priest."

"I was driven to it by that man's unmitigated arrogance."

"You must apologize! Immediately, before they invoke the wrath of their gods upon you!"

"Why do you fear this so? It is yourself you should be concerned about–not me. Remember, you are not untainted before the gods–the death of Tizoc has seen to that."

"Yes, and I have done my best to make amends for it through proper reverence. I strongly urge you to do the same."

His words reached Ahuitzotl, and the monarch's rage abated somewhat; he slumped back into his throne and gazed directly at the cleric he had insulted. The priest still possessed a stunned expression and shied away from the Revered Speaker's glance while the rest of his members remained open-mouthed in their disbelief.

"You must excuse my disparaging remark," Ahuitzotl said. "If as damaging as you consider it, this was because I also found your interrogation demeaning to me. I will not be blatantly lectured as some pervenu unacquainted with the requirements of his office–I reacted adversely to how I perceived your words. If I erred, I apologize for it. I trust you will take this into account when you consult with your gods."

The priest was still too dazed to answer him, but another one stepped forward and spoke for him. "You apology is accepted, Lord. The error is ours; the questioning was indeed tactless and irreverent to you–your perception of it as such cannot be faulted. However, my lord should be cautioned that he has offended the gods this day, and they will not be as easily appeased."

"I shall make my amends to them, but in my own way, as I have done once before."

"How will we know this, Lord?"

"By the victories Huitzilopochtli will grant me. Will you accept that as a sign?"

"I will, Lord." said the priest as he walked back to where his peers were standing.

Although Ahuitzotl wanted to discuss additional material relevant to his proposed operation, the atmosphere had been sufficiently soured by his open confrontation with the priest that it seemed pointless for him to go on. His advisors had been so unnerved over the incident that their subsequent answers directed themselves more towards appeasing the Revered speaker's wrath than at providing useful information. Frustrated and disgusted over how things were proceeding, Ahuitzotl terminated the meeting and dismissed those present while he himself retired to his quarters. The hall emptied quickly with only Tlohtzin, Motecuhzoma, and Cihuacoatl remaining; all three were visibly disturbed over what had happened.

"Did you hear what he called the priest?" Tlohtzin commented. "He comes ever closer to incurring their hostility if he has not done so already, to say nothing of their gods."

"What prompted him to do it?" Motecuhzoma asked. "I did not think the priest's questioning unreasonable."

"He is determined to destroy Cocijoeza," Cihuacoatl informed them. "It has poisoned his mind."

"Cocijoeza?" Tlohtzin questioned. "We plan a war on Soconusco. He said nothing about the Zapotecs."

"Soconusco is but a pretext–do not speak to anyone of this if you value your positions. The Revered Speaker would condemn me if he discovered I said this to you. His real objective is Tehuantepec."

Tlohtzin and Motecuhzoma glanced at each other quite bewildered over why Ahuitzotl should be reluctant to tell them that. It made more sense to attack Tehuantepec; no one was satisfied with their truce in spite of the tributes and concessions obtained from that city–the humiliation was not only the Revered Speaker's.

"Why keep that a secret?" Motecuhzoma mused. "We would all prefer to avenge the indignity dealt us by Cocijoeza."

"He does not want word of this to reach Cocijoeza so he can catch him by surprise before he can move to his bastion at Giengola. Also there is Pelaxilla."

"His mistress?"

"He sent her to Tehuantepec to gain Cocijoeza's confidence so that he would reveal his defenses to her, but she has not provided any information yet, and now the Zapotecan means to marry her. This has very much upset him–No! Obsessed him!-and intensifies his resolve to destroy Cocijoeza."

"He risks such a perilous journey without adequate preparation because of a woman?" Tlohtzin responded, most astounded.

"No ordinary woman, Tlohtzin, but one who has completely possessed him."

"No matter. Is this what one can expect from a Revered Speaker?"

"I wish I could tell you otherwise," Cihuacoatl replied in his disdain, "I met Pelaxilla once, and, believe me, I cannot understand how she has managed to so dominate him. Unfortunately, this indeed appears to be the case."

On that discouraging note, Tlohtzin and Motecuhzoma left the palace hall to the minister who remained to brood over the present state of affairs. It must have been a source of extreme exasperation to Cihuacoatl. He had, at the peril of his life, done away with one unworthy ruler and replaced him with a far more capable one, and yet not an entirely satisfactory selection. No one could deny what prestige and glory Ahuitzotl had brought back to the Mexica at a time it was most needed, but this was not done without its price. Cihuacoatl tired of having to endure Ahuitzotl's wrath and unpredictability, his frequent emotional harangues, of incessantly reminding him of ceremonial obligations, and now this, the final indignity-his obsession to destroy an enemy not for the sake of the realm, but because of a woman. He questioned if Tenochtitlan was ever to see the perfect ruler.

VI

T he war council called by Ahuitzotl endorsed his plan to march against Soconusco. Its members were reluctant at first, the vast distance presenting itself as a formidable obstacle, and only through the Revered Speaker's strong insistance was concurrence at last obtained. The question troubling most was whether the rewards to be acquired on a journey of this magnitude would be of sufficient quantity to justify its undertaking. Ahuitzotl pursuaded them it would, emphasizing that failure to act would not only deprive Anahuac of the tributes to be gained from Soconusco, but also those of Tehuantepec and other southern cities which were certain to default on their own payments if they concluded that the Mexica were daunted from further such enterprises by the long travels involved. His account was convincing and the council granted him the approval he was after; he left feeling great satisfaction—his determined showdown with Cocijoeza had passed its first major hurdle.

He refrained from mentioning anything to the council about his ulterior plan to attack Tehuantepec, thinking it would oppose such action because the city was already honoring its tributes, even though Ahuitzotl deemed the amount inconsequential, in addition to minimizing the security risk its revelation posed. As far as getting his army to assault it, he saw no problems there; the promise of booty would readily entice his warriors into sacking the city once they were in its vicinity.

A more pressing concern for him was if he should inform Pelaxilla of his intentions. He remained confused over her loyalties; his inclination was to say she was, and always would be, true to him, yet he was at a loss to explain her failure to communicate. He was especially incensed over the reports that she had refused to see the pochteca he specifically sent to her-this greatly heightened his dilemma and left him baffled by her actions. Indeed, he had no way of knowing where Pelaxilla's allegiance lay, a dilemma greatly intensifying his doggedness to reclaim her. He agonized over this at length, discussing it with both Tlalalca and Cihuacoatl on a number of occasions. For the empress, the answer was clear. She believed Pelaxilla remained loyal to Tenochtitlan and that her marriage to Cocijoeza was forced on her; the only proper course was that she should be told of his plans and given advance warnings.

"She will need to protect herself," Tlalalca advised Ahuitzotl, "If your warriors sack the city, how are they to know who she is? You must alert her."

"You raise a good point," he replied. "This means I will have to be the first one to enter the palace."

"If she is there. Cocijoeza could place her elsewhere when he sees his city attacked."

She convinced him of the necessity to let Pelaxilla know, but he still held nagging doubts about such notification falling into the wrong hands and alerting Cocijoeza instead. When he presented the problem to his minister, he received a considerable different reaction.

"You must be mad!" Cihuacoatl declared in his exacerbation, losing sight of his courtly etiquette. "You would reveal your secret intentions to your enemy's wife?"

"She is his wife in name only; her allegiance is with us."

"What evidence do you have of that? Indeed, Lord, this woman has caused you to lose grasp of your sound judgment. Has she sent any of the reports you requested from her? Has she listened to the messengers you sent to her? On what basis can you conclude she is loyal to you?"

"She would never betray me. I know this."

"I'm too old to be swayed by such ridiculous sentimentality, Lord. As minister, I am trained to consider the facts and to give appropriate counsel regarding them. My advice is to refrain from such absurd notions and assure yourself that you catch Cocijoeza by surprise. Do not reveal your plans to anyone!"

"How will I insure her safety if I don't give her an advance warning?" Ahuitzotl worried. "She could be killed during the attack."

"Thoroughly brief your commanders on it. Issue orders that no woman is to be harmed. That would make considerably more sense, given these circumstances, then relying on this-this woman to keep your plans secret from her husband."

"That would not guarantee her safety. You know how it is-there are always some warriors who fail to receive the word."

"I am at an utter loss by what evidence your faith in her allegiance is warranted; nothing in her conduct leads me to such a conclusion. All the indications point to the contrary."

"She is true to me. I assure it."

"I'm wasting my time. You will do as you have a mind to, but I must be honest, Lord, that this time I seriously question your judgment. I am most disillusioned."

"I expect you to give me the counsel that you perceive correct; I won't censure you for this. But you will see, in this case, you are wrong."

"So you will send her word of your plan."

"I must! I cannot risk possible injury or death to her."

Cihuacoatl recognized the futility of persisting in his opposition to the notion, and while still incensed, he had no desire to alienate his master any further through obtuse recalcitrance. Plagued with extreme reservations, he reluctantly changed his mood and assumed a supportive stance on Ahuitzotl's misguided proposal.

"Shall I call for a messenger, Lord? I presume you will want to instruct him personally on the words he is to convey to Lady Pelaxilla."

"Yes," Ahuitzotl answered, gratified that the minister now saw things his way. "It must be carried by one of our lords so that it will be received in Cocijoeza's court."

Cihuacoatl understood; the message had to be served in a capacity that commanded official access to the highest circles in Tehuantepec, a condition not guaranteed by a mere courier. As luck would have it, Cocijoeza's formal request for assistance in moving against Soconusco had also been received and lent a legitimacy to the expectation of a message from Anahuac. The minister obtained his courier from the lords trained in diplomacy who worked with the ambassadors and delegates sent to various nations. He soon returned, bringing a young noble before the Revered Speaker.

"His name is Tezomoc," the minister said. "He is the eldest son of our ambassador to Cholula and comes highly recommended. He can be relied upon to do all you ask, Lord."

Ahuitzotl first studied the young noble, a handsome man who ought to give a good account of himself, then handed him a folded parchment which a scribe had written while the minister was out.

"In your hands is an important message which is to go to one person, and that person only," Ahuitzotl began. "It is of such importance that you must yourself give it to that person. You will carry it to Tehuantepec as swiftly as possible. There is a Mexicatl empress at the palace of the Zapotec lord, Cocijoeza; her name is Pelaxilla-to her alone you will give this parchment. So that you are received by the Zapotec ruler and have access to his court, you will also bear a second message-a verbal one-which he will eagerly expect and welcome. You will inform him that our war council has convened and agreed to assist him in subjugating Soconusco. We will march from Anahuac on the day Tochtli next month. This gives you nearly a month's start on us. Have you any questions regarding your assignment?"

"How will I know this Pelaxilla, Lord?" Tezomoc asked. "And what if I do not see her?"

"She is their queen. If the Zapotecans adhere to their custom, the good news you bring Cocijoeza will prompt him to invite you, as a noble, to a feast in his palace. There you should meet her. She is surrounded by her Mexica handmaidens; if you address these ladies in our tongue, they will certainly direct you to her. But approach them with subtleness—discretion is necessary. I rely on your tact to accomplish this. If, in spite of this, you are unable to meet with her, you will have to use your initiative to somehow make contact with her. The message is crucial and must reach her."

"I shall do my best, Lord," Tezomoc answered confidently. "You can depend on me."

"Good! And if Pelaxilla has any messages for me, you can intercept us on your return journey to Anahuac. The route to Tehuantepec, while quite long, is essentially under our control; I do not see any difficulties for you."

Tezomoc rendered a respectful bow and left the palace with Cihuacoatl who arranged for a small escort with Tlohtzin. Early at dawn on the following day, the party was on its way, leaving Tenochtitlan across its southern causeway to Ixtapalapa.

Ahuitzotl viewed its departure overwhelmed with a sense of grave uncertainty. He had committed himself irreversibly to an act which defied all sound military logic and was having his troubles reconciling this as a proper move. Cihuacoatl was correct in emphasizing that there was nothing in Pelaxilla's conduct which supported a claim she that still retained an allegiance to Tenochtitlan, or to him. Yet the slightest probability that she no longer loved him was utterly unthinkable to him, so horrible to contemplate, that he could not bring himself towards acknowledging its acceptance, and while he was at a loss to explain her behavior, he believed Tlalalca in her supposition that Pelaxilla simply was not afforded the opportunity to contact him. He had to believe this. What else could it be? She loved him, and he loved her, a love deep and eternal; nothing would ever come between them to change that. Yes, he had done the right thing, he repeatedly said to himself; if anything were to happen to his dear Pelaxilla as a consequence of his failure to adequately prepare her for his coming, he would never be able to forgive himself. His satisfaction thus restored, Ahuitzotl walked back to the palace to seek comfort from Tlalalca.

VII

ochtli, the eighth day of the month, came early to Tenochtitlan, its dawn being heralded by the deep, thunderous pounding of the giant panhuehuetl calling the armies into formation. The Revered Speaker issued a directive that none be permitted to absent themselves from this undertaking except the aged, maimed, women, and children and selected priests and other officials required to keep the city functioning. The order was not actually necessary as it had been nearly two years since the citizenry had occasion to engage in warfare and enthusiasm ran high. Even the prospect of an eight-hundred league march served as no deterrent to the eagerness demonstrated by the warriors.

If the soldiers of Tenochtitlan embraced the coming campaign, the rulers of its allied cities did not share in their excitement. Chimalpopoca assured Ahuitzotl that his chief commander, Colotl, would lead the Tepanecs, but he himself abstained-he was too old for this trek and had no confidence that he would ever return to Anahuac if he dared to undertake it. Ahuitzotl was not surprised by this and, although he did his best to encourage the Tepanec lord-he tried to force his hand by sending him the arms and unit insignia only a monarch could carry-he could understand Chimalpopoca's reluctance for the long march. The lord of Tlacopan had over twenty years on him, and it could readily be discerned that his actions were indeed slowed, to say nothing of his zeal. It might be better that he stayed behind as his lack of ardor could impart a negative impression on his warriors-so Ahuitzotl rationalized Chimalpopoca's absence.

With Nezahualpilli, Ahuitzotl was less likely to tolerate any shirking of what he considered a paramount duty. He had received no word from the Texcocan if he meant to lead his army but accepted that his association with Texcoco was still at a low over the execution of Nenetzin. In fact, to some extend this operation offered a test to ascertain how things stood between the two monarchs and whether the hostilities remained. Nezahualpilli made no promises over his participation in the venture and left Ahuitzotl wondering about it up to the day the expedition was scheduled to leave. In all his reports to Tenochtitlan, he carefully avoided mentioning the Acolhua leader by name–the Revered Speaker was not to find this out for certain until the armies merged in Cholula-giving Ahuitzotl ample reasons for suspecting the worst. He would have to prepare himself for another setback, Ahuitzotl thought as Tochtli arrived and he had not yet received any confirmation out of his Texcocan ally.

Ahuitzotl's army took the road over the Eagle Pass pass between the snow-capped peaks of Iztaccihuatl and Popocatepetl, a long upward climb that wearied its warriors and slowed their pace. Ordinarily, Ahuitzotl might have found this trek to his liking, awed by the magnificent green forests and natural beauty of the open glades between them, but as a result of his impatience in arriving at Tehuantepec, the pass now posed a major obstacle for him, exasperating him with its endless winding trail as it led higher and higher.

"Will it take us forever to reach the summit?" Ahuitzotl groaned. "I did not remember it being this long."

"We've always given ourselves at least two full days to get there, Lord," Tlohtzin reminded him. "Why the hurry, Lord? Soconusco will not disappear if we lose a day's march."

"I was not aware of my haste."

"You are flustered by the long climb; you push our forward elements to hasten their step; you move as fast as possible without actually running. Yes, it is apparent."

"You've kept up well enough."

"I've maintained my burden quietly, Lord. The fact is that I'm driven to exhaustion and am at the point of collapsing."

Tlohtzin's words focused Ahuitzotl's attention back to the welfare of his warriors, a concern he always took into high regard but presently overlooked in his preoccupation over getting to his destination. He scanned over his porters and nearby soldiers, taking notice of their laborious breathing and excessive perspiration. "Give the lead chieftain word to set up a campsite at the first clearing," Ahuitzotl directed. "Our journey is long. There's no point in expending ourselves in its early stages."

Ahuitzotl may have thought this at the end of the day's march, moved to compassion when he saw his servants toiling under the weight of their baggage, but the next morning, after breaking camp, the army proceeded as rapidly as before. The uphill climb along the road rising between the two mountain peaks was strenuous, lasting an entire day, and yet the army was prodded continuously to maintain the furious pace set by its restless monarch. Not until dusk came upon them did this relentless drive offer the warriors a respite; their present campsite was set up a few leagues after they crossed the summit. At this high altitude, the night air was frigid and bonfires were lit to keep warm, and in front of his fire at the command post, Ahuitzotl was huddled with a blanket about him and in the accompaniment of Tlohtzin and Motecuhzoma.

"Might I ask, Lord, why we move at such a pace?" Tlohtzin inquired, still annoyed over the arduous day's trek. "You drive us as if propelled ahead by some unreasonable force."

Ahuitzotl stared blankly into the flickering flames seemingly oblivious of what was around him. Tlohtzin doubted that his master heard him and glanced at Motecuhzoma who seemed equally puzzled over his strange comportment.

"I have endured all the humiliation I can take from this vile Zapotecan, Cocijoeza," Ahuitzotl at last replied still glaring into the fire. "If I move with urgency, it's because I wish to bring my struggle with him to a close as soon as possible. As long as he continues to rule in Tehuantepec, he stands as a power in opposition to me-and I will not have it!"

He had confirmed what Cihuacoatl said, but Tlohtzin nevertheless feigned surprise. "I thought we are on the way to assist him in defeating Soconusco," he said. "Yet you speak as if our conflict is with him. Is it proper to ask why you want to do this?"

"Why?" Ahuitzotl replied and then hesitated in searching for a suitable answer. "Because he alone, of all the monarchs I have warred on, has managed to battle us to a draw and can boast of it. His arrogance exists as a thorn in my side, and I mean to put an end to it."

"You should have told us, Lord. This will require revisions in our plans-the commanders should be briefed on it."

"Not yet. Cocijoeza must be taken by complete surprise: he must suspect nothing. It's better our warriors believe they are on the way to assist him-the enemy has his ears everywhere. No one must know otherwise until the right moment arrives."

"How will we amass our armies for the assault on Tehuantepec if we are divided by a day's interval all the way there? He keeps a large army there."

"He must assemble it first. Remember, he thinks we are coming to assist him and will welcome us with open arms as befits the custom. He will be caught unprepared to counter us if we unexpectedly turn on him."

"A treacherous act-one not likely to grant us honor."

"You may condemn the method, but not its necessity. Cocijoeza humiliated us—I seek retribution."

After two more days of marching, although now at a more reasonable pace as Ahuitzotl conceded his exertions strained his force, the Mexica arrived at Cholula where the local ruler treated their principals to a regal feast in his palace. While camped outside the city, Ahuitzol received a messenger from Texcoco confirming Nezahualpilli had chosen to remain in his city and left the command of the Acolhuacan army to his eldest son, Coanacoch. Even though Ahuitzotl had suspected all along that his ally meant to stay away, the news nevertheless embittered him.

"Nezahualpilli will not lead his army," he said to Tlohtzin. "There is still ill feeling between us, as I feared."

"Why regret it?" Motecuhzoma interjected scornfully. "We are better off without him."

"I expected to hear that from you," Ahuitzotl grumbled. "You harbor a lasting grudge against him for what he has done to Nenetzin. I warn you-let the matter rest. Nezahualpilli did what any lord in his position would have done-even you."

"I disagree, Lord. He went far beyond what was prudent and capitalized on the occasion to direct personal insults upon us. Exonerate him if you wish, but as long as I live, I shall hold him accountable for that."

The tension was mounting between Ahuitzotl and Motecuhzoma, much to the former's irritation, but he refrained from denouncing his commander on the basis that it was too early in the expedition to have friction arising among its leaders. When he retired that night, Ahuitzotl sensed a recalcitrance developing in Motecuhzoma that did not sit well with him, and he pondered how much of this he should abide before putting the youngster in his place.

Following a day of resting at Cholula, the army resumed its march across the high plateau characterizing its vicinity and proceeded in a southeasterly direction for Tochtepec, the Mixtec city taken by Ahuitzotl during his previous incursion through this region. Ahuitzotl again pushed his army as much as was feasible, taking full advantage of the last clear and level stretch along the journey to Tehuantepec; once past Tochtepec, the road veered south to Mixtlan over terrain that was rugged and marked by sinuous trails crossing one valley after another. Upon arriving there, they were accorded a favorable reception-Ahuitzotl's earlier coming was well remembered and no one dared risk offending the Mexica warlord.

Ahuitzotl rested for two days at Tochtepec. In part, he was troubled over having forced his warriors to move at the exhausting pace he set for them. They became dispirited and their grumbling reached the ears of their commanders who feared they would not be able to subdue the rising discontent; the days of relaxation would remedy this situation. Also he was interested in seeing what had been accomplished in the way of rebuilding the city. His forces had dealt severely with it in their initial encounter with its inhabitants suffering horrible losses; Ahuitzotl was impressed that the Mixtecs actually decided on resettling there. While the townspeople may have trembled on hearing of his second coming, this time he was amiably disposed towards them and strove to allay their fears, refusing to allow his warriors to commit abuses of any kind.

Even after his resting period in Tochtepec, the Army of Tepaneca had not caught up with Ahuitzotl's force, an indication of how forceful he had been urging his warriors onward. He debated on whether to give his army one more day's respite and decided against it, his anxiousness getting the best of him. Before departing, he left the local ruler with the distasteful news that there would be two more armies to feed and restock with provisions following his own-Tochtepec would be emptied of its food reserve and was in no position to deny its 'guests' what they wanted. Even as peaceful visitors, the Mexica created problems for the Mixtecs.

Ahuitzotl's army retraced the route it took when it devastated the Mixtec nation prior to becoming stalemated in battling the Zapotecs at Giengola. From Tochtepec, it moved southerly through the narrow valleys and dense forests distinguishing its passage toward the next city of any consequence, the Mixtec capital, Mixtlan. There the Mexica were heralded with all the dignity and gala the local populace could offer. To Ahuitzotl's amazement, none other than the Mixtec monarch, Tezacoalco, his previous antagonist, now was hosting him in his palace. Ahuitzotl had believed Tezacoalco died in the fighting at Giengola as none of the later reports he received when exacting tributes from the Mixtecs alluded to any supposition that his former enemy was alive. Their meeting was of keen interest to both men, and each made a lengthy assessment of the other. Tezacoalco was decidedly at a disadvantage, his empire having been subjugated and consigned a tribute state to Anahuac; Ahuitzotl understood his predicament and made it clear to him his purpose was directed elsewhere. Still, he wished to learn of Tezacoalco's relationship with Cocijoeza, his one-time ally.

"The old rivalries and hostilities are returning," Tezacoalco said to Ahuitzotl through an interpreter. "Our unity was effective only while we faced a common opponent—you. Since then, we find ourselves pressured by continuous inroads into our regions by the Zapotecs, as it has been for many generations. There is no feeling of kinship among us; quite the opposite in fact, we very much despise them."

"I assume Cocijoeza shares your viewpoint."

"He is most powerful, and a resourceful ruler, Great Lord. Like you, he has aims of expanding his domain and will resort to whatever means available to enhance his own glory and position. You say you are to help him take Soconusco-no doubt he had much to do with generating this state of affairs. That is typical of how Cocijoeza operates."

"You suggest that I err in trusting him."

"He is the devious sort. Whatever designs he has in mind, you can be assured he intends to come out the winner."

"These are harsh words for a former ally; however, I shall consider your assessment and will keep on the alert for any deception. No one will come out ahead of me in my own enterprises."

"Good. Perhaps you will do something about the inequitable manner in which my nation is treated as compared with Zapoteca."

"Inequitable?"

"The tributes you demand from us are triple those you exact from them. What have we done to deserve this? Cocijoeza fought you as hard as we did; yet he was hardly touched by you—his cities were spared while mine were gutted. If I seem bitter, Great Lord, you must agree I have my justifications."

Ahuitzotl studied his host, impressed with his bearing; it took nerve to sit in the presence of the ruler who conquered his nation and insist he was being unfairly treated. Yet his point was valid, Ahuitzotl thought, and he would have liked giving him his assurance the situation would soon change but deemed it too risky at present to reveal his own deception of Cocijoeza.

"I shall address your grievance when I return," Ahuitzotl said. "We can do something about it, I'm sure."

"That makes my burdens more bearable, Lord. I do not like Cocijoeza scoffing at me. He makes a grand show of his new wife and how she confirms his friendship with you."

Ahuitzotl turned ashen; this was the first time he heard of her since his departure from Anahuac. "Do you speak of Pelaxilla?" he asked nervously.

"That is her-the woman you sent to him."

"You have seen her?"

"I was at the wedding. Cocijoeza boasts of her as if she represented his most brilliant triumph. His masterstroke he calls it. She is a most attractive woman, to be sure, but that ought not give the man cause to scorn the rest of us. He has made abundant use of her to promote his prestige among his lords."

"Believe me, that was not my purpose in sending her to him. But tell me, did she seem happy to you? What did you make of her disposition?"

Tezacoalco thought the questions peculiar when his translator conveyed them to him, and he eyed his guest curiously before responding. "She seemed most happy, Lord," he presently said. "She had wonderful, shining eyes-I stood next to her-and she warmed us with her gleaming smile. A lovely lady she is and yes, quite content I would say."

Ahuitzotl tensed. This was the very thing he did not want to hear and it aroused in him grave suspicions about Pelaxilla; his heartbeat accelerated and he was overwhelmed by the feverish hot flashes that always struck him when he sensed she was lost to him.

"So nothing in her behavior led you to believe that she regretted this marriage," Ahuitzotl continued.

"Certainly not, Lord. She was very happy."

This was too much for Ahuitzotl and he sank into his chair feeling weak. His appetite ruined, he barely touched the plate of food in front of him and was in no mood to enjoy the singers and dancers Tezacoalco had entertaining his guests. He sat brooding and seething, making his commanders uncomfortable with his dour and dispirited nature. "I will destroy him," Ahuitzotl muttered to himself audibly enough to be heard by those next to him, including Tezacoalco and his interpreter. "By Huitzilopochtli! If I live to do one more act, it must be to destroy him!"

"Of whom does my lord speak?" asked Tezacoalco after these words were related to him.

Ahuitzotl gave his host a wild look; his eyes glowed as fire and his entire face was contorted to present him in a disagreeable posture. He rose from his chair, too taut and restless to remain seated. "I must take my leave, Tezacoalco," he said under heavy breath. "I regret that you and I did not meet under more favorable circumstances. We might have become friends."

Tlohtzin, Motecuhzoma, and the other chieftains arose with intentions of leaving with their master, but Ahuitzotl halted them. "Stay here," he advised them. "Do Tezacoalco the honor of his hospitality. I need to be by myself."

They were delighted in hearing this-the feasting was joyous and the food delicious-and willingly resumed their dining as they watched their troubled master depart. Tezocoalco remained mystified over this. "Have I offended your lord?" he asked Tlohtzin who sat at his opposite side.

"Not you, Lord," answered the commander, "but rather Cocijoeza. His animosity is for the Zapotecan."

"Indeed?" replied an amazed Tezacoalco. "And yet he goes to help him war on Soconusco. Your motivations are, if you will pardon my saying so, somewhat peculiar to me."

"In truth, Lord, I am often confused by them myself."

Tezacoalco liked Tlohtzin's reply; a glint of humor shone in his eyes and he smiled. "The man your lord must destroy-I assume he speaks of Cocijoeza. A strange sort of alliance you Mexica have with the Zapotecs."

"It was struck up solely between our Revered Speaker and the Zapotecan monarch, and somehow involved Pelaxilla. I say to you, Lord, that she is the major source of his problems. She was his favorite mistress, you know."

"If that was so, why did he give her to Cocijoeza?"

"It makes no sense to me, Lord. But I say too much over a matter I am not clear on. Certainly something seems amiss."

Tezacoalco leaned back in his chair and brought a goblet to his lips, and after he drained its contents and set it back down, a smirk was seen on his face. He did not have to be told anything; he had understood it all. He knew.

From Mixtlan, the army continued marching south, again prodded rapidly forward by Ahuitzotl whose desperation to reach Tehuantepec was approaching the breaking point. The terrain posed a tortuous obstacle, with the trail winding back and forth across repeated ridges and through deep and narrow valleys, and in passing each successive range, the elevation lowered with a corresponding rise in temperature; the warriors remembered how hot and miserable the region seemed to them the last time.

At the mouth of one of those defiles, they came across the fortress city of Xaltepec and saw it looming over the vicinity in a shattering ruin, standing out as a stark reminder of the cruel fashion in which Ahuitzotl had ordered its destruction. Desolate with its torn down walls gloomily accented against the hillside, it apparently had not been considered worthwhile for the Mixtecs to rebuild, even though Ahuitzotl viewed its location strategic in guarding the southern approach to Mixtlan and thought its reoccupation essential. Perhaps Tezocoalco could not pursuade anyone to settle there for exactly that reason: it stood out as a target city and no one wished facing a repeated slaughter such as occurred there. Ahuitzotl's army camped beneath the ruins and when he walked alone through the burned out palaces and temples that afternoon, he pondered over how Tezacoalco managed to suppress the rage he must have surely felt towards him for having done this. He sensed a sadness in it; he did not want his destruction to be lasting-there was no point in that.

The next day, the army continued on its march and a week later reached Itzcuintepec. When the Mexica came upon the city's outer perimeter, the local ruler, along with his principal lords, stepped forth to greet Ahuitzotl and to invite him to a gala held in his honor. They were lavishly regaled, dining on spicy, succulent dishes while entertained by wrestlers and a group of acrobats. Tlohtzin and Motecuhzoma thought the show delightful, considering the resources available, but Ahuitzotl was too restive to engross himself in the performances and preoccupied with reaching his next destination, Tototepec, where he would enter Zapoteca. Now that he was this close to the border, he became even more obsessed over making that final and long awaited contact with Cocijoeza. The despised monarch had dominated all his thinking since their last encounter and as the moment of truth was nearing, Ahuitzotl needed a release from all his pent up energies and so, as in Mixtlan, he excused himself early from the fete to walk by himself back to the campsite under a moonlit sky.

He was only a week from the Zapotec domain and twenty days from its capital, and his excitement mounted at its mere contemplation. He could hardly wait for the dawn-the night was too long for him-when he would continue his advance. Tototepec was but a transitory site of minor importance to him-his destiny lay in Tehuantepec. At long last, he would learn of the truths behind his Pelaxilla's enigmatic behavior.

VIII

n arduous trek lay between Itzcuintepec and Tototepec—more so than Ahuitzotl had remembered from his previous journey over the route. The valleys were low and their insect infested forests so dense that they blocked out the sun, and the road was narrow and sinuous, often nothing more than a trodden path, with Ahuitzotl's army stretched out along it for miles as warriors moved in columns of no more than two abreast. Internal communicated was difficult with security of the flanks all but neglected as patrols had to hack through the jungle undergrowth as they advanced.

More annoying than the terrain was the temperature, oppressively hot in this lower altitude, and for the Mexica who spent their entire lives in the cooler highlands of Anahuac, an adjustment far from easy. The dampness caused their cotton tunics and armor to stick to their perspiring bodies and insects stung at their exposed flesh, buzzing irritatingly about their heads; a climate inhospitable in the extreme and they could not comprehend how anyone could live in it.

Halfway into their sixth day after leaving Itzcuintepec, the valley began to widen and its roadway extended ahead in a fairly straight direction making the journey considerably lighter for them. Ahuitzotl believed they were now in Zapoteca, reasoning that the ranges they crossed over constituted a natural barrier defining its borders, but as yet he had not seen any signs of villages or agricultural development which might have denoted a population center. But if his movement seemed to go unnoticed that afternoon, things turned out quite differently on the following day. After breaking camp and proceeding onward that morning, the forward elements of the army were soon met by a scout from the advance party who had been sent back to alert the main body that it would encounter a Zapotec force. He was taken to Ahuitzotl and repeated his story.

"You say the Zapoteca wait for us?" Ahuitzotl asked.

"Yes, Lord, just before their city, Tototepec. We spotted them as we moved into the clearing."

"How many are there?"

"Not many, but we could not tell; there appeared to be more of them waiting in the city."

"A welcoming delegation perhaps," Tlohtzin guessed. "They knew we were coming."

"So it seems, but why?"

"My guess is that Cocijoeza means to provide us with guides to take us to Tehuantepec."

"I don't like it. There's a conniving behind this," Ahuitzotl muttered. A cold sensation came over him, as if he realized something was drastically wrong here. Although Cocijoeza expected the Mexica to assist in his efforts against Soconusco, why should this in itself call for a delegation, especially with Tehuantepec still a week's journey away? Such an overture was rarely done unless requested-clearly it represented an unusual action.

Ahuitzotl and Tlohtzin moved to the head of the column so as to get a first-hand look at what was in store for them when they reached Tototepec. After arriving there, Ahuitzotl directed the force to continue on its advance. With worried impatience, he set a hurried pace for his army as it proceeded on until he could see a clearing ahead. When he and his warriors emerged from the forests, they were greeted by a stunning sight.

In front of them, in a cleared plain before Tototepec, stood the entire Zapotec army in full battle gear and massed along two lines extending as far as the eye could see with an open pathway centered between them. Ahuitzotl stared at the grand spectacle in stunned amazement, unable to give expression to his astonishment.

"The whole Zapotec army is here!" Tlohtzin exclaimed.

"It cannot be!" Ahuitzotl gulped, disbelieving what he was seeing.

"If that's not them, then perhaps you had best relieve me of my duties, Lord."

"What can it mean?"

"We'll know soon enough. Their commander is approaching us."

A richly attired warrior wearing a headdress of plumages extending half his body height above his head walked in the company of several other captains equally splendorously adorned. Ahuitzotl and Tlohtzin moved out to meet them midway between the armies while Mexica warriors stood poised, prepared for the unexpected. Ahuitzotl did not see Cocijoeza among the officials coming to see him, but the chief commander had all the regal bearing of high nobility about him and the Revered Speaker surmised he was of the royal family. There was a sober demeanor about them; if they were here to greet the Mexica, they regarded their task with grave seriousness. The chief commander spoke first.

"I am here to welcome the Mexica sovereign, Lord Ahuitzotl, to Zapoteca upon the request of my master, Lord Cocijoeza. Is it he I am addressing?

"It is," Ahuitzotl affirmed.

"I am Cochija, younger brother of Lord Cocijoeza and commander of our army. I am instructed to escort you and your army to Tehuantepec and beyond, to the borders of Soconusco, where I am to help in conquering that realm as agreed on by the terms send to us."

"Why does Lord Cocijoeza find this necessary?" Ahuitzotl asked, not at all pleased over Cochija's orders. "I did not request an escort."

"He extends this special honor to you for rendering him assistance. We will provide a similar escort for each of your armies so that none will feel slighted. My master did not think you would object; indeed, he knew you would appreciate it."

Ahuitzotl turned red and was at a temporary loss for words. Clearly Cocijoeza distrusted him, but how could he have known what treachery had been planned for him? The only person who knew of these plans was Pelaxilla; she could not possibly have confided them in him-or could she? No, that was not possible! Maybe Tezomoc revealed them, having read the parchment given him. But that did not make sense-he had no cause to do that. It must have been Pelaxilla. One thing was absolutely certain: with his Zapotecan escort, his scheme could not be implemented.

"Inform your lord we are grateful for his concern," Ahuitzotl finally replied, "but the Mexica are capable of conducting their own campaigns and do not require an escort. We can use some of his warriors as guides but think his army can be put to better use under his independent leadership."

"Am I to tell him that you spurn the honor he grants you?"

Ahuitzotl sensed his temperature rising as he suppressed an inclination to burst forth in a volley of vehemence, but was forced to constrain himself. For one thing, the move was highly imprudent with his warriors outnumbered by what seemed ever increasing proportions as more and more Zapotec units emerged from Tototepec. Although fuming within, he feigned a skillful demonstration of gratitude. "I suppose that would be callous of us," he answered. "It's not our wish to undermine Lord Cocijoeza's well-meaning gesture; after all, we have a partnership in this venture. Are we to meet him?"

"You are, Great Lord. He has an invitation for you and your chieftains and priests to a royal reception. He expects you to remain there for several days of resting after your long journey."

What Cocijoeza had in mind, Ahuitzotl surmised, was to keep his army there long enough until it merged with those of his allies so he could maintain them all under his surveillance while his own army stood intact to protect him. In extreme exasperation, Ahuitzotl could see his scheme unraveling-all his planning, all his hopes for destroying Cocijoeza and reclaiming his honor, all the effort exerted in its implementation were dashed to pieces. Worse, he had now something far greater to worry about: why had Pelaxilla done this to him?

"Very well," Ahuitzotl declared, "Lead us to Tehuantepec."

Cochija said something to one of his chieftains who hastily sped toward the Zapotecan units and passed the words on to various commanders. Immediately thereupon, the entire body of assembled warriors on both sides of the divided pathway shouted out a thunderous applause meant to gratify their deliverers. Thousands of voices rang out as the soldiers raised their spears and shields over their heads and greeted the Mexica.

To the Mexica warriors, who knew nothing of their monarch's deceptive aims, this reception was heartily received as they soaked up the ingratiating laudations; they soon joined their 'allies' in the merriment, whooping and cheering and in general relishing the honors accorded them. As prodigious and glorious a welcome as they had ever encountered, they expressed their elation in the smiles and satisfied glances they gave each other. Amid the persisting applause, the Mexica advanced toward their generous host and, with the Zapotecs on both sides of them, began the trek to Tehuantepec under their benign escort.

Everywhere they marched, the populace embraced the Mexica with persistent roars of approval. After resting in Tototepec for a day, under the watchful eyes of their host, girls placed flowers on their tunics as they paced through the streets on their way to the capital, giving them heartwarming smiles and profusely thanking them for having come so far to help their own warriors. Ahuitzotl's soldiers could not help but be seduced by such an acclamation-it constituted an extension of friendship never previously rendered to them and they reacted with pride and exhiliration to it. Even Tlohtzin and Motecuhzoma were impressed by the spectacle and seemed to relish in it; only one person in the Mexica force was displeased: the Revered Speaker.

For Ahuitzotl, the reception spelled doom for any plan to defeat his wily adversary, and as the two armies proceeded, he remained in a state of shocked agitation trying to piece together the events that had brought this about. He could no longer deny that Pelaxilla had a hand in it, no matter how horrifying that prospect struck him-she had alerted Cocijoeza to the deception planned for him. But why? How could she do this to him? He feared the answer was the most unthinkable of all possibilities: Pelaxilla, his one great love, who swore she would always love him, was lost to him. Against all expectations, she had rejected him in favor of Cocijoeza.

The more he dwelled on this subject, the greater rose his vehemence for the Zapotec monarch. He was not even a handsome man, decidedly fat with his excessively wrinkled face dominated by a disproportionately large aquiline nose. What did Pelaxilla, the most beautiful of women, see in such a man? His frustration was aggravated by a perception that he was unable to do anything about this situation-with his escort, which was in actuality a bodyguard for Cocijoeza rather than an augmentation force, he could do nothing. He was, in every respect, within Cocijoeza's palm.

The journey lasted ten days from Tototepec to the Zapotecan capital-long days which strained Ahuitzotl's impatience to the extreme brink. He ached for Pelaxilla; he knew once he saw her and talked to her, he could dissuade her from the course she had set upon. If she saw him, she would again remember how much she truly loved him and would want to return to Tenochtitlan with him. As each successive day passed, Ahuitzotl's anxieties turned more and more toward regaining his Pelaxilla than from seeking vengeance on Cocijoeza. He now all but abandoned his plan to destroy the Zapotecan and was preoccupied only with getting Pelaxilla back as no more hope existed for the former, but he knew once he talked with her he would again succeed in recapturing devotion. The deep love they had for each other was sure to reassert itself. He yearned for the reception gala arranged for him-there he would at last meet her.

The welcome bestowed on Ahuitzotl's warriors at Tehuantepec exceeded anything they had ever experienced. The entire population was lined along the main avenue leading to the central plaza roaring out its professed approval with deafening consistency. "Ahuitzotl! Ahuitzotl! Ahuitzotl!" the crowds poured out over and over, each time louder than before, in a stunning display of exuberance.

"See how they honor you, Lord?" Tlohtzin commented. "Tenochtitlan has never equaled this. Truly they appreciate our help in taking Soconusco."

"It has nothing to do with Soconusco!" Ahuitzotl snarled. "This entire exhibition is designed to keep us in check. Cocijoeza has my warriors exactly where he wants them-tamed by flattery and under his control."

"I'm loathe to say it, but Cocijoeza has conceived a masterly ploy. We shall have to be content with Soconusco. Obviously we can no longer attack Tehuantepec after this."

"Finally you begin to understand. I have been betrayed!"

"Betrayed? By whom, Lord?"

"The only person who knew of what I planned–Pelaxilla."

"You revealed your plan to her?" Tlohtzin replied in a manner suggesting it was the most foolish act that could ever have been perpetrated.

"How could I have known? After all, she was sent here to help me defeat Cocijoeza."

"It seems her loyalties were misplaced. I see why you were distrustful of our reception. It all makes sense now."

"I fear I must prepare myself for a greater setback."

"Worse than being betrayed?"

"I may have lost her," Ahuitzotl fretted.

"Lost her? You confound me, Lord. I should think you would seek to punish her for this."

How could Tlohtzin know? Ahuitzotl had never confided his personal life to the commander and saw how his concern over losing Pelaxilla must have seemed paradoxical to him. "It's a complex affair," Ahuitzotl said in almost complete resignation. "To presently relate it gives it an absurd dimension-I doubt if it would be understandable."

By now they had arrived in the city's plaza. Ahead of them rested the double-storied palace of Cocijoeza. Enormous and magnificent, it rivaled any such structure in Tenochtitlan, rendering its surrounding buildings diminutive in comparison; only the temple to the rain god, Cojico, the principal deity of the Zapotecs, loomed more massively over the square. Ahuitzotl's heartbeat quickened as he neared the steps leading to the main doorway of Cocijoeza's residence; he noticed a group of prominent figures atop the stairway awaiting his arrival. Among them, at their center, was a corpulent man dressed in a white tunic and golden loincloth which extended to knee level. A deep blue cape was slung over his shoulder and reached to his ankles behind him and he wore a golden crown edged by blue feathers rising two head-lengths above him. Even from a distance of still fifty paces, Ahuitzotl knew this was Cocijoeza.

When Ahuitzotl reached the base of the steps, he stopped and looked up at the Zapotec monarch and his ministers who stood glaring down at him. Although Cocijoeza cut an impressive profile in his finery, Ahuitzotl still regarded him with notable contempt, thinking him too fat and disagreeable in features to be an influential ruler. But, begrudgingly, he had to acknowledge the Zapotecan's cunning and resourcefulness as he was the only enemy leader to battle him to a stalemate, an extraordinary achievement by any account-Ahuitzotl could not deny him that distinction. Cocijoeza nodded his head-a gesture amplified by the huge plumage of his headdress-to indicate that he was ready to receive his guest.

"My master bids you to meet him," Cochija said to Ahuitzotl. "He wishes to speak to you."

Ahuitzotl and Tlohtzin started up the steps, while Cocijoeza and two of his ministers stepped down, so that they would meet in the middle. The Revered Speaker's eyes never left his host as he tried to ascertain what qualities this ruler possessed which might have attracted Pelaxilla. He did not understand it-certainly not the man's appearance could have captured her fascination, for when they faced each other, Ahuitzotl detected the many wrinkles and furrowed lines in the Zapotecan's face. In addition to being considerably heavier than Ahuitzotl, he was also older.

"I welcome you to Tehuantepec," Cocijoeza spoke out in a fluent Nahuatl tongue; his eyes emitted a warm glow which focused attention to them-was it this that captivated Pelaxilla?-but he gave a smirk which Ahuitzotl perceived with resentment. "I trust you had a good journey."

"An uneventful one," answered Ahuitzotl. "I hope our march to Soconusco will be more promising."

"It will, but we can discuss this later. Now it is better that you bathe and wash off the dust of your travels. We have prepared a banquet for your pleasure this evening and I would have you join me and my lovely wife at my table."

His words cut into Ahuitzotl like a knife. "I assume you speak of the lady Pelaxilla," he said.

"I do." Cocijoeza grinned, causing Ahuitzotl to seethe. "She was the most wonderful present you could have possibly sent to me, and I must not neglect to show my gratitude. But do not let me detain you from cleaning up; the comforts of my palace are at your disposal. Your warriors will camp next to my own on the eastern edge of the city, if this meets your approval."

"It is agreeable to me," Ahuitzotl replied, realizing there was little choice in the selection of the site. "I may remain with my warriors during the night, as is my habit; however, I do accept your offer to use your facilities."

"As ever, the warrior-king. I shall see you tonight then; my servants will guide you to the place. Before you enter, I request that you turn about and face my people gathered below. Let us raise our joined hands together to symbolize our partnership in this venture."

Ahuitzotl acceded to the ruler's wishes, and he turned to gaze over the crowded plaza. Momentarily ignoring the abhorrence he held for his host, he extended his right hand to Cocijoeza who clasped it tightly with his own fleshy palm and elevated it over his head. The multitude burst forth with exuberant jubilation, including the cohorts of warriors, Mexica and Zapotec, assembled with the townspeople. An impressive demonstration of cohesiveness it was-who out there could have known the weak connection which kept it in place? After savoring the laudation delivered them, Cocijoeza lowered his hand and released his grip. The applause gradually subsided as each party then set about to prepare themselves for the evening's gala.

Tlohtzin placed his subordinate commanders in charge of establishing the camp while he joined his master in the palace; lady servants provided for their care as they bathed in a communal pool reserved for honored guests. A short time Later, Motecuhzoma also joined them after having supervised setting up the command post. For Ahuitzotl, the pleasures afforded by the soothing lavation, while welcome enough, were but short-lived comforts to the greater complication possessing him, contributing little to ease the tenseness that beset him, and the afternoon dragged on agonizingly slow as he, in near desperation, waited for the banquet to begin. But he was finally in Tehuantepec, here, to where his destiny led him, where he would find the answers to all the questions that for so long tormented him—tonight he would learn the truth. The prospect held frightening ramifications, leaving him in a state of suspenseful duress, for it might confirm his deepest fears, and he was not certain how he would react to such a revelation. At long last, he was to again see Pelaxilla.

IX

The sun had set when Ahuitzotl, Tlohtzin, Motecuhzoma, and several of the ranking Mexica chieftains and priests came to the palace door. Although still daylight, braziers and torches already illuminated the interior halls shedding an inviting glow off the reddish plaster. An attendant greeted them and bade them to follow him; they were led into a cavernous room as spacious as any in Anahuac that easily held a hundred guests. When Ahuitzotl made his entrance, one of the dignitaries announced his coming; a temporary hush fell upon the celebrants who paused to see this famed conqueror-then the talking resumed as the guests continued their pleasure.

Cocijoeza, a broad smile covering his whole face, proceeded to where Ahuitzotl was standing in order to offer his visitor an appropriate welcome. He seemed quite delighted that the Mexica had arrived and started to introduce members of his royal family and Tehuantepec's leading nobles to them. He was justly proud of his sons, handsome men who had distinguished themselves in numerous battles, and spoke of each one's heroics. Ahuitzotl tried his best to give the monarch his undivided attention, but his interest remained focused elsewhere as he strained to see Pelaxilla; she was not present, or he did not see her as yet. Cocijoeza noticed the Revered Speaker's distraction. "I see that I bore you," he said. "You are looking for another member of my family."

"Is she here?" Ahuitzotl asked, certain Cocijoeza knew what he wanted.

"She will be-when we have seated ourselves for dinner."

"Why do you hide her from me until then? I see several other ladies present."

Cocijoeza stopped his walking to look directly into Ahuitzotl's eyes with a fierce penetration that almost had him reeling in its intensity. "Hear me, friend," Cocijoeza spoke out soberly, "She has told me of the love she once bore you, and for many days I truly feared this eventual encounter between you and her. At first I was adamant in keeping her out of your sight, but she has given me her assurances that things would no longer be the same between you two. I trust her, and have agreed to let you see her, and so you shall. You will have your moments of privacy with her-after we have completed our meal."

"Do you fear that our meeting will spoil the dinner for you?"

"No, Great Lord." Cocijoeza slowly emphasized. "I fear it will spoil the dinner for you."

Ahuitzotl turned pale; the certainty in which Cocijoeza uttered his words told him that things could indeed be as bad as he had feared. The Zapotecan might just as well have said Pelaxilla was lost to him-he clearly implied as much-and while he may not have realized it, he had already spoiled the dinner for his guest. Yet, even now, Ahuitzotl moved on the shred of hope that if he was offered the chance to see Pelaxilla, he could somehow rectify the situation and win her back. "You will allow me to speak with her in private?" Ahuitzotl wanted to be sure he heard it right.

"In one of my chambers. She expressed a desire to explain herself to you."

Ahuitzotl was not used to having his own time dictated by anyone; he still found it incomprehensible that Pelaxilla was now Cocijoeza's wife and he had no more influence over her. "I appreciate this," he said, trying hard to be the ingratiating guest. "It is important to me."

"I do this for her sake," Cocijoeza reminded Ahuitzotl. "You understand she belongs to me now, and I trust you to treat her accordingly."

His words offended Ahuitzotl-it seemed inconceivable that anyone but he could lay a claim on Pelaxilla-but he hid his displeasure. He had to accept it, he said to himself, no matter how the notion filled him with repugnance. He nodded his assent.

"Then I have nothing to fear," Cocijoeza responded, "Let us not dwell on the subject. We have more urgent thing to discuss-the operations against our common adversary, Soconusco."

And so their conversation was directed to the Soconusco campaign, and although a joint battle plan was developed as they spoke, Ahuitzotl found his concentration waning as he was anxiously awaiting Pelaxilla and, try as he might, could not divert his attention from this. Cocijoeza's noted his ally's hungry anticipation and decided not to delay any further in serving the dinner. He informed a servant to call his guests to their seats.

Court etiquette demanded that the Revered Speaker seat himself next to his host; this meant that Pelaxilla would be seated on Cocijoeza's left with him between them, and it was Cochija who was on her opposite side- Ahuitzotl had hoped he could have that distinction. He waited for his host to seat himself when he saw Pelaxilla entering the hall from one of its side portals. He stood entranced by her beauty as she approached them; she was even lovelier than he remembered and he was overcome with horrible regrets that he ever parted with her. Now that he saw her, all his desire for her again engulfed him and his heart ached for her.

Pelaxilla's eyes widened to two big bulbs when she saw Ahuitzotl. He thought a glow emanated from them but she did not smile or say anything and simply walked around the standing dignitaries in the direction of the Revered Speaker. She avoided looking at him when she passed by him; Ahuitzotl kept on beholding her, transfixed in his longing for her, until she stood beside her husband and waited for him to seat himself.

When Cocijoeza saw that all his guests had taken their place, he sat down, encouraging the rest into following his example, and soon the servants brought forth the first of many aromatic and tasty dishes. In typical fashion, the feasting began as a solemn occasion, but soon rejoicing and merrymaking inevitably ensued out of the conversation and comradeship. Even the more sober Mexica, who feared too much carousing could invoke envy out of the gods, joined in the revelry. Through a number of interpreters and the lady attendants who accompanied Pelaxilla to these regions, lighthearted humor was exchanged making for an atmosphere marked by congeniality. Cocijoeza led much of the hilarity, sharing his joking with Pelaxilla who responded with quiet and warm glances.

But Ahuitzotl did not enjoy the gaiety as he was highly discomfited at having Pelaxilla so near and yet not being able to possess her, and in many ways she was also quite restrained by his presence. Seemingly, both of them wanted, and needed, to speak out all the emotional conflicts which had taken hold of them. Ahuitzotl continued gazing at her, dazzled by her loveliness and yearning to speak to her. She would give him a quick glance and then, seeing how he was enraptured by her, straighten her head and proceed on her meal while pretending not to be moved by it, only to glance at him again. Clearly she was not altogether uninterested in Ahuitzotl-a vestige of her former desires still remained with her.

Cocijoeza was not unaware of their silent restraint and may have felt somewhat uneasy about it; he recognized Pelaxilla was a rare prize for him and any remote possibility of her former romantic inclinations being rekindled would have dismayed him. He thus deemed it appropriate to intervene in their quietude and by so doing perhaps spoil any chances of a recurrence of earlier passions. "You do not eat, friend," he remarked. "You do not speak, nor do you appear to enjoy yourself. Am I failing in hosting my guest properly?"

At first, Ahuitzotl did not even realize he was being spoken to; then he came back to the present. "You need not worry," he replied. "My chieftains are having the time of their lives."

"And you?"

"I do not have to explain my predicament to you. You said that your wife has fully apprised you of it."

"So she has, but she too is strangely quiet this evening. I may have erred in permitting her to see you after dinner."

"You did not err," Ahuitzotl tried to assure Cocijoeza, fearing he might change his mind. "She is your wife; nothing I can do will alter that. You have nothing to concern yourself about."

"Then I must trust you, friend. In the meantime, you should try to enjoy your meal. Your time with her will come soon enough."

Ahuitzotl wondered how Cocijoeza could have meant that. If Pelaxilla had revealed his plan to sieze Tehuantepec to him, it remained questionable if the Zapotecan could ever trust him. Perhaps now that he had effectively eliminated its chance of success, he had nothing more to fear from him.

The feasting proceeded as more dishes were introduced and entertainment was provided. A number of singers and dancers portrayed the regional songs and choreography prevalent through the nation, each group representing a particular variation. These were followed by acrobats who deftly performed their daring-dos in the hall's center floor from where its seated guests could observe their renditions. They put on a delightful show, and everyone appeared highly amused with it-except Ahuitzotl, and perhaps also Pelaxilla. The Revered Speaker was becoming increasingly anxious in his anticipation for the promised time alone with the empress;

all this frolicking was but a diversion to his true desires. He gripped his goblet in a futile attempt to alleviate his restlessness.

Somehow he managed to maintain his composure, after enduring moments when he feared he would explode in a burst of rage, until the feast finally drew to a close. After the concluding oblations were recited and the guests started to leave, Ahuitzotl at last felt a degree of relief from pressures that he thought would crush him.

"I shall see you later at the camp," Ahuitzotl told his companions. "I must see someone first."

"We can wait for you," replied Tlohtzin.

"No. I can't tell how long this will take."

"Is it wise to walk the city by yourself? This is not Tenochtitlan."

"No harm will come to me."

"As you wish, Lord." Tlohtzin said and then began to walk away with Motecuhzoma.

Ahuitzotl remained in the hall with Pelaxilla and Cocijoeza. He gave her a nervous glance, and she returned it with one of equal apprehensiveness; for both, this was a moment of extreme emotional intensity-one long sought and yet feared. Ahuitzotl's heart palpitated in his throat.

"She will take you to one of the chambers," Cocijoeza said. "Take as long as you like, but know that guards will be nearby; I will not have my wife's safety jeopardized."

Ahuitzotl thought this demeaning. He had already given Cocijoeza his word that he considered Pelaxilla his wife-as such, she was untouchable to him no matter how much he might have wished the contrary. "You do not have to belabor the point," Ahuitzotl answered. "I said you have nothing to fear."

"Then say what you must; I will not intrude on your privacy."

Cocijoeza stayed in the hall and watched as Pelaxilla departed with Ahuitzotl. She walked silently through a dimly lit corridor with him directly behind her. Her long black hair spread lustrously down her back stopping at her narrow waist, and the voluptuous swaying of her hips underneath her skirt enthralled him; for an instant, he entertained the thought of lifting her in his arms, as he had done so often before, and carrying her to bed. He fought off these notions, but they resurfaced repeatedly, testing his resolve.

She entered a room through a portal covered by a thickly woven curtain reaching to the floor. Once inside, she moved all the way to the opposite wall, then turned around and stood facing him. He again suppressed impulses to rush up to her and embrace her as they remained standing there in an inhibited hushed nervousness gazing at one another. His eyes spoke louder than anything he could have stated at that moment—the longing and hoping that she would once more be attracted to him was defined in them. And there was more: she saw the puzzlement, the disappointment, and even the anger over all that had happened since he last saw her. And there was frightful worry—the dread that he would have to accept what he could not cope with.

Pelaxilla's eyes spoke of sadness. She still found Ahuitzotl appealing and tried to repress strong emotional urges which overcame whenever she was in his presence. There was also fear, but of a different kind—she feared his wrath at having betrayed him. At length, the stillness became intolerable for her and she felt compelled to initiate the conversation. "Well?" she said, her voice quivering, "Say to me what you will, but do not torment me with this oppressive silence. That I cannot endure."

"You know what I want to talk about," he responded. "I must have an answer to this doubt torturing me all these months."

"I am prepared to answer all your questions."

"What has happened to us? Why did you refuse contact with me once you came here? You must have known the unbearable suffering this caused me."

"You should never have sent me here."

"Why?"

"At first, I was so heartsick at what you had done to me, and wished to hurt you in return for it. I wanted my silence to cause you torment—this I thought all the while as I was on that horribly long journey to this place. I was even more despondent when I at last glimpsed at the man you sent me to, Cocijoeza. I thought him old and repulsive, but then, when he began to speak to me and console me in my grief, and to see to my comfort here, something happened that I never expected. My heart reached out for him and I began to grow fond of him."

"No! Do not tell me this!" Ahuitzotl anguished.

"What could I do? It is the work of Xochiquetzal, and we are powerless when the goddess touches us."

"What are you saying? That you love this-this Zapotecan?"

"Yes, as I have never loved anyone before."

"You cannot mean it."

"He is a good man, and more affectionate and considerate of my needs than you have ever been. He has done more to help me and comfort me than you would have even thought about. Xochiquetzal has done her contrivance on me. I love this man."

Ahuitzotl was in shock; he thought it utterly incomprehensible that she could regard such a man with any kind of warmth. He considered Cocijoeza's appearance alone a deterrent to any possibility of affection arising out of their meeting; in his wildest dreams he would never have expected Pelaxilla to regard him in a favorable light. And now for her to declare that she loved him? This was too much. His initial astonishment gave way to enmity.

"You love him? But what of your love for me?"

"I cannot love two men with equal intensity. Xochiquetzal somehow does not allow for that. The love of one man always supersedes that of another, and so it is between us now. My love for Cocijoeza has overcome whatever feelings I once bore for you."

"You can say this to me even as I now stand before you?"

"What else can I say to you? I cannot revive something that is no longer in me. Cocijoeza has replaced you in my heart."

"That fat, pompous slob!" Ahuitzotl bellowed out, unable to check his mounting rage. "You spurn my love for such a man!"

Pelaxilla momentarily recoiled at his outburst, and then she struck back. "You ridicule the man. I tell you that his qualities far outshine yours in almost every respect, and if you mean to engage in a barrage of insults against him, I shall immediately leave."

"You shall...? By the gods! It is I, Ahuitzotl, Lord of the Mexica, you are speaking to. You do not give me directives!"

"Who is the pompous one now?" she snapped back at him. "You forget yourself. I am not the Pelaxilla of old you speak to, but the wife of Cocijoeza, empress of Tehuantepec. If you flaunt your title against me, I will thrust mine upon you."

Her reaction startled him, but also it made him reflect over his conduct and he recognized that he was exceeding his authority, especially as it related to her-she was correct in asserting her position: he had no more claim on her.

"You have betrayed me," he declared in a more subdued voice.

"What did you expect? Did you think I would be a party to seeing my own husband deceived by you and perhaps even killed by you? Can you not understand the difficulty your scheme placed me in? It was much like someone asking me to help in bringing about your downfall."

"Then you revealed my purpose in coming here to him."

"Of course I did! And were you to ask me again, I would again do so!"

"Is it possible?" Ahuitzotl roared out. "Is it possible that you would contrive to work against me-and against your people!"

"I am sorry," she replied. "I had no one to turn to."

"You had a mission!" Ahuitzotl nearly yelled. "You were sent here to perform a duty! You had obligations to your people-to me!"

His anger alarmed her, and when he came nearer to her, she was overcome with fear. "Do not attempt anything you will regret," she alerted him. "I have only to scream and the palace guards will have you surrounded."

Her warning had its effect; Ahuitzotl backed off, suppressing a rage he felt surging within him. "You betrayed me!" he repeated.

"It was your ambition and greed that betrayed you," she cried out. "I did not ask to be sent here. I begged you over and over not to send me here, as did Tlalalca. How was I to know what fate had in store for me? It is Xochiquetzal who exacts her vengeance on you-this is her way of punishing you for having deprecated the love she generated between us. Don't you see? Our love was a blessing from the goddess, and you chose to demean it by making me an instrument of your hatred for Cocijoeza. You offended her, and she turned my eyes to Cocijoeza, the man you wanted to destroy, because of this. It was you, not I, who brought about the betrayal."

Her words quieted him. He had indeed tampered with powers beyond his control, and what she said made sense. With much reluctance, he was forced to conclude that he had truly created the cause of his own misfortune, and now he was overwhelmed with horror that she was actually lost to him. "How shall I live without you?" he moaned.

"I said those same words when you sent me away from Tenochtitlan-do you remember it? And look what has happened. In her own way, Xochiquetzal sees to it that we are somehow helped out of our difficulties. She will do the same for you."

This offered little comfort to Ahuitzotl who could only think of the despair in living without his adored Pelaxilla. "She will not help me," he sorrowfully declared. "No one can. My love for you is too intense to be so readily dismissed. It transcends everything that I live for; it's what makes my life tolerable. Without it, I am lost."

Pelaxilla was deeply touched by his lamentation and nearly on the verge of breaking out in tears. Had she not herself undergone the transition a year earlier, she might have likewise agreed that he was lost-but now she knew otherwise. Even this, the most horribly painful of all human experiences, can be surmounted.

"You must have more faith," she tried to allay his apprehensions. "All is never lost; you have only to see it in your own court. Look at how dearly Tlalalca loves you. There was a time when she bitterly reviled you and also feared you; surely you can appreciate the wondrous thing that has been at work there. Xochiquetzal sees to our needs."

"This does not help, Pelaxilla; you do not know how deeply I love you. The prospect of never seeing you again is too frightening to contemplate. I don't believe I can survive it."

"I spoke almost those exact words once. Strange, isn't it, how things happen to us in spite of all that we think? You will discover, once you return to Tenochtitlan, that you will see Tlalalca in a different way which will even surprise you."

"Why do you keep bringing up Tlalalca? It's you I am concerned about."

"I'm trying to help you. You've never appreciated Tlalalca to the extend that you should have. She is a most noble woman, so beautiful, and yet you have always placed her in a secondary position to me. With me removed from that, your affections will be devoted exclusively to her and both your lives will be enriched as a result of that."

"You are trying to make me forget you, Pelaxilla, and it's useless. It's not possible. Besides, I remember when you yourself had nothing good to say about Tlalalca, so why extol her virtues to me now?"

Tears came to Pelaxilla's eyes as she paused over what he had just said, recalling a behavior that now embarrassed her.

"I was blinded by my jealousy and envy-all over you. That is how much I loved you then. I'm relieved that such anxieties no longer torment me, and I have Tlalalca to thank for that. When she told me how she had come to love you, but could not confide it in you and had to resign herself to be content with always being second in your heart to me, I became aware for the first time of the terrible suffering she must have endured through all these years. Do you know what that can do to a person? She gave me true understanding, and a lifelong shame of how cruelly I thought of her for so long, and I shall never forget her for it. If only I could get you to see her as I now see her-I love her and honor her. How fortunate you are to have her as your empress."

"You have changed. You are not the Pelaxilla I once knew."

"My life has changed-and you were responsible for that-how could I not be affected by it?"

"It was a mistake. Had I known this would happen, I would never have sent you here. Who could have imagined that you would be attracted to-to Cocijoeza?"

"Perhaps a mistake for you, but for me it was fortuitous. I am happier here than I have ever been in Tenochtitlan."

"Please, Pelaxilla, do not say this. You don't realize how painful it is for me to hear that."

"It's true. Did you know I am carrying Cocijoeza's child?"

Ahuitzotl felt a lump in his throat, as if the final fatal blow had been dealt him on top of the total disappointments already delivered. He was now overcome with a deep sadness as nothing remained left to him by which he might yet regain her affection-it was over for him. "There is no more hope for me," he muttered brokenly, "I have in truth lost you."

Tears trickled down Pelaxilla's face, for she had never seen him like this and understood his grief. And she also knew there was nothing she could do to alleviate it-he would have to undergo that painful process himself.

"I am truly sorry for you," she wept. "This was not my doing, but Xochiquetzal's. I hope you remember this when you think of me."

"I shall never see you again." Ahuitzotl groaned as the horror of this realization sank in.

She moved up to him and placed her hands on both sides of his head, then she lowered it and kissed him on the lips for the last time. Ahuitzotl was too shaken to even embrace her.

"It's over," she said through her tears when she released her hold on him. "Even you cannot change that. Do not think unkindly of me. I did not betray you out of malice, but to protect my husband. I was placed in such a horrible quandary."

Ahuitzotl was torn with remorse. He stood there with watery eyes having at last come face to face with the reality that he had denied himself all these recent months. Never had he felt such grief. Of what use was it now to try and destroy his adversary? She would never be his again, holding such a deed forever against him, and her child would exist as a permanent reminder of a love she once possessed–a love he took from her. The mighty warrior-king, who had always taken by will what he could not obtain otherwise, now stood pitiful and helpless against forces he was unable to control-forces that had deprived him of what he desired most in life. She was so beautiful to him now, but she was no longer his; he lost the most important battle of his life. His dreams, his hopes, his expectations, everything lay in permanent ruin. He had come to Tehuantepec fearing the worst-and he had found it.

Their eyes met at length one more time. Ahuitzotl thought he saw her reaching for him through her gaze, and he was siezed with an impulse to rush to her and glasp her firmly in his arms, but then conceded that he was deluding himself. Neither of them could say anything more-he was paralyzed in his stark confrontation with undeniable truth; she was afraid that whatever else was said would only draw out the torment which had already lasted too long. They spoke with their eyes-and they understood.

"I could never think unkindly of you," Ahuitzotl gulped out at last. "I cannot erase this love I have for you. It will exist to haunt me the rest of my life."

He then turned around and slowly proceeded for the door; she gazed after him with her large dilated pupils and slumped to her knees. She was left in the room weeping.

Grief-stricken and dazed, Ahuitzotl staggered through the narrow corridor utterly crushed. His entire world had collapsed on him; the heartache he felt was more agonizing than anything he had ever experienced or believed possible and his neck and face burned from hot flashes which swept over him at recurring intervals. The unmitigated nightmare of Pelaxilla's loss repeated itself over and over in his mind, and he knew he would never recover from this unparalleled shock-he feared how he was to survive it.

Heartsick, despondent, and defeated, a lonely monarch walked clumsily and slowly along the city's darkened, vacant streets to the campsite. Tears were streaming down his face.

X

The Mexica stayed in Tehuantepec for a full week until they were united into one composite force while the Zapotecs retained a vigilance over them, still not trustful of Ahuitzotl's motivations. They need not have troubled themselves; Ahuitzotl was so badly dejected over his meeting with Pelaxilla that nothing more existed to bring him out of his despondency. Even the battle plans finalized during this time were completed without his presence. Tlohtzin and Motecuhzoma visited Cocijoeza in his stead and later apprised him on the details covered, but the Revered Speaker seemed to have lost all interest in the campaign, and it was only through persistence that the chieftains managed to obtain his assessment on these.

During each of the nights the Mexica remained camped outside Tehauntepec, Cocijoeza held a feast for their leaders. Ahuitzotl stayed away from all of them except the last one when he was again gripped with a powerful yearning to see Pelaxilla once more. But this time no ladies were present and Ahuitzotl knew that he had lost his chance to see her; he could not bring himself to plead with Cocijoeza for permission to have another audience with her, thinking it demeaning enough to have lost her to the Zapotecan, so that he was not about to endure the additional humiliation such an entreaty entailed. Besides, he now recognized this would be of no avail; Pelaxilla clarified her position to him and he failed to distract her from it the last time. What hope did he have that he could succeed with yet another meeting?

When the time came for commencing the expedition to Soconusco, Ahuitzotl recovered from his dolorous state to some degree as the excitement of a march into heretofore unknown regions now worked its seductiveness to override all other considerations. His commanders, and particularly Tlohtzin, were elated to see their warlord's enthusiasm revitalized; his long depression having had an enervating effect on all of them.

The Mexica resorted to their usual practice of preceding an invasion with customary diplomatic gestures. Hence, even before they arrived in Tehuantepec, they already had dispatched envoys to Soconusco to warn its reigning monarch of the impending crisis and offer him an opportunity to capitulate and accept the conditions imposed on him, or suffer horrible and inevitable consequences. The lords of Soconusco must have been genuinely alarmed that the Mexica would come so far to chastise them for their mockery-they had believed the vast distances a secure deterrent-and pondered over the ultimatum. But Ahuitzotl meant to have his battles-he did not embark on such a long journey to have his enemy readily concede to him-and thus advised his emissaries to be as arrogant and offensive in their demands as their conduct allowed. The ploy worked, and the indignant lords, angered at the haughtiness and threats of these brazen envoys, rejected all conditions offered them and hurled insults of their own upon the Mexica. Thus the course of events had been shaped; Ahuitzotl received word of Soconusco's rejection from his couriers while he rested at Tehuantepec.

Tehuantepec's inhabitants lined the streets to give the departing armies a farewell acclamation as still part of Cocijoeza's plan to flatter the shrewd conqueror whom he distrusted, and the Zapotec army remained to act as an escort for the men of Anahuac while in their domain lest Ahuitzotl should change his mind and attempt yet to turn on his host. To the warriors, this ostentatious display demonstrated the unity of their alliance with Zapoteca; Ahuitzotl's decision not to inform them of his plan to sieze Tehauntepec now prudently paid off for him. His own men would never know of his degradation.

Three large armies moved on Soconusco. The armies of Tenochtitlan and Tlatelolco were combined into one force, and those of Acolhuacan and Tepaneca merged into the second element, while the Zapotecs comprised the third element. A huge contingent of Zapotec warriors remained attached to Ahuitzotl's army to keep watch on him; most of them would rejoin Cocijoeza once it reached the eastern boundary of Zapoteca, with a few staying to serve as guides. This was not an unwise move on the part of Cocijoeza, for even at this stage, Ahuitzotl harbored thoughts of finding an opportunity to slay the monarch during the confusion of battle. This likelihood was greatly reduced by his remaining with his own army. But if he were to somehow become separated from it during the fighting, Ahuitzotl was thinking, such a possibility might present itself. Or maybe the Zapotecan, through a stroke of fortune, might already be claimed by the gods to perish in combat. If this happened, Pelaxilla might yet be his.

The invading armies, divided by a day's march, moved along the primary merchant's trail skirting the coastline. It ran mostly in a straight path over flattened plains between the sea and mountains, occasionally snaking around sloping ridges descending to the water's edge at intermittent areas separating the valleys. Terrain was not the major headache for the Mexica here as they had expected, but rather it was the stifling heat and dense forests ridden with insects, particularly annoying mosquitoes. Most of the warriors shed their cotton armor as they could not stand it clinging to their sweating bodies-they carried these slung over their shoulders together with their shields. And ever present were the insects, buzzing about their heads, mercilessly stinging them, and numberless. To the highland Mexica, these discomforts were most irritating–the dry, cool, and essentially insect free valley of Anahuac was a paradise on earth compared to this.

The first enemy stronghold they came upon was Amaxtlan, a thriving city near the sea marking Soconusco's western frontier; they arrived there after being on the trail for two weeks. The Soconuscans, awaiting this invasion, had assembled an enormous army that was camped around the city-scouts alerted them to the allied advance and when Ahuitzotl reached the plain west of the city, they were poised for attack.

A sense of urgency prevailed among the Mexica as trumpets signaled the warriors into their battle order. Hastily, they donned their protective head gear and armored tunics and took up their battle stations under their banners and insignia. The Soconuscans, adhering to custom, waited for their attackers to complete the configuration. Undismayed by the numerical superiority of his enemy, Ahuitzotl issued directives to initiate an assault upon his command as soon as the priests had finished their divinations. When the time was at hand, he called for the attack to commence and his lines advanced on a broad front. To the Soconuscans, who knew they possessed the greater numbers, this boldness was a startling sight. Not to be undone, they ordered their own lines to move out and meet the aggressor.

Ahuitzotl relied on his proven ruse of archers hidden behind a front wall of warriors, their purpose remaining, as in previous battles, not primarily to inflict casualties but to disrupt the opponent's cohesion and create turmoil. The Soconuscans, unaware of this maneuver, were caught totally unprepared when a hail of arrows descended on them; their leading warriors fell into disorder as they tried to shield their heads and bodies and were temporarily blinded–the moment chosen by the Mexica to charge. They stormed ahead like frenzied beasts, wildly shouting out their war whoops in their assault against a shocked forward line. In an instant, Mexica soldiers came crashing into their rows and slashing at them with their deadly maquauhuitl; so fierce was the onslaught that the enemy's leading units literally fell beneath it, cut down before they could recoup from their setback. Screaming as they were struck under, with blood spewing forth from gruesome wounds, they collapsed in gory, contorted heaps while trampled over by attackers in pursuit of their comrades who were still in disarray.

Behind the lines, alarmed Soconuscan commanders called on the battalions held in reserve to assist their beleaguered combatants. They risked everything on this desperate action, leaving nothing in depth to counter a potential enemy breakthrough, reasoning that with their edge in warriors, they could contain the aggressor at the lines by weight of numbers. As it turned out, such was the case on this day; with the entire front of his army committed to battle, Ahuitzotl had no room in which to make a countermove and the contest invariably evolved into a gigantic slugging match with unit hammering away at unit across the width of the plain.

Furious at himself for having fallen into this predicament, Ahuitzotl knew that in such kind of confrontation strength in numbers would eventually dominate; he had no intentions of allowing the Soconuscans their advantage. "Sound the retreat!" he shouted to the chief priest accompanying him. "There are too many of them!"

Reluctantly the warriors disengaged themselves after hearing the trumpet call, but the Soconuscans, having suffered severe losses in the Mexica assualt, were too shaken to give pursuit. With no units in reserve, they were highly vulnerable and dangerously exposed and therefore prudently decided to sound out their own withdrawal. The first day's battle thus ended in a stalemate.

Late that afternoon, the second army arrived and Ahuitzotl spent a major portion of the evening deriving tomorrow's battle plan with its commanders, Colotl and Coanacoch. He was determined to fight the upcoming battle somewhat differently so that he could conduct a number of maneuvers which would strike a decisive blow to the Soconuscans, especially if they again ventured to rely on their reserve components to assist their lines. Not everyone thought this was necessary.

"Tomorrow we have the Acolhuas and Tepanecs with us," Motecuhzoma boldly interjected, "and it will not matter because we'll have the superior numbers."

"Why lose thousands in a battle when we can win it with less casualties?" Ahuitzotl replied. "These head-on confrontations are too costly-better to vary our methods. It is demoralizing to be attacked from two directions at the same time, and dispirited warriors are easier to defeat."

"If the gods have already predetermined who is to die, of what use are these applications?"

This was the sort of annoying question Ahuitzotl thoroughly despised, for it required him to apply caution in answering lest he offend the priests who believed in its infallibility. "We seek to destroy the enemy," Ahuitzotl said, "and we will do whatever most expeditiously achieves this end. I will not have our force depleted in the opening phase of this operation"

The priests may have found a cause for objecting to this, but none of the commanders disputed their warlord. On the battlefield, the Revered Speaker reigned supreme–Ahuitzotl had brought them their greatest triumphs and many of these were achieved through his deviating from the proscriptions defining their war doctrines. Motecuhzoma sat justifiably red-faced over his hasty comment-a remark not welcomed by Ahuitzotl.

On the following morning, the armies again faced each other, and after the rituals were completed in their usual precision, the battle resumed. As yesterday, Ahuitzotl initiated the attack, but not on a broad front; his right wing, mainly comprised of the Tepanecs under Colotl, launched the assault. By contrast, the Soconuscans repeated their advance along the entire width of the field and had their warriors spaced equitably throughout their formation. Not used to the unorthodox approach presented by Ahuitzotl, the enemy commander recognized his force was not strong enough at his flank to counter Colotl's attack. Alarmed, he felt compelled to bolster it and issued immediate orders for a number of units on his right flank to move to his left and augment that portion of his line. Ahuitzotl had cunningly anticipated this deployment and was set to deal his counterblow.

"It's time!" he shouted to a messenger. "Send word to Coanacoch and Motecuhzoma to attack their right!"

On receiving the message, the Acolhuas, augmented by the bulk of the Tlatelolco army under Motecuhzoma, launched a heated charge against the reduced Soconusco right flank. Before any warrior made contact, the maneuver which determined the outcome of the battle had been completed. With thousands of Soconuscans caught halfway between the two extreme wings, and unable to bolster neither, the Mexica exerted their concentrated energy against those two weak points. They crashed with rapacious fury into their stunned opponents, almost instantly smashing through their thinner lines and threatening to entrap the whole of their army in a sweeping envelopment. To further confuse the enemy commander, Ahuitzotl now advanced his center against his adversary.

The victory was not to be easy, however; in a frantic move, the enemy commander ordered his numerically superior center to assault Ahuitzotl who was weaker in the middle because of the units he had transferred to his flanks. A horrific slaughter ensued as these opposing forces met; the Mexica held their position, slaying one enemy warrior after another, but fell in large numbers under the clubs and spears of their assailants. Ahuitzotl and Tlohtzin were in the thick of it, wielding their weapons with deadly efficiency and striking down the enemy soldiers attacking them, but things looked bleak as the heaps of fallen warriors piled higher.

But help was on its way. First from Motecuhzoma, who quickly assessed the Soconuscan commander's move when he drove on the Mexica center, and then from Colotl on the right, who had already penetrated the enemy's opposing wall of resistance. Instantly, they issued orders directing their squadrons to wheel inward and strike the Soconuscans in the center from behind. Once the drives were initiated, the trapped enemy warriors abandoned their hopes of victory and one by one bolted from their ranks to escape the carnage. Those wedged in too deeply between their enclosing foe and unable to flee lost the will to fight on; one after another dropped his arms and submitted to capture with its inevitable fate-being sacrificed. By midday, the battle was over and Amaxtlan stood at the mercy of Ahuitzotl.

It had been a stunning, although bloody, triumph. The bulk of Amaxtlan's manhood lay dead, wounded, or captured at the hands of the Mexica, counting in the thousands. Amaxtlan paid a terrible penalty for its staunch resistance and was next gutted in an orgy of lust, brutality, and fire by warriors exacting a cruel vengeance for the heavy losses they had suffered, who vented their rage on the defenseless inhabitants in an unchecked exhibition of savagery.

The Mexica remained encamped around the smoldering ruins of Amaxtlan the next day, recuperating from the costly fighting, when Cocijoeza came upon the scene leading his Zapotec army. This was the first time the shocked monarch had seen the work of his ally; he was horrified at the sight of so many dead, especially those of noncombatants, piled on wooden stacks for burning. Such would have been the fate of Tehuantepec, he thought, had he not been alerted to the danger by Pelaxilla-truly he was indebted to her.

"I see I come too late," Cocijoeza said to Ahuitzotl.

"We could have used you," answered Ahuitzotl, "but they chose not to wait."

"You have made grim work of Amaxtlan."

"Does it disturb you?"

"I see no honor or purpose in slaying the innocent, and will not allow my warriors to do so."

"Enraged warriors who expect to be rewarded by plunder are difficult to restrain. We took a heavy toll in the hard fought battle. I don't like it either, but it happens."

Cocijoeza was not convinced of that, and Ahuitzotl seemed embarrassed over his skepticism; he did not wish the Mexica to be known as mere butchers. Yet he grasped the value of shock effect upon an enemy's disposition and, in general, permitted one or two such slaughters to take place in order to hasten an opponent's surrender. He reasoned that in the long run such a tactic saved more innocent victims than a protracted war of attrition. Not all lords agreed with that, considering the sack of a city as unworthy conduct for warriors and a besmirch on their honor, but it was Ahuitzotl who was the conqueror-and what was death, after all, but a mere transfer from this, the worst of all possible worlds, to a better place.

"Perhaps the next time you can postpone battle so my army can participate in it," said Cocijoeza soberly. "We have as much at stake in taking Soconusco as you do."

"You will have your opportunity," Ahuitzotl affirmed.

More strongholds fell to the allied armies as they advanced on Soconusco, but the resistance that met them was unexpectedly severe at each site and their progress was significantly slowed as a result. To the Mexica, who had now been ceaselessly on the move for nearly six months, except for their intermittent periods of resting at the major cities along their route, the repeated battles and marches began to exact its price. Weariness and fatigue dampened their enthusiasm, sapping strength and spirits alike, to say nothing of the meager rewards they obtained for their efforts; vocal discontent prevailed among their ranks and many questioned if this far-off campaign was worth the effort.

This was a new kind of war the Mexica were confronted with; they were not only battling enemy armies, but also entire populations, and in each of the strongholds, they encountered armed opposition by women and children as well as warriors, and it took days to seize them. At Mapachtepec, a major city between Amaxtlan and Soconusco itself, they struggled for two entire weeks before the city fell into their hands, and when it was finally captured, the spoils to be obtained were engulfed in the same flames which destroyed it—there was nothing left for the conquerors.

It required them four months to reach Soconusco-months of hard fighting and marching-and when the Mexica saw the size of the enemy army that awaited them there, they were dismayed. By now they were exhausted and could only view the prospect of another major battle with much disdain. Even though Soconusco looked as if it might offer some riches, Ahuitzotl would have preferred to come to terms with its lords rather than engage in a lengthy and costly endeavor against them, and as both armies settled in their campsites for the inevitable clash, he instructed his envoys to be both generous in their surrender terms as well as diplomatic in issuing these in order to induce the Soconuscans into capitulation. In actuality, it made no difference-the enemy lords were not about to concede without a fight.

As this was to be the decisive engagement between the powers, Ahuitzotl was not about to initiate it without all his forces present and delayed in his attack until the Zapotecan army joined his own. The Soconuscans, always on the defensive throughout this campaign, were unnerved over Ahuitzotl's previous successes and did not dare make the first move out of fear of falling into a trap, reasoning that it was better to wait for their formidable adversary to make the preliminary moves and then determine what measures were available to counter them. The antagonists were thus camped within sight of each other on opposite ends of the plain around the city for the next three days as each side was being augmented to its full complements.

On the third day, the Zapotecs arrived and Ahuitzotl stood at maximum strength levels. Soconusco in the meantime was also reinforced by numerous elements from its neighboring communities, but in total numbers they remained at a disadvantage as they never sufficiently recovered from the staggering losses they sustained at Amaxtlan and Mapachtepec. Since those encounters, they had only fought a regressive war unable to halt the steady advance of the invaders. They banked their hopes on a strong stand, believing their warriors would be inspired to perform at optimum level in defending their capital.

At his council on the last night before the crucial contest, Ahuitzotl informed Cocijoeza and his commanders of the details entailing this imminent battle. Even at this late stage, he held out some hope the enemy might yield to him if offered another opportunity-a move he rarely, if ever, considered. "While the priests make their preparations tomorrow, we will send our envoys to the Soconuscans one more time to give them an opportunity to surrender," he said.

"Of what use is that?" Motecuhzoma protested. "Why waste our time when we already have their answer?"

"They are fighting for their homes, and the opposition will be fierce," Ahuitzotl replied. "If you thought Mapachtepec was a hard-fought contest, I tell you it was nothing compared to what we can expect here. If we can attain our aims by avoiding this, we should do so."

A murmur arising from the gathering strongly emphasized that they opposed the notion and expressed considerable astonishment that their renowned warlord would even suggest this.

"Can it be," Motecuhzoma continued, "you would consider such a proposal? Our warriors did not come this far to be now deprived of the spoils that can be had by taking Soconusco."

"As I have heard, they are weary of this protracted operation and desire nothing more than to have it ended so that we can return to Anahuac. Perhaps you have heard something else."

Motecuhzoma fell silent; such indeed was the nature of their warriors' grumbling-he did not realize Ahuitzotl knew this.

"I run this campaign," Ahuitzotl sternly advised the impetuous young Motecuhzoma. "Do not forget that!"

Motecuhzoma's obtuseness was a sign of the general malcontent spreading throughout the Mexica force over this operation, and it presented a serious challenge to Ahuitzotl's leadership. He had enticed his warriors onward during the early stages of their undertaking with promises of riches, and now that it was apparent to everyone these were not forthcoming, he faced a problem of declining motivation and a waning will to continue the enterprise. Soconusco offered a prospect of wealth, but by now there was cause for doubting if the men would battle for it.

Cocijoeza, a shrewd commander in his own right, recognized the growing deteriorating morale among the Mexica which he attributed to a combination of physical exhaustion and disappointment over the lack of profitable return in proportion to the exertion and distances involved. As he observed Ahuitzotl arguing with his subordinates, he came to the conclusion that he had nothing more to fear from his former adversary, and he questioned if the men of Anahuac would ever again take on an expedition of this scope and range. He even dared to think that there was reason to be optimistic about an eventual rebellion to throw off the Mexica yoke. Ahuitzotl noted the smirk on his Zapotecan ally's face and fully knew what he was thinking; he seethed over Motecuhzoma's lack of discretion-his discontent should have been announced in private audience, not before Cocijoeza. To avoid exposing further weakness in the command structure, Ahuitzotl terminated the meeting.

Ahuitzotl's second attempt at encouraging the Soconuscans to surrender proved futile; they contemptuously rejected the envoy's final offerings and sent him back to the Mexica lines under a typical barrage of insults and well known abusive gestures. When this rejection was received by the monarch, he became determined to make them pay for their insolence. His honest effort at conciliation snubbed, he would now destroy Soconusco as he did Amaxtlan-with no quarter given.

Ahuitzotl planned for his Mexica to lead the assault while keeping the Zapotecs in reserve until he felt it necessary to deploy them. This was not intended as a slur on Cocjioeza, although he may have perceived it as such, but rather because Ahuitzotl recognized this battle required the kind of discipline he could only depend on his warriors to give him. He also wanted to minimize the chances of a communication breakdown, a possibility always existing when there was a need for translating orders. Cocijoeza understood this well enough but still resented the secondary role relegated to his army; Ahuitzotl had to resort upon his utmost diplomatic skills to placate his allied lord.

Unlike the other battles fought with the Soconuscans, Ahuitzotl did not expect his enemy to move out against him; this caution dictated a defensive posture for them, which meant the Mexica would have to dislodge them from their barriers, always a high-risk proposition. If such was to be the case, it would preclude deceptive maneuvers and traps from being exercised; that called for a battle of attrition, invariably hard fought and costly and what the Revered Speaker wanted to avoid.

When the oblations to the war-favoring deities were completed, trumpets signaled the onset of the Mexica attack; it began in Ahuitzotl's characteristic 'style'-with a concentrated drive initiated by the right wing under Colotl and his Tepanecs. "If this does not cause them to shift their lines," Ahuitzotl said to Tlohtzin, "then we'll be forced into another slugging match. It will pit our discipline and strength against their resolve to defend their city."

"I see another Mapachtepec," answered Tlohtzin grimly. "Nothing to be relished."

The charging Tepaneca squadrons plunged into contact, with warriors crashing down on the city's defenders and breaching their front ranks but then becoming mired in the fearsome resistance. Ahuitzotl and Tlohtzin scanned the enemy position but detected no movement in it; the Soconusccans had learned their lesson and were not inclined to weaken some other sector of their line, apparently feeling secure that their flank could hold out against the assault. "They won't deploy!" declared Ahuitzotl. "Prepare to move on them!"

Successive commands prodded the remaining force into action, presenting the defenders with an awesome spectacle of thousands of warriors, brilliantly adorned in plumages and armaments, rushing at them under their unit standard bearers. Even from behind the wooden and stone barricades which they had erected when the Mexica arrival was imminent, the Soconuscans felt an imperilment in the fury of their opponent's charge.

Ahuitzotl again made use of his archers, but this time not to confuse or break the enemy ranks, which would have been unlikely behind their barriers; instead he employed them to hide his massing the center warriors into that formidable wedge adopted from Zozoltin. While the Soconuscans hid behind their shields for cover from the deadly hail of missiles, this maneuver was completed and the formation advanced on the defender's center. Once more the enemy was confronted with an unfamiliar deployment of forces, but they could not afford to be cowed by it and refused to balk at the attack. However, the Soconuscan commander discerned that he had to strengthen his lines to repulse this drive and called on reserves to buttress his front-line units.

A vociferous collision of arms echoed across the battlefield when the Mexica came crashing into the unyielding Soconuscans. They hurled their lances into the enemy's ranks, then charged furiously on them, using their shields as battering rams as well as body protection. Their momentum carried them past the first wall of defenders, smashing readily through it, but when they forged deeper in their penetration and met the reserve components, their progress came to a grinding halt. The combatants became tightly constricted as they hacked at each other, and the resultant slaughter was frightful. Blood flowed freely from ripped-open bodies and sliced-off limbs; enraged soldiers clawed at their attackers and tumbled over fallen comrades only to be cut down an instant later as they lost their balance. As soon as one fell, another took his place, and Ahuitzotl was in the midst of the melee, encroached from every direction by a determined foe bent on repulsing the attack and fighting for his life.

An audacious enemy soldier hacked a pathway passed the last Eagle knight standing between him and Ahuitzotl. He bashed his stone-headed club into the knight's skull with one powerful stroke that split it wide open, spilling out parts of the brain. Ahuitzotl stopped the soldier's next blow with his shield, reeling under the impact, but then swung his own maquauihuitl deftly into his opponent's neck, nearly severing the head from its body. A second warrior aimed his spear for the monarch, but

Tlohtzin struck him down with his warclub before he could release it. More Soconuscans pierced the wall of Eagles protecting their master only to be hacked under by Ahuitzotl and Tlohtzin who faced them with their backs to each other to avoid anyone blindsiding them. Additional Eagles joined the bodyguard force and for the moment held back the foe, allowing Ahuitzotl the pause he needed to properly assess the situation.

Their advance was stalled at every point along the field.. Amid ever higher heaps of bodies, the warriors replacing them seemed endless, and with their forward inertia completely halted, they were now desperately holding the ground gained from rapacious opponents who fought with a tenacity such as the Mexica had rarely encountered.

At this critical juncture, Ahuitzotl sent a messenger to Cocijoeza urging him to commit his Zapotecs to battle and concentrate on reinforcing the heavily engaged center. The waiting monarch, who was eager to get his warriors into action, expected this when he saw the two forces locked in their struggle and unable to break the stalemate. Responding to his ally's call, he led the bulk of his army against the hard-pressed sector. Shouting out their battle cries, the Zapotecs sallied forth thundering across the field, bursting with pride and enthusiastic over being called upon to assist the invincible Mexica. Fresh and rested, they burst upon the scene as a most welcome relief to the weary Mexica who had driven themselves to near exhaustion battering against the immovable Soconuscan lines for most of the contested day.

The Zapotecs gave a good account of themselves, attacking the thickest concentration of enemy warriors and gradually driving them back to the confines of their city. Many acts of individual heroics stood out; one bold Zapotec soldier faught off a number of opponents to rescue a Mexica chieftain about to be taken only to be himself pierced through the vitals with a spear; another killed a dozen enemy warriors in leading his squadron to relieve Ahuitzotl himself. The Soconuscans fought with equal bravery and skill but eventually gave way to the greater pressures hammering at them, and by late afternoon, following an entire day of ceaseless battle, their depleted lines faltered. Trumpets directed the defenders deeper into their city where they assembled around its various temples and palaces to make a stand.

Ahuitzotl gave them no respite and ordered his warriors in hot pursuit; Cocijoeza was now with him, having reached his entrenched ally at a timely moment just as he was about to be overwhelmed, so a significantly larger force was at the Revered Speaker's disposal. The Zapotecan monarch, however, became alarmed that a massacre was about to ensue–Mexica warriors were beginning to sack several sections of the beleaguered city. "What will you do?" he argued with Ahuitzotl. "We came here to increase our tributes and to subjugate them. Will you now destroy them?"

"They had their chance," Ahuitzotl growled. "Now they must pay for their folly."

"To annihilate them is to negate the reasons we came here. I implore you-strike an accord with them and be done with this campaign."

"It's too late for that. I must placate my warriors."

"I want no part of any cruel slaughter," Cocijoeza denounced the Revered Speaker angrily. "This is not why I undertook this mission, or called for your assistance. It does neither of us any good to have them killed."

Ahuitzotl knew Cocijoeza was correct, and as his warriors surrounded each of the strongholds where the defenders meant to fight to the last, he directed them to desist in further battle. His commanders encountered bitter protests when they enforced his instructions; in some units they faced outright mutiny and had to threaten their subordinate chieftains with severe penalties before they could obtain a compliance. Momentarily order was established, but on a fragile premise. Ahuitzotl had to act quickly if he was to prevent an eruption of unchecked wrath.

An emissary was sent to the temple stronghold in the city's central plaza to bring the Soconuscan lords into a conference with their conquerors-they were promised safe conduct to the meeting. Soconusco's ruler accepted the offer and soon came forward, accompanied by a number of his principals that included the chief ministers, the army's commander, and members of the tribal council; he appreciated this second chance at concluding their affair and knew these were rarely granted by Ahuitzotl. Interpreters attended both parties when they met in the open square amid impatient armies.

"You have requested to see me," he said through his translator, "and I have come. I hope to have a worthwhile exchange."

"That is up to you," declared Ahuitzotl. "We both know victory is in our hands. You have battled us honorably and have nothing to be ashamed of, however, it's futile to persist in your opposition as we are in your city.

We strongly suggest that you formally concede defeat and by so doing terminate the hostility between us."

"What can we expect from you if we do?"

"You will acknowledge us as your overlords and will submit to us, and Tehuantepec, the tributes determined by our assessors. We will not burden you with excessive quotas, demanding only a proportion consistent with the amounts we levy on other kingdoms. You are to open your regions to trade, providing our merchants the same protection you render your own. The captives we have taken we will retain and take with us to Anahuac, but we will ask no more from those warriors who surrender with you. You must also establish the diplomatic exchanges with us that we maintain with all realms, adhering to the courtesies and obligations that entails, extending these to Tehuantepec as well. The details will be worked out."

The terms were not harsh and, under the circumstances, quite reasonable; the lords of Soconusco fared considerably better than they dared hope. "That is it?" their surprised lord answered.

"There is one more thing. My warriors have come a long way and are customarily rewarded for the hardships they endure by the plunder taken from the cities we sieze. If you surrender and accept out terms, it means they have to forego the booty they expected in taking Soconusco. Ordinarily this would pose no problem, but this has been a far more arduous undertaking than usual; I fear if they are not compensated by some special gifts or favors there may be rebellion among them. I consider it a prudent act on your part to offer them some form of restitution."

"I understand," replied the ruler. "I shall do what I can. Your terms are accepted; we will do as you say."

Their accord being struck, Ahuitzotl and Cocijoeza then turned over the details of the surrender to their subordinate chieftains. Occasional outcries were heard in some units over being deprived of the spoils in sacking the city, but for the most part, the promises of presents succeeded in alleviating their anger, and most warriors were gratified that this lengthy operation was ended.

Soconusco was thus spared and its grateful ruler hosted his conquerors to royal feasting in his palace during their stay here. Ahuitzotl's switch from hostility to conciliation perplexed even those closest to him-Cocijoeza deemed the surrender terms too easy-but possibly he was too dispirited to continue on this campaign and wanted nothing more than to have it ended as hastily as he could promulgate its conclusion. Soconusco had, after all, been a secondary objective for him-he had failed in his primary one, siezing Tehuantepec and its lord, Cocijoeza-and there was no more inducement to prolong this conflict; whatever might be gained from it was trivial in comparison. Yet Ahuitzotl did find his curiosity notably aroused when his host spoke of great empires lying to the east and north of his realm during their last feast together prior to the scheduled departure day.

"The region to the east is called Cuautemallah," he said, "and it is dominated by the kingdoms of the Quiche and Cakchiquel. In the north are Mactun and Xicallanca. These are no mean kingdoms, Lord. There are riches in them beyond anything possessed by us or the Zapotecs. They have great cities and well-maintained stone roadways which connect them, and their merchants deal in highly prized commodities."

"I have heard such talk before," answered Ahuitzotl in his skepticism. "It's been my experience that the more the tales speak of wealth existing in these far-off regions, the greater has been my disappointment when I arrived there."

"Ah, but not these, Great Lord. Here, take a look at this jade knife." The ruler handed Ahuitzotl an exquisitely carved knife made wholly of jade, the most valued of all stones, and trimmed with a bejewelled handle.

"Magnificent!" exclaimed Ahuitzotl. "Superb craftsmanship. I've never seen anything so beautifully done."

"It comes from Mactun-an example of what these kingdoms are capable of doing. We have been at continuous war with the people of Cuautemallah. With your assistance, we could dominate them once and for all. Together, they could not stand against us."

The notion was not without its appeal, but Ahuitzotl seriously doubted whether his warriors possessed an inclination to venture even more distances from Anahuac, especially into these jungle regions where the forests, insects, and temperatures proved bothersome irritants. "My army is spent," he concluded with genuine regret. "I would not be able to induce its participation into such a venture."

"A pity. Think of all the empires out there ripe for our taking. You could be master of the earth."

"It will have to be with a new army. I have you to thank for wearing out this one. Had you not fought us so tenaciously, and offered me your proposal earlier, things might have been different. Wouldn't you agree, Tlohtzin?"

Ahuitzotl laughed as he said this, and looked at Tlohtzin for a mutual agreement, but his smile quickly vanished when he noticed his commander's startled countenance. "What's wrong?" Ahuitzotl reacted with alarm. "Why do you look at me like that?"

"My mind is playing tricks on me, Lord," replied Tlohtzin. "I thought I saw something different about you, but it appears I was mistaken."

"Do not play games with me, Tlohtzin," Ahuitzotl said, disturbed over his evasion. "Tell me what you saw."

"Are you feeling well, Lord?" Tlohtzin asked with noticeable concern.

"Of course. A little fatigued perhaps, like the rest of the warriors. Why?"

"Your face. For a moment there it looked somewhat thinner to me than I thought it should, but now it appears as usual. I don't know what gave me that impression."

Almost involuntarily, Ahuitzotl brought his right hand to his face and stroked the contours of his cheeks and chin; he also initially thought it felt less fleshy and was struck with a sober disquietude as he recalled Tlohtzin's astonishment. Then, after more of his probing, he dispelled his fears deducing that he had not eaten as much as he should have and, consequently, lost some weight as a result.

Yet, something like this could not be dismissed so readily, and even if Ahuitzotl minimized its importance at present, the concern remained and was to manifest itself periodically by coming to the forefront and gripping him with anxiety. He pondered if this Soconusco expedition would not eventually exact a greater price on him.

XI

For almost two years the Mexica armies had been away from Anahuac, and when they at last returned to parade triumphantly along Tenochtitlan's main avenues, they were accorded the usual fanfare reserved for such occasions. But the jubilation and applause was subdued significantly by the anguish and severe disappointment felt from seeing the many sons, husbands, and relatives who no longer made up its ranks. The Soconuscan campaign had taken a frightening toll among the conquerors with some of the units entering the capital reduced by as much as one-half of their original numbers. Joy and regret, elation and grief, happiness and heartbreak, the entire gamut of emotional range wrapped up in such an occurrance, greeted the weary warriors marching solemnly toward the square. But they were home-it had been a long venture.

Ahuitzotl felt the same sense of relief expressed by his warriors when he approached his residence after having dismissed the army, but there was also an acute bitterness in him. He looked upon this, the most arduous and exhausting expedition ever undertaken by any monarch, as a dismal failure. Its primary purpose was foiled because of Pelaxilla's betrayal, and then succeeded by the most devasted setback of them all-her loss. Soconusco had been but a backdrop for the greater struggle between him and his rival, Cocijoeza, whom he believed having won the battle-the people acclaimed his accomplishments and hailed him their greatest conqueror, but he had lost the war.

Ahuitzotl never again saw Pelaxilla after that final meeting with her. Even though he and his army rested again at Tehuantepec on the return march, and there were numerous feasts honoring their successes in Cocijoeza's palace, Pelaxilla demurred from attending them and refused to see Ahuitzotl. For him, this was the ultimate and most painful blow, coming when he had once more been bolstered by notions that he could regain her if he saw her and spoke with her just one more time-to have these opportunities denied crushed him. Perhaps Pelaxilla knew better and saw its futility, and meant to spare him additional explanations which would only serve to disappoint him more-this was what her servants related to him. Whatever the reasons, it dealt him a terrible blow, leaving him feeling utterly dejected, and during the journey back to Anahuac, he fell into long bouts of depression and moodiness, speaking to and seeing no-one and demoralizing those accompanying him and attending to his needs.

Not until he reached Tenochtitlan did Ahuitzotl snap out of his doldrums, and as he walked up the palace steps and noted his minister waiting for him at the top, he was in a better frame of mind than had been his comportment through most of the return trek-but clearly he was not his former self. With his hopes vanquished, Ahuitzotl himself was a casualty of the Soconusco war.

To make matters worse, he now bore the signs Tlohtzin first mentioned at Soconusco and was increasingly self-conscious about it. He imagined people eyeing him peculiarly, giving credence to his fears that something was wrong, even if he did not feel bad physically, and was curious if Cihuacoatl would notice what others had observed in him.

"Welcome back, Lord." Cihuacoatl greeted his master. "It must have been a strenuous campaign for you."

"Why do you say that?" Ahuitzotl quickly asked.

"You have lost weight-a considerable amount, I would say-since I last saw you. It's quite noticeable."

Cihuacoatl could not have known how disturbing those words sounded to Ahuitzotl, reinforcing the worries about his well-being. "It was not easy." he answered. "Did you receive the dispatches I sent you?"

"I have, Lord. I was heartsick to learn what that woman had done to you. You should have heeded my advice, but then, who could have known?"

"It came as a profound shock to me. I failed in my objective."

"You are wrong to perceive it as a failure, Lord. You have extended our influence farther than anyone before you, and undoubtedly any successor ever will. Your name is enshrined among the chroniclers. Who has done as much?"

"I have learned that some things are more important than the glories of conquest. A hard lesson for me—losing the person who meant more to me than life itself. Had it not been for this drive to dominate, to attain fame and glory, to do more than anyone else had done, she would still be with me. It has been a lesson, I tell you. I shall never recover from it."

"Am I hearing correctly? Our greatest warlord mopes over the loss of a single woman? Forget her, Lord. No woman is worth that kind of trouble. You can have any woman in the realm you desire-why allow one to bring you such despair?"

"Pelaxilla was special to me. None can take her place."

"Apparently not special enough to keep you from using her to destroy your enemy."

Ahuitzotl glared at his minister, and the hatred reflected in his eyes gave Cihuacoatl a jolt. "I warn you, minister," he said at length, "Never again mention my mistake to me. I comprehend fully what I have done and seek no reminder of it."

"Excuse this old man's insolence, Lord," Cihuacoatl hastily retracted, remembering the sway the mistress had held over his master. "I did not mean to minimize her importance to you, or to cause you any further duress, but rather my intention was to to emphasize your unequalled successes instead of your perceived failures. I apologize."

"My successes?" Ahuitzotl scowled. "And what are those?"

"You belittle what you have done, Lord. Think of it. You have been gone from Anahuac for nearly two years and not one of our subject states dared to rise in rebellion against us-not one! This is no mean achievement, Lord. Indeed, our chroniclers claim it has never happened before during the reign of any Revered Speaker. You should not underestimate this accomplishment."

The minister was right; no other monarch could have absented himself for such a length of time without being faced with numerous revolts. Ahuitzotl found gratification in that and his frown turned to a smile. "You excel in conciliation, Cihuacoatl," he said. "I err in keeping you here when I go on my expeditions; your talent would have greatly assisted me on this one."

"I would have preferred it to remaining here, Lord. Do you know what it is like presiding over a city devoid of men?"

Ahuitzotl laughed as he could well visualize his minister's frustrations-had he been a younger man, he might have made better use of the situation.

"You did not enjoy the companionship of all those women?"

Cihuacoatl eyed his master somberly, then retorted, "Believe me, Lord, they no longer excite me as they once used to. If you possessed some of my reservations towards them, and I had some of your desire for them, we might come to a better understanding."

"It's worth talking about, but not at present. I want to clean up. I shall call you to brief me later."

Ahuitzotl then proceeded into his palace, which seemed more inviting to him than he remembered, and after he passed through the main door, he saw Tlalalca there waiting for him, holding the hand of their young son who stood beside her. He smiled at Cuauhtemoc, who appeared quite happy at seeing him even if he was essentially a stranger to the boy, his long absences having negated any bonding in these formative years. When Ahuitzotl tried to lift him into his arms, Cuauhtemoc resisted, shying away from the attempt, although not crying out.

"He does not know his father," Tlalalca said, beaming brightly. "You will have to amend that situation." She then directed Cuauhtemoc to seek out his usual caretaker–now no longer Xoyo, but one the other mistresses residing in the palace-in one of the adjacent rooms and he, familiar with the request, scampered off.

A faint smile came to Ahuitzotl as he nodded his concurrence. Then his eyes turned to her; he scanned over her, beginning at her face and covering the slender features of her body draped in the traditional skirt and triangular sleeveless cotton blouse. Her glossy long black hair was stretched back from her forehead and hung loosely down her back. she looked exceedingly attractive to him-he had been so completely absorbed in Pelaxilla that he rarely thought of Tlalalca. Now that she was standing there with her eyes gleaming and a wide smile on her face, he found himself quite enticed by her, and he returned her smile with a warm glow of his own.

"I've missed you," Tlalalca spoke first. "It's been a long time."

There was a sadness in his smile; the empress knew this was a bittersweet return for him. "I've heard about Pelaxilla, from Cihuacoatl," she continued, "It must have been difficult for you."

Hearing Pelaxilla's name mentioned brought back the heartache he had felt throughout the return journey, and he tried to repress his pain but failed in this effort; his eyes turned glassy and his voice was trembling. "She is lost to me," he muttered, overcome with a chill now familiar to him. "I shall never see her again."

"It's so sad. She became a close friend to me. I dearly wanted her back with us."

"She spoke words of kindness about you, such as I would not have expected to hear from her. She said that she is indebted to you for giving her understanding about many things and that she loves you and honors you."

Tlalalca was overcome with sorrow; tears came to her, but she bore them quietly and refrained from crying out.

Ahuitzotl walked up to her and wiped the tears off her face with his hand and then gently embraced her. Even while sharing this moment of mutual comfort from their grief, the scent of her perfumed hair stimulated his senses; he felt his heartbeat quickening and a burning in his loins-he was consumed with an overpowering urge to release his pent up energies. Her heavy breathing told him that she was also in an impassioned state and desired to make love as much as he did. His hand reached under her blouse and cupped the smooth roundness of her breasts, and he felt the hardness of her nipples with his fingertips.

"Come," he said softly, "and join me in my bath."

Tlalalca was more than willing, his stroking having aroused her to a feverish pitch and it had been almost two years since she last enjoyed the pleasures of sensual contact. Together they ambled into the bathing chamber which had already been prepared for him by servants who, in their habitual manner, filled the cistern with tepid water and set out towels and other items and then left so he might have his privacy. Ahuitzotl took off his clothes under the longing eyes of the empress, then helped her remove her skirt, and when she was naked before him, she nestled against him and ran her hands along his side fondling his muscular frame.

"Your ribs are showing," she said. "You've lost weight."

Again this worrisome feature was brought to his attention; he was not aware of having reduced the amount of food he ate by any significant degree and was at a loss to explain his lesser weight. It had been because of the energy expended on his long operation, he thought-that accounted for it. "We drove ourselves relentlessly," he said, more to convince himself than her. "I spent all my time on my feet. Now that I'm back, I will undoubtedly regain it."

"I hope so; you looked better with the extra weight."

Momentarily concerned, he soon dismissed his fretting in his enflamed ardor. Highly excited at seeing her nudity, he lifted Tlalalca into his arms and carried her to the cistern, descending into its waters slowly at first and then plunging in when halfway down the steps. Only after being completely submerged did he release his hold on her.

They frolicked merrily in the water, rubbing themselves, touching their heated flesh, and fondling their most delicate parts in relishment. Ahuitzotl caressed her everywhere, feeling every contour of her silky skin, sliding his hands between her legs and through the folds of her buttocks, and delighting in its delectable softness. His tongue lapped at the protrusion of her brownish nipples and he enclosed his lips over them to fully savor its deliciousness. She was beside herself with pleasure and moaned out her ecstatic pleasure.

Unable to further restrain his impulses, Ahuitzotl flung Tlalalca in his arms and quickly emerged from the tub. They hurriedly dried themselves and moved to the adjacent room to lie on its mats. Instantly he was on top of her, his phallus instinctively finding the orifice affording it a snug fit. Then began the spasmodic rhythmic movements increasing in intensity at every motion until attaining a climactic surge of exquisite gratification.

They panted, they gasped, they groaned in ecstatic delight-every pore of their bodies responded to the excitement; goose-bumps surfaced over Tlalalca's flesh as she moaned out her exquisitely intense satisfaction under his heated frame. A love such as neither had ever experienced before, magnified in its exhilaration beyond all conception and intoxicating in its erotic stimulation, and when it culminated in an explosion of orgasmic thrill, they believed that they had undergone the most gratifying event of their lives. They nestled into an embrace in their total exhaustion, taking deep gulps of air to recuperate from the exotic ordeal.

Drained of strength, they lay on their backs and allowed the coolness of a gentle breeze to kiss their naked bodies, saying nothing as this was far too pleasurable a moment to mar by spoken words and was better enjoyed in silence. Enervated and overcome with drowsiness, Ahuitzotl soon fell asleep; Tlalalca stayed awake for awhile longer, soothingly content and warmed by what she had experienced. At last she also lapsed into a blissful slumber at his side. It had been their finest homecoming.

XII

The joy of Ahuitzotl's homecoming soon faded and was replaced by a deep depression as the irreversibility of Pelaxilla's loss began to sink into his brain. For days he moped within the confines of his palace seeing no one and overcome with notions of how things might have ended differently had he been more forceful in his meeting with her. He often wandered about the corridors late at night cursing himself for having failed in his attempt to reclaim her and more than once shouted out for her into the darkness as if entreating the gods to show pity on him and to bring into being events through which he might again possess her. In spite of his pleadings, their ears were closed to him and the situation remained as hopeless as before: she was gone—forever.

And there were moments of intense rage-the uncontrollable vehemence he felt for Cocijoeza over having won Pelaxilla from him which pursued him without mercy and relentlessly refused to grant him a respite. He stormed against his adversary aloud, shouting abuses and insults upon him, and visualizing the injuries he should have inflicted upon him. He should have killed him, he said to himself repeatedly; he had frequent opportunities to do so at Soconusco and let them slip away from him. Pelaxilla may have damned him for it at first, but in time she would have diminished its importance if not forgotten it. What a fool he had been for not killing him! He visualized the fat Zapotecan seated in his throne and laughing at him-and he was red with rage.

His melancholy and angry moods were a source of much discomfort to those nearest to him, alienating them from him—even his son avoided him-and making them reluctant to associate with him, so that, as a consequence, he was left increasingly by himself to brood over his misfortunes. Cihuacoatl had all but given up trying to see him. Thus it transpired that Ahuitzotl spent several weeks alone in his residence without a single visitor except for

Tlalalca whose concern for him compelled her to frequently break into his disquietude and attempt to alleviate, if not end, his despondency.

"You cannot continue like this," she begged during one of her visits to his chamber. "It's destroying you and the relationships you must maintain as Revered Speaker. And you have not gotten any closer to Cuauhtemoc."

Ahuitzotl glanced at her; he was quite aware of this but found himself powerless to overcome the dejection he felt.

"You make it difficult," Tlalalca persisted. "I try my best to help you surmount your depression and my efforts are wasted. It causes me to feel as though I mean nothing to you at all."

"Do not think that," he told her; she was relieved to finally hear his voice.

"What else am I to think when you will not hear me, will not speak to me, and will not respond to the affection I try to give you? You make me feel that I am somehow the source of your bitterness and depression."

"Is this what I have done?" said Ahuitzotl, at last showing some regard over how his behavior had affected his wife and now genuinely regretting his selfishness. "It's unintentional. You have in fact been a great help to me in this crisis. I don't want you to think I'm not grateful."

"If that's so, then why can't you relate this to me, so I am not left in despair pondering over how I have offended or hurt you."

"It's not that I haven't thought about it. I have, and quite often, but I'm unable to express it to you."

"I'm your wife. Why should you have any reservations in sharing your torments with me?"

"Because it concerns Pelaxilla, and a wife does not want her husband so troubled over the loss of another woman."

"I've been a party to this affection you have for her all these years and it's never bothered you before."

"Perhaps I recognize the futility of my mourning her loss and do not want others to bring it to my attention. My mind tells me what foolishness this is, but my heart will not permit me to accept it-I can't seem to surmount this deprivation I feel."

"It's not that you can't accept it, but that you won't."

"Because I fear this kind of advice, I refrain from telling anyone about this," he reacted harshly. "I've said those very words to myself often enough, and yet the agony remains–it has a will of its own. How can I make anyone understand?"

"You can say that? I won't deny you have suffered a great loss, but do not behave as though your case is so unique. Do you think you're the only one to mourn losing a beloved? Many are so afflicted, and if they have recovered from their torment, then also will you."

She was angry with him, and for ample reasons; he had himself caused her an enormous amount of grief which she quietly endured for years. Ahuitzotl sank back on his cushions and reflected on this. Her words were the same ones he had said enough times, but it was different hearing them from her–much as if a mirror had been propped up in front of him and what was seen was not appreciated and she rendered an absurdity to his brooding. "I suppose you're right," he acknowledged. "My behavior has not been particularly noteworthy for a monarch."

"Indeed it has not," she agreed. "You have sulked alone in these halls for so long it's a wonder you know what is going on in your realm. Certainly others have asked themselves that."

"What do you mean?"

"Your ministers, especially Cihuacoatl, have made frequent inquiries into your state of health. They have become greatly distressed by your behavior."

"Cihuacoatl would never understand the nature of my affliction. His sole preoccupation is with matters of state."

"He's not the only one. There's general speculation as to whether you have taken leave of your senses. I've been embarrassed to hear what's said."

"What's this you say?" Ahuitzotl grew alarmed. "There's talk that I am demented?"

"It has been mentioned by some."

"By who?"

"I can't name anyone specifically. It's the sort of thing whispered among the lords and servants when they are unable to see you or communicate with you."

Ahuitzotl's face reddened; at last he was shaken from his listless state. Whether calculated or not, Tlalalca had successfully rekindled his interest in matters he had neglected, even if not with the best of intentions, for he was determined to put an end to rumors questioning his reason. He called out for a messenger who quickly ran to his presence. "Send for Cihuacoatl," Ahuitzotl instructed him, "Have him gather my chief advisors in the reception hall as soon as possible. Let me know when they arrive."

A wave of Ahuitzotl's hand sent the messenger scurrying off toward the administrative center where the ministers held their offices.

"So they say that I am mad," said Ahuitzotl as he paced his quarters, an indication of his agitation. "They will be amazed how informative my madness can be."

Ordinarily his display of anger would have upset Tlalalca, but after so many weeks of sullenness, it came as a promising change for her: at last he lived in the present. "Will you be angry with them?" she asked.

He did not answer, and his silence confirmed his intent.

"Must you always look for ways to hold your ministers in suspense?" she continued. "Wouldn't it be better to show some friendliness after your long absence from them?"

"Do you now tell me how I should conduct my official duties?"

"I'm pleased you mean to busy yourself in them, for this will help dispel your miseries. But you approach this matter with seeming vindictiveness; I cannot see how this will settle things with your detractors."

Her counsel impressed him. She had a way of clarifying the implications of his conduct and she excelled in making him see its foolishness. "Perhaps you're right," he conceded. "It's unwise to begin my sessions with them in a confrontation. I have no wish to confirm their suspicions about my 'madness' to them."

"I ought not have mentioned it. You've become obsessed with the opinions others have of you. Its gnawing at you."

Before he could answer, the messenger reappeared at his chamber door and informed him that the ministers were ready for him. Ahuitzotl gave Tlalalca a sharp glance suggesting he understood and meant to comply with her wishes, but with him, one never knew, she thought; she had been misled by him too often in the past to make a conclusive assessment. Then he departed for the conference.

The ministers were elated to see their monarch, manifesting itself in the courtesies granted him as he entered; at first they applauded, and then they bowed their heads in respect as he passed by them on his way to the royal seat. Cihuacoatl was particularly delighted over his master's presence-he had missed the briefings he was used to giving him on a regular basis; the dignity and importance of his office seemed diminished without having a superior to report to. "It has been many weeks, Lord," the minister beamed. "You have given us cause to be concerned over your health."

"Yes, I've heard of your concerns, but as you can see, I am here and well. You may dispense with your fears about my health."

"We are gratified to see it. I assume this is why you have summoned us together-so we might witness your recovery."

"You are wrong. That is not why I called for this meeting."

"Indeed?" Cihuacoatl felt himself becoming tense. "I would have thought this. What, then, is the purpose of our gathering?"

"I want to check on the projects I proposed before going on our Soconusco campaign. Mainly, I'm interested in the aqueduct I wanted built from the springs of Coyoacan to Tenochtitlan. Is the work in progress?"

"But Lord," Cihuacoatl replied nervously, "The work has not even begun. You did not tell us to initiate its construction."

"You knew this is my prized project," Ahuitzotl snapped at his minister. "Must I lead you by the hand to start something I wish to have done? At the least, stones from the quarries should have been extracted and set aside for shaping and transport. Not one of you has taken the initiative to proceed on this while I was away?"

"We could not, Lord."

"Why not?"

"Tzutzumatzin, the Lord of Coyoacan, still opposes the construction of such an aquaduct. Without his consent, no phase of the project can commence. We have no authority to overrule his decision-only you can do that."

"You mean this entire project has been in abeyance for two years because Tzutzumatzin will not agree to it?"

"If you will recall, Lord, no decision was reached when you last spoke with him on it."

"Tzutzumatzin defies me still. I thought I had conveyed the necessity of this project for Tenochtitlan's growth to him. How is it that he can continue to thwart my plans?"

"He is persuasive in his declaration that the project poses a danger for the city. He has our interests at heart."

"Our interests!" Ahuitzotl arose, bellowing. "Fools! It is Coyoacan's interests he wishes to protect! He wants the spring for his own use, perhaps in the hope that Coyoacan will someday grow as rapidly as Tenochtitlan. This is not likely to happen, and it's our growth which he is jeopardizing by his obstinacy. We cannot permit him to stand in the way of a project of such vital importance to us."

"As I am told, Lord, the nature of his concerns are legitimately based. Many of our own engineers share his belief that this aqueduct entails great risks for us."

"Ridiculous. Don't you know that for every engineer who tells you this, there is another who disagrees with him? Who are these engineers you speak of? Name them to me."

Cihuacoatl was shocked at the demand; he knew if he were to mention them to his angry master, they faced potential retaliatory action at his hands. He chose to be evasive. "It is but opinions they hold, Lord, and not as though they meant to oppose your plans. They expressed concern over how we would regulate the increased volume of water entering Tenochtitlan with our existing system of causeways and dikes not designed to contain any overflow."

Ahuitzotl detected his minister's reluctance to identify the dissenting builders but hesitated to make a point of it; his real opposition remained Tztzumatzin whom he suspected of being jealous of Tenochtitlan's prosperity.

"The engineers I spoke with have told me that a system of troughs and gates can be built into the aqueduct to control its flow," Ahuitzotl explained. "These fears are unfounded. What do you think the water will be used for-creating a giant reservoir inside the city? No! It will be consumed by the people."

"If you say so, Lord. You have consulted with these experts and know of what they speak."

"Let us confront Tzutzumatzin on this matter once and for all. Send a messenger to him and have him report to this council so we may all understand the reasons behind his obstinacy."

"Do you mean to send a messenger directly to him?"

"That's what I said," Ahuitzotl declared.

"What of Chimalpopoca? He is Tzutzumatzin's master, and has an interest in this."

"It's not necessary to involve him. I have no desire to get mired in the ceaseless abyss of indecision and haggling that would come out of this. We have had enough delays."

"My lord, I must caution you. This constitutes a serious breach of etiquette with Tlacopan. Coyoacan is a subject city of Chimalpopoca, and its ruler is a highly respected member of his royal house. For you to summon for Tzutzumatzin directly and possibly berate him for opposing your project would be to usurp Chimalpopoca's authority. He will not stand for this."

"Why do you defy me at every turn? My dispute is with Tzutzumatzin, no one else, and it is he who I will castigate for it if I choose to."

"As head minister, I am compelled to advise you against this drastic action. It will not be well received by Chimalpopoca, nor any other lords of Anahuac who respect the accords that bind our cities."

"I don't think you quite understand, Cihuacoatl. There is a calculated intent behind this. It will demonstrate our position of dominance over our alliance cities-and rather effectively at that. The message is that when it comes to the welfare of Tenochtitlan and its populace, I will not tolerate any kind of opposition."

"I beseech you, Lord, to weight the wisdom of this carefully. The move is fraught with dangers."

"I'm aware of that, but if we are successful, the benefits will be great-our supremacy will be firmly established."

"You would be so rash as to risk our alliance over this?"

"I would," Ahuitzotl gloated. "Send the messenger."

The assignment was exceedingly distasteful to a worried Cihuacoatl; he was convinced that his master failed to comprehend the gravity of his proposal or cared so little for the alliance that he could toy with the fabric which held it in place. Neither condition was desirable for the old minister who strongly believed in the sanctity of established protocol as the enduring bond that solidified the compacts and interrelationship existing between powers. Beset with the gravest of misgiving, he sensed that a monumental blunder was in the making of which he was an unwilling party, and only in great reluctance did he sent a courier to Tzutzumatzin's court. It seemed to him as though nothing had changed, and even after his months of absence, the Revered Speaker's strong will asserted itself and dominated over the council's members. He stood as headstrong as ever and they, against their better judgment, bowed to his will.

XIII

huitzotl was correct when he informed his minister that the request for Tzutzumatzin to appear before Tenochtitlan's council in actuality amounted to a demonstration of the power the capital exerted over its allied cities. And so it was perceived by the ruler of Coyoacan. The demand posed a serious dilemma for Tzutzumatzin who recognized that it contravened the established formalities and yet was gravely concerned over offending Anahuac's mightiest monarch. He deliberated at some length over all its implications and cautiously decided it would be best to comply with Ahuitzotl's directive. But first, he took the necessary measure to inform his overlord of the order the Revered Speaker had issued him and his intent to adhere to it. He did not wait for Chimalpopoca's reply-the directive made it clear his presence was to be immediate-proceeding instead for Ahuitzotl's palace with a number of his advisors. When he arrived later that afternoon, Cihuacoatl reconvened the council and send word of its session to his master.

Tzutzumatzin was quite apprehensive about this meeting; he could sense his palms sweating and a weakness in his knees. Cihuacoatl took note of his discomfort and felt a degree of sympathy for the ruler; he tried to allay his fears. "Do you know why you have been summoned?" he asked him.

"Yes," Tzutzumatzin nervously replied. "It is the aqueduct he wants to build. He wants my concurrence on it."

"Will you accede to his wishes?"

"My position remains the same. I see it as a threat to your city and oppose its construction."

"Then we shall be in for a hard time. I hoped there might be some latitude for compromise, but I fear neither of you will be so inclined. Enough said-here comes the Revered Speaker."

Ahuitzotl walked briskly in, took a brief glance at Tzutzumatzin which gave no hint of his disposition, and seated himself in his royal chair. "I shall come straight to the point, Tzutzumatzin," he began. "Even before we undertook our Soconusco operation, I sent you word that I expected your fullest cooperation on a project I placed the greatest priority on—the aqueduct. Two years later I find nothing has been done, allegedly because you continue to defy me. Why?"

"I do not defy you, Lord," Tzutzumatzin indignantly replied. "I see a danger to your city in this project and deem it my duty to inform you of it."

"Many disagree with that assessment. I am among them."

"They do not understand the nature of the springs at Coyoacan. The flow emanating from there is extremely inconsistent; during times of much rainfall, it swells to a virtual torrent and no amount of masonry will check its surging waters."

"Do not bore me with your fine details. My own engineers have studied all aspects of it and affirm the waters can be controlled with a well-designed system of channels and bypasses. There is no need to reiterate this. You have been apprised of it often enough. We both know that the aqueduct is no longer the issue, Tzutzumatzin. What is in question here is your open defiance of me. That is your unpardonable transgression of which you must give an account for."

"I protest this!" Tzutzumatzin replied, now much alarmed as he sensed the gravity of his situation. "My intentions have been honorable and I will not be castigated for it."

"All Anahuac knows Tenochtitlan is in need of water, and that it has been my declared objective to fulfill this need. Yet you have stood in opposition to this purpose from the beginning and continue to do so, and, worse, you have been outspoken in your resistance and have made a public display of it. Do you deny this?"

"I admit my disagreement has been vocal, but it always centered around the inherent risks of the project itself-never has it been directed against you personally!"

"That is not how it has been perceived," Ahuitzotl roared out, "nor is it presently seen as such. Instead, it is seen by everyone as a confrontation of Coyoacan against Tenochtitlan and as a sign of your professed rebellion against my authority."

"That is preposterous!" Tzutzumatzin angrily retorted. "For a mere suburban town like Coyoacan to challenge the capital of our realm is ludicrous! How could we hope to ever win such a contest? Everyone knows this is absurd."

"What everyone knows is that this amounts to a test of will between you and I. Hear me, Tzutzumatzin, and take heed. I will not be defied as Tizoc was, and if there is a dispute existing between myself and my subject lords, I must and will prevail. Do you understand this?"

"Your authority has never been disputed by me."

"By the gods! Can you be so blind? You dispute it when you counteract my wishes, especially when you do this publicly. The damage has been done, and Anahuac has been witness to it, so now you atone for your insubordination."

"Atone for pointing out the dangers your project entails?"

"There is no danger!" Ahuitzotl shouted at him. "Get that through your thick skull!"

Tzutzumatzin recoiled in fright, as did the ministers in attendance, including Cihuacoatl; never had they seen an allied ruler so severely censured by the Revered Speaker. Ahuitzotl, on seeing their consternation, paused and awkwardly attempted to regain his composure by leaning back in his throne. He breathed heavily as he glared at the fearful Coyoacan lord.

"You will publicly retract all the statements you have made in reference to this project which counteracted my desires," Ahuitzotl continued. "Further, you will declare before everyone your support of this project. Then, to fully demonstrate your support, you will announce the number of laborers Coyoacan will assign to work on it. This is what I direct you to do. You are strongly urged to obey. Are these instructions clear to you?"

"Quite clear, Lord."

"Then I can be assured of your compliance?"

"I must speak with the priests. You ask me to give consent on something which contradicts all my experience and learning as a builder. I must see what the gods direct me to do."

Ahuitzotl tensed; he thinned his lips, pressing them tightly together, and his head quivered. "You defy me still!" he exclaimed. "Can it be we heard you correctly?"

Tzutzumatzin had been badly shaken by this entire encounter and was too frightened to say anything more lest it provoke the Revered Speaker to greater wrath. The tension hung oppressively over the assembly and no one dared utter a word-one could hear the ministers gasping for their breath. Afraid to answer, Tzutzumatzin waited for Ahuitzotl to resume their conversation.

"Do not delay in consulting with your gods, Tzutzumatzin," Ahuitzotl instructed him. "Send word by tomorrow on what they advise. You may go."

Anxious to be out of the hall, Tzutzumatzin and his alarmed ministers needed no prodding to hasten their exit. "Remember, Tzutzumatzin," Ahuitzotl yelled after him, "We are in need of this water. See to it that the gods are informed of this."

The council remained in session on the following afternoon after having completed much of its business awaiting word from Tzutzumatzin. Most of the ministers expected Coyoacan's ruler to acquiesce to the demand given him by the Revered Speaker which they did not think unreasonable. After all, Tzutzumatzin had been quite outspoken in his criticism of Ahuitzotl's pet project and, even if for good intentions, this nonetheless amounted to an open challenge of his supremacy. The monarch was justified in seeking atonement, and most felt that Tzutzumatzin escaped in relatively good shape, if a bit unnerved-he could have fared much worse.

The message was delivered by a member of Coyoacan's royal house, being too important to be entrusted to merely a courier; everyone assembled eagerly anticipated it. "Give us Lord Tzutzumatzin's words," Ahuitzotl instructed. "We have waited patiently to hear them."

The young prince was at a momentary loss on whether to face the council or the Revered Speaker; Cihuacoatl motioned for him to speak to the monarch. He then began.

"These are my master's words: I shall do what my overlord asks. He has insisted on my compliance to his orders and I, as a subject monarch, must obey. I shall therefore announce my support of this project, as I have been directed, and will provide my lord with the numbers he desires to labor over it. I shall even retract publicly to having opposed this work; however, I will not renounce my misgivings over its wisdom and will continue to alert those who ask me about its dangers. The risks in harnessing the springs of Coyoacan exist, and will continue to exist, in spite of all that is said. They will not go away and cease to be merely because it is so wished. These are my words to my master and Tenochtitlan's council."

All eyes turned on the Revered Speaker. Ahuitzotl glasped the arms of his throne tightly and appeared as a crouched jaguar in a stance ready to pounce upon its prey. "He dared!" Ahuitzotl exclaimed. "He dared to alter my orders to him!"

"But, Lord," Cihuacoatl said after dismissing the courier, "He does everything you ask."

"Everything but what is most important. He persists in his claim that I and my engineers are wrong. He still opposes us."

Nobody could refute this; Tzutzumatzin's reply startled even his most staunchest defenders at the council-they could not believe he would be so brash as to readily assert his continued recalcitrance. His fate now rested with the angry monarch.

"He is an impediment to all I want to accomplish," Ahuitzotl slowly went on. "Can I risk to have him, when the slightest miscalculation or error takes place, even if it has nothing to do with his premonitions, wave this over my head and cry out 'I told you so'? Am I, master of Anahuac, to endure this kind of public humiliation from some minor local ruler? No. I tell you I will not. Tzutzumatzin has exceeded his discretions by snubbing the conciliatory measures I offered; he should have given greater consideration towards this stranglehold he has on me and recognized I could not allow myself to be so constrained. He has, by his own action, forced my hand and sealed his fate."

"What do you suggest, Lord?" Cihuacoatl asked, dreading his answer.

"His death!-the penalty for defying a Revered Speaker."

The ministers were shocked; to kill a rebellious sovereign of a foreign power or an enemy state amounted to one thing, but to order the death of a local lord who was a kinsman of Chimalpopoca, ruler of Tlacopan of the Triple Alliance, and moreover, a highly respected noble, was quite another matter. Certainly Tzutzumatzin had gone too far, but he did not merit death-that constituted a punishment out of all proportion to the nature of the offense. Yet none of the ministers dared to protest this action and Ahuitzotl, who possessed an instinct for capitalizing on such fears, added to their intimidation. "Well?" he asked, You seem strangely quiet about it.

Do you object? If so, state your reasons for it now so I might know who disagrees with my and why."

No one raised an objection, as Ahuitzotl expected.

"Understand this," he continued. "I consider this matter closed and will have no more attention drawn to it." With this terse comment, and before the full significance of his words grasped anyone, Ahuitzotl arose from his throne and exited from the hall, leaving Cihuacoatl with instructions to dismiss the council.

The next day, a squadron of warriors under Motecuhzoma marched across the southern causeway for Coyoacan and on arriving there surrounded Tzutzumatzin's palace. When the guards refused them entry, Motecuhzoma ordered his soldiers to break in. They rammed down the gate and entered but were unable to find the object of their search.

"Where is he?" Motecuhzoma asked the captain of the palace guard force.

"He was alerted on your coming and fled," came his reply.

"Where did he go?"

"He did not tell me."

"If you like, I can send your entire guard force to Tenochtitlan before Lord Ahuitzotl. That will not be a pleasant experience I can assure you. Now tell me, where is Tzutzumatzin?"

"I swear it before the gods. I do not know."

An oath such as this was beyond question, and Motecuhzoma had no cause to doubt the captain; only a demented man who had no fear of the hereafter would utter a false statement.

"Very well," Motecuhzoma said, "I will leave for further instructions, but understand, I shall come back. It will do no good for your nobles to hide Tzutzumatzin from us. Relate this to your lord when you see him again. The Revered Speaker will be sure to have his way."

Ahuitzotl flushed indignantly when Motecuhzoma reported to him that Tzutzumatzin had gone into hiding, apparently with the cooperation of the lords of Coyoacan, and was nowhere to be found.

"You searched the palace?" Ahuitzotl asked.

"He was not there, Lord."

"This entire sordid affair has gone on too long and must be terminated. Send messengers to the leading families of Coyoacan that you will again, in two days, appear at Tzutzumatzin's palace and that he had better be there. If he is not, I will not hesitate to sieze Coyoacan with my army. By harboring him, they are accessories to his treasonous crimes and will accordingly suffer the full consequences. Let them think on that for awhile."

The messengers were sent, and at the designated time, Motecuhzoma again came to Coyoacan's regal residence with another squadron. This time their reception was more direct—they were led straight to the monarch who had waited for them. He was seated in his royal chair at the end of the council hall and calmly faced his approaching executioners.

"Do you know why we have come?" Motecuhzoma spoke first.

"I do," Tzutzumatzin slowly answered; now that his fate was inevitable, he seemed prepared to accept it and his demeanor was surprisingly calm. "Your master drives a hard bargain-my life for that of my city's-and all this over what I regarded to be in his best interest. Tezcatlipoca must have had a strange purpose in this."

"Do not bring the gods into this. The fate befalling you is of your own making. You should have declared your opposition privately."

"Yes, that was a mistake. I admit to it, but once expressed, there was no way to amend it without suffering personal indignity. Such is the nature of these offices we hold that we have to continue on the course we have set upon in spite of ourselves."

"What foolish talk is that? You could have changed your position as the Revered Speaker requested."

"It is not so easy, young man, especially when you know yourself to be correct and the position called upon to uphold as false. One day you may discover the truth of this. What fate has your master decreed for me?"

"You are to be hanged. At this very moment the noose is being set up in the courtyard."

"I see. An ignoble end for one who merely tried to warn his lord of the dangers in the mad project he contemplates."

"We are ready for you," Motecuhzoma cut off his conversation, tiring of further delays in a task he was not enthusiastic about to begin with.

Tzutzumatzin's attendants bedecked him in his royal robe of bejeweled bird feathers. Then he bade his young executioner to lead the way, and his only outburst of anger came when Motecuhzoma tried to station two warriors at his side. "Do not treat me as though I were a common criminal," he rebuked Motecuhzoma sharply. "I will make my own way to the place of execution. If the gods have decreed that I must die, I accept my destiny."

Embarrassed, Motecuhzoma acceded to his wishes and ordered the guards to leave, and only he walked with Tzutzumatzin into the courtyard. At the far end of the enclosure, a rope had been flung over one of the stone lintels which jutted out from the second story of a palace adjunct. Most of the squadron warriors stood about the vicinity awaiting the doomed monarch's arrival; three of them held on the end of the rope in readiness to pull their victim into the air.

Tzutzumatzin stood gazing at the noose in front of him as if in a trance. He grabbed it with both hands, then turned to face Motecuhzoma and his companions. "Tell your Lord Ahuitzotl that I prophesize this fate for him. Before long, when he has completed his grand aqueduct and makes use of it, Tenochtitlan will be flooded and possibly destroyed. The fault for this will be his for having spurned by advice. Know then who to blame when this disaster befalls you."

Tzutzumatzin next put the rope around his own neck and nodded for the warriors to string him up. They looked toward Motecuhzoma who momentarily hesitated and waited until he too indicated his consent; then they pulled on the rope and raised Tzutzumatzin upward where he dangled and squirmed for a while before falling lifeless. After watching the body swaying to and fro with its head twisted grotesquely to one side, the warriors secured the rope in place to a post and soon departed leaving the dead monarch hanging there to be disposed of by his family.

XIV

The assassination of Tzutzumatzin, for that is what it was, struck like a thunderbolt throughout Anahuac, being perceived as a serious abuse of power on the part of the Revered Speaker and outraging the lords of the Triple Alliance. For the first time, hostile criticism was hurled at Ahuitzotl, denouncing this breach of etiquette. In Tlacopan, Chimalpopoca had to be forcefully restrained from making a public condemnation of his overlord and openly insulting him; he was furious over having had his authority usurped while torn with remorse over the death of one of his favored relatives. In his court, he shouted out abuses against Ahuitzotl, cursing him for what he had done; he threatened to terminate his compact with Tenochtitlan as long as Ahuitzotl ruled but was curtailed from this certain suicidal course by cooler heads that prevailed. Weeping tears of rage, the old monarch sank back into his royal chair utterly disconsolate in his helplessness as he looked back over the bizarre sequence of events leading to his noble subject's murder in stunned disbelief. To his deep dismay, the realization struck him that Tlacopan no longer held sway over Tenochtitlan's ascendancy in power and now existed as nothing more than a mere vassal state in its association with the prevailing force in Anahuac, as did all other cities. The confederacy of the Triple Alliance remained so in name only—in reality, Tenochtitlan dominated.

Nezahualpilli, who had maintained virtually no contact with the Revered Speaker since the execution of Nenetzin, was so distressed over the news that he was prompted to make an appearance in Tenochtitlan to demand an explanation. Ahuitzotl, never inclined to justify his actions to anyone, admittedly did not look forward to the meeting; however, he could not refuse the Texcocan his attention, although he was determined not to be castigated by his ally. Their relationship remained badly strained, and this latest episode was not going to help in rectifying that. If Ahuitzotl held out for any hopes about discussing his aqueduct with Nezahualpilli, a reputed master builder whose advice he would have highly valued, these quickly evaporated when he found the irate Texcocan interested only in learning of the reasons for Tzutzumatzin's death.

"If you could identify his crime to me," Nezahualpill fumed, "I should be more disposed to consider your motives for killing him and let the matter rest. As it is, you make it difficult for me to see your actions in a favorable light."

"As Revered Speaker, it should be enough for you that I say he offended me and was the cause of his own death," Ahuitzotl coldly stated.

"Great Lord, I am not an minor underling to be dismissed with such casual indifference. There are grave accusations being made to which I must provide satisfactory answers. Tzutzumatzin's execution has created a furor throughout the realm. It is important for us to settle the questions being asked."

"What sort of questions?"

"What crime has Tzutzumatzin committed? In what way did he err? Did he conspire against your royal crown? Was he a traitor? A thief? Or a murderer? Was he an adulterer?"

"His crime was treason. Disobediance to the Revered Speaker amounts to treasonous conduct, as you well know. Death is the appropriate and defined penalty."

"Treason! Is it treasonous now to caution you of the perils entailed in your project?"

"To specify such dangers to me—no. But to persist in opposition to me after being presented with evidence to the contrary, to close one's eyes to that evidence, and to make a public platform of this resistance-that indeed constitutes a challenge to my authority and is tantamount to treason. He was offered abundant chances to redeem himself but chose, instead, to continue in his disobediance. I'll not allow a subordinate ruler to openly defy me or to deprecate me-and neither would you! You have slain a son for less a reason as I had for killing Tzutzumatzin-you are the last person to speak to me of my errors!"

His last statement struck a raw nerve, and Nezahualpilli reacted angrily to it. "The lords do not question my son's death; it is Tzutzumatzin's that is being disputed. He was a ruler like us, and elected by a council that thought him pious and honorable. And like us, he represented the divine workings of the gods on earth. What you have done amounts to an offense against the gods and–you must surely be aware of this!-it is their retribution you have to look out for."

Ahuitzotl tensed under the Texcocan's incessant questioning, finding it irritating, and neared the breaking point. "All right!" he shouted. "Perhaps I did act hastily and should have tempered my anger with more prudence. Is that what you want to hear? I admit it. But the deed has been done and I cannot reverse what has happened. Most certainly I did not seek to offend the gods."

"But you have."

"Do not play the righteous monarch with me, Nezahualpilli. Your own conduct is not entirely untainted, you know. Your indignant and vile display of Nenetzin was not an exercise of prudence on your part."

Nezahualpilli deemed it appropriate to pause and cool their conversation which was attaining a heated confrontation; he did not come to Tenochtitlan to further aggravate frictions already existing between them. "Yes," he at length conceded, "that was an imprudent act, and I have since come to regret it. You are poper to remind me of its folly; things have never been the same between us since that affair. We both have our burdens to carry, although I adjudge yours the graver misdeed."

"If I could amend my mistake, I would," Ahuitzotl conceded. "I could not believe this deed would lead to such an uproar among the lords. Tzutzumatzin's defiance was clear enough to my council and should have been similarly regarded by Chimalpopoca and his court."

"My advice is to make a public demonstration of remorse over what you did and hope this gesture will be gratefully received by the Tepanec nobles."

"And how am I supposed to do that?"

"You don't know? Have you lost your capacity to show compassion? If so, you will be seen as a pitiful monarch indeed."

Ahuitzotl was silenced as he deliberated over Nezahualpilli's inference. Even under the current strain of their relationship, he still possessed a deep-seated, if somewhat begrudging, respect for his ally's counsel.

"Yes, you're right." Ahuitzotl presently acknowledged. "I am distressed over this and have wished many times that I had not acted so rashly.

Perhaps if I offered my apologies and provided Tzutzumatzin's heirs with compensation-that would be better than pretending nothing happened."

"They will appreciate it, if it is done with sincerity."

"Why shouldn't it be? I am a man of my word."

"You are a better judge of that than I; if you say what you mean, the lords will know it and have no reason to doubt you."

"Yes, it must be done. If for no other purpose than to ease my own self-loathing over it. I truly did not mean for it to end this way. Had it not been for the importance of this project, I would never have dreamed of committing such an act."

Nezahualpilli remained skeptical; he was too familiar with Ahuitzotl's impetuous nature to be swayed by this kind of rhetoric and he questioned if the Revered Speaker actually believed it. Now that attention had been focused on the project which was the source of Tzutzumatzin's demise, Nezahualpilli began to inquire into it.

Ahuitzotl was more than eager to entertain his colleague with all the details and intricacies of his proposed aqueduct in the hope he would illicit a positive reaction from the famed builder who had in his day achieved renown for erecting some of the grandest structures in Anahuac. He described all aspects of the project, specifying the volume of water which would travel through the conduit-almost boasting of its quantity-and how the flow was to be regulated by an elaborate system of sluice gates and channels and numerous bypasses that were to divert the main stream to various areas of the city. The conception was ambitious, challenging in its complexity and scope, and the expenditure of manpower and masonry involved exceeded the construction of the Great Temple, although Ahuitzotl meant for it to be completed in a year's time. To do that, no less than fifty thousand laborers, drawn from every city bordering the lakeshore and working in continuous shifts, were to be employed. The figures were impressive, but to Ahuitzotl's exasperation, Nezahualpilli was decidedly lacking in enthusiasm over the enterprise. Nothing else could have been more disappointing for Ahuitzotl than having the Texcocan minimize what he regarded the crowning achievement of his reign, much as if a greatly respected teacher contemptuously cut off the eagerness of an admiring student trying to please him. Ahuitzotl suppressed the seething pressures he felt surging within him as he finished explaining the details.

"Well?" he concluded, "What do you think of it?"

"An engineering marvel." Nezahualpilli replied in a tedious tone which belied the description. "Certainly it ought to solve the water shortage in Tenochtitlan."

"That's all you can say about it?"

"The problem I see is not with the aqueduct itself, but with the run-off required once it carries all that water into your city."

"Why is that a problem? The water will be consumed by the people and used in the chinampas. Whatever amount is left after that will flow through the gates in the causeways into the lake."

"Just how much water do you estimate will be consumed from a flow that is continuous? The dimensions of your aqueduct will make it difficult to stop the flow once begun."

"Two hundred thousand people will make short work of it. It will all be used."

"Yes, and deposited back into the drains. Remember, Lord, that Nezahualcoyotl's dam retains the waters of the lake itself and does not allow for a natural outlet. I would caution you to contruct a method of cutting off the water's flow at its source-by the springs of Coyoacan. You must devise a means of preventing the flow from being continuous; it will not help if you cut off the run to a particular section of the city when the overflow still enters the lake."

"Do you think my engineers failed to take this into account? Everything you speak of has been incorporated into their plans and given the necessary attention."

"See to it that they have, Lord; otherwise you will have a disaster on your hands."

"I already said they have," Ahuitzotl emphasized, becoming irritated that Nezahualpilli doubted it. "You do not have to belabor the point as if I were incapable of understanding it."

"I meant no offense, but merely wished to make certain you fully grasped the significance of what I was saying."

"It has been sufficiently stressed to where I don't need your advice."

"Then I had best refrain from saying more."

"Do that. I do not favor your criticizing my greatest project."

"What will you do to me? Perchance kill me as you did Tzutzumatzin?"

Nezahualpilli had gone too far and knew it; Ahuitzotl's face swelled and reddened as if he was about to unleash a torrent of fury, but he managed to restrain himself and kept his poise despite the provocation. "You make a mockery of my treatment of Tzutzumatzin," Ahuitzotl snarled. "You know full well that he, unlike you, chose to make his dissent an overt public challenge of my powers. I was justified in doing what I did."

Nezahualpilli was relieved the Revered Speaker's admonishment was no worse than this; he decided to use this as a means of extricating himself from the mired situation he inadvertantly created. "I erred, Lord. I came here to learn the truth behind what happened and you have provided it for me. It's not my desire to leave with our association in no better condition than when I arrived. Perhaps it is best if I left now rather than remain here and let my rash tongue destroy what I set out to do."

"That will benefit us both," agreed Ahuitzotl. "I can see we need more time to reconcile our differences."

"Then I shall go. Before leaving, let me once more say that I applaud your decision to offer restitution to Tzutzumatzin's family. It's important that we maintain our harmony with the lords of Tepaneca. I have heard that Chimalpopoca is extremely distraught over this incident, especially at having his hegemony over Coyoacan usurped. You are correct in trying to regain his good graces."

Nezahualpilli could not have known the Revered Speaker's true feelings on this matter and meant by this expression of concern to prod him towards the favorable action. As it was, Ahuitzotl's misgivings over Tzutzumatzin's death were genuine, and he voiced no objections to the reminder even though he read the Texcocan's intentions clearly. "I share your concern," Ahuitzotl replied. "You won't find my efforts wanting."

Satisfied, Nezahualpilli exited leaving Ahuitzotl to reflect over their discussion. Patching up the strained alliance existing between their three cities was crucial if he was to count on their future cooperation, Ahuitzotl knew, and if he failed to make progress with Nezahualpilli, at least he might succeed with Chimalpopoca. Above all, the way was now open for beginning the work on the aqueduct-nothing more existed to further intervene with its implementation.

XV

Ahuitzotl's aqueduct was a stupendous undertaking conceived as nothing less than the ultimate achievement of his reign-his great and everlasting contribution to Tenochtitlan, a legacy for the ages. A huge labor force was conscripted for the construction, with each of the cities on the waters of Lake Texcoco tasked for a specified number of workers and sectionally apportioned its own assignment. Those from the western shore cities–Azcapotzalco, Tolpetlac, Tenayuca, Tlacopan, Coyoacan, and Tizaapan-worked on the dam complex at the springs through which the water was to be harnessed and fed into various feeder ducts leading to the primary conduit. Crews from the southern cities–from Xochimilco, Cuitlahuac, Chalco, Culhuacan, and Ixtapalapa-labored on the main trough crossing the lake, while those of Tenochtitlan erected the dispersal network through which the water was channeled into the capital's multitudinous precincts. The workers resembled more an enormous army than a labor force, but with the diverse tasks distributed through the composite whole, they were well organized and constantly occupied.

In addition to the workers themselves, a large supporting complement was required to quarter and feed them, and to provide a constant supply of tools, ropes, and other material entailed in the construction. Temporary houses, made of wooden frames and covered with thick drapery, were set up; eating facilities established; latrines, with the necessary canoes to carry human waste products to the chinampas for use as fertilizer, were emplaced in proximity to the major working areas; everything was designed to minimize the time lost and to insure the project's completion as early as possible. Wives, daughters, and other relatives cooked, brought water for drinking, and laundered while husbands and sons towed stones, chiselled, and emplaced mortar.

The aqueduct functioned on the gravity principle, with its source on the mainland at a higher elevation than the flat grounds of the island capital; it descended at a slight angle from there and maintained a steady slope throughout its length, although this was not perceptible to the eye. Designed to cross the lake rested upon stone pylons anchored at measured intervals to permit for the proper weight distribution of its massive masonry, it would extend for almost two leagues over the water. It did not run parallel to the Coyoacan-Ixtapalapa causeway, but rather approached it obliquely from a spot nearly a full league's distance away from it on the mainland; not until it reached the southernmost section of the capital, the Acachinanco precinct, would it bend and run adjacent to the causeway. From there, it was to run for another league parallel to the avenue until, just south of the main plaza, it met its terminus where it branched into smaller channels extending to the different sectors of the city; one was to lead to Ahuitzotl's palace, another fed a fountain planned for the central square, while the rest fed the numerous reservoirs.

The main conduit was basically a trough, enclosed on all sides but the top and approximately the width of a man's stretched out arms with the same depth and a square if viewed from a cross-section. Its masonry was supported upon evenly spaced uprights to keep it at a higher plane than its surrounding area and still allow for a slight descend. Rafts and canoes were utilized to carry the stone blocks, mortar, and scaffolding over the lake.

At its source, an elaborate system of dams and channels was planned so that the water emanating from the springs could be diverted into the aperture of the main conduit. Dams were to regulate the water level so only the desired amount flowed through the duct, anticipated to be about half of its depth. This way the flow could be shut off by inserting oaken boards into grooved vertical ridges, both at the beginning and end of the main line. This was, to Ahuitzotl's eyes, as Nezahualpilli aptly described it-an engineering marvel-and he felt immense pride as he watched the structure coming steadily into form under the toil of the thousands of laborers.

Ahuitzotl made daily inspections of his dream project with his minister. There permeated an element of exhiliration associated in an undertaking of such magnitude, not much different from the excitement he felt when leading his army into battle. He enjoyed doing things on a gigantic scale; it filled him with a sense of gratification to see the seemingly impossible mastered under his set direction and sponsorship. He relished having his builders describing all the intricacies of the system and fancied himself as their equal in comprehending the underlying principles which necessitated doing something one way as opposed to another. This was, after all, his grand project, and he would know every aspects of it.

Cihuacoatl, who knew of his master's deficiencies and lack of formal training in the construction arts, was not taken in by this demonstration of knowledge and often detected when a point was made in error. Yet he thought it prudent not to correct Ahuitzotl, who had made it plain enough that he would not have his favored development criticized, and refrained from drawing undue attention to the faulty declarations. Like the monarch, the minister placed his trust in the demonstrated expertise of the designers and builders; it made for an agreeable, if not very informative, relationship.

In part, Ahuitzotl's frequent visits to the building sites were meant to counteract his tendency to regress into a plethora of self-pity and depression over his missed Pelaxilla. He hoped, by immersing himself completely in this enterprise, he would be able to put an end to the feelings of deprivation which continued to overwhelm him at recurring intervals. This only worked to some degree; there were still those long agonizing periods when his mind repeatedly turned to his beloved mistress and he was afflicted with the deepest grief and despair over how he could possibly have lost her. And with the sorrow came also the hate-the intense, extreme, all-consuming, overpowering hate he bore for Cocijoeza over his success. Against his better judgment, these emotions persisted to torment him, and he often feared how much longer he could endure such misery without succumbing to it.

Tlalalca, who had grown accustomed to Ahuitzotl's behavior, always seemed to know what troubled him. She cherished the time he now spent with her, and certainly he was not lacking in the affection he granted her, for he obviously preferred her to the other women of the court and relinquished nearly all of his private moments to her. Yet it distressed her that all her applications to please him could not erase the memory of Pelaxilla.

"You must forget her," Tlalalca told him. "This endless preoccupation with her can only bring you pain and sorrow."

"So you know when I'm thinking of her."

"It's plain enough. You hardly speak; you eat by yourself; you walk the halls alone, and there's that expression on your face-that lost and fearful look. Always it is the same."

"There's no use denying it. Yes, I was thinking of her. No matter how much I delve into other things and try to keep myself busy, she comes back to me-and I react with the same fears, the burning sensations, and the horrible longing. How can I fight that?"

"It can be done-if you will it strongly enough."

"I've tried everything, all to no avail. Do you realize I have even thought of her while making love to you, visualizing it was her I was making love to. That's how bad this is."

Tlalalca's eyes widened and a look of stunned dismay came over her. "How can you say such a thing to me?" she decried, severely jolted by his admission and upset over his callousness. "Your confession borders on outright cruelty."

"I'm being honest with you. I did not think you to be offended by it."

"Honest it may well be, but most certainly it does not make me feel any better to learn our lovemaking has been but a sham to you. And you have the nerve to suggest I shouldn't be offended by this? I would have preferred your silence to this!"

"I thought we knew each other well enough by now where I could be open and truthful about how I feel. If I did not believe this, I would never have mentioned it to you. You know I do not want to intentionally cause you any anguish."

"What comfort is it to me knowing that all the time when I thought you were enjoying yourself with me, when I believed you delighted in the tenderness I gave you, when I believed I pleased you, you pretended I was Pelaxilla? I suppose you feigned your moans of pleasure also."

"You exaggerate it. It was not all the time-indeed, not even most of the time-only in rare instances when I found my longing for her too strong to overcome."

"Exaggerate you say? How am I to detect which those moments might be? From my perspective, it may as well be all of the time."

"What would you have me do? Tell you each time I have such thoughts? The woman has possessed me. I cannot erase her memory so readily."

She was too distraught to answer at once; his revelation mortified her, not so much because she felt herself belittled by it or professed an envy for Pelaxilla, but rather because she had actually believed she gratified him and that he appreciated it. If she had been asked at what times she was assured that she superseded Pelaxilla in his thoughts, she would have unequivocally sworn it was during her lovemaking with him. She believed this so completely that she was convinced Pelaxilla was all but forgotten-to discover this was not the case came as a profound shock.

"Indeed you are obsessed with her," she almost wept, "so that you have no regard how you treat anyone else. You assert that you would not want to cause me anguish, but how you have failed. If only you could feel the pain you have inflicted on me."

"Don't be so sentimental. You know you are my favorite lady in the court and I have not neglected you."

"A small comfort for being, after all, your wife."

"It's true. I'm quite happy with you."

"Are you? Don't flatter yourself by rendering such compliments. You are so cold that you cannot see how you've shaken my deepest convictions about us. Cruel man! Of what use are such statements to me when I know it's Pelaxilla you are thinking of? You're not talking to me-you're talking to her!"

Ahuitzotl was discouraged that he could not make her understand the depth of his obsession with Pelaxilla; he feared whatever else he added would only be distorted and was reluctant to go on. "Perhaps I ought to leave you for the present," he said. "I don't enjoy seeing you like this."

"Why your sudden concern for me? All you did was destroy the last shred of promise I clung to that we might somehow find love for one another. It's nothing to you."

"You who brought up the subject. Why must I be made to suffer for what you took upon yourself?"

"You suffer? What of me? Do you concern yourself with me?"

"This is too much. I will not be castigated for what I have long demonstrated. You are well aware that you are my favorite here. What more do you want?"

"What every woman wants-an assurance that she is loved. You have shattered all that for me tonight," she bitterly denounced him. "Your words mean nothing to me after what you have confessed to me. You have no capacity to know what I feel-you care nothing about what you do to others. All you think about is yourself and your own sorrows."

He felt uncomfortable over her reproachment; there was more than a hint of truth in it and Tlalalca had reasons for her indignation. But if he came across as insensitive, that was a misperception, for he did indeed care about Tlalalca. He knew it was wrong that Pelaxilla came first, even now that she was lost to him, yet such were his emotions that he would indeed jeopardize his present relationship for one that could never be. Xochiquetzal did not bestow any of her benevolence upon him-she damned him!

"Please believe me when I say I do not wish to see you hurt," Ahuitzotl said. "You mean much to me and, if through this obsession with Pelaxilla, I cause you grief, it's not intentional."

"Still you do not tell me what I want to hear," Tlalalca sobbed. "You have never told me what I long for, hope for, pray for, to hear you say."

"What is that?"

She could not believe that he was so unfeeling and felt almost foolish for telling him. "You've never told me that you loved me," she sadly declared, hopelessly resigned that she was unlikely to ever hear this coming from his lips. How could he when he so loved Pelaxilla? And even if he were to do so now, bereft of his own choosing, his sincerity would be suspect. Indeed, to hear those words uttered now after what he had confided this night would have seemed quite ludicrous.

He prudently spared her the hollowness of those words by withholding from expressing them; however, in his eyes was a message as vividly contradictory to what he had spoken as could have been possibly perceived. She saw in them a look of intense longing, which she thought was for her but feared she might be misinterpreting the signs as she had often done before.

The encounter had been tense for Ahuitzotl, and he wanted no more of it on this day; he placed his hands on her shoulders and drew her towards him to kiss her lips-she melted within his grasp. "You must be patient with me," he strove to comfort her. "I need more time to recover from my loss; soon things with properly amend themselves." Then he released her and walked from the chamber leaving Tlalalca torn with anguish.

"I...love...you." she spoke out brokenly amid her tears, but he was already gone and did not hear it. As so many other times, her most heartfelt sentiments fell upon emptiness.

The wound he gave her that night had cut deep, and Tlalalca would bear its scars for a long time, and their relationship, which had moved steadily closer and warmer in the recent months, was once again severely tested. She reacted to her injury in the usual way–involuntarily feeling a tenseness when in his presence, and unable to maintain a meaningful conversation with him. She also needed time to recover from the jolt. But recover she would, and it was Ahuitzotl, amazingly enough, who felt most assured of this.

Ahuitzotl, in contrast to what might have been expected from him, was far more patient with Tlalalca than she dared hope and did his best to make amends for the damage his reckless tongue inflicted on her. He devoted most of his nights to her, soothing her anxieties and directing all his energies towards satisfying her, both physically and in spirit. He resolved never again to mention Pelaxilla's name in her presence and kept to himself whenever he was overcome with those recurring pangs of intense yearning for his lost mistress. And so, as the days and weeks wore on, he eventually succeeded in restoring her faith in his affection; she even came to believe that perhaps he truly loved her after all–and no other conviction was more important to her.

Ahuitzotl could, of course, seek escapism from his troubles through the frequent inspection tours he made on the building of his aqueduct. At first, such visits offered him relief not only from Pelaxilla, but also from Tlalalca whom he could not face for a number of days after his painful revelation to her. As the days passed, and he managed to regain Tlalalca's confidence to some degree, his visits became rarer; however, other requisites of his office occupied him and afforded him less and less time to reflect on his previous misfortunes. Gradually, but steadily, events were doing their part in breaking him away from the past and pulling him out of his disconsolation.

In this connection, Ahuitzotl made it a point to spend more time with his son, Cuauhtemoc, regularly stopping by to see him. He took sufficient care to shield the boy from negative influences, maintaining a pleasant disposition in his presence, and suppressing any signs of frustration or anger ensuing out of his duties or mood swings that might be adversely received. He succeeded quite well in engendering a warm relationship with the youngster, who soon longed for his father's visits, and took an active interest in the his well-being, playing with him whenever the opportunity presented itself, and actually enjoying these moments, much to his own surprise. He took delight in hearing Cuauhtemoc gain language skills and learning to elucidate newly found discoveries that excited him. He never believed that he would derive pleasures in parenthood, deeming this as effete and not worthy of true manliness, and was frequently amused over his adaptation to an activity affording him relaxation from the daily grind.

Weeks turned to months, and the work on the aqueduct progressed without respite; both ends of the project had now been completed, and only the center portion-the long conduit over the waters of Lake Texcoco-remained. This was, in many ways, the most difficult and cumbersome, and certainly the most time-consuming, section to erect. Each of the stone blocks, the containers holding the mortar, and the beams required to erect the scaffolding that spanned the trough between the pylons, had to be transported out to the worksite on rafts. Crews spread outward to meet at some point in the lake about equidistant from their starting locations-thus the aqueduct now extended over the water from both Coyoacan and Tenochtitlan and only about a half-league gap separated it.

While this work proceeded on course, Ahuitzotl was also kept busy with the many ceremonial duties demanded of his office. The world had to be kept in existence and the gods and goddesses fully nourished to keep the cycle going. Sacrifices had to be offered; blood—red, sacred, and life-giving blood had to be spilled from man so that the gods might live. Each month which elapsed had its own deity to be served and a specific sacrificial need: Tlacaxipehualiztli, the second month, dedicated to the god of youthful spring, Xipe Totec, required victims to be flayed and their removed skin worn by his priests; Tozoztontli, the third month, belonged to Chicomecoatl, the mother of corn, and Tlaloc, who brought the life-giving rains—both needed their share of blood; the fourth month, Hueytozoztli, again honored Tlaloc, as well as the corn god, Cinteotl, and the fifth month, Toxcatl, was devoted to the chief god in the pantheon, Tezcatlipoca, who represented the great mysteries of life; on it went, up to the eighteenth and final month, Izcalli, which called for the grisly fire sacrifices to Xiuhtecuhtli, Lord of Time and Fire. It had all been developed through generations of priests and rulers, and constituted the mainstay of their life, the purpose of their being-all a necessary function to keep the fifth Sun, Tonatiuh, and thus the world, alive.

There was also Ahuitzotl's requirement to attend the sacred games-the tlachtli-held in the great ball courts in every major city. More than a game, this drama depicting the daily struggle of day over night, and was presided over by the gods themselves-attendance for the Revered Speaker was mandatory. Tlachtli was Huitzilopochtli's game, and Ahuitzotl boasted enough times that he was that god's most devoted servant: he would never have absented himself from the contests.

In this way, with the ceaseless and repeated ritual demands which faced him, did Ahuitzotl spend more than a year in Tenochtitlan-a rare achievement for the dynamic warrior-king who had in the previous years of his reign carved out a trail of conquests and left such business to his Vice-Ruler, Cihuacoatl. He was becoming more cautious in his approach towards these sacred duties, for he believed the adversities he suffered as of late were due to the angry gods extracting their vengeance for his years of belittling them, as the priests had so often suggested and warned him about, and even went so far as to have them tutor him on the significations of their rites. There were those who thought it too late for him, especially after the murder of Tzutzumatzin, and Ahuitzotl was not left without significant consternation over this. He began having troubling notions about whether the prognostications of the priests might not be correct.

As if things were not bad enough, Ahuitzotl also began feeling increased anxiousness over his physical being. He continued to lose weight in spite of indulging himself in regular meals and not having undergone the rigors of a strenuous march in over a year, but now, on recurring occasions, he also felt sensations of pain in his chest and abdomen. His court physicians appeared baffled by these symptoms and were unable to diagnose the ailment, although the herb juices they recommended did help in alleviating his suffering. Still, its persistence plagued him, and if he did not openly relate this to Tlalalca or Cihuacoatl, he nonetheless found himself more and more preoccupied over it. He had ample justifications for worrying about the wrath of the gods. What if the priests were right?

XVI

The day came when the finishing slab of stone was lifted into place to complete the final linkage along the aqueduct. Ahuitzotl had himself and his court entourage oared out to the spot in the lake where this last connection was made. He beamed with pride at his wondrous accomplishment as he gazed in both directions to assess the total length of the conduit; it seemed to stretch as far as the eye could see.

"It is done," Ahuitzotl exulted, glancing at Cihuacoatl who shared in the moment's glory. "I ask you, have you ever seen anything like it?"

"A majestic feat, Lord." proclaimed the minister, equally impressed. "As magnificent as the Great Temple itself."

"So it is. And both exist as lasting monuments to my reign. There has never been any greater than mine, as these imposing structures will attest. Let Tizoc have his stone and calendar. What are they compared to this?"

An unfair attack, thought Cihuacoatl; after all, most of the Great Temple had been erected under Tizoc, and it was only by Ahuitzotl's unparalleled and never-to-be-forgotten slaughter of thousands upon its sacrificial blocks that he forever stole the temple from Tizoc by forging his own stamp into its pre-eminence. While finding it necessary to rid the realm of Tizoc's ineffective rule, Cihuacoatl resented Ahuitzotl's continued deprecation of him.

"You have nothing to say?" Ahuitzotl commented. "Have my accomplishments left you speechless?"

"They do inspire a sense of awe, Lord."

"How true. In two days, the ceremonial opening of the aqueduct will commence. We must go over our part in the rites once more so nothing will go wrong. These, more than any others, must gratify Tlaloc and the Water Goddess, Chalchihuitlicue."

Rowers took them back to the palace where Ahuitzotl sent for the chief priests of these water deities so he could be assured all would go well. He remembered the aftermath of the Great Temple's dedication and this time was on uncertain footing, for he knew he had committed a grievous error in ordering Tzutzumatzin's death. The world was watching this, to see if the Coyoacan's prediction would prove accurate, and Ahuitzotl understood that his prestige and reputation, and even his future effectiveness in dealing with the lords of Anahuac, was at stake here. Everything that possibly could be done to insure the success of the ceremony had to be considered.

When the day for the dedication arrived-the ninth day of the month, Atl, named for water-the stage was set for a dignified and impressive observance. The finished work was to be consecrated to Tlaloc and Chalchihuitlicue amidst a splendorous aquatic show replete with all the symbols of rain and water that were identified with these elements. The main rites were to take place in two separate vicinities: one at the springs of Coyoacan where the floodgates would be opened to release the flow; the other at the opposite end of the conduit, in Tenochtitlan, where its principal artery fed into numerous sub-channels leading to the city's major precincts. Ahuitzotl and Cihuacoatl took their place at the terminus while Chimalpopoca, now reconciled with the Revered Speaker after the latter's show of remorse in offering compensation to Tzutzumatzin's family, and lords of the leading western shore cities were at the source.

"Look at the sky, Lord." Cihuacoatl pointed out as he walked with his master toward the platform erected adjacent to the conduit just before it divided into its multiple lines. "It is overcast and portents a rainfall. Tlaloc is pleased."

"An auspicious beginning," Ahuitzotl said through his wide smile. "This day will be remembered."

They were accompanied by priests, dressed in blue, the color representing their water deities, and with them was a small child-one of four-six years old, which was to be sacrificed. Chalchihuitlicue was not a particularly demanding goddess of victims, but her tastes ran for the young. A child was to be offered along the four key sections of the aqueduct as its water passed each of these points so that the blood could mingle with it and bless its course.

When all the participants had stationed themselves at their designated places, the ceremony was ready to commence. A brazier was ignited at the terminus location and a powder tossed into its flame which emitted dense clouds of bluish smoke, the signal for those celebrants at the aqueduct's source to initiate the rites.

"Let us begin." Chimalpopoca informed the head priest.

Chalchihuitlicue's chief priest approached the dam structure; he was dressed as the Water Goddess herself, wearing a blue cloak and a diadem of heron feathers. His face was blackened with melted rubber smeared over it and his forehead was painted blue; he wore green gemstones in his ears, lips, and wrists. All his vestments had a symbolic significance directly associated with the goddess and her consort, Tlaloc. He was in the accompaniment of several other votaries who wore similar adornments and paints, but otherwise were almost naked. When he arrived at the deep waters retained behind the dams, he cupped his hands into it and brought its cold, sweet taste to his lips. He repeated this several more times and after having ingested the water, he then spoke to the pool as if he were addressing the goddess.

"Precious Lady. We are gratified that you have come in this most welcome fashion and wish to direct you to the path you are to follow from here. So it is that I, representing your likeness, come to receive you and greet you, and to guide you to your new arrival. This is the day, dear lady, of your coming to Tenochtitlan, and we are most deeply honored."

He next sprinkled maize-flour on the waters and motioned for his seconds to cast their offerings, symbols of rain and water, into the pool. While a group of musicians played and singers voiced their renditions devoted to Tlaloc and Chalchihuitlicue, earthenware jars of fishes, frogs, water snakes, and leeches were emptied into the water. Then the priests grabbed the first of the little girls to be offered.

"Release the flow," Chimalpopoca directed.

Selected personnel pulled on ropes and raised the numerous floodgates inserted along the dam. At first, the water flowed towards the mouth of the conduit in a smooth, steady stream, and as it passed by the head priest, his assistants flung the girl over a sacrificial block and he speedily cut out her beating heart. Blood gushed forth from the gaping hole in her chest and her lifeless body was cast into the current so that water and blood ran as one. The heart was placed on a platter to be carried later to the idol of the goddess.

More gates were pulled open, and what started out as a steady stream now rushed along the troughs feeding the main conduit in a torrent. "It comes too fast!" the priest shouted, growing alarmed. "Too much water enters into the main channel. Stem the flow!"

Chimalpopoca ordered his crews to close the gates. To their shock and dismay, they were unable to do so; as they tried to push the oaken barriers back into the slots, all their combined strength could not overcome the flowing surge. To make matters worse, the level of the pond could not be reduced as it was filled by its springs in a continuous outpouring of fresh water. In an instant, a roaring cascade came rushing down the many troughs and crashed like thunder into the bottleneck presented by the main duct; its spray spewed upward like a waterspout and rained down upon priests and lords alike.

Water shot through the main conduit at a frightening speed; the very walls of the structure trembled where its line angled toward the lake. Even as the torrent was rampaging towards the terminus, Ahuitzotl had already begun his obeisance to Chalchihuitlicue. After finishing his orisons amid the priestly chanting, he lifted the girl selected for the Water Goddess into the air to show her to his audience-she was heavily drugged and quite oblivious to her condition-and then laid her on the altar-stone where she was held down by two priests. The initial smaller stream, red from the blood of the three prior victims now flowed by him, and he raised his knife above his head and plummeted it into the exposed chest, slicing a deep horizontal gash across it. He deftly reached into the gory cavity and ripped out the pulsating organ within. The priests hurriedly carried the body to the duct's edge and were proceeding to set it into the stream when a wall of water, reaching to the top of the trough, came upon them.

The force of the gushing stream snatched the small body from them and carried it along the chute and over its end into a sub-channel while a stunned Ahuitzotl watched. He stood aghast as he saw this flow roaring out of the main duct and thunderously crashing in a huge spray against the divided stone walls separating the various troughs. So powerful spewed its outburst that it broke through the first retaining wall smashing stone and water into the successive channel embankments. As the flow continuously gushed forth, it poured over the rims of these walls and streamed into the surrounding area; at last, Ahuitzotl regained his wits. "What is the matter with them?" he shouted at Cihuacoatl. "Why can't they control this flow?"

"Something must have gone drastically wrong, Lord! Surely this could not have been anticipated."

Fear gripped Ahuitzotl as he recalled Tzutzumatzin's warning; he called for a messenger. "Tell Chimalpopoca to stop this flow!" he told the courier. "We are on the verge of having a flood. Inform him this is most urgent!"

As the messenger sped off, Ahuitzotl stared with stark disbelief at the powerful cascade splashing ceaselessly over the retaining walls and sending a raging stream down the avenue toward the central plaza, carrying chunks of debris and masonry from the broken walls with it. Everywhere people hastily climbed the steps of the base platforms supporting administrative buildings and temples to avoid its flow; cries of dismay arose when the swift water rushed around and through houses forcing their occupants to flee.

"How can this be?" Ahuitzotl muttered in near panic. "How is this possible?"

To Cihuacoatl, the answer was apparent: Ahuitzotl was damned by the gods-they were wreaking their revenge upon the unfortunate monarch and, if this was the case, nothing could save him. If ever there was a patent sign of their displeasure, this had to be it. He was suddenly overcome with a dread that everyone in Tenochtitlan may come to suffer on his account. "The gods are angry with you, Lord!" Cihuacoatl fearfully declared. "You have offended them once too often."

"Don't tell me that!" Ahuitzitl snapped back contemptuously. "There was a miscalculation at the source-nothing more. It should soon be corrected."

But the torrent continued, spilling relentlessly out from the conduit with a crushing energy that pounded incessantly at the broken retaining wall, crashing over it into the next wall until it too, under the constant pressure, gave way. With nothing more to funnel the water, it ran like a river in the streets, all of it now pouring from the duct flowed freely into the city.

When the messenger came to the spring, he found Chimalpopoca frantically directing his crews to halt the current swelling forth from the floodgates. He could see this exertion was largely futile, yet dutifully passed on the Revered Speaker's message, much to Chimalpopoca's chagrin.

"Tell our master," Chimalpopoca informed the messenger, "we cannot stop the flow; the spring will not go down but keeps the same level no matter how much water is drained from it."

Ahuitzotl paled when he heard these words; there was no hope left for him. He, mightiest of the Mexica conquerors, had met his downfall within sight of his palace. For the first time, he feared the wrath of the populace–they would never forgive him for this havoc he caused them. "Do you mean to say that Chimalpopoca can do nothing about this?" he strained to ask.

"That is what he told me, Lord," replied the messenger.

"It can't be. My engineers stated repeatedly that the waters could be controlled. None of them warned me of this."

"Tzutzumatzin did, Lord," declared Cihuacoatl, "and you had him killed for it."

"Damn you, minister. Never say that to me again!"

Ahuitzotl looked down the avenue that was rapidly being vacated by frantic people scrambling for higher ground as they tried to escape the flood; as far as he could see, there was water–and still it came spewing forth from the conduit. He scanned the destroyed retaining walls through which the water rushed virtually unobstructed–a veritable river running into the great plaza–and no words could adequately describe his mortification. Defeated, soaked to the skin from the spray, and horribly dejected, Ahuitzotl seemed to be in a daze as he surveyed the damage. He felt totally helpless in this situation; he probed his mind on how to fight this battle, but no answers came to him. He was lost.

Cihuacoatl, unable to make sense out of a condition he had never before experienced, rushed to his master's side and sought advice.

"What will you do?" he asked. "We must stop this flood."

"Don't you think I'm aware of that?" Ahuitzotl shouted furiously at the shaken minister. "And why do you ask me that? Am I an engineer? Why not ask the priests of Chalchihuitlicue why the goddess is angry and what we can do to appease her?"

"Ask her priests? Do you see the frightened look in them? They cannot help us!"

"Of what use are they then? As always, I find their functions wanting at a time when I need them the most. All their collective knowledge is worthless to me."

Cihuacoatl failed to hide his fear over the balsphemous outburst; even under pressures such as this, one had to be careful about addressing the gods. For a Revered speaker already at grave risk in being unfavorably regarded by them, his was an unpardonable declaration fraught with dangers. "What you say is frightening," he warned his master. "Take heed, Lord!"

"Then give me counsel I can use! What do you suggest I do?"

"You must consult with your engineers, Lord. Surely they will know what to do."

"Will they? The fools should have foreseen this. How much value can I place on their judgment after this?"

"Some of them ought to have ideas worth considering."

"I have no choice. Yes, send for them. Have them meet me at the palace."

"At the palace?"

"What am I to do here? I can't put a stop to this, and evidently, from what you say, neither can the priests despite of all their divinations. I see no point in my staying here."

Even as he thus spoke these words, a clap of thunder rolled across the darkened sky and rain began to fall. Cihuacoatl gazed horror-stricken at the monarch; this was insult being heaped upon injury. "Tlaloc!" he cried out and in that single word send a quiver of abject fear through Ahuitzotl.

The rain started out in hefty, interspersed droplets which struck like small pellets upon the face and splattered, one here, another there, until the tempo quickened and no spot was left dry. Then it suddenly happened-as if a dam had burst in the clouds-and it poured hard and heavy, coming down in a deluge and sounding like a million drumbeats when striking the water all around them in the streets. For Ahuitzotl, this was the final calamity-the world was collapsing on him.

"I am cursed!" Ahuitzotl screamed out in his distress. "What more can possibly happen?"

There was no more doubt. If ever proof was required for a situation, it was now patently offered, and everyone in Tenochtitlan must have been struck with the same thought: their ruler was damned by the gods and would bring the nation to ruin. Priests, lords, laymen, and slaves alike all feared they would suffer the fate of their accursed Revered Speaker–they shrank back in horror as he passed by them.

He had had enough. With his clothes and plumed headdress dripping wet, a disheveled Ahuitzotl sloshed through ankle-deep water for the palace. Nobody met him at the doorway, but when he reached his chamber Tlalalca came and handed him a towel so he could dry himself.

"You are not afraid?" Ahuitzotl asked her as he changed his clothes. "You do not hide your face in shame at seeing me?"

"What are you talking about?"

"Haven't you seen what's happened? The city is being flooded by my aqueduct. There is water everywhere, and now it's raining on top of all that. My subjects tremble when they see me and are too frightened to look at me. They are all thinking I have brought this catastrophe to them because of my irreverence."

"Have they told you this?"

"They don't have to. I can plainly read it in their fear-ridden faces. Only Cihuacoatl has mentioned it, but I'm certain he is voicing the concerns of everyone. Tzutzumatzin's prophesy is being fulfilled and the entire world is a witness to it."

For once, Tlalalca could not help him in his despair; she knew little of the nature of the aqueduct and less of the fate of Tzutzumatzin. The rumors were rife, of course, but Ahuitzotl had maintained a tight lip over this and related nothing to his family on the events surrounding the present situation.

"What will you do?" she asked.

"I am to meet with my engineers to find out how we can stop the flooding. They should be arriving here about now; I must go to receive them."

He left for the reception hall where a number of the builders had already entered and were awaiting his presence; Cihuacoatl was also there with them. Ahuitzotl paced the floor nervously searching for some appropriate introductory words and, finding none, came straight to the point in his usual blunt fashion. "You know the problem," he said, "and there is but one answer I seek. I now ask you-how do we stop the water's flow from the aqueduct?"

They remained silent, each afraid to voice his opinions on the matter; Ahuitzotl deduced it was because they had no answers–his patience was being severely strained. "Well?" he fumed, "Is there nothing you can tell me? It was in accordance with your plans and directions that the aqueduct was built. I took your advice over the Coyoacan lord, Tzutzumatzin, because you spoke of, and convinced me, on the merit of your design. Why is it that now, when I am again in need of your advice, you will not give it?"

Reluctantly, a spokesman for the builders dared to step forward and speak. "We cannot give an answer you would appreciate, Lord," he said. "This defies all our calculations and should not have occurred. There are greater forces at work here."

"Explain what you mean," Ahuitzotl demanded, curious if his answer would match the general prevailing consensus.

"It's as if Chalchihuitlicue meant, indeed contrived, to have things go awry. If this is so, we are totally at her mercy-our designs are of no consequence."

"Is this what I can expect from men learned in the building arts? When their plans prove faulty, and their advice misdirected, they attempt to hide these shortcomings by attributing them to Chalchihuitlicue? Not one of you will claim a responsibility in this affair?"

"There is more to this, Lord. Look at the rain. We have not had such a downpour in years, if ever; yet it strikes us now when we are in dire straits with the aqueduct. Tlaloc is intent on telling us something."

"And what might that be?"

The spokesman found himself awkwardly placed in relating his deepest convictions on this; he deemed the monarch's insistance extremely bothersome but knew he could not escape it. "There is talk Tlaloc is angry with you, Lord," he said. "He means to punish you for killing Tzutzumatzin. What good are our measures against the power of Tlaloc?"

Ahuitzotl flushed in his embarrassment, but also was seized with an apprehensiveness, for the builder merely phrased what he knew to be a basic fear among his people. Yet he deeply resented the engineers leaning on this to escape their own culpability and the erroneous information they had given him.

"It's because of you that I chose to ignore Tzutzumatzin's warnings," he castigated them, "and was eventually forced to even silence him. If you are bent on blaming me for what has happened, let me caution you that I hold all of you as much accountable for it. If the gods seek to punish me, be assured, I will impart some of that punishment upon you. Do you understand?"

Trembling, they muttered their comprehension; the monarch instilled deep fears when aroused to fury.

"Now," Ahuitzotl continued, "what is your sum advice on how to remedy this situation?"

They babbled anxiously among themselves, groping frantically for methods on how to obtain a solution; there were arguments, disagreements, and demonstrations of incoherence and resignation-but in actuality none of them knew what to do. Ahuitzotl observed their discord for awhile, becoming increasingly annoyed over the unproductive spectacle, until he grew impatient with their indecision. The thought came to him that he should perhaps sacrifice them to the water deities-at least this might bring results. "Well?" Ahuitzotl finally spoke out. "Am I to wait all day? What is your counsel?"

"We must examine the project in its entirety," the spokesman tensely replied, "from the springs to its ending so we might learn what to make of it. Only then will we know how to proceed."

This response was not to Ahuitzotl's liking, for it meant additional delays to a problem that demanded immediate action, but he saw no alternative. He did not know how grave a threat he faced or if he had sufficient time to allow for such a review. "How long will that take?" he asked.

"The rest of the day at least," came the reply, "By then we should be able to suggest a solution."

"Very well. We will meet again tonight-and there had better be some answers!"

He consented to their leaving and they hastily proceeded on their assignment discomfited in the knowledge that they faced as much a threat in their master as in the faulty project.

Ahuitzotl sank back in his royal chair and sulked over the day's events, pondering the adversities besetting him, and he feared the consequences of his engineers' failure to stem the flood. How was he to face his people after this? In this present crisis, who would remember the glorious achievements of his reign? "I can still hear it raining," he said to Cihuacoatl soberly. "It will not abate. What's it like out there?"

"The reservoirs are filling, and will soon overflow. Already the lake's level has risen noticeably. I fear if the engineers do not act quickly, we shall face a major calamity."

"Such a rain! Why does it come now? What does it mean?"

"I think you know," the minister coldly surmised. "The builders were correct when they said greater forces are at work here."

"What can I do?"

"I suggest you send for Nezahualpilli, Lord."

"I see. I am to come crawling to him and submit myself to his derision. He would relish such a moment. I can just see him grinning from ear to ear as he reminds me of having scorned his advice. Why should I undergo such a humiliation?"

"To save the city, Lord!" Cihuacoatl harshly emphasized. "He is, after all, Anahuac's master builder and most likely knows what to do here. I would not hesitate in seeking his counsel if I were you-there's not that much time available to us before..."

"Before what?"

"Before we will have to inform the people to evacuate Tenochtitlan. The water continues to rise."

This prospect held terrible ramifications, not only from the standpoint of the personal effects lost or damaged in such an event, but more importantly, for the consternation and lack of confidence this would engender against the monarch. It was natural for Ahuitzotl to balk at the suggestion. "Do you think that will be necessary?" he fretted.

"I hope not, Lord. It depends largely on what we are told by the engineers this evening."

"That I should live to see such a day. One is left totally defenseless when faced with angry gods-especially when the priests cannot say what must be done to placate them."

His words came as an impassioned plea seeking for an answer to a horrid nightmare defying comprehension. Cihuacoatl was sympathetic to his master's plight, but like everyone else, he could do very little. He remained with him to await the counsel from the builders and to offer him what small consolation he could in the face of this disaster. This was, to use the Revered Speaker's own words, a day to be remembered.

XVII

Ahuitzotl's meeting with the engineers proved useless; none of them could offer any productive solutions to the problems and only succeeded in incurring his wrath upon their heads. In a moment of unchecked fury, he ordered half of them to be sacrificed in the flimsy hope such an act might induce the goddess Chalchihuitlicue to relent in her punishment. They met their deaths calmly, recognizing the harm they had brought upon Tenochtitlan and believing that by surrendering their lives they might somehow bring this calamity to an end. Ahuitzotl himself cut out their hearts and in desperation offered them to the goddess. The rains stopped shortly thereafter, as if giving credence to his action, but the aqueduct remained a threat, pouring water unrestrained into the city.

Days turned to weeks, and still the water gushed profusely and unchecked from the conduit, having long spilled over all the reservoirs and channels, and rising even higher. Without being told-Ahuitzotl still declined on issuing an evacuation order-people began moving out of the city which was gradually being inundated. Canoes transported them and their belongings to the mainland where relief stations had been set up by the adjacent city rulers; many lost articles of value-booty collected in the campaigns-in their hectic attempts to leave submerged homes. And through it all, the aqueduct continued spewing out its enormous volume that swept unabated into the central square. The water level now reached to half the first tier of the Great Temple, immersing all streets and leaving the temples, palaces, and administrative buildings upon their base platforms like islands in a sea. Houses, chinampas, and gardens were flooded-and fear reigned supreme.

Still Ahuitzotl was reluctant to send for Nezahualpilli, the only man deemed able to save the situation. This came as a source of extreme vexation for Cihuacoatl who now looked to the Texcocan as Tenochtitlan's salvation. "Why do you refuse to call for him?" he asked, his irritation evident. "Your efforts to end this crises have failed, and yet you do not call on the one man in Anahuac who might know what to do. Why?"

"He will make a pompous display of his admonishment and announce to the world how he told me of the hazards entailed in my project. How I failed to adhere to his advice."

"I would not worry about him announcing this to the world, Lord. If nothing is done soon, you and I will be the only people left in Tenochtitlan."

"He will humiliate me. This event offers him the opportunity he has so long wished for. He will exploit it to the fullest to enhance his own stature and diminish mine. He longs for this."

Cihuacoatl thought it inconceivable that, even in this crisis situation, his master actually placed a greater priority on his personal prestige than on the welfare of his capital. He could no longer retain his exasperation and exploded in a vehement harangue that stunned Ahuitzotl. "Are you so blind that you cannot see the seriousness of our predicament?" he shouted at him. "Do you mean to tell me you would rather have our city destroyed than ask for help from the only man who can save it because of your vanity? Where is your duty to your subjects? I thought you a greater man than this! Indeed, your pettiness makes Tizoc appear as a paragon of virtue! I thought we had appointed a ruler as his successor; it is obvious I was mistaken."

Ahuitzotl was stung by the minister's outburst, a castigation Cihuacoatl never openly dared before, and he was amazed at his effectiveness. His face reddened, and he was overcome with a sense of shame as he realized the minister was justified in rebuking him for neglecting his duties. As for Cihuacoatl, he knew he had exceeded the bounds of appropriate conduct and fully expected to be severely chided for it. To his astonishment, Ahuitzotl assented.

"Thank you, minister," the monarch replied, "for revealing my selfishness to me. You are correct in asserting I am remiss in my duties—I did not think you had it in you—and I accede to your counsel. Yes, go and send for Nezahualpilli; perhaps he will succeed where the others have so miserably failed."

This time, Cihuacoatl appreciated carrying out his master's orders. A boat was immediately dispatched to transmit an urgent appeal to Texcoco where Nezahualpilli was appraised of what had occurred and requested to help resolve Tenochtitlan's crisis. He welcomed the opportunity to come to Ahuitzotl's assistance, an act by which he believed he could patch up the flagging alliance between their cities, but would also make the most of it and give his rival the reproofs he was long overdue. Such circumstances were rare in the offing and could not be left to slip by unmentioned.

Nezahualpilli arrived by boat the next day and met his ally as he was seated in his hall before the members of his council.

"You have surveyed the damage?" Ahuitzotl asked.

"I have, Lord."

Ahuitzotl did not want to give Nezahualpilli the floor to say whatever he liked, but found it impossible under the watchful eyes of the ministers and counselors to prevent him from doing so, for all were eager to hear what the Texcocan could impart on them. Reluctantly, Ahuitzotl opened the way for him do do just that.

"So what is your assessment?" Ahuitzotl continued, fully expecting to hear a long, bombastic discourse over how he had erred. Nezahualpilli did not disappoint him.

"Great Lord," began the Texcocan. "You have dallied long in seeking counsel. When it was given to you by the Lord of Coyoacan, Tzutzumatzin, you diminished its importance—only now that your city faces destruction, and you have been gripped with fear, do you pay heed to the advice you should have considered long before. The element that faces you now is water, and you will not be able to vanquish or expel it by your valor as you would your other enemies. How will you be able to resist and repair the situation?"

Nezahualpilli paused momentarily to scan over his audience; he noticed that he had the full, undivided attention of every individual present in the hall and savored their focus on him. Then he went on.

"Recognize, Mighty Lord, that you have sinned against the gods and have offended them in slaying Tzutzumatzin, whose likeness this judicious ruler represented, and who was entrusted by them to carry out their obligations in governing his realm. For your crime, the Lord of Creation now permits your city to be destroyed. What will your enemies make of this, when they see your city being emptied and you and your lords forced to flee as an eternal vengeance upon you? What will they say, seeing the city built by your ancestors after they so long labored on it, destroyed in forty days on your account?"

Ahuitzotl winced when the Texcocan spoke these words, and he questioned how much longer he was going to be able to endure this harangue. He could see everyone's eyes riveted upon him as if carefully weighing his reaction to the speech. Nezahualpilli must have his moment, he thought bitterly, but he wished his colleague would get to the crux of his discourse and spare him this useless diatribe.

"It is my opinion," Nezahualpilli continued, "that the waters must be cut off at its source–at the springs of Coyoacan. To do this, you must demolish the network of dams you have constructed there so that the water can follow its previous course. Also to appease the wrath of Chalchihuitlecue, I propose that a solemn sacrifice should be offered which should include many prized jewels and feathers of numerous quail, and simultaneously some children of which she is so fond. In this way, we may be able to restrain her springs so that less water will pour forth from them. I shall render all the assistance I can until the problem is corrected."

His last statement particularly pleased the lords and they felt gratified that a builder of Nezahualpilli's stature condescended to offer them his own services. Only Ahuitzotl remained less than impressed, regarding the entire gesture as a ploy on the Texcocan's part to ingratiate himself to the Revered Speaker after having humiliated him to the extent that he did. But for once, Ahuitzotl could not speak his mind. The lords judged him in this affair and would have rebelled if had jeopardized the aid being offered–he had to act as the grateful recipient of Texcoco's assistance.

"We are obviously indebted to your magnanimity, Nezahualpilli," Ahuitzotl proclaimed. "What compensation will you seek for this?"

"To see Tenochtitlan spared from this disaster will be reward enough for me, Lord."

Again murmurs resounded throughout the hall as the lords embraced this goodwill gesture and voiced their hearty approvals. Ahuitzotl disdained over their adulation. "You overwhelm us with your benevolence," he said. "You appear certain you can remedy this calamitous situation."

"I shall do what I can, Lord," Nezahualpilli grinned. "I hope you can obtain divers for me who are quite familiar with the spring."

"They shall be provided."

"I would also suggest, Lord, that, to insure full atonement for the many wrongs committed, you offer Chalchijuitlicue more sacrifices in addition to the children-perhaps a few leading nobles of your city."

The council fell silent as this was a proposal which suddenly sent chills into those present; if the monarch acquiesced to the suggestions, some of them were sure to pay the price. In an instant, Nezahualpilli's popularity all but vanished.

Ahuitzotl stared into the eyes of his ally and understood, for through this deliberate threat against the council members, Nezahualpilli has shrewdly given the Revered Speaker an opportunity to regain some of the good graces of his alienated lords. There was a silent smile on the Texcocan's face, and Ahuitzotl responded in kind indicating his comprehension: without a single word being spoken, the message had been conveyed. "I don't think that will be necessary," Ahuitzotl answered. "Let us see how you proceed on your repairs before contemplating such drastic action."

The council breathed easier, and Ahuitzotl acquired a new-found respect for his compatriot ruler, having greatly appreciated the gesture.

Almost immediately upon termination of the meeting, the salvage work was initiated. Nezahualpilli, accompanied by the Revered Speaker, proceeded by boat to Coyoacan where messengers had been dispatched to gather up divers acquainted with the spring-these were for the most part the very same workers employed in constructing the dam complex that diverted its waters into the aqueduct months earlier. Under Nezahualpilli's trained eye, they searched for sections of the spring where its flow might be stemmed or diverted by inserting huge boulders and building a series of new trenches leading away from the existing troughs. Earthworks were erected to redirect the water toward that portion of the lake not obstructed by the causeways or Nezahualcoyotl's dike where natural outlets permitted the runoff to escape. The objective was that, once the spring was brought under control and the flood waters had receded, the aqueduct could be repaired and put back into service through a rebuilt system of gates designed by Nezahualpilli.

An undertaking of such importance could not proceed without the necessary invocations to the gods and the priests performed their valuable functions in this regard. They came daily to the springs while the work was in progress, decked out as the water deities with their faces and bodies painted blue, and sang out their intones after which they offered up a selected victim. The first day Ahuitzotl himself inaugurated these rites by sacrificing a six-year old girl and allowing her blood to mingle freely with the spring waters. Even the divers engaged in the salvaging operations were painted blue to honor Chalchihuitlicue. No act could be carried out without assuring it had the full approval of the goddess and her consort, Tlaloc.

Their work would last for weeks and, to Ahuitzotl's credit, he allowed Nezahualpilli a free hand in directing the reconstruction under his skilled hands. This was not because the monarch had no wish to insert his own ideas into the project, but rather due to the frightful results of the last fiasco having had their humbling effect on him. He could serve his cause better by remaining in the background and limiting his activities to the frequent visits he made for the purpose of having Nezahualpilli update him on the progression of this work. Indeed, the catastrophe had inculcated deep fears in him-fears he rarely, if ever, considered earlier-that he was walking on a tightrope in his relationship with the gods. The man who once exuded with the confidence which led him to speak for the gods now cringed in horrid anxiety of them and had to weigh every decision he made in the context of how it might be received by them.

In the meantime, the water had its damaging effect on the city. At first gushing forth in swift motion under the thrust of spewing from the damaged main conduit, its currents swept incessantly against the mortar and underpinnings of many structures, striking these with rocks, logs, and other debris carried along with the rapid flow, and by this action eroded the understructure which anchored them in place. Then, when the water level rose, these foundations, already damaged to some degree, were further weakened by dampening inner mortar not designed to withstand such an inundation. Collapsing first were the smaller houses whose adobe walls simply dissolved under the liquid battering, but later, when the waters repeatedly surged back and forth, whipped up by wind and current, some of the larger stone structures, their foundations gnawed away, began to tilt, initially sinking at the weakest point and then losing a wall or two when their upper mass lost their support from the lopsided buttresses.

Most of Tenochtitlan's citizens had evacuated their residences and were offered shelter by a sympathetic population in the neighboring mainland cities, although some of these centers closer to the lake's edge were likewise flooded. But a number of them remained in the capital, chiefly among them priests who resided in their higher level temple structures and their adjuncts as well as the Revered Speaker and his family. Many of the administrative and ceremonial buildings rested atop large base platforms and despite of presently standing as islands in the water, they remained essentially intact. Ahuitzotl's new palace was an exception, where the base portion of the edifice supporting that section spanning the canal was directly exposed to the flooding; the palace had been particularly severely battered there because of the initial currents spilling water into the canal after it flowed across the plaza. This, however, did not deter the royal family from continuing to reside in the upper story where its living quarters had always been, but food had to be shipped by boats because the kitchens in the lower floor remained flooded.

The disciplined nature of the society allowed for organization of parties set up to cater to the needs of the monarch and his priests and ministers, and they were not left wanting in spite of remaining marooned within their island platforms. Daily, supplies of produce, water, and news from the mainland reached them-the fires of the temples braziers could not be extinguished, nor the ceremonial duties interrupted. Even certain protocol had to be maintained under these austere conditions; as his own palace kitchen was not serviceable, Ahuitzotl regaled his Texcocan guest in the former palace, that of Motecuhzoma Ilhuicamina, which stood atop a higher platform and was largely unscathed in the deluge.

"What is the general mood of the populace?" Ahuitzotl asked Nezahualpilli after they had finished their meal. "Do they blame me for this?"

"They're not pleased with you, and they fear for you," the Texcocan confided. "They speak often of the plague that followed the Great Temple's dedication, and of your murdering Tzutzumatzin, and believe that the gods will not accept your offerings to them."

"None of them speak of the glories I have brought to them? Of my many conquests and the prestige I gained for our people?"

"I have not heard these mentioned, Lord."

"This mean all my accomplishments were for naught-flooded out of my people's memories as surely as this aqueduct flooded Tenochtitlan."

Nezahualpilli detected the grave concern this gave Ahuitzotl, and he sympathized with him-no man had done more to stabilize and expand the realm, and the Mexica eagle never soared more brilliantly than under his rule. To have all this diminished or even forgotten because of the trepidations of the gods was a horrible fate indeed-an inglorious summation of Ahuitzotl's reign.

"Is this what you fear?" Nezahualpilli asked.

"I fear anonymity," Ahuitzotl admitted. "All my life I have struggled against this fear; everything I have done has been directed at achieving fame and glory-not always for our domain, you understand, but for my personal gain. This drive has differentiated me from others."

"Such self claim to fortune and glory necessarily undermines the importance of the gods and has no place in our world which exists by their grace. This has been your incalculable mistake, Lord, and you are indeed not like others in that respect."

"Then your conclusion is that the gods are justified in turning their wrath upon me."

"It is, Lord."

Nezahualpilli's lack of hesitancy startled Ahuitzotl, for it made the answer appear as incontrovertible. "So by inference, my life's work has been wasted on my people," he determined soberly.

"Not necessarily. The nature of men is to preoccupy themselves in their present miseries when things are going badly for them. You will find, however, that once the flood is gone and your aqueduct functions properly to supply them with plentiful water—I guarantee you it will-their respect for you, as well as their recollections of what you have done for the realm, will again be fully restored. Be assured of it."

Ahuitzotl felt some hope as Nezahualpilli's words elevated him out of his morose state. "I am relieved to hear that," he said. "When all this is over, we shall have to work on bringing our alliance to its former amiable standing. I have a plan on how to do it."

"Please do not send me another Nenetzin."

Ahuitzotl laughed, as did Nezahualpilli, this bespeaking of their renewed friendship, demonstrating the gratitude which the Revered Speaker felt towards his Texcocan colleague; earlier such a remark would have been adjudged a gross insult.

"No man alive could have satisfied her cravings. I should have known better—an unreasonable expectation of love's power prompted me to sent her to you. We all believed she truly loved you. But no, my plan is to rid ourselves of our traditional enemy, the Tlaxcalans. I shall present you with its details when this crisis is over."

Nezahualpilli was more than mildly interested in such a proposition, and their meeting that evening concluded on a more congenial and promising footing than had been the case in several years. Ahuitzotl, much revitalized in spirit after speaking with his ally, now eagerly sought the pleasures which Tlalalca would give him as he was being oared back to his palace. He thought about all her efforts in easing his terrible anxieties and how she comforted him in his most perilous moments, and that he had never expressed his full appreciation for it-tonight he would make this abundantly clear to her. He sensed his pulse accelerating in his anticipation.

Oarsmen steered his canoe to that section of the palace where the main doorway met the steps leading to the upper floor; they rowed directly to them as the lower level was still partially submerged, and as they held the vessel steady against a stone upright, Ahuitzotl stepped out and thanked them for their services. He then started upstairs, his excitement mounting with every step he ascended. But when he walked along the dimly visible corridor toward the chamber where Tlalalca would be waiting, he heard a sudden low creaking sound and thought he felt the floor vibrating beneath his feet. He paused to listen, straining to make out its source-it was the sound of stones scraping against the timbers holding them in place: a crunching, grating sound.

Just then there was a loud crack-a major support beam had snapped under the weight of the masonry resting upon it. In a resounding, thunderous crash, the floor of the hallway in front of him abruptly caved in, stones and beams tumbling into the exposed waters of the canal below. With the collapse of the floor went the main buttressing timbers supporting numerous vertical uprights and, in rapid succession, the walls toppled inward into the gaping hole which had opened beneath them. Ensuing screams of frightened women and children were drowned out by the sonorous rumbling of the collapsing edifice; some of them fell into the abyss that had been the corridor; others were crushed by debris and rubble falling from the crumbling roof.

"Tlalalca!" Ahuitzotl shouted, horror-stricken when he saw a wall section crashing into her chamber. He ran for it, sidestepping the holes opening under his feet and dodging the falling stones.

Then, as he was about to enter the chamber, he was struck on the head by a segment of a crossbeam that had loosened from the roof, along with the bits of masonry that had held it in place. The jagged piece of rafter slammed heavily into him, cutting a terrible gash in his forehead from which the blood spurted forth-he cried out in his agony. Reeling under the blow, his head throbbing with violent spasms of intense pain and its accompanying blackouts, Ahuitzotl stumbled into the room as more chunks of debris fell in him—he was momentarily knocked unconscious.

Pulsating aches piercing repeatedly through his brain revived him. In dizziness, and only dimly comprehending what had happened, Ahuitzotl staggered to his feet, falling and having to raise himself up again. His body convulsed in pain, but he probed ahead through the rubble resting on the chamber's floor and inched his way ahead. Then he saw her, her face and body horribly scraped and cut, lying bleeding and nearly buried under a heap of rock.

His head still throbbing and resisting the wobbliness which swept over him, he managed, with tremendous exertion, to toss aside the debris covering much of her until his hands were bloodied in the frantic effort. He then clasped her in his arms-she murmered out low moans, broken and whimpering, besieged by her injuries.

"Pelaxilla!" Ahuitzotl cried and held her close to him as he winced in his pain.

"Pelaxilla!" he repeated and wept, "My dear Pelaxilla."

Tlalalca's eyes opened wide in an expression of utmost horror. This was the final and ultimate shock for her-in one long, dreadful anguished scream, she released the torment of a lifetime that she had suffered at his hands, and then broke into low whimpering sobs, painfully emitted under her laborious breathing, until she lapsed into unconsciousness, leaving him bewildered and dazed over her strange reaction.

XVIII

That was how rescuers found them-the confused Revered Speaker babbling incoherently to the empress lying unconscious in his arms amid the rubble. They arrived as quickly as they could. When the oarsmen who had dropped off their master at his residence saw its center section collapsing, they hurriedly searched for help, first seeking it in the old palace where Nezahualpilli was staying, and then an adjacent structure to get Cihuacoatl. The rumbling of the falling edifice and screams of its occupants had already alerted them to what was happening and it remained a matter of marshalling the canoes and personnel to begin the rescue effort. This was accomplished within minutes, and soon a flotilla sped for the partially destroyed palace to recover its inhabitants who were heard crying out in the darkness.

Both sections of the palace which rested on the solid banks of the canal remained intact; only the lengthy center portion bridging the water had fallen in, although in the collapse parts of the northern half's upper level were dragged along with it. Cihuacoatl, knowing his master's chamber was in that section over the canal, feared the worst. But when they came nearer, he saw that part of the chamber still hung precariously attached to the southern end of the structure-there was some hope this is where might find the monarch. Nezahualpilli noted the minister's consternation when they landed their canoes. "You look worried," he said. "It appears that in spite of your regret over the ills he has brought to Tenochtitlan, you are not ready to do without him."

"This is true, Lord," answered Cihuacoatl. "I've grown accustomed to his methods and have acquired a familiarity with them. I'm not ready to exchange this for a newcomer whom we haven't even considered yet. For all his faults, there is greatness in him. He has done much for us-more than anyone else in my memory."

They ascended the stairs while others in nearby canoes fished out the women and children who had fallen into the water or lay injured amid the debris scattered about-their moans echoed grimly in the dark leading the rescuers to them. When Cihuacoatl and Nezahualpilli, along with Motecuhzoma, came to the entrance of the Revered Speaker's chamber-more than a third of which had broken off-they saw him there weeping as he gently wiped the blood from Tlalalca's face. The scene gave them pause; she appeared dead to them and his own wounds were quite severe, yet he spoke to comfort her as if she could hear him even as the blood continued to seep from the gash in his forehead.

"My Lord," Cihuacoatl cried out in his relief.

Ahuitzotl turned his head in the direction of the voice, but looked uncomprehendingly at the minister, then resumed talking to Tlalalca, stroking back her hair and clasping her firmly against him.

"He appears not to know you," Nezahualpilli told the minister. "What is he saying to her?"

"I can make no sense out of it–listen."

"Forgive me. Forgive me." Ahuitzotl repeated over and over. "Please forgive me."

They crept ahead, insecure over how to approach their monarch over the creaking, quivering floor, but despite its seemingly fragile condition, it held, and when they reached his side, they tried to lift him away from his empress.

"No!" Ahuitzotl moaned. "Leave me with her."

He held her even closer and was unwilling to have them remove her from his clasp; Cihuacoatl could not decide what to do and looked to Nezahualpilli and Motecuhzoma for guidance. They continued to gaze benumbed at the pitiful sight, until at last, Nezahualpilli grabbed the monarch under his shoulders and thrust him upward. "My Lord," he soberly exclaimed, "You must allow us to help you."

Initially, Ahuitzotl had a befuddled expression about him and did not know who was speaking to him; then a spark came to his eyes-he understood. "Ne-Nezahualpilli?" he uttered.

"Yes, Lord. You must let us take you from here. You are gravely injured."

Ahuitzotl nodded, and thereupon fainted; Nezahualpilli clung on to him to keep him from falling. Then he and Motecuhzoma carried their master from the chamber while Cihuacoatl checked on Tlalalca. Tears of joy came to him when he detected the small but distinguishable rising and lowering of her chest under her faint respiration.

"She lives!" Cihuacoatl wept aloud. "The empress lives."

But his momentary exhiliration vanished when he lifted her out of the rubble and saw the extent of her injuries. Her lacerations were severe and the bleeding profuse, and to his horror, he felt a wooden stake under her side-she had been impaled by a piece of crossbeam that had splintered when it snapped from the ceiling. Fearful that he would be unable to stop the blood flow if he pulled this terrible fragment from her, Cihuacoatl ripped off a portion of his cloak and wrapped it securely around the sliver's edge to prevent more seepage of her blood. He lifted her up and carried her from the room when he was met by a grief-stricken Xoyo.

The old woman's tears ran like small rivulets down her deeply wrinkled cheeks and fell in drops from her chin. Momentarily stopped as he viewed the pitiful sight, the minister then moved around her. "Come with us, old woman," he said as he passed by. "She'll be in need of you."

Holding her hand over her mouth as if to keep herself from emitting a horrid scream, Xoyo followed Cihuacoatl down the steps to the waiting canoes. The monarch had already been placed upon folded blankets when Cihuacoatl handed Tlalalca to Nezahualpilli in the boat—both he and Motecuhzoma were momentarily stunned when they saw her wound. They laid her next to Ahuitzotl and covered them both with additional blankets; Xoyo seated herself next to Tlalalca and held her lady's head in her lap. Quickly, the rowers proceeded to the old palace where physicians waited.

Ahuitzotl awoke to find himself among a number of lords and ministers, including Cihuacoatl, Nezahualpilli, Tlohtzin, and Motecuhzoma. Also present were his personal servants and court physician, Tezotzin. He could feel a dull pounding inside his head, painfully stabbing him with every pulsation of his heartbeat; he reached up and felt the bandage which had been wrapped over his wound. Recurring blackouts flashed over his eyes; his vision was blurred and he had to take long glances to affix an image in his mind. His tongue felt somewhat heavy when he wanted to speak.

"How long?" he slurred.

"A full day, Lord," Cihuacoatl answered, greatly relieved that his master understood.

Ahuitzotl peered blankly at his minister-a look so devoid of any sign of recognition that Cihuacoatl doubted his previous conclusion. He continued his staring and seemed to alternate between bouts of cognizance and incomprehension-some of the time a sparkle radiated from his eyes which appeared to denote an awareness of who he was observing, but other times he was quite expressionless and apparently saw nothing in spite of having his eyes wide open and fixed on an object. Cihuacoatl eyed Tezotzin, who returned the gaze and shook his head: the indications were disturbing.

Then the Revered Speaker gave them cause to breath a little easier when his eyes again demonstrated a perception of his surroundings; he looked searchingly from person to person as if meaning to speak to each one of them until he focused back on the minister.

"Tlalalca?" he asked him.

"In the adjacent room, Lord," Cihuacoatl replied, hesitant to say more, but revealing his apprehensions in this evasion.

"How is she?"

The minister could not defer from answering; he would have preferred a more auspicious time to inform his master of her condition, for it was not good and he did not want his lord to fall back into some kind of relapse spawned by disappointment. "She is badly injured, Lord," he said. "The physicians are doing their best, but fear for her. Yet she lives, and there is hope."

Ahuitzotl slowly closed his eyes and turned red as if somehow ashamed, and when he opened them again, a frightening comportment engulfed him. He tried to rise from the mats, but in this attempt found his throbbing pain so intensified that he fell back and held his jaw tightly shut to repress his crying out until the aches subsided.

"You must rest, Lord," Tezotzin cautioned him, "if you mean to recover from your injury. These things cannot be rushed."

"I must see her. I must speak to her." Ahuitzotl babbled wildly. "There is something important I must say to her."

"It will have to wait, Lord," Cihuacoatl said.

"No. I must speak to her."

"My Lord," the minister sharply jolted his memory. "She cannot hear you."

"But-but you said she lives."

"She does, Lord, but she is unconscious; she cannot hear you."

The words reached him, but his fear remained; he glared at the ceiling and everyone in the room saw that his mind was in turmoil-whatever he wished to say to the empress bore heavily on him. Unable to attain his purpose, and racked with the relentless headaches magnified when he tried to rise, Ahuitzotl appeared to by groping to remain focused in the present and keep from drifting into oblivion. His eyes glanced nervously about as he searched for additional matters of concern.

"My son, Cuauhtemoc?" he asked.

"Unharmed, Lord."

Ahuitzotl emitted a subdued sigh of relief, but then slipped into another semi-conscious state which left his onlookers worried. At last he closed his eyes and fell asleep.

When he again awoke, Ahuitzotl saw the darkened chamber dimly lit by a small burning brazier and the physician assigned to watch him was dozing under its flickering light-the rest of the group had gone. For a considerable time he simply lay there unmoving, having his thoughts disrupted by throes of pain shooting through him at repeated intervals, but after he adjusted to enduring these spasms, he began to think of Tlalalca-he needed to speak to her. He remembered having been told about her unconsciousness but believed that, if he spoke with her, she would hear him. Slowly, not wanting to wake the attending physician, he arose, sitting up and then rising to his feet. He was about to take his first step when he was overwhelmed with a rushing dizziness; spots flashed before his eyes and his vision clouded up. Almost immediately, he fell crashing back upon the layered mats, startling the physician.

"My Lord!" he exclaimed. "What means this?"

He tried to get up again; the physician sprang to his side determined to stop him, but Ahuitzotl was adamant. "I must see her," he said. "You must help me to my wife's chamber."

The physician balked. While against his professional judgment to expose a patient to possible greater shocks, this was the Revered Speaker entreating him for assistance. How could he refuse? Hesitating only for an instant, he flung one of Ahuitzotl's arms over his shoulder and lifted him up using his own body as a crudge for his master, and so, half-walking and half-carrying, the physician took him to the adjacent room.

They saw Xoyo sitting on cushions adjacent to the bedding upon which the empress lay; she raised her head to glare at the intruders with her moist eyes. Ahuitzotl motioned for the physician to move closer until they stood next to Tlalalca, then requested that he and Xoyo wait outside the chamber as he wanted to be alone with her. Although averse to leaving their charges, both adhered to his wishes.

She lay covered with white cotton sheets save for her head which rested on a soft pillow; her face had been washed clean and showed no scars or cuts and her eyes were closed, as were her lips. Ahuitzotl felt a lump in his throat as he gazed upon her, finding it difficult to believe that so gentle a sight masked so grave an injury, and he was struck by her serene beauty. She was lovelier than he remembered her in any previous encounter. Why had he not realized it before? He thought about his treatment of her and how, in her last conscious moment, he called her Pelaxilla. What an unspeakable shock that must have been. Overcome with remorse, Ahuitzotl sank to his knees and openly wept.

"How beautiful you look," he spoke to the motionless empress, his voice trembling. "I have been so cruel to you. You have been so understanding, so tolerant of my faults, while I was pitiless in my callousness. Only now do I realize how much I love you, and yet have never spoken these words to you. If only you could know. I say them to you now, in the hope that somehow, by the grace of Xochiquetzal, you will hear them. I love you, Tlalalca. I love you."

He scanned her reposed face in anticipation that he would detect some kind of response—a faint smile, a blink of the eye, a twitch, however slight, anything, but some sign-that she heard him. There was nothing; his anxieties heightened in his desperation to have her realize his deepest feelings. He stroked her hair and touched her soft face. "You must hear me," he entreated. "I must know you will forgive me for what I have done to you. I beg that you forgive me."

He continued hoping to see a sign coming from her, but she remained as motionless as before; he leaned his head on her abdomen, burying it in the sheets so his weeping might be muffled. His grief was heartfelt, for he truly now adored her and needed her. "You are all I have left that I cherish," he moaned. "Without you, I am lost."

The physician reentered the chamber after hearing Ahuitzotl's cries and, recognizing the futility of his efforts, concluded this suffering was of no benefit to his health-indeed it was fraught with risks-and decided to bring it to an end. "Come, Lord," he said as he put his hands on his master's shoulders and lifted him away from the bed. "You must refrain from this-your depression will not help in your recovery. Let us return to your chamber."

Ahuitzotl offered no resistance, sensing that he could do nothing more, and they staggered from the room leaving the shattered Xoyo with her empress. The old woman meticulously reshuffled the sheets where Ahuitzotl had wrinkled them and smoothened the folds. Then, after carefully looking over her lady to see that everything was comfortably arranged for her, she resumed her seat and began to hum a song she knew-a prayer to the Mother of the Gods, Teteoinnan-and patiently remained at her vigil as she had done throughout so much of her lifetime.

Under the care of Tenochtitlan's finest physicians and many servants who saw to all his needs, Ahuitzotl made steady progress and was soon able to move about. He was given various herb potions which accelerated his improvement, but was afflicted by recurring spells in which he seemed to fade into a kind of oblivious state where he was out of contact with his surroundings. To court observers, it appeared as some sort of trance, and it seemed to come in waves, overwhelming him and then subsiding, and lasting of short duration; its coming was unpredictable and at irregular intervals, sometimes repeatedly within a single morning, and then not again for two or more days. What mystified the physicians most was that they could discover no phenomenon which triggered its onset-it came and went quite randomly as it pleased.

Rarely having seen such a malady, the healers scanned their texts for descriptions and remedies which may have been recorded. They grew alarmed when their inquiries proved unsuccessful and sent messengers to the far regions of the realm in search of fellow physicians of repute who might be able to impart their knowledge or experience on the subject. The consensus among them was unfavorable-they feared these trances prognosticated a form of dementia that would, in time, grow progressively worse. In private, they were concerned for him; in public, they gave him encouragement.

During one of his lucid periods a few days later, Ahuitzotl decided to return to Tlalalca's chamber to check on her. Although no longer under the constant watch of the physicians, he was still kept company by his servants and others who remained to meet his requirements, and it chanced that Cihuacoatl was with him on this day. The minister, who felt that the torment these visits caused him greatly aggravated his unstable condition, tried to dissuade him from his purpose.

"She is still unconscious, Lord. Would it not be better to leave her in her peace?"

To Ahuitzotl, whose frequent visitations were made in the belief that he was helping her, the words were hollow. "No, Cihuacoatl," he answered. "I tell you, she hears me. I must continue to speak to her, to tell her how much I long to have her return to me. She will listen and come back to me."

Cihuacoatl knew otherwise. Each day Tlalalca remained in her comatose state imperiled her further, for she could not eat or drink and was growing ever weaker. But only physical restraint could have put a stop to his master's determination, and the minister was not about to apply that effort to prevent him from his intentions. Reluctantly, he was prepared to follow him when a protracted, agonizing shriek echoed through the palace corridor.

"What was that?" Ahuitzotl reacted tensely.

"Xoyo!" replied Cihuacoatl, and immediately sensed a horror.

They rushed into the adjacent room-Ahuitzotl's heart pounded the linings of his throat-and saw the old woman on her knees beside the bed clutching the empress in her shaking arms; she was sobbing hysterically. Tezotzin was there, leaning against the wall and covering his face in his elbow while trembling in anguish.

"Wh-what?" Ahuitzotl gulped.

He knew. Mortified, he stood frozen as his greatest nightmare-the thing he dreaded above all possibilities-now confronted him. Too dazed for words, he slowly approached the mats. It could not be, he said to himself: it could not happen to him-not after all he had said to her; not after how he implored her forgiveness; not when he so sincerely wanted her. The gods could not possibly take her from him after all his impassioned pleading.

When he stood beside her, he looked down at her pallid face, lovelier and more serene than even before, remaining in its final repose with eyes and lips closed. She looked as if she was only sleeping, he thought-how peacefully she rested. She was surely the most beautiful woman ever to enter Tlalocan, the South Heaven; already the gods and goddesses were welcoming her. Tlalocan was a happy place where people sang and danced and had no more worries-why, then, was he so torn with remorse? He should be rejoicing for her-she was at last free from the suffering he had caused her. Why did he feel such unbelievable sorrow?

Tlalalca had died without ever regaining consciousness, and when the full consequence of its meaning struck him-horribly, with devastating and brutal severity-an icy chill tore into his body leaving him shuddering under its impact. He glared with stunned incomprehension at the body lying there; tears swelled in his eyes and ran down his cheeks, and he swallowed his compulsion to cry out. Worst of all, he had that terrible last scream to live with-he was never to know if she had forgiven him for that final act of cruelty on her. How was he ever to erase that from his memory?

He ran his trembling fingers over her face-already her lips were cold-to feel her delicate softness one more time. Then he could no longer control his repressed emotions; he clamped his hands over his mouth and rushed from the chamber, and when he was alone in the corridor, he slumped against its walls sliding down under his weakening knees and released a tortured cry that shook the palace.

"Tlalalca!" he screamed in his anguish, drowning out everything in its volume. "Tlalalca!"

Cihuacoalt, himself in tears as he grieved over the loss of Tlalalca whom he genuinely adored, tried to remove Xoyo from her clasp on the empress. She wailed out and refused to be budged, and the minister gave up in his attempts and instead went to the physician.

"When?" he asked.

"This morning," answered the distraught Tezotzin. "Evidently while the old woman slept. Perhaps that is why she cannot be consoled."

"Truly sad," commented Cihuacoatl. "Never have I experienced so sorrowful a time."

When the minister joined his master in the corridor, he found him sitting in his trance-like state staring blankly into nothingness ahead of him. He called for the physician's help and together they carried Ahuitzotl back to his own chamber and settled him on his bed. The shock had been extreme, and they wondered if he would recover from it.

Later that day, Tlalalca's body was removed from the palace and taken to the funery to be prepared for the burial. Unlike the usual rite in which dead nobility were burned on pyres, she had to be interred because she met death by accident at the hands of the water deities, or as a horrid consequence of their actions. The servants who came for her had to forceably remove Xoyo, who clung tenaciously against being separated from her life-long charge; they left the bereft old woman sobbing and alone in the empty chamber.

That evening, long after the sun had set and the palace corridors were lit up by the fires of numerous braziers, Xoyo at last arose from her crouched position and walked about the chambers, halls, and bathing rooms which were so familiar to her. She had devoted almost her entire adult lifetime in service of Tlalalca, nursing her as a baby and watching her grow into the wonderful woman that she became for her-forty years she had been with her, caring for her, loving and admiring her. It seemed incomprehensible that she should no longer be with her; for the first time Xoyo felt the pangs of loneliness and was deeply frightened by it. She glanced over the furnishings and memorabilia that had become so much part of her over the years, yet even these exuded a hollowness without the empress to fawn over them and comment on them. It all was so meaningless now-not even the memory of Tlalalca could give life to the emptiness in which the old woman found herself.

What would she do? With Tlalalca there was a purpose to her living; the empress retained the services of an ungainly aged woman who had long outlived her usefulness to anyone else—whether she did this out of pity or habit did not matter. What was important was that Xoyo found a meaning to her life in the employ of her lady. But it ran deeper than that— much deeper-for Xoyo loved Tlalalca as if she had been her own daughter; never having married or experienced the pleasures of love, she found her consolation in tending to her empress, a fulltime occupation for her which she cherished. To undergo the misfortune of outliving her charge was a horror that Xoyo never in her wildest imagination dared to contemplate: the cruelest of fate had befallen her. Her only hope was that they would now sacrifice her in conformance with the funeral rites, so that she might serve her lady in the afterlife.

As prescribed by custom, Tlalalca lay on a low cot adorned in her finest clothing and jewelry in the palace reception hall for four days so that the lords and ladies from thoughout Anahuac who were her friends could make their visitations. She had been bathed in aromatic oils and perfumed to make the encounter pleasant for the guests; flowers were abundantly placed about her and added their own pleasing fragrances. They arrived and brought various gifts, mostly garments, ornaments, and containers of food, so that the empress might not enter her journey to Tlalocan impoverished. Many guests appeared; in her unassuming way, Tlalalca had attained a popularity which extended beyond the limits of the capital—she did this so effortlessly that it came as a surprise to the nobles of Tenochtitlan. She was greatly venerated, and her loss was keenly felt and touched nearly everyone.

Ahuitzotl made nightly appearances after the visitors had retired to their quarters; he was finally resigned to her fate, and spoke to wish her joy in the afterlife. He consoled his sorrow by noting the large number of gifts presented to Tlalalca for her new journey, and he knew that she would be much happier in Tlalocan than here; this knowledge conforted him and he reminded himself of it whenever overcome with grief.

When the time came to inter the empress and designate those attendants who would be sacrificed to continue their service to her in Tlalocan, Xoyo received her second mortal shock when she was not selected-ironically, her age now worked against her.

"You are too old, Xoyo," Cihuacoatl informed her. "The empress would find your services wanting."

Her only hope of rejoining her lady snatched from her, Xoyo understood the bleak kind of life which lay ahead. She would walk the palace halls by herself unheeded, unwanted, and unnoticed: her isolation would be complete. She desperately pleaded her case with the minister.

"My lady did not find my service wanting in life," she begged. "Why should she do so now? Please, Lord Minister, do not deprive me of caring for her."

"It's useless to persist," Cihuacoatl reproached her. "The priests have decided. I have no say in the matter."

Failing in her attempts to secure her happiness, a dismayed Xoyo slunk from his presence and slipped quietly from the scene to continue her aimless wandering about the palace grounds.

The spot chosen for the burial was an open plot within the royal garden behind the palace-only a few paces from where Tizoc drank his fatal potion-and, with numerous dignitaries in attendance, the solemn observance proceeded as declared by the priests of Mictlancihuatl, the Death Goddess. Five servants who had spent much of their time in caring for the empress while she lived were also honored to accompany her in her new life-the chief stewart, her personal priest, two close female attendants, and a dwarf. All met their deaths without complaint-indeed, privileged-by having their throats cut in front of the body of their lady. After they were thus slain, they were placed alongside their queen within the grave while contrite priests chanted mournful songs and wished them eternal bliss in Tlalocan. The members of the royal family stood by, many weeping in sorrow, but not Ahuitzotl; he simply remained in a dazed stupor and silent throughout the rite's duration. Perhaps he did grasp what was happening or, if he did, was reconciled to his continued punishment meted out by vengeful gods.

When the ceremony was over, work crews, under the direction of a lower ranking priest, began to throw dirt into the pit to cover up the deceased. A variety of flowers were planted into this fresh soil so the entire burial spot became hidden in their glowing blooms; soon it blended in so perfectly with its surrounding growth that it became invisible as a gravesite. Yet to everyone who witnessed the burial and who had known the empress, this was a sacred plot of ground-to be looked upon with reverence to her memory and in sorrow. In time, the memories would fade, as would the sorrow, but the many flowers would continue to blossom brightly and beautifully-it remained an altogether fitting monument to Tlalalca.

The funeral rites did not end with the burial but went on for a total of ten days, with more ceremonies eulogizing the virtues of the empress and the traditional feasting that was part of such an occasion. And through it all, Ahuitzotl kept his own participation to the essential minimum demands and hid from view the remaining time. Word circulated that he was too grief-stricken to indulge in the feasting, finding the death of his empress very difficult to endure, and could not bear to see his friends while in this despondent state. But others also said that he was no longer himself and had, in fact, lost his faculties, and that his few appearances were during rare moments of lucidness. There were insiders who knew, Cihuacoatl among them, but refused to mention anything, and this contributed to making the situation rife for rumors. When the rites finally ended, the minister, not the Revered Speaker, bade the guests farewell and a good journey home.

Each day that passed saw Xoyo sitting for hours before the flower patch marking Tlalalca's gravesite, singing out sad melodies to her departed lady. To all but the most callous observer, this was truly a pitiful, heart-rendering scene-the solitary old woman seated by herself in that quiet garden extending expression to her grief in the only way she knew how. Soon enough this became so familiar a sight that it was largely ignored by the palace residents, most dismissing it as the fancies of a foolish woman incapable of letting go of the past. It therefore came as a surprise one afternoon, several weeks later, when there emanated a significant commotion among the ladies of the court while the minister made one of his periodic visits to check on his master's health. He heard them screaming and saw them running from the garden.

"What is it?" Cihuacoatl asked a fleeing girl.

"It is the old one, Xoyo," replied the frightened girl. "She has hanged herself!"

Cihuacoatl peered into the garden where he saw Xoyo's limp body swaying slightly to-and-fro under the branch of a tree and the strewn blocks of wood which had previously been stacked to make a platform. A touch of remorse came over him, and he regretted that this poor old woman was not permitted to join her lady by sacrifice as she so dearly had wished. What astounded him was the all-out exertion the weakened aged Xoyo had applied in her endeavor-her sheer determination to see it through. Did she believe she would be reunited with her lady in Tlalocan? Or was she so horribly miserable in her loneliness and uselessness that nothing else mattered except to end it all? He looked toward the monarch to see what he might be thinking-Ahuitzotl appeared indifferent to the affair; apparently he had not understood what happened.

The flood subsided soon after Coyoacan's spring waters had been diverted and a program was initiated to rebuild the capital. Because it had been mostly the old and dilapidated buildings which were damaged or destroyed, the single exception being Ahuitzotl's unusual new palace, these were rehabilitated or torn down to make way for entirely new structures. An edict was issued by Cihuacoatl, allegedly under the auspices of the Revered Speaker, that placed minimal restrictions on the design or dimensions of these new facilities thus permitting the wealthy nobles and others to erect their houses in the manner they saw fit-the hope was that this would expedite the city's reconstruction. They built and painted their new homes to suit their individual fancies, with beautiful extensions of green gardens and magnificent patios, more original and elegant in styling and construction than what was replaced. The metropolis that emerged from the disaster was therefore far more colorful and spectacular than what had been, with its many canals bordered by embankments and lined with willow and poplar trees.

This transformation did not occur overnight, but mainly in the year after the disaster. The initial stage for it was set when Nezahualpilli completed his reconstruction of the dams which harnessed the springs at Coyoacan and brought the aqueduct under control. He next supervised the rebuilding of the channel retaining walls damaged at the conduit's terminus. He remained in the capital for six months as the work assumed its final stages under his guidance, and when he was finished, the aqueduct functioned as it had originally been designed to do, bringing the sweet, clear life-giving water into Tenochtitlan. Ahuitzotl rewarded the Texcocan with prized gifts and high praise, quite out of his character since, to some degree, Nezahualpilli's work stood out as a public repudiation and personal humiliation of the Revered Speaker-the disaster and its tragic aftermath had at last humbled the once proud and arrogant monarch. As

Nezahualpilli listened to the laudations conferred upon him, he adjudged them so out of context with the Revered Speaker he was used to hearing that he almost preferred to have him as he formerly was. He believed Ahuitzotl had publicly affected his ingratiating display, and on the day when he prepared to return to his own city, he met with his colleague in order to learn the truth

"You saved the city," Ahuitzotl told him, "a munificent gesture on your part. Tenochtitlan is grateful to you."

"What of Tenochtitlan's ruler?" Nezahualpilli could not resist asking. "Is he as grateful?"

"Why shouldn't he be?"

"You don't know? Or is it that you no longer care."

"I assume you allude to the the degradation your rescue effort represents on my person."

"I am. I can understand how you might make a fine public demonstration of your gratitude, for the people must see how you are penitent over the misery you have caused them, but I would leave here a happier man if I knew what you are really thinking."

"Is this important to you?"

"Yes. So I know with whom I am dealing and how I am to pursue my associations with him. I want no more deceptions going on between us and wish to have an understanding with my colleague that is, above all, forthright and honest."

"Then hear me out so that you may make your judgment on me. I am walking on an uncertain pathway with the gods-this is what is believed, especially by the priests-and am not clear as to how I should react to the charities given me. Were I to show any ingratitude, I might suffer worse at their hand that I already have-as if such a thing was possible. You see me now, and hear me, in one of my intelligible periods. I'm told that I often lapse into what could appropriately be called a demented state. Such is my penalty for having spoken and acted as I saw fit, and by that behavior, having offended the gods who now conspire to bring about my defeat. I have lost the two persons who meant more to me than life itself. My beloved Pelaxilla I lost to that....fat Zapotecan, Cocijoeza, and my dear Tlalalca was taken from me by Chalchihuitlicue. My city I caused to be flooded and nearly destroyed; my people are angry with me and will not face me-they remember only the ill fortunes I have brought to them. My own body is being ravaged by a malady the physicians are unable to diagnose. So you see, Nezahualpilli, it is not that I no longer care, but that I fear. I fear to say what I think lest I bring even greater injury upon myself and my subjects. How could I endure more suffering? I have paid for my folly in full. Do you understand?"

Nezahualpilli nodded, deeply touched by his words, and felt compassion for Ahuitzotl. Yet, even under all the misfortunes which befell him, there remained a disturbing aspect to his interpretations of it; Nezahualpilli was amazed to find the Revered Speaker's fears still misdirected. "But my lord," he said, "the gods do not only know what you speak-they know what you think."

The shock was visible on Ahuitzotl's face, as if at last the actual circumstances of his downfall were fully revealed to him.

"Then I am lost!" he exclaimed.

In sorrow, Nezahualpilli left the unhappy monarch to reflect on this within his quarters while he bade farewell to the lords and craftsmen who had labored with him these many weeks. The occasion was a sad one-they had grown accustomed to the Texcocan's method of doing things and had come to know him on a personal basis, and had grown fond of him. As frequently happens when men are brought together in an enterprise demanding their combined exertions and cooperation, comraderies are formed and, when the functions which forged these unions are finally ended, a sense of loss overcomes its participants-there is even regret that the work is concluded. Cihuacoatl was the last to declare his sendoff to the Texcocan.

"He has changed," Nezahualpilli informed the minister before making his departure. "I'm not convinced it is for the better."

"He's brought grievous harm to himself as well as to others," replied Cihuacoatl. "Such misfortunes leave their scars."

"You will not find the decisive and resolute Revered Speaker of old who broke the patterns of accepted conventions and applied this to secure great successes for the realm. In his place, you have a frightened, insecure, and hesitant lord who may not rule as effectively."

"These deviations you speak of also led to his ruin, for they turned our gods against him, and there's reason to question their overall value to us.

But to be fair, he has already done so much more than any other monarch and these feats will certainly not be forgotten. His place is secure enough among the chroniclers and poets. He has done well."

"Truly it is as you say. However, I must look to other things which now beckon me. Let me wish you and your lord well as I take my leave."

With that, Nezahualpilli and his entourage set out on their march home. Cihuacoatl remained at the palace steps gazing after him with notable sadness; like so many others, he felt he was losing a close friend.

In the months that followed, the numerous new buildings which arose gave Tenochtitlan a clean magnificence that surely must have aroused the envy of its neighboring cities. It gleamed splendidly in the sunshine with its brilliantly painted houses and varied architecture. There was much of what could be justly described as a foreign influence characterizing this new look of the capital-in his far-reaching conquests, Ahuitzotl had brought back hundreds of artisans from many kingdoms whose talents and skills were soon apparent to the captors and who now applied their energies into the new construction. Thus a beautiful cosmopolitan center grew out of the wreckage of the disaster and took on its resplendent appearance.

One structure was not rebuilt, but merely modified to some limited extent-Ahuitzotl's recent palace whose central section had collapsed. The largely intact southern portion of the building-the part facing the central square-was converted onto an administrative complex, its back wall overlooking the canal plastered over so no trace was left of the innovative overhang which once spanned the water. The northern section on the opposite bank was torn down and its stones used to erect an apartment house. Thus Ahuitzotl and the royal family members resided back in the palace built by his famed grandfather, Motecuhzoma Ilhuicamina.

Ahuitzotl's public appearances became much less frequent following the disaster, and even rarer as the months passed during which the city was being rebuilt. He made his required ceremonial presence known when he could, and continued to open the sacrificial rites as his duties demanded, but they were of short duration and he departed as soon as he had fulfilled his role in the proceedings; often Cihuacoatl took his place when it was said he was ailing. To the people, remembering their carousing Revered Speaker of old who enjoyed being in the public's eye, this gave rise to substantial speculation as well as consternation. Now that the flood had long gone, and that they looked with civic pride upon the new image of their capital, they were prepared to forgive their monarch-rumor had it that he hid from them because he could not bear to face them after the calamity he brought upon them-and again recalled the many campaigns they engaged in under his singular dynamic leadership and the scores of victories he gave them. Even to this day, those captives taken during the Soconusco operation still provided Tenochtitlan's priests with the victims for their ceremonial demands. He was, after all, their famed Revered Speaker and commanded their respect. Also, many warriors lusted for new adventures-a considerable length of time had passed since their last war.

Inside the palace, the situation was very different from what the people knew, for their warlord's torment, unlike that of the city's, was not ended. In addition to the deteriorating reasoning powers ensuing from his head injury, his physical condition was also rapidly degenerating. None of the physicians, who were sworn to secrecy under a threat of death, could find a remedy, or even identify the nature of this sickness afflicting him. The symptoms were evident: his flesh was being slowly eaten away from internally leaving the skin clinging loosely to the bones, much like someone dying of starvation, with the resultant gaunt and emaciated appearance. The gradual wasting away of the flesh was also accompanied by agonizing pains, but these the physicians were able to alleviate through the application of a variety of potions and drugs.

This decaying process had actually gone on steadily since its first signs were noticed after Ahuitzotl returned from Soconusco; because it progressed imperceptibly slowly in the beginning, it remained essentially diagnostically obscure. That something was in fact amiss could not be denied, however, for his pain intensified and, no matter how much food he ate, he continued to lose weight. But in the aftermath of the flood, with the terrible physical and psychological injuries it caused him, his deterioration accelerated. Ahuitzotl woke up one morning-or so it seemed to him-during one of his lucid states a short time after Tlalalca's funeral and glared at himself in a mirror; he was horror-stricken over what he saw. He appeared a much older man, with sagging eyelids and stark features; he touched his face repeatedly feeling its thinned flesh and protruding cheekbones. He screamed out in ghastly dismay, bringing a servant to his side. "My Lord!" exclaimed the valet after entering. "What is it?"

"Do you see this?" Ahuitzotl groaned, barely able to catch his breath and trembling violently as he still gazed in the mirror. "Can this be my face? I hardly recognize it!"

"But Lord, this is how you have looked for days."

Horrified, Ahuitzotl sent out another long, agonizing howl; he could not conceive that the gods meant for him to suffer even more, after all the misery they had already inflicted upon him. "How can I face my people looking like this?" Ahuitzotl wept. "I cannot let them see me! I am a prisoner within my own palace!"

And so he was. The monarch who had taken the Mexica eagle over greater distances and to more remote frontiers than anyone before him, the mightiest of their conquerors, the warrior-king incarnate, now had to pass his days confined within the narrow walls of his residence in self-imposed isolation spawned by this blow to his vanity. He met his ceremonial requirements with the help of cosmeticians who did their best to conceal the degenerating influences and the elaborately plumed headdresses he wore. But the anxieties resulting from the shock upon learning of the extent of his sickness only worsened his condition, adding increased strain to an already severely stressful situation.

As progressed this malady, so also did the mental lapses the physicians had prognosticated in their initial assessments. They now occurred with more frequent consistency and lasted longer, so that the hapless monarch was often seen wandering aimlessly about in his palace and its adjacent garden babbling incoherently and trailed by attendants to care for his even most basic bodily functions. This was a most ignoble and inglorious manner for the great warlord to conclude his remarkable reign, and for all practical purposes, his rule was ended. It became a source of acute embarrassment for the ministers and members of the royal family to behold the disgraceful spectacle and they avoided seeing him. Cihuacoat assumed more of his master's duties as each month passed and then eventually ruled as regent while the interclan council met periodically to address the problem of selecting a successor when the time came.

And yet, while he lived, the domain remained stable, making Cihuacoatl's regency correspondingly easier-such was the power and the legacy he left for his people that the very mention of his name invoked such awe among the nations he conquered that none dared to rise in rebellion.

This, more than any other aspect of Ahuitzotl's reign, was his greatest contribution to the realm. All through its brief history of dominance over Anahuac and regions beyond, begun by Itzcoatl only three generations ago, the Mexica had been faced with constant and repeated uprisings among their subjugated dominions; almost all of Tizoc's wars entailed suppressing revolts in regions that had previously been conquered by Motecuhzoma Ilhuicamina and Axayacatl. It constituted a major problem that frustrated every Mexica ruler and appeared to offer no solutions. But under Ahuitzotl, whose brutal and thorough method of subjugation was firmly implanted into the vanquished's memory, there were no insurrections and this despite the kingdom spanning to greater horizons and comprising more cities and nations than ever before. It was undeniably a noteworthy achievement, and Cihuacoatl never lost sight of it or failed to appreciate it.

A difficulty remained with the powerful independent nations, many in close proximity to Anahuac, the principal examples of these being Tlaxcala, only a two day's journey from Lake Texcoco's eastern shores, and the Tarascan state, Michoacan, in the west. There was little doubt that Ahuitzotl deemed these powers a thorn in the Mexica's side and anticipated for their eventual conquest. He had already drawn up plans for taking on Tlaxcala, the more annoying of the two states, and had suggested such a venture to Nezahualpilli. The martial spirit which motivated him and forged the pattern of his life remained with him and continued to manifest itself during his lucid moments. Once he even expressed the notion that he would again conquer Tehuantepec to Cihuacoatl-he did not specify his reasons for it; the Zapotecs were presently staunch allies of the Mexica-but the minister had his suspicions why such a move was being contemplated, and it was not for the benefit of the nation.

But all these plans faded as the months elapsed and in their passing took their increased toll on the unfortunate monarch. The wasting disease ravaged his flesh pitilessly, shriveling his skin until it nearly touched his bones. Ahuitzotl must have known by now that there was no hope for him-when he was clearheaded, he looked with dread upon the debased condition which ceaselessly followed, a condition so undignified for the great warrior-king that he would certainly have preferred death, and only his horror over further alienating the gods deterred him from ordering his own killing.

He had disappeared from the public eye; Cihuacoatl had taken over all his ceremonial tasks now and there were few left in Tenochtitlan who did not hear of their lord's affliction. To silence the rampant rumors, Cihuacoatl was forced to issue a formal declaration regarding the nature and gravity of Ahuitzotl's malady; many a warrior was devastated by these news-they had never known so great a warlord and could not even imagine of anyone taking his place.

Nearing the end, when Ahuitzotl lay on his mats too weakened to rise, he sent for Cihuacoatl during a period of lucidity which he feared would not last much longer. When the old minister arrived at his side, he was received by that warm glow so familiar to him—even through his emaciated face, he still exuded a radiance that moved men. "The Lord of Death, Mictlantecuhtli, calls me," Ahuitzotl began, his words coming out slowly, interrupted by pauses when he gasped for air and suppressed his pains. "The gods have seen to that. I must know, Cihuacoatl, what will become of me. Will I be accepted into the East Paradise after having angered them so?"

"Indeed yes, Lord," Cihuacoatl affirmed. "We shall take the appropriate measures to assure you of it. The gods will be pleased. They would never reject so great a warrior as you."

"Rarely have I known fear, but I fear now. I readily admit it to you. I am afraid that the harm I have brought to our people is not ended. I had a horrible vision in which I saw our glorious Huitzilopochtli toppled from his pedestal and flung from the Great Temple amid fire and blood, and I heard the wailing of our people. They were crying out—pleading to our gods who no longer protected them. I do not know what it means, but I fear the retribution I have suffered will be wreaked upon Tenochtitlan. Who rules after me?"

"We are undecided, Lord. The most promising candidate is your nephew, Motecuhzoma. He has impressed many speakers of the council with his pious conduct, to say nothing of his abilities."

Ahuitzotl appeared reflective over the prospect, not convinced that the choice was desireable. "He is of such sober disposition," he said at length. "I would have judged him too severe. But then, who else is there? I suppose his kind of serious piety will please the gods more than what I have done, but he will live in my shadow, and this will greatly offend him."

"Perhaps, but as my lord said-who else is there?"

Ahuitzotl's countenance turned grim; the sparkle vanished in his eyes and he appeared troubled again. "Where did I go wrong, Cihuacoatl?" he muttered. "Was it the great sacrifice?"

"I believe so, Lord."

"But if so, why did Huitzilopochtli grant me my victories following it?"

"The ways of the gods are not for our conjecture, Lord, but I believe Huitzilopochtli became envious when you corrupted the purpose of that sacrifice into an exhibition to your personal glory, rather than to honor him. Was that not why slew all those captives-to eclipse the accomplishments of Tizoc so the people would venerate you instead? As to the subsequent victories, I could not even guess what his design was on these. Perhaps he himself could not decide; he so favored you."

Ahuitzotl closed his eyes and appeared to slip into a sleeplike trance; possibly he strained to comprehend the methods by which he brought about his destruction, or he may have simply reacted to the differing drugs administered to alleviate his pains. He may have even been on the threshold of that strange form of dementia which now dominated him. Whatever it was, it led the minister to conclude that the monarch was finished with him; he was about to go when his master's words halted him. "Don't leave me-please," he pleaded.

Cihuacoatl resumed his position by the Revered Speaker's side somewhat discomfited in hearing his belabored breathing and seeing him wincing in his agony. Also, without that glow in his eyes, the raw ugliness of his wrinkled, shallow face seemed accentuated; Cihuacoatl could hardly bear to glance at it. Then he heard some low murmuring-Ahuitzotl was saying more, but so faintly that it was barely distinguishable. Cihuacoatl leaned closer to him.

"She was a good woman," Ahuitzotl spoke brokenly. "Without her, I would not have enjoyed a long life anyway."

Pelaxilla again, Cihuacoatl thought, sensing a mounting anger within him; in many ways, she, even more than the gods, was the instrument of his undoing. He wished the Revered Speaker had never set his eyes upon her-how different things might have been.

"I have never treated her with proper devotion," he went on. "Even when I knew how much she loved me, I ignored it and even rebuked her for it. It was cruel of me-so cold."

Now the minister was not certain of whom his master was thinking about. "Who, Lord?" he asked.

"Tlalalca," he answered.

Cihuacoatl saw the tears streaming down his gaunt face. He uttered no sound, and yet in his quiet weeping expressed a sorrow so deep in conviction that the minister was moved to great pity and fought back his own tears-he felt the remorse that had torn at his lord since that terrible day when she died and offered him no respite in his despair, robbing him of any chance to redeem himself. He closed his eyes again, and when he reopened them, he was possessed of that blank definition in his face which told the minister he had lapsed into his dementia.

"My Lord?" spoke Cihuacoatl.

No reply came as the monarch gazed at some indefinite fixed point in the distant trees seen through the windows and was quite heedless of Cihuacoatl's presence. He apparently again resided within his own peculiar realm which afforded no contact with the realities around him. Seeing no more purpose in remaining, Cihuacoatl arose from his seat, keeping his eyes on his master for an indication of awareness in him as to his situation-there was none. Before departing, however, Cihuacoatl lingered to study the frail, broken man lying there so helplessly, and as he did, a thousand recollections of Ahuitzotl's former lordliness raced through his mind. What a bold, proud man he had been! What a king! How frightening a spectacle to see so great a warlord reduced to this miserably wretched remnant of his previous self. The gods were brutal in their retribution.

Ahuitzotl never again regained his clear-headedness; he lingered in his oblivious condition for a while longer, but no longer grasped the efforts of his attendants to feed or nurse him or to clean up after him. He suffered excruciating pain-whenever the effects of the drugs wore off, his screams were heard at the farthest end of the palace and spurred the court physicians into administering additional dosages. Only under this heavy sedation was his existence kept in tolerable protraction. In this manner, he lived out his remaining days.

Death came mercifully to Ahuitzotl midway into the second year after the flood. He died during the darkness of night-so peacefully that the dozing guardians around him were not even aware of the transition-a quiet departure vividly contrasting the turbulent life he had led.

XX

Even though Ahuitzotl's death had long been expected, when it actually transpired there was no reduced amount of shock or grief in spite of its anticipation. There burst forth a prodigious outpouring of lamentation, not only among the members of the royal house, but among the people of Tenochtitlan and Anahuac as a whole. Forgotten were the adversities he brought upon them, and they now remembered him for his genius and generosity; they spoke of his many impressive victories with admiration and each warrior denoted with pride over having served in his campaigns and fought at his side. And they spoke of the gifts he so liberally bestowed upon them, ignoring that often these gestures were prompted by his trying to avert their mutinies. But mostly, in their recollections, they marvelled at the extent of his conquests and the enormous prestige and power he attained for the realm. In truth, the Mexica eagle had never soared to such dazzling heights.

Ahuitzotl lay in state for four days inside the palace reception hall to allow Anahuac's lords, their ladies, and dignitaries the opportunity to gaze upon their acclaimed warrior-king for the last time. His body was annointed in sweet-smelling perfumes and oils which retarded the decaying process; aromatic incense burners enveloped the setting, providing for a pleasant encounter. The morticians skillfully touched up his face so that, despite its fleshless state, they recreated a firmness and serenity which would have pleased him. Luckily, they could hide the emaciated body under rich clothing-it would not have been possible to reconstitute it to its former condition as they managed to do with the head.

So numerous were the visiting guests that temporary lodging had to be set aside for them as the palaces of Axayacatl and Moquihuix in Tlatelolco were inadequate to house them all. Such was Ahuitzotl's fame and reputation that none wished to be absent from the funeral and sought to pay appropriate homage to him and present him with their valued possessions. These gifts were placed adjacent to the cot upon which the body rested and soon filled the hall. Many of the veteran campaigners who had undergone such arduous expeditions with the mighty warlord wept openly when they saw him in death-he had seemed invincible to them and they could not believe that he would never again lead them into battles.

The funeral ceremony arranged for Ahuitzotl surpassed those of any other sovereign in solemnity and pomp. More gifts were presented, more dignitaries in attendance, and a greater number of orations delivered than ever before; no singular event more effectively and dramatically demonstrated the prestige of the Mexica kingship. Not one of the participants failed to notice the majesty and significance of this: in death, as in life, Ahuitzotl commanded respect-he was the eagle personified.

The site of Ahuitzotl's funeral pyre was at the base of the Great Temple, but the procession taking him there left from the palace and passed through Tenochtitlan's major avenues in a more circuitous route to give its populace a full glimpse of the somber proceedings. It was headed by the litter bearers who carried the deceased monarch cloaked in seventeen mantles representing the principal deities and covered with a mask. The outer cloak was turquoise-the color of Huitzilopochtli-and the mask was formed of greenish-blue jadestone mosaic pieces fashioned into a reasonable likeness of the monarch's face. His body sat upright in the litter with its knees folded to the chest and the arms wrapped around them and secured in place so that the seated position could be maintained.

Immediately behind the grim-faced litter bearers walked the chief minister, Cihuacoatl, Vice-Ruler of Tenochtitlan and presently regent until the interclan council could select Ahuitzotl's successor. He was colorfully clad in a magnificently plumed headdress and the jaguar-skin tunic of his office; his feathered cloak glistened as sunlight reflected off its embedded gemstones. He in turn was followed by the rulers of the Triple Alliance, Chimalpopoca of Tlacopan, and Nezahualpilli of Texcoco, also attired in their most elegant finery, and after them came the rulers of the other major cities in Anahuac and its allied kingdoms. Also with this group were the ambassadors and dignitaries of foreign powers, including the enemy nations of Tlaxcala and Huexotzinco, closest to Anahuac. The death of so noted a monarch demanded a truce between these traditional antagonists and obligated their lords to join in mourning-if not themselves, then their representative. This was the only time in which they could walk openly with the Mexica, for to render them harm constituted a defilement of the sacred rites.

Behind these lords came the members of the royal house which included Motecuhzoma, his half-brother Cuitlahuac, the monarch's older children, and the ladies of the court who served as his mistresses-the younger children, among them Cuauhtemoc, now six years old, remained under a caretaker at the palace. A single drummer marched alongside them beating out the dull thuds by which the cortage kept some semblance of a cadence as it proceeded along.

After the royal family came the numerous priests, counselors, and ministers, as well as the chief nobles of the city and the visiting rulers. Many of the priests chanted dirges to their eparted lord sounding as low drones broken only by the drumbeat. These were followed by several squadrons of Order of the Eagles and Order of the Jaguar knights, all seasoned veterans who had participated in the campaigns led by Ahuitzotl and headed by Tlohtzin. Trailing them was a large entourage of palace servants, slaves, and spared captives who, for some reason or other, found the Revered Speaker's favor and came to serve him; they carried the many gifts and personal belongings of Ahuitzotl-his battle attire, insignia, shield, and weapons-items which were to go with him into his afterlife.

All along the avenues, people assembled to watch the solemn procession, most standing in hushed reverence, but some wailing out their lamentation while others joined in the humming of the priestly chants. In this stark munificent expression of sobriety they mourned over their great departed lord: no-one had witnessed anything like it.

When all the parties returned to the main plaza, the Revered Speaker's litter was set beneath the steps of the Great Temple and immediately surrounded by wooden shafts and dried reeds. The principal speakers stationed themselves next to this pyre while the remaining procession formed into a semi-circle about them and the gift bearers deposited their wares against the wooden pile, stacking it outward as additional items were heaped on it. Ahuitzotl's valets, cooks, and mistresses-the latter being difficult to select as few knew which of the ladies he preferred after Pelaxilla and Tlalalca-stood by to await being sent with their lord into the hereafter.

Nezahualpilli, as ruler of Texcoco, the administrative city of the realm, was the first to speak.

"Great Lord and Conqueror! The glory you have brought to us, the nations you have subjugated, the tributes they now render us, all these things will be forever remembered in our hearts and remind us of your passage upon this world. What can we say about the time you spent with us? You came upon us much like a falling star, of equal short duration, yet in the brief period of your shining, you impressed us with your brilliance. Even as you now enter paradise, to come into the presence of the Lord of Creation in whose house you will meet your noble ancestors and forebearers, we are left to ponder your deeds and to bemoan our loss. Now is covered with dust the seat of the almighty god, the royal throne, which you kept clean, whose likeness you represented, and in whose name you governed our realm. Who can we name to fill this seat who will shine as brightly for us? You have ruled us well, Mighty Lord; your exploits are ever on our lips and fill us with admiration and awe. May you relish the bliss of paradise. So that you may be comforted there, we have selected your favorites in court to join you so you may continue to enjoy their services. Farewell, Lord, our hearts are with you."

After Nezahualpilli, Chimalpopoca, reconciled over the slaying of his cousin, Tzutzumatzin, by the generous restitution Ahuitzotl rendered, gave his presentation, a likewise moving speech entreating for the departed monarch to find happiness in his paradise and reminding him that it was the living who were the more unfortunate and endured the greatest suffering. The Tepanecan was followed by a number of other speakers who continued the trend started by Nezahualpilli: originality came rarely in such prescribed rituals.

When the speech-making was ended, the honored victims chosen to accompany their lord were led up to the priests tasked to do the cutting and, one by one, knelt in front of them to have their bare throats slit. Thus dispatched, their bodies were cast upon the heap like so much additional kindling along with the stacked gifts, and when the pyre was ready to be ignited, Nezahualpilli nodded for the torch bearers to proceed.

Within minutes, a torrent of hot flames shot into the sky, sizzling and crackling loudly and giving off blueish-gray clouds of smoke. While the fire roared, the priests chanted their mournful intones, even more voluminously than before in order to drown out the noisy combustion, and on-lookers stood awe-struck as they watched their lord being consumed in its intense blaze. They remained until the fire expended itself as the material which fueled it was educed to smoldering embers. By late afternoon, when the sun had already gone down behind the western mountains, the fire flickered out and Ahuitzotl's ashes were collected and put in an urn which would be placed in the Stone of the Sun atop the Great Temple. The prominant lords and visitors then partook of their traditional feasting in the palace that comprised an integral function of the ceremony-a solemn occasion conducted under a grim pall of contrition, not the joyous event commemorating a victory in battle. With this sober feast ended the major segment of the funeral to Ahuitzotl.

A few days later, Cihuacoatl made an appearance at the palace and asked to see Prince Motecuhzoma. The young heir, when told of the minister's visit, had some notion as to its purpose; rumors were rife that the interclan council was to meet this week to determine a successor and it was well known among the ruling circles that Motecuhzoma was the preferred candidate for that exalted position. He had, over the last two years, assumed a posture of grave piety and modesty-some thought it feigned, especially Tlohtzin who was familiar with the man's behavior-and spent an inordinate portion of his time in the temples administering to the needs of the gods by supervising their cleaning and care. That he was an accomplished military figure was firmly established; in campaign after campaign, he had distinguished himself with acts of personal bravery and leadership-qualities essential in a candidate nominated for the royal seat.

Yet Motecuhzoma must have had some reservations about the exact nature of the minister's call; after all. the council was not yet in session-why should Cihuacoatl trouble himself to seeing him? Surely not to make any more personal assessments-he knew Motecuhzoma well enough. Regardless of his reasons, it was imprudent to keep the minister in waiting as he was the council's ranking member and therefore most influential, and Motecuhzoma hurried to the reception hall where he saw Cihuacoatl standing adjacent to the empty eagle feather and jaguar-skinned throne. "You wished to see me, Lord Minister?" Motecuhzoma said upon entering.

Cihuacoatl turned to face his prospective candidate, studying the young prince carefully. He had a noble bearing about him, the minister thought, even if a bit affected, and exuded a confidence typical of members of the royal family clan. His moves were graceful and methodical, and he commanded the same regal presence that characterized his worthy predecessor-a notable quality the minister adjudged reserved for those nobles born to rule. His spirit on the battlefield was indefatigable and he excelled in the art of warfare. In sum, he possessed all the attributes which set him apart from his peers and placed him in a superior standing-it was not out of any shortage of abilities and talent that he stood as the leading prospect for the kingship. But there was another reason that Cihuacoatl wished to speak to him.

"On the matter of succession," the minister began, wasting no time in arriving at the point of the meeting. "Certainly it should come as no surprise to you that the members of our council consider you their favorite to fulfill the position. And as you know, I have considerable weight in that body and, more than anyone else, can determine the outcome of its decisions. There are concerns I must have satisfied to my mind if I am to reach my own conclusions about the man I will select. I trust you will not reproach me for the inquiry I intend to-indeed, must-unfold on you."

"Is it an interrogation I am asked to consent to?"

"You may call it that; it will have significant preponderance over my opinion on the ascendancy. You are not the only candidate whom I wish to question."

"Then say what you must, Lord Minister. I shall endeavor to satisfy your doubts."

"How did you regard our last Revered Speaker?" Cihuacoatl began on his inquisition.

The question puzzled Motecuhzoma, but he assumed the minister had his purpose for asking it and did not delay in answering. "Certainly he was our most prodigious conqueror, and ruled supreme in the battle. I deem it a great personal honor to have served under his command. He has taught me much. There are things I might have done differently had I led our forces, but then Lord Ahuitzotl usually triumphed and it is difficult to berate success."

"Yet you seem to be critical of this, his most accomplished and recognized feat."

"He deviated greatly from the accepted doctrines. Tailoring his tactics to suit his conception of waging war-this was a heretofore unknown precept. It's much like taking that prerogative away from the gods who predetermine such outcomes. I am not altogether comfortable with it."

"So you feel he was remiss in some aspects of his duties. In what respect?"

"I am in agreement with the assessments held by many of our priests—that Lord Ahuitzotl had a tendency to underestimate their functions and neglected to give them the attention and respect they were due. He was, if you will permit my saying so, quite arrogant in that he selected the deities he would worship. There are those who think this is what brought about his downfall. It was a dangerous thing to do, as he discovered to his dismay."

"Then you agree that the Revered Speaker's first and foremost duty is to the gods."

"To whom he owes his appointment to begin with, of course. The matter is undisputed."

A glint came to the minister's eyes; his questions were being answered very much to his satisfaction-and without the slightest hint of hesitation. Motecuhzoma not only provided the kind of opinions sought, but expressed an absolute certainty about it. Cihuacoatl liked that.

"As you know, Lord Ahuitzotl came to an early and quite horrifying end. What is your conclusion about that?"

"The gods exacted vengeance upon him-of that I'm convinced, although I could not tell you what specific act he committed which offended them. I think mainly his overall belittling of them. I've seen it all, Lord Minister. His presumptions and driving ambition had to be his undoing, to say nothing of his obsession over this-this mistress of his, Pelaxilla, who so fouly betrayed him. An evil and unworthy woman she must have been. Yet somehow she managed to possess my uncle with her sinister charms-something I have never understood. There were other things too. Lord Ahuitzotl had no conception of modesty; everything he did seemed, to me at least, done for attaining personal glory and his own self-serving goals. It had to be only a matter of time before the gods would weary of this and seek to put an end to it. In truth, I can't say I was surprised."

He was hard on his relative, the minister thought; but his notions were not much different from those held by himself.

"How would you do things differently?" Cihuacoatl asked.

"For one thing, I would never allow any woman to make me lose sight of my better judgment. I have my wives, and am quite content with them, but I will not consult with them or employ them on matters pertaining to the realm. Such affairs are none of their concern."

Cihuacoatl's pleasure was apparent when he heard this, and it brought back sobering recollections he wished he could forget. For like Motecuhzoma, the minister believed Ahuitzotl's obsession with Pelaxilla contributed greatly to the adversities he eventually came to face. Even now, Cihuacoatl could not forgive his former master for having rejected his counsel on desisting from notifying her of his planned seizure of Tehuantepec-the most damaging of Ahuitzotl's actions in the eyes of the minister, one which defied all the rules of good statesmanship and deeply invoked his anger and bitterness. It very much pleased Cihuacoatl that Motecuhzoma shared this view.

"Yes," Cihuacoatl wanted to hear more. "Go on."

"I would honor all the gods with equal devotion and sacrifice. My uncle clearly favored Huitzilopochtli, and while I also revere him, I would certainly not be lacking in my allegiance to the others. It's not in our judgment that we make ourselves the arbiters of the gods whom we favor and propitiate above the rest-that amounts to the worst kind of blasphemy. Who am I to say which is greater, Quetzalcoatl or Huitzilopochtli, or Tezcatlipoca, or the goddess Coatlicue? It does astound me how Lord Ahuitzotl dared to take that kind of decision upon himself-that is what I meant when I said he was presumptuous. Are not all our deities vital to our survival? But in fairness, I must confess that it was through his experience I learned this important lesson. Had I not seen with my own eyes the terrible retribution the gods inflicted upon him-so relentlessly, one awful disaster heaped upon another, utterly without pity-the lesson might also have been lost on me. But I saw and I learned from it."

Cihuacoatl was impressed. Motecuhzoma presented his points well-he was saying all the right things, exactly what the minister wished to hear, and knew it.

"Indeed that is commendable," the minister could not resist interjecting. "And it brings us to the quality I most seek in the man I will select for the crown. He must demonstrate a willingness to propitiate all our gods and goddesses to their satisfaction; in this respect he must differ from Ahuitzotl. If we can get a brilliant military leader as well, so much the better, for the tasks entrusted to us by the glorious Huitzilopochtli certainly calls for that, but primarily it is a monarch favored by the gods I seek. We cannot, ever again, afford to submit ourselves to the grave risks we endured at the hands of your uncle. In spite of his genius, he nearly destroyed us."

"You need not worry about me on that account," Motecuhzoma confidently asserted. "Nor am I lacking in military abilities, as my record attests. I fear no living man, Lord Minister, but the gods I fear. I have seen what they can do. Only a fool would dare to provoke their wrath upon his head."

"Thank you, Lord," Cihuacoatl declared, indicating that the meeting was concluded. "This has been an interesting encounter for me-quite enlightening. Perhaps we shall have more to do with each other in the coming days."

There was a lightness to the minister as he later departed from the palace and proceeded across the plaza. He felt his discussion with Motecuhzoma had been most rewarding, and the burdens of the decision which faced him earlier seemed substantially eased. He was at last convinced he had found that harmonious combination he so avidly searched for in a monarch and which had eluded him throughout his ministership, and he knew what course he would take.

As he walked along, he passed under the shadow cast upon the pavement by the Great Temple; he paused to gaze up its steep double stairway. The memory of that immense sacrifice on its inauguration lingered in his mind, a vision imprinted in him as vividly as if it had occurred but yesterday, and he gravely pondered over it. This enormous edifice stood as a personification which was both the progenitor and destroyer of Lord Ahuitzotl, he thought; it induced his motivation to excel and was the impetus promoting all his aspirations, and then led to his eventual ruin by the excesses he committed upon it. How ironic it was that Huitzilopochtli's self-proclaimed most devoted servant should meet his destruction over the temple dedicated to that god's glory. Yet he felt humbled standing beneath its sheer massiveness and sensed a manifestation of an eternal presence bespeaking of some greater power, and he understood how this structure could have so predominately shaped the destiny of his former lord. While he so reflected over this, a sudden cold chill overcame the minister and he tightened his cloak about his neck as he was struck with a curious notion: he wondered if there might not be a sinister smile on that idol's stone face.

EPILOGUE

Ahuitzotl, Water Dog, the eighth Revered Speaker, died in the year Ten Rabbit. This was in 1502. That same year, a small band of Spaniards, under the fourth voyage of Christopher Columbus, stopped at a native outpost on the mouth of the Ulua River in present day Honduras and made contact with the Mayan civilization. News of their arrival struck like a thunderbolt-the God, Quetzalcoatl, had returned–as promised! The days of the Mexica-Tenocha, who would later be called the Aztecs, were numbered.

THE AFTERMATH

Motecuhzoma Xocoyotzin ruled from 1502 until 1520 and became known to history as Montezuma II, the Aztec monarch who met the Spaniards under Cortez. In many respects, his own story is even more tragic that Ahuitzotl's, but it is one often related and does not bear repeating here. It will be sufficient to say that Motecuhzoma's indecision, spawned by his doubts and fears over who the Spaniards were and associating them with, if not Quetzalcoatl himself, at least that god's emissaries, caused him to vaccilate and defer military contact until Cortez managed to enter Tenochtitlan and was virtually handed over the empire by the troubled ruler. His people subsequently rebelled over this betrayal and when the Spaniards attempted to use the monarch to placate their fury, he was mortally wounded by stones and arrows hurled upon him (by some native accounts, he was stabbed to death by Cortez). He was then succeeded by his half-brother, Cuitlahuac, who died after a mere eighty-day reign from the effects of small pox which the invaders introduced to Anahuac.

Nezahualpilli ruled in Texcoco until he died in 1515, spending the later years of his reign in frequent, and no doubt stressful, struggles to prevent Motecuhzoma's encroachment on Texcoco's autonomy. Motecuhzoma never forgave him for the base execution of Chalchiuhnenetzin and, following his death, exacted vengeance on the Acolhuas by passing up Nezahualpilli's elder sons and appointing Cacama, a son born to Chalchiuhnenetzin, as successor-an act which both symbolically and politically reduced Acolhuacan to a subordinate state of Tenochtitlan. The consequences of Motecuhzoma's interference were far-reaching in that Nezahualpilli's legitimate heirs, never accepting Cacama as ruler, would eventually ally themselves with Cortez against the Mexica-Tenocha.

Ironically, Motecuhzoma was also to destroy Cacama who initially approved of permitting Cortez to enter Tenochtitlan, but became disgusted over Motecuhzoma's subservile obeisance to the Spaniards and plotted a rebellion against them. Motecuhzoma revealed this plan to Cortez who imprisoned Cacama and later executed him.

Tlilpopocatzin, the Cihuacoatl, Woman Snake, died a year after Ahuitzotl in 1503. He was succeeded by his son, Tlacaelel II; because he himself was the son of Tlacaelel, a most remarkable figure in Aztec chronicles, some confusion exists regarding his ministership and many scholars believe that only one Tlacaelel remained as Cihuacoatl from the time of Itzcoatl until late into Ahuitzotl's reign.

Chimalpopoca's fate is shrouded in obscurity, but it is established that when Motecuhzoma embarked on his own campaign against Soconusco in 1504, a new Revered Speaker ruled in Tlacopan. Presumedly this was the year of his death. It should also be noted that Tlacopan's name was changed to Tacuba earlier in Chimalpopoca's reign.

Cuitlahuac was succeeded by Cuauhtemoc, the son of Ahuitzotl and last Aztec emperor. Cuauhtemoc. By all accounts, he defended Tenochtitlan heroically against the Spaniards and their allies, and after a seventy-nine day siege of the capital, was taken captive by Cortez on August 13, 1521. While with Cortez on an expedition into Honduras in 1524, Cuauhtemoc was accused of plotting an insurrection by a local chieftain and executed. The Spanish chronicler Bernal Diaz expressed profound sorrow over his death saying it "...was very unjust and made a bad impression on all present." He remains one of his nation's most revered heroes and his monument stands where Mexico City's magnificent Paseo de la Reforma intersects with the Avenida Insurgentes.

The Zapotecs were led by a monarch named Cocijopij when they fell to the Spaniards. He recognized their military superiority and at first collaborated with them and agreed to build churches and convents for them, but he maintained a loyalty to his own gods, continuing his prayers to them while also embracing the Christian faith. This dual practice was unacceptable to the conquerors and he was turned over to the regional Inquisition for his paganism where he was physically and financially broken, and was made to watch as his priests were slain before him. He died in impoverishment and alone. Cocijopij was the son of Cocijoeza and his Mexicatl wife, Pelaxilla.

AFTERWORD

Water Dog was conceived from the beginning as a romantic tragedy in its true classical sense, that is, where a protagonist brings about his own downfall through his excessive pride and arrogance and through his suffering evokes pity out of an observer. Fortunately, Ahuitzotl's reign lends itself well to such an interpretation as he has an incipient stage of great successes to be then followed by disasters on the home front within sight of his own palace. He was without question the greatest of the Aztec warrior-kings, a title fitting him better than any other of their monarchs, who spread his conquests to the farthest regions of their 'empire', reaching to present day Guatemala, and yet his murder of Tzutzumatzin over the construction of the aqueduct, and its subsequent flooding of Tenochtitlan are well described events that humbled the proud ruler and even caused his death–some accounts say he struck his head on a lintel as he tried to flee from the torrent causing the brain damage that was to kill him later. Others say he suffered from a 'wasting' disease that ravaged his flesh leaving him emaciated and horrible to look at. That he came to a dreadful end is clear, and the conclusion that the Gods sought their vengeance upon him may actually have been the prevailing belief among his subjects. He was known for his ferocity, which is to say that he would have been idolized by his people as this was their calling, their reason for being, and that may make him somewhat unappealing to the present reader, but I strove to give him a sympathetic cord, especially through his eventual grief and remorse over what his actions led to.

The enormous sacrifice at the dedication of the Great Temple in Tenochtitlan is a matter of record, with some sources attributing as many as 80,000 victims to that event. I rejected this count on the basis of it being a physical impossibility for the four days allotted to this slaughter–even

20,000 strains the sheer logistics of undertaking such a task. That the victims voluntarily submitted to their fate appears to have been actually the case, that being decided through the act of being taken captive, although, as suggested in this novel, its excessiveness may have led to horrible misgivings among them. It is unlikely that the numbers slain where based on the reason stated in this novel—out of Ahuitzotl's intent to erase the memory of Tizoc from his people's minds thereby marking it as an event to his own glory—an exposition of his ultimate pride-a conception purely fictional but pivotal to heightening the tragic outcome of his ultimate fate.

On the subject of religion, it is difficult, perhaps even impossible, for the western mind to grasp the significance that the sacrificial rituals held for meso-American cultures. Solemnity and desperation best describes the nature of these rites—the belief was that the fifth and last sun had to be kept in existence through nourishment—blood-a sacred debt owed to the Gods by humankind, and a failure to meet this demand meant a collapse of their universe. This obligation appears to be very deeply ingrained in the people's psyche so that even today, animal sacrifices still occur out of a conviction that the shedding of the blood is essential to maintain life. Theirs was probably the most egocentric religion ever created, with the entire external universe, the cosmos and all, existing solely through the actions taken by humans on earth. Because their pantheon was comprised of many deities, as well as their avatars, the requirement to nourish them all became ever more burdensome until it attained monumental proportions among the Aztecs alienating them from their neighbors who kept their own sacrificial demands on a more subdued level. Motecuhzoma's statement to Cortez that "We fear our Gods" was totally accurate.

My novel is, first and foremost, a love story, and I concentrated on the relationship between Ahuitzotl and Pelaxilla and Tlalalca, placing a greater priority on this than on the accuracy of the events and locations described. While the number of campaigns and cities taken in these actually took place and were placed in the chronological sequence of their occurance, the circumstances surrounding these, although given a plausibility, are fictitious. To distinguish Ahuitzotl's 'genius' on the battlefield, I admittedly 'westernized' his tactics, that is, I had him apply the maneuvers, such as envelopments, deceptions, concentrated fire-power, which have characterized brilliant military leaders in our history. He may have utilized such tactics to assure the successes he achieved, but this is by no means known; the primary objective in war was to secure captives, which suggests that the numbers of warriors slain in battles would have been low. But there were notable exceptions to this, the most renowned being the virtual annihilation of the Aztec army by the Tarascans when the sixth Revered Speaker, Axayacatl, invaded Michoacan–it is said that 25,000 Aztec warriors were slain in a major battle. Using this example as a cue, I envisioned Ahuitzotl's battles, especially his conquest of the Huaxtecs, as bloody affairs entailing significant casualty counts, where the seizing of territory and cities prevailed over the taking of captives as the primary objective of the war.

As for the love interests of Ahuitzotl, very little is known about the two primary female characters of this novel. Pelaxilla is mentioned by name in only one source out of all the books I read in my research, and that is in Frederick Peterson's *Ancient Mexico* where she is described as a princess in Ahuitzotl's court. Some historians maintain that she was his daughter without giving her name. What is known about her is that she was sent to Cocijoeza to spy on him because Ahuitzotl was dissatisfied with the truce he had concluded with the Zapotecan king and that she did betray Ahuitzotl, having fallen in love with Cocijoeza. I chose to make Ahuitzotl and Pelaxilla lovers, again to enhance the anguish that a tragic figure must undergo, and what I wrote about her is purely fictitious, such as her being a mistress to Tizoc and not of royal descent. The reader may question how a lover could possibly send the object of his love to a foreign ruler, as Ahuitzotl does with Pelaxilla, and my answer to this is to say that I believe that would be very consistent with the thinking of a megalomaniac, such as Ahuitzotl was. He would reason that because he himself was so smitten by Pelaxillla, and his own judgment was infallible, a similar reaction would possess anyone else. Having these tendencies, his determination to defeat Cocijoeza became his paramount objective, even if it was to be at the expense of foregoing his beloved woman–truly a situation of hatred taking precedence over love, and Ahuizotl appropriately suffers for it.

Tlalalcapatl, shortened to Tlalaca in this novel, is an even more remote figure. In fact, I have no book source for her. During the twentieth anniversary of the Seattle World's Fair, several square riggers visited our city. One of them was the Mexican naval training ship, the *Cuauhtemoc,* and it was moored on the waterfront where I visited it. There was a sign next to the gangplank saying the ship was named for the last Aztec emperor who was the son of the Emperor Ahuitzotl and Princess Tlalalcapatl (I have a photograph as proof of this). I was unsuccessfully searching for the name of the mother of Cuauhtemoc when I came upon this sign. When Hugh Thomas came out with his great book, *Conquest*, he identified Cuauhtemoc's mother as Tiacapantzin; this caused some consternation in me and I questioned if I should change Tlalalca's name, but I decided to stick with it, although I have no references as to how the Mexican navy arrived at her name. Everything about her in my book is fiction, except for a claim to being Cuauhtemoc's mother, but she remains a key figure in the tragedy coming to Ahuitzotl. She is one of those creations that a writer comes to love, and in truth I loved her more than Pelaxilla even though that was not my original intent, a development arising out of the story quite by accident. She is herself a very tragic figure, her unrequited love for Ahuitzotl meant to tear at the reader's heartstrings, and it was painful to depict her misfortune as I did, but that is the nature of tragedies–the protagonist must suffer.

Chalchuinenetzen, shortened to Nenetzin, by the accounts rendered on her, appears to have been a nymphomaniac and was actually executed by Nezahaulpilli for her adultry, along with three of her paramours. In real life, she was even more sinister than depicted in this novel, having had many of her lovers executed after tiring of her affairs with them over her many years in Texcoco. My possible deviation from the historical data is in that she may have been sent to Nezahualpilli's court by her father, Axayacatl, rather than by Ahuitzotl. I chose to have it happen under Ahuitzotl to emphasize his mercurial relationship with his allied monarchs, and also his trust in Tlalalca's judgement even when she is wrong. A major theme of this novel is Ahuitzotl's love-hate relationship with Nezahualpilli, a man he deeply admires and yet is often in a confrontational stance with; Nenetzon serves as the catalyst by which this affiliation is presented to the reader. This also makes Motecuhzoma's concern for her more plausible–she would have been a mere child if Axayacatl presented her to Nezahualpilli and not really well known to him. It is possible that Motecuhzoma could have used her death as a pretext for declaring his dominance over Texcoco after Nezahualpilli's death without actually knowing her, but that seems unlikely.

The reader may have considered the many orations and speeches delivered in this novel as tedious and it should be clarified that such rhetoric was a very important aspect of Aztecan life. All references allude to their love of language and seeking every opportunity to see its beauty presented, in oratory and poetry. The exactness of the spoken word, in enunciation as well as meaning would have been constantly emphasized and declared by them, and hearing this properly displayed was highly valued. The Nahuatl language does have a nice ring to it, with so many of its words ending with the letter i, that it must have lent itself well for these purposes. My inclusion in depicting this was aimed at demonstrating this point.

The characters based on people who actually existed included Ahuitzotl, Chimalpopoca, Cihuacoatl, Cocijoeza, Coanacoch, Lady of Tula, Motecuhzoma, Nenetzin, Nezahualpilli, Pelaxilla, Tizoc, Tlalalca, and Tzutzumatzin. Fictitious characters were Alotl, Colotl, Huactli, Nopalzin, Tezacoalco, Tezotzin, Tlohtzin, Xaman Utec, Xoyo, and Zozoltin. I have tried to re-create the world of the Aztecs as best as possible, trying to be accurate in my depictions of its rites and what life would have been like in it, drawing from many sources written about them to achieve this end, but it must be kept in mind that I am not a scholar or historian and do not claim to have expertise in that field. Nor am I an expert in construction, as the astute reader may have deduced in my depiction of the aqueduct's failure and the collapse of part of Ahuitzot's new palace. My primary purpose was to create a moving love story, conceived as a tragedy, and to meet this end, I concentrated on the relationship between Ahuitzotl and the two predominant women in his life, Pelaxilla and Tlalalca, as well as their interconnection to each other. Also I meant to present Ahuitzotl in that context, with the greatness and weakness that marked his character, bringing about his ruin through personal actions and ultimately coming to terms with this. This novel should be appreciated as such, and not on the exactness of the world presented.

This was a novel literally three decades in the making, twenty-six years of it languishing in a closet untouched. Job demands that entailed much overtime work prevented my further devotion to it after an initial period of being rejected repeatedly by publishers and agents. I retired at age sixty-two (in March, 2006) so that I might once more work on it and place it on line and when I believed it to be ready, I was again faced with new rejections and saw this cycle repeating itself. It was at this point (in 2008) that I decided to write the novel, *Polyxena*, in order to 'test the waters' of the print-on-demand publishers. *Polyxena*, my second novel, was thus conceived as the vehicle by which *Ahuitzotl*, my first novel, was to come to the market and owes its creation to this purpose. Life is full of ironies.

—H. Allenger